R. P. Cuff
Central Michigan College
Mt. Pleasant, Michigan

1948

The Story Survey

The Story Survey

Edited by

HAROLD BLODGETT

Assistant Professor of English
Union College

J. B. LIPPINCOTT COMPANY

CHICAGO   PHILADELPHIA   NEW YORK

528

ACKNOWLEDGMENTS

M ANY of the stories in this anthology are protected by copyright, as indicated by credit lines in the body of the book. I am most grateful to the publishers, authors, and agents who have so courteously given permission to include them.

For their generous assistance in translating several stories I am greatly indebted to my colleagues, Dr. Gordon R. Silber and Dr. Charles H. Stubing of Union College, to Barbara Coney Silber, and to my wife, Dorothy Blodgett, whose constant interest has lightened the whole work.

While the responsibility for the choice of stories is mine alone, I am indeed grateful for the suggestions of many friends, especially Dr. Dale Mitchell of Bradford Junior College, Dr. Desmond Powell of Colorado College, Mr. Lynn Montross of Sanbornton, New Hampshire, Professor Sidney Cox of Dartmouth College, Mr. Helmer Webb, Librarian of Union College, and Dr. Harrison C. Coffin of Union College. And finally may I express my deep appreciation to Dr. Burges Johnson, chairman of the Field of English, Union College, for his good counsel and encouragement.

H. B.

CONTENTS

The Story Survey

INTRODUCTION

No COLLECTION of short stories can hope to be completely representative of a period, a type, or a country. Neither can it hope, without a good deal of editorial presumption, to be thought a collection of the "best" stories. The anthologist does not fulfill an ideal—either his own or that of his readers—but he does try to justify a certain plan in his mind, a plan to meet a need and to achieve a practicable result.

The plan of this book is to bring together a generous number of good stories which have given pleasure to many readers—stories with sufficient imaginative power and technical versatility to reveal the many possibilities of the art. In time the selection is limited to stories of the last hundred years or so, and in place to the literature of the western world. It seemed fitting that for an American audience half of the selection should be devoted to American stories; and that in turn the European selection should be divided equally between stories of England and Ireland, and stories of the Continent. Necessarily such an arrangement scants the representation of stories from France, Germany, Italy, Russia, and other foreign countries, but an omnibus volume of the stories of all nations is not the intent of this collection. It is hoped that what the selection may lose in inclusiveness it gains in practical adaptation to the needs of a group. Its design is to be useful both for the college classes whose primary purpose is the writing of the short story, and those whose first aim is the appreciative study of the short story as literature. The two aims are, of course, often combined within a single program of instruction.

In the editor's opinion the art of reading needs more than ever to be cherished and encouraged in these days when emphasis upon the divine right of self-expression has become so clamorous. The art of writing has many—probably too many—votaries, and nothing is more certain than that no lack of encouragement is ever going to balk the destined author. But it is worth remembering that this destined author will need the discriminating audience that shall spur him to the best use of his art. All of us have the privilege of becoming this audience

3

by cultivating our powers of appreciation. To be a good reader is an enviable accomplishment which this collection seeks to foster. To try to write one's own stories is a pleasing and instructive exercise, but to try to appreciate the great writing of others is a pleasure no less absorbing.

The making of short stories has increased enormously within the last twenty years, becoming almost a phenomenon of mass industry, and the general level of sheer technical dexterity is high. In numbers stories are abundant today, but it is as hard—and as exciting—as ever to find the wisdom and beauty which alone justifies their preservation. Many of the stories in this collection have outlasted their generation to become classics; and some of them, written more recently, will be the classics of the future. They are, no doubt, already familiar to the devotee of the short story. The editor has not sought to exclude stories merely because of their familiarity or because they have already appeared in other anthologies; yet he has felt free to exclude certain universally known classics, such as Irving's "The Legend of Sleepy Hollow" or Harte's "The Luck of Roaring Camp" to make a place for other tales not so certain to be listed in every educational syllabus.

All literature is a report—often a minority report—of man upon his cosmic predicament. Sometimes he turns from what he sees to construct another world full of a life remote or strange or wonderful, and somehow more satisfying. Sometimes he turns to the faithful interpretation of the world he already knows. Whether he is moved by a romantic impulse to escape "real life," or the realistic impulse to record actualities, he is making a pronouncement, and receives pleasure from the indomitable will for expression. He may also receive, as Joseph Conrad reminded us, that glimpse of truth for which he has forgotten to ask. The short story, like all other literary forms, shares this unceasing fluctuation between the romantic and the realistic impulse, changing with the changing fashions of successive generations. Literary criticism, recording this change, must employ labels which can never be adequate to the task. Unquestionably there is in the brutal and sordid realism of many stories a romantic impulse to disturb and shock the reader with the presentation of sensational acts. There is, conversely, a realistic appetite for exact observation of dress, manners, and custom in many a tale commonly called romantic. Critics have occasionally resorted to the label "romantic realism" in their efforts to designate accurately the quality of a story. "Realistic romanticism" should find an equal number of uses.

The good story can never be wholly classified by an "ism," either of form or of content. If it rejects the form that has come to be called traditional, it achieves a vital form of its own. It is never inconclusive. Even if its purpose is to reveal the apparent purposelessness or haphazardness of life itself, its revelation will have a harmony of proportion which justifies it as a work of art. If it rejects traditional materials of story telling in an attempt to get closer to things of present meaning and use, it still will not forget to tell a story. Even if it is accused of being propaganda—a familiar charge these days—it will, like the writing of Ignazio Silone, derive so intimately, so legitimately from the writer's own deeply felt experience that it becomes art interpreting a way of life. There is no reason whatever why the short story should not at times act as a powerful instrument of social reform, but if the story is good such an agency is incidental, however effective, and is not achieved at all unless its power be the power of telling a story well. The short story writer has but one obligation—to move and interest the reader by his narrative skill—and the good story is the creature of no "ism" whatever.

It is always tempting to generalize upon the progress of so lively a medium as the short story. Edward J. O'Brien, who has been offering annual collections of the best stories for more than twenty years, remarked in *Story* for December, 1935, that "there is as much difference between the American short story of 1914 and the American short story of 1935 as there is between the poetry of Pope and the poetry of Keats." A difference, yes—especially in the striking subjection of the story to all manner of experimentation. Whether or not the difference is also an advance in quality is a matter of opinion. Just as—to extend O'Brien's comparison—Lord Byron liked Pope's poetry better than Keats', so some readers today may prefer the older stories to the new. But just as the poetry of Keats seems to most readers today to be more "poetical" than that of Pope, so the present-day short story seems more expressive of the potentialities of the form than ever before.

Something of the excitement aroused by these potentialities is expressed by the English writer, H. E. Bates, who remarked some years ago that after the World War "the short story more than any other form was the perfect outlet for the creative energy of any poet who was born in a world of bitterness and blood and yet had life before him. . . . The post-war short story writer made the discovery that Chekhov and Maupassant had made before him, that the short story was the most flexible of all prose forms, that it could be anything from a prose-poem without a plot or character to an analysis of the most complex human emotions. . . ." A similar testimony was given at about the same time by Gleb Struve, writing of the short story in Russia after the Revolution. The interest of young Russians in the short story resulted, Struve said, in "a rich crop of so-called 'dynamic' prose, reflecting the civil war and the first turbulent years of the Revolution, at once romantic and realistic, in which lyrical emotions and detachment verging on cruelty were strangely mingled."

It is interesting that both of these observations associate the short story with lyrical expression, and unquestionably the most conspicuous characteristic in the literary revolution of the short story since the World War has been the subjective and personal note of emotional release. The great strength of this characteristic has been its eloquent expression of the modern temper: interest in the springs of behavior, endless self-analysis, the attempt to find meaning in life, the search for objectives, impatience with illusion—all that the disenchanted soul in an indifferent universe can find to support its hope for dignity and integrity. Its great weakness, on the other hand, has been a surrender to mere brooding, aimlessness of mood, morbid introspection, and an overwhelming sense of bewilderment and frustration leading some-times to violent or senseless acts. This is why a listing of many modern stories, reduced to synopsis, reads like a catalogue of horrors. This is why editors, looking for stories that people will read, occasionally wonder if a sense of humor has deserted the tribe of authors.

Lately there have been signs of rebellion against the story that does nothing more than project a mood—signs that many a reader believes it not unreasonable to ask that a story be first a story, the dramatic narration of event. The curiosity to know what is going to happen next is fundamental in human nature, and in the past the great masters of story telling have always satisfied it. The need is not, and will not be forgotten by the masters of the short story today and tomorrow. And besides the satisfaction of his narrative curiosity the good reader asks for something more. Call it beauty, call it significance, call it power—or whatever—it responds to the hunger of the spirit. Each of the stories in this collection makes an answer of its own.

THE TECHNIQUE OF THE SHORT STORY

A First Word

A<small>LL ACHIEVEMENT</small> in the arts is self-accomplishment, and no amount of wishful, or wistful, thinking, no beating of the wings of desire, no poring over "How to do it" articles, no enrollment in "You can *write!*" courses, no study of formulas or systems, however confidently advertised, is in itself the slightest guarantee of success in the art of the short story. After all, story writers are born, not made, a truism that needs constant reiteration in our time because our time is distinguished by an almost hysterical over-emphasis upon writing as a profession. One can hardly pick up a magazine or a newspaper without finding somewhere the announcement that anybody can write a good short story, if properly trained, and that there is a lot of money waiting for the product. The situation calls for a good astringent—such as Ring Lardner's inimitable preface on "How to Write Short Stories" in his book of the same title. Lardner remarks that "you can't find no school . . . which can make a great author out of a born druggist."

Does this mean that all treatises on the art of fiction are useless? By no means. There are good treatises, and bad ones; and the good ones, without exception, insist that the writer *look to himself,* that he examine his own imagination and his own experience to see, first, whether he has anything interesting and significant to tell, and, second, in what way he can tell it most effectively. And then they insist— these good treatises—that the only way to learn to write is to write, that work, and more work, is almost everything. This amounts to saying that while story writing can not be taught, it can be learned. The impetus must proceed, always, from the student. He has his experience to work upon, and it can belong to no one else. Out of what Conrad called "an obscure inner necessity," he will, if he is a true writer, compel his imagined experience to assume form. He may be interested in a conflict of circumstance, a childhood reminiscence, a character engaged in vital struggle; a memory of sharp loneliness; a time of triumph, an illuminating idea, an unforgettable adventure— it matters not what. He tries to put it in story form. He stumbles and

7

fails again and again; and here is precisely the point at which he can be helped. The wise teacher can tell him what *not* to do. The teacher can point out certain errors in technique. He can put his finger on a fatal shift in point of view, or a lapse in emotional force, or an implausibility in character interpretation, or an absurdity in plot construction. This is not to say that the hard-working aspirant will not find these errors for himself. The teacher is simply a consultant, another mind to criticize, perhaps to criticize all the more effectively for not being involved in the toils of creative invention.

It may seem a paradox that the teacher, who is often not himself a creative writer, may have something useful to say to the story-teller. It is sometimes forgotten that the good teacher is creative in his criticism. Besides, there is always another consultant at hand if you have a row of books—the successful professional writer. Occasionally he will allow us a more than generous glimpse into his workshop. The prefaces of Henry James, the writing of Edith Wharton on the art of fiction, the frank comment of Somerset Maugham on his own work, the journals of Katherine Mansfield, or Nathaniel Hawthorne, or Arnold Bennett—to name but a few instances—richly repay all the study a student can give to them. And, finally, nothing is more productive in the discipline of writing—except the practice itself!—than close, concentrated attention to the finished work—the stories of the masters.

What Makes a Story

A generation ago it was common for treatises on the art of the short story to assume that its form had been perfected, that the principles of its composition had been first fully expounded and illustrated by Edgar Allan Poe, and that his successors had explored its resources so exhaustively that nothing remained for the literary aspirant but to follow the rules.

The aspirant could of course hope for originality in theme and material, but structure and form had been settled. The short-story (Brander Matthews was responsible for the hyphen) was as exact a literary form as the sonnet. If you broke its rules, you were not writing a story, just as George Meredith was not writing a sonnet when he invented his sixteen-line stanza for *Modern Love,* which, otherwise, is strangely like a sonnet sequence.

From this point of view the logic of form could become as beautifully rigid as the logic of a proposition by Euclid. Indeed some enthusiasts went so far as to propound the corollary that a story of character must begin only with dialogue revealing character, a story of plot with an incident, and a story of atmosphere with a "bit" of setting. For one kind of critical temperament Poe's "Philosophy of Composition" was too heady a drink.

To make exclusions by definitions is an exercise in which critics have always been more interested than story tellers. Now Poe, who was both critic and story teller, had an extraordinary absorption in exact analysis. "He is popularly regarded as the type of the imaginative man," says Mr. Padraic Colum, "but those who have come into contact with his mind have reason to believe that his critical faculties were in excess of his imaginative and creative faculties." No one can deny that Poe's famous analysis of the short story in his review of Hawthorne's *Twice-Told Tales* was one of the most useful, as well as most quoted, statements of principle ever delivered by a critic. It was lucid and dogmatic, and it conferred exact consciousness of purpose upon an art that had been all too unconscious of its exact aims. But he did not invent the short story; neither did he establish its limits. He did brilliantly enunciate its artistic necessity—singleness of purpose, singleness of effect—which holds true for all good stories everywhere.

Can not the short story hold true to Poe's principle, and still remain perhaps the most flexible of prose forms? Many writers of our day have pleaded for its liberation from the single exact type held in editors' or critics' minds. "If America continues to be the land of *the* short story," Miss Ruth Suckow has said, "it will ultimately lose its short stories." Surely it is the life of art that the creative imagination is always in advance of the theorists, conforming to its own severe discipline, establishing at times a certain pattern, as Poe did, for other writers to follow, and then dropping the pattern to advance to further conquest.

Unquestionably the "new freedom" which the short story has taken to itself has been greatly abused. It furnishes a license to undisciplined writers who do not need license, but a sense of form. It seems to offer an excuse for writers who have not really thought out their purpose, but only want a chance to let loose a pent-up flood of reverie, reflection, and recollection without limit and without selection. The editor of *The Forum,* Henry Goddard Leach, has complained bitterly that "more and more the stories in magazines and collections seem to lack plot and evidence of an ability to handle the more normal themes of human experience; and they become mere character sketches, analyses of subnormal behavior, or exhibitions of eccentric style."

He confesses to a longing for an old-fashioned yarn with plot and meaning.

Yet there seems no likelihood that Mr. Leach will ever run out of old-fashioned yarns. They are legion. It would be regrettable if story writers were to forget that the aim of all fiction is to tell a story and that its purpose is entertainment. But let not "story" and "entertainment" be arbitrarily circumscribed. Mr. Goddard might complain with equal point about the vast quantities of empty, machine-made, "contrived" stories which also flood the magazines, stories which exactly follow a certain formula—a chief character overcoming successive hurdles on the way to his happy ending—but which are as hollow as jugs.

Let us not worry too greatly about whether or not a story is merely an episode, or a sketch, or a "frozen moment" or an essay or a tone-poem in masquerade. Let us be concerned that it adheres everywhere to one central purpose, that it is single in its effect, that it is artistically satisfying in its imaginative grasp of event or character or setting.

STRUCTURE OF THE STORY

To get to fundamentals, a story is narrative, and all narrative is a recital of happenings. If the narrative is a mere relation of given events—that and nothing more—we call it an anecdote. Somerset Maugham has reminded his readers not to forget that the anecdote is the basis of fiction. But the short story goes beyond the mere recital of circumstance. It *integrates* its events, selects and arranges them to produce some dominant effect felt by the artist and intended for the reader. Here the quoting of Poe becomes inevitable:

A skilful literary artist has constructed a tale. If wise, he has not fashioned his thoughts to accommodate his incidents; but having conceived, with deliberate care, a certain unique or single *effect* to be wrought out, he then invents such incidents,—he then combines such events as may best aid him in establishing this preconceived effect. If his very initial sentence tend not to the outbringing of this effect, then he has failed in his first step. In the whole composition there should be no word written, of which the tendency, direct or indirect, is not to the one pre-established design. And by such means, with such care and skill, a picture is at length painted which leaves in the mind of him who contemplates it with the kindred art, a sense of the fullest satisfaction. Undue brevity is just as exceptionable here as in the poem; but undue length is yet more to be avoided.

Although Poe does not use the words "economy" and "emphasis" in this paragraph, he implies these qualities in every sentence. *Only* such incidents may be used as will bear on the effect. The effect itself must give the fullest satisfaction. Now life itself—or a "slice" of it— does not yield a narrative effect with economy or emphasis except by accident. The story writer must impose his pattern by a process of selection, a process that many a yarn-spinner early in the history of the story refused to go through; he just rambled.

You can not select until you have decided what you want to do. What is your story *for?* This question brings us to the three basic elements of the short story: *character, action,* and *setting.* Is your story intended *primarily* to engage the reader's interest in the qualities of people? Or is it intended *primarily* to interest the reader in a complication of events? Or is it intended *primarily* to express a mood or an atmosphere? Do not be misled into thinking that the listing of these elements means that all stories are to be pigeon-holed in three compartments. They are merely useful in designating the writer's focus. It would be hard to find a "pure" example of any one of them. It is doubtful if many story writers of today would be as dogmatic as Robert Louis Stevenson in insisting on the distinction between them. Stevenson's biographer, Mr. Graham Balfour, writes:

Either on that day or about that time I remember very distinctly his saying to me: "There are, so far as I know, three ways, and three ways only, of writing a story. You may take a plot and fit characters to it, or you may take a character and choose incidents and situations to develop it, or lastly—you must bear with me while I try to make this clear"— (here he made a gesture with his hand as if he were trying to shape something and give it outline and form)—"you may take a certain atmosphere and get action and persons to express it and realize it. I'll give you an example—'The Merry Men.' There I began with the feeling of one of those islands on the west coast of Scotland, and I gradually developed the story to express the sentiment with which the coast affected me."

Some theorists insist upon a fourth "element"—*theme*—and point to a type of story whose chief intent is to reveal some truth about life. But *all* stories worth reading have some underlying significance, some judgment about life implied in the narrative (a possible exception might be the pure adventure story; the only "theme" of Wilkie Collins' "A Terribly Strange Bed" is that young gamblers in a strange gambling house are likely to get into trouble). In his "Weaving the Short Story"

Douglas Bement is very sensible as well as ingenious in comparing the *theme* of the short story to the warp; and *action, character,* and *setting* to the woof of the fabric which is the short story.

The truth is that nearly every good story combines all these elements into an artistic entity, and the reader, captured by its illusion, does not ask himself about the author's focus. He feels it, nevertheless, and it is useful to the aspirant to attempt to detect it. It is a valuable exercise to turn to each of the stories in this collection and ask yourself: What is the author's dominant idea? Is he interested *chiefly* in character, in action, in setting, in theme, or in two or more of these elements together?

There seems no doubt, for instance, that in writing about the little son of Jean Blin in "The Manuscript of a Village Doctor," Anatole France was chiefly concerned with presenting the portrait of a child genius. But not that alone. He is also interested in showing us how the detachment of a scientist is shaken by the spectacle of death wantonly destroying a precocious child. In "Taking the Veil" Katherine Mansfield is chiefly interested in presenting a young girl in a mood of extravagant reverie, brought on by a "crush" over an actor. But in O. Henry's "Roads of Destiny" or Munro's "Lady Packletide's Tiger," or Hawthorne's "Mr. Higginbotham's Catastrophe," we are chiefly interested, not in character or in place, but in *what happens*. A clear instance of the "setting" or "atmosphere" story, one in which the atmosphere is actually the chief character, so to speak, is hard to find. To some readers the so-called "regional" story is mainly interesting, not for what happens, or for its people, but for its impression of place and time. For example Josephine Johnson's "Arcadia Recalled" invokes an idyllic summer on a farm; and James Still's "Job's Tears" brings vividly to us the picture of a small mountain family living through a hard winter. But to call either of these "atmosphere stories" is perhaps to depend too trustfully on labels.

In Walter Edmond's "Blind Eve" is the author mainly interested in the evocation of times past—the atmosphere, so to speak,—or in the story of how Perry Joslin went sparking, or in the personalities of Perry and blind Eve? And in "Mrs. Ripley's Trip" is Hamlin Garland mainly interested in depicting the Middle Border country, or in telling the story of how a woman had her way, or in interpreting the characters of Jane and Ethan Ripley? Such questions may seem a little pedantic in the way they tear a story apart, but they help to fix the student's attention upon the essential problem of *focus*.

PLOT

Having decided what your story is *for,* your next problem is that of design; the arrangement of events or the *plan* of action. *Plot* is not to be identified with action itself, or with idea. The plot is the blue-print of the story; some amateurs seem to ignore it altogether—archi-tects by intuition alone. We shall see that the plot of the so-called traditional story is indeed far easier to indicate than the plot of many modern stories which are not so concerned with solving a situation as with presenting it. But *all* good stories, traditional or "modern," have design. Let us concern ourselves with the traditional form first.

We call short stories *dramatic* narratives in order to distinguish them from mere sequences of events. Now drama occurs when human nature is in conflict, or in collision with some force. Out of this collision grows the plot, or the design. The struggle may be entirely within oneself: in Chekhov's "Grief" a cab-driver, Iona Potapov, is torn with grief over the death of his son; in Arnold Zweig's "The Parcel" Dr. Rohme is fearful that his own indecisiveness will turn his beloved against him; in Sherwood Anderson's "Sophistication" a boy and a girl struggle toward spiritual maturity and an understanding with each other. Sometimes the struggle is between one person and another. In H. H. Munro's "Mrs. Packletide's Tiger" we have the diverting spectacle of two ladies competing for the spotlight; in Sudermann's "New Year's Eve Confession" is an ingenious variation of the im-memorial situation of two men in love with the same woman. And often the struggle is between a character and impersonal forces—the physical environment, or public opinion, or convention, or Death, or the overriding power which we call Destiny. In James Joyce's "A Little Cloud" we see little Chandler's futile struggle against the con-fining bonds of dreary domesticity; in Ambrose Bierce's "One of the Missing" a soldier fights against Death and loses; in Silone's "The Trap" a liberal pits himself against the forces of Fascism.

Sometimes the real struggle, or the real "story," is concealed beneath a more apparent conflict. The *real* conflict in Garland's "Mrs. Ripley's Trip" is not so much between husband and wife, as between both of them and the harsh poverty of prairie life. The *real* conflict in Marjorie Rawling's "The Pardon" is not so much between the pardoned convict and his wife as between the convict and the pressure of social opinion which makes him a lonely outcast.

In the traditional story the design which grows out of this conflict takes a well-defined form: In the *beginning* of the story the *initial situation* is presented, in which we find the chief character involved. In the *middle,* or the body of the story, we have the rising action that brings us to the *climax,* or the point at which the opposing force either conquers, or is conquered. Note that this climax is merely structural; it may or may not coincide with the climax of emotional interest. The *climax* also indicates the *turning point* at which the action begins to fall. In the *end* or the conclusion of the story, we have the *denouement* or conclusive act which finishes the narrative. Sometimes there is also a *sequel* or *aftermath* which may point the significance of the story. An interesting *sequel* may be found in Ring Lardner's "There Are Smiles." Here the story proper is concerned with the growing interest of a traffic cop in an attractive young girl whose incorrigibly reckless driving brings inevitable tragedy. The sequel is a brief three paragraphs wherein we see how profoundly the tragedy has affected the cop's disposition.

It is common in discussions of the short story to represent this design graphically by a single line, beginning with the initial situation, rising through two-thirds of its length to the climax, and falling in the last third to level again at the denouement. Rather than to make graphs, it would be useful for the student to decide which of the stories in this collection naturally lend themselves to such a design, and then to write paragraphs summarizing the various stages.

The Story of Untraditional Pattern

The student will find that many modern stories do not conform to traditional pattern. Instead of presenting a single situation and then resolving it, a story may be concerned solely with a moment of significance, or with illuminating a situation, a crisis in the life of a character, without attempt at solution. Sometimes the implication is that there *is* no solution, or that it is sufficient to record the experience. This is the sort of story to which some theorists refuse the name of story. There are several in this collection. Yet each one of them abides by some principle of artistic completion which is satisfying to the reader's sense of fitness. In William Saroyan's "A Cold Day" a young man writes a letter complaining bitterly about how cold it is in San Francisco, so cold that he can't write a good story; so he writes a complaint instead. But the complaint is in itself an artistic entity: the depiction of a struggle between a writer and his environment, conveying a single effect of half-humorous indignation. In Hemingway's "After the

Storm" we are told about a beachcomber's attempt to break into a sunken liner, fresh after a wreck with the dead inside her. There is no complication; he simply fails, but the story is complete in its implication of cold horror and avarice. In "Your Obituary, Well Written" Conrad Aiken is not interested in a complication of circumstances, but in evoking a moment of awareness, a "rapprochement" between two sensitive people.

One further word on this problem of design. A successful short story writer once told the editor that a good way for the beginner to grasp the problem of design is simply to take one or two admired stories and *copy them*. The sheer drudgery of transferring a story from book or magazine to typed pages would, he believes, reveal more about proportion and form than all the outlines in the manuals.

The Action of the Story

In its broadest sense *action* is what *takes place* in the story to make it worth the telling. You have decided on your theme, you have your design in mind, and now you are faced with the problem of setting down the story. If the chief interest of the story lies in event, as in the adventure yarn, this action is bound to be mostly physical and outward. Your chief character is in a predicament from which he attempts to extricate himself. The story is a record of his successive set-backs and advances up to the turning point, or climax, at which the issue is decided for good or for ill. For example, in Ambrose Bierce's "One of the Missing," the main situation shows the soldier, Jerome Searing, caught in a trap, imprisoned beneath fallen timbers. When he recovers consciousness, he attempts to dislodge himself. Then a fresh danger occurs: he realizes that his rifle, also caught in the débris, is aimed directly at his forehead. He knows that his slightest movement may discharge the rifle. He stops his struggle to await a rescue party, and tries to fall asleep. Presently he meets another hazard; rats scampering about may touch off the trigger of the rifle! He renews his efforts, trying to wedge a board so that it may deflect the bullet, should the rifle be discharged. This plan also fails. Then in the composure of despair he makes up his mind to end the suspense by deliberately shooting himself! He tries to thrust the strip of board against the trigger, and final irony!, there is no explosion because the rifle is *already discharged! But the soldier does not know this;* and, as the author sardonically remarks, the rifle does its work.

Much can be learned by careful study of such stories. You will see that the author keeps the reader constantly in suspense about the outcome of each successive set-back and advance. *The reader wants to know what will happen next.* The continual posing of this question in the mind of the reader is the means by which the drama of the story is created. Note, too, that the author constantly *repeats* and *varies* his incidents—on the one hand always hammering home the predicament of the chief character by creating fresh hazards, and on the other, always ingeniously changing them.

Indeed the more the student analyzes good stories, the more he will realize that *repetition* is a basic principle of story telling, whether the interest be chiefly in event, in character, or in setting. The expert author never allows a point to lapse, never gives the reader too much credit for remembering. "As I was saying," the story teller remarks, and then he *tells us again.*

The beginner is often puzzled by the sheer ingenuity of action in the so-called complication story. He is inclined to ask, "How do you 'think up' plots, how do you invent surprising situations and dazzling solutions of them?" There is no real answer. Such writers as H. C. Bunner, O. Henry, and H. H. Munro seemed to have a natural ability for what Galsworthy called stories with a sting in the tail, seemed to have a lively and curious instinct for playing delightfully upon oddity of circumstance. Their story-telling intuition worked that way. Mere ingenuity, mere surprise is in itself a comparatively unimportant quality. In their best stories O. Henry and Munro and all dealers in literary fireworks give us more than surprise. They say something interesting about life, something that reveals their own view.

So far we have dealt with action in but one kind of story—that in which outward event is the chief interest. But it is obvious that in many great stories outward "physical" action is not the real story. The real action is within; the real drama goes on within the minds and hearts of the characters. The greatest development of the short story since Poe, and its greatest contributions, have come from recognition of its "psychological" possibilities. What people do in the world is so often less interesting than what they are, and the whole intent of such writers as Sherwood Anderson, Chekhov, and D. H. Lawrence is to explore the realm of personality. The outward action of Lawrence's "The Blind Man" is simple: A man and his wife are awaiting a visitor; he comes and they spend the evening together. But these three personalities react powerfully upon each other; and Lawrence is concerned with expressing the drama of their relationship. And something happens, something intensely interesting, but it happens within the spirit. In Conrad Aiken's "Your Obituary, Well Written" the outward action is exceedingly simple: the meeting of a man and a woman, and a second meeting at tea. But the real story is the revelation of how these meetings are, for the man at least, moments which caught up all the "scanty poetry" of his life. To be sure, outward action is often plentiful in stories whose chief interest is not in event. It is in Ferner Nuhn's "Ten." A boy earns a fifty cent piece, loses it, and finds it again. We follow the boy through two active days, but our interest abides not so much in what the boy *does* as in the evocation of boyhood engaged in its own important concerns.

Fortunately there is no formula for plotting action in good stories. Each has its own lively individuality. It is one thing to put an adventurer through a series of suspense-provoking crises; it is another to make a voyage of discovery among the shallows and depths of human relationship. It may be useful, however, to offer advice on one or two problems:

(1) *Dramatize, don't outline.* The first efforts of beginning writers are nearly always a *telling about* instead of a *telling* of a story. The story must be *presented;* it is character in action. The first story is likely to be a synopsis of a much longer story. The writer has not succeeded in limiting it to the point where it becomes effective; and he uses a great many adjectives and adverbs to describe a character or an incident instead of revealing them. He says that the big-league pitcher, knocked out in the fifth inning, walked disconsolately off the mound. He does not show us the pitcher striding off to the boos of the fans, eyes studying the ground, lips moving in disgust, his glove dangling.

It may help the writer to think of his story as a series of scenes, as if he were to present it on the stage before an audience. Considered in this way, he will find that his story naturally divides itself into those episodes which might be directly staged—unified in time, in place, and action—and those which are, so to say, "running scenes"—carrying the story from one place to another. In Miss Suckow's "Golden Wedding" our first "scene" presents the Willeys at home getting ready for their golden wedding celebration; the second "running scene" is the bobsled ride to their son George's home, and the arrival; then follows the long scene of the dinner and celebration; then the afternoon sleighride; the return to the house again; the journey home; and the final scene in which the old couple prepare for bed.

Such an analysis is useful in considering structure alone, and has nothing to do with the skillful interpretation which makes a great story. And stories will not necessarily lend themselves to this sort of treatment. In Frances Newman's "Rachel and Her Children," for instance, the actual scene—a church funeral—is merely "setting" while the story itself is conveyed in the sardonic reflections of Mrs. Overton and the review of her life. Nevertheless structural analysis in terms of "scene" will often be helpful in eliminating the unnecessary comment, explanation, and moralizing with which beginning writers clutter up their stories. It will help, also, to solve the troublesome problem of *transitions*. The writer will wonder how to get his story from one place to another, and he will discover that often he doesn't have to. The best advice about transitions, says a well-known writer, is "Ignore them."

(2) *How to Begin.*   Advice on this point is probably useless. What the story writer actually does is to search for the natural, inevitable way to begin the sort of story he has in mind. The search will not uncommonly require a dozen tries, and opening paragraphs will be rejected again and again. Sometimes the story doesn't start at all, and must be abandoned for some future attempt. F. Scott Fitzgerald, whose stories often seem so superbly casual, has written engagingly of his own false starts in one of those too rare articles which permit us to enter the workshop.[1]

It will be interesting although it may not solve the difficulty of starting one's own story, to study the beginnings of stories in this collection. "Golden Wedding," like many good stories, begins with dialogue—a good lead because it attracts attention, starts the action, and reveals character. "Deep Water Man" begins with a statement about the character. So does "The Horses." Many stories lead off with the character in action, as do "One of the Missing" and "After the Storm." Some stories reveal the intent of the whole story in the very first sentence, as in "Mrs. Packletide's Tiger" and "The Cask of Amontillado." Occasionally as in "A Day in New York"—the author will begin with an epigrammatic reflection. In "Your Obituary, Well Written" Conrad Aiken goes much further and writes a beginning which practically amounts to a complete informal essay. And very often a story will find its best beginning in a description of its setting,

---

[1] "One Hundred False Starts" by F. Scott Fitzgerald, *The Saturday Evening Post*, March 4, 1933. Mr. Fitzgerald uses this title in a general sense to mean not "starts" merely, but the whole effort to make a story come clear.

as in "With the Fog," whose first paragraph gives us "the known world of the average Brushy Mountain family."

A device to gain dramatic suspense is to start a story in the very midst of its action, leaving the explaining to do later. The method has obvious advantages, but the novice will find that it is not easy, after the dramatic scene is over, to acquaint the reader naturally and unobtrusively with the necessary antecedent information. Taking time out of its natural order in the structure of the story has been called "the flash-back." It doesn't always occur at the beginning. In "A Day in New York" we are at first interested in a remark about gallantry in women, and in the character, Dan Byrd. Then we see Dan Byrd and his wife excitedly preparing for a trip to New York. Then after they are on the platform waiting for the train, the author "flashes back" in time to tell us how "Many things had happened to make this vacation possible." If the student will study the time scheme of the stories in this collection, he will notice that most of them are in chronological, sharply-limited time order. Sometimes retrospect will illuminate the whole theme—witness "Rachel and Her Children"—but the shift in time is indicated without obtrusiveness. If the "flash-back" is a mere trick, the structure will appear obviously contrived; if it fits naturally in the story telling the absorbed reader will not even notice that it is a device at all.

CHARACTER

Today many writers would object to Stevenson's phrase about taking a plot and fitting characters to it. They would point out that even in the story whose chief interest is event the *plot must fit the characters;* the action must seem inevitably to occur because the chief character is the kind of man he is. John Galsworthy, talking about the drama, says "A human being is the best plot there is; it may be impossible to see why he is a good plot, because the idea within which he was brought forth cannot be fully grasped; but it is plain that *he is a good plot.*" [2] The editor has heard Sherwood Anderson complain bitterly about "the poison plot"—poison because if a writer thinks in terms of "plot" he is tempted to twist his story characters to fit it. Anderson reflects upon a character—say George Willard in "Winesburg, Ohio"—and forms his design from what George Willard is bound to think and say and do.

---

[2] "Some Platitudes Concerning Drama" from *The Inn of Tranquility,* Charles Scribner's Sons, 1912.

It is not likely that Stevenson would object to the views of Anderson and Galsworthy. In Stevenson's own first published story, "A Lodging for the Night,"—surely a story full of action and event—the design is determined by the highly individual character of Villon. He is no ordinary vagabond; no ordinary vagabond would defend his honor so spiritedly before the lord of Brisetout. What Stevenson probably had in mind was the truth that in the "event" story the character may be less an individual than he is a *type* of character. Irving's German student is a romantic *type*—any young, sensitive idealist of the "Werther" tradition. Ambrose Bierce's Jerome Searing is a type of the courageous, hardy soldier. H. H. Munro's Mrs. Packletide is a type of social climber and sensation monger. Notice, however, that the great writer will make even his "types" interesting. The tyro, thinking only of some odd complication or twist of event, is likely to fill his story with mere wooden "stooges"—the dashing soldier of fortune, the beautiful, but coy heroine, the sinister, smooth-seeming villain. Many stories which proceed from a current fashion suffer from such ventriloquists' characters.

Sometimes great stories may be concerned not so much with an individual character as with a *personified trait*. The narrator in Poe's "The Cask of Amontillado" is the very spirit of concentrated revenge. The husband in James Stephens' delightful story "The Horses" is not a henpecked husband so much as he is *all* henpecked husbands. Thomas Mann's powerful story "The Hungry" is not so much concerned with the individuality of Detlef as with his standing for a dominant trait in the artistic temperament. Sometimes the individuality of even strongly-drawn characters seems to vanish, and our minds are occupied not with two people—witness the girl and the physician in Turgenev's "The District Doctor"—but with two forces—Love and Death—contending with each other. The cab-driver, Iona Potapov, grieving for his little son, becomes a symbol of all suffering humanity. So great art tends always toward the universal.

But suppose the creative imagination is prompted, not by some unusual sequence of events happening to "typical" people nor by a theme which seems to personify a dominant trait, but by the recollection of *an individual* in a revealing time of crisis or struggle. Many great stories, especially in our time, are so impelled. In his penetrating essay on Ivan Turgenev, Henry James writes: "The first form in which a tale appeared to him was as the figure of an individual, or a combination of individuals, whom he wished to see in action, being sure that such people must do something very special and interesting."

Something about this individual is of special interest—some dominating trait—and the imagination realizes that he can act in no other way than he does. Character is destiny! In a novel we might show him developing and changing under the vicissitudes of living. But the story is too brief for that. The short story presents an individual whose character is already formed, and whose actions, when he is confronted by a particular situation, seem *inevitable*. This situation need not be at all unusual. It can be, and often is, as "everyday" as Sherwood Anderson's story of George Willard and Helen White walking out in the evening. Anton Chekhov said: "Why write about a man getting into a submarine and going to the North Pole to reconcile himself to the world, while his beloved at that moment throws herself with a hysterical shriek from the belfry? All this is untrue and does not happen in real life. One must write about simple things: how Peter Semionovich married Marie Ivanovna. That is all."

That is the way Chekhov's imagination worked. But the same principle works when the situation is highly unusual, as in Galsworthy's "Salta Pro Nobis" where a dancer, condemned to death, reveals the white flame of her spirit in a last dance upon the eve of execution. The important thing is that character and action *must fit;* and in reading the story we say to ourselves unconsciously: "That is the sort of thing he *would* do." In Joyce's "A Little Cloud" a frustrated young clerk is swept, feebly protesting, down the tide of mediocrity. In Walter de la Mare's "The Nap," Mr. Thripp, whose whole heart is loyalty, remains a bulwark of strength for the family whose shortcomings his mind recognizes only too clearly.

Notice that the author's *focus* is nearly always directed to a single chief character even in those stories in which two or more persons seem to appeal equally to our attention. In Arnold Zweig's "The Parcel" we are as interested in Claudia as in Doctor Rohme, but the story is told from Doctor Rohme's point of view. Other instances are "Golden Wedding" with the focus upon Mrs. Willey, and "The District Doctor" with the focus upon the physician. Indeed, to think of a short story as having a single chief character acting at a moment of crisis is a good limiting principle, but not all stories can be brought within it. The two old friends of Maupassant's grim story "A Fishing Party" are of equal significance, and sometimes a writer—as in Josephine

Johnson's "Arcadia Recalled"—focuses her attention upon a whole group.

A common mistake of beginning writers is to allow the development of their story to depend upon a sudden change in the dominant trait of their chief character. It is true that there is often a striking change in attitude—Ambrose Bierce's courageous soldier is reduced to paralyzing fear and Ring Lardner's jovial traffic cop becomes a surly grouch—but these are changes to which, given the conditions, all humanity is subject. A fundamental change in essential character is rarely, if ever, convincing within the limits of a short story.

For example the editor once received a student story about a newspaper editor whose dominant characteristic was his professional callousness to the suffering caused by unfavorable publicity. "If it is news it must be printed" was his unbreakable rule. But under the humanizing influence of a wistful girl-reporter, he was persuaded in one-half hour to kill a story whose release might have meant unbearable anguish to a mother. He "came to realize" that the necessities of humanity are greater than those of journalism. Countless college stories have been written about an athlete, sulking in his tent, who "comes to realize" all that Alma Mater means to him and goes out at the last minute to push the ball over for the winning touchdown. The phrase itself "come to realize" is aptly employed by Thomas Uzzell to label this type of story. It may appeal sometimes to the tender-minded who like to think of last minute repentance, and who confuse, as Mr. Uzzell points out, the use of the word "character" in its moral sense with its use in the psychological sense.[3]

The student of story writing has advanced toward artistic maturity when he summarily rejects all such tricks for interpreting character, when he recognizes that genuine traits of character furnish an infinite variety of fascinating incident without resort to improbable changes of heart or "surprise" characteristics sprung upon the reader at the last minute. Students who make these mistakes are invariably those who like to write of remote or peculiar people who never existed for them save in the memory of the cinema screen or a magazine page.

Let the beginner look to the life about him, to the people he knows. If he can't sense a story in the mailman who lugs back his rejected manuscripts, or in the shoe cobbler down the street, or in the pretty girl who dashes by him in the blue convertible coupe at precisely 9:20 A.M.

---

[3] See pp. 475–478 of Uzzell's *Narrative Technique,* Harcourt, Brace, and Company, 1934.

every day, or the barber who hums a passage from Chopin while he
wets the hair,—then the chances are that he does not have the experiencing temperament, the observing imagination which makes the
writer. He will not be able to write of how Peter Semionovich married
Maria Ivanovna. To tell him to look to himself, too, is probably gratuitous advice in the face of all the bounding and deep-breathing egos
which have been released by the passionate imitation of William
Saroyan. But let him take to heart the fine advice of Frances Newman:
"My only theories are that a writer must choose people and places he
knows all about, that he must be painfully careful about choosing his
point of view and sticking to it, that he must go down deeply enough
into himself—to the point where he becomes different from every other
human being. . . ."[4]

Probably most story tellers would agree with Turgenev that their
fiction characters are suggested by living models, but it does not follow
that the creation of the character depends upon a factual reporting of
the appearance, habits, and conversation of a real person. The imagination does not work that way, and those who make a game of discovering the originals in a piece of fiction are often deceived. In fact
an actual person does not come to life in fiction; he does not fit in
with the illusion of reality which *seems* more real than the actual. The
fictitious character is a sort of composite of traits observed in actual
life; and if he is truly imagined, he will take to himself a "real" life of
his own. Sometimes the story teller will come to a point in the story
where the character begins, as it were, to take over the story and
"dictate" its development.

Character is best revealed in action, and the student will observe that
most of the stories in this collection rely very little upon direct exposition. Of course the author will often characterize or describe—as
Stevenson writes of Villon that "Greed had made folds about his eyes,
evil smiles had puckered his mouth"—but lengthy passages "about" a
character were commoner in the day when the short story was more a
hybrid of the eighteenth century essay than a literary form in its own
right. Washington Irving, as much essayist as story teller, tells us that
"Gottfried Wolfgang was a young man of good family" and then goes
on with a long paragraph of characterization,—this in a story whose
chief interest is anecdotal.

It seems more natural now to allow the action of the story the fullest

---

[4] P. 263, *The Letters of Frances Newman*, edited by Hansell Baugh, Horace Liveright
Company, 1929.

possible freedom in speaking for character. "Ah, Tony was a sort o' man!" we are told, and Hardy's presentation of Tony Syke's escapades leaves no doubt about what sort he was. The rich pattern of incident in such stories as Coppard's "The Handsome Lady," de la Mare's "The Nap," Brace's "Deep Water Man," or Edmond's "Blind Eve" is such excellent characterization that one does not think of having to be told by the author what kind of person the chief character is. Even when the story is told *by* the chief character, there is an implied, sometimes unconscious characterization of himself although his telling deals only with action. When the narrator of "After the Storm" complains that "Even the birds got more out of her than I did" we are left in no doubt about him.

Of course what a man says is quite as revealing as what he does. The two are concomitants, and in some stories characterization is revealed almost entirely through dialogue. The gesture of body, the intonation of voice, the expression of the face, the thing said, the thing done—all become a natural tightly-woven pattern. It will repay the student to study the stories of Ring Lardner, whose genius was especially happy in revealing character through dialogue.

In some stories characterization through *what one says to oneself*— whether it be simple self-prompting, or reverie, or daydreaming, or the "stream of consciousness"—is almost the whole excitement of the composition. Through this medium we understand the spiritual hunger of the artist in Thomas Mann's story, the sentimental abnegation of the young girl in "Taking the Veil," the wistful ambitions of young Chandler in "A Little Cloud," the anguish of the young mother in Nancy Hale's story. . . . Indeed the most significant, the most deeply interesting of all stories for our time are those which are full of self-questioning because the increase of our civilization is an increase in trouble of the spirit. Sometimes this kind of story appears deceptively easy to the beginner because of its air of frank spontaneity. Actually it can be the most difficult of all forms because it makes more demands, not only upon wisdom and understanding, but upon technical knowledge of the way the mind works, than many a young writer is able to give to it. As Dorothy Scarborough has said so well, "The 'interior monologue' with its unedited thoughts, the ragbag of recollections unsorted, has proved a vast bore in the writing of the unskilled."[5] The young writer, rashly venturing upon this method, may recall the modesty of Sherwood Anderson who confesses of Helen White that

[5] Introduction, p. x, *Selected Short Stories of Today,* Farrar and Rinehart, 1935.

"there is no way of knowing what woman's thoughts went through her mind."

When a writer engages in direct characterization, whether in extended exposition or in a brief phrase, we take his word for it if he is persuasive. And when we overhear the thoughts of a character, we are privileged to make our own judgment upon the sort of person he is. But the illumination cast most commonly on a character comes from another person within the story. We understand the character in the light of the conversation, action, and attitudes of other people. Among great modern writers Henry James commands a phenomenal dexterity in the intricate analysis of character through the comprehension of other minds. Always he keeps the author out of it, making no direct comment. In "Paste" the moral evasiveness of Arthur Prime is seen through the fastidious honesty of the girl, Charlotte. We see the fussiness and grumbling of old Mr. Willey in "Golden Wedding" through the patient eyes of his wife. Both Anatole France and Turgenev make memorable studies of personality through the mind of a physician. In Arthur Schnitzler's story two brothers are poignantly revealed in a mutual dependence so deep-rooted that without it life has no meaning. D. H. Lawrence was so profoundly concerned with "awareness" in personal relationship that it became a major theme in all he wrote. It was Chekhov's also, although Chekhov was impressed with the lack of understanding between human beings, with the essential loneliness of the individual.

SETTING

Stevenson, it will be recalled, said that the inspiration for "The Merry Men" began with "the feeling of one of those islands on the west coast of Scotland," and that he developed the story to express the sentiment with which the coast affected him. If in thinking of his story the writer is chiefly moved by considerations of its place and time, if the whole spatial and temporal environment is its most memorable attribute, then he is justified in calling it a tale of atmosphere or setting. But the term "tale of atmosphere" has always been a label rather loosely applied, and its attachment to any particular story becomes a matter of personal judgment. For instance Brander Matthews called Hamlin Garland's "Return of the Private" a tale of atmosphere, but many a reader thinks of this story chiefly in terms of character and incident. It has already been remarked that that story is rare indeed whose setting is in fact its chief actor. Usually it is simply the *medium* through which the story grows just as the biological medium—if the figure is not too inappropriate—is the nutritive mixture for a culture.

In preliminary work upon his novels Sinclair Lewis takes elaborate care with "laying out" the story. For the writing of "Babbitt" he made detailed maps of the streets and outlying districts of Zenith City. He knew Babbitt's house and office building to every exact detail, including the arrangement of the furniture. He could have told you not only about the familiar haunts of the characters he actually used, but about those he didn't use, and about the environment of the whole swarming city.

Just so the expert short story writer, working with perhaps but a single episode, will fix the setting in his mind before he writes a word. The season of the year, the year itself, the time of day, the place, the climate, the weather, the social milieu—all these elements may play a part in great or small degree. He knows the setting so well that he, like Sinclair Lewis, could construct a model of it. It might be the single room of William Saroyan's "A Cold Day" with its books, its small phonograph, its old tub, and above all, its cold. It might be a rural village, such as A. E. Coppard's genial but angular parish of Tull with its grey church and churchyard, its northern prospect of farm and forest. It may evoke the whole quality of a countryside—Garland's harsh, windy Iowa prairie in November, Kathleen Morehouse's Carolina mountain valley in April flowering; Walter Edmond's canal lock in the Kill Gorge at the close of winter before the feeling of spring had come; William Faulkner's southern town in the days before paving and city laundry; Josephine Johnson's lovely Arcadia on the farm, recalled in childhood memory. . . .

But always the setting must be strictly integrated to the underlying purpose of the story. It is never mere décor, something furnished, something laid on, something extrinsic. Perhaps the whole environment, as in "The Pardon" or "With the Fog" or "Job's Tears," stands in vital, inseparable relation to character and conduct. Perhaps a single impression of some object—like the double-red thorn tree in Conrad Aiken's "Your Obituary, Well Written"—will seem in recollection to intensify an emotional crisis, will seem even to act as symbol of the emotion. Or perhaps the setting will be merely a back-drop, as in Henry James' "Paste," to a drama not primarily concerned with place and time. Whatever his purpose is, the expert writer will never introduce the extraneous; every single object will have its place in the harmony of the composition. The beginner, forgetting that after all description is not narration, is often overenthusiastic about the possibilities of lush and striking passages. Chekhov, writing to his brother, Alexander about writing problems, advised him always to seize upon the little particulars. "For instance," he said, "you will get the full effect of a moonlight night if you write that on the mill-dam a little glowing star-point flashed from the neck of a broken bottle, and the round, black shadow of a dog, or a wolf, emerged and ran. . . ."

Point of View

We have seen that the planning of a short story becomes a process of eliminations. To achieve a single narrative effect with economy of means and the utmost emphasis—to borrow the phraseology of Clayton Hamilton's oft-quoted definition—is ruthlessly to reject. Over-characterization, superfluous incident, and unnecessary description will corrupt that magical power of evocation which marks the achieved story. Another principle of limitation, another fascinating discipline which in fact determines the whole form of the story, is the decision the author must make upon the story's point of view. From what vantage shall he present his narrative? All such positions or "angles of narration," as they are sometimes called, resolve themselves into either the first or the third person, and it is convenient so to consider them although the classification obviously goes beyond a merely grammatical distinction.

If you tell your story in the first person, you speak either as the chief actor or a minor actor in the events to be related. Sometimes a writer assumes this point of view with such skillful illusion that it seems as if he must actually be relating experiences of his own. Indeed Somerset Maugham felt compelled in his preface to *East and West* to caution his readers against this assumption. The use of the first person has the great advantage of naturalness, of casual off-handedness. You imply: "This thing happened to me. I know it because I was there, and what I don't know I'm under no obligation to explain. Take it or leave it." It also has obvious disadvantages. You can not very gracefully characterize yourself in terms of praise, and you must not be implausibly knowing about matters outside your ken. But this is not always much of a disadvantage, not in the first-person adventure story, for instance, because here the "I" of the narrative is a general type, like the young man in "A Terribly Strange Bed." Also it is possible—as in "After the Storm"—to achieve a subtle *unconscious* characterization of the narrator.

The first person is the most effective point of view for the recollected story in which the narrator—as in Faulkner's "That Evening Sun" or Still's "Job's Tears" or Gorki's "One Autumn Night"—tells of something that happened in childhood or youth. The whole quality of the telling is that of personal reminiscence. And the first person is especially effective in throwing an air of plausibility around the unusual tale, the thing that, believe it or not, happened one time. Balzac's "A Passion in the Desert" and Dickens' "The Signal Man" are good instances. The story-within-a-story or the "framed story," as it is often called, lends itself most naturally to this point of view. In "The District Doctor" the first "I" is apparently that of the author who introduces us to the second "I"—the district doctor from whom we hear the story. Why could not Turgenev have dispensed with the "frame," begun the story directly with the doctor, and still have preserved the first-person point of view? He could, but then he would have lost both the opportunity of the first "I" to characterize the doctor and that air of verisimilitude which comes from a story told by word of mouth. In this story we, the readers, are in effect listening to a conversation with all a conversation's opportunities for persuading a listener to believe. A more intricate arrangement of the framed story is exemplified in Sudermann's "The New Year's Eve Confession." Here the tale begins in the first person also. A gentleman is talking to a lady, and in order to illustrate a point he recounts a conversation which, related in the third person, becomes the story. Usually a shift in point of view is a confession of technical weakness, but here the "frame" and the story proper are ingeniously related to each other.

There is a kind of first-person narrative which has all the effect of third-person, and could be so conveyed with little change of direction. The "I" is the mere "I" of the author intruding himself now and then as Bret Harte does in "Tennessee's Partner" or Owen Francis when he refers to "a group of us" in "The Ladies Call on Mr. Pussick." It is a mere quibble to call this "angle" a first-person point of view. It has precisely the same effect as that of Ring Lardner's third-person "There Are Smiles" in which the author does not actually introduce himself but conveys an illusion of talking to you off-handedly as if he might enter the story at any moment.

If you tell your story in the third person, you must decide whether you as author are going to enter into the minds of your characters, or whether you are to remain outside, an observer but not a mind reader. If the former, you have a further choice to make: Shall you enter into one mind alone, interpreting the story from the point of view of that single mind, or shall you be free to enter into the minds of any of your characters at your own will?

The first alternative need detain us but briefly. It is rare indeed to find a *purely* objective story, a story in which the author, never permitting himself an interpretive phrase, simply shows us the characters acting and talking, allowing us to make all inferences from the spectacle. But it is not hard to find stories in which the treatment is predominantly objective. Notice, for example, the superb self-restraint of the story "A Trip to Czardis." The author does not *tell* us what the little boys, Daniel and Jim, are thinking. We just see them going through their extraordinary day; we hear them talk and see what they do, and we realize at the end that the terrible implications of that day have struck home to the older boy. In such a story all commentary is futile, and would be a weakness. This point of view is a powerful asset in those stories which depend for their effect upon the reader's gradual awareness of what is happening. The meaning of the happening can be concealed until the events themselves bring it clear, and the emotional significance is likewise quietly controlled until its full force breaks at the end of the story. The laconic restraint of the objective story, its essential cleanliness of structure, makes it a desirable discipline for those writers who tend to "editorialize" too much, who tell *about* instead of telling. The objective story has been popular with the "hard" school of fiction associated with Ernest Hemingway and the other realists of the "lost generation." Such fiction deals with vivid, colorful action and with characters who do not bother with the rhetoric of thought. Its danger is that it can so easily become mannered and a little inhuman.

It must be clear that for most story themes the advantage of subjective treatment is too great to be ignored. If your imagination is stirred by some interior excitement or struggle of mind—that is to say, by some dramatic aspect of human character—then you, as writer, will want to be more than the seeing eye, the hearing ear, the recording hand. You may find that for its most effective presentation your story must be interpreted through the consciousness of your chief character. Your story becomes his private world. This limitation upon your story is precisely the same as that given it if your chief character were to tell the story in first person. From both points of view the writer of the story is limited to the experience of his chief character, to the "angle" from which the character sees the story. But while the third-person point of view loses the naturalness and plausibility of the "I" telling the story, it gains enormously in scope. It can interpret the consciousness of the chief character without the embarrassment of an "I" looking on himself and explaining his own qualities. In Chekhov's "Grief" it is enormously more natural for us to see the story through the lonely mind of the cab-driver than it would be to listen to him lamenting in the first person as William Saroyan does in "A Cold Day." Why? Because the cab-driver, unlike the freezing author in "A Cold Day," is humble and comparatively inarticulate.

All this amounts to saying that a story must take the form most natural to it, a form by no means always immediately apparent to the writer, but arrived at by trial and error. In our collection those third-person stories which are written from the point of view of a single character show that character to be the very nub of the story; sometimes other people are almost as important to the story's outcome, but they are never its generating force. It is little Chandler we are interested in, and it is his mind we enter when we read "A Little Cloud"; Gallaher swaggers his way through most of the story, but we need none of his thoughts.

Sometimes the author goes a further step, and not only enters the mind of his chief character, but *becomes* that mind. The story is then a direct recording of mood as it is made articulate by the image-making faculty of a troubled consciousness. In Nancy Hale's "No One My Grief Can Tell" a mother's mind is a torment of emotions—possessive love for her child, the realization that he will grow and leave her, a part of herself no longer; and above and beyond this the sharp consciousness of the growing indifference of her husband. Most of the story becomes reverie, a swiftly moving series of images floating in the mind of the mother and dictated by her turbulent grief. Katherine Mansfield employs the same technique in "Taking the Veil" except that here the reverie takes the form of make-believe story rather than a procession of images moving in a wild harmony.

It is a brilliant device, this telling the story through recording the stream of consciousness of the main character, but it is as limited as it is brilliant. It is of little use in stories which depends upon outward event for their interest, and it does little to illuminate our understanding of the so-called "normal" character who seems to be in cheerful command of his faculties. For the exploration of the neurotic mind, the day-dreaming mind, the rationalizing mind, the subconscious mind, and even the sufficiently mysterious work-a-day mind of the ordinary situation, the device of recording the stream-of consciousness, is in expert hands a tool of extraordinary versatility. But let the beginner have respect for it. Let him ask himself what he actually knows of the discoveries of modern psychology, what he knows of the process he so confidently employs. And let him ask himself if his story may not be successfully presented without resort to psychoanalytic technique. Mark Twain's "My Platonic Sweetheart" is a persuasive and charming study of the life of dreams without benefit of Freud; it is probably just as well that he does not know what the Freudians would make of it.

We come, finally, to the third-person which does not limit itself to the "angle" of any one character, but is free to enter the minds of all or any of the characters; is free, also, to move at will in time and space. This is the god-like, omniscient point of view of the traditional novelist, and it is still the favorite of the short story writer also. It is equally adaptable to the swift, objective action story, the psychological study of character, and to the story of fantasy or atmosphere. In "Roads of Destiny" O. Henry is free to manipulate fate as he wishes; his hero is his puppet, illustrating a theme. In "Sophistication," Sherwood Anderson enters the minds of George Willard, of Helen White, and Helen White's escort, the college instructor, with equal facility, and he is also at liberty to digress with a general dissertation upon sophistication and youth. When James Stephens writes "The Horses," the thoughts of a horse or a dog are as open to him as the thoughts of his human characters. In "One of the Missing" Ambrose Bierce does not hesitate to review the past life of an artillery officer whose only function in the story is to fire the shot which ultimately settles the fate of Jerome Searing. It is not necessary to multiply instances. The omniscient point of view is the most flexible of all points of view, and just because it is, the writer must be careful not to abuse that flexibility. He must play fair with the reader and avoid the creation of false suspense by withholding vital information which he, as omniscient author, knows about. As in the legitimate mystery story, he must not drag red herrings across the trail.

Let the writer, then, choose his point of view and stick to it as Frances Newman recommended. It is conceivable, but not probable, that a given story might also be successful from another point of view than that employed by the author. It would be an interesting finger-exercise to attempt such a transformation with one of the stories in this volume: to tell, for instance, Silone's story "The Trap" in the first person from the point of view of Daniel. The failure to achieve effectiveness by such a transformation would in itself be proof that there is only one "right" point of view, and that when it is found, the story will spring into form like the pattern of iron filings before a magnet.

A Final Word

A thorough study of technical aspects of the short story will confirm the student's understanding that technique, while fundamental, is not enough. No skillfulness in craft can in itself make a memorable story. Above all, a story must *interest,* and it interests because of a vital way of telling. Vitality, freshness, originality, individuality—all these can and often do find expression through an entirely traditional technique; they also often break an established technique. They are greater than the rule.

Little has been said in this account about style or manner of telling, but it is plain enough that the great stories in this collection are great because their authors have written out of a distinctive quality of personality which gives savor to their work. Style, Proust remarks, is a function of vision, not of technique. It is achieved when the creative relationship—or communicating power—between a writer's mind and the outside world has become unique and his own, when the writer has something interesting to say which no one else can say in just his way.

It sometimes seems as if a beginning author has to make a choice between two paths at the start, a choice demanded by the fact that many stories which go to market and stay there are not literature. The beginner may say to himself: "I want to sell my stories as soon as possible, and my first concern is to study the trade until I know the kind of product in demand. Then I shall produce that product." Or the beginner can say: "I'm interested in doing my best to interpret what interests me. I'm going to work out my own manner, and if the public likes it, well and good." It is this second choice that Thornton Wilder had in mind when he was reported as saying to an interviewer: "I feel that for good or for ill you should talk to yourself in your own private language and be willing to sink or swim on the hope that your private language has nevertheless sufficient correspondence with that of persons of some reading and some experience." [6]

---

[6] From "Novelist into Playwright," Ross Parmenter, *Saturday Review of Literature,* June 11, 1938.

Unquestionably Wilder's point of view is that of the artist in fiction; and only the artist will endure. Instead of turning to the immediate study of the market, it would be time better spent for the ambitious beginner to study the great masters—Maupassant or Chekhov or Poe— to read such books as Katherine Mansfield's *Journal,* to experiment long with one's own stories, and to keep a voluminous journal or notebook of one's own. Let him remember that many distinctive story writers whose names are now potent in the market began by "talking to themselves" in the pages of those magazines which are hospitable to experiment.

But too sharp an insistence upon this choice would result in a false dichotomy. In some writers there probably is no choice. They are those fortunate people whose own true vision of reality happens to be the vision of the majority. There is no essential reason why commercially successful writing should not be synonymous with artistically successful writing. Such story-tellers as Ring Lardner, P. G. Wodehouse, and— let us say, Walt Disney—have the happy skill of an artistry which commands a wide appeal. And, further, it may be that a legitimate compromise between the two choices is possible: that is, one can strive for the popular audience and also strive to avoid the mediocrity that is associated with mass production. There is snobbery in the charge that the "big" magazines do not print first-rate stories. There is resentment in the counter-charge that the "little" magazines are dull. And critical talk is always inclined to become preternaturally solemn. The beginning writer, intent on trying out his own abilities, will not pay too much attention to criticism; he will get cheerfully to work.

American Stories

Washington Irving

Although Irving says in his preface to Tales of a Traveller that he values stories for their sound morals, his avowal is not to be taken too seriously. The writer who gave us the first two great American classics of story telling—"The Legend of Sleepy Hollow" and "Rip Van Winkle"—was mindful of many values. Irving's Sketch Book (1819) was an announcement that a pioneer had established new claims to a form of which one can find the intimation in Addison, the fuller realization in Irving, Hawthorne, and Poe. Tales of a Traveller, appearing five years later, dug more ore from a vein whose richness was diminishing.

With a pen as versatile as it was genial, Washington Irving wrote many other works, among them the Spanish sketches of The Alhambra (1832) and the biographies of Columbus, Oliver Goldsmith, and George Washington. He was born in New York in 1783, spent many fruitful years abroad as a literary ambassador to the Old World, and rounded out his last honored years at Tarrytown in the Hudson valley whose legends had haunted him. He died in 1830.

THE ADVENTURE OF THE GERMAN STUDENT *

Washington Irving

On a stormy night, in the tempestuous times of the French revolution, a young German was returning to his lodgings, at a late hour, across the old part of Paris. The lightning gleamed, and the loud claps of thunder rattled through the lofty narrow streets—but I should first tell you something about this young German.

Gottfried Wolfgang was a young man of good family. He had

* From Tales of a Traveller by Washington Irving, 1824. Reprinted by courtesy of G. P. Putnam's Sons.

studied for some time at Göttingen, but being of a visionary and enthusiastic character, he had wandered into those wild and speculative
doctrines which have so often bewildered German students. His se-
cluded life, his intense application, and the singular nature of his
studies, had an effect on both mind and body. His health was im-
paired; his imagination diseased. He had been indulging in fanciful
speculations on spiritual essences, until, like Swedenborg, he had an
ideal world of his own around him. He took up a notion, I do not
know from what cause, that there was an evil influence hanging over
him; an evil genius or spirit seeking to ensnare him and ensure his
perdition. Such an idea working on his melancholy temperament,
produced the most gloomy effects. He became haggard and despond-
ing. His friends discovered the mental malady preying upon him, and
determined that the best cure was a change of scene; he was sent,
therefore, to finish his studies amidst the splendors and gayeties of
Paris.

Wolfgang arrived at Paris at the breaking out of the revolution.
The popular delirium at first caught his enthusiastic mind, and he
was captivated by the political and philosophical theories of the day:
but the scenes of blood which followed shocked his sensitive nature,
disgusted him with society and the world, and made him more than
ever a recluse. He shut himself up in a solitary apartment in the *Pays
Latin,* the quarter of students. There, in a gloomy street not far from
the monastic walls of the Sorbonne, he pursued his favorite speculations. Sometimes he spent hours together in the great libraries of
Paris, those catacombs of departed authors, rummaging among their
hoards of dusty and obsolete works in quest of food for his unhealthy
appetite. He was, in a manner, a literary ghoul, feeding in the charnel-
house of decayed literature.

Wolfgang, though solitary and recluse, was of an ardent temperament, but for a time it operated merely upon his imagination. He was
too shy and ignorant of the world to make any advances to the fair,
but he was a passionate admirer of female beauty, and in his lonely
chamber would often lose himself in reveries on forms and faces
which he had seen, and his fancy would deck out images of loveliness
far surpassing the reality.

While his mind was in this excited and sublimated state, a dream
produced an extraordinary effect upon him. It was of a female face of
transcendent beauty. So strong was the impression made, that he
dreamt of it again and again. It haunted his thoughts by day, his

slumbers by night; in fine, he became passionately enamoured of this shadow of a dream. This lasted so long that it became one of those fixed ideas which haunt the minds of melancholy men, and are at times mistaken for madness.

Such was Gottfried Wolfgang, and such his situation at the time I mentioned. He was returning home late one stormy night, through some of the old and gloomy streets of the Marais, the ancient part of Paris. The loud claps of thunder rattled among the high houses of the narrow streets. He came to the Place de Grève, the square where public executions are performed. The lightning quivered about the pinnacles of the ancient Hôtel de Ville, and shed flickering gleams over the open space in front. As Wolfgang was crossing the square, he shrank back with horror at finding himself close by the guillotine. It was the height of the reign of terror, when this dreadful instrument of death stood ever ready, and its scaffold was continually running with the blood of the virtuous and the brave. It had that very day been actively employed in the work of carnage, and there it stood in grim array, amidst a silent and sleeping city, waiting for fresh victims.

Wolfgang's heart sickened within him, and he was turning shuddering from the horrible engine, when he beheld a shadowy form, cowering as it were at the foot of the steps which led up to the scaffold. A succession of vivid flashes of lightning revealed it more distinctly. It was a female figure, dressed in black. She was seated on one of the lower steps of the scaffold, leaning forward, her face hid in her lap; and her long dishevelled tresses hanging to the ground, streaming with the rain which fell in torrents. Wolfgang paused. There was something awful in this solitary monument of woe. The female had the appearance of being above the common order. He knew the times to be full of vicissitude, and that many a fair head, which had once been pillowed on down, now wandered houseless. Perhaps this was some poor mourner whom the dreadful axe had rendered desolate, and who sat here heart-broken on the strand of existence, from which all that was dear to her had been launched into eternity.

He approached, and addressed her in the accents of sympathy. She raised her head and gazed wildly at him. What was his astonishment at beholding, by the bright glare of the lightning, the very face which had haunted him in his dreams. It was pale and disconsolate, but ravishingly beautiful.

Trembling with violent and conflicting emotions, Wolfgang again accosted her. He spoke something of her being exposed at such an hour of the night, and to the fury of such a storm, and offered to conduct her to her friends. She pointed to the guillotine with a gesture of dreadful signification.

"I have no friend on earth!" said she.

"But you have a home," said Wolfgang.

"Yes—in the grave!"

The heart of the student melted at the words.

"If a stranger dare make an offer," said he, "without danger of being misunderstood, I would offer my humble dwelling as a shelter; myself as a devoted friend. I am friendless myself in Paris, and a stranger in the land; but if my life could be of service, it is at your disposal, and should be sacrificed before harm or indignity should come to you."

There was an honest earnestness in the young man's manner that had its effect. His foreign accent, too, was in his favor; it showed him not to be a hackneyed inhabitant of Paris. Indeed, there is an eloquence in true enthusiasm that is not to be doubted. The homeless stranger confided herself implicitly to the protection of the student.

He supported her faltering steps across the Pont Neuf, and by the place where the statue of Henry the Fourth had been overthrown by the populace. The storm had abated, and the thunder rumbled at a distance. All Paris was quiet; that great volcano of human passion slumbered for a while, to gather fresh strength for the next day's eruption. The student conducted his charge through the ancient streets of the *Pays Latin,* and by the dusky walls of the Sorbonne, to the great dingy hotel which he inhabited. The old portress who admitted them stared with surprise at the unusual sight of the melancholy Wolfgang with a female companion.

On entering his apartment, the student, for the first time, blushed at the scantiness and indifference of his dwelling. He had but one chamber—an old-fashioned saloon—heavily carved, and fantastically furnished with the remains of former magnificence, for it was one of those hotels in the quarter of the Luxembourg palace, which had once belonged to nobility. It was lumbered with books and papers, and all the usual apparatus of a student, and his bed stood in a recess at one end.

When lights were brought, and Wolfgang had a better opportunity of contemplating the stranger, he was more than ever intoxicated by her beauty. Her face was pale, but of a dazzling fairness, set off by a profusion of raven hair that hung clustering about it. Her eyes were large and brilliant, with a singular expression approaching almost to wildness. As far as her black dress permitted her shape to be seen, it was of perfect symmetry. Her whole appearance was highly striking, though she was dressed in the simplest style. The only thing approaching to an ornament which she wore, was a broad black band round her neck, clasped by diamonds.

The perplexity now commenced with the student how to dispose of the helpless being thus thrown upon his protection. He thought of abandoning his chamber to her, and seeking shelter for himself elsewhere. Still he was so fascinated by her charms, there seemed to be such a spell upon his thoughts and senses, that he could not tear himself from her presence. Her manner, too, was singular and unaccountable. She spoke no more of the guillotine. Her grief had abated. The attentions of the student had first won her confidence, and then, apparently, her heart. She was evidently an enthusiast like himself, and enthusiasts soon understand each other.

In the infatuation of the moment, Wolfgang avowed his passion for her. He told her the story of his mysterious dream, and how she had possessed his heart before he had even seen her. She was strangely affected by his recital, and acknowledged to have felt an impulse towards him equally unaccountable. It was the time for wild theory and wild actions. Old prejudices and superstitions were done away; every thing was under the sway of the "Goddess of Reason." Among other rubbish of the old times, the forms and ceremonies of marriage began to be considered superfluous bonds for honorable minds. Social compacts were the vogue. Wolfgang was too much of a theorist not to be tainted by the liberal doctrines of the day.

"Why should we separate?" said he: "our hearts are united; in the eye of reason and honor we are as one. What need is there of sordid forms to bind high souls together?"

The stranger listened with emotion: she had evidently received illumination at the same school.

"You have no home nor family," continued he; "let me be every thing to you, or rather let us be every thing to one another. If form is necessary, form shall be observed—there is my hand. I pledge myself to you for ever."

"For ever?" said the stranger, solemnly.

"For ever!" repeated Wolfgang.

The stranger clasped the hand extended to her: "then I am yours," murmured she, and sank upon his bosom.

The next morning the student left his bride sleeping, and sallied forth at an early hour to seek more spacious apartments suitable to the change in his situation. When he returned, he found the stranger lying with her head hanging over the bed, and one arm thrown over it. He spoke to her, but received no reply. He advanced to awaken her from her uneasy posture. On taking her hand, it was cold—there was no pulsation—her face was pallid and ghastly.—In a word she was a corpse.

Horrified and frantic, he alarmed the house. A scene of confusion ensued. The police was summoned. As the officer of police entered the room, he started back on beholding the corpse.

"Great heaven!" cried he, "how did this woman come here?"

"Do you know any thing about her?" said Wolfgang eagerly.

"Do I?" exclaimed the officer: "she was guillotined yesterday."

He stepped forward; undid the black collar round the neck of the corpse, and the head rolled on the floor!

The student burst into a frenzy. "The fiend! the fiend has gained possession of me!" shrieked he: "I am lost for ever."

They tried to soothe him, but in vain. He was possessed with the frightful belief that an evil spirit had reanimated the dead body to ensnare him. He went distracted, and died in a mad-house.

Here the old gentleman with the haunted head finished his narrative.

"And is this really a fact?" said the inquisitive gentleman.

"A fact not to be doubted," replied the other. "I had it from the best authority. The student told it to me himself. I saw him in a mad-house in Paris."

Nathaniel Hawthorne

WHERE IRVING found half-humorous legend in his country's past, Hawthorne found the struggle between good and evil within the Puritan soul. His sombre genius needed the novel for its fullest range, but in his Twice-Told Tales (1837, 1842) he advanced the short story so far that Poe, reviewing his accomplishment, announced its theory. Hawthorne's Note-Books, filled with story ideas, show that his imagination was usually set at work by some intense moral situation which he would clothe in plot and character. He eschewed Irving's diffusiveness; when his tales succeeded, they glowed with a steady concentrated fire. "Mr. Higginbotham's Catastrophe" is evidence that not all of his stories are morality tales, that he had, among other qualities, a quizzical appreciation of Yankee eccentricities.

Hawthorne was born in Salem, Massachusetts, in 1804, graduated from Bowdoin with Longfellow, then spent twelve solitary years at home in Salem attempting to perfect his writing. "I have seen so little of the world," he wrote to Longfellow, "that I have nothing but thin air to concoct my stories of. . . ." But he was building better than he knew. His first publications were his stories and sketches; then with the middle of the century came his great romances, The Scarlet Letter and The House of the Seven Gables. Like Irving, he knew Europe well. He died at Plymouth, New Hampshire, in 1864 with three of his romances left incomplete.

MR. HIGGINBOTHAM'S CATASTROPHE *

Nathaniel Hawthorne

A YOUNG FELLOW, a tobacco peddler by trade, was on his way from Morristown, where he had dealt largely with the Deacon of the Shaker settlement, to the village of Parker's Falls, on Salmon River. He had a neat little cart, painted green, with a box of cigars depicted on each side panel, and an Indian chief, holding a pipe and a golden tobacco stalk, on the rear. The peddler drove a smart little mare, and was a young man of excellent character, keen at a bargain, but none the worse liked by the Yankees; who, as I have heard them say, would rather be shaved with a sharp razor than a dull one. Especially was he beloved by the pretty girls along the Connecticut, whose favor he used to court by presents of the best smoking tobacco in his stock; knowing well that the country lasses of New England are generally great performers on pipes. Moreover, as will be seen in the course of my story, the peddler was inquisitive, and something of a tattler, always itching to hear the news and anxious to tell it again.

After an early breakfast at Morristown, the tobacco peddler, whose name was Dominicus Pike, had traveled seven miles through a solitary piece of woods, without speaking a word to anybody but himself and his little gray mare. It being nearly seven o'clock, he was as eager to hold a morning gossip as a city shopkeeper to read the morning paper. An opportunity seemed at hand when, after lighting a cigar with a sun-glass, he looked up, and perceived a man coming over the brow of the hill, at the foot of which the peddler had stopped his green cart. Dominicus watched him as he descended, and noticed that he carried a bundle over his shoulder on the end of a stick, and traveled with a weary, yet determined pace. He did not look as if he had started in the freshness of the morning, but had footed it all night, and meant to do the same all day.

"Good morning, mister," said Dominicus, when within speaking distance. "You go a pretty good jog. What's the latest news at Parker's Falls?"

The man pulled the broad brim of a gray hat over his eyes, and answered, rather suddenly, that he did not come from Parker's Falls,

* From *Twice-Told Tales* by Nathaniel Hawthorne, second series, 1842. First printed anonymously in *The New England Magazine,* December, 1834. Reprinted by courtesy of the Houghton Mifflin Company.

which, as being the limit of his own day's journey, the peddler had naturally mentioned in his inquiry.

"Well then," rejoined Dominicus Pike, "let's have the latest news where you did come from. I'm not particular about Parker's Falls. Any place will answer."

Being thus importuned, the traveler—who was as ill looking a fellow as one would desire to meet in a solitary piece of woods—appeared to hesitate a little, as if he was either searching his memory for news, or weighing the expediency of telling it. At last, mounting on the step of the cart, he whispered in the ear of Dominicus, though he might have shouted aloud and no other mortal would have heard him.

"I do remember one little trifle of news," said he. "Old Mr. Higginbotham, of Kimballton, was murdered in his orchard, at eight o'clock last night, by an Irishman and a nigger. They strung him up to the branch of a St. Michael's pear-tree, where nobody would find him till the morning."

As soon as this horrible intelligence was communicated, the stranger betook himself to his journey again, with more speed than ever, not even turning his head when Dominicus invited him to smoke a Spanish cigar and relate all the particulars. The peddler whistled to his mare and went up the hill, pondering on the doleful fate of Mr. Higginbotham whom he had known in the way of trade, having sold him many a bunch of long nines, and a great deal of pigtail, lady's twist, and fig tobacco. He was rather astonished at the rapidity with which the news had spread. Kimballton was nearly sixty miles distant in a straight line; the murder had been perpetrated only at eight o'clock the preceding night; yet Dominicus had heard of it at seven in the morning, when, in all probability, poor Mr. Higginbotham's own family had but just discovered his corpse, hanging on the St. Michael's pear-tree. The stranger on foot must have worn seven-league boots to travel at such a rate.

"Ill news flies fast, they say," thought Dominicus Pike; "but this beats railroads. The fellow ought to be hired to go express with the President's Message."

The difficulty was solved by supposing that the narrator had made a mistake of one day in the date of the occurrence; so that our friend did not hesitate to introduce the story at every tavern and country store along the road, expending a whole bunch of Spanish wrappers among at least twenty horrified audiences. He found himself invariably the first bearer of the intelligence, and was so pestered with questions that he could not avoid filling up the outline, till it became quite a respectable narrative. He met with one piece of corroborative evidence. Mr. Higginbotham was a trader; and a former clerk of his, to whom Dominicus related the facts, testified that the old gentleman was accustomed to return home through the orchard about nightfall, with the money and valuable papers of the store in his pocket. The clerk manifested but little grief at Mr. Higginbotham's catastrophe, hinting, what the peddler had discovered in his own dealings with him, that he was a crusty old fellow, as close as a vice. His property would descend to a pretty niece who was now keeping school in Kimballton.

What with telling the news for the public good, and driving bargains for his own, Dominicus was so much delayed on the road that he chose to put up at a tavern, about five miles short of Parker's Falls. After supper, lighting one of his prime cigars, he seated himself in the bar-room, and went through the story of the murder, which had grown so fast that it took him half an hour to tell. There were as many as twenty people in the room, nineteen of whom received it all for gospel. But the twentieth was an elderly farmer, who had arrived on horseback a short time before, and was now seated in a corner smoking his pipe. When the story was concluded, he rose up very deliberately, brought his chair right in front of Dominicus, and stared him full in the face, puffing out the vilest tobacco smoke the peddler had ever smelt.

"Will you make affidavit," demanded he, in the tone of a country justice taking an examination, "that old Squire Higginbotham of Kimballton was murdered in his orchard the night before last, and found hanging on his great pear-tree yesterday morning?"

"I tell the story as I heard it, mister," answered Dominicus, dropping his half-burnt cigar; "I don't say that I saw the thing done. So I can't take my oath that he was murdered exactly in that way."

"But I can take mine," said the farmer, "that if Squire Higginbotham was murdered night before last, I drank a glass of bitters with his ghost this morning. Being a neighbor of mine, he called me into his store, as I was riding by, and treated me, and then asked me to do a little business for him on the road. He didn't seem to know any more about his own murder than I did."

"Why, then, it can't be a fact!" exclaimed Dominicus Pike.

"I guess he'd have mentioned, if it was," said the old farmer; and he removed his chair back to the corner, leaving Dominicus quite down in the mouth.

Here was a sad resurrection of old Mr. Higginbotham! The peddler had no heart to mingle in the conversation any more, but comforted himself with a glass of gin and water, and went to bed where, all night long, he dreamed of hanging on the St. Michael's pear-tree. To avoid the old farmer (whom he so detested that his suspension would have pleased him better than Mr. Higginbotham's), Dominicus rose in the gray of the morning, put the little mare into the green cart, and trotted swiftly away towards Parker's Falls. The fresh breeze, the dewy road, and the pleasant summer dawn, revived his spirits, and might have encouraged him to repeat the old story had there been anybody awake to hear it. But he met neither ox team, light wagon chaise, horseman, nor foot traveler, till, just as he crossed Salmon River, a man came trudging down to the bridge with a bundle over his shoulder, on the end of a stick.

"Good morning, mister," said the peddler, reining in his mare. "If you come from Kimballton or that neighborhood, may be you can tell me the real fact about this affair of old Mr. Higginbotham. Was the old fellow actually murdered two or three nights ago, by an Irishman and a nigger?"

Dominicus had spoken in too great a hurry to observe, at first, that the stranger himself had a deep tinge of negro blood. On hearing this sudden question, the Ethiopian appeared to change his skin, its yellow hue becoming a ghastly white, while, shaking and stammering, he thus replied:—

"No! no! There was no colored man! It was an Irishman that hanged him last night, at eight o'clock. I came away at seven! His folks can't have looked for him in the orchard yet."

Scarcely had the yellow man spoken, when he interrupted himself, and though he seemed weary enough before, continued his journey at a pace which would have kept the peddler's mare on a smart trot. Dominicus started after him in great perplexity. If the murder had not been committed till Tuesday night, who was the prophet that had foretold it, in all its circumstances, on Tuesday morning? If Mr. Higginbotham's corpse were not yet discovered by his own family, how came the mulatto, at above thirty miles' distance, to know that he was hanging in the orchard, especially as he had left Kimballton before the unfortunate man was hanged at all? These ambiguous circumstances, with the stranger's surprise and terror, made Dominicus think of raising a hue and cry after him, as an accomplice in the murder; since a murder, it seemed, had really been perpetrated.

"But let the poor devil go," thought the peddler. "I don't want his black blood on my head; and hanging the nigger wouldn't unhang Mr. Higginbotham. Unhang the old gentleman! It's a sin, I know; but I should hate to have him come to life a second time, and give me the lie!"

With these meditations, Dominicus Pike drove into the street of Parker's Falls, which, as everybody knows, is as thriving a village as three cotton factories and a slitting mill can make it. The machinery was not in motion, and but a few of the shop doors unbarred, when he alighted in the stable yard of the tavern, and made it his first business to order the mare four quarts of oats. His second duty, of course, was to impart Mr. Higginbotham's catastrophe to the hostler. He deemed it advisable, however, not to be too positive as to the date of the direful fact, and also to be uncertain whether it were perpetrated by an Irishman and a mulatto, or by the son of Erin alone. Neither did he profess to relate it on his own authority, or that of any one person; but mentioned it as a report generally diffused.

The story ran through the town like fire among girdled trees, and became so much the universal talk that nobody could tell whence it had originated. Mr. Higginbotham was as well known at Parker's Falls as any citizen of the place, being part owner of the slitting mill, and a considerable stockholder in the cotton factories. The inhabitants felt their own prosperity interested in his fate. Such was the excitement, that the Parker's Falls Gazette anticipated its regular day of publication, and came out with half a form of blank paper and a column of double pica emphasized with capitals, and headed HORRID MURDER OF MR. HIGGINBOTHAM! Among other dreadful details, the printed account described the mark of the cord round the dead man's neck, and stated the number of thousand dollars of which he had been robbed; there was much pathos also about the affliction of his niece, who had gone from one fainting fit to another, ever since her uncle was found hanging on the St. Michael's pear-tree with his pockets inside out. The village poet likewise commemorated the young lady's grief in seventeen stanzas of a ballad. The selectmen held a meeting, and, in consideration of Mr. Higginbotham's claims on the town, determined to issue handbills, offering a reward of five hundred dollars for the apprehension of his murderers, and the recovery of the stolen property.

Meanwhile the whole population of Parker's Falls, consisting of shopkeepers, mistresses of boarding-houses, factory girls, millmen, and school boys, rushed into the street and kept up such a terrible loquacity as more than compensated for the silence of the cotton machines, which refrained from their usual din out of respect to the deceased. Had Mr. Higginbotham cared about posthumous renown, his untimely ghost would have exulted in this tumult. Our friend Dominicus, in his vanity of heart, forgot his intended precautions, and mounting on the town pump, announced himself as the bearer of the authentic intelligence which had caused so wonderful a sensation. He immediately became the great man of the moment, and had just begun a new edition of the narrative, with a voice like a field preacher, when the mail stage drove into the village street. It had traveled all night, and must have shifted horses at Kimballton, at three in the morning.

"Now we shall hear all the particulars," shouted the crowd.

The coach rumbled up to the piazza of the tavern, followed by a thousand people; for if any man had been minding his own business till then, he now left it at sixes and sevens, to hear the news. The peddler, foremost in the race, discovered two passengers, both of whom had been startled from a comfortable nap to find themselves in the center of a mob. Every man assailing them with separate questions, all propounded at once, the couple were struck speechless, though one was a lawyer and the other a young lady.

"Mr. Higginbotham! Mr. Higginbotham! Tell us the particulars about old Mr. Higginbotham!" bawled the mob. "What is the coroner's verdict? Are the murderers apprehended? Is Mr. Higginbotham's niece come out of her fainting fits? Mr. Higginbotham! Mr. Higginbotham!"

The coachman said not a word, except to swear awfully at the hostler for not bringing him a fresh team of horses. The lawyer inside had generally his wits about him even when asleep; the first thing he did, after learning the cause of the excitement, was to produce a large, red pocket-book. Meantime Dominicus Pike, being an extremely polite young man, and also suspecting that a female tongue would tell the story as glibly as a lawyer's, had handed the lady out of the coach. She was a fine, smart girl, now wide awake and bright as a button, and had such a sweet pretty mouth, that Dominicus would almost as lief have heard a love tale from it as a tale of murder.

"Gentlemen, and ladies," said the lawyer to the shopkeepers, the millmen, and the factory girls, "I can assure you that some unaccountable mistake, or, more probably, a willful falsehood, maliciously contrived to injure Mr. Higginbotham's credit, has excited this singular uproar. We passed through Kimballton at three o'clock this morning, and most certainly should have been informed of the murder had any been perpetrated. But I have proof nearly as strong as Mr. Higginbotham's own oral testimony, in the negative. Here is a note relating to a suit of his in the Connecticut courts, which was delivered me from that gentleman himself. I find it dated at ten o'clock last evening."

So saying, the lawyer exhibited the date and signature of the note, which irrefragably proved, either that this perverse Mr. Higginbotham was alive when he wrote it, or—as some deemed the more probable case, of two doubtful ones—that he was so absorbed in worldly business as to continue to transact it even after his death. But unexpected evidence was forthcoming. The young lady, after listening to the peddler's explanation, merely seized a moment to smooth her gown and put her curls in order, and then appeared at the tavern door, making a modest signal to be heard.

"Good people," said she, "I am Mr. Higginbotham's niece."

A wondering murmer passed through the crowd on beholding her so rosy and bright; that same unhappy niece, whom they had supposed, on the authority of the Parker's Falls Gazette, to be lying at death's door in a fainting fit. But some shrewd fellows had doubted, all along, whether a young lady would be quite so desperate at the hanging of a rich old uncle.

"You see," continued Miss Higginbotham, with a smile, "that this strange story is quite unfounded as to myself; and I believe I may affirm it to be equally so in regard to my dear uncle Higginbotham. He has the kindness to give me a home in his house, though I contribute to my support by teaching a school. I left Kimballton this morning to spend the vacation of commencement week with a friend, about five miles from Parker's Falls. My generous uncle, when he heard me on the stairs, called me to his bedside, and gave me two dollars and fifty cents to pay my stage fare, and another dollar for my extra expenses. He then laid his pocket-book under his pillow, shook hands with me, and advised me to take some biscuit in my bag, instead of breakfasting on the road. I feel confident, therefore, that I left my beloved relative alive, and trust that I shall find him so on my return."

The young lady courtesied at the close of her speech, which was so sensible and well worded, and delivered with such grace, and propriety, that everybody thought her fit to be preceptress of the best academy in the State. But a stranger would have supposed that Mr. Higginbotham was an object of abhorrence at Parker's Falls, and that a thanksgiving had been proclaimed for his murder; so excessive was the wrath of the inhabitants on learning their mistake. The millmen resolved to bestow public honors on Dominicus Pike, only hesitating whether to tar and feather him, ride him on a rail, or refresh him with an ablution at the town pump, on the top of which he had declared himself the bearer of the news. The selectmen, by advice of the lawyer, spoke of prosecuting him for a misdemeanor, in circulating unfounded reports, to the great disturbance of the peace of the Commonwealth. Nothing saved Dominicus, either from mob law or a court of justice, but an eloquent appeal made by the young lady in his behalf. Addressing a few words of heartfelt gratitude to his benefactress, he mounted the green cart and rode out of town, under a discharge of artillery from the schoolboys, who found plenty of ammunition in the neighboring clay-pits and mudholes. As he turned his head to exchange a farewell glance with Mr. Higginbotham's niece, a ball, of the consistence of hasty pudding, hit him slap in the mouth, giving him a most grim aspect. His whole person was so bespattered with the like filthy missiles, that he had almost a mind to ride back, and supplicate for the threatened ablution at the town pump; for, though not meant in kindness, it would now have been a deed of charity.

However, the sun shone bright on poor Dominicus, and the mud, an emblem of all stains of undeserved opprobrium, was easily brushed off when dry. Being a funny rogue, his heart soon cheered up; nor could he refrain from a hearty laugh at the uproar which his story had excited. The handbills of the selectmen would cause the commitment of all the vagabonds in the State; the paragraph in the Parker's Falls Gazette would be reprinted from Maine to Florida, and perhaps form an item in the London newspapers; and many a miser would tremble for his money bags and life, on learning the catastrophe of Mr. Higginbotham. The peddler meditated with much fervor on the charms of the young schoolmistress, and swore that Daniel Webster never spoke nor looked so like an angel as Miss Higginbotham, while defending him from the wrathful populace at Parker's Falls.

Dominicus was now on the Kimballton turnpike, having all along determined to visit that place, though business had drawn him out of the most direct road from Morristown. As he approached the scene of the supposed murder, he continued to revolve the circumstances in his mind, and was astonished at the aspect which the whole case assumed. Had nothing occurred to corroborate the story of the first traveler, it might now have been considered as a hoax; but the yellow man was evidently acquainted either with the report or the fact; and there was a mystery in his dismayed and guilty look on being abruptly questioned. When, to this singular combination of incidents, it was added that the rumor tallied exactly with Mr. Higginbotham's character and habits of life; and that he had an orchard, and a St. Michael's pear-tree, near which he always passed at nightfall: the circumstantial evidence appeared so strong that Dominicus doubted whether the autograph produced by the lawyer, or even the niece's direct testimony, ought to be equivalent. Making cautious inquiries along the road, the peddler further learned that Mr. Higginbotham had in his service an Irishman of doubtful character, whom he had hired without a recommendation, on the score of economy.

"May I be hanged myself," exclaimed Dominicus Pike aloud, on reaching the top of a lonely hill, "if I'll believe old Higginbotham is unhanged till I see him with my own eyes, and hear it from his own mouth! And as he's a real shaver, I'll have the minister or some other responsible man for an indorser."

It was growing dusk when he reached the toll-house on Kimballton turnpike, about a quarter of a mile from the village of this name. His little mare was fast bringing him up with a man on horseback, who trotted through the gate a few rods in advance of him, nodded to the toll-gatherer, and kept on towards the village. Dominicus was acquainted with the tollman, and, while making change, the usual remarks on the weather passed between them.

"I suppose," said the peddler, throwing back his whiplash, to bring it down like a feather on the mare's flank, "you have not seen anything of old Mr. Higginbotham within a day or two?"

"Yes," answered the toll-gatherer. "He passed the gate just before you drove up, and yonder he rides now, if you can see him through the dusk. He's been to Woodfield this afternoon, attending a sheriff's sale there. The old man generally shakes hands and has a little chat with me; but to-night, he nodded,—as if to say, 'Charge my toll,' and jogged on; for wherever he goes, he must always be at home by eight o'clock."

"So they tell me," said Dominicus.

"I never saw a man look so yellow and thin as the squire does," continued the toll-gatherer. "Says I to myself, to-night, he's more like a ghost or an old mummy than good flesh and blood."

The peddler strained his eyes through the twilight, and could just discern the horseman now far ahead on the village road. He seemed to recognize the rear of Mr. Higginbotham; but through the evening shadows, and amid the dust from the horse's feet, the figure appeared dim and unsubstantial; as if the shape of the mysterious old man were faintly molded of darkness and gray light. Dominicus shivered.

"Mr. Higginbotham has come back from the other world, by way of the Kimballton turnpike," thought he.

He shook the reins and rode forward, keeping about the same distance in the rear of the gray old shadow, till the latter was concealed by a bend of the road. On reaching this point, the peddler no longer saw the man on horseback, but found himself at the head of the village street, not far from a number of stores and two taverns, clustered round the meeting-house steeple. On his left were a stone wall and a gate, the boundary of a wood-lot, beyond which lay an orchard, farther still, a mowing field, and last of all, a house. These were the premises of Mr. Higginbotham, whose dwelling stood beside the old highway, but had been left in the background by the Kimballton turnpike. Dominicus knew the place; and the little mare stopped short by instinct; for he was not conscious of tightening the reins.

"For the soul of me, I cannot get by this gate!" said he, trembling. "I never shall be my own man again, till I see whether Mr. Higginbotham is hanging on the St. Michael's pear-tree!"

He leaped from the cart, gave the rein a turn round the gate post, and ran along the green path of the wood-lot as if Old Nick were chasing behind. Just then the village clock tolled eight, and as each deep stroke fell, Dominicus gave a fresh bound and flew faster than before, till dim in the solitary centre of the orchard, he saw the fated pear-tree. One great branch stretched from the old contorted trunk across the path, and threw the darkest shadow on that one spot. But something seemed to struggle beneath the branch!

The peddler had never pretended to more courage than befits a man of peaceable occupation, nor could he account for his valor on this awful emergency. Certain it is, however, that he rushed forward, prostrated a sturdy Irishman with the butt end of his whip, and found—not indeed hanging on the St. Michael's pear-tree, but trembling beneath it, with a halter round his neck—the old, identical Mr. Higginbotham!

"Mr. Higginbotham," said Dominicus tremulously, "you're an honest man, and I'll take your word for it. Have you been hanged or not?"

If the riddle be not already guessed, a few words will explain the simple machinery by which this "coming event" was made to "cast its

shadow before." Three men had plotted the robbery and murder of
Mr. Higginbotham; two of them, successively, lost courage and fled,
each delaying the crime one night by their disappearance; the third
was in the act of perpetration, when a champion, blindly obeying the
call of fate, like the heroes of old romance, appeared in the person of
Dominicus Pike.

It only remains to say, that Mr. Higginbotham took the peddler
into high favor, sanctioned his addresses to the pretty schoolmistress,
and settled his whole property on their children, allowing themselves
the interest. In due time, the old gentleman capped the climax of his
favors, by dying a Christian death, in bed, since which melancholy
event Dominicus Pike has removed from Kimballton, and established
a large tobacco manufactory in my native village.

Edgar Allan Poe

EDGAR ALLAN POE was born in Boston in 1809, but is associated with the literature of the South. When he died in Baltimore in 1849, he had established his genius in three fields: poetry, criticism, and the short story.

Although he regarded "Ligeia" as his greatest story, other critics have named other stories for this honor—for example, "The Fall of the House of Usher," "The Pit and the Pendulum," "The Purloined Letter" or "The Cask of Amontillado." The variety of choice is in itself a tribute. In all of his stories Poe sought for the one intense impression, the one overwhelming effect of beauty or terror or analytic power.

He is the great master of the contrived story. He deals always with the exceptional, and fundamentally he interpreted no human character but himself. Nevertheless the springs of the motives in his stories reside in all human hearts, and few can be unresponsive to his strange words: "Nor was I indeed ignorant of the flowers and the vine, but the hemlock and the cypress overshadowed me night and day."

THE CASK OF AMONTILLADO *
Edgar Allan Poe

THE THOUSAND injuries of Fortunato I had borne as I best could, but when he ventured upon insult I vowed revenge. You, who so well know the nature of my soul, will not suppose, however, that I gave utterance to a threat. *At length* I would be avenged; this was a point definitely settled—but the very definitiveness with which it was resolved precluded the idea of risk. I must not only punish but punish

* From *Tales of Mystery and Imagination* by Edgar Allan Poe. First published in *Godey's Lady's Book,* November, 1846.

with impunity. A wrong is unredressed when retribution overtakes its redresser. It is equally unredressed when the avenger fails to make himself felt as such to him who has done the wrong.

It must be understood that neither by word nor deed had I given Fortunato cause to doubt my good will. I continued, as was my wont, to smile in his face, and he did not perceive that my smile *now* was at the thought of his immolation.

He had a weak point—this Fortunato—although in other regards he was a man to be respected and even feared. He prided himself on his connoisseurship in wine. Few Italians have the true virtuoso spirit. For the most part their enthusiasm is adopted to suit the time and opportunity, to practise imposture upon the British and Austrian *millionaires*. In painting and gemmary, Fortunato, like his countrymen, was a quack, but in the matter of old wines he was sincere. In this respect I did not differ from him materially;—I was skillful in the Italian vintages myself, and bought largely whenever I could.

It was about dusk, one evening during the supreme madness of the carnival season, that I encountered my friend. He accosted me with excessive warmth, for he had been drinking much. The man wore motley. He had on a tight-fitting parti-striped dress, and his head was surmounted by the conical cap and bells. I was so pleased to see him that I thought I should never have done wringing his hand.

I said to him—"My dear Fortunato, you are luckily met. How remarkably well you are looking to-day. But I have received a pipe of what passes for Amontillado, and I have my doubts."

"How?" said he. "Amontillado? A pipe? Impossible! And in the middle of the carnival!"

"I have my doubts," I replied; "and I was silly enough to pay the full Amontillado price without consulting you in the matter. You were not to be found, and I was fearful of losing a bargain."

"Amontillado!"

"I have my doubts."

"Amontillado!"

"And I must satisfy them."

"Amontillado!"

"As you are engaged, I am on my way to Luchresi. If any one has a critical turn it is he. He will tell me—"

"Luchresi cannot tell Amontillado from Sherry."

"And yet some fools will have it that his taste is a match for your own."

"Come, let us go."

"Whither?"

"To your vaults."

"My friend, no; I will not impose upon your good nature. I perceive you have an engagement. Luchresi—"

"I have no engagement;—come."

"My friend, no. It is not the engagement, but the severe cold with which I perceive you are afflicted. The vaults are insufferably damp. They are encrusted with nitre."

"Let us go, nevertheless. The cold is merely nothing. Amontillado! You have been imposed upon. And as for Luchresi, he cannot distinguish Sherry from Amontillado."

Thus speaking, Fortunato possessed himself of my arm; and putting on a mask of black silk and drawing a *roquelaure* closely about my person, I suffered him to hurry me to my palazzo.

There were no attendants at home; they had absconded to make merry in honour of the time. I had told them that I should not return until the morning, and had given them explicit orders not to stir from the house. These orders were sufficient, I well knew, to insure their immediate disappearance, one and all, as soon as my back was turned.

I took from their sconces two flambeaux, and giving one to Fortunato, bowed him through several suites of rooms to the archway that led into the vaults. I passed down a long and winding staircase, requesting him to be cautious as he followed. We came at length to the foot of the descent, and stood together upon the damp ground of the catacombs of the Montresors.

The gait of my friend was unsteady, and the bells upon his cap jingled as he strode.

"The pipe," he said.

"It is farther on," said I; "but observe the white web-work which gleams from these cavern walls."

He turned towards me, and looked into my eyes with two filmy orbs that distilled the rheum of intoxication.

"Nitre?" he asked, at length.

"Nitre," I replied. "How long have you had that cough?"

"Ugh! ugh! ugh!—ugh! ugh! ugh!—ugh! ugh! ugh!—ugh! ugh! ugh!—ugh! ugh! ugh!"

My poor friend found it impossible to reply for many minutes.

"It is nothing," he said, at last.

"Come," I said, with decision, "we will go back; your health is precious. You are rich, respected, admired, beloved; you are happy, as once I was. You are a man to be missed. For me it is no matter. We will go back; you will be ill, and I cannot be responsible. Besides, there is Luchresi—"

"Enough," he said; "the cough is a mere nothing; it will not kill me. I shall not die of a cough."

"True—true," I replied; "and, indeed, I had no intention of alarming you unnecessarily—but you should use all proper caution. A draught of this Medoc will defend us from the damps."

Here I knocked off the neck of a bottle which I drew from a long row of its fellows that lay upon the mould.

"Drink," I said, presenting him the wine.

He raised it to his lips with a leer. He paused and nodded to me familiarly, while his bells jingled.

"I drink," he said, "to the buried that repose around us."

"And I to your long life."

He again took my arm, and we proceeded.

"These vaults," he said, "are extensive."

"The Montresors," I replied, "were a great and numerous family."

"I forget your arms."

"A huge human foot d'or, in a field azure; the foot crushes a serpent rampant whose fangs are imbedded in the heel."

"And the motto?"

"Nemo me impune lacessit."

"Good!" he said.

The wine sparkled in his eyes and the bells jingled. My own fancy grew warm with the Medoc. We had passed through long walls of piled skeletons, with casks and puncheons intermingling, into the inmost recesses of catacombs. I paused again, and this time I made bold to seize Fortunato by an arm above the elbow.

"The nitre!" I said; "see, it increases. It hangs like moss upon the vaults. We are below the river's bed. The drops of moisture trickle among the bones. Come, we will go back ere it is too late. Your cough—"

"It is nothing," he said; "let us go on. But first, another draught of the Medoc."

I broke and reached him a flagon of De Grâve. He emptied it at a breath. His eyes flashed with a fierce light. He laughed and threw the bottle upwards with a gesticulation I did not understand.

I looked at him in surprise. He repeated the movement—a grotesque one.

"You do not comprehend?" he said.

"Not I," I replied.

"Then you are not of the brotherhood."

"How?"

"You are not of the masons."

"Yes, yes," I said; "yes, yes."

"You? Impossible! A mason?"

"A mason," I replied.

"A sign," he said, "a sign."

"It is this," I answered, producing from beneath the folds of my *roquelaure* a trowel.

"You jest," he exclaimed, recoiling a few paces. "But let us proceed to the Amontillado."

"Be it so," I said, replacing the tool beneath the cloak and again offering my arm. He leaned upon it heavily. We continued our route in search of the Amontillado. We passed through a range of low arches, descended, passed on, and descending again, arrived at a deep crypt, in which the foulness of the air caused our flambeaux rather to glow than flame.

At the most remote end of the crypt there appeared another less spacious. Its walls had been lined with human remains, piled to the vault overhead, in the fashion of the great catacombs of Paris. Three sides of this interior crypt were still ornamented in this manner. From the fourth side the bones had been thrown down, and lay promiscuously upon the earth, forming at one point a mound of some size. Within the wall thus exposed by the displacing of the bones, we perceived a still interior crypt or recess, in depth about four feet, in width three, in height six or seven. It seemed to have been constructed for no especial use within itself, but formed merely the interval between two of the colossal supports of the roof of the catacombs, and was backed by one of their circumscribing walls of solid granite.

It was in vain that Fortunato, uplifting his dull torch, endeavoured to pry into the depth of the recess. Its termination the feeble light did not enable us to see.

"Proceed," I said; "herein is the Amontillado. As for Luchresi—"

"He is an ignoramus," interrupted my friend, as he stepped unsteadily forward, while I followed immediately at his heels. In an instant he had reached the extremity of the niche, and finding his progress arrested by the rock, stood stupidly bewildered. A moment more and I had fettered him to the granite. In its surface were two iron staples, distant from each other about two feet, horizontally. From one of these depended a short chain, from the other a padlock. Throwing the links about his waist, it was but the work of a few seconds to secure it. He was too much astounded to resist. Withdrawing the key I stepped back from the recess.

"Pass your hand," I said, "over the wall; you cannot help feeling the nitre. Indeed, it is *very* damp. Once more let me *implore* you to return. No? Then I must positively leave you. But I must first render you all the little attentions in my power."

"The Amontillado!" ejaculated my friend, not yet recovered from his astonishment.

"True," I replied; "the Amontillado."

As I said these words I busied myself among the pile of bones of which I have before spoken. Throwing them aside, I soon uncovered a quantity of building stone and mortar. With these materials and with the aid of my trowel, I began vigorously to wall up the entrance of the niche.

I had scarcely laid the first tier of the masonry when I discovered that the intoxication of Fortunato had in a great measure worn off. The earliest indication I had of this was a low moaning cry from the depth of the recess. It was *not* the cry of a drunken man. There was then a long and obstinate silence. I laid the second tier, and the third, and the fourth; and then I heard the furious vibrations of the chain. The noise lasted for several minutes, during which, that I might hearken to it with more satisfaction, I ceased my labours and sat down upon the bones. When at last the clanking subsided, I resumed the trowel, and finished without interruption the fifth, the sixth, and the seventh tier. The wall was now nearly upon a level with my breast. I again paused, and holding the flambeaux over the mason-work, threw a few feeble rays upon the figure within.

A succession of loud and shrill screams, bursting suddenly from the throat of the chained form, seemed to thrust me violently back. For a brief moment I hesitated, I trembled. Unsheathing my rapier, I began to grope with it about the recess; but the thought of an instant reassured me. I placed my hand upon the solid fabric of the catacombs, and felt satisfied. I reapproached the wall; I replied to the yells of him who clamoured. I re-echoed, I aided, I surpassed them in volume and in strength. I did this, and the clamourer grew still.

It was now midnight, and my task was drawing to a close. I had completed the eighth, the ninth, and the tenth tier. I had finished a portion of the last and the eleventh; there remained but a single stone to be fitted and plastered in. I struggled with its weight; I placed it partially in its destined position. But now there came from out the niche a low laugh that erected the hairs upon my head. It was succeeded by a sad voice, which I had difficulty in recognising as that of the noble Fortunato. The voice said—

"Ha! ha! ha!—he! he! he!—a very good joke, indeed—an excellent jest. We shall have many a rich laugh about it at the palazzo—he! he! he!—over our wine—he! he! he!"

"The Amontillado!" I said.

"He! he! he!—he! he! he!—yes, the Amontillado. But is it not getting late? Will not they be awaiting us at the palazzo, the Lady Fortunato and the rest? Let us be gone."

"Yes," I said, "let us be gone."

"For the love of God, Montresor!"

"Yes," I said, "for the love of God!"

But to these words I hearkened in vain for a reply. I grew impatient. I called aloud—

"Fortunato!"

No answer. I called again—

"Fortunato!"

No answer still. I thrust a torch through the remaining aperture and let it fall within. There came forth in return only a jingling of the bells. My heart grew sick; it was the dampness of the catacombs that made it so. I hastened to make an end of my labour. I forced the last stone into its position; I plastered it up. Against the new masonry I re-erected the old rampart of bones. For the half of a century no mortal has disturbed them. *In pace requiescat!*

Bret Harte

THE CHRONICLER of the Argonauts of '49 was born in Albany in 1836. His removal to California in his teens and his absorption in the character portrayals of Dickens were strong determinants in a career which made him the pioneer local colorist of America. The publication of "The Luck of Roaring Camp" in 1868 brought him eastward to accept fame and to find disillusionment. Stories poured from his pen. "The Outcasts of Poker Flat" and "Tennessee's Partner" were as novel and romantic as "The Luck." But the vein grew thin, Harte fell into difficulties, and the last thirty years of his life, most of them spent abroad, were anticlimactic. Up to his death in London in 1901, he continued to work doggedly, producing stories that fell more captivatingly on British ears than American.

Harte was a first-rate craftsman, a greatly gifted story teller, but he was so insistent with his paradoxes, so picturesque with his pioneers that his portrayals often failed in essential honesty. Those readers who wanted their villains to be villains, their heroes, heroes, were dazzled by his manipulations. But although he mixed the ingredients he did not alter the values; there was still the familiar foil of vice versus virtue, the same draining of human naturalness from human character. Yet it will not be forgotten that he contributed two or three enduring classics to American story telling.

TENNESSEE'S PARTNER *
Bret Harte

I DO NOT think that we ever knew his real name. Our ignorance of it certainly never gave us any social inconvenience, for at Sandy Bar in 1854 most men were christened anew. Sometimes these appellatives

* From *The Luck of Roaring Camp and Other Tales* by Bret Harte. Reprinted by courtesy of the Houghton Mifflin Company.

were derived from some distinctiveness of dress, as in the case of "Dungaree Jack;" or from some peculiarity of habit, as shown in "Saleratus Bill," so called from an undue proportion of that chemical in his daily bread; or from some unlucky slip, as exhibited in "The Iron Pirate," a mild, inoffensive man, who earned that baleful title by his unfortunate mispronunciation of the term "iron pyrites." Perhaps this may have been the beginning of a rude heraldry; but I am constrained to think that it was because a man's real name in that day rested solely upon his own unsupported statement. "Call yourself Clifford, do you?" said Boston, addressing a timid newcomer with infinite scorn; "hell is full of such Cliffords!" He then introduced the unfortunate man, whose name happened to be really Clifford, as "Jaybird Charley,"—an unhallowed inspiration of the moment that clung to him ever after.

But to return to Tennessee's Partner, whom we never knew by any other than this relative title. That he had ever existed as a separate and distinct individuality we only learned later. It seems that in 1853 he left Poker Flat to go to San Francisco, ostensibly to procure a wife. He never got any farther than Stockton. At that place he was attracted by a young person who waited upon the table at the hotel where he took his meals. One morning he said something to her which caused her to smile not unkindly, to somewhat coquettishly break a plate of toast over his upturned, serious, simple face, and to retreat to the kitchen. He followed her, and emerged a few moments later, covered with more toast and victory. That day week they were married by a justice of the peace, and returned to Poker Flat. I am aware that something more might be made of this episode, but I prefer to tell it as it was current at Sandy Bar,—in the gulches and bar-rooms,—where all sentiment was modified by a strong sense of humor.

Of their married felicity but little is known, perhaps for the reason that Tennessee, then living with his partner, one day took occasion to say something to the bride on his own account, at which, it is said, she smiled not unkindly and chastely retreated,—this time as far as Marysville, where Tennessee followed her, and where they went to housekeeping without the aid of a justice of the peace. Tennessee's Partner took the loss of his wife simply and seriously, as was his fashion. But to everybody's surprise, when Tennessee one day returned from Marysville, without his partner's wife,—she having smiled and retreated with somebody else,—Tennessee's Partner was the first man to shake his hand and greet him with affection. The boys who had gathered in the cañon to see the shooting were naturally indignant. Their indignation might have found vent in sarcasm but for a certain look in Tennessee's Partner's eye that indicated a lack of humorous appreciation. In fact, he was a grave man, with a steady application to practical detail which was unpleasant in a difficulty.

Meanwhile a popular feeling against Tennessee had grown up on the Bar. He was known to be a gambler; he was suspected to be a thief. In these suspicions Tennessee's Partner was equally compromised; his continued intimacy with Tennessee after the affair above quoted could only be accounted for on the hypothesis of a copartnership of crime. At last Tennessee's guilt became flagrant. One day he overtook a stranger on his way to Red Dog. The stranger afterward related that Tennessee beguiled the time with interesting anecdote and reminiscence, but illogically concluded the interview in the following words: "And now, young man, I'll trouble you for your knife, your pistols, and your money. You see your weppings might get you into trouble at Red Dog, and your money's a temptation to the evilly disposed. I think you said your address was San Francisco. I shall endeavor to call." It may be stated here that Tennessee had a fine flow of humor, which no business preoccupation could wholly subdue.

This exploit was his last. Red Dog and Sandy Bar made common cause against the highwayman. Tennessee was hunted in very much the same fashion as his prototype, the grizzly. As the toils closed around him, he made a desperate dash through the Bar, emptying his revolver at the crowd before the Arcade Saloon, and so on up Grizzly Cañon; but at its farther extremity he was stopped by a small man on a gray horse. The men looked at each other a moment in silence. Both were fearless, both self-possessed and independent, and both types of a civilization that in the seventeenth century would have been called heroic, but in the nineteenth simply "reckless."

"What have you got there?—I call," said Tennessee quietly.

"Two bowers and an ace," said the stranger as quietly, showing two revolvers and a bowie-knife.

"That takes me," returned Tennessee; and, with this gambler's epigram, he threw away his useless pistol and rode back with his captor.

It was a warm night. The cool breeze which usually sprang up with the going down of the sun behind the chaparral-crested mountain was that evening withheld from Sandy Bar. The little cañon was stifling with heated resinous odors, and the decaying driftwood on the Bar sent forth faint sickening exhalations. The feverishness of day and its fierce passions still filled the camp. Lights moved restlessly along the bank of the river, striking no answering reflection from its tawny current. Against the blackness of the pines the windows of the old loft above the express-office stood out staringly bright; and through their curtainless panes the loungers below could see the forms of those who were even then deciding the fate of Tennessee. And above all this, etched on the dark firmament, rose the Sierra, remote and passionless, crowned with remoter passionless stars.

The trial of Tennessee was conducted as fairly as was consistent with a judge and jury who felt themselves to some extent obliged to justify, in their verdict, the previous irregularities of arrest and indictment. The law of Sandy Bar was implacable, but not vengeful. The excitement and personal feeling of the chase were over; with Tennessee safe in their hands, they were ready to listen patiently to any defense, which they were already satisfied was insufficient. There being no doubt in their own minds, they were willing to give the prisoner the benefit of any that might exist. Secure in the hypothesis that he ought to be hanged on general principles, they indulged him with more latitude of defense than his reckless hardihood seemed to ask. The Judge appeared to be more anxious than the prisoner, who, otherwise unconcerned, evidently took a grim pleasure in the responsibility he had created. "I don't take any hand in this yer game," had been his invariable but good-humored reply to all questions. The Judge—who was also his captor—for a moment vaguely regretted that he had not shot him "on sight" that morning, but presently dismissed this human weakness as unworthy of the judicial mind. Nevertheless, when there was a tap at the door, and it was said that Tennessee's Partner was there on behalf of the prisoner, he was admitted at once without question. Perhaps the younger members of the jury, to whom the proceedings were becoming irksomely thoughtful, hailed him as a relief.

For he was not, certainly, an imposing figure. Short and stout, with a square face, sunburned into a preternatural redness, clad in a loose duck "jumper" and trousers streaked and splashed with red soil, his aspect under any circumstances would have been quaint, and was now even ridiculous. As he stooped to deposit at his feet a heavy carpetbag he was carrying, it became obvious, from partially developed legends and inscriptions, that the material with which his trousers had been patched had been originally intended for a less ambitious covering. Yet he advanced with great gravity, and after shaking the hand of each person in the room with labored cordiality, he wiped his serious perplexed face on a red bandana handkerchief, a shade lighter than his complexion, laid his powerful hand upon the table to steady himself, and thus addressed the Judge:—

"I was passin' by," he began, by way of apology, "and I thought I'd just step in and see how things was gittin' on with Tennessee thar,— my pardner. It's a hot night. I disremember any sich weather before on the Bar."

He paused a moment, but nobody volunteering any other meteorological recollection, he again had recourse to his pocket-handkerchief, and for some moments mopped his face diligently.

"Have you anything to say on behalf of the prisoner?" said the Judge finally.

"Thet's it," said Tennessee's Partner, in a tone of relief. "I come yar as Tennessee's pardner,—knowing him nigh on four year, off and on, wet and dry, in luck and out o' luck. His ways ain't aller my ways, but thar ain't any p'ints in that young man, thar ain't any liveliness as he's been up to, as I don't know. And you sez to me, sez you,—confidential-like, and between man and man,—sez you, 'Do you know anything in his behalf?' and I sez to you, sez I,—confidential-like, as between man and man,—'What should a man know of his pardner?'"

"Is this all you have to say?" asked the Judge impatiently, feeling, perhaps, that a dangerous sympathy of humor was beginning to humanize the court.

"Thet's so," continued Tennessee's Partner. "It ain't for me to say anything agin' him. And now, what's the case? Here's Tennessee wants money, wants it bad, and doesn't like to ask it of his old pardner. Well, what does Tennessee do? He lays for a stranger, and he fetches that stranger; and you lays for *him,* and you fetches *him;* and the honors is easy. And I put it to you, bein' a fa'r-minded man, and to you, gentlemen all, as fa'r-minded men, ef this isn't so."

"Prisoner," said the Judge, interrupting, "have you any questions to ask this man?"

"No! no!" continued Tennessee's Partner hastily. "I play this yer hand alone. To come down to the bed-rock, it's just this: Tennessee, thar, has played it pretty rough and expensive-like on a stranger, and on this yer camp. And now, what's the fair thing? Some would say more, some would say less. Here's seventeen hundred dollars in coarse gold and a watch,—it's about all my pile,—and call it square!" And before a hand could be raised to prevent him, he had emptied the contents of the carpetbag upon the table.

For a moment his life was in jeopardy. One or two men sprang to their feet, several hands groped for hidden weapons, and a suggestion to "throw him from the window" was only overridden by a gesture from the Judge. Tennessee laughed. And apparently oblivious of the excitement, Tennessee's Partner improved the opportunity to mop his face again with his handkerchief.

When order was restored, and the man was made to understand, by the use of forcible figures and rhetoric, that Tennessee's offense could not be condoned by money, his face took a more serious and sanguinary hue, and those who were nearest to him noticed that his rough hand trembled slightly on the table. He hesitated a moment as he slowly returned the gold to the carpetbag, as if he had not yet entirely caught the elevated sense of justice which swayed the tribunal, and was perplexed with the belief that he had not offered enough. Then he turned to the Judge, and saying, "This yer is a lone hand, played alone, and without my pardner," he bowed to the jury and was about to withdraw, when the Judge called him back:—

"If you have anything to say to Tennessee, you had better say it now."

For the first time that evening the eyes of the prisoner and his strange advocate met. Tennessee smiled, showed his white teeth, and saying, "Euchred, old man!" held out his hand. Tennessee's Partner took it in his own, and saying, "I just dropped in as I was passin' to see how things was gettin' on," let the hand passively fall, and adding that "it was a warm night," again mopped his face with his handkerchief, and without another word withdrew.

The two men never again met each other alive. For the unparalleled insult of a bribe offered to Judge Lynch—who, whether bigoted, weak, or narrow, was at least incorruptible—firmly fixed in the mind of that mythical personage any wavering determination of Tennessee's fate; and at the break of day he was marched, closely guarded, to meet it at the top of Marley's Hill.

How he met it, how cool he was, how he refused to say anything, how perfect were the arrangements of the committee, were all duly reported, with the addition of a warning moral and example to all future evil-doers, in the "Red Dog Clarion," by its editor, who was present, and to whose vigorous English I cheerfully refer the reader. But the beauty of that midsummer morning, the blessed amity of earth and air and sky, the awakened life of the free woods and hills, the joyous renewal and promise of Nature, and above all, the infinite serenity that thrilled through each, was not reported, as not being a part of the social lesson. And yet, when the weak and foolish deed was done, and a life, with its possibilities and responsibilities, had passed out of the misshapen thing that dangled between earth and sky, the birds sang, the flowers bloomed, the sun shone, as cheerily as before; and possibly the "Red Dog Clarion" was right.

Tennessee's Partner was not in the group that surrounded the ominous tree. But as they turned to disperse, attention was drawn to the singular appearance of a motionless donkey-cart halted at the side of the road. As they approached, they at once recognized the venerable "Jenny" and the two-wheeled cart as the property of Tennessee's Partner, used by him in carrying dirt from his claim; and a few paces distant, the owner of the equipage himself, sitting under a buckeye-tree, wiping the perspiration from his glowing face. In answer to an inquiry, he said he had come for the body of the "diseased," "if it was all the same to the committee." He didn't wish to "hurry anything;" he could "wait." He was not working that day; and when the gentlemen were done with the "diseased," he would take him. "Ef thar is any present," he added, in his simple, serious way, "as would care to jine in the fun'l, they kin come." Perhaps it was from a sense of humor, which I have already intimated was a feature of Sandy Bar,—perhaps it was from something even better than that, but two thirds of the loungers accepted the invitation at once.

It was noon when the body of Tennessee was delivered into the hands of his partner. As the cart drew up to the fatal tree, we noticed that it contained a rough oblong box,—apparently made from a section of sluicing,—and half filled with bark and the tassels of pine. The cart was further decorated with slips of willow and made fragrant with buckeye-blossoms. When the body was deposited in the box, Tennessee's Partner drew over it a piece of tarred canvas, and gravely mounting the narrow seat in front, with his feet upon the shafts, urged the little donkey forward. The equipage moved slowly on, at that decorous pace which was habitual with Jenny even under less solemn circumstances. The men—half curiously, half jestingly, but all good-humoredly—strolled along beside the cart, some in advance, some a little in the rear of the homely catafalque. But whether from the narrowing of the road or some present sense of decorum, as the cart passed on, the company fell to the rear in couples, keeping step, and otherwise assuming the external show of a formal procession. Jack Folinsbee, who had at the outset played a funeral march in dumb show upon an imaginary trombone, desisted from a lack of sympathy and appreciation,—not having, perhaps, your true humorist's capacity to be content with the enjoyment of his own fun.

The way led through Grizzly Cañon, by this time clothed in funereal drapery and shadows. The redwoods, burying their moccasined feet in the red soil, stood in Indian file along the track, trailing an uncouth benediction from their bending boughs upon the passing bier. A hare, surprised into helpless inactivity, sat upright and pulsating in the ferns by the roadside as the cortège went by. Squirrels hastened to gain a secure outlook from higher boughs; and the blue-jays, spreading their wings, fluttered before them like outriders, until the outskirts of Sandy Bar were reached, and the solitary cabin of Tennessee's Partner.

Viewed under more favorable circumstances, it would not have been a cheerful place. The unpicturesque site, the rude and unlovely outlines, the unsavory details, which distinguish the nest-building of the California miner, were all here with the dreariness of decay superadded. A few paces from the cabin there was a rough inclosure, which, in the brief days of Tennessee's Partner's matrimonial felicity, had been used as a garden, but was now overgrown with fern. As we approached it, we were surprised to find that what we had taken for a recent attempt at cultivation was the broken soil about an open grave.

The cart was halted before the inclosure, and rejecting the offers of assistance with the same air of simple self-reliance he had displayed throughout, Tennessee's Partner lifted the rough coffin on his back, and deposited it unaided within the shallow grave. He then nailed down the board which served as a lid, and mounting the little mound of earth beside it, took off his hat and slowly mopped his face with his handkerchief. This the crowd felt was a preliminary to speech, and they disposed themselves variously on stumps and boulders, and sat expectant.

"When a man," began Tennessee's Partner slowly, "has been running free all day, what's the natural thing for him to do? Why, to come home. And if he ain't in a condition to go home, what can his best friend do? Why, bring him home. And here's Tennessee has been running free, and we brings him home from his wandering." He paused and picked up a fragment of quartz, rubbed it thoughtfully on his sleeve, and went on: "It ain't the first time that I've packed him on my back, as you see'd me now. It ain't the first time that I brought him to this yer cabin when he couldn't help himself; it ain't the first time that I and Jinny have waited for him on yon hill, and picked him up and so fetched him home, when he couldn't speak and didn't know me. And now that it's the last time, why"—he paused and rubbed the quartz gently on his sleeve—"you see it's sort of rough on his pardner. And now, gentlemen," he added abruptly, picking up his long-handled shovel, "the fun'l's over; and my thanks, and Tennessee's thanks, to you for your trouble."

Resisting any proffers of assistance, he began to fill in the grave, turning his back upon the crowd, that after a few moments' hesitation gradually withdrew. As they crossed the little ridge that hid Sandy Bar from view, some, looking back, thought they could see Tennessee's Partner, his work done, sitting upon the grave, his shovel between his knees, and his face buried in his red bandana handkerchief. But it was argued by others that you couldn't tell his face from his handkerchief at that distance, and this point remained undecided.

In the reaction that followed the feverish excitement of that day, Tennessee's Partner was not forgotten. A secret investigation had cleared him of any complicity in Tennessee's guilt, and left only a suspicion of his general sanity. Sandy Bar made a point of calling on him, and proffering various uncouth but well-meant kindnesses. But from that day his rude health and great strength seemed visibly to decline; and when the rainy season fairly set in, and the tiny grass-blades were beginning to peep from the rocky mound above Tennessee's grave, he took to his bed.

One night, when the pines beside the cabin were swaying in the storm and trailing their slender fingers over the roof, and the roar and rush of the swollen river were heard below, Tennessee's Partner lifted his head from the pillow, saying, "It is time to go for Tennessee; I must put Jinny in the cart;" and would have risen from his bed but for the restraint of his attendant. Struggling, he still pursued his singular fancy; "There, now, steady, Jinny,—steady, old girl. How dark it is! Look out for the ruts,—and look out for him, too, old gal. Sometimes, you know, when he's blind drunk, he drops down right in the trail. Keep on straight up to the pine on the top of the hill. Thar! I told you so!—thar he is,—coming this way, too,—all by himself, sober, and his face a-shining. Tennessee! Pardner!"

And so they met.

Ambrose Bierce

It is a critical commonplace to compare Bierce's story telling with that of Poe, but the comparison is not very enlightening. Their favorite province was the tale of terror, but where Poe was morbid and moody, Bierce was chill and bitter. Yet both were lonely men at odds with their world; both were often savage in their criticism. For many years Bierce's stories did not win as much appreciation as they deserve. Now he is regarded, and rightly so, as a great story writer. His chief distinction is his style which, in the phrase of George Sterling, "is as crystal clear, yet as disquieting, as the waters of a haunted well."

Ambrose Bierce was born in Ohio in 1842, served throughout the Civil War, being brevetted major for bravery, was a journalist and columnist in London and San Francisco, wrote several volumes of stories, poems, and essays, and finally disappeared in Mexico in 1913 where it is assumed he was killed by Mexican revolutionists. Besides In the Midst of Life (1899) he wrote a volume of stories of the supernatural entitled Can Such Things Be? (1893).

ONE OF THE MISSING *

Ambrose Bierce

JEROME SEARING, a private soldier of General Sherman's army, then confronting the enemy at and about Kennesaw Mountain, Georgia, turned his back upon a small group of officers with whom he had been talking in low tones, stepped across a light line of earthworks, and disappeared in a forest. None of the men in line behind the works had said a word to him, nor had he so much as nodded to them in passing, but all who saw understood that this brave man had been intrusted

---

* From *In the Midst of Life* by Ambrose Bierce. Reprinted by permission of A. & C. Boni, Inc.

with some perilous duty. Jerome Searing, though a private, did not serve in the ranks; he was detailed for service at division headquarters, being borne upon the rolls as an orderly. "Orderly" is a word covering a multitude of duties. An orderly may be a messenger, a clerk, an officer's servant—anything. He may perform services for which no provision is made in orders and army regulations. Their nature may depend upon his aptitude, upon favor, upon accident. Private Searing, an incomparable marksman, young, hardy, intelligent and insensible to fear, was a scout. The general commanding his division was not content to obey orders blindly without knowing what was in his front, even when his command was not on detached service, but formed a fraction of the line of the army; nor was he satisfied to receive his knowledge of his *vis-à-vis* through the customary channels; he wanted to know more than he was apprised of by the corps commander and the collisions of pickets and skirmishers. Hence Jerome Searing, with his extraordinary daring, his woodcraft, his sharp eyes, and truthful tongue. On this occasion his instructions were simple: to get as near the enemy's lines as possible and learn all that he could.

In a few moments he had arrived at the picket-line, the men on duty there lying in groups of two and four behind little banks of earth scooped out of the slight depression in which they lay, their rifles protruding from the green boughs with which they had masked their small defenses. The forest extended without a break toward the front, so solemn and silent that only by an effort of the imagination could it be conceived as populous with armed men, alert and vigilant— a forest formidable with possibilities of battle. Pausing a moment in one of these rifle-pits to apprise the men of his intention Searing crept stealthily forward on his hands and knees and was soon lost to view in a dense thicket of underbrush.

"That is the last of him," said one of the men; "I wish I had his rifle; those fellows will hurt some of us with it."

Searing crept on, taking advantage of every accident of ground and growth to give himself better cover. His eyes penetrated everywhere, his ears took note of every sound. He stilled his breathing, and at the cracking of a twig beneath his knee stopped his progress and hugged the earth. It was slow work, but not tedious; the danger made it exciting, but by no physical signs was the excitement manifest. His pulse was as regular, his nerves were as steady as if he were trying to trap a sparrow.

"It seems a long time," he thought, "but I cannot have come very far; I am still alive."

He smiled at his own method of estimating distance, and crept forward. A moment later he suddenly flattened himself upon the earth and lay motionless, minute after minute. Through a narrow opening in the bushes he had caught sight of a small mound of yellow clay—one of the enemy's rifle-pits. After some little time he cautiously raised his head, inch by inch, then his body upon his hands, spread out on each side of him, all the while intently regarding the hillock of clay. In another moment he was upon his feet, rifle in hand, striding rapidly forward with little attempt at concealment. He had rightly interpreted the signs, whatever they were; the enemy was gone.

To assure himself beyond a doubt before going back to report upon so important a matter, Searing pushed forward across the line of abandoned pits, running from cover to cover in the more open forest, his eyes vigilant to discover possible stragglers. He came to the edge of a plantation—one of those forlorn, deserted homesteads of the last years of the war, upgrown with brambles, ugly with broken fences and desolate with vacant buildings having blank apertures in place of doors and windows. After a keen reconnoissance from the safe seclusion of a clump of young pines Searing ran lightly across a field and through an orchard to a small structure which stood apart from the other farm buildings, on a slight elevation. This he thought would enable him to overlook a large scope of country in the direction that he supposed the enemy to have taken in withdrawing. This building, which had originally consisted of a single room elevated upon four posts about ten feet high, was now little more than a roof; the floor had fallen away, the joists and planks loosely piled on the ground below or resting on end at various angles, not wholly torn from their fastenings above. The supporting posts were themselves no longer vertical. It looked as if the whole edifice would go down at the touch of a finger.

Concealing himself in the débris of joists and flooring, Searing looked across the open ground between his point of view and a spur of Kennesaw Mountain, a half-mile away. A road leading up and across this spur was crowded with troops—the rear-guard of the retiring enemy, their gun-barrels gleaming in the morning sunlight.

Searing had now learned all that he could hope to know. It was his duty to return to his own command with all possible speed and report his discovery. But the gray column of Confederates toiling up the mountain road was singularly tempting. His rifle—an ordinary "Springfield," but fitted with a globe sight and hair-trigger—would easily send its ounce and a quarter of lead hissing into their midst. That would probably not affect the duration and result of the war, but it is the business of a soldier to kill. It is also his habit if he is a good soldier. Searing cocked his rifle and "set" the trigger.

But it was decreed from the beginning of time that Private Searing was not to murder anybody that bright summer morning, nor was the Confederate retreat to be announced by him. For countless ages events had been so matching themselves together in that wondrous mosaic to some parts of which, dimly discernible, we give the name of history, that the acts which he had in will would have marred the harmony of the pattern. Some twenty-five years previously the Power charged with the execution of the work according to the design had provided against that mischance by causing the birth of a certain male child in a little village at the foot of the Carpathian Mountains, had carefully reared it, supervised its education, directed its desires into a military channel, and in due time made it an officer of artillery. By the concurrence of an infinite number of favoring influences and their preponderance over an infinite number of opposing ones, this officer of artillery had been made to commit a breach of discipline and flee from his native country to avoid punishment. He had been directed to New Orleans (instead of New York), where a recruiting officer awaited him on the wharf. He was enlisted and promoted, and things were so ordered that he now commanded a Confederate battery some two miles along the line from where Jerome Searing, the Federal scout, stood cocking his rifle. Nothing had been neglected—at every step in the progress of both these men's lives, and in the lives of their contemporaries and ancestors, and in the lives of the contemporaries of their ancestors, the right thing had been done to bring about the desired result. Had anything in all this vast concatenation been overlooked Private Searing might have fired on the retreating Confederates that morning, and would perhaps have missed. As it fell out, a Confederate captain of artillery, having nothing better to do while awaiting his turn to pull out and be off, amused himself by sighting a field-piece obliquely to his right at what he mistook for some Federal officers on the crest of a hill, and discharged it. The shot flew high of its mark.

As Jerome Searing drew back the hammer of his rifle and with his eyes upon the distant Confederates considered where he could plant his shot with the best hope of making a widow or an orphan or a childless mother,—perhaps all three, for Private Searing, although he had repeatedly refused promotion, was not without a certain kind of ambition,—he heard a rushing sound in the air, like that made by the wings of a great bird swooping down upon its prey. More quickly than he could apprehend the gradation, it increased to a hoarse and horrible roar, as the missile that made it sprang at him out of the sky, striking with a deafening impact one of the posts supporting the confusion of timbers above him, smashing it into matchwood, and bringing down the crazy edifice with a loud clatter, in clouds of blinding dust!

When Jerome Searing recovered consciousness he did not at once understand what had occurred. It was, indeed, some time before he opened his eyes. For a while he believed that he had died and been buried, and he tried to recall some portions of the burial service. He thought that his wife was kneeling upon his grave, adding her weight to that of the earth upon his breast. The two of them, widow and earth, had crushed his coffin. Unless the children should persuade her to go home he would not much longer be able to breathe. He felt a sense of wrong. "I cannot speak to her," he thought; "the dead have no voice; and if I open my eyes I shall get them full of earth."

He opened his eyes. A great expanse of blue sky, rising from a fringe of the tops of trees. In the foreground, shutting out some of the trees, a high, dun mound, angular in outline and crossed by an intricate, patternless system of straight lines; the whole an immeasurable distance away—a distance so inconceivably great that it fatigued him, and he closed his eyes. The moment that he did so he was conscious of an insufferable light. A sound was in his ears like the low, rhythmic thunder of a distant sea breaking in successive waves upon the beach, and out of this noise, seeming a part of it, or possibly coming from beyond it, and intermingled with its ceaseless undertone, came the articulate words: "Jerome Searing, you are caught like a rat in a trap—in a trap, trap, trap."

Suddenly there fell a great silence, a black darkness, an infinite tranquillity, and Jerome Searing, perfectly conscious of his rathood, and well assured of the trap that he was in, remembering all and nowise alarmed, again opened his eyes to reconnoitre, to note the strength of his enemy, to plan his defense.

He was caught in a reclining posture, his back firmly supported by a solid beam. Another lay across his breast, but he had been able to shrink a little away from it so that it no longer oppressed him, though it was immovable. A brace joining it at an angle had wedged him against a pile of boards on his left, fastening the arm on that side. His legs, slightly parted and straight along the ground, were covered upward to the knees with a mass of débris which towered above his narrow horizon. His head was as rigidly fixed as in a vise; he could move his eyes, his chin—no more. Only his right arm was partly free. "You must help us out of this," he said to it. But he could not get it from under the heavy timber athwart his chest, nor move it outward more than six inches at the elbow.

Searing was not seriously injured, nor did he suffer pain. A smart rap on the head from a flying fragment of the splintered post, incurred simultaneously with the frightfully sudden shock to the nervous system, had momentarily dazed him. His term of unconsciousness, including the period of recovery, during which he had had the strange fancies, had probably not exceeded a few seconds, for the dust of the wreck had not wholly cleared away as he began an intelligent survey of the situation.

With his partly free right hand he now tried to get hold of the beam that lay across, but not quite against, his breast. In no way could he do so. He was unable to depress the shoulder so as to push the elbow beyond that edge of the timber which was nearest his knees; failing in that, he could not raise the forearm and hand to grasp the beam. The brace that made an angle with it downward and backward prevented him from doing anything in that direction, and between it and his body the space was not half so wide as the length of his forearm. Obviously he could not get his hand under the beam nor over it; the hand could not, in fact, touch it at all. Having demonstrated his inability, he desisted, and began to think whether he could reach any of the débris piled upon his legs.

In surveying the mass with a view to determining that point, his attention was arrested by what seemed to be a ring of shining metal immediately in front of his eyes. It appeared to him at first to surround some perfectly black substance, and it was somewhat more than a half-inch in diameter. It suddenly occurred to his mind that the blackness was simply shadow and that the ring was in fact the muzzle of his rifle protruding from the pile of débris. He was not long in satisfying himself that this was so—if it was a satisfaction. By closing either eye he could look a little way along the barrel—to the point where it was hidden by the rubbish that held it. He could see the one side, with the corresponding eye, at apparently the same angle as the other side with the other eye. Looking with the right eye, the weapon seemed to be directed at a point to the left of his head, and *vice versa*. He was unable to see the upper surface of the barrel, but could see the under surface of the stock at a slight angle. The piece was, in fact, aimed at the exact centre of his forehead.

In the perception of this circumstance, in the recollection that just previously to the mischance of which this uncomfortable situation was the result he had cocked the rifle and set the trigger so that a touch would discharge it, Private Searing was affected with a feeling of uneasiness. But that was as far as possible from fear; he was a brave man, somewhat familiar with the aspect of rifles from that point of view, and of cannon too. And now he recalled, with something like amusement, an incident of his experience at the storming of Missionary Ridge, where, walking up to one of the enemy's embrasures from which he had seen a heavy gun throw charge after charge of grape among the assailants he had thought for a moment that the piece had been withdrawn; he could see nothing in the opening but a brazen circle. What that was he had understood just in time to step aside as it pitched another peck of iron down that swarming slope. To face firearms is one of the commonest incidents in a soldier's life— firearms, too, with malevolent eyes blazing behind them. That is what a soldier is for. Still, Private Searing did not altogether relish the situation, and turned away his eyes.

After groping, aimless, with his right hand for a time he made an ineffectual attempt to release his left. Then he tried to disengage his head, the fixity of which was the more annoying from his ignorance of what held it. Next he tried to free his feet, but while exerting the powerful muscles of his legs for that purpose it occurred to him that a disturbance of the rubbish which held them might discharge the rifle; how it could have endured what had already befallen it he could not understand, although memory assisted him with several instances in point. One in particular he recalled, in which in a moment of mental abstraction he had clubbed his rifle and beaten out another gentleman's brains, observing afterward that the weapon which he had been diligently swinging by the muzzle was loaded, capped, and at full cock—knowledge of which circumstance would doubtless have cheered his antagonist to longer endurance. He had always smiled in recalling that blunder of his "green and salad days" as a soldier, but now he did not smile. He turned his eyes again to the muzzle of the rifle and for a moment fancied that it had moved; it seemed somewhat nearer.

Again he looked away. The tops of the distant trees beyond the bounds of the plantation interested him: he had not before observed how light and feathery they were, nor how darkly blue the sky was, even among their branches, where they somewhat paled it with their green; above him it appeared almost black. "It will be uncomfortably hot here," he thought, "as the day advances. I wonder which way I am looking."

Judging by such shadows as he could see, he decided that his face was due north; he would at least not have the sun in his eyes, and north—well, that was toward his wife and children.

"Bah!" he exclaimed aloud, "what have they to do with it?"

He closed his eyes. "As I can't get out I may as well go to sleep. The rebels are gone and some of our fellows are sure to stray out here foraging. They'll find me."

But he did not sleep. Gradually he became sensible of a pain in his forehead—a dull ache, hardly perceptible at first, but growing more and more uncomfortable. He opened his eyes and it was gone—closed them and it returned. "The devil!" he said, irrelevantly, and stared again at the sky. He heard the singing of birds, the strange metallic note of the meadow lark, suggesting the clash of vibrant blades. He fell into pleasant memories of his childhood, played again with his brother and sister, raced across the fields, shouting to alarm the sedentary larks, entered the sombre forest beyond and with timid steps followed the faint path to Ghost Rock, standing at last with audible heart-throbs before the Dead Man's Cave and seeking to penetrate its awful mystery. For the first time he observed that the opening of the haunted cavern was encircled by a ring of metal. Then all else vanished and left him gazing into the barrel of his rifle as before. But whereas before it had seemed nearer, it now seemed an inconceivable distance away, and all the more sinister for that. He cried out and, startled by something in his own voice—the note of fear—lied to himself in denial: "If I don't sing out I may stay here till I die."

He now made no further attempt to evade the menacing stare of the gun barrel. If he turned away his eyes an instant it was to look for assistance (although he could not see the ground on either side the ruin), and he permitted them to return, obedient to the imperative fascination. If he closed them it was from weariness, and instantly the poignant pain in his forehead—the prophecy and menace of the bullet —forced him to reopen them.

The tension of nerve and brain was too severe; nature came to his relief with intervals of unconsciousness. Reviving from one of these he became sensible of a sharp, smarting pain in his right hand, and when he worked his fingers together, or rubbed his palm with them, he could feel that they were wet and slippery. He could not see the hand, but he knew the sensation; it was running blood. In his delirium he had beaten it against the jagged fragments of the wreck, had clutched it full of splinters. He resolved that he would meet his fate more manly. He was a plain, common soldier, had no religion and not much philosophy; he could not die like a hero, with great and wise last words, even if there had been some one to hear them, but he could die "game," and he would. But if he could only know when to expect the shot!

Some rats which had probably inhabited the shed came sneaking and scampering about. One of them mounted the pile of débris that held the rifle; another followed and another. Searing regarded them at first with indifference, then with friendly interest; then, as the thought flashed into his bewildered mind that they might touch the trigger of his rifle, he cursed them and ordered them to go away. "It is no business of yours," he cried.

The creatures went away; they would return later, attack his face, gnaw away his nose, cut his throat—he knew that, but he hoped by that time to be dead.

Nothing could now unfix his gaze from the little ring of metal with its black interior. The pain in his forehead was fierce and incessant. He felt it gradually penetrating the brain more and more deeply, until at last its progress was arrested by the wood at the back of his head. It grew momentarily more insufferable: he began wantonly beating his lacerated hand against the splinters again to counteract that horrible ache. It seemed to throb with a slow, regular recurrence, each pulsation sharper than the preceding, and sometimes he cried out, thinking he felt the fatal bullet. No thoughts of home, of wife and children, of country, of glory. The whole record of memory was effaced. The world had passed away—not a vestige remained. Here in this confusion of timbers and boards is the sole universe. Here is immortality in time—each pain an everlasting life. The throbs tick off eternities.

Jerome Searing, the man of courage, the formidable enemy, the strong, resolute warrior, was as pale as a ghost. His jaw was fallen; his eyes protruded; he trembled in every fibre; a cold sweat bathed his entire body; he screamed with fear. He was not insane—he was terrified.

In groping about with his torn and bleeding hand he seized at last a strip of board, and, pulling, felt it give way. It lay parallel with his body, and by bending his elbow as much as the contracted space would permit, he could draw it a few inches at a time. Finally it was altogether loosened from the wreckage covering his legs; he could lift it clear of the ground its whole length. A great hope came into his mind; perhaps he could work it upward, that is to say backward, far enough to lift the end and push aside the rifle; or, if that were too tightly wedged, so place the strip of board as to deflect the bullet. With this object he passed it backward inch by inch, hardly daring to breathe lest that act somehow defeat his intent, and more than ever unable to remove his eyes from the rifle, which might perhaps now hasten to improve its waning opportunity. Something at least had been gained: in the occupation of his mind in this attempt at self-defense he was less sensible of the pain in his head and had ceased to wince. But he was still dreadfully frightened and his teeth rattled like castanets.

The strip of board ceased to move to the suasion of his hand. He tugged at it with all his strength, changed the direction of its length all he could, but it had met some extended obstruction behind him and the end in front was still too far away to clear the pile of débris and reach the muzzle of the gun. It extended, indeed, nearly as far as the trigger guard, which, uncovered by the rubbish, he could imperfectly see with his right eye. He tried to break the strip with his hand, but had no leverage. In his defeat, all his terror returned, augmented tenfold. The black aperture of the rifle appeared to threaten a sharper and more imminent death in punishment of his rebellion. The track of the bullet through his head ached with an intenser anguish. He began to tremble again.

Suddenly he became composed. His tremor subsided. He clenched his teeth and drew down his eyebrows. He had not exhausted his means of defense; a new design had shaped itself in his mind— another plan of battle. Raising the front end of the strip of board, he carefully pushed it forward through the wreckage at the side of the rifle until it pressed against the trigger guard. Then he moved the end slowly outward until he could feel that it had cleared it, then, closing his eyes, thrust it against the trigger with all his strength!

There was no explosion; the rifle had been discharged as it dropped from his hand when the building fell. But it did its work.

Lieutenant Adrian Searing, in command of the picket-guard on that part of the line through which his brother Jerome had passed on his mission, sat with attentive ears in his breastwork behind the line. Not the faintest sound escaped him; the cry of a bird, the barking of a squirrel, the noise of the wind among the pines—all were anxiously noted by his overstrained senses. Suddenly, directly in front of his line, he heard a faint, confused rumble, like the clatter of a falling building translated by distance. The lieutenant mechanically looked at his watch. Six o'clock and eighteen minutes. At the same moment an officer approached him on foot from the rear and saluted.

"Lieutenant," said the officer, "the colonel directs you to move forward your line and feel the enemy if you find him. If not, continue the advance until directed to halt. There is reason to think that the enemy has retreated."

The lieutenant nodded and said nothing; the other officer retired. In a moment the men, apprised of their duty by the non-commissioned officers in low tones, had deployed from their rifle-pits and were moving forward in skirmishing order, with set teeth and beating hearts.

This line of skirmishers sweeps across the plantation toward the mountain. They pass on both sides of the wrecked building, observing nothing. At a short distance in their rear their commander comes. He casts his eyes curiously upon the ruin and sees a dead body half buried in boards and timbers. It is so covered with dust that its clothing is Confederate gray. Its face is yellowish white; the cheeks are fallen in, the temples sunken, too, with sharp ridges about them, making the forehead forbiddingly narrow; the upper lip, slightly lifted, shows the white teeth, rigidly clenched. The hair is heavy with moisture, the face as wet as the dewy grass all about. From his point of view the officer does not observe the rifle; the man was apparently killed by the fall of the building.

"Dead a week," said the officer curtly, moving on and absently pulling out his watch as if to verify his estimate of time. Six o'clock and forty minutes.

Henry James

WITH HENRY JAMES the short story was a study in manners, a subtle analysis of temperament revealed in the reactions of his characters to some psychologically interesting situation. Much influenced by Hawthorne's own preoccupation with dilemmas of the mind, he was less intense, less portentous than Hawthorne, but wider in range and inclined, unlike the transcendentalists, to find his themes among the occurrences of conventional society. Henry James' skill in exposing human nature is brilliant and restless. Some of his best writing is in the short story form although he was primarily a novelist and confessed that "it was a relief to escape from the frail craft of the short story, where he ever felt the danger of running aground."

Henry James was born in New York City in 1843, the younger brother of William James, the philosopher. He was educated in private schools abroad and at Harvard. He returned to Europe in 1869, and after occasional sojourns to America, settled in England where he died in 1916, having become a British subject the year before. The list of his stories and novels is too long to be listed here, but the student will be especially interested in such stories as "A Passionate Pilgrim" (1871), "The Madonna of the Future" (1873), "The Real Thing" (1893), and "The Turn of the Screw" (1898).

PASTE *

Henry James

"I'VE FOUND a lot more things," her cousin said to her the day after the second funeral; they're up in her room—but they're things I wish *you'd* look at."

---

* From *The Author of Beltraffio and Other Tales* by Henry James. Reprinted by permission of The Macmillan Company, publishers.

The pair of mourners, sufficiently stricken, were in the garden of the vicarage together, before luncheon, waiting to be summoned to that meal, and Arthur Prime had still in his face the intention, she was moved to call it rather than the expression, of feeling something or other. Some such appearance was in itself of course natural within a week of his stepmother's death, within three of his father's; but what was most present to the girl, herself sensitive and shrewd, was that he seemed somehow to brood without sorrow, to suffer without what she in her own case would have called pain. He turned away from her after this last speech—it was a good deal his habit to drop an observation and leave her to pick it up without assistance. If the vicar's widow, now in her turn finally translated, had not really belonged to him it was not for want of her giving herself, so far as he ever would take her; and she had lain for three days all alone at the end of the passage, in the great cold chamber of hospitality, the dampish greenish room where visitors slept and where several of the ladies of the parish had, without effect, offered, in pairs and successions, piously to watch with her. His personal connexion with the parish was now slighter than ever, and he had really not waited for this opportunity to show the ladies what he thought of them. She felt that she herself had, during her doleful month's leave from Bleet, where she was governess, rather taken her place in the same snubbed order; but it was presently, none the less, with a better little hope of coming in for some remembrance, some relic, that she went up to look at the things he had spoken of, the identity of which, as a confused cluster of bright objects on a table in the darkened room, shimmered at her as soon as she had opened the door.

They met her eyes for the first time, but in a moment, before touching them, she knew them as things of the theatre, as very much too fine to have been with any verisimilitude things of the vicarage. They were too dreadfully good to be true, for her aunt had had no jewels to speak of, and these were coronets and girdles, diamonds, rubies and sapphires. Flagrant tinsel and glass, they looked strangely vulgar, but if after the first queer shock of them she found herself taking them up it was for the very proof, never yet so distinct to her, of a far-off faded story. An honest widowed cleric with a small son and a large sense of Shakespeare had, on a brave latitude of habit as well as of taste—since it implied his having in very fact dropped deep into the "pit"—conceived for an obscure actress several years older than himself an admiration of which the prompt offer of his reverend name and hortatory hand was the sufficiently candid sign. The response had perhaps in those dim years, so far as eccentricity was concerned, even bettered the proposal, and Charlotte, turning the tale over, had long since drawn from it a measure of the career renounced by the un-distinguished comédienne—doubtless also tragic, or perhaps panto-mimic, at a pinch—of her late uncle's dreams. This career couldn't have been eminent and must much more probably have been comfort-less.

"You see what it is—old stuff of the time she never liked to mention."

Our young woman gave a start; her companion had after all re-joined her and had apparently watched a moment her slightly scared recognition. "So I said to myself," she replied. Then to show in-telligence, yet keep clear of twaddle: "How peculiar they look!"

"They look awful," said Arthur Prime. "Cheap gilt, diamonds as big as potatoes. These are trappings of a ruder age than ours. Actors do themselves better now."

"Oh now," said Charlotte, not to be less knowing, "actresses have real diamonds."

"Some of them." Arthur spoke dryly.

"I mean the bad ones—the nobodies too."

"Oh some of the nobodies have the biggest. But mamma wasn't of that sort."

"A nobody?" Charlotte risked.

"Not a nobody to whom somebody—well, not a nobody with diamonds. It isn't all worth, this trash, five pounds."

There was something in the old gewgaws that spoke to her, and she continued to turn them over. "They're relics. I think they have their melancholy and even their dignity."

Arthur observed another pause. "Do you care for them?" he then asked. "I mean," he promptly added, "as a souvenir."

"Of you?" Charlotte threw off.

"Of me? What have I to do with it? Of your poor dead aunt who was so kind to you," he said with virtuous sternness.

"Well, I'd rather have them than nothing."

"Then please take them," he returned in a tone of relief which ex-pressed somehow more of the eager than of the gracious.

"Thank you." Charlotte lifted two or three objects up and set them down again. Though they were lighter than the materials they imitated they were so much more extravagant that they struck her in truth as rather an awkward heritage, to which she might have preferred even a matchbox or a penwiper. They were indeed shameless pinchbeck. "Had you any idea she had kept them?"

"I don't at all believe she *had* kept them or knew they were there, and I'm very sure my father didn't. They had quite equally worked off any tenderness for the connexion. These odds and ends, which she thought had been given away or destroyed, had simply got thrust into a dark corner and been forgotten."

Charlotte wondered. "Where then did you find them?"

"In that old tin box"—and the young man pointed to the receptacle from which he had dislodged them and which stood on a neighbouring chair. "It's rather a good box still, but I'm afraid I can't give you *that*."

The girl took no heed of the box; she continued only to look at the trinkets. "What corner had she found?"

"She hadn't 'found' it," her companion sharply insisted; "she had simply lost it. The whole thing had passed from her mind. The box was on the top shelf of the old school-room closet, which, until one put one's head into it from a step-ladder, looked, from below, quite cleared out. The door's narrow and the part of the closet to the left goes well into the wall. The box had stuck there for years."

Charlotte was conscious of a mind divided and a vision vaguely troubled, and once more she took up two or three of the subjects of this revelation; a big bracelet in the form of a gilt serpent with many twists and beady eyes, a brazen belt studded with emeralds and rubies, a chain, of flamboyant architecture, to which, at the Theatre Royal Little Peddlington, Hamlet's mother must have been concerned to attach the portrait of the successor to Hamlet's father. "Are you very sure they're not really worth something? Their mere weight alone—!" she vaguely observed, balancing a moment a royal diadem that might have crowned one of the creations of the famous Mrs. Jarley.

But Arthur Prime, it was clear, had already thought the question over and found the answer easy. "If they had been worth anything to speak of she would long ago have sold them. My father and she had unfortunately never been in a position to keep any considerable value locked up." And while his companion took in the obvious force of this he went on with a flourish just marked enough not to escape her: "If they're worth anything at all—why you're only the more welcome to them."

Charlotte had now in her hand a small bag of faded figured silk— one of those antique conveniences that speak to us, in terms of evapo-

rated camphor and lavender, of the part they have played in some
personal history; but though she had for the first time drawn the
string she looked much more at the young man than at the question-
able treasure it appeared to contain. "I shall like them. They're all I
have."

"All you have—?"

"That belonged to her."

He swelled a little, then looked about him as if to appeal—as against
her avidity—to the whole poor place. "Well, what else do you want?"

"Nothing. Thank you very much." With which she bent her eyes on
the article wrapped, and now only exposed, in her superannuated
satchel—a string of large pearls, such a shining circle as might once
have graced the neck of a provincial Ophelia and borne company to
a flaxen wig. "This perhaps *is* worth something. Feel it." And she
passed him the necklace, the weight of which she had gathered for
a moment into her hand.

He measured it in the same way with his own, but remained quite
detached. "Worth at most thirty shillings."

"Not more?"

"Surely not if it's paste?"

"But *is* it paste?"

He gave a small sniff of impatience. "Pearls nearly as big as filberts?"

"But they're heavy," Charlotte declared.

"No heavier than anything else." And he gave them back with an
allowance for her simplicity. "Do you imagine for a moment they're
real?"

She studied them a little, feeling them, turning them round.
"Mightn't they possibly be?"

"Of that size—stuck away with that trash?"

"I admit it isn't likely," Charlotte presently said. "And pearls are
so easily imitated."

"That's just what—to a person who knows—they're not. These have
no lustre, no play."

"No—they *are* dull. They're opaque."

"Besides," he lucidly inquired, "how could she ever have come by
them?"

"Mightn't they have been a present?"

Arthur stared at the question as if it were almost improper. "Because
actresses are exposed—?" He pulled up, however, not saying to what,
and before she could supply the deficiency had, with the sharp ejacula-

tion of "No, they mightn't!" turned his back on her and walked away. His manner made her feel she had probably been wanting in tact, and before he returned to the subject, the last thing that evening, she had satisfied herself of the ground of his resentment. They had been talking of her departure the next morning, the hour of her train and the fly that would come for her, and it was precisely these things that gave him his effective chance. "I really can't allow you to leave the house under the impression that my stepmother was at *any* time of her life the sort of person to allow herself to be approached—"

"With pearl necklaces and that sort of thing?" Arthur had made for her somehow the difficulty that she couldn't show him she understood him without seeming pert.

It at any rate only added to his own gravity. "That sort of thing, exactly."

"I didn't think when I spoke this morning—but I see what you mean."

"I mean that she was beyond reproach," said Arthur Prime.

"A hundred times yes."

"Therefore if she couldn't, out of her slender gains, ever have paid for a row of pearls—"

"She couldn't, in that atmosphere, ever properly have had one? Of course she couldn't. I've seen perfectly since our talk," Charlotte went on, "that that string of beads isn't even as an imitation very good. The little clasp itself doesn't seem even gold. With false pearls, I suppose," the girl mused, "it naturally wouldn't be."

"The whole thing's rotten paste," her companion returned as if to have done with it. "If it were *not,* and she had kept it all these years hidden—"

"Yes?" Charlotte sounded as he paused.

"Why I shouldn't know what to think!"

"Oh I see." She had met him with a certain blankness, but adequately enough, it seemed, for him to regard the subject as dismissed; and there was no reversion to it between them before, on the morrow, when she had with difficulty made a place for them in her trunk, she carried off these florid survivals.

At Bleet she found small occasion to refer to them and, in an air charged with such quite other references, even felt, after she had laid them away, much enshrouded, beneath various piles of clothing, that they formed a collection not wholly without its note of the ridiculous. Yet she was never, for the joke, tempted to show them to her pupils, though Gwendolen and Blanche in particular always wanted, on her return, to know what she had brought back; so that without an accident by which the case was quite changed they might have appeared to enter on a new phase of interment. The essence of the accident was the sudden illness, at the last moment, of Lady Bobby, whose advent had been so much counted on to spice the five days' feast laid out for the coming of age of the eldest son of the house; and its equally marked effect was the despatch of a pressing message, in quite another direction, to Mrs. Guy, who, could she by a miracle be secured—she was always engaged ten parties deep—might be trusted to supply, it was believed, an element of exuberance scarcely less potent. Mrs. Guy was already known to several of the visitors already on the scene, but she wasn't yet known to our young lady, who found her, after many wires and counter-wires had at last determined the triumph of her arrival, a strange charming little red-haired black-dressed woman, a person with the face of a baby and the authority of a commodore. She took on the spot the discreet, the exceptional young governess into the confidence of her designs and, still more, of her doubts; intimating that it was a policy she almost always promptly pursued.

"To-morrow and Thursday are all right," she said frankly to Charlotte on the second day, "but I'm not half-satisfied with Friday."

"What improvement, then, do you suggest?"

"Well, my strong point, you know, is *tableaux vivants*."

"Charming. And what is your favourite character?"

"Boss!" said Mrs. Guy with decision; and it was very markedly under that ensign that she had, within a few hours, completely planned her campaign and recruited her troop. Every word she uttered was to the point, but none more so than, after a general survey of their equipment, her final inquiry of Charlotte. She had been looking about, but half-appeased, at the muster of decoration and drapery. "We shall be dull. We shall want more colour. You've nothing else?"

Charlotte had a thought. "No—I've *some* things."

"Then why don't you bring them?"

The girl weighed it. "Would you come to my room?"

"No," said Mrs. Guy—"bring them to-night to mine."

So Charlotte, at the evening's end, after candlesticks had flickered through brown old passages bedward, arrived at her friend's door with the burden of her aunt's relics. But she promptly expressed a fear. "Are they too garish?"

When she had poured them out on the sofa Mrs. Guy was but a

minute, before the glass, in clapping on the diadem. "Awfully jolly—
we can do Ivanhoe!"

"But they're only glass and tin."

"Larger than life they are, *rather!*—which is exactly what's wanted
for tableaux. *Our* jewels, for historic scenes, don't tell—the real thing
falls short. Rowena must have rubies as big as eggs. Leave them with
me," Mrs. Guy continued—"they'll inspire me. Good-night."

The next morning she was in fact—yet very strangely—inspired.
"Yes, *I'll* do Rowena. But I don't, my dear, understand."

"Understand what?"

Mrs. Guy gave a very lighted stare. "How you come to have such
things."

Poor Charlotte smiled. "By inheritance."

"Family jewels?"

"They belonged to my aunt, who died some months ago. She was
on the stage a few years in early life, and these are a part of her trappings."

"She left them to you?"

"No; my cousin, her stepson, who naturally has no use for them,
gave them to me for remembrance of her. She was a dear kind thing,
always so nice to me, and I was fond of her."

Mrs. Guy had listened with frank interest. "But it's *he* who must
be a dear kind thing!"

Charlotte wondered. "You think so?"

"Is *he*," her friend went on, "also 'always so nice' to you?"

The girl, at this, face to face there with the brilliant visitor in the
deserted breakfast-room, took a deeper sounding. "What is it?"

"Don't you know?"

Something came over her. "The pearls—?" But the question fainted
on her lips.

"Doesn't *he* know?"

Charlotte found herself flushing. "They're *not* paste?"

"Haven't you looked at them?"

She was conscious of two kinds of embarrassment. *"You* have?"

"Very carefully."

"And they're real?"

Mrs. Guy became slightly mystifying and returned for all answer:
"Come again, when you've done with the children, to my room."

Our young woman found she had done with the children that morning so promptly as to reveal to them a new joy, and when she reap-

peared before Mrs. Guy this lady had already encircled a plump white throat with the only ornament, surely, in all the late Mrs. Prime's— the effaced Miss Bradshaw's—collection, in the least qualified to raise a question. If Charlotte had never yet once, before the glass, tied the string of pearls about her own neck, this was bcause she had been capable of no such stoop to approved "imitation"; but she had now only to look at Mrs. Guy to see that, so disposed, the ambiguous objects might have passed for frank originals. "What in the world have you done to them?"

"Only handled them, understood them, admired them and put them on. That's what pearls want; they want to be worn—it wakes them up. They're alive, don't you see? How *have* these been treated? They must have been buried, ignored, despised. They were half-dead. Don't you *know* about pearls?" Mrs. Guy threw off as she fondly fingered the necklace.

"How *should* I? Do *you?*"

"Everything. These were simply asleep, and from the moment I really touched them—well," said their wearer lovingly, "it only took one's eye!"

"It took more than mine—though I did just wonder; and than Arthur's," Charlotte brooded. She found herself almost panting. "Then their value—?"

"Oh their value's excellent."

The girl, for a deep contemplative moment, took another plunge into the wonder, the beauty and the mystery. "Are you *sure?*"

Her companion wheeled round for impatience. "Sure? For what kind of an idiot, my dear, do you take me?"

It was beyond Charlotte Prime to say. "For the same kind as Arthur—and as myself," she could only suggest. "But my cousin didn't know. He thinks they're worthless."

"Because of the rest of the lot? Then your cousin's an ass. But what —if, as I understood you, he gave them to you—has he to do with it?"

"Why if he gave them to me as worthless and they turn out precious—!"

"You must give them back? I don't see that—if he was such a noodle. He took the risk."

Charlotte fed, in fancy, on the pearls, which decidedly were exquisite, but which at the present moment somehow presented themselves much more as Mrs. Guy's than either as Arthur's or her own. "Yes—

he did take it; even after I had distinctly hinted to him that they looked to me different from the other pieces."

"Well then!" said Mrs. Guy with something more than triumph—with a positive odd relief.

But it had the effect of making our young woman think with more intensity. "Ah you see he thought they couldn't be different, because—so peculiarly—they shouldn't be."

"Shouldn't? I don't understand."

"Why how would she have got them?"—so Charlotte candidly put it.

"She? Who?" There was a capacity in Mrs. Guy's tone for a sinking of persons—!

"Why the person I told you of: his stepmother, my uncle's wife—among whose poor old things, extraordinarily thrust away and out of sight, he happened to find them."

Mrs. Guy came a step nearer to the effaced Miss Bradshaw. "Do you mean she may have stolen them?"

"No. But she had been an actress."

"Oh well then," cried Mrs. Guy, "wouldn't that be just how?"

"Yes, except that she wasn't at all a brilliant one, nor in receipt of large pay." The girl even threw off a nervous joke. "I'm afraid she couldn't have been our Rowena."

Mrs. Guy took it up. "Was she very ugly?"

"No. She may very well, when young, have looked rather nice."

"Well then!" was Mrs. Guy's sharp comment and fresh triumph.

"You mean it was a present? That's just what he so dislikes the idea of her having received—a present from an admirer capable of going such lengths."

"Because she wouldn't have taken it for nothing? *Speriamo*—that she wasn't a brute. The 'length' her admirer went was the length of a whole row. Let us hope she was just a little kind!"

"Well," Charlotte went on, "that she was 'kind' might seem to be shown by the fact that neither her husband, nor his son, nor I, his niece, knew or dreamed of her possessing anything so precious; by her having kept the gift all the rest of her life beyond discovery—out of sight and protected from suspicion."

"As if, you mean"—Mrs. Guy was quick—"she had been wedded to it and yet was ashamed of it? Fancy," she laughed while she manipulated the rare beads, "being ashamed of *these!*"

"But you see she had married a clergyman."

"Yes, she must have been 'rum! But at any rate he had married *her*. What did he suppose?"

"Why that she had never been of the sort by whom such offerings are encouraged."

"Ah my dear, the sort by whom they're *not*—!" But Mrs. Guy caught herself up. "And her stepson thought the same?"

"Overwhelmingly."

"Was he then, if only her stepson—"

"So fond of her as that comes to? Yes; he had never known, consciously, his real mother, and, without children of her own, she was very patient and nice with him. And *I* liked her so," the girl pursued, "that at the end of ten years, in so strange a manner, to 'give her away'—"

"Is impossible to you? Then don't!" said Mrs. Guy with decision.

"Ah but if they're real I can't keep them!" Charlotte, with her eyes on them, moaned in her impatience. "It's too difficult."

"Where's the difficulty, if he has such sentiments that he'd rather sacrifice the necklace than admit it, with the presumption it carries with it, to be genuine? You've only to be silent."

"And keep it? How can *I* ever wear it?"

"You'd have to hide it, like your aunt?" Mrs. Guy was amused. "You can easily sell it."

Her companion walked round her for a look at the affair from behind. The clasp was certainly, doubtless intentionally, misleading, but everything else was indeed lovely. "Well, I must think. Why didn't *she* sell them?" Charlotte broke out in her trouble.

Mrs. Guy had an instant answer. "Doesn't that prove what they secretly recalled to her? You've only to be silent!" she ardently repeated.

"I must think—I must think!"

Mrs. Guy stood with her hands attached but motionless. "Then you want them back?"

As if with the dread of touching them Charlotte retreated to the door. "I'll tell you to-night."

"But may I wear them?"

"Meanwhile?"

"This evening—at dinner."

It was the sharp selfish pressure of this that really, on the spot, determined the girl; but for the moment, before closing the door on the question, she only said: "As you like!"

They were busy much of the day with preparation and rehearsal, and at dinner that evening the concourse of guests was such that a place among them for Miss Prime failed to find itself marked. At the time the company rose she was therefore alone in the school-room, where, towards eleven o'clock, she received a visit from Mrs. Guy. This lady's white shoulders heaved, under the pearls, with an emotion that the very red lips which formed, as if for the full effect, the happiest opposition of colour, were not slow to translate. "My dear, you should have seen the sensation—they've had a success!"

Charlotte, dumb a moment, took it all in. "It *is* as if they knew it—they're more and more alive. But so much the worse for both of us! I can't," she brought out with an effort, "be silent."

"You mean to return them?"

"If I don't I'm a thief."

Mrs. Guy gave her a long hard look: what was decidedly not of the baby in Mrs. Guy's face was a certain air of established habit in the eyes. Then, with a sharp little jerk of her head and a backward reach of her bare beautiful arms, she undid the clasp and, taking off the necklace, laid it on the table. "If you do you're a goose."

"Well, of the two—!" said our young lady, gathering it up with a sigh. And as if to get it, for the pang it gave, out of sight as soon as possible, she shut it up, clicking the lock, in the drawer of her own little table; after which, when she turned again, her companion looked naked and plain without it. "But what will you say?" it then occurred to her to demand.

"Downstairs—to explain?" Mrs. Guy was after all trying at least to keep her temper. "Oh I'll put on something else and say the clasp's broken. And you won't of course name *me* to him," she added.

"As having undeceived me? No—I'll say that, looking at the thing more carefully, it's my own private idea."

"And does he know how little you really know?"

"As an expert—surely. And he has always much the conceit of his own opinion."

"Then he won't believe you—as he so hates to. He'll stick to his judgement and maintain his gift, and we shall have the darlings back!" With which reviving assurance Mrs. Guy kissed her young friend for good-night.

She was not, however, to be gratified or justified by any prompt event, for, whether or no paste entered into the composition of the ornament in question, Charlotte shrank from the temerity of despatch-

ing it to town by post. Mrs. Guy was thus disappointed of the hope of
seeing the business settled—"by return," she had seemed to expect—
before the end of the revels. The revels, moreover, rising to a frantic
pitch, pressed for all her attention, and it was at last only in the
general confusion of leave-taking that she made, parenthetically, a
dash at the person in the whole company with whom her contact had
been most interesting.

"Come, what will you take for them?"

"The pearls? Ah, you'll have to treat with my cousin."

Mrs. Guy, with quick intensity, lent herself. "Where then does he
live?"

"In chambers in the Temple. You can find him."

"But what's the use, if *you* do neither one thing nor the other?"

"Oh I *shall* do the 'other,'" Charlotte said: "I'm only waiting till I
go up. You want them so awfully?" She curiously, solemnly again,
sounded her.

"I'm dying for them. There's a special charm in them—I don't know
what it is: they tell so their history."

"But what do you know of that?"

"Just what they themselves say. It's all *in* them—and it comes out.
They breathe a tenderness—they have the white glow of it. My dear,"
hissed Mrs. Guy in supreme confidence and as she buttoned her glove—
"they're things of love!"

"Oh!" our young woman vaguely exclaimed.

"They're things of passion!"

"Mercy!" she gasped, turning short off. But these words remained,
though indeed their help was scarce needed, Charlotte being in private
face to face with a new light, as she by this time felt she must call it,
on the dear dead kind colourless lady whose career had turned so
sharp a corner in the middle. The pearls had quite taken their place as
a revelation. She might have received them for nothing—admit that;
but she couldn't have kept them so long and so unprofitably hidden,
couldn't have enjoyed them only in secret, for nothing; and she had
mixed them in her reliquary with false things in order to put curiosity
and detection off the scent. Over this strange fact poor Charlotte in-
terminably mused: it became more touching, more attaching for her
than she could now confide to any ear. How bad or how happy—in
the sophisticated sense of Mrs. Guy and the young man at the temple—
the effaced Miss Bradshaw must have been to have had to be so mute!
The little governess at Bleet put on the necklace now in secret sessions;

she wore it sometimes under her dress; she came to feel verily a haunting passion for it. Yet in her penniless state she would have parted with it for money; she gave herself also to dreams of what in this direction it would do for her. The sophistry of her so often saying to herself that Arthur had after all definitely pronounced her welcome to any gain from his gift that might accrue—this trick remained innocent, as she perfectly knew it for what it was. Then there was always the possibility of his—as she could only picture it—rising to the occasion. Mightn't he have a grand magnanimous moment?—mightn't he just say, "Oh I couldn't of course have afforded to let you have it if I had known; but since you *have* got it, and have made out the truth by your own wit, I really can't screw myself down to the shabbiness of taking it back."?

She had, as it proved, to wait a long time—to wait till, at the end of several months, the great house of Bleet had, with due deliberation, for the season, transferred itself to town; after which, however, she fairly snatched at her first freedom to knock, dressed in her best and armed with her disclosure, at the door of her doubting kinsman. It was still with doubt and not quite with the face she had hoped that he listened to her story. He had turned pale, she thought, as she produced the necklace, and he appeared above all disagreeably affected. Well, perhaps there was reason, she more than ever remembered; but what on earth was one, in close touch with the fact, to do? She had laid the pearls on his table, where, without his having at first put so much as a finger to them, they met his hard cold stare.

"I don't believe in them," he simply said at last.

"That's exactly then," she returned with some spirit, "what I wanted to hear!"

She fancied that at this his colour changed; it was indeed vivid to her afterwards—for she was to have a long recall of the scene—that she had made him quite angrily flush. "It's a beastly unpleasant imputation, you know!"—and he walked away from her as he had always walked at the vicarage.

"It's none of *my* making, I'm sure," said Charlotte Prime. "If you're afraid to believe they're real—"

"Well?"—and he turned, across the room, sharp round at her.

"Why it's not my fault."

He said nothing more, for a moment, on this; he only came back to the table. "They're what I originally said they were. They're rotten paste."

"Then I may keep them?"

"No. I want a better opinion."

"Than your own?"

"Than *your* own." He dropped on the pearls another queer stare; then, after a moment, bringing himself to touch them, did exactly what she had herself done in the presence of Mrs. Guy at Bleet—gathered them together, marched off with them to a drawer, put them in and clicked the key. "You say I'm afraid," he went on as he again met her; "but I shan't be afraid to take them to Bond Street."

"And if the people say they're real—?"

He had a pause and then his strangest manner. "They won't say it! They shan't!"

There was something in the way he brought it out that deprived poor Charlotte, as she was perfectly aware, of any manner at all. "Oh!" she simply sounded, as she had sounded for her last word to Mrs. Guy; and within a minute, without more conversation, she had taken her departure.

A fortnight later she received a communication from him, and toward the end of the season one of the entertainments in Eaton Square was graced by the presence of Mrs. Guy. Charlotte was not at dinner, but she came down afterwards, and this guest, on seeing her, abandoned a very beautiful young man on purpose to cross and speak to her. The guest displayed a lovely necklace and had apparently not lost her habit of overflowing with the pride of such ornaments.

"Do you see?" She was in high joy.

They were indeed splendid pearls—so far as poor Charlotte could feel that she knew, after what had come and gone, about such mysteries. The poor girl had a sickly smile. "They're almost as fine as Arthur's."

"Almost? Where, my dear, are your eyes? They *are* 'Arthur's'!" After which, to meet the flood of crimson that accompanied her young friend's start: "I tracked them—after your folly, and, by miraculous luck, recognised them in the Bond Street window to which he had disposed of them."

"*Disposed* of them?" Charlotte gasped. "He wrote me that I had insulted his mother and that the people had shown him he was right—had pronounced them utter paste."

Mrs. Guy gave a stare. "Ah I told you he wouldn't bear it! No. But I had, I assure you," she wound up, "to drive my bargain!"

Charlotte scarce heard or saw; she was full of her private wrong. "He wrote me," she panted, "that he had smashed them."

Mrs. Guy could only wonder and pity. "He's really morbid!" But it wasn't quite clear which of the pair she pitied; though the young person employed in Eaton Square felt really morbid too after they had separated and she found herself full of thought. She even went the length of asking herself what sort of a bargain Mrs. Guy had driven and whether the marvel of the recognition in Bond Street had been a veracious account of the matter. Hadn't she perhaps in truth dealt with Arthur directly? It came back to Charlotte almost luridly that she had had his address.

Henry Cuyler Bunner

A STORY TELLER with a superb gift for the provocative situation and the surprising conclusion, H. C. Bunner did for New York City and the Eastern Seaboard what H. H. Munroe was later to do for England. Both men had the lively, satiric eye which finds joy in observing the foibles of middle-class society; both had great technical skill. Bunner's interest in the art of the story led him to analyse carefully the work of the masters, especially that of Maupassant to whose plots he gave "a United States twist."

During his editorship of Puck in the Nineties, Bunner was famous not only for his stories but for the graceful lyrics, essays, and parodies which he turned out with a sure hand. With him the distinction ordinarily drawn between journalism and literature did not hold; he was always the man of letters. In his short life he managed to produce much pleasurable reading. His short stories are collected in the volumes Short Sixes (1890), Zadoc Pine (1891), More Short Sixes (1894), and Made in France (1893), the last being a re-telling of a few of Maupassant's best known tales.

H. C. Bunner was born in Oswego, New York, in 1855. Obliged to forego the advantages of a college education, he quickly made a name in New York journalism, contributing to several magazines and eventually assuming the editorship of Puck, which he held until his death in 1896.

THE TWO CHURCHES OF 'QUAWKET *

H. C. Bunner

THE REVEREND Colton M. Pursly, of Aquawket, (commonly pronounced 'Quawket,) looked out of his study window over a remarkably pretty New England prospect, stroked his thin, grayish
side-whiskers, and sighed deeply. He was a pale, sober, ill-dressed
Congregationalist minister of forty-two or three. He had eyes of
willow-pattern blue, a large nose, and a large mouth, with a smile of
forced amiability in the corners. He *was* amiable, perfectly amiable
and innocuous—but that smile sometimes made people with a strong
sense of humor want to kill him. The smile lingered even while he
sighed.

Mr. Pursly's house was set upon a hill, although it was a modest
abode. From his window he looked down one of those splendid
streets that are the pride and glory of old towns in New England—a
street fifty yards wide, arched with grand Gothic elms, bordered with
houses of pale yellow and white, some in the homelike, simple yet
dignified colonial style, some with great Doric porticos at the street
end. And above the billowy green of the tree-tops rose two shapely
spires, one to the right, of granite, one to the left, of sand-stone. It was
the sight of these two spires that made the Reverend Mr. Pursly sigh.

With a population of four thousand five hundred, 'Quawket had
an Episcopal Church, a Roman Catholic Church, a Presbyterian
Church, a Methodist Church, a Universalist Church, (very small,) a
Baptist Church, a Hall for the "Seventh-Day Baptists," (used for
secular purposes every day but Saturday,) a Bethel, and—"The Two
Churches"—as every one called the First and Second Congregational
Churches. Fifteen years before, there had been but one Congregational
Church, where a prosperous and contented congregation worshiped in
a plain little old-fashioned red brick church on a side-street. Then, out
of this very prosperity, came the idea of building a fine new free-stone
church on Main Street. And, when the new church was half-built, the
congregation split on the question of putting a "rain-box" in the new
organ. It is quite unnecessary to detail how this quarrel over a handful
of peas grew into a church war, with ramifications and interlacements
and entanglements and side-issues and under-currents and embroil-

---

* From *Short Sixes* by Henry Cuyler Bunner. Charles Scribner's Sons, 1891. Reprinted
by permission of Charles Scribner's Sons.

ments of all sorts and conditions. In three years there was a First
Congregational Church, in free-stone, solid, substantial, plain, and a
Second Congregational Church in granite, something gingerbready,
but showy and modish—for there are fashions in architecture as there
are in millinery, and we cut our houses this way this year and that way
the next. And these two churches had half a congregation apiece, and
a full-sized debt, and they lived together in a spirit of Christian unity,
on Capulet and Montague terms. The people of the First Church
called the people of the Second Church the "Sadduceeceders," because
there was no future for them, and the people of the Second Church
called the people of the First Church the "Pharisee-me"s. And this
went on year after year, through the Winters when the foxes hugged
their holes in the ground within the woods about 'Quawket, through
the Summers when the birds of the air twittered in their nests in the
great elms of Main Street.

If the First Church had a revival, the Second Church had a fair. If
the pastor of the First Church exchanged with a distinguished preacher
from Philadelphia, the organist of the Second Church got a celebrated
tenor from Boston and had a service of song. This system after a time
created a class in both churches known as "the floats," in contradis-
tinction to the "pillars." The floats went from one church to the other
according to the attractions offered. There were, in the end, more floats
than pillars.

The Reverend Mr. Pursly inherited this contest from his predecessor.
He had carried it on for three years. Finally, being a man of logical
and precise mental processes, he called the head men of his congregation together, and told them what in worldly language might be set
down thus:

There was room for one Congregational Church in 'Quawket, and
for one only. The flock must be reunited in the parent fold. To do this
a master stroke was necessary. They must build a Parish House. All
of which was true beyond question—and yet—the church had a debt
of $20,000 and a Parish House would cost $15,000.

And now the Reverend Mr. Pursly was sitting at his study window,
wondering why all the rich men *would* join the Episcopal Church.
He cast down his eyes, and saw a rich man coming up his path who
could readily have given $15,000 for a Parish House, and who might
safely be expected to give $1.50, if he were rightly approached. A shade
of bitterness crept over Mr. Pursly's professional smile. Then a look
of puzzled wonder took possession of his face. Brother Joash Hitt

was regular in his attendance at church and at prayer-meeting; but he kept office-hours in his religion, as in everything else, and never before had he called upon his pastor.

Two minutes later, the minister was nervously shaking hands with Brother Joash Hitt.

"I'm very glad to see you, Mr. Hitt," he stammered, "very glad—I'm—I'm—"

"S'prised?" suggested Mr. Hitt, grimly.

"Won't you sit down?" asked Mr. Pursly.

Mr. Hitt sat down in the darkest corner of the room, and glared at his embarrassed host. He was a huge old man, bent, heavily-built, with grizzled dark hair, black eyes, skin tanned to a mahogany brown, a heavy square under-jaw, and big leathery dew-laps on each side of it that looked as hard as the jaw itself. Brother Joash had been all things in his long life—sea-captain, commission merchant, speculator, slave-dealer even, people said—and all things to his profit. Of late years he had turned over his capital in money-lending, and people said that his great claw-like fingers had grown crooked with holding the tails of his mortgages.

A silence ensued. The pastor looked up and saw that Brother Joash had no intention of breaking it.

"Can I do any thing for you, Mr. Hitt?" inquired Mr. Pursly.

"Ya-as," said the old man. "Ye kin. I b'leeve you gin'lly git sump'n over'n' above your sellery when you preach a fun'l sermon?"

"Well, Mr. Hitt, it—yes—it is customary."

"How much?"

"The usual honorarium is—h'm—ten dollars."

"The—*whut?*"

"The—the fee."

"Will you write me one for ten dollars?"

"Why—why—" said the minister, nervously; "I didn't know that any one had—had died—"

"There hain't no one died, ez I know. It's *my* fun'l sermon I want."

"But, my dear Mr. Hitt, I trust you are not—that you won't—that—"

"Life's a rope of sand, parson—you'd ought to know that—nor we don't none of us know when it's goin' to fetch loost. I'm most ninety now, 'n' I don't cal'late to git no younger."

"Well," said Mr. Pursly, faintly smiling; "when the time *does* come—"

"No, *sir!*" interrupted Mr. Hitt, with emphasis; "when the time *doos* come, I won't have no use for it. Th' ain't no sense in the way most folks is berrid. Whut's th' use of puttin' a man into a mahog'ny coffin, with a silver plate big's a dishpan, an' preachin' a fun'l sermon over him, an' costin' his estate good money, when he's only a poor deef, dumb, blind fool corpse, an' don't get no good of it? *Naow,* I've be'n to the undertaker's, an' hed my coffin made under my own sooperveesion—good wood, straight grain, no knots—nuthin' fancy, but doorable. I've hed my tombstun cut, an' chose my text to put onto it—'we brung nuthin' into the world, an' it is certain we can take nuthin' out'—an' now I want my fun'l sermon, jes' as the other folks is goin' to hear it who don't pay nuthin' for it. Kin you hev it ready for me this day week?"

"I suppose so," said Mr. Pursly, weakly.

"I'll call fer it," said the old man. "Heern some talk about a Perrish House, didn't I?"

"Yes," began Mr. Pursly, his face lighting up.

" 'T ain't no sech a bad *i*dee," remarked Brother Joash. "Wal, good day." And he walked off before the minister could say anything more.

One week later, Mr. Pursly again sat in his study, looking at Brother Joash, who had a second time settled himself in the dark corner.

It had been a terrible week for Mr. Pursly. He and his conscience, and his dream of the Parish House, had been shut up together working over that sermon, and waging a war of compromises. The casualties in this war were all on the side of the conscience.

"Read it!" commanded Brother Joash. The minister grew pale. This was more than he had expected. He grew pale and then red and then pale again.

"Go ahead!" said Brother Joash.

"Brethren," began Mr. Pursly, and then he stopped short. His pulpit voice sounded strange in his little study.

"Go ahead!" said Brother Joash.

"We are gathered together here to-day to pay a last tribute of respect and affection—"

"Clk!" There was a sound like the report of a small pistol. Mr. Pursly looked up. Brother Joash regarded him with stern intentness.

"—to one of the oldest and most prominent citizens of our town, a pillar of our church, and a monument of the civic virtues of probity, industry and wisdom, a man in whom we all took pride, and—"

"Clk!" Mr. Pursly looked up more quickly this time, and a faint suggestion of an expression just vanishing from Mr. Hitt's lips awakened in his unsuspicious breast a horrible suspicion that Brother Joash had chuckled.

"—whose like we shall not soon again see in our midst. The children on the streets will miss his familiar face—"

"Say!" broke in Brother Joash, "how'd it be for a delegation of child'n to foller the remains, with flowers or sump'n? They'd volunteer if you give 'em the hint, wouldn't they?"

"It would be—unusual," said the minister.

"All right," assented Mr. Hitt, "only an *i*dee of mine. Thought they might like it. Go ahead!"

Mr. Pursly went ahead, haunted by an agonizing fear of that awful chuckle, if chuckle it was. But he got along without interruption until he reached a casual and guarded allusion to the widows and orphans without whom no funeral oration is complete. Here the metallic voice of Brother Joash rang out again.

"Say! Ef the widders and orphans send a wreath—or a Gates-Ajar—*ef* they do, mind ye!—you'll hev it put a-top of the coffin, where folks'll see it, wun't ye?"

"Certainly," said the Reverend Mr. Pursly, hastily; "his charities were unostentatious, as was the whole tenor of his life. In these days of spendthrift extravagance, our young men may well—"

"Say!" Brother Joash broke in once more. "Ef any one wuz to git up right there, an' say that I wuz the derndest meanest, miserly, penurious, parsimonious old hunks in 'Quawket, you wouldn't let him talk like that, would ye?"

"Unquestionably not, Mr. Hitt!" said the minister, in horror.

"Thought not. On'y thet's whut I heern one o' your deacons say about me the other day. Didn't know I heern him, but I did. I thought you wouldn't allow no such talk as that. Go ahead!"

"I must ask you, Mr. Hitt," Mr. Pursly said, perspiring at every pore, "to refrain from interruptions—or I—I really—can not continue."

"All right," returned Mr. Hitt, with perfect calmness. "Continner."

Mr. Pursly continued to the bitter end, with no further interruption that called for remonstrance. There were soft inarticulate sounds that seemed to him to come from Brother Joash's dark corner. But it might have been the birds in the *Ampelopsis Veitchii* that covered the house.

Brother Joash expressed no opinion, good or ill, of the address. He

paid his ten dollars, in one-dollar bills, and took his receipt. But as
the anxious minister followed him to the door, he turned suddenly
and said:

"You was talkin' 'bout a Perrish House?"

"Yes—"

"Kin ye keep a secret?"

"I hope so—yes, certainly, Mr. Hitt."

"The' 'll be one."

"I feel," said the Reverend Mr. Pursly to his wife, "as if I had
carried every stone of that Parish House on my shoulders and put it
in its place. Can you make me a cup of tea, my dear?"

The Summer days had begun to grow chill, and the great elms of
'Quawket were flecked with patches and spots of yellow, when, early
one morning, the meagre little charity-boy whose duty it was to
black Mr. Hitt's boots every day—it was a luxury he allowed himself
in his old age—rushed, pale and frightened, into a neighboring
grocery, and cried:

"Mist' Hitt's dead!"

"Guess not," said the grocer, doubtfully. "Brother Hitt's gut th'
Old Nick's agency for 'Quawket, 'n' I ain't heerd th't he's been discharged for inattention to dooty."

"He's layin' there smilin'," said the boy.

"Smilin'?" repeated the grocer. "Guess I'd better go 'n' see."

In very truth, Brother Joash lay there in his bed, dead and cold,
with a smile on his hard old lips, the first he had ever worn. And a
most sardonic and discomforting smile it was.

The Reverend Mr. Pursly read Mr. Hitt's funeral address for the
second time, in the First Congregational Church of 'Quawket. Every
seat was filled; every ear was attentive. He stood on the platform, and
below him, supported on decorously covered trestles, stood the coffin
that enclosed all that was mortal of Brother Joash Hitt. Mr. Pursly
read with his face immovably set on the line of the clock in the middle
of the choir-gallery railing. He did not dare to look down at the
sardonic smile in the coffin below him; he did not dare to let his
eye wander to the dark left-hand corner of the church, remembering
the dark left-hand corner of his own study. And as he repeated each
complimentary, obsequious, flattering platitude, a hideous, hysterical

fear grew stronger and stronger and stronger within him that suddenly he would be struck dumb by the "clk!" of that mirthless chuckle that had sounded so much like a pistol-shot. His voice was hardly audible in the benediction.

The streets of 'Quawket were at their gayest and brightest when the mourners drove home from the cemetery at the close of the noon-tide hour. The mourners were principally the deacons and elders of the First Church. The Reverend Mr. Pursly lay back in his seat with a pleasing yet fatigued consciousness of duty performed and martyr-dom achieved. He was exhausted, but humbly happy. As they drove along, he looked with a speculative eye on one or two eligible sites for the Parish House. His companion in the carriage was Mr. Uriel Hankinson, Brother Joash's lawyer, whose entire character had been aptly summed up by one of his fellow-citizens in conferring on him the designation of "a little Joash for one cent."

"Parson," said Mr. Hankinson, breaking a long silence, "that was a fust-rate oration you made."

"I'm glad to hear you say so," replied Mr. Pursly, his chronic smile broadening.

"You treated the deceased right handsome, considerin'," went on the lawyer Hankinson.

"Considering what?" inquired Mr. Pursly, in surprise.

"Considerin'—well, *considerin'*—" replied Mr. Hankinson, with a wave of his hand. "You must feel to be reel disapp'inted 'bout the Parish House, I sh'd s'pose."

"The Parish House?" repeated the Reverend Mr. Pursly, with a cold chill at his heart, but with dignity in his voice. "You may not be aware, Mr. Hankinson, that I have Mr. Hitt's promise that we should have a Parish House. And Mr. Hitt was—was—a man of his word." This conclusion sounded to his own ears a trifle lame and impotent.

"Guess you had his promise that there *should* be a Parish House," corrected the lawyer, with a chuckle that might have been a faint echo of Brother Joash's.

"Well?"

"Well—the Second Church gits it. I draw'd his will. Good day, parson, I'll 'light here. Air's kind o' cold, ain't it?"

Mark Twain

MARK TWAIN (Samuel Langhorne Clemens) was not an artisan of the short story, and when he wrote a successful one, it was something of a tour de force. He sometimes confessed a humorous despair in managing his plots and characters, and his work shop was filled with manuscript pages which came to nothing. Even his published stories were likely to depend upon outlandish or grotesque situations—witness "The £1,000,000 Bank Note" or "The Esquimau Maiden's Romance"—and his most ambitious short story "The Man Who Corrupted Hadleyburg" creaks with complicated manipulation.

But he was a man of genius, and his failures were more interesting than the successes of lesser writers. And he didn't always fail. "The Celebrated Jumping Frog" and "Jim Baker's Blue Jay Yarn" are classics of folk-lore, and the story included here "My Platonic Sweetheart," a tale which reads like a personal record, is indeed memorable for its wistfulness, its haunting tenderness not betrayed into sentimentality.

Mark Twain's career needs no annotation here. In his seventy-five years from 1835 to 1910 he developed a stature unsurpassed in American letters. His four greatest books, in the editor's opinion, are Innocents Abroad (1869), Roughing It (1872), Life on the Mississippi (1883), and Huckleberry Finn (1884).

MY PLATONIC SWEETHEART *
Mark Twain

I MET HER first when I was seventeen and she fifteen. It was in a dream. No, I did not meet her; I overtook her. It was in a Missourian village which I had never been in before, and was not in

---

* From *The Mysterious Stranger and Other Stories* by Mark Twain. Harper & Brothers. Reprinted by permission of Harper & Brothers.

at that time, except dreamwise; in the flesh I was on the Atlantic seaboard ten or twelve hundred miles away. The thing was sudden, and without preparation—after the custom of dreams. There I was, crossing a wooden bridge that had a wooden rail and was untidy with scattered wisps of hay, and there she was, five steps in front of me; half a second previously neither of us was there. This was the exit of the village, which lay immediately behind us. Its last house was the blacksmith-shop; and the peaceful clinking of the hammers— a sound which nearly always seems remote, and is always touched with a spirit of loneliness and a feeling of soft regret for something, you don't know what—was wafted to my ears over my shoulder; in front of us was the winding country road, with woods on one side, and on the other a rail fence, with blackberry vines and hazel bushes crowding its angles; on an upper rail a bluebird, and scurrying toward him along the same rail, a fox-squirrel with his tail bent high like a shepherd's crook; beyond the fence a rich field of grain, and far away a farmer in shirtsleeves and straw hat wading knee-deep through it; no other representatives of life, and no noise at all; everywhere a Sabbath stillness.

I remember it all—and the girl, too, and just how she walked, and how she was dressed. In the first moment I was five steps behind her; in the next one I was at her side—without either stepping or gliding; it merely happened; the transfer ignored space. I noticed that, but not with any surprise; it seemed a natural process.

I was at her side. I put my arm around her waist and drew her close to me, for I loved her; and although I did not know her, my behavior seemed to me quite natural and right, and I had no misgivings about it. She showed no surprise, no distress, no displeasure, but put an arm around my waist, and turned up her face to mine with a happy welcome in it, and when I bent down to kiss her she received the kiss as if she was expecting it, and as if it was quite natural for me to offer it and her to take it and have pleasure in it. The affection which I felt for her and which she manifestly felt for me was a quite simple fact; but the quality of it was another matter. It was not the affection of brother and sister—it was closer than that, more clinging, more endearing, more reverent; and it was not the love of sweethearts, for there was no fire in it. It was somewhere between the two, and was finer than either, and more exquisite, more profoundly contenting. We often experience this strange and gracious thing in our dream-loves; and we remember it as a feature of our childhood-loves, too.

We strolled along, across the bridge and down the road, chatting like the oldest friends. She called me George, and that seemed natural and right, though it was not my name; and I called her Alice, and she did not correct me, though without doubt it was not her name. Everything that happened seemed just natural and to be expected. Once I said, "What a dear little hand it is!" and without any words she laid it gracefully in mine for me to examine it. I did it, remarking upon its littleness, its delicate beauty, and its satin skin, then kissed it; she put it up to her lips without saying anything and kissed it in the same place.

Around a curve of the road, at the end of half a mile, we came to a log house, and entered it and found the table set and everything on it steaming hot—a roast turkey, corn in the ear, butterbeans, and the rest of the usual things—and a cat curled up asleep in a splint-bottomed chair by the fireplace; but no people; just emptiness and silence. She said she would look in the next room if I would wait for her. So I sat down, and she passed through a door, which closed behind her with a click of the latch. I waited and waited. Then I got up and followed, for I could not any longer bear to have her out of my sight. I passed through the door, and found myself in a strange sort of cemetery, a city of innumerable tombs and monuments stretching far and wide on every hand, and flushed with pink and gold lights flung from the sinking sun. I turned around, and the log house was gone. I ran here and there and yonder down the lanes between the rows of tombs, calling Alice; and presently the night closed down, and I could not find my way. Then I woke, in deep distress over my loss, and was in my bed in Philadelphia. And I was not seventeen, now, but nineteen.

Ten years afterward, in another dream, I found her. I was seventeen again, and she was still fifteen. I was in a grassy place in the twilight deeps of a magnolia forest some miles above Natchez, Mississippi; the trees were snowed over with great blossoms, and the air was loaded with their rich and strenuous fragrance; the ground was high, and through a rift in the wood a burnished patch of the river was visible in the distance. I was sitting on the grass, absorbed in thinking, when an arm was laid around my neck, and there was Alice sitting by my side and looking into my face. A deep and satisfied happiness and an un-wordable gratitude rose in me, but with it there was no feeling of sur-prise; and there was no sense of a time-lapse; the ten years amounted to hardly even a yesterday; indeed, to hardly even a noticeable fraction of it. We dropped in the tranquilest way into affectionate caressings and pettings, and chatted along without a reference to the separation; which was natural, for I think we did not know there had been any that one might measure with either clock or almanac. She called me Jack and I called her Helen, and those seemed the right and proper names, and perhaps neither of us suspected that we had ever borne others; or, if we did suspect it, it was probably not a matter of consequence.

She had been beautiful ten years before; she was just as beautiful still; girlishly young and sweet and innocent, and she was still that now. She had blue eyes, a hair of flossy gold before; she had black hair now, and dark-brown eyes. I noted these differences, but they did not suggest change; to me she was the same girl she was before, absolutely. It never occurred to me to ask what became of the log house; I doubt if I even thought of it. We were living in a simple and natural and beautiful world where everything that happened was natural and right, and was not perplexed with the unexpected or with any forms of surprise, and so there was no occasion for explanations and no interest attaching to such things.

We had a dear and pleasant time together, and were like a couple of ignorant and contented children. Helen had a summer hat on. She took it off presently and said, "It was in the way; now you can kiss me better." It seemed to me merely a bit of courteous and considerate wisdom, nothing more; and a natural thing for her to think of and do. We went wandering through the woods, and came to a limpid and shallow stream a matter of three yards wide. She said:

"I must not get my feet wet, dear; carry me over."

I took her in my arms and gave her my hat to hold. This was to keep my own feet from getting wet. I did not know why this should have that effect; I merely knew it; and she knew it, too. I crossed the stream, and said I would go on carrying her, because it was so pleasant; and she said it was pleasant to her too, and wished we had thought of it sooner. It seemed to me a pity that we should have walked so far, both of us on foot, when we could have been having this higher enjoyment; and I spoke of it regretfully, as a something lost which could never be got back. She was troubled about it, too, and said there must be some way to get it back; and she would think. After musing deeply a little while she looked up radiant and proud, and said she had found it.

"Carry me back and start over again."

I can see, now, that that was no solution, but at the time it seemed luminous with intelligence, and I believed that there was not another little head in the world that could have worked out that difficult problem with such swiftness and success. I told her that, and it pleased her; and she said she was glad it all happened, so that I could see how capable she was. After thinking a moment she added that it was "quite atreous." The words seemed to mean something, I do not know why: in fact, it seemed to cover the whole ground and leave nothing more to say; I admired the nice aptness and the flashing felicity of the phrase, and was filled with respect for the marvelous mind that had been able to engender it. I think less of it now. It is a noticeable fact that the intellectual coinage of Dreamland often passes for more there than it would fetch here. Many a time in after years my dream-sweetheart threw off golden sayings which crumbled to ashes under my pencil when I was setting them down in my note-book after breakfast.

I carried her back and started over again; and all the long afternoon I bore her in my arms, miles upon miles, and it never occurred to either of us that there was anything remarkable in a youth like me being able to carry that sweet bundle around half a day without some sense of fatigue or need of rest. There are many dream-worlds, but none is so rightly and reasonably and pleasantly arranged as that one.

After dark we reached a great plantation-house, and it was her home. I carried her in, and the family knew me and I knew them, although we had not met before; and the mother asked me with ill disguised anxiety how much twelve times fourteen was, and I said a hundred and thirty-five, and she put it down on a piece of paper, saying it was her habit in the process of perfecting her education not to trust important particulars to her memory; and her husband was offering me a chair, but noticed that Helen was asleep, so he said it would be best not to disturb her; and he backed me softly against a wardrobe and said I could stand more easily now; then a negro came in, bowing humbly, with his slouch-hat in his hand, and asked me if I would have my measure taken. The question did not surprise me, but it confused me and worried me, and I said I should like to have advice about it. He started toward the door to call advisers; then he and the family and the lights began to grow dim, and in a few moments the place was pitch dark; but straightway there came a flood of moonlight and a gust of cold wind, and I found myself crossing a frozen lake, and my arms were empty. The wave of grief that swept through me woke me up, and I was sitting at my desk in the news-paper office in San Francisco, and I noticed by the clock that I had been asleep less than two minutes. And what was of more consequence, I was twenty-nine years old.

That was 1864. The next year and the year after I had momentary glimpses of my dream-sweetheart, but nothing more. These are set down in my note-books under their proper dates, but with no talks nor other particulars added; which is sufficient evidence to me that there were none to add. In both of these instances there was the sudden meeting and recognition, the eager approach, then the instant disappearance, leaving the world empty and of no worth. I remember the two images quite well; in fact, I remember all the images of that spirit, and can bring them before me without help of my note-book. The habit of writing down my dreams of all sorts while they were fresh in my mind, and then studying them and rehearsing them and trying to find out what the source of dreams is, and which of the two or three separate persons inhabiting us is their architect, has given me a good dream-memory—a thing which is not usual with people, for few drill the dream-memory—and no memory can be kept strong without that.

I spent a few months in the Hawaiian Islands in 1866, and in October of that year I delivered my maiden lecture; it was in San Francisco. In the following January I arrived in New York, and had just completed my thirty-first year. In that year I saw my platonic dream-sweetheart again. In this dream I was again standing on the stage of the Opera House in San Francisco, ready to lecture, and with the audience vividly individualized before me in the strong light. I began, spoke a few words, and stopped, cold with fright; for I discovered that I had no subject, no text, nothing to talk about. I choked for a while, then got out a few words, a lame, poor attempt at humor. The house made no response. There was a miserable pause, then another attempt, and another failure. There were a few scornful laughs; otherwise the house was silent, unsmilingly austere, deeply offended. I was consuming with shame. In my distress I tried to work upon its pity. I began to make servile apologies, mixed with gross and ill-timed flatteries, and to beg and plead for forgiveness; this was too much, and the people broke into insulting cries, whistlings, hoot-ings, and cat-calls, and in the midst of this they rose and began to struggle in a confused mass toward the door. I stood dazed and helpless, looking out over this spectacle, and thinking how everybody would be talking about it next day, and I could not show myself in the streets. When the house was become wholly empty and still, I sat down on the only chair that was on the stage and bent my head down on the reading-desk to shut out the look of that place. Soon that familiar dream-voice spoke my name, and swept all my troubles away:

"Robert!"

I answered:

"Agnes!"

The next moment we two were lounging up the blossomy gorge called the Iao Valley, in the Hawaiian Islands. I recognized, without any explanations, that Robert was not my name, but only a pet name, a common noun, and meant "dear"; and both of us knew that Agnes was not a name, but only a pet name, a common noun, whose spirit was affectionate, but not conveyable with exactness in any but the dream-language. It was about the equivalent of "dear," but the dream-vocabulary shaves meanings finer and closer than do the world's day-time dictionaries. We did not know why those words should have those meanings; we had used words which had no existence in any known language, and had expected them to be understood, and they were understood. In my note-books there are several letters from this dream-sweetheart, in some unknown tongue—presumably dream-tongue—with translations added. I should like to be master of that tongue, then I could talk in shorthand. Here is one of those letters—the whole of it:

"Rax oha tal."

Translation.—"When you receive this it will remind you that I long to see your face and touch your hand, for the comfort of it and the peace."

It is swifter than waking thought; for thought is not thought at all, but only a vague and formless fog until it is articulated into words.

We wandered far up the fairy gorge, gathering the beautiful flowers of the ginger-plant and talking affectionate things, and tying and retying each other's ribbons and cravats, which didn't need it; and finally sat down in the shade of a tree and climbed the vine-hung precipices with our eyes, up and up and up toward the sky to where the drifting scarfs of white mist clove them across and left the green summits floating pale and remote, like spectral islands wandering in the deeps of space; and then we descended to earth and talked again.

"How still it is—and soft, and balmy, and reposeful! I could never tire of it. You like it, don't you, Robert?"

"Yes, and I like the whole region—all the islands. Maui. It is a darling island. I have been here before. Have you?"

"Once, but it wasn't an island then."

"What was it?"

"It was a sufa."

I understood. It was the dream-word for "part of a continent."

"What were the people like?"

"They hadn't come yet. There weren't any."

"Do you know, Agnes—that is Haleakala, the dead volcano, over there across the valley; was it here in your friend's time?"

"Yes, but it was burning."

"Do you travel much?"

"I think so. Not here much but in the stars a great deal."

"Is it pretty there?"

She used a couple of dream-words for "You will go with me some time and you will see." Non-committal, as one perceives now, but I did not notice it then.

A man-of-war bird lit on her shoulder; I put out my hand and caught it. Its feathers began to fall out, and it turned into a kitten; then the kitten's body began to contract itself to a ball and put out hairy, long legs, and soon it was a tarantula; I was going to keep it, but it turned into a star-fish, and I threw it away. Agnes said it was not worth while to try to keep things; there was no stability about them. I suggested rocks; but she said a rock was like the rest; it wouldn't stay. She picked up a stone, and it turned into a bat and flew away. These curious matters interested me, but that was all; they did not stir my wonder.

While we were sitting there in the Iao gorge talking, a Kanaka came along who was wrinkled and bent and white-headed, and he stopped and talked to us in the native tongue, and we understood him without trouble and answered him in his own speech. He said he was a hundred and thirty years old, and he remembered Captain Cook well, and was present when he was murdered; saw it with his own eyes, and also helped. Then he showed us his gun, which was of strange make, and he said it was his own invention and was to shoot arrows with, though one loaded it with powder and it had a percussion lock. He said it would carry a hundred miles. It seemed a reasonable statement; I had no fault to find with it, and it did not in any way surprise me. He loaded it and fired an arrow aloft, and it darted into the sky and vanished. Then he went his way, saying that the arrow would fall near us in half an hour, and would go many yards into the earth, not minding the rocks.

I took the time, and we waited, reclining upon the mossy slant at the base of a tree, and gazing into the sky. By and by there was a hissing sound, followed by a dull impact, and Agnes uttered a groan. She said, in a series of fainting gasps:

"Take me to your arms—it passed through me—hold me to your heart—I am afraid to die—closer—closer. It is growing dark—I cannot see you. Don't leave me—where are you? You are not gone? You will not leave me? I would not leave you."

Then her spirit passed; she was clay in my arms.

The scene changed in an instant and I was awake and crossing Bond Street in New York with a friend, and it was snowing hard. We had been talking, and there had been no observable gaps in the conversation. I doubt if I had made any more than two steps while I was asleep. I am satisfied that even the most elaborate and incident-crowded dream is seldom more than a few seconds in length. It would not cost me very much of a strain to believe in Mohammed's seventy-year dream, which began when he knocked his glass over, and ended in time for him to catch it before the water was spilled.

Within a quarter of an hour I was in my quarters, undressed, ready for bed, and was jotting down my dream in my note-book. A striking thing happened now. I finished my notes, and was just going to turn out the gas when I was caught with a most strenuous gape, for it was very late and I was very drowsy. I fell asleep and dreamed again. What now follows occurred while I was asleep; and when I woke again the gape had completed itself, but not long before, I think, for I was still on my feet. I was in Athens—a city which I had not then seen, but I recognized the Parthenon from the pictures, although it had a fresh look and was in perfect repair. I passed by it and climbed a grassy hill toward a palatial sort of mansion which was built of red terra-cotta and had a spacious portico, whose roof was supported by a rank of fluted columns with Corinthian capitals. It was noonday, but I met no one. I passed into the house and entered the first room. It was very large and light, its walls were of polished and richly tinted and veined onyx, and its floor was a pictured pattern in soft colors laid in tiles. I noted the details of the furniture and the ornaments—a thing which I should not have been likely to do when awake—and they took sharp hold and remained in my memory; they are not really dim yet, and this was more than thirty years ago.

There was a person present—Agnes. I was not surprised to see her, but only glad. She was in the simple Greek costume, and her hair and eyes were different as to color from those she had had when she died in the Hawaiian Islands half an hour before, but to me she was exactly her own beautiful little self as I had always known her, and she was still fifteen, and I was seventeen once more. She was sitting on an ivory settee, crocheting something or other, and had her crewels in a shallow willow work-basket in her lap. I sat down by her and we began to chat in the usual way. I remembered her death, but the pain and the grief and the bitterness which had been so sharp and so desolating to me at the moment that it happened had wholly passed from me now, and had left not a scar. I was grateful to have her back, but there was no realizable sense that she had ever been gone, and so it did not occur to me to speak about it, and she made no reference to it herself. It may be that she had often died before, and knew that there was nothing lasting about it, and consequently nothing important enough in it to make conversation out of.

When I think of that house and its belongings, I recognize what a master in taste and drawing and color and arrangement is the dream-artist who resides in us. In my waking hours, when the inferior artist in me is in command, I cannot draw even the simplest picture with a pencil, nor do anything with a brush and colors; I cannot bring before my mind's eye the detail image of any building known to me except my own house at home; of St. Paul's, St. Peter's, the Eiffel Tower, the Taj, the Capitol at Washington, I can reproduce only portions, partial glimpses; the same with Niagara Falls, the Matter-horn, and other familiar things in nature; I cannot bring before my mind's eye the face or figure of any human being known to me; I have seen my family at breakfast within the past two hours; I cannot bring their images before me, I do not know how they look; before me, as I write, I see a little grove of young trees in the garden; high above them projects the slender lance of a young pine, beyond it is a glimpse of the upper half of a dull-white chimney covered by an A-shaped little roof shingled with brown-red tiles, and half a mile away is a hill-top densely wooded, and the red is cloven by a curved, wide vacancy, which is smooth and grass-clad; I cannot shut my eyes and reproduce that picture as a whole at all, nor any single detail of it except the grassy curve, and that but vaguely and fleetingly.

But my dream-artist can draw anything, and do it perfectly; he can paint with all the colors and all the shades, and do it with delicacy and truth; he can place before me vivid images of palaces, cities, hamlets, hovels, mountains, valleys, lakes, skies, glowing in sunlight or moonlight, or veiled in driving gusts of snow or rain, and he can set before me people who are intensely alive, and who feel, and express their feelings in their faces, and who also talk and laugh, sing and swear. And when I wake I can shut my eyes and bring back those people, and the scenery and the buildings; and not only in general view, but often in nice detail. While Agnes and I sat talking in that grand Athens house, several stately Greeks entered from another part of it, disputing warmly about something or other, and passed us by with courteous recognition; and among them was Socrates. I recognized him by his nose. A moment later the house and Agnes and Athens vanished away, and I was in my quarters in New York again and reaching for my note-book.

In our dreams—I know it!—we do make the journeys we seem to make; we do see the things we seem to see; the people, the horses, the cats, the dogs, the birds, the whales, are real, not chimeras; they are living spirits, not shadows; and they are immortal and inde-structible. They go whither they will; they visit all resorts, all points of interest, even the twinkling suns that wander in the wastes of space. That is where those strange mountains are which slide from under our feet while we walk, and where those vast caverns are whose bewildering avenues close behind us and in front when we are lost, and shut us in. We know this because there are no such things here, and they must be there, because there is no other place.

This tale is long enough, and I will close it now. In the forty-four years that I have known my Dreamland sweetheart, I have seen her once in two years on an average. Mainly these were glimpses, but she was always immediately recognizable, notwithstanding she was so given to repair herself and getting up doubtful improvements in her hair and eyes. She was always fifteen, and looked it and acted it; and I was always seventeen, and never felt a day older. To me she is a real person, not a fiction, and her sweet and innocent society has been one of the prettiest and pleasantest experiences of my life. I know that to you her talk will not seem of the first intellectual order; but you should hear her in Dreamland—then you would see!

I saw her a week ago, just for a moment. Fifteen, as usual, and I seventeen, instead of going on sixty-three, as I was when I went to sleep. We were in India, and Bombay was in sight; also Windsor Castle, its towers and battlements veiled in a delicate haze, and from it the Thames flowed, curving and winding between its swarded banks, to our feet. I said:

"There is no question about it, England is the most beautiful of all countries."

Her face lighted with approval, and she said, with that sweet and earnest irrelevance of hers:

"It is, because it is so marginal."

Then she disappeared. It was just as well; she could probably have added nothing to that rounded and perfect statement without damaging its symmetry.

This glimpse of her carries me back to Maui, and that time when I saw her gasp out her young life. That was a terrible thing to me at the time. It was preternaturally vivid; and the pain and the grief and the misery of it to me transcended many sufferings that I have known in waking life. For everything in a dream is more deep and strong and sharp and real than is ever its pale imitation in the unreal life which is ours when we go about awake and clothed with our artificial selves in this vague and dull-tinted artificial world. When we die we shall slough off this cheap intellect, perhaps, and go abroad into Dreamland clothed in our real selves, and aggrandized and enriched by the command over the mysterious mental magician who is here not our slave, but only our guest.

Hamlin Garland

THE ENDURING power of Hamlin Garland's first book of stories Main-Travelled Roads rests upon their exemplification of his own advice: "Write of those things for which you care most and of which you know the most." Those stories came out of the bitterness which he felt against the poverty and loneliness of farm life in the Middle Border when he returned to his father's farm near Ordway, South Dakota, in the summer of 1887 after three years in Boston. The first of these stories was "Mrs. Ripley's Trip." Its underlying humor, its appreciation of the pathos and dignity of character under the burden of drudgery, marked Hamlin Garland as a great artist inspired by important themes. To call him a local-colorist would be inaccurate; he is a realist and historian.

Hamlin Garland was born in Wisconsin in 1860. During his boyhood he moved with his parents to Iowa and the Dakotas where he did the work of a farmer. In 1884 he moved to Boston and began his studies for a literary career. He tells his own story in a great series of autobiographical works, the most important of which is A Son of the Middle Border (1917). Main-Travelled Roads (1890) was supplemented by Other Main-Travelled Roads in 1910, and several other of Mr. Garland's works contain excellent short stories.

MRS. RIPLEY'S TRIP *

Hamlin Garland

THE NIGHT was in windy November, and the blast, threatening rain, roared around the poor little shanty of Uncle Ripley, set like a chicken-trap on the vast Iowa prairie. Uncle Ethan was mending his

* From *Main-Travelled Roads* by Hamlin Garland. Harper & Brothers. Reprinted by permission of the author.

old violin, with many York State "dums!" and "I gol darns!" totally oblivious of his tireless old wife, who, having "finished the supper dishes," sat knitting a stocking, evidently for the little grandson who lay before the stove like a cat.

Neither of the old people wore glasses, and their light was a tallow candle; they couldn't afford "none o' them new-fangled lamps." The room was small, the chairs were wooden, and the walls bare—a home where poverty was a never-absent guest. The old lady looked pathetically little, weazened, and hopeless in her ill-fitting garments (whose original color had long since vanished), intent as she was on the stocking in her knotted, stiffened fingers, and there was a peculiar sparkle in her little black eyes, and an unusual resolution in the straight line of her withered and shapeless lips.

Suddenly she paused, stuck a needle in the spare knob of her hair at the back of her head, and looking at Ripley, said decisively: "Ethan Ripley, you'll haff to do your own cooking from now to New Year's. I'm goin' back to Yaark State."

The old man's leather-brown face stiffened into a look of quizzical surprise for a moment; then he cackled, incredulously: "Ho! Ho! har! Sho! be y', now? I want to know if y' be."

"Well, you'll find out."

"Goin' to start to-morrow, mother?"

"No, sir, I ain't; but I am on Thursday. I want to get to Sally's by Sunday, sure, an' to Silas's on Thanksgivin'."

There was a note in the old woman's voice that brought genuine stupefaction into the face of Uncle Ripley. Of course in this case, as in all others, the money consideration was uppermost.

"Howgy 'xpect to get the money, mother? Anybody died an' left yeh a pile?"

"Never you mind where I get the money, so 's 't *you* don't haff to bear it. The land knows if I'd 'a' waited for *you* to pay my way—"

"You needn't twit me of bein' poor, old woman," said Ripley, flaming up after the manner of many old people. "I've done *my* part t' get along. I've worked day in and day out—"

"Oh! *I* ain't done no work, have I?" snapped she, laying down the stocking and levelling a needle at him, and putting a frightful emphasis on "I."

"I didn't say you hadn't done no work."

"Yes, you did!"

"I didn't neither. I said—"

"I *know* what you said."

"I said I'd done *my part!*" roared the husband, dominating her as usual by superior lung power. "I didn't *say* you hadn't done your part," he added with an unfortunate touch of emphasis.

"I know y' didn't *say* it, but y' meant it. I don't know what y' call doin' my part, Ethan Ripley; but if cookin' for a drove of harvest hands and threshin' hands, takin' care o' the eggs and butter, 'n' diggin' 'taters an' milkin' ain't *my* part, I don't expect to do my part, 'n' you might as well know it fust's last.

"I'm sixty years old," she went on, with a little break in her harsh voice, dominating him now by woman's logic, "an' I've never had a day to myself, not even Fourth o' July. If I've went a-visitin' 'r to a picnic, I've had to come home an' milk 'n' get supper for you menfolks. I ain't been away t' stay overnight for thirteen years in this house, 'n' it was just so in Davis County for ten more. For twenty-three years, Ethan Ripley, I've stuck right to the stove an' churn without a day or night off."

Her voice choked again, but she rallied, and continued impressively, "And now I'm a-goin' back to Yaark State."

Ethan was vanquished. He stared at her in speechless surprise, his jaw hanging. It was incredible.

"For twenty-three years," she went on, musingly, "I've just about promised myself every year I'd go back an' see my folks." She was distinctly talking to herself now, and her voice had a touching, wistful cadence. "I've wanted to go back an' see the old folks, an' the hills where we played, an' eat apples off the old tree down by the well. I've had them trees an' hills in my mind days and days—nights, too—an' the girls I used to know, an' my own folks—"

She fell into a silent muse, which lasted so long that the ticking of the clock grew loud as a gong in the man's ears, and the wind outside seemed to sound drearier than usual. He returned to the money problem; kindly, though.

"But how y' goin' t' raise the money? I ain't got no extra cash this time. Agin Roach is paid, an' the interest paid, we ain't got no hundred dollars to spare, Jane, not by a jugful."

"Wal, don't you lay awake nights studyin' on where I'm a-goin' to get the money," said the old woman, taking delight in mystifying him. She had him now, and he couldn't escape. He strove to show his indifference, however, by playing a tune or two on the violin.

"Come, Tukey, you better climb the wooden hill," Mrs. Ripley said, a half-hour later, to the little chap on the floor, who was beginning to get drowsy under the influence of his grandpa's fiddling. "Pa, you orta 'a' put that string in the clock to-day—on the 'larm side the string is broke," she said, upon returning from the boy's bed-room. "I orta git up early to-morrow, to git some sewin' done. Land knows, I can't fix up much, but they is a little I c'n do. I want to look decent."

They were alone now, and they both sat expectantly.

"You 'pear to think, mother, that I'm agin yer goin'."

"Wal, it would kinder seem as if y' hadn't hustled yerself any t' help me git off."

He was smarting under the sense of being wronged. "Wal, I'm just as willin' you should go as I am for myself, but if I ain't got no money I don't see how I'm goin' to send—"

"I don't want ye to send; nobody ast ye to, Ethan Ripley. I guess if I had what I've earnt since we came on this farm I'd have enough to go to Jericho with."

"You've got as much out of it as I have," he replied gently. "You talk about your goin' back. Ain't I been wantin' to go back myself? And ain't I kep' still 'cause I see it wa'n't no use? I guess I've worked jest as long and as hard as you, an' in storms an' in mud an' heat, ef it comes t' that."

The woman was staggered, but she wouldn't give up; she must get in one more thrust.

"Wal, if you'd 'a' managed as well as I have, you'd have some money to go with." And she rose and went to mix her bread and set it "raisin'."

He sat by the fire twanging his fiddle softly. He was plainly thrown into gloomy retrospection, something quite unusual for him. But his fingers picking out the bars of a familiar tune set him to smiling, and whipping his bow across the strings, he forgot all about his wife's resolutions and his own hardships. "Trouble always slid off his back like punkins off a haystack, anyway," his wife said.

The old man still sat fiddling softly after his wife disappeared in the hot and stuffy little bedroom off the kitchen. His shaggy head bent lower over his violin. He heard her shoes drop—*one, two.* Pretty soon she called:

"Come, put up that squeakin' old fiddle, and go to bed. Seems as if you orta have sense enough not to set there keepin' everybody in the house awake."

"You hush up," retorted he. "I'll come when I git ready and not till. I'll be glad when you're gone—"

"Yes, I warrant *that.*"

With which amiable good-night they went off to sleep, or at least she did, while he lay awake pondering on "where under the sun she was goin' t' raise that money."

The next day she was up bright and early, working away on her own affairs, ignoring Ripley entirely, the fixed look of resolution still on her little old wrinkled face. She killed a hen and dressed and baked it. She fried up a pan of doughnuts and made a cake. She was engaged in the doughnuts when a neighbor came in, one of these women who take it as a personal affront when any one in the neighborhood does anything without asking their advice. She was fat, and could talk a man blind in three minutes by the watch. Her neighbor said:

"What's this I hear, Mis' Ripley?"

"I dun know. I expect you hear about all they is goin' on in this neighborhood," replied Mrs. Ripley, with crushing bluntness; but the gossip did not flinch.

"Well, Sett Turner told *me* that her husband told *her* that Ripley told *him* this mornin' that you was goin' back East on a visit."

"Wal, what of it?"

"Well, air yeh?"

"The Lord willin' an' the weather permittin', I expect I be."

"Good land, I want to know! Well, well! I never was so astonished in my whole life. I said, ses I, 'It can't be.' 'Well,' ses 'e, 'tha's what *she* told me,' ses 'e. 'But,' ses I, 'she is the last woman in the world to go gallavantin' off East,' ses I. 'An',' ses he, 'but it comes from good authority,' ses he. 'Well, then, it must be so,' ses I. But, land sakes! do tell me all about it. How come you to make up y'r mind? All these years you've been kind a' talkin' it over, an' now y'r actshelly goin'— well, I *never!* 'I s'pose Ripley furnishes the money,' ses I to him. 'Well, no,' ses 'e. 'Ripley ses he'll be blowed if he sees where the money's coming from,' ses 'e; and ses I, 'But maybe she's jest jokin',' ses I. 'Not much,' he ses. S' 'e: 'Ripley believes she's goin' fast enough. He's jest as anxious to find out as we be—' "

Here Mrs. Doudney paused for breath; she had walked so fast and rested so little that her interminable flow of "ses I's" and "ses he's" ceased necessarily. She had reached, moreover, the point of most vital interest—the money.

"An' you'll find out jest 'bout as soon as he does," was the dry response from the figure hovering over the stove; and with all her manoeuvering that was all she got.

All day Ripley went about his work exceedingly thoughtful for him. It was cold blustering weather. The wind rustled among the corn-stalks with a wild and mournful sound, the geese and ducks went sprawling down the wind, and the horses' coats were ruffled and backs raised.

The old man was husking all alone in the field, his spare form rigged out in two or three ragged coats, his hands inserted in a pair of gloves minus nearly all the fingers, his thumbs done up in "stalls," and his feet thrust into huge coarse boots. The "down ears" wet and chapped his hands, already worn to the quick. Toward night it grew colder and threatened snow. In spite of all these attacks he kept his cheerfulness, and though he was very tired, he was softened in temper.

Having plenty of time to think matters over, he had come to the conclusion that the old woman needed a play-spell. "I ain't likely to be no richer next year than I am this one; if I wait till I'm able to send her she won't never go. I calc'late I c'n git enough out o' them shoats to send her. I'd kind a' lotted on eat'n' them pigs done up in sassengers, but if the ol' woman goes East, Tukey and me'll kind a' haff to pull through without 'em. We'll have a turkey f'r Thanksgivin', an' a chicken once 'n a while. Lord! but we'll miss the gravy on the flap-jacks." (He smacked his lips over the thought of the lost dainty.) "But let'er rip! We can stand it. Then there is my buffalo overcoat. I'd kind a' calc'lated on havin' a buffalo—but that's gone up the spout along with them sassengers."

These heroic sacrifices having been determined upon, he put them into effect at once.

This he was able to do, for his corn-rows ran along the road leading to Cedarville, and his neighbors were passing almost all hours of the day.

It would have softened Jane Ripley's heart could she have seen his bent and stiffened form among the corn-rows, the cold wind piercing to the bone through his threadbare and insufficient clothing. The rising wind sent the snow rattling among the moaning stalks at intervals. The cold made his poor dim eyes water, and he had to stop now and then to swing his arms about his chest to warm them. His voice was hoarse with shouting at the shivering team.

That night as Mrs. Ripley was clearing the dishes away she got to thinking about the departure of the next day, and she began to soften.

She gave way to a few tears when little Tewksbury Gilchrist, her grandson, came up and stood beside her.

"Gran'ma, you ain't goin' away to stay always, are yeh?"

"Why, course not, Tukey. What made y' think that?"

"Well, y' ain't told us nawthin' 't all about it. An' yeh kind o' look 's if yeh was mad."

"Well, I ain't mad; I'm jest a-thinkin', Tukey. Y' see, I come away from them hills when I was a little girl a'most; before I married y'r grandad. And I ain't never been back. 'Most all my folks is there, sonny, an' we've been s' poor all these years I couldn't seem t' never git started. Now, when I'm 'most ready t' go, I feel kind a queer—'s if I'd cry."

And cry she did, while little Tewksbury stood patting her trembling hands. Hearing Ripley's step on the porch, she rose hastily and, drying her tears, plunged at the work again.

Ripley came in with a big armful of wood, which he rolled into the wood-box with a thundering crash. Then he pulled off his mittens, slapped them together to knock off the ice and snow, and laid them side by side under the stove. He then removed cap, coat, blouse, and finally his boots, which he laid upon the wood-box, the soles turned toward the stove-pipe.

As he sat down without speaking, he opened the front doors of the stove, and held the palms of his stiffened hands to the blaze. The light brought out a thoughtful look on his large, uncouth, yet kindly, visage. Life had laid hard lines on his brown skin, but it had not entirely soured a naturally kind and simple nature. It had made him penurious and dull and iron-muscled; had stifled all the slender flowers of his nature; yet there was warm soil hid in his heart.

"It's snowin' like all p'ssessed," he remarked finally. "I guess we'll have a sleigh-ride to-morrow. I calc'late t' drive y' daown in scrumptious style. If you must leave, why, we'll give yeh a whoopin' old send-off—won't we, Tukey?"

Nobody replying, he waited a moment. "I've ben a-thinkin' things over kind o' t'-day, mother, an' I've come t' the conclusion that we *have* been kind o' hard on yeh, without knowin' it, y' see. Y' see I'm kind o' easy-goin', an' little Tuke he's only a child, an' we ain't c'nsidered how you felt."

She didn't appear to be listening, but she was, and he didn't appear, on his part, to be talking to her, and he kept his voice as hard and dry as he could.

"An' I was tellin' Tukey t'-day that it was a dum shame our crops hadn't turned out better. An' when I saw ol' Hatfield go by I hailed him, an' asked him what he'd gimme for two o' m' shoats. Wal, the upshot is, I sent t' town for some things I calc'late you'd need. An' here's a ticket to Georgetown, and ten dollars. Why, ma, what's up?"

Mrs. Ripley broke down, and with her hands all wet with dishwater, as they were, covered her face, and sobbed. She felt like kissing him, but she didn't. Tewksbury began to whimper too; but the old man was astonished. His wife had not wept for years (before him). He rose and walking clumsily up to her timidly touched her hair—

"Why, mother! What's the matter? What've I done now? I was calc'latin' to sell them pigs anyway. Hatfield jest advanced the money on 'em."

She hopped up and dashed into the bedroom, and in a few minutes returned with a yarn mitten, tied around the wrist, which she laid on the table with a thump, saying: "I don't want yer money. There's money enough to take me where I want to go."

"Whee—ew! Thunder and gimpsum root! Where 'd ye get that? Didn't dig it out of a hole?"

"No, I jest saved it—a dime at a time—see!"

Here she turned it out on the table—some bills, but mostly silver dimes and quarters.

"Thunder and scissors! Must be two er three hundred dollars there," he exclaimed.

"They's jest seventy-five dollars and thirty cents; jest about enough to go back on. Tickets is fifty-five dollars, goin' and comin'. That leaves twenty dollars for other expenses, not countin' what I've already spent, which is six-fifty," said she, recovering her self-possession. "It's plenty."

"But y' ain't calc'lated on no sleepers nor hotel bills."

"I ain't goin' on no sleeper. Mis' Doudney says it's jest scandalous the way things is managed on them cars. I'm goin' on the old-fashioned cars, where they ain't no half-dressed men runnin' around."

"But *you* needn't be afraid of them, mother; at your age—"

"There! you needn't throw my age an' homeliness into my face, Ethan Ripley. If I hadn't waited an' tended on you so long, I'd look a little more's I did when I married yeh."

Ripley gave it up in despair. He didn't realize fully enough how the proposed trip had unsettled his wife's nerves. She didn't realize it herself.

"As for the hotel bills, they won't be none. I ain't agoin' to pay them pirates as much for a day's board as we'd charge for a week's, and have nawthin' to eat but dishes. I'm goin' to take a chicken an' some hard-boiled eggs, an' I'm goin' right through to Georgetown."

"Wal, all right, mother; but here's the ticket I got."

"I don't want yer ticket."

"But you've got to take it."

"Well, I hain't."

"Why, yes, ye have. It's bought, an' they won't take it back."

"Won't they?" she was perplexed again.

"Not much they won't. I ast 'em. A ticket sold is sold."

"Wal, if they won't—"

"You bet they won't."

"I s'pose I'll haff to use it." And that ended it.

They were a familiar sight as they rode down the road toward town next day. As usual, Mrs. Ripley sat up straight and stiff as "a half-drove wedge in a white-oak log." The day was cold and raw. There was some snow on the ground, but not enough to warrant the use of sleighs. It was "neither sleddin' nor wheelin'." The old people sat on a board laid across the box, and had an old quilt or two drawn up over their knees. Tewksbury lay in the back part of the box (which was filled with hay), where he jounced up and down, in company with a queer old trunk and a brand-new imitation-leather hand-bag.

There is no ride quite so desolate and uncomfortable as a ride in a lumber-wagon on a cold day in autumn, when the ground is frozen, and the wind is strong and raw with threatening snow. The wagon-wheels grind along in the snow, the cold gets in under the seat at the calves of one's legs, and the ceaseless bumping of the bottom of the box on the feet is almost intolerable.

There was not much talk on the way down, and what little there was related mainly to certain domestic regulations, to be strictly followed, regarding churning, pickles, pancakes, etc. Mrs. Ripley wore a shawl over her head, and carried her queer little black bonnet in her hand. Tewksbury was also wrapped in a shawl. The boy's teeth were pounding together like castanets by the time they reached Cedarville, and every muscle ached with the fatigue of shaking.

After a few purchases they drove down to the station, a frightful little den (common in the West), which was always too hot or too cold. It happened to be too hot just now—a fact which rejoiced little Tewksbury.

"Now git my trunk *stamped,* 'r *fixed,* 'r whatever they call it," she said to Ripley, in a commanding tone, which gave great delight to the inevitable crowd of loafers beginning to assemble. "Now remember, Tukey, have grandad kill that biggest turkey night before Thanksgivin', an' then you run right over to Mis' Doudney's—she's got a nawful tongue, but she can bake a turkey first-rate—an' she'll fix up some squash-pies for yeh. You can warm up one o' them mince-pies. I wish ye could be with me, but ye can't; so do the best ye can."

Ripley returning now, she said: "Wal, now, I've fixed things up the best I could. I've baked bread enough to last a week, an' Mis' Doudney has promised to bake for yeh—"

"I don't like her bakin'."

"Wal, you'll haff to stand it till I get back, 'n' you'll find a jar o' sweet pickles an' some crab-apple sauce down suller, 'n' you'd better melt up some brown sugar for 'lasses, 'n' for goodness' sake don't eat all them mince-pies up the fust week, 'n' see that Tukey ain't froze goin' to school. An' now you'd better get out for home. Good-by! an' remember them pies."

As they were riding home, Ripley roused up after a long silence. "Did she—a—kiss you good-by, Tukey?"

"No sir," piped Tewksbury.

"Thunder! didn't she?" After a silence: "She didn't me, neither. I guess she kind a' sort a' forgot it, bein' so flustrated, y' know."

One cold, windy, intensely bright day, Mrs. Stacey, who lives about two miles from Cedarville, looking out of the window, saw a queer little figure struggling along the road, which was blocked here and there with drifts. It was an old woman laden with a good half-dozen parcels, which the wind seemed determined to wrench from her.

She was dressed in black, with a full skirt, and her cloak being short, the wind had excellent opportunity to inflate her garments and sail her off occasionally into the deep snow outside the track, but she held out bravely till she reached the gate. As she turned in, Mrs. Stacey cried:

"Why! it's Grandma Ripley, just getting back from her trip. Why! how do you do? Come in. Why! you must be nearly frozen. Let me take off your hat and veil."

"No, thank ye kindly, but I can't stop," was the given reply. "I must be gittin back to Ripley. I expec' that man has jest let ev'rything go six ways f'r Sunday."

"Oh, you *must* sit down just a minute and warm."

"Wal, I will; but I've got to git home by sundown sure. I don't suppose they's a thing in the house to eat," she said solemnly.

"Oh, dear! I wish Stacey was here, so he could take you home. An' the boys at school—"

"Don't need any help, if 't wa'nt for these bundles an' things. I guess I'll jest leave some of 'em here, an'—Here! take one of these apples. I brought 'em from Lizy Jane's suller, back to Yaark State."

"Oh! they're delicious! You must have had a lovely time."

"Pretty good. But I kep' thinkin' of Ripley an' Tukey all the time. I s'pose they have had a gay time of it" (she meant the opposite of gay). "Wal, as I told Lizy Jane, I've had my spree, an' now I've got to git back to work. They ain't no rest for such as we are. As I told Lizy Jane, them folks in the big houses have Thanksgivin' dinners every day of their lives, and men an' women in splendid clo's to wait on 'em, so 't Thanksgivin' don't mean anything to 'em; but we poor critters, we make a great to-do if we have a good dinner onct a year. I've saw a pile o' this world, Mrs. Stacey—a pile of it! I didn't think they was so many big houses in the world as I saw b'tween here an' Chicago. Wal, I can't sit here gabbin'." She rose resolutely. "I must get home to Ripley. Jest kind o' stow them bags away. I'll take two an' leave them three others. Good-by! I must be gittin' home to Ripley. He'll want his supper on time."

And off up the road the indomitable little figure trudged, head held down to the cutting blast—little snow-fly, a speck on a measureless expanse, crawling along with painful breathing, and slipping, sliding steps—"Gittin' home to Ripley an' the boy."

Ripley was out to the barn when she entered, but Tewksbury was building a fire in the old cook-stove. He sprang up with a cry of joy, and ran to her. She seized him and kissed him, and it did her so much good she hugged him close, and kissed him again and again, crying hysterically.

"Oh, gran'ma, I'm so glad to see you! We've had an awful time since you've been gone."

She released him, and looked around. A lot of dirty dishes were on the table, the table-cloth was a "sight to behold" (as she afterward said), and so was the stove—kettle-marks all over the table-cloth, splotches of pancake batter all over the stove.

"Wal, I sh'd say as much," she dryly assented, untying her bonnet-strings.

When Ripley came in she had her regimentals on, the stove was brushed, the room swept, and she was elbow-deep in the dish-pan. "Hullo mother! Got back, hev yeh?"

"I sh'd say it was about *time*," she replied curtly, without looking up or ceasing work. "Has ol' 'Crumpy' dried up yet?" This was her greeting.

Her trip was a fact now; no chance could rob her of it. She had looked forward twenty-three years toward it, and now she could look back at it accomplished. She took up her burden again, never more thinking to lay it down.

O. Henry

CRITICISM has not dealt impartially with O. Henry since his death in 1910. Underestimation has succeeded overpraise, and the man who used to be miscalled the American Maupassant has been more recently called a trickster, a mere gymnast of the short story, while on his head have been heaped the sins of his imitators. He was a purveyor of wares, and he created no great characters nor did he impress mankind with profundity of insight. His greatest weakness was a certain stridency and cheapness of tone.

Having admitted these defects, one should be as quick to acknowledge his great virtues. His sheer power of invention was prodigal in originality, and hardly surpassed in the whole history of story-telling. His best stories are not dependent on tricks; and he had the great richness of sympathy necessary to the creation of a whole city of his own—Baghdad-on-the-Subway. He could be a mighty artificer, and the story here included—"Roads of Destiny"—is one which Stevenson could have been proud to sign.

The outlines of O. Henry's career are well-known. Born William Sidney Porter in 1862 at Greensboro, North Carolina, he received but the rudiments of an education, spent sixteen years in Texas, was unjustly indicted in an embezzlement case, fled to South America, returned to serve a prison sentence in Ohio, and came on to New York City where he dazzled the journalistic world with his amazing output of stories, writing in three years' time more than one hundred and fifty for one market alone.

ROADS OF DESTINY *

O. Henry

I go to seek on many roads
What is to be.
True heart and strong, with love to light—
Will they not bear me in the fight
To order, shun or wield or mould
My Destiny?

Unpublished Poems of David Mignot.

The song was over. The words were David's; the air, one of the countryside. The company about the inn table applauded heartily, for the young poet paid for the wine. Only the notary, M. Papineau, shook his head a little at the lines, for he was a man of books, and he had not drunk with the rest.

David went out into the village street, where the night air drove the wine vapour from his head. And then he remembered that he and Yvonne had quarrelled that day, and that he had resolved to leave his home that night to seek fame and honour in the great world outside.

"When my poems are on every man's tongue," he told himself, in a fine exhilaration, "she will, perhaps, think of the hard words she spoke this day."

Except the roysterers in the tavern, the village folk were abed. David crept softly into his room in the shed of his father's cottage and made a bundle of his small store of clothing. With this upon a staff, he set his face outward upon the road that ran from Vernoy.

He passed his father's herd of sheep huddled in their nightly pen— the sheep he herded daily, leaving them to scatter while he wrote verses on scraps of paper. He saw a light yet shining in Yvonne's window, and a weakness shook his purpose of a sudden. Perhaps that light meant that she rued, sleepless, her anger, and that morning might—But, no! His decision was made. Vernoy was no place for him. Not one soul there could share his thoughts. Out along that road lay his fate and his future.

Three leagues across the dim, moonlit champaign ran the road, straight as a ploughman's furrow. It was believed in the village that the road ran to Paris, at least; and this name the poet whispered often to himself as he walked. Never so far from Vernoy had David travelled before.

The Left Branch

Three leagues, then, the road ran, and turned into a puzzle. It joined with another and a larger road at right angles. David stood, uncertain, for a while, and then took the road to the left.

Upon this more important highway were, imprinted in the dust, wheel tracks left by the recent passage of some vehicle. Some half an hour later these traces were verified by the sight of a ponderous carriage mired in a little brook at the bottom of a steep hill. The driver and postilions were shouting and tugging at the horses' bridles. On the road at one side stood a huge, black-clothed man and a slender lady wrapped in a long, light cloak.

David saw the lack of skill in the efforts of the servants. He quietly assumed control of the work. He directed the outriders to cease their clamour at the horses and to exercise their strength upon the wheels. The driver alone urged the animals with his familiar voice; David himself heaved a powerful shoulder at the rear of the carriage, and with one harmonious tug the great vehicle rolled up on solid ground. The outriders climbed to their places.

David stood for a moment upon one foot. The huge gentleman waved a hand. "You will enter the carriage," he said, in a voice large, like himself, but smoothed by art and habit. Obedience belonged in the path of such a voice. Brief as was the young poet's hesitation, it was cut shorter still by a renewal of the command. David's foot went to the step. In the darkness he perceived dimly the form of the lady upon the rear seat. He was about to seat himself opposite, when the voice again swayed him to its will. "You will sit at the lady's side."

The gentleman swung his great weight to the forward seat. The carriage proceeded up the hill. The lady was shrunk, silent, into her corner. David could not estimate whether she was old or young, but a delicate, mild perfume from her clothes stirred his poet's fancy to the belief that there was loveliness beneath the mystery. Here was an adventure such as he had often imagined. But as yet he held no key to it, for no word was spoken while he sat with his impenetrable companions.

In an hour's time David perceived through the window that the vehicle traversed the street of some town. Then it stopped in front of a closed and darkened house, and a postilion alighted to hammer impatiently upon the door. A latticed window above flew wide and a nightcapped head popped out.

"Who are ye that disturb honest folk at this time of night? My house is closed. 'Tis too late for profitable travellers to be abroad. Cease knocking at my door, and be off."

"Open!" spluttered the postilion, loudly; "open for Monseigneur the Marquis de Beaupertuys."

"Ah!" cried the voice above. "Ten thousand pardons, my lord. I did not know—the hour is so late—at once shall the door be opened, and the house placed at my lord's disposal."

Inside was heard the clink of chain and bar, and the door was flung open. Shivering with chill and apprehension, the landlord of the Silver Flagon stood, half clad, candle in hand, upon the threshold.

David followed the marquis out of the carriage. "Assist the lady," he was ordered. The poet obeyed. He felt her small hand tremble as he guided her descent. "Into the house," was the next command.

The room was the long dining-hall of the tavern. A great oak table ran down its length. The huge gentleman seated himself in a chair at the nearer end. The lady sank into another against the wall, with an air of great weariness. David stood, considering how best he might now take his leave and continue upon his way.

"My lord," said the landlord, bowing to the floor, "h-had I expected this honour, entertainment would have been ready. T-t-there is wine and cold fowl and m-m-maybe—"

"Candles," said the marquis, spreading the fingers of one plump white hand in a gesture he had.

"Y-yes, my lord." He fetched half a dozen candles, lighted them, and set them upon the table.

"If monsieur would, perhaps, deign to taste a certain Burgundy— there is a cask—"

"Candles," said monsieur, spreading his fingers.

"Assuredly—quickly—I fly, my lord."

A dozen more lighted candles shone in the hall. The great bulk of the marquis overflowed his chair. He was dressed in fine black from head to foot save for the snowy ruffles at his wrist and throat. Even the hilt and scabbard of his sword were black. His expression was one of sneering pride. The ends of an upturned moustache reached nearly to his mocking eyes.

The lady sat motionless, and now David perceived that she was young, and possessed of pathetic and appealing beauty. He was startled from the contemplation of her forlorn loveliness by the booming voice of the marquis.

"What is your name and pursuit?"

"David Mignot. I am a poet."

The moustache of the marquis curled nearer to his eyes.

"How do you live?"

"I am also a shepherd; I guarded my father's flock," David answered, with his head high, but a flush upon his cheek.

"Then listen, master shepherd and poet, to the fortune you have blundered upon to-night. This lady is my niece, Mademoiselle Lucie de Varennes. She is of noble descent and is possessed of ten thousand francs a year in her own right. As to her charms, you have but to observe for yourself. If the inventory pleases your shepherd's heart, she becomes your wife at a word. Do not interrupt me. Tonight I conveyed her to the *château* of the Comte de Villemaur, to whom her hand had been promised. Guests were present; the priest was waiting; her marriage to one eligible in rank and fortune was ready to be accomplished. At the altar this demoiselle, so meek and dutiful, turned upon me like a leopardess, charged me with cruelty and crimes, and broke, before the gaping priest, the troth I had plighted for her. I swore there and then, by ten thousand devils, that she should marry the first man we met after leaving the *château,* be he prince, charcoal-burner, or thief. You, shepherd, are the first. Mademoiselle must be wed this night. If not you, then another. You have ten minutes in which to make your decision. Do not vex me with words or questions. Ten minutes, shepherd; and they are speeding."

The marquis drummed loudly with his white fingers upon the table. He sank into a veiled attitude of waiting. It was as if some great house had shut its doors and windows against approach. David would have spoken, but the huge man's bearing stopped his tongue. Instead, he stood by the lady's chair and bowed.

"Mademoiselle," he said, and he marvelled to find his words flowing easily before so much elegance and beauty. "You have heard me say I was a shepherd. I have also had the fancy, at times, that I am a poet. If it be the test of a poet to adore and cherish the beautiful, that fancy is now strengthened. Can I serve you in any way, mademoiselle?"

The young woman looked up at him with eyes dry and mournful. His frank, glowing face, made serious by the gravity of the adventure, his strong, straight figure and the liquid sympathy in his blue eyes, perhaps, also, her imminent need of long-denied help and kindness, thawed her to sudden tears.

"Monsieur," she said, in low tones, "you look to be true and kind. He is my uncle, the brother of my father, and my only relative. He loved my mother, and he hates me because I am like her. He has made my life one long terror. I am afraid of his very looks, and never before dared to disobey him. But to-night he would have married me to a man three times my age. You will forgive me for bringing this vexation upon you, monsieur. You will, of course, decline this mad act he tries to force upon you. But let me thank you for your generous words, at least. I have had none spoken to me in so long."

There was now something more than generosity in the poet's eyes. Poet he must have been, for Yvonne was forgotten; this fine, new loveliness held him with its freshness and grace. The subtle perfume from her filled him with strange emotions. His tender look fell warmly upon her. She leaned to it, thirstily.

"Ten minutes," said David, "is given me in which to do what I would devote years to achieve. I will not say I pity you, mademoiselle; it would not be true—I love you. I cannot ask love from you yet, but let me rescue you from this cruel man, and, in time, love may come. I think I have a future; I will not always be a shepherd. For the present I will cherish you with all my heart and make your life less sad. Will you trust your fate to me, mademoiselle?"

"Ah, you would sacrifice yourself from pity!"

"From love. The time is almost up, mademoiselle."

"You will regret it, and despise me."

"I will live only to make you happy, and myself worthy of you."

Her fine small hand crept into his from beneath her cloak.

"I will trust you," she breathed, "with my life. And—and love—may not be so far off as you think. Tell him. Once away from the power of his eyes I may forget."

David went and stood before the marquis. The black figure stirred, and the mocking eyes glanced at the great hall clock.

"Two minutes to spare. A shepherd requires eight minutes to decide whether he will accept a bride of beauty and income! Speak up, shepherd, do you consent to become mademoiselle's husband?"

"Mademoiselle," said David, standing proudly, "has done me the honour to yield to my request that she become my wife."

"Well said!" said the marquis. "You have yet the making of a courtier in you, master shepherd. Mademoiselle could have drawn a worse prize, after all. And now to be done with the affair as quick as the Church and the devil will allow!"

He struck the table soundly with his sword hilt. The landlord came, knee-shaking, bringing more candles in the hope of anticipating the great lord's whims. "Fetch a priest," said the marquis, "a priest; do you understand? In ten minutes have a priest here, or—"

The landlord dropped his candles and flew.

The priest came, heavy-eyed and ruffled. He made David Mignot and Lucie de Varennes man and wife, pocketed a gold piece that the marquis tossed him, and shuffled out again into the night.

"Wine," ordered the marquis, spreading his ominous fingers at the host.

"Fill glasses," he said, when it was brought. He stood up at the head of the table in the candlelight, a black mountain of venom and conceit, with something like the memory of an old love turned to poison in his eye, as it fell upon his niece.

"Monsieur Mignot," he said, raising his wineglass, "drink after I say this to you: You have taken to be your wife one who will make your life a foul and wretched thing. The blood in her is an inheritance running black lies and red ruin. She will bring you shame and anxiety. The devil that descended to her is there in her eyes and skin and mouth that stoop even to beguile a peasant. There is your promise, monsieur poet, for a happy life. Drink your wine. At last, mademoiselle, I am rid of you."

The marquis drank. A little grievous cry, as if from a sudden wound, came from the girl's lips. David, with his glass in his hand, stepped forward three paces and faced the marquis. There was little of a shepherd in his bearing.

"Just now," he said, calmly, "you did me the honour to call me 'monsieur.' May I hope, therefore, that my marriage to mademoiselle has placed me somewhat nearer to you in—let us say, reflected rank— has given me the right to stand more as an equal to monseigneur in a certain little piece of business I have in mind?"

"You may hope, shepherd," sneered the marquis.

"Then," said David, dashing his glass of wine into the contemptuous eyes that mocked him, "perhaps you will condescend to fight me."

The fury of the great lord outbroke in one sudden curse like a blast from a horn. He tore his sword from its black sheath; he called to the hovering landlord: "A sword there, for this lout!" He turned to the lady, with a laugh that chilled her heart, and said: "You put much labour upon me, madame. It seems I must find you a husband and make you a widow in the same night."

"I know not sword-play," said David. He flushed to make the confession before his lady.

"'I know not sword-play,'" mimicked the marquis. "Shall we fight like peasants with oaken cudgels? *Hola!* Francois, my pistols!"

A postilion brought two shining great pistols ornamented with carven silver, from the carriage holsters. The marquis tossed one upon the table near David's hand. "To the other end of the table," he cried; "even a shepherd may pull a trigger. Few of them attain the honour to die by the weapon of a De Beaupertuys."

The shepherd and the marquis faced each other from the ends of the long table. The landlord, in an ague of terror, clutched the air and stammered: "M-M-Monseigneur, for the love of Christ! not in my house!—do not spill blood—it will ruin my custom—" The look of the marquis, threatening him, paralyzed his tongue.

"Coward," cried the lord of Beaupertuys, "cease chattering your teeth long enough to give the word for us, if you can."

Mine host's knees smote the floor. He was without a vocabulary. Even sounds were beyond him. Still, by gestures, he seemed to beseech peace in the name of his house and custom.

"I will give the word," said the lady, in a clear voice. She went up to David and kissed him sweetly. Her eyes were sparkling bright, and colour had come to her cheek. She stood against the wall, and the two men levelled their pistols for her count.

"*Un—deux—trois!*"

The two reports came so nearly together that the candles flickered but once. The marquis stood, smiling, the fingers of his left hand resting, outspread, upon the end of the table. David remained erect, and turned his head very slowly, searching for his wife with his eyes. Then, as a garment falls from where it is hung, he sank, crumpled, upon the floor.

With a little cry of terror and despair, the widowed maid ran and stooped above him. She found his wound, and then looked with her old look of pale melancholy. "Through his heart," she whispered. "Oh, his heart!"

"Come," boomed the great voice of the marquis, "out with you to the carriage! Daybreak shall not find you on my hands. Wed you shall be again, and to a living husband, this night. The next we come upon, my lady, highwayman or peasant. If the road yields no other, then the churl that opens my gates. Out with you to the carriage!"

The marquis, implacable and huge, the lady wrapped again in the mystery of her cloak, the postilion bearing the weapons—all moved out to the waiting carriage. The sound of its ponderous wheels rolling away echoed through the slumbering village. In the hall of the Silver Flagon the distracted landlord wrung his hands above the slain poet's body, while the flames of the four and twenty candles danced and flickered on the table.

THE RIGHT BRANCH

Three leagues, then, the road ran, and turned into a puzzle. It joined with another and a larger road at right angles. David stood, uncertain, for a while, and then took the road to the right.

Whither it led he knew not, but he was resolved to leave Vernoy far behind that night. He travelled a league and then passed a large château which showed testimony of recent entertainment. Lights shone from every window; from the great stone gateway ran a tracery of wheel tracks drawn in the dust by the vehicles of the guests.

Three leagues farther and David was weary. He rested and slept for a while on a bed of pine boughs at the roadside. Then up and on again along the unknown way.

Thus for five days he travelled the great road, sleeping upon Nature's balsamic beds or in peasants' ricks, eating of their black, hospitable bread, drinking from streams or the willing cup of the goatherd.

At length he crossed a great bridge and set his foot within the smiling city that has crushed or crowned more poets than all the rest of the world. His breath came quickly as Paris sang to him in a little undertone her vital chant of greeting—the hum of voice and foot and wheel.

High up under the eaves of an old house in the Rue Conti, David paid for lodging, and set himself, in a wooden chair, to his poems. The street, once sheltering citizens of import and consequence, was now given over to those who ever follow in the wake of decline.

The houses were tall and still possessed of a ruined dignity, but many of them were empty save for dust and the spider. By night there was the clash of steel and the cries of brawlers straying restlessly from inn to inn. Where once gentility abode was now but a rancid and rude incontinence. But here David found housing commensurate to his scant purse. Daylight and candlelight found him at pen and paper.

One afternoon he was returning from a foraging trip to the lower world, with bread and curds and a bottle of thin wine. Halfway up his dark stairway he met—or rather came upon, for she rested on the stair—a young woman of a beauty that should balk even the justice of a poet's imagination. A loose, dark cloak, flung open, showed a rich gown beneath. Her eyes changed swiftly with every little shade of thought. Within one moment they would be round and artless like a child's, and long and cozening like a gypsy's. One hand raised her gown, undraping a little shoe, high-heeled, with its ribbons dangling, untied. So heavenly she was, so unfitted to stoop, so qualified to charm and command! Perhaps she had seen David coming, and had waited for his help there.

Ah, would monsieur pardon that she occupied the stairway, but the shoe!—the naughty shoe! Alas! it would not remain tied. Ah! if monsieur *would* be so gracious!

The poet's fingers trembled as he tied the contrary ribbons. Then he would have fled from the danger of her presence, but the eyes grew long and cozening, like a gypsy's, and held him. He leaned against the balustrade, clutching his bottle of sour wine.

"You have been so good," she said, smiling. "Does monsieur, perhaps, live in the house?"

"Yes, madame. I—I think so, madame."

"Perhaps in the third story, then?"

"No, madame; higher up."

The lady fluttered her fingers with the least possible gesture of impatience.

"Pardon. Certainly I am not discreet in asking. Monsieur will forgive me? It is surely not becoming that I should inquire where he lodges."

"Madame, do not say so. I live in the—"

"No, no, no; do not tell me. Now I see that I erred. But I cannot lose the interest I feel in this house and all that is in it. Once it was my home. Often I come here but to dream of those happy days again. Will you let that be my excuse?"

"Let me tell you, then, for you need no excuse," stammered the poet. "I live in the top floor—the small room where the stairs turn."

"In the front room?" asked the lady, turning her head sidewise.

"The rear, madame."

The lady sighed, as if with relief.

"I will detain you no longer, then, monsieur," she said, employing the round and artless eye. "Take good care of my house. Alas! only the memories of it are mine now. Adieu, and accept my thanks for your courtesy."

She was gone, leaving but a smile and a trace of sweet perfume. David climbed the stairs as one in slumber. But he awoke from it, and the smile and the perfume lingered with him and never afterward did either seem quite to leave him. This lady of whom he knew nothing drove him to lyrics of eyes, chansons of swiftly conceived love, odes to curling hair, and sonnets to slippers on slender feet.

Poet he must have been, for Yvonne was forgotten; this fine, new loveliness held him with its freshness and grace. The subtle perfume about her filled him with strange emotions.

On a certain night three persons were gathered about a table in a room on the third floor of the same house. Three chairs and the table and a lighted candle upon it was all the furniture. One of the persons was a huge man, dressed in black. His expression was one of sneering pride. The ends of his upturned moustache reached nearly to his mocking eyes. Another was a lady, young and beautiful, with eyes that could be round and artless, like a child's, or long and cozening, like a gypsy's, but were now keen and ambitious, like any other conspirator's. The third was a man of action, a combatant, a bold and impatient executive, breathing fire and steel. He was addressed by the others as Captain Desrolles.

This man struck the table with his fist, and said, with controlled violence:

"To-night. To-night as he goes to midnight mass. I am tired of the plotting that gets nowhere. I am sick of signals and ciphers and secret meetings and such *baragouin*. Let us be honest traitors. If France is to be rid of him, let us kill in the open, and not hunt with snares and traps. To-night, I say. I back my words. My hand will do the deed. To-night, as he goes to mass."

The lady turned upon him a cordial look. Woman, however wedded to plots, must ever thus bow to rash courage. The big man stroked his upturned moustache.

"Dear captain," he said, in a great voice, softened by habit, "this time I agree with you. Nothing is to be gained by waiting. Enough of the palace guards belong to us to make the endeavour a safe one."

"To-night," repeated Captain Desrolles, again striking the table. "You have heard me, marquis; my hand will do the deed."

"But now," said the huge man, softly, "comes a question. Word must be sent to our partisans in the palace, and a signal agreed upon. Our staunchest men must accompany the royal carriage. At this hour what messenger can penetrate so far as the south doorway? Ribout is stationed there; once a message is placed in his hands, all will go well."

"I will send the message," said the lady.

"You, countess?" said the marquis, raising his eyebrows. "Your devotion is great, we know, but—"

"Listen!" exclaimed the lady, rising and resting her hands upon the table; "in a garret of this house lives a youth from the provinces as guileless and tender as the lambs he tended there. I have met him twice or thrice upon the stairs. I questioned him, fearing that he might dwell too near the room in which we are accustomed to meet. He is mine, if I will. He writes poems in his garret, and I think he dreams of me. He will do what I say. He shall take the message to the palace."

The marquis rose from his chair and bowed. "You did not permit me to finish my sentence, countess," he said. "I would have said: 'Your devotion is great, but your wit and charm are infinitely greater.'"

While the conspirators were thus engaged, David was polishing some lines addressed to his *amorette d'escalier*. He heard a timorous knock at his door, and opened it, with a great throb, to behold her there, panting as one in straits, with eyes wide open and artless, like a child's.

"Monsieur," she breathed, "I come to you in distress. I believe you to be good and true, and I know of no other help. How I flew through the streets among the swaggering men! Monsieur, my mother is dying. My uncle is a captain of guards in the palace of the king. Some one must fly to bring him. May I hope—"

"Mademoiselle," interrupted David, his eyes shining with the desire to do her service, "your hopes shall be my wings. Tell me how I may reach him."

The lady thrust a sealed paper into his hand.

"Go to the south gate—the south gate, mind—and say to the guards there, 'The falcon has left his nest.' They will pass you, and you will go to the south entrance to the palace. Repeat the words, and give this letter to the man who will reply 'Let him strike when he will.' This is the password, monsieur, entrusted to me by my uncle, for now when the country is disturbed and men plot against the king's life, no one without it can gain entrance to the palace grounds after nightfall. If you will, monsieur, take him this letter so that my mother may see him before she closes her eyes."

"Give it me," said David, eagerly. "But shall I let you return home through the streets alone so late? I—"

"No, no—fly. Each moment is like a precious jewel. Some time," said the lady, with eyes long and cozening, like a gypsy's, "I will try to thank you for your goodness."

The poet thrust the letter into his breast, and bounded down the stairway. The lady, when he was gone, returned to the room below.

The eloquent eyebrows of the marquis interrogated her.

"He is gone," she said, "as fleet and stupid as one of his own sheep, to deliver it."

The table shook again from the batter of Captain Desrolles's fist.

"Sacred name!" he cried; "I have left my pistols behind! I can trust no others."

"Take this," said the marquis, drawing from beneath his cloak a shining, great weapon, ornamented with carven silver. "There are none truer. But guard it closely, for it bears my arms and crest, and already I am suspected. Me, I must put many leagues between myself and Paris this night. Tomorrow must find me in my *château*. After you, dear countess."

The marquis puffed out the candle. The lady, well cloaked, and the two gentlemen softly descended the stairway and flowed into the crowd that roamed along the narrow pavements of the Rue Conti.

David sped. At the south gate of the king's residence a halberd was laid to his breast, but he turned its point with the words: "The falcon has left his nest."

"Pass, brother," said the guard, "and go quickly."

On the south steps of the palace they moved to seize him, but again the *mot de passe* charmed the watchers. One among them stepped forward and began: "Let him strike—" but a flurry among the guards told of a surprise. A man of keen look and soldierly stride suddenly pressed through them and seized the letter which David held in his hand. "Come with me," he said, and led him inside the great hall. Then he tore open the letter and read it. He beckoned to a man uniformed as an officer of musketeers, who was passing. "Captain Tetreau, you will have the guards at the south entrance and the south gate arrested and confined. Place men known to be loyal in their places." To David he said: "Come with me."

He conducted him through a corridor and an anteroom into a

spacious chamber, where a melancholy man, sombrely dressed, sat brooding in a great, leather-covered chair. To that man he said:

"Sire, I have told you that the palace is as full of traitors and spies as a sewer is of rats. You have thought, sire, that it was my fancy. This man penetrated to your very door by their connivance. He bore a letter which I have intercepted. I have brought him here that your majesty may no longer think my zeal excessive."

"I will question him," said the king, stirring in his chair. He looked at David with heavy eyes dulled by an opaque film. The poet bent his knee.

"From where do you come?" asked the king.

"From the village of Vernoy, in the province of Eure-et-Loir, sire."

"What do you follow in Paris?"

"I—I would be a poet, sire."

"What did you in Vernoy?"

"I minded my father's flock of sheep."

The king stirred again, and the film lifted from his eyes.

"Ah! in the fields!"

"Yes, sire."

"You lived in the fields; you went out in the cool of the morning and lay among the hedges in the grass. The flock distributed itself upon the hillside; you drank of the living stream; you ate your sweet, brown bread in the shade, and you listened, doubtless, to blackbirds piping in the grove. Is not that so, the shepherd?"

"It is, sire," answered David, with a sigh; "and to the bees at the flowers, and, maybe, to the grape gatherers singing on the hill."

"Yes, yes," said the king, impatiently; "maybe to them; but surely to the blackbirds. They whistled often, in the grove, did they not?"

"Nowhere, sire, so sweetly as in Eure-et-Loir. I have endeavoured to express their song in some verses that I have written."

"Can you repeat those verses?" asked the king, eagerly. "A long time ago I listened to the blackbirds. It would be something better than a kingdom if one could rightly construe their song. And at night you drove the sheep to the fold and then sat, in peace and tranquillity, to your pleasant bread. Can you repeat those verses, shepherd?"

"They run this way, sire," said David, with respectful ardour:

> " 'Lazy shepherd, see your lambkins
> Skip, ecstatic, on the mead;
> See the firs dance in the breezes,
> Hear Pan blowing at his reed.

"Hear us calling from the tree-tops,
    See us swoop upon your flock;
    Yield us wool to make our nests warm
    In the branches of the—' "

"If it pleases your majesty," interrupted a harsh voice, "I will ask a question or two of this rhymester. There is little time to spare. I crave pardon, sire, if my anxiety for your safety offends."

"The loyalty," said the king, "of the Duke d'Aumale is too well proven to give offence." He sank into his chair, and the film came again over his eyes.

"First," said the duke, "I will read you the letter he brought:

" 'Tonight is the anniversary of the dauphin's death. If he goes, as is his custom, to midnight mass to pray for the soul of his son, the falcon will strike, at the corner of the Rue Esplanade. If this be his intention, set a red light in the upper room at the southwest corner of the palace, that the falcon may take heed.'

"Peasant," said the duke, sternly, "you have heard these words. Who gave you this message to bring?"

"My lord duke," said David, sincerely, "I will tell you. A lady gave it me. She said her mother was ill, and that this writing would fetch her uncle to her bedside. I do not know the meaning of the letter, but I will swear that she is beautiful and good."

"Describe the woman," commanded the duke, "and how you came to be her dupe."

"Describe her!" said David with a tender smile. "You would command words to perform miracles. Well, she is made of sunshine and deep shade. She is slender, like the alders, and moves with their grace. Her eyes change while you gaze into them; now round, and then half shut as the sun peeps between two clouds. When she comes, heaven is all about her; when she leaves, there is chaos and a scent of hawthorn blossoms. She came to me in the Rue Conti, number twenty-nine."

"It is the house," said the duke, turning to the king, "that we have been watching. Thanks to the poet's tongue, we have a picture of the infamous Countess Quebedaux."

"Sire and my lord duke," said David earnestly, "I hope my poor words have done no injustice. I have looked into that lady's eyes. I will stake my life that she is an angel, letter or no letter."

The duke looked at him steadily. "I will put you to the proof," he said, slowly. "Dressed as the king, you shall, yourself, attend mass in his carriage at midnight. Do you accept the test?"

David smiled. "I have looked into her eyes," he said. "I had my proof there. Take yours how you will."

Half an hour before twelve the Duke d'Aumale, with his own hands, set a red lamp in a southwest window of the palace. At ten minutes to the hour, David, leaning on his arm, dressed as the king, from top to toe, with his head bowed in his cloak, walked slowly from the royal apartments to the waiting carriage. The duke assisted him inside and closed the door. The carriage whirled away along its route to the cathedral.

On the *qui vive* in a house at the corner of the Rue Esplanade was Captain Tetreau with twenty men, ready to pounce upon the conspirators when they should appear.

But it seemed that, for some reason, the plotters had slightly altered their plans. When the royal carriage had reached the Rue Christopher, one square nearer than the Rue Esplanade, forth from it burst Captain Desrolles, with his band of would-be regicides, and assailed the equipage. The guards upon the carriage, though surprised at the premature attack, descended and fought valiantly. The noise of conflict attracted the force of Captain Tetreau, and they came pelting down the street to the rescue. But, in the meantime, the desperate Desrolles had torn open the door of the king's carriage, thrust his weapon against the body of the dark figure inside, and fired.

Now, with loyal reinforcements at hand, the street rang with cries and the rasp of steel, but the frightened horses had dashed away. Upon the cushions lay the dead body of the poor mock king and poet, slain by a ball from the pistol of Monseigneur, the Marquis de Beaupertuys.

The Main Road

Three leagues, then, the road ran, and turned into a puzzle. It joined with another and a larger road at right angles. David stood, uncertain, for a while, and then sat himself to rest upon its side.

Whither those roads led he knew not. Either way there seemed to lie a great world full of chance and peril. And then, sitting there, his eye fell upon a bright star, one that he and Yvonne had named for theirs. That set him thinking of Yvonne, and he wondered if he had not been too hasty. Why should he leave her and his home because a few hot words had come between them? Was love so brittle a thing that jealousy, the very proof of it, could break it? Mornings always brought a cure for the little heartaches of evening. There was yet time for him to return home without any one in the sweetly sleeping village of Vernoy being the wiser. His heart was Yvonne's; there where he had lived always he could write his poems and find his happiness.

David rose, and shook off his unrest and the wild mood that had tempted him. He set his face steadfastly back along the road he had come. By the time he had retravelled the road to Vernoy, his desire to rove was gone. He passed the sheepfold, and the sheep scurried, with a drumming flutter, at his late footsteps, warming his heart by the homely sound. He crept without noise into his little room and lay there, thankful that his feet had escaped the distress of new roads that night.

How well he knew woman's heart! The next evening Yvonne was at the well in the road where the young congregated in order that the *curé* might have business. The corner of her eye was engaged in a search for David, albeit her set mouth seemed unrelenting. He saw the look; braved the mouth, drew from it a recantation and, later, a kiss as they walked homeward together.

Three months afterward they were married. David's father was shrewd and prosperous. He gave them a wedding that was heard of three leagues away. Both the young people were favourites in the village. There was a procession in the streets, a dance on the green; they had the marionettes and a tumbler out from Dreux to delight the guests.

Then a year, and David's father died. The sheep and the cottage descended to him. He already had the seemliest wife in the village. Yvonne's milk pails and her brass kettles were bright—*ouf!* they blinded you in the sun when you passed that way. But you must keep your eyes upon her yard, for her flower beds were so neat and gay they restored to you your sight. And you might hear her sing, aye, as far as the double chestnut tree above Père Gruneau's blacksmith forge.

But a day came when David drew out paper from a long-shut drawer, and began to bite the end of a pencil. Spring had come again and touched his heart. Poet he must have been, for now Yvonne was well-nigh forgotten. This fine new loveliness of earth held him with its witchery and grace. The perfume from her woods and meadows stirred him strangely. Daily had he gone forth with his flock, and brought it safe at night. But now he stretched himself under the hedge and pieced words together on his bits of paper. The sheep strayed, and the wolves, perceiving that difficult poems make easy mutton, ventured from the woods and stole his lambs.

David's stock of poems grew larger and his flock smaller. Yvonne's nose and temper waxed sharp and her talk blunt. Her pans and kettles grew dull, but her eyes had caught their flash. She pointed out to the poet that his neglect was reducing the flock and bringing woe upon the household. David hired a boy to guard the sheep, locked himself in the little room in the top of the cottage, and wrote more poems. The boy, being a poet by nature, but not furnished with an outlet in the way of writing, spent his time in slumber. The wolves lost no time in discovering that poetry and sleep are practically the same; so the flock steadily grew smaller. Yvonne's ill temper increased at an equal rate. Sometimes she would stand in the yard and rail at David through his high window. Then you could hear her as far as the double chestnut tree above Père Gruneau's blacksmith forge.

M. Papineau, the kind, wise, meddling old notary, saw this, as he saw everything at which his nose pointed. He went to David, fortified himself with a great pinch of snuff, and said:

"Friend Mignot, I affixed the seal upon the marriage certificate of your father. It would distress me to be obliged to attest a paper signifying the bankruptcy of his son. But that is what you are coming to. I speak as an old friend. Now, listen to what I have to say. You have your heart set, I perceive, upon poetry. At Dreux, I have a friend, one Monsieur Bril—Georges Bril. He lives in a little cleared space in a houseful of books. He is a learned man; he visits Paris each year; he himself has written books. He will tell you when the catacombs were made, how they found out the names of the stars, and why the plover has a long bill. The meaning and the form of poetry is to him as intelligent as the baa of a sheep is to you. I will give you a letter to him, and you shall take him your poems and let him read them. Then you will know if you shall write more, or give your attention to your wife and business."

"Write the letter," said David, "I am sorry you did not speak of this sooner."

At sunrise the next morning he was on the road to Dreux with the precious roll of poems under his arm. At noon he wiped the dust from his feet at the door of Monsieur Bril. That learned man broke the seal of M. Papineau's letter, and sucked up its contents through his gleaming spectacles as the sun draws water. He took David inside to his study and sat him down upon a little island beat upon by a sea of books.

Monsieur Bril had a conscience. He flinched not even at a mass of manuscript the thickness of a finger length and rolled to an incorrigible curve. He broke the back of the roll against his knee and began to read. He slighted nothing; he bored into the lump as a worm into a nut, seeking for a kernel.

Meanwhile, David sat, marooned, trembling in the spray of so much literature. It roared in his ears. He held no chart or compass for voyaging in that sea. Half the world, he thought, must be writing books.

Monsieur Bril bored to the last page of the poems. Then he took off his spectacles and wiped them with his handkerchief.

"My old friend, Papineau, is well?" he asked.

"In the best of health," said David.

"How many sheep have you, Monsieur Mignot?"

"Three hundred and nine, when I counted them yesterday. The flock has had ill fortune. To that number it has decreased from eight hundred and fifty."

"You have a wife and a home, and lived in comfort. The sheep brought you plenty. You went into the fields with them and lived in the keen air and ate the sweet bread of contentment. You had but to be vigilant and recline there upon nature's breast, listening to the whistle of the blackbirds in the grove. Am I right thus far?"

"It was so," said David.

"I have read all your verses," continued Monsieur Bril, his eyes wandering about his sea of books as if he conned the horizon for a sail. "Look yonder, through that window, Monsieur Mignot; tell me what you see in that tree."

"I see a crow," said David, looking.

"There is a bird," said Monsieur Bril, "that shall assist me where I am disposed to shirk a duty. You know that bird, Monsieur Mignot; he is the philosopher of the air. He is happy through submission to his lot. None so merry or full-crawed as he with his whimsical eye and rollicking step. The fields yield him what he desires. He never grieves that his plumage is not gay, like the oriole's. And you have heard, Monsieur Mignot, the notes that nature has given him? Is the nightingale any happier, do you think?"

David rose to his feet. The crow cawed harshly from his tree.

"I thank you, Monsieur Bril," he said, slowly. "There was not, then, one nightingale note among all those croaks?"

"I could not have missed it," said Monsieur Bril, with a sigh. "I read every word. Live your poetry, man; do not try to write it any more."

"I thank you," said David, again. "And now I will be going back to my sheep."

"If you would dine with me," said the man of books, "and overlook the smart of it, I will give you reasons at length."

"No," said the poet, "I must be back in the fields cawing at my sheep."

Back along the road to Vernoy he trudged with his poems under his arm. When he reached his village he turned into the shop of one Zeigler, a Jew out of Armenia, who sold anything that came to his hand.

"Friend," said David, "wolves from the forest harass my sheep on the hills. I must purchase firearms to protect them. What have you?"

"A bad day, this, for me, friend Mignot," said Zeigler, spreading his hands, "for I perceive that I must sell you a weapon that will not fetch a tenth of its value. Only last week I bought from a peddler a wagon full of goods that he procured at a sale by a *commissionaire* of the crown. The sale was of the *château* and belongings of a great lord—I know not his title—who has been banished for conspiracy against the king. There are some choice firearms in the lot. This pistol —oh, a weapon fit for a prince!—it shall be only forty francs to you, friend Mignot—if I lose ten by the sale. But perhaps an arquebuse—"

"This will do," said David, throwing the money on the counter. "Is it charged?"

"I will charge it," said Zeigler. "And for ten francs more, add a store of powder and ball."

David laid his pistol under his coat and walked to his cottage. Yvonne was not there. Of late she had taken to gadding much among the neighbours. But a fire was glowing in the kitchen stove. David opened the door of it and thrust his poems in upon the coals. As they blazed up they made a singing, harsh sound in the flue.

"The song of the crow!" said the poet.

He went up to his attic room and closed the door. So quiet was the village that a score of people heard the roar of the great pistol. They flocked thither, and up the stairs where the smoke, issuing, drew their notice.

The men laid the body of the poet upon his bed, awkwardly arranging it to conceal the torn plumage of the poor black crow. The women chattered in a luxury of zealous pity. Some of them ran to tell Yvonne.

M. Papineau, whose nose had brought him there among the first, picked up the weapon and ran his eye over its silver mountings with a mingled air of connoisseurship and grief.

"The arms," he explained, aside, to the *curé,* "and crest of Monsiegneur, the Marquis de Beaupertuys."

Ring Lardner

IN WRITING stories, Ring Lardner—to use his own idiom—was a natural. He told them so effortlessly that their great technical skill is taken as a matter of course. His characters—baseball players, housewives, bell-hops, bridge players, cops, song writers, vaudeville actors, and the ordinary man—talk the common speech, and their predicaments arise from the everyday ordinary occurrences which make up the pattern of American life. Years ago H. L. Mencken was one of the first publicly to call attention to Lardner's competence and accuracy in writing authentic American.

Lardner will be remembered, not only for his gaiety and outrageous humor, but for his unerring ability to set down life's small vanities and cruelties, and underlying tragedy. He was born in Michigan in 1885, worked as a sports reporter on newspapers in Chicago, St. Louis, and Boston; and then turned to columning and free-lance writing. He died in 1933. His occasional pieces may be found in First and Last (1934), his collected stories in Round Up (1929).

THERE ARE SMILES *

Ring Lardner

AT THE BUSY corner of Fifth Avenue and Forty-sixth Street there was, last summer, a traffic policeman who made you feel that he didn't have such a terrible job after all. Lots of traffic policemen seem to enjoy abusing you, sadistic complex induced by exposure to bad weather and worse drivers, and, possibly, brutal wives. But Ben Collins just naturally appeared to be having a good time whether he was scolding you or not; his large freckled face fairly beamed with

---

* From *Round Up* by Ring Lardner. Charles Scribner's Sons, 1929. Reprinted by permission of Charles Scribner's Sons.

joviality and refused to cloud up even under the most trying conditions.

It heartened you to look at him. It amused you to hear him talk. If what he said wasn't always so bright, the way he said it was.

Ben was around thirty years old. He was six feet four inches tall and weighed two hundred and eighteen pounds. This describes about eighty per cent of all the traffic officers between Thirty-second Street and the Park. But Ben was distinguished from the rest by his habitual good humour and—well, I guess you'd have to call it his subtlety.

For example, where Noonan or Wurtz or Carmody was content with the stock "Hey! Get over where you belong!" or "Where the hell do you think you're going?" Ben was wont to finesse.

"How are you, Barney?" he would say to a victim halted at the curb.

"My name isn't Barney."

"I beg your pardon. The way you was stepping along, I figured you must be Barney Oldfield."

Or, "I suppose you didn't see that red light."

"No."

"Well, what did you think the other cars was stopped for? Did you think they'd all ran out of gas at once?"

Or, "What business are you in?"

"I'm a contractor."

"Well, that's a good, honorable business and, if I was you, I wouldn't be ashamed of it. I'd quit trying to make people believe I was in the fire department."

Or, "How do you like London?"

"Me? I've never been there."

"I thought that's where you got the habit of driving on the wrong side of the street."

Transgressions at Ben's corner, unless they resulted seriously, were seldom punished beyond these sly rebukes, which were delivered in such a nice way that you were kind of glad you had done wrong.

Off duty he was "a big good-natured boy," willing to take Grace to a picture, or go over to the Arnolds' and play cards, or just stay at home and do nothing.

And then one morning in September, a dazzlingly new Cadillac roadster, blue with yellow trimmings, flashed down from the north, violating all the laws of common sense and of the State and City of New York. Shouts and whistles from Carmody and Noonan, at Forty-eighth and Forty-seventh, failed to check its crazy career, but Ben, first planting his huge bulk directly in its path, giving the driver the choice of slackening speed or running into him, and then, with an alertness surprising in one so massive, sidestepping and jumping onto the running-board, succeeded in forcing a surrender at the curb half-way between his post and Forty-fifth Street.

He was almost mad and about to speak his mind in words beginning with capitals when he got his first look at the miscreant's face. It was the prettiest face he had ever seen and it wore a most impudent, ill-timed, irresistible smile, a smile that spoiled other smiles for you once for all.

"Well—" Ben began falteringly; then recovering something of his stage presence: "Where's your helmet?"

She made no reply, but continued to smile.

"If you're in the fire department," said Ben, "you ought to wear a helmet and a badge. Or paint your car red and get a sireen."

Still no reply.

"Maybe I look like a bobby. Maybe you thought you was in London where they drive on the left side of the street."

"You're cute," she said, and her voice was as thrilling as her smile. "I could stay here all morning and listen to you. That is I could, but I can't. I've got a date down on Eighth Street and I'm late for it now. And I know you're busy, too. So we mustn't keep each other any longer now. But I'd like to hear your whole line some day."

"Oh, you would!"

"Where do you live?"

"At home."

"That isn't very polite, is it? I was thinking you might live in the Bronx—"

"I do."

"—and that's on the way to Rye, where I live, so I might drive you."

"Thanks. When I die, I want to die of old age."

"Oh, I'm not a bad driver, really. I do like to go fast, but I'm careful. In Buffalo, where we lived before, the policemen all knew I was careful and they generally let me go as fast as I wanted to."

"This ain't Buffalo. And this ain't no speedway. If you want to go fast, stay off Fifth Avenue."

The girl looked him right in the eye. "Would you like that?"

"No," said Ben.

She smiled at him again. "What time are you through?"

"Four o'clock," said Ben.

"Well," said the girl, "some afternoon I may be going home about then—"

"I told you I wasn't ready to die."

"I'd be extra careful."

Ben suddenly realized that they were playing to a large staring audience and that for once, he was not the star.

"Drive on!" he said in his gruffest tone. "I'm letting you go because you're a stranger, but you won't get off so easy next time."

"I'm very, very grateful," said the girl. "Just the same I don't like being a stranger and I hope you won't excuse me on that ground again."

Which remark, accompanied by her radiant smile, caused Mr. Collins, hitherto only a bathroom singer, to hum quite loudly all the rest of his working day snatches of a gay Ohman and Arden record that his wife had played over and over the night before.

His relief, Tim Martin, appeared promptly at four, but Ben seemed in no hurry to go home. He pretended to listen to two new ones Tim had heard on the way in from Flushing, one about a Scotchman and some hotel towels and one about two Heebs in a night club. He managed to laugh in the right place, but his attention was on the northbound traffic, which was now none of his business.

At twenty minutes past four he said good-bye to Martin and walked slowly south on the east side of the street. He walked as far as Thirty-sixth, in vain. Usually he caught a ride home with some Bronx or north suburban motorist, but now he was late and had to pay for his folly by hurrying to Grand Central and standing up in a subway express.

"I was a sucker!" he thought. "She probably drove up some other street on purpose to miss me. Or she might have come in on one of them cross streets after I'd walked past it. I ought to stuck at Forty-fourth a while longer. Or maybe some other fella done his duty and had her locked up. Not if she smiled at him, though."

But she wouldn't smile like that at everybody. She had smiled at him because she liked him, because she really thought he was cute. Yes, she did! That was her regular line. That was how she had worked on them Buffalo fellas. "Cute!" A fine word to use on a human Woolworth Building. She was kidding. No, she wasn't; not entirely. She'd liked his looks as plenty other gals had, and maybe that stuff about the fire department and London had tickled her.

Anyway, he had seen the most wonderful smile in the world and he still felt warm from it when he got home, so warm that he kissed his wife with a fervor that surprised her.

When Ben was on the day shift, he sometimes entertained Grace at supper with an amusing incident or two of his work. Sometimes his stories were pure fiction and she suspected as much, but what difference did it make? They were things that ought to have happened even if they hadn't.

On this occasion he was wild to talk about the girl from Rye, but he had learned that his wife did not care much for anecdotes concerning pretty women. So he recounted one-sided arguments with bungling drivers of his own sex which had very little foundation in fact.

"There was a fella coming south in a 1922 Buick and the light changed and when it was time to go again, he thought he was starting in second, and it was reverse instead, and he backed into a big Pierce from Greenwich. He didn't do no damage to the Pierce and only bent himself a little. But they'd have held up the parade ten minutes talking it over if I hadn't bore down.

"I got the Buick fella over to the curb and I said to him, 'What's the matter? Are you homesick?' So he said what did I mean, homesick, and I said, 'Well, you was so anxious to get back to wherever you come from that you couldn't even wait to turn around.'

"Then he tried to explain what was the matter, just like I didn't know. He said this was his first trip in a Buick and he was used to a regular gear shift.

"I said, 'That's fine, but this ain't no training-camp. The place to practice driving is four blocks farther down, at Forty-second. You'll find more automobiles there and twice as many pedestrians and policemen, and besides, they've got street-cars and a tower to back into.'

"I said, 'You won't never learn nothing in a desert like this.' You ought to heard the people laugh."

"I can imagine!" said Grace.

"Then there was a Jordan, an old guy with a gray beard. He was going to park right in front of Kaskel's. He said he wouldn't be more than half an hour. I said, 'Oh, that's too bad! I wished you could spend the weekend.' I said, 'If you'd let us know you was coming, we'd have arranged some parties for you.' So he said, 'I've got a notion to report you for being too fresh.'

"So I said, 'If you do that, I'll have you arrested for driving without your parents' consent.' You ought to have heard them laugh. I said, 'Roll, Jordan, roll!' You ought to have heard them."

"I'll bet!" said Grace.

Ben fell into a long, unaccustomed silence.

"What are you thinking about?"

It came out against his better judgment. "There was a gal in a blue Cadillac."

"Oh! There was! What about her?"

"Nothing. Only she acted like it was her Avenue and I give her hell."

"What did you say to her?"

"I forget."

"Was she pretty?"

"I didn't notice. I was sore."

"You!"

"She all but knocked me for a corpse."

"And you probably just smiled at her."

"No. She done the smiling. She smiled—" He broke off and rose from the table. "Come on, babe. Let's go to the Franklin. Joe Frisco's there. And a Chaplin picture."

Ben saw nothing of the blue Cadillac or its mistress the rest of that week, but in all his polemics he was rehearsing lines aimed to strengthen her belief in his "cuteness." When she suddenly appeared, however, late on the following Tuesday afternoon, he was too excited to do anything but stare, and he would have lost an opportunity of hearing her enchanting voice if she hadn't taken the initiative. Northbound, she stopped at the curb a few feet above his corner and beckoned to him.

"It's after four," she said. "Can't I drive you home?"

What a break! It was his week on the late shift.

"I just come to work. I won't be off till midnight."

"You're mean! You didn't tell me you were going to change."

"I change every week. Last week, eight to four; this week, four to twelve."

"And next week eight to four?"

"Yes'm."

"Well, I'll just have to wait."

He couldn't say a word.

"Next Monday?"

He made an effort. "If you live."

She smiled that smile. "I'll live," she said. "There's an incentive."

She was on her way and Ben returned to his station, dizzy.

"Incentive, incentive, incentive," he repeated to himself, memorizing it, but when he got home at half past one, he couldn't find it in Grace's abridged Webster; he thought it was spelled with an *s*.

The longest week in history ended. A little before noon on Monday the Cadillac whizzed past him going south and he caught the word "later." At quitting time, while Tim Martin was still in the midst of his first new one about two or more Heebs, Ben was all at once aware that she had stopped right beside him, was blocking the traffic, waiting for him.

Then he was in her car, constricting his huge bulk to fit it and laughing like a child at Tim's indelicate ejaculation of surprise.

"What are you laughing at?"

"Nothing. I just feel good."

"Are you glad to be through?"

"Yes. Today."

"Not always?"

"I don't generally care much."

"I don't believe you do. I believe you enjoy your job. And I don't see how you can because it seems to me such a hard job. I'm going to make you tell me all about it as soon as we get out of this jam."

A red light stopped them at Fifty-first Street and she turned and looked at him amusedly.

"It's a good thing the top is down," she said. "You'd have been hideously uncomfortable in one more fold."

"When I get a car of my own," said Ben, "it'll have to be a Mack, and even then I'll have to hire a man to drive it."

"Why a man?"

"Men ain't all crazy."

"Honestly, I'm not crazy. Have I come near hitting anything?"

"You've just missed everything. You drive too fast and you take too many chances. But I knew it before I got in, so I can't kick."

"There isn't room for you to, anyway. Do you want to get out?"

"No."

"I doubt if you could. Where do you live?"

"Hundred and sixty-fourth, near the Concourse," said Ben.

"How do you usually go home?"

"Like this."

"And I thought I was saving you from a tiresome subway ride or something. I ought to have known you'd never lack invitations. Do you?"

"Hardly ever."

"Do the people ask you all kinds of questions?"

"Yes."

"I'm sorry. Because I wanted to and now I can't."

"Why not?"

"You must be tired of answering."

"I don't always answer the same."

"Do you mean you lie to people, to amuse yourself?"

"Sometimes."

"Oh, that's grand! Come on, lie to me! I'll ask you questions, probably the same questions they all ask, and you answer them as if I were a fool. Will you?"

"I'll try."

"Well, let's see. What shall I ask first? Oh, yes. Don't you get terribly cold in winter?"

He repeated a reply he had first made to an elderly lady, obviously a visitor in the city, whose curiosity had prompted her to cross-examine him for over twenty minutes on one of the busiest days he had ever known.

"No. When I feel chilly, I stop a car and lean against the radiator."

His present interviewer rewarded him with more laughter than was deserved.

"That's wonderful!" she said. "And I suppose when your ears are cold, you stop another car and borrow its hood."

"I'll remember that one."

"Now what next? Do you ever get hit?"

"Right along, but only glancing blows. I very seldom get knocked down and run over."

"Doesn't it almost kill you, standing on your feet all day?"

"It ain't near as bad as if it was my hands. Seriously, Madam, I get so used to it that I sleep that way nights."

"Don't the gasoline fumes make you sick?"

"They did at first, but now I can't live without them. I have an apartment near a public garage so I can run over there any time and re-fume myself."

"How tall are you?"

"Six feet ten."

"Not really!"

"You know better, don't you? I'm six feet four, but when women ask me, I tell them anything from six feet eight to seven feet two. And they always say, 'Heavens!' "

"Which do you have the most trouble with, men drivers or women drivers?"

"Men drivers."

"Honestly."

"Sure. There's fifty times as many of them."

"Do lots of people ask you questions?"

"No. You're the first one."

"Were you mad at me for calling you cute the other day?"

"I couldn't be mad at you."

A silence of many blocks followed. The girl certainly did drive fast and Ben might have been more nervous if he had looked ahead, but mostly his eyes were on her profile which was only a little less alluring than her smile.

"Look where we are!" she exclaimed as they approached Fordham Road. "And you live at a Hundred and sixty-fourth! Why didn't you tell me?"

"I didn't notice."

"Don't get out. I'll drive you back."

"No, you won't. I'll catch a ride. There's a fella up this way I want to see."

"You were nice to take a chance with me and not to act scared. Will you do it again?"

"Whenever you say."

"I drive in once a week. I go down to Greenwich Village to visit my sister. Generally on Mondays."

"Next Monday I'll be on the late shift."

"Let's make it the Monday after."

"That's a long ways off."

"The time will pass. It always does."

It did, but so haltingly! And the day arrived with such a threat of rain that Ben was afraid she wouldn't come in. Later on, when the threat was fulfilled and the perils of motoring trebled by a steady drizzle and slippery pavements, he was afraid she would. Prudence, he knew, was not in her make-up and if she had an engagement with her sister, nothing short of a flood would prevent her keeping it.

Just before his luncheon time, the Cadillac passed, going south. Its top was up and its squeegee flying back and forth across the front glass.

Through the rain he saw the girl smile and wave at him briefly. Traffic was thick and treacherous and both must keep their minds on it.

It was still drizzling when she reappeared and stopped for him at four.

"Isn't this a terrible day?" she said.

"Not now!"

She smiled, and in an instant he forgot all the annoyance and discomfort of the preceding hours.

"If we leave the top up, you'll get stoop-shouldered, and if we take it down, we'll be drowned."

"Leave it up. I'm all right."

"Do you mind if we don't talk much? I feel quiet."

He didn't answer and nothing more was said until they turned east at Mount Morris Park. Then:

"I could find out your name," she said, "by remembering your number and having somebody look it up. But you can save me the trouble by telling me."

"My name is Ben Collins. And I could learn yours by demanding to see your driver's license."

"Heavens! Don't do that! I haven't any. But my name is Edith Dole."

"Edith Dole. Edith Dole," said Ben.

"Do you like it?"

"It's pretty."

"It's a funny combination. Edith means happiness and Dole means grief."

"Well," said Ben, "you'll have plenty of grief if you drive without a license. You'll have it anyway if you drive fast on these kind of streets. There's nothing skiddier than car-tracks when it's raining."

They were on upper Madison and the going was dangerous. But that was not the only reason he wanted her to slow down.

Silence again until they were on the Concourse.

"Are you married?" she asked him suddenly.

"No," he lied. "Are you?"

"I will be soon."

"Who to?"

"A man in Buffalo."

"Are you stuck on him?"

"I don't know. But he wants me and my father wants him to have me."

"Will you live in Buffalo?"

"No. He's coming here to be my father's partner."

"And yours."

"Yes. Oh, dear! Here's a Hundred and sixty-fourth and I mustn't take you past it today, not in this weather. Do you think you can extricate yourself?"

He managed it with some difficulty.

"I don't suppose I'll see you again for two weeks."

"I'm afraid not," she said.

He choked down the words that wanted to come out. "Miss Dole," he said, "take my advice and don't try for no records getting home. Just loaf along and you'll be there an hour before your supper's ready. Will you? For that guy's sake in Buffalo?"

"Yes."

"And my sake, too."

Gosh! What a smile to remember!

He must walk slow and give himself a chance to calm down before he saw Grace. Why had he told the girl he wasn't married? What did she care?

Grace's greeting was a sharp command. "Take a hot bath right away! And wear your bath-robe afterwards. We won't be going anywhere tonight."

She and Mary Arnold had been in Mount Vernon at a card-party. They had got soaked coming home. She talked about it all through supper, thank the Lord!

After supper he tried to read, but couldn't. He listened awhile to the Ohman and Arden record which his wife couldn't get enough of. He went to bed, wishing he could sleep and dream, wishing he could sleep two weeks.

He was up early, early enough to look at the paper before breakfast. "Woman Motorist Killed By Street-Car in Bronx." His eyes felt funny as he read: "Miss Edith Dole, twenty-two, of Rye, was instantly killed when the automobile she was driving skidded and struck a street-car at the corner of Fordham Road and Webster Avenue, the Bronx, shortly after four-thirty yesterday afternoon.

"Grace," he said in a voice that was not his own, "I forgot. I'm supposed to be on the job at seven this morning. There's some kind of a parade."

Out of the house, alone, he talked aloud to himself for the first time since he was a kid.

"I can't feel as bad as I think I do. I only seen her four or five times. I can't really feel this bad."

Well, on an afternoon two or three weeks later, a man named Hughes from White Plains, driving a Studebaker, started across Forty-sixth Street out of turn and obeyed a stern order to pull over to the curb.

"What's your hurry?" demanded the grim-faced traffic policeman. "Where the hell do you think you're going? What's the matter with you, you so-and-so!"

"I forgot myself for a minute. I'm sorry," said Mr. Hughes. "If you'll overlook it, I'll pick you up on my way home and take you to the Bronx. Remember, I give you a ride home last month? Remember? That is, it was a fella that looked like you. That is, he looked something like you. I can see now it wasn't you. It was a different fella."

Conrad Aiken

CONRAD AIKEN'S distinguished contributions to the short story are those of a sensitive mind engaged by the mind's own subtleties. As a story writer he is wont to explore the sometimes delicate, sometimes violent variations of human behavior with the clinical curiosity of a psychoanalyst. As a poet he brings to his writing the poet's power of evoking mood. In much of his expression there is the inescapable sadness of a mind caught and entranced by chaos.

He was born in Georgia in 1889, and graduated from Harvard in the class of 1911 which included T. S. Eliot, John Hall Wheelock, Van Wyck Brooks, Walter Lippmann, and John Reed. Aiken was class poet. Since college he has devoted himself entirely to letters in this country and abroad. His Selected Poems won the Pulitzer Prize in 1929. His collections of short stories are Costumes by Eros (1928), Bring! Bring! (1925), and Among the Lost People (1934). His novels include Blue Voyage (1927), Great Circle (1933), and King Coffin (1935).

YOUR OBITUARY, WELL WRITTEN *
Conrad Aiken

A COUPLE of years ago I saw in the "agony column" of *The Times* a very curious advertisement. There are always curious things in that column—I have always been fascinated by that odd little company of forlorn people who so desperately and publicly wear their hearts on their sleeves for daws to peck at. Some of them appear there over and over again—the person who signs himself, or herself, "C.," for example: who regularly every three months or so inserts the message *"Tout*

---

* From *Costumes By Eros* by Conrad Aiken. Charles Scribner's Sons, 1928. Reprinted by permission of Charles Scribner's Sons.

passe, l'amitié reste." What singular and heartbreaking devotion does that brief legend convey? Does it ever reach the adored being for whom it is intended, I wonder? Does he ever see it, does he ever reply? Has he simply abandoned her? Were they sundered by some devastating tragedy which can never be healed? And will she go on till she dies, loosing these lovely flame-colored arrows into an utterly unresponsive void? . . .

I never tire of reflecting on these things; but the advertisement of which I have just spoken was of a different sort altogether. This was signed "Journalist," and merely said: "Your obituary? Well written, reviewed by yourself, and satisfaction thus insured." My first response to this oddity was mere amusement. How extraordinarily ingenious of this journalist! It seemed to me that he had perhaps found a gold-mine —I could well imagine that he would be inundated with orders for glowing eulogies. And what an astonishing method of making a living —by arranging flowers, as it were, for the about-to-be-dead! That again was fascinating—for it made me wonder what sort of bird this journalist might be. Something wrong with him, no doubt—a kind of sadist, a gloomy creature who perhaps revelled rather unhealthily in the mortuary; even, perhaps, a necrophile. Or was he, on the other hand, perfectly indifferent and detached about it, a mere hack-writer who had, by elimination, arrived at a rather clever idea? . . . But from these speculations I went on to others, and among them the question— to me a highly interesting one—of what, exactly, one would want put into one's own obituary. What would this be? Would one want just the usual sort of thing—the "he was born," "he lived in Rome," "he was a well-known connoisseur of the arts, and a patron of painting," "conspicuous in the diplomatic society of three countries," "a brilliant amateur archaeologist," "died intestate" sort of thing? . . . Or would one prefer to have one's personal qualities touched on—with perhaps a kindly reference to one's unfailing generosity, one's warmth of heart, and one's extraordinary equableness of disposition? . . .

By neither alternative did it seem to me that my "satisfaction could be insured." Neither for those who knew me, nor for those who did not, could any such perfunctory *eulogium* be in the least evocative. In what respect would these be any better than the barest of tombstone engravings, with its "born" and "died" and "he was a devoted father"? Mrs. X. or Mr. Z., reading of me that I was an amateur archaeologist and a kind old fellow, a retired diplomatic secretary, would form no picture of me, receive from such bare bones of statement not the faintest impression of what I might call the "essence" of my life: not the faintest. But if not these, what then? And it occurred to me suddenly that the best, and perhaps the only, way of leaving behind one a record of one's life which might be, for a world of strangers, revelatory, was that of relating some single episode of one's history: some single, and if possible central, episode in whose small prism all the colors and lights of one's soul might be seen. Seen just for a flash, and then gone. Apprehended, vividly, and then forgotten—if one ever *does* forget such things. And from this, I proceeded to a speculation as to just which one, of all the innumerable events of a well-filled life, I would choose as revelatory. My meeting with my wife at a ball in Calcutta, for example? Some incident of our unhappy life together—perhaps our quarrel in Venice, at the Lido? The effect of her suicide upon me, her drowning in the Mediterranean—the news of which came to me, while I was dining at the Reform Club, from the P. & O. Company? . . . I considered all of these, only to reject them. Possibly I rejected them—to some extent, anyway—simply because they were essentially painful. I don't know. Anyway, whatever the reasons, I did reject them, and at last found myself contemplating my odd little adventure with Reine Wilson, the novelist. Just why I fastened upon this, it would be hard to say. It was not an adventure at all: it was hardly even an episode. It was really nothing but the barest of encounters, as I see it now, or as any *third* person would see it. If I compare it with my protracted love-affair with Mrs. M., for example, or even with my very brief infatuation with Hilda K., it appears to be a mere nothing, a mere fragrance.

A mere fragrance! . . . Yes, it was that; and it is for that reason, I see now, that it is so precious to me. Volatile and swift as it was, it somehow caught into itself all the scanty poetry of my life. If I may be pardoned for appearing a little bit "romantic" about myself, I might say that it was as if I were a tree, and had, in this one instance, put forth a single blossom, a blossom of unique beauty, perhaps a sort of "sport," which, unlike my other blossoms, bore no fruit, but excelled all the others in beauty and sweetness. That sounds, in the prosaic statement, rather affected, I am afraid; but it is as nearly a literal statement of the truth as I can find.

It happened when I was a young man, about four years after I had married. I was already unhappy and restless. I wasn't wholly aware of this—I had, at all events, no conscious desire, as yet, to go in search of adventure. All the same, it is obvious to me now that I was, *uncon-*

sciously, in search of some sort of escape or excitement. I went about a
good deal—and I went about alone. My own tastes being mildly
literary, and my wife's not, I made rather a specialty of literary teas
and "squashes," and had soon made a considerable number of acquaintances among the younger writers who lived in London at that
time. Among these was a group of young folk who ran a small
monthly magazine called *The Banner*—a magazine which, like many
other such things, ran a brilliant but sporadic course for a year or two
and then went bankrupt. My friend Estlin first told me about this, and
called my attention to the work of Reine Wilson, whose first novel
was coming out serially in *The Banner,* and whose husband was
assistant-editor of it. I read the first two chapters of "Scherzo," and I
was simply transported by it. It seemed to me the most exquisite prose
I had ever read—extraordinarily alive, extraordinarily poetic, and exquisitely feminine. It was the prose of a woman who was, as it were,
all sensibility—of a soul that was all a tremulous awareness. Could one
have—I asked Estlin—so ethereally delicate a consciousness, a consciousness so easily wounded, and *live?* And he horrified me by replying "No," and by telling me that Reine Wilson was—to all intents
—dying. She had a bad heart, and had been definitely "given up." She
might die at any minute. And she ought, by rights, to be dead already.

This shocked me, and also made me very curious; and when Estlin
asked me, one day, to come to lunch with himself and the Wilsons, I
needed no urging. We were to meet them at a little French place in
Wardour Street—long since gone, I regret to say—and on our way
thither we stopped at a pub for a glass of sherry. It was there that, by
way of preface to the encounter, Estlin told me that there was something "queer" in the Wilson situation.

"Queer?" I said.

"Yes, queer. Nobody can make it out. You see, they lived together
before they married—when they were both writing for *The Times.*
For about three years. But then, all of a sudden, they married: and the
minute they were properly married—presto!—they separated. She took
a flat in Hampstead—and he took one in Bloomsbury. Once a week,
they held a reception together at her flat—and they still do. But so far
as any one knows, they've never lived together from that day to this.
He doesn't seem to be in love with any one else—and neither does she.
They are perfectly friendly—even affectionate. But they live apart. And
she always refers to him simply as 'Wilson.' She even *calls* him Wilson.
Damned funny."

I agreed with him, and I pondered. Was it—I asked—because she had a bad heart? too much of a strain for her? . . . Estlin thought not; though he wasn't sure. He even thought that the bad heart had developed *after* the separation. He shook his head over it, and said "Rum!" and we went to meet them. He added, inconsequentially, that he thought she would like me.

She did like me—and I liked her. At first sight. I find it difficult to describe the impression she made upon me—I think I was first struck by the astonishing frailty of her appearance, an other-world fragility, almost a *transparent* spiritual quality, as if she were already a disembodied soul. She was seated at a small table, behind a pot of ferns, which half concealed her face. Her brown eyes, under a straight bang of black hair, were round as a doll's, and as intense.

"Isn't it like meeting in a *jungle?*" she said. She made the tiniest of gestures toward the fern; and I was struck by the restraint with which she did this, and by the odd way in which her voice, though pitched very low, and very carefully controlled, nevertheless contrived to reveal a burning intensity of spirit such as I have never elsewhere encountered. There was something gingerly about her self-control: and also something profoundly terrifying. It seemed to me that I had never met any one whose hold on life was so terribly *conscious*. It was as if she held it—this small, burning jewel—quite literally in her hands; as if she felt that at any instant it might escape her; or as if she felt that, if it didn't escape, it might, if not firmly held, simply burn itself away in its own sheer aliveness. And to sit with her, to watch the intense restraint of all her gestures and expressions, and above all to listen to the feverish controlledness with which she spoke, was at once to share in this curious attitude toward life. Insensibly, one became an invalid. One felt that the flame of life was burning low—and burning low for *every one*—but burning with all the more beauty and pure excellence for that; and one entered into a strange and secret conspiracy to guard that precious flame with all one's power.

II

I had little opportunity, during that luncheon-party, for any "private" talk with Reine: the conversation was general. Not only that, but it was, as was to be expected, pretty literary, and I, perforce, took an inconspicuous part in it. Wilson struck me as a rather opinionated person, rather loud-voiced, rather sprawling, and I felt myself somewhat affronted by the excessiveness of his "Oxford manner." In fact,

I disliked him, and thought him rather a fool. How on earth—I wondered—had he managed to attract so exquisite a creature as his wife? What on earth had she seen in him? . . . For there was something coarse in him, and also, I felt sure, something dishonest. He seemed to me hypocritical. He seemed to me to be merely *posing* as a literary man. And I thought that his loud enthusiasms were the effort of the insincere to make an impression, to carry conviction. Was it possible that Reine didn't see through this? Or was it possible—and this idea really excited me—that she *did* see through him, and that it was for this reason that they had separated? . . .

I found myself setting myself in a kind of opposition to him: not by anything so obvious as contradiction, but, simply, by being very quiet. I quite definitely exaggerated my usual quietness and restraint of speech, endeavoring at the same time to make it very pungent and concise; simply because I felt that this was what she wanted and needed. And she rewarded me by being, in our few interchanges, extraordinarily nice to me. I remember, when Wilson had been declaiming against the enormous emptiness of Henry James, and his total lack of human significance, that I waited for a pause and then said, very gently, that I could not agree: that James seemed to me the most consummate analyst of the influence of character upon character, particularly in situations of a profound moral obliquity, that there had ever been. Reine looked at me, on this, as if I had been a kind of revelation to her: her eyes positively brimmed with light and joy.

"Isn't he?" she whispered. She leaned forward, intently, with her small pointed chin resting upon her clasped hands; and then added: "No one else—*no* one—has made such beauty, and such *intricate* beauty, out of the iridescence of moral decay!" . . .

I don't remember what I said in reply to this—I am not sure that I said anything; but I do remember that I felt, at this moment, as if an accolade had been bestowed upon me. It was as if, abruptly, Reine and I were alone together—as if her husband, "Wilson," and my friend young Estlin, had somehow evaporated. I think I blushed; for I was conscious that suddenly she was looking at me in an extraordinarily penetrating way—appraisingly, but also with unmistakable delight. We had discovered a bond—or *she* had discovered one—and we were going to be friends. Obviously. A subtle something-or-other at once took place between us, and it was as much "settled" as if we had said it in so many words. And when we got up to separate, after the lunch,

it was almost as a matter of course that she invited me to come to tea
with her on the following Sunday. She was, in fact, deliciously firm
about it—as if she were determined to stand no nonsense. It was to me
she turned and not to Estlin (Estlin was much amused), and it was to
me she first put out her hand.

"You *will* come to tea, won't you? Next Sunday? And bring Mr.
Estlin with you? . . ."

I murmured that I would be delighted—we smiled—and then, taking
Wilson's arm for support (my heart ached when I saw this) she turned
and went slowly out through the glass doors to Wardour Street.

Estlin was smiling to himself, and shaking his head.

"You're a terrible fellow," he said—"a terrible fellow!"

"Me?" I said. "Why?"

I knew perfectly well why, of course—but it pleased me to have
Estlin say that I had made an unusual impression on Reine Wilson.

"And you may not know it," he added, "but she's damned hard to
please. *Damned* hard to please. In fact, a good deal of an intellectual
snob, and excessively cruel to those she dislikes. You just wait! . . .
If she catches you admiring the wrong thing . . . !"

I laughed, a little discomfited—for I had already foreseen for myself
that possibility. How could I, an amateur, keep it up? It was all very
well to make one lucky shot about Henry James—but sooner or later
I was bound to give myself away as, simply, not of her kin. . . .
Or *was* I? . . . For I admit I was vain enough to hope that I might
really be enough of a person, fine and rich and subtle enough, to
attract her. How much was I presuming in hoping this? She had liked
me—she had been excited by that remark—we had certainly *met* each
other in a rather extraordinary way, of which she had shown herself to
be thrillingly conscious. And I was myself, I must confess, very much
excited by all this. She was, in every respect, the most remarkable
woman I had ever met. I do not know how to explain this—for it was
not that she had *said,* at lunch, anything especially remarkable: it was,
rather, what she *was,* and *how* she said things. Her burning intensity
of spirit, the sheer naked honesty with which she felt things, and
the wonderful and terrible way in which she could appear so vividly
and joyfully, and yet so precariously, alive—all this, together with her
charming small oddity of appearance, the doll-like seriousness of face
and doll-like eyes, combined to make a picture which was not merely

enchanting. It was, for me, terribly disturbing. I was going to fall in love with her—and I was going to fall hard and deep.

Going to. I used the phrase advisedly. For there is always, in these affairs, a point at which one can say that one is *going* to fall in love, but has not yet done so: a point at which one feels the powerful and seductive fascination of this other personality, feels drawn to it almost irresistibly, and knows that *unless* one resists one is going to be enslaved. Nevertheless, it *is,* at this point, still possible to resist. One can turn one's back on the Siren, turn one's ship away from Circe's Isle, sail away—if one only has a little courage and good sense. Good sense? No. *That* phrase, I am afraid, has crept down to me from the Victorians. What I would prefer to call it now, in my own case, is cowardice. Or, if you like, caution. Or again, respect for the conventions. For I am sure that is what it was. . . . During the five days which intervened between the luncheon-party and my engagement for tea, I did a lot of thinking about this. I knew perfectly well that if I were to let myself go, I could fall in love. But did I want to fall in love? And suppose I did. Quite apart from my own domestic complications—and the situation with my wife was already quite sufficiently unpleasant—what good would it do me? For I was desperately, horribly, miserably sure of one thing and one thing only: that Reine Wilson would not fall in love with me. Or if she did, that she would fall out again in double-quick time. And there, hung up for the crows to peck at, I would be. . . .

I thought about this—and thought and thought. But I didn't—as the hours crept toward Sunday—find any solution. Of course, I would go to tea—there was no question about that. So much rope I would grant myself, and no more. No harm could come of that—or at any rate, no greater harm than was done already. One is ingenious, when one is falling in love, at finding good excuses for meetings with one's beloved. Yes, I would go to tea—and *then* I would make up my mind as to the future. A good deal would depend on what happened at tea. If I should disgrace myself—if she were to find me out—or, as was only too likely, if she simply found me uninteresting, a nice young fellow, no doubt, with an idea or two, but not at all on *The Banner* level— well, that would be the end of it. But if, on the other hand, our mutual attraction should deepen—if, somehow, by hook or by crook, I should manage to keep up the deception—or even, actually, to prove a sufficient match for her—what then? . . . What would happen to us? . . . What about my wife? . . . What about that detestable "Wilson"? . . . And, above all, what about her bad heart? . . .

III

The new number of *The Banner* came out on Saturday, and it contained of course another instalment of "Scherzo." I read this—and it seemed to me even more delightful and more obviously a work of first-rate genius, than the chapters which had gone before. It was in this instalment that the description of the picnic occurred. This entranced me. Never, it seemed to me, had an *al fresco* party been so beautifully done in prose. The gaiety, the coltish rompings of the young girls, that marvellously described wood, and the cries of the children in it, playing hide-and-seek—the solemn conversation of the two little boys who had discovered a dead vole, and were wondering how most magnificently to dispose of it—the arrival of Grandma Celia with the basket—and above all, Underhill's dream. It seemed to me a stroke of the finest genius to have poor Underhill, at that crisis of his life, dragged into such a party—frisked about, romped over, made to tell stories and to light fires; and then, when he sneaked away and found a clearing in the gorse and slept, having that marvellous dream . . . ! The dream was so vivid and so terrifying that I felt as if I had dreamt it myself. It was I who had been in that cottage during the thunderstorm—it was I who tried vainly to shut the rattling windows and doors against the torrents of rain and hail, hoping to protect those mysterious "other people"—and it was I who finally, disheartened, despairing, had set out to climb the black mountain valley toward the storm. And the description of that Alpine valley, with its swishing pines and firs, and the terrible white cloud which hung at the upper end of it! My blood froze as I moved toward that cloud and saw the death-lightning which shot from it unceasingly. It hung there portentously: like death itself. And I, who had at first moved toward it as if voluntarily, now felt myself being drawn off the ground and into the air—I floated at first a foot or two off the path and then a little higher—I was on a level with the tops of the trees, and every second drawing nearer to the dense white cloud—I could see, at last, that it was a magnificent cold arch of greenish ice, impenetrable and hostile—its cold vapor blew upon me—and then came a final flash and I knew that I was already dead. . . . It was superb, it was annihilating. And only the most daring of genius would have presumed to expand a mere dream, in the midst of a realistic narrative, to such proportions and to concentrate in it all the agony and tragedy of a torn soul.

I was still in a fever of excitement about this when I was shown into

Reine Wilson's sitting-room by a young woman who seemed to combine the functions of house-keeper and trained-nurse. Reine rose to
greet me, rose slowly and weakly and with conscious effort, and then,
having given me her hand, was assisted by the young woman to her
chair by the tea-table. The young woman brought in the teapot and
the hot scones, and then withdrew. I had seated myself on a couch by
the open window. A double-red thorn-tree was in blossom in the small
garden, and its fragrance filled the room.

"I've just been reading—" I said—in a voice that I am afraid shook a
little—"your new instalment of 'Scherzo.' I think it's perfectly en-
trancing."

Reine looked at me, I thought with a trace of hostility—I was certain
that my approach had been too blunt.

"Oh, *do* you?" she said. And then immediately added, with a kind of
careful lightness: "One lump or two, Mr. Grant? . . . Is this too
weak for you?"

I stood up and moved to the tea-table for my cup of tea, and for the
hot scone which she offered me; and suddenly I felt horribly shy. I had
ruined myself at the outset—I had rushed in too fast and too far. I
ought to have known better. I ought to have known that I must leave
the lead to her, and follow up the controlled reticence of manner with
which I had made such a success at the luncheon-party. A violent
outbreak like that! With a creature so exquisitely sensitive!—I felt
clumsy and coarse and miserably ashamed. And I sank onto the couch
again very much humiliated and very conscious of my hands and
feet.

But Reine, to my astonishment, had mercy on me.

"I'm *so* glad you liked it!" she said. And she said it with such an air
of relief, and with a voice so rich in delight, that I felt a shock of
returning confidence as vivid and intense as, a moment since, its departure had been. And I had an instant and heavenly conviction that I
could now throw all caution to the winds. She looked at me with wide-
open eyes—it was almost as if she looked at me with wide-open soul.
We had, abruptly, "met" again: and we had met more intimately than
before. It was strange, at that moment, how everything seemed to be
conspiring to make this mutual recognition complete: the long room
lined with bookcases; the high mantel of cream-colored wood and the
pale Dutch tiles which surrounded the fireplace; the worn Khelim rug
which stretched between us, and the open window, which it seemed
not improbable that the thorn-tree itself had opened, in order that its

fragrance and the London spring might come in to us—all these details were vividly and conspiratorially present to me, as if they were indeed a part of the exquisite mingling of our personalities at that poised instant of time. Was not I myself in this room, this rug, that mantel, the tea-table spread with tea-things, and the inquisitive thorn-tree? Was not I myself Reine Wilson, entertaining a strange young man in whom I felt a subtle and bewildering and intoxicating attraction? Destiny was in this—aeons of patient evolution and change, wars and disasters and ages of darkness, the sandlike siftings of laws and stars, had all worked for the fulfilment of this ultimate minute, this perfect flowering of two meeting minds. I could not be mistaken in my belief that it was the same for her as for me. With the deep tremor in my own soul, I could feel the tremor in hers. If it were not true, she could not possibly be holding her teacup as she did, or frowning slightly as she did, or withholding, as she deliciously did, the smile of delighted confession which I knew she was near to giving me.

"You know—" I then added—"I think that dream is marvellous—simply marvellous."

"*Do* you!" she cried. "But how lovely! You *really* liked it? You didn't think there was too much of it? . . ."

She leaned toward me with the eagerness of a schoolgirl, her eyes wide with intensity.

"Too much of it! Heavens no. I was never so enthralled by anything in my life."

"But do you *mean* it? . . . Why, you know, Wilson wanted me to 'cut' it. He said it was far, far too long. And everybody on *The Banner* has said so. . . . But *you* think it's all right? . . ."

"It's much more than all right. It couldn't possibly be anything but what it is. It seems to me to be the very *soul* of the thing—the centre and source of light. It *had* to be that, hadn't it? . . . I mean, a glowing symbol for the whole thing. For Underhill's Gethsemane. . . ."

She looked at me, after this, for a long moment, and then she drew in her breath very slowly and deeply, subtly relaxing.

"Heavens!" she said—"you *are* a miracle."

"Am I?"

"You know you are. I hadn't *dared* to suppose that any one would see what I intended by that. Or would like it, even if they did. . . . Isn't it extraordinary!"

She gave an odd light little laugh, not without a trace of bitterness, and then, with a smile still charmingly lighting her small face, gazed downward abstractedly at the Khelim rug. I knew what she meant by "extraordinary"—she meant that it was extraordinary that two minds should find each other as swiftly and easily as ours did. I knew also that she would not want the strangeness of this, and its beauty, too explicitly noted. For that would be to spoil it.

"Yes," I sighed, "it is. . . . Can I steal another scone?"

"Do! . . . Have one of the underneath ones—they're hotter!"

I took one, and returned to the couch. The room had suddenly darkened—it had clouded up—and a momentary patter of drops on the leaves of the thorn-tree sounded in the silence, as if it were inside the room.

"Rain!" I said. . . . "I love it! Don't you?"

"You mean the sound of it? . . ."

"No—everything. The sound, yes, but also the light—rain has always had for me, ever since I can remember, a special sort of *magic*. On rainy days I experience a special kind of delicious melancholy—a melancholy that is happy, if that means anything to you. I brood, my imagination is set free, I am restless and depressed, and yet at the same time it is as if something inside me wanted to sing. . . . Don't I sound like a sentimental idiot?"

"Oh!" she said, "how *nice* of you!"

She rose, very gingerly, and coming to the end of the couch rested her two hands on the blue-canvas arm, one hand on top of the other. As she looked out through the window at the thorn-tree, watching the small leaves courtsey and genuflect to the raindrops, and then spring up again released, I felt as if I were going to tremble. I found myself thinking about her heart again—she looked so astonishingly frail. How could so frail a body, a body so ethereally and transparently slight, contain a spirit so vivid? One felt that with the slightest flutter the bright bird might escape and be gone.

"Yes," she said, in almost a whisper, as if to herself, "it is beautiful . . . beautiful. It does make one want to sing. And how the thrushes adore it!"

"I remember—" I said—"how once, when I was a small boy, I went bathing in the sea on a darkish day. While I was swimming, it began to rain. I was at first astonished—almost frightened. The water was smooth—there was no sound of waves—and all about me arose a delicate and delicious *seething*, the low sound of raindrops on the sea. It was a ghostly and whispering sound—there was something sinister in it, and also something divinely soothing. I lay on my back and floated, letting the drops fall on my face while I looked up at the clouds—and then I swam very softly, so as to be able to listen. I don't believe I was ever happier in my life. It was as if I had gone into another world. . . . And then, when I went ashore, I remember how I *ran* to the bathing-hut, for fear of getting wet! . . ."

"Of course!" she cried. "Of course you would! . . ."

She sank down on the couch, facing me. And then she went on:

"You've given me back something I had forgotten. . . . It must have been when I was eleven or twelve. It was raining very hard—it was pouring—and when I went down to the library to practise at the piano the room was dark, with that kind of morning darkness that engulfs one. The French windows were open onto the garden, but the curtains hung perfectly still, for there was no wind, no current of air. One of those heavy, straight rains, on a quiet day—a rain as solid and serried as rain in a Japanese print. . . . I went into the room and closed the door behind me—and it seemed to me, so massive and insistent was the sound of the rain from the garden, with all its multitudinous patter and spatter, that the room itself was full of rain. The sounds were the sound of water, the light was the light of water—it was as if I were a fish in a darkened aquarium. I stood still for a long while, just drinking it in and staring out at the drenched garden, where all the trees and shrubs were bowed down under the unrelenting downpour. Not long before, I had seen somewhere some photographs greatly enlarged, of raindrops falling into water: and now, as I went to the open French windows, I watched the large bright eave-drops splashing into the puddles on the brick terrace, and I was enchanted to see that *my* drops were exactly like those. They made the most exquisite little silvery water-spouts and umbrellas and toadstools, and all with such a heavenly clucking and chuckling and chirruping. The bubbles winked and were gone—is there anything so evanescent as a rain-bubble?—and other bubbles came, sliding a fraction of an inch to right or left before they burst. . . . I had a strange feeling, then, as I turned to go to the piano—I felt as if I belonged to the rain, or as if I were the rain itself. I had a sensation in my throat that was like sadness, but was also ecstatic—something like your desire to sing. I looked at the glossy black grand piano—and that too had a watery look, like a dark pool gleaming under a heavy overhang of foliage. And when I sat down on the cool piano-stool, and touched timidly my fingers to the keys, the keys too were cold, and it was as if I were dipping my hands into the clearest of rain-water. . . . Is it any wonder that the music sounded to me like the drops pattering and spattering in the garden? I was delighted to the point of obsession with this idea. I played a little sonata through three times, luxuriating in its arpeggios and runs, which I took pianissimo, and feeling as if I were helping the rain to rain. . . . Good heavens! If I had only known the Handel Water-Music Suite! The illusion would have been perfect. . . ."

"It's so perfect for me," I said, "that I am tempted to look at your hands to see if they are still wet."

We smiled at each other, then, our eyes meeting with a shyness that was not altogether a shyness; and after a moment, by a common impulse, turned to look out at the red-blossomed tree, from which arose a soft irregular patter. We were silent for a long while. In fact, I think we sat there in complete silence till the nurse-companion came back again for the tea-things; and I remember noticing everything, every minutest detail, in the small brick-walled garden. A laburnum-tree at the farther end with long pendulous blossoms, of so bright a yellow that it gave one the illusion of sunlight against the dark wall. And a row of lupins along a flagged path, with a bright eye of water in every one of the dark hand-shaped leaves. . . . These things are still vivid in my memory. But what we said to each other after that I cannot recall. I don't think we said very much. We felt, I think, that we had already said all that was essential. I do remember Reine's saying that "Wilson" had gone off somewhere to play cricket: and also she said something about a dismal female tea-party to which she had gone in Earl's Court the day before. But that, I think, was all; and not long afterward I rose and came away.

IV

I never saw her again. In the first place, I funked it—I was afraid that I couldn't keep it up. The thing was so exquisite as it stood, so perfect—and besides, what could I do? It seemed to me that almost anything after that, would be an anticlimax. If I were to go again, there might be some one else there—we should have to be stiff and distant with each other—or we wouldn't be able to talk to each other at all. Wilson might be there, with his loud fake enthusiasms and his horrible Oxford manner and his sprawling tweed legs. . . .

At bottom, however, it was a kind of terror that kept me away. I was in love with her, and I had more than a hope that she was very nearly in love with me. But hadn't we already had the finest of it? The thing, as it stood, was all bloom and fragrance; and mightn't it be only too appallingly easy by some unguarded shaking of the tree, to destroy the whole rare miracle? . . . Wouldn't I—to use a less poetic image—let the cat out of the bag, if I were to go again? And then there was her bad heart, and the fact that we were both, alas, married. The complications and miseries, if we *did* allow the meeting to go further, might well be fatal to both of us.

Even so, I am not sure that I wouldn't have gone, had not fate in the guise of the Foreign Office intervened. I was sent, only a few weeks later, to Rome, where my duties kept me for a year and a half. It was while I was there that "Scherzo" came out in book-form. Estlin sent me a copy—and I at once sat down and wrote a letter to Reine, a brief one, telling her again of the incomparable delight it gave me. It was a month or more before I heard from her—and then came a short note from Seville. It was rather cool, rather cryptic, distinctly guarded. She thanked me formally, she was glad I liked the dream so much, she felt, as I did, that the ending was perhaps a shade "tricky," or a "surprise" sort which didn't quite "go" with the tone of the rest. That was all. But there was also a postscript at the bottom of the page, which seemed to me to be in a handwriting a little less controlled— as if she had hesitated about adding it, and had then, impulsively, dashed it in at the last minute. This was simply: "I always think of you as the man who loves rain." . . . That was all.

It was only a few weeks after this, when, opening *The Times* in a small café in the Via Tritoni, I was shocked to see her name in the column of death announcements. "Suddenly, at Paris, on the 18th of March." . . . Suddenly, at Paris, on the 18th of March! . . . I sat and stared stupidly at the announcement, leaving untouched on the little table before me my *granita di cafe con pana.* . . . Reine Wilson was dead—Reine was dead. That little girl who had stood in the dark room by the French windows, her sleeve brushing the stirless curtains, watching the rain—who had dipped her hands through the clearest rain-water to the white piano keys—and seen the little umbrellas of silver—was dead. I got up and walked out blindly into the bright street. Without knowing how I got there, I found myself presently in the Borghese Gardens. There was a little pond, in which a great number of ducks were sailing to and fro, gabbling and quacking, and children were throwing bread into the water. I sat down on a bench under a Judas-tree—it was in blossom, and the path under it was littered with purple. An Italian mother slapped the hand of her small boy who was

crying, and said harshly *"Piangi! . . . Piangi! . . ."* Cry! . . . Cry!
. . . And I too felt like weeping, but I shed no tears. Reine Wilson the
novelist was still alive; but Reine Wilson the dark-haired little girl
with whom I had fallen in love was dead, and it seemed to me that
I too was dead.

Wilbur Daniel Steele

ADMIRERS of Wilbur Daniel Steele do not find it hard to understand why his stories have won many prizes, including four O. Henry Memorial awards, and why he received a special award in 1921 for maintaining the highest level of merit for three years among American short story writers. Powerful in theme, often melodramatic in situation, his stories satisfy the reader's longing for something to happen, and they are equally impressive for their evoking of atmosphere and plausible delineation of unusual characters. Twenty years ago Edward J. O'Brien said of Land's End, an early collection of his tales, that "almost without exception, they represent the best that is being accomplished in America today by a literary artist." Since that date Steele's mastery of the resources of the short story has produced even better work. Among his great stories, appearing in several collections, are "Blue Murder," "The Woman at Seven Brothers," "The Man Who Saw Through Heaven," "Bubbles," "When Hell Froze," and the story here printed. Mr. Steele has also written several novels and a collection of one-act plays.

Wilbur Daniel Steele was born in Greensboro, North Carolina, in 1886. He graduated from the University of Denver, where his father taught Biblical literature, studied painting in Boston, Paris, and New York, and has travelled in far regions which have furnished much material for his writing. Many of his stories deal with experiences of the New England sea coast. He now lives in Old Lyme, Connecticut.

HOW BEAUTIFUL WITH SHOES *
Wilbur Daniel Steele

By the time the milking was finished, the sow, which had farrowed the past week, was making such a row that the girl spilled a pint of the warm milk down the trough-lead to quiet the animal before taking the pail to the well-house. Then in the quiet she heard a sound of hoofs on the bridge, where the road crossed the creek a hundred yards below the house, and she set the pail down on the ground beside her bare, barn-soiled feet. She picked it up again. She set it down. It was as if she calculated its weight.

That was what she was doing, as a matter of fact, setting off against its pull toward the well-house the pull of that wagon team in the road, with little more of personal wish or will in the matter than has a wooden weathervane between two currents in the wind. And as with the vane, so with the wooden girl—the added behest of a whip-lash cracking in the distance was enough; leaving the pail at the barn door, she set off in a deliberate, docile beeline through the cow-yard, over the fence, and down in a diagonal across the farm's one tilled field toward the willow brake that walled the road at the dip. And once under way, though her mother came to the kitchen door and called in her high flat voice, 'Amarantha, where you goin', Amarantha?' the girl went on apparently unmoved, as though she had been as deaf as the woman in the doorway; indeed, if there was emotion in her it was the purely sensuous one of feeling the clods of the furrows breaking softly between her toes. It was springtime in the mountains.

'Amarantha, why don't you answer me, Amarantha?'

For moments after the girl had disappeared beyond the willows the widow continued to call, unaware through long habit of how absurd it sounded, the name which that strange man her husband had put upon their daughter in one of his moods. Mrs. Doggett had been deaf so long she did not realize that nobody else ever thought of it for the broad-fleshed, slow-minded girl, but called her Mary or, even more simply, Mare.

Ruby Herter had stopped his team this side of the bridge, the mules' heads turned into the lane to his father's farm beyond the road. A big-barreled, heavy-limbed fellow with a square, sallow, not unhandsome face, he took out youth in ponderous gestures of masterfulness;

* From *Harper's Magazine*, August, 1932. Reprinted by permission of the author.

it was like him to have cracked his whip above his animals' ears the
moment before he pulled them to a halt. When he saw the girl getting
over the fence under the willows he tongued the wad of tobacco out of
his mouth into his palm, threw it away beyond the road, and drew a
sleeve of his jumper across his lips.

'Don't run yourself out o' breath, Mare; I got all night.'

'I was comin'!' It sounded sullen only because it was matter of fact.

'Well, keep a-comin' and give us a smack.' Hunched on the wagon
seat, he remained motionless for some time after she had arrived at the
hub, and when he stirred it was but to cut a fresh bit of tobacco, as if
already he had forgotten why he threw the old one away. Having
satisfied his humor, he unbent, climbed down, kissed her passive mouth,
and hugged her up to him, roughly and loosely, his hands careless of
contours. It was not out of the way; they were used to handling
animals both of them; and it was spring. A slow warmth pervaded
the girl, formless, nameless, almost impersonal.

Her betrothed pulled her head back by the braid of her yellow hair.
He studied her face, his brows gathered and his chin out.

'Listen, Mare, you wouldn't leave nobody else hug and kiss you,
dang you!'

She shook her head, without vehemence or anxiety.

'Who's that?' She hearkened up the road. 'Pull your team out,' she
added, as a Ford came in sight around the bend above the house,
driven at speed. 'Geddap!' she said to the mules herself.

But the car came to a halt near them, and one of the five men
crowded in it called, 'Come on, Ruby, climb in. They's a loony loose
out o' Dayville Asylum, and they got him trailed over somewheres
on Split Ridge, and Judge North phoned up to Slosson's store for
ever'body come help circle him—come on, hop the runnin'-board!'

Ruby hesitated, an eye on his team.

'Scared, Ruby?' The driver raced his engine. 'They say this boy's a
killer.'

'Mare, take the team in and tell pa.' The car was already moving
when Ruby jumped it. A moment after it had sounded on the bridge
it was out of sight.

'Amarantha, Amarantha, why don't you come, Amarantha?'

Returning from her errand, fifteen minutes later, Mare heard the
plaint lifted in the twilight. The sun had dipped behind the back
ridge, and though the sky was still bright with day, the dusk began
to smoke up out of the plowed field like a ground-fog. The girl had

returned through it, got the milk, and started toward the well-house before the widow saw her.

'Daughter, seems to me you might!' she expostulated without change of key. 'Here's some young man friend o' yourn stopped to say howdy, and I been rackin' my lungs out after you. . . . Put that milk in the cool and come!'

Some young man friend? But there was no good to be got from puzzling. Mare poured the milk in the pan in the dark of the low house over the well, and as she came out, stooping, she saw a figure waiting for her, black in silhouette against the yellowing sky.

'Who are you?' she asked, a native timidity making her sound sulky.

'"Amarantha!"' the fellow mused. 'That's poetry.' And she knew then that she did not know him.

She walked past, her arms straight down and her eyes front. Strangers always affected her with a kind of muscular terror simply by being strangers. So she gained the kitchen steps, aware by his tread that he followed. There, taking courage at sight of her mother in the doorway, she turned on him, her eyes down at the level of his knees.

'Who are you and what d'y' want?'

He still mused. 'Amarantha! Amarantha in Carolina! That makes me happy!'

Mare hazarded one upward look. She saw that he had red hair, brown eyes, and hollows under his cheek-bones, and though the green sweater he wore on top of a gray overall was plainly not meant for him, sizes too large as far as girth went, yet he was built so long of limb that his wrists came inches out of the sleeves and made his big hands look even bigger.

Mrs. Doggett complained. 'Why don't you introduce us, daughter?'

The girl opened her mouth and closed it again. Her mother, unaware that no sound had come out of it, smiled and nodded, evidently taking to the tall, homely fellow and tickled by the way he could not seem to get his eyes off her daughter. But the daughter saw none of it, all her attention centered upon the stranger's hands.

Restless, hard-fleshed, and chap-bitten, they were like a countryman's hands; but the fingers were longer than the ordinary, and slightly spatulate at their ends, and these ends were slowly and continuously at play among themselves.

The girl could not explain how it came to her to be frightened and at the same time to be calm, for she was inept with words. It was simply that in an animal way she knew animals, knew them in health and ailing, and when they were ailing she knew by instinct, as her father had known, how to move so as not to fret them.

Her mother had gone in to light up; from beside the lampshelf she called back, 'If he's aimin' to stay to supper you should've told me, Amarantha, though I guess there's plenty of the side-meat to go 'round, if you'll bring me in a few more turnips and potatoes, though it is late.'

At the words the man's cheeks moved in and out. 'I'm very hungry,' he said.

Mare nodded deliberately. Deliberately, as if her mother could hear her, she said over her shoulder, 'I'll go get the potatoes and turnips, ma.' While she spoke she was moving, slowly, softly, at first, toward the right of the yard, where the fence gave over into the field. Unluckily her mother spied her through the window.

'Amarantha, where *are* you goin'?'

'I'm goin' to get the potatoes and turnips.' She neither raised her voice nor glanced back, but lengthened her stride. 'He won't hurt her,' she said to herself. 'He won't hurt her; it's me, not her,' she kept repeating, while she got over the fence and down into the shadow that lay more than ever like a fog on the field.

The desire to believe that it actually did hide her, the temptation to break from her rapid but orderly walk grew till she could no longer fight it. She saw the road willows only a dash ahead of her. She ran, her feet floundering among the furrows.

She neither heard nor saw him, but when she realized he was with her she knew he had been with her all the while. She stopped, and he stopped, and so they stood, with the dark open of the field all around. Glancing sidewise presently, she saw he was no longer looking at her with those strangely importunate brown eyes of his, but had raised them to the crest of the wooded ridge behind her.

By and by, 'What does it make you think of?' he asked. And when she made no move to see, 'Turn around and look!' he said, and though it was low and almost tender in its tone, she knew enough to turn.

A ray of the sunset hidden in the west struck through the tops of the topmost trees, far and small up there, a thin, bright hem.

'What does it make you think of, Amarantha? . . . Answer!'

'Fire,' she made herself say.

'Or blood.'

'Or blood, yeh. That's right, or blood.' She had heard a Ford going up the road beyond the willows, and her attention was not on what she said.

The man soliloquized. 'Fire and blood, both; spare one or the other, and where is beauty, the way the world is? It's an awful thing to have to carry, but Christ had it. Christ came with a sword. I love beauty, Amarantha. . . . I say, I love beauty!'

'Yeh, that's right, I hear.' What she heard was the car stopping at the house.

'Not prettiness. Prettiness'll have to go with ugliness, because it's only ugliness trigged up. But beauty!' Now again he was looking at her. 'Do you know how beautiful you are, Amarantha, "Amarantha sweet and fair"?' Of a sudden, reaching behind her, he began to unravel the meshes of her hair-braid, the long, flat-tipped fingers at once impatient and infinitely gentle. ' "Braid no more that shining hair!" '

Flat-faced Mare Doggett tried to see around those glowing eyes so near to hers, but wise in her instinct, did not try too hard. 'Yeh,' she temporized. 'I mean, no, I mean.'

'Amarantha, I've come a long, long way for you. Will you come away with me now?'

'Yeh—that is—in a minute I will, mister—yeh. . . .'

'Because you want to, Amarantha? Because you love me as I love you? Answer!'

'Yeh—sure—uh . . . *Ruby!*'

The man tried to run, but there were six against him, coming up out of the dark that lay in the plowed ground. Mare stood where she was while they knocked him down and got a rope around him; after that she walked back toward the house with Ruby and Older Haskins, her father's cousin.

Ruby wiped his brow and felt of his muscles. 'Gees, you're lucky we come, Mare. We're no more'n past the town, when they came hollerin' he'd broke over this way.'

When they came to the fence the girl sat on the rail for a moment and rebraided her hair before she went into the house, where they were making her mother smell ammonia.

Lots of cars were coming. Judge North was coming, somebody said. When Mare heard this she went into her bedroom off the kitchen and got her shoes and put them on. They were brand new two-dollar shoes with cloth tops, and she had only begun to break them in last Sunday; she wished afterwards she had put her stockings on too, for they would have eased the seams. Or else that she had put on the old button pair, even though the soles were worn through.

Judge North arrived. He thought first of taking the loony straight through to Dayville that night, but then decided to keep him in the lock-up at the courthouse till morning and make the drive by day. Older Haskins stayed in, gentling Mrs. Doggett, while Ruby went out to help get the man into the Judge's sedan. Now that she had them on, Mare didn't like to take the shoes off till Older went; it might make him feel small, she thought.

Older Haskins had a lot of facts about the loony.

'His name's Humble Jewett,' he told them. 'They belong back in Breed County, all them Jewetts, and I don't reckon there's none on 'em that's not a mite unbalanced. He went to college though, worked his way, and he taught somethin' 'rother in some academy-school a spell, till he went off his head all of a sudden and took after folks with an axe. I remember it in the paper at the time. They give out one while how the Principal wasn't goin' to live, and there was others—there was a girl he tried to strangle. That was four—five year back.'

Ruby came in guffawing. 'Know the only thing they can get him to say, Mare? Only God thing he'll say is, "Amarantha, she's goin' with me." . . . Mare!'

'Yeh, I know.'

The cover of the kettle the girl was handling slid off the stove with a clatter. A sudden sick wave passed over her. She went out to the back, out into the air. It was not till now she knew how frightened she had been.

Ruby went home, but Older Haskins stayed to supper with them, and helped Mare do the dishes afterward; it was nearly nine when he left. The mother was already in bed, and Mare was about to sit down to get those shoes off her wretched feet at last, when she heard the cow carrying on up at the barn, lowing and kicking, and next minute the sow was in it with a horning note. It might be a fox passing by to get at the henhouse, or a weasel. Mare forgot her feet, took a broom-handle they used in boiling clothes, opened the back door, and stepped out. Blinking the lamplight from her eyes, she peered up toward the outbuildings, and saw the gable end of the barn standing like a red arrow in the dark, and the top of a butternut tree beyond it drawn in skeleton traceries, and just then a cock crowed.

She went to the right corner of the house and saw where the light came from, ruddy above the woods down the valley. Returning into the house, she bent close to her mother's ear and shouted, 'Somethin's a-fire down to the town, looks like,' then went out again and up to the barn. 'Soh! Soh!' she called in to the animals. She climbed up and stood on the top rail of the cow-pen fence, only to find she could not locate the flame even there.

Ten rods behind the buildings a mass of rock mounted higher than their ridgepoles, a chopped-off buttress of the back ridge, covered with oak scrub and wild grapes and blackberries, whose thorny ropes the girl beat away from her skirt with the broom-handle as she scrambled up in the wine-colored dark. Once at the top, and the brush held aside, she could see the tongue-tip of the conflagration half a mile away at the town. And she knew by the bearing of the two church steeples that it was the building where the lock-up was that was burning.

There is a horror in knowing animals trapped in a fire, no matter what the animals.

'Oh, my God!' Mare said.

A car went down the road. Then there was a horse galloping. That would be Older Haskins probably. People were out at Ruby's father's farm; she could hear their voices raised. There must have been another car up from the other way, for lights wheeled and shouts were exchanged in the neighborhood of the bridge. Next thing she knew, Ruby was at the house below, looking for her probably.

He was telling her mother. Mrs. Doggett was not used to him, so he had to shout even louder than Mare had to.

'What y' reckon he done, the hellion! he broke the door and killed Lew Fyke and set the courthouse afire! . . . Where's Mare?'

Her mother would not know. Mare called. 'Here, up the rock here.'

She had better go down. Ruby would likely break his bones if he tried to climb the rock in the dark, not knowing the way. But the sight of the fire fascinated her simple spirit, the fearful element, more fearful than ever now, with the news. 'Yes, I'm comin',' she called sulkily, hearing feet in the brush. 'You wait; I'm comin'.'

When she turned and saw it was Humble Jewett, right behind her among the branches, she opened her mouth to screech. She was not quick enough. Before a sound came out he got one hand over her face and the other arm around her body.

Mare had always thought she was strong, and the loony looked gangling, yet she was so easy for him that he need not hurt her. He made no haste and little noise as he carried her deeper into the undergrowth. Where the hill began to mount it was harder though. Presently he set her on her feet. He let the hand that had been over her mouth slip down to her throat, where the broad-tipped fingers wound, tender as yearning, weightless as caress.

'I was afraid you'd scream before you knew who 'twas, Amarantha. But I didn't want to hurt your lips, dear heart, your lovely, quiet lips.'

It was so dark under the trees she could hardly see him, but she felt his breath on her mouth, near to. But then, instead of kissing her, he said, 'No! No!' took from her throat for an instant the hand that had held her mouth, kissed its palm, and put it back softly against her skin.

'Now, my love, let's go before they come.'

She stood stock still. Her mother's voice was to be heard in the distance, strident and meaningless. More cars were on the road. Nearer, around the rock, there were sounds of tramping and thrashing. Ruby fussed and cursed. He shouted, 'Mare, dang you, where are you, Mare?' his voice harsh with uneasy anger. Now, if she aimed to do anything, was the time to do it. But there was neither breath nor power in her windpipe. It was as if those yearning fingers had paralyzed the muscles.

'Come!' The arm he put around her shivered against her shoulder blades. It was anger. 'I hate killing. It's a dirty, ugly thing. It makes me sick.' He gagged, judging by the sound. But then he ground his teeth. 'Come away, my love!'

She found herself moving. Once when she broke a branch underfoot with an instinctive awkwardness he chided her. 'Quiet, my heart, else they'll hear!' She made herself heavy. He thought she grew tired and bore more of her weight till he was breathing hard.

Men came up the hill. There must have been a dozen spread out, by the angle of their voices as they kept touch. Always Humble Jewett kept caressing Mare's throat with one hand; all she could do was hang back.

'You're tired and you're frightened,' he said at last. 'Get down here.'

There were twigs in the dark, the overhang of a thicket of some sort. He thrust her in under this, and lay beside her on the bed of groundpine. The hand that was not in love with her throat reached across her; she felt the weight of its forearm on her shoulder and its fingers among the strands of her hair, eagerly, but tenderly, busy. Not once did he stop speaking, no louder than breathing, his lips to her ear.

'*"Amarantha sweet and fair—Ah, braid no more that shining hair. . . ."*'

Mare had never heard of Lovelace, the poet; she thought the loony was just going on, hardly listened, got little sense. But the cadence of it added to the lethargy of all her flesh.

'*"Like a clew of golden thread—Most excellently ravelléd. . . ."*'

Voices loudened; feet came tramping; a pair went past not two rods away.

'*". . . Do not then wind up the light—In ribbands, and o'ercloud in night . . ."*'

The search went on up the woods, men shouting to one another and beating the brush.

'*". . . But shake your head and scatter day!"* I've never loved, Amarantha. They've tried me with prettiness, but prettiness is too cheap, yes, it's too cheap.'

Mare was cold, and the coldness made her lazy. All she knew was that he talked on.

'But dogwood blowing in the spring isn't cheap. The earth of a field isn't cheap. Lots of times I've lain down and kissed the earth of a field, Amarantha. That's beauty, and a kiss for beauty.' His breath moved up her cheek. He trembled violently. 'No, no, not yet!' He got to his knees and pulled her by an arm. 'We can go now.'

They went back down the slope, but at an angle, so that when they came to the level they passed two hundred yards to the north of the house, and crossed the road there. More and more her walking was like sleep-walking, the feet numb in their shoes. Even where he had to let go of her, crossing the creek on stones, she stepped where he stepped with an obtuse docility. The voices of the searchers on the back ridge were small in distance when they began to climb the face of Coward Hill, on the opposite side of the valley.

There is an old farm on top of Coward Hill, big hay-fields as flat as tables. It had been half-past nine when Mare stood on the rock above the barn; it was toward midnight when Humble Jewett put aside the last branches of the woods and let her out on the height, and half a moon had risen. And a wind blew there, tossing the withered tops of last year's grasses, and mists ran with the wind, and ragged shadows with the mists, and mares'-tails of clear moonlight among the shadows, so that now the boles of birches on the forest's edge beyond the fences were but opal blurs and now cut alabaster. It struck so cold against the girl's cold flesh, this wind, that another wind of shivers blew through her, and she put her hands over her face and eyes. But the madman stood with his eyes open wide and his mouth open, drinking the moonlight and the wet wind.

His voice, when he spoke at last, was thick in his throat.

'Get down on your knees.' He got down on his and pulled her after. 'And pray!'

Once in England a poet sang four lines. Four hundred years have forgotten his name, but they have remembered his lines. The daft man knelt upright, his face raised to the wild scud, his long wrists hanging to the dead grass. He began simply:

> ' "O western wind, when wilt thou blow
> "That the small rain down can rain?" '

The Adam's-apple was big in his bent throat. As simply he finished.

> ' "Christ, that my love were in my arms
> "And I in my bed again!" '

Mare got up and ran. She ran without aim or feeling in the power of the wind. She told herself again that the mists would hide her from him, as she had done at dusk. And again, seeing that he ran at her shoulder, she knew he had been there all the while, making a race of it, flailing the wind with his long arms for joy of play in the cloud of spring, throwing his knees high, leaping the moon-blue waves of the brown grass, shaking his bright hair; and her own hair was a weight behind her, lying level on the wind. Once a shape went bounding ahead of them for instants; she did not realize it was a fox till it was gone.

She never thought of stopping; she never thought anything, except once, 'Oh, my God, I wish I had my shoes off!' And what would have been the good in stopping or in turning another way, when it was only play? The man's ecstasy magnified his strength. When a snake-fence came at them he took the top rail in flight, like a college hurdler and, seeing the girl hesitate and half turn as if to flee, he would have releaped it without touching a hand. But then she got a loom of buildings, climbed over quickly, before he should jump, and ran along the lane that ran with the fence.

Mare had never been up there, but she knew that the farm and the house belonged to a man named Wyker, a kind of cousin of Ruby Herter's, a violent, bearded old fellow who lived by himself. She could not believe her luck. When she had run half the distance and Jewett had not grabbed her, doubt grabbed her instead. 'Oh, my God, go careful!' she told herself. 'Go slow!' she implored herself, and stopped running, to walk.

Here was a misgiving the deeper in that it touched her special knowledge. She had never known an animal so far gone that its instincts failed it; a starving rat will scent the trap sooner than a fed one. Yet, after one glance at the house they approached, Jewett paid it no further attention, but walked with his eyes to the right, where the cloud had blown away, and wooded ridges, like black waves rimed with silver, ran down away toward the Valley of Virginia.

'I've never lived!' In his single cry there were two things, beatitude and pain.

Between the bigness of the falling world and his eyes the flag of her hair blew. He reached out and let it whip between his fingers. Mare was afraid it would break the spell then, and he would stop looking away and look at the house again. So she did something almost incredible; she spoke.

'It's a pretty—I mean—a beautiful view down that-a-way.'

'God Almighty beautiful, to take your breath away. I knew I'd never loved, Belovéd—' He caught a foot under the long end of one of the boards that covered the well and went down heavily on his hands and knees. It seemed to make no difference. 'But I never knew I'd never lived,' he finished in the same tone of strong rapture, quadruped in the grass, while Mare ran for the door and grabbed the latch.

When the latch would not give, she lost what little sense she had. She pounded with her fists. She cried with all her might: 'Oh—hey— in there—hey—in there!' Then Jewett came and took her gently between his hands and drew her away, and then, though she was free, she stood in something like an awful embarrassment while he tried shouting.

'Hey! Friend! whoever you are, wake up and let my love and me come in!'

'No!' wailed the girl.

He grew peremptory. 'Hey, wake up!' He tried the latch. He passed to full fury in a wink's time; he cursed, he kicked, he beat the door till Mare thought he would break his hands. Withdrawing, he ran at it with his shoulder; it burst at the latch, went slamming in, and left a black emptiness. His anger dissolved in a big laugh. Turning in time to catch her by a wrist, he cried joyously, 'Come, my Sweet One!'

'No! No! Please—aw—listen. There ain't nobody there. He ain't to home. It wouldn't be right to go in anybody's house if they wasn't to home, you know that.'

His laugh was blither than ever. He caught her high in his arms. 'I'd do the same by his love and him if 'twas my house, I would.' At the threshold he paused and thought, 'That is, if she was the true love of his heart forever.'

The room was the parlor. Moonlight slanted in at the door, and another shaft came through a window and fell across a sofa, its covering dilapidated, showing its wadding in places. The air was sour, but both of them were farm-bred.

'Don't, Amarantha!' His words were pleading in her ear. 'Don't be so frightened.'

He set her down on the sofa. As his hands let go of her they were shaking.

'But look, I'm frightened too.' He knelt on the floor before her, reached out his hands, withdrew them. 'See, I'm afraid to touch you.' He mused, his eyes rounded. 'Of all the ugly things there are, fear is the ugliest. And yet, see, it can be the very beautifulest. That's a strange queer thing.'

The wind blew in and out of the room, bringing the thin, little bitter sweetness of new April at night. The moonlight that came across Mare's shoulders fell full upon his face but hers it left dark, ringed by the aureole of her disordered hair.

'Why do you wear a halo, Love?' He thought about it. 'Because you're an angel, is that why?' The swift, untempered logic of the mad led him to dismay. His hands came flying to hers, to make sure they were of earth; and he touched her breast, her shoulders, and her hair. Peace returned to his eyes as his fingers twined among the strands.

' "Thy hair is as a flock of goats that appear from Gilead. . . ." ' He spoke like a man dreaming. ' "Thy temples are like a piece of pomegranate within thy locks." '

Mare never knew that he could not see her for the moonlight.

'Do you remember, Love?'

She dared not shake her head under his hand. 'Yeh, I reckon,' she temporized.

'You remember how I sat at your feet, long ago, like this, and made up a song? And all the poets in all the world have never made one to touch it, have they, Love?'

'Ugh-ugh—never.'

' "How beautiful are thy feet with shoes. . . ." Remember?'
'Oh, my God, what's he sayin' now?' she wailed to herself.

> ' *"How beautiful are thy feet with shoes, O prince's daughter! the*
> *joints of thy thighs are like jewels, the work of the hands of a*
> *cunning workman.*
> *"Thy navel is like a round goblet, which wanteth not liquor; thy*
> *belly is like a heap of wheat set about with lilies.*
> *"Thy two breasts are like two young roes that are twins." '*

Mare had not been to church since she was a little girl, when her
mother's black dress wore out. 'No, no!' she wailed under her breath.
'You're awful to say such awful things.' She might have shouted it;
nothing could have shaken the man now, rapt in the immortal, passionate periods of Solomon's Song.

> ' *". . . now also thy breast shall be as clusters of the vine, and the*
> *smell of thy nose like apples." '*

Hotness touched Mare's face for the first time. 'Aw, no, don't talk
so!'

> ' *"And the roof of thy mouth like the best wine for my belovéd . . .*
> *causing the lips of them that are asleep to speak." '*

He had ended. His expression changed. Ecstasy gave place to anger,
love to hate. And Mare felt the change in the weight of the fingers in
her hair.

'What do you mean, I mustn't say it like that?' But it was not to
her his fury spoke, for he answered himself straightway. 'Like poetry,
Mr. Jewett; I won't have blasphemy around my school.'

'Poetry! My God! if that isn't poetry—if that isn't music—' . . .
'It's Bible, Jewett. What you're paid to teach here is *literature.*'

'Doctor Ryeworth, you're the blasphemer and you're an ignorant
man.' . . . 'And your Principal. And I won't have you going around
reading sacred allegory like earthly love.'

'Ryeworth, you're an old man, a dull man, a dirty man, and you'd
be better dead.'

Jewett's hands had slid down from Mare's head. 'Then I went to
put my fingers around his throat, so. But my stomach turned, and I
didn't do it. I went to my room. I laughed all the way to my room.
I sat in my room at my table and I laughed. I laughed all afternoon

and long after dark came. And, then, about ten, somebody came and stood beside me in my room.'

' "Wherefore dost thou laugh, son?"

'Then I knew who He was, He was Christ.

' "I was laughing about that dirty, ignorant, crazy old fool, Lord."

' "Wherefore dost thou laugh?"

'I didn't laugh any more. He didn't say any more. I kneeled down, bowed my head.

' "Thy will be done! Where is he, Lord?"

' "Over at the girls' dormitory, waiting for Blossom Sinckley."

'Brassy Blossom, dirty Blossom . . .'

It had come so suddenly it was nearly too late. Mare tore at his hands with hers, tried with all her strength to pull her neck away.

'Filthy Blossom! and him an old filthy man, Blossom! and you'll find him in Hell when you reach there, Blossom. . . .'

It was more the nearness of his face than the hurt of his hands that gave her power of fright to choke out three words.

'I—ain't—Blossom!'

Light ran in crooked veins. Through the veins she saw his face bewildered. His hands loosened. One fell down and hung; the other he lifted and put over his eyes, took it away again and looked at her.

'Amarantha!' His remorse was fearful to see. 'What have I done!' His hands returned to hover over the hurts, ravening with pity, grief and tenderness. Tears fell down his cheeks. And with that, dammed desire broke its dam.

'Amarantha!, my love, my dove, my beautiful love—'

'And I ain't Amarantha neither, I'm Mary! Mary, that's my name!'

She had no notion what she had done. He was like a crystal crucible that a chemist watches, changing hue in a wink with one adeptly added drop; but hers was not the chemist's eye. All she knew was that she felt light and free of him; all she could see of his face as he stood away above the moonlight were the whites of his eyes.

'Mary!' he muttered. A slight paroxysm shook his frame. So in the transparent crucible desire changed its hue. He retreated farther, stood in the dark by some tall piece of furniture. And still she could see the whites of his eyes.

'Mary! Mary Adorable!' A wonder was in him. 'Mother of God!'

Mare held her breath. She eyed the door, but it was too far. And already he came back to go on his knees before her, his shoulders so bowed and his face so lifted that it must have cracked his neck, she thought; all she could see on the face was pain.

'Mary Mother, I'm sick to my death. I'm so tired.'

She had seen a dog like that, one she had loosed from a trap after it had been there three days, its caught leg half gnawed free. Something about the eyes.

'Mary Mother, take me in your arms . . .'

Once again her muscles tightened. But he made no move.

'. . . and give me sleep.'

No, they were worse than the dog's eyes.

'Sleep, sleep! why won't they let me sleep? Haven't I done it all yet, Mother? Haven't I washed them yet of all their sins? I've drunk the cup that was given me; is there another? They've mocked me and reviled me, broken my brow with thorns and my hands with nails, and I've forgiven them, for they knew not what they did. Can't I go to sleep now, Mother?'

Mare could not have said why, but now she was more frightened than she had ever been. Her hands lay heavy on her knees, side by side, and she could not take them away when he bowed his head and rested his face upon them.

After a moment he said one thing more. 'Take me down gently when you take me from the Tree.'

Gradually the weight of his body came against her shins, and he slept.

The moon streak that entered by the eastern window crept north across the floor, thinner and thinner; the one that fell through the southern doorway traveled east and grew fat. For a while Mare's feet pained her terribly and her legs too. She dared not move them, though, and by and by they did not hurt so much.

A dozen times, moving her head slowly on her neck, she canvassed the shadows of the room for a weapon. Each time her eyes came back to a heavy earthenware pitcher on a stand some feet to the left of the sofa. It would have had flowers in it when Wyker's wife was alive; probably it had not been moved from its dust-ring since she died. It would be a long grab, perhaps too long; still it might be done if she had her hands.

To get her hands from under the sleeper's head was the task she set herself. She pulled first one, then the other, infinitesimally. She waited. Again she tugged a very, very little. The order of his breathing was not disturbed. But at the third trial he stirred.

'Gently! gently!' His own muttering waked him more. With some drowsy instinct of possession he threw one hand across her wrists, pinning them together between thumb and fingers. She kept dead quiet, shut her eyes, lengthened her breathing, as if she too slept.

There came a time when what was pretense grew a peril; strange as it was, she had to fight to keep her eyes open. She never knew whether or not she really napped. But something changed in the air, and she was wide awake again. The moonlight was fading on the doorsill, and the light that runs before dawn waxed in the window behind her head.

And then she heard a voice in the distance, lifted in maundering song. It was old man Wyker coming home after a night, and it was plain he had had some whiskey.

Now a new terror laid hold of Mare.

'Shut up, you fool you!' she wanted to shout. 'Come quiet, quiet!' She might have chanced it now to throw the sleeper away from her and scramble and run, had his powers of strength and quickness not taken her simple imagination utterly in thrall.

Happily the singing stopped. What had occurred was that the farmer had espied the open door and, even befuddled as he was, wanted to know more about it quietly. He was so quiet that Mare began to fear he had gone away. He had the squirrel-hunter's foot, and the first she knew of him was when she looked and saw his head in the doorway, his hard, soiled, whiskery face half up-side-down with craning.

He had been to the town. Between drinks he had wandered in and out of the night's excitement; had even gone a short distance with one search party himself. Now he took in the situation in the room. He used his forefinger. First he held it to his lips. Next he pointed it with a jabbing motion at the sleeper. Then he tapped his own forehead and described wheels. Lastly, with his whole hand, he made pushing gestures, for Mare to wait. Then he vanished as silently as he had appeared.

The minutes dragged. The light in the east strengthened and turned rosy. Once she thought she heard a board creaking in another part of the house, and looked down sharply to see if the loony stirred. All she could see of his face was a temple with freckles on it and the sharp ridge of a cheekbone, but even from so little she knew how deeply and peacefully he slept. The door darkened. Wyker was there again. In one hand he carried something heavy; with the other he beckoned.

'Come jumpin'!' he said out loud.

Mare went jumping, but her cramped legs threw her down halfway to the sill; the rest of the distance she rolled and crawled. Just as she tumbled through the door it seemed as if the world had come to an end above her; two barrels of a shotgun discharged into a room make a noise. Afterwards all she could hear in there was something twisting and bumping on the floorboards. She got up and ran.

Mare's mother had gone to pieces; neighbor women put her to bed when Mare came home. They wanted to put Mare to bed, but she would not let them. She sat on the edge of her bed in her lean-to bedroom off the kitchen, just as she was, her hair down all over her shoulders and her shoes on, and stared away from them, at a place in the wallpaper.

'Yeh, I'll go myself. Lea' me be!'

The women exchanged quick glances, thinned their lips, and left her be. 'God knows,' was all they would answer to the questionings of those that had not gone in, 'but she's gettin' herself to bed.'

When the doctor came though he found her sitting just as she had been, still dressed, her hair down on her shoulders and her shoes on.

'What d' y' want?' she muttered and stared at the place in the wallpaper.

How could Doc Paradise say, when he did not know himself?

'I didn't know if you might be—might be feeling very smart, Mary.'

'I'm all right. Lea' me be.'

It was a heavy responsibility. Doc shouldered it. 'No, it's all right,' he said to the men in the road. Ruby Herter stood a little apart, chewing sullenly and looking another way. Doc raised his voice to make certain it carried. 'Nope, nothing.'

Ruby's ears got red, and he clamped his jaws. He knew he ought to go in and see Mare, but he was not going to do it while everybody hung around waiting to see if he would. A mule tied near him reached out and mouthed his sleeve in idle innocence; he wheeled and banged a fist against the side of the animal's head.

'Well, what d' y' aim to do 'bout it?' he challenged its owner.

He looked at the sun then. It was ten in the morning. 'Hell, I got work!' he flared, and set off down the road for home. Doc looked at Judge North, and the Judge started after Ruby. But Ruby shook his head angrily. 'Lea' me be!' He went on, and the Judge came back.

It got to be eleven and then noon. People began to say, 'Like enough

she'd be as thankful if the whole neighborhood wasn't camped here.'
But none went away.

As a matter of fact they were no bother to the girl. She never saw
them. The only move she made was to bend her ankles over and rest
her feet on edge; her shoes hurt terribly and her feet knew it, though
she did not. She sat all the while staring at that one figure in the
wallpaper, and she never saw the figure.

Strange as the night had been, this day was stranger. Fright and
physical pain are perishable things once they are gone. But while pain
merely dulls and telescopes in memory and remains diluted pain,
terror looked back upon has nothing of terror left. A gambling chance
taken, at no matter what odds, and won was a sure thing since the
world's beginning; perils come through safely were never perilous.
But what fright does do in retrospect is this—it heightens each sensuous
recollection, like a hard, clear lacquer laid on wood, bringing out the
color and grain of it vividly.

Last night Mare had lain stupid with fear on groundpine beneath
a bush, loud foot-falls and light whispers confused in her ear. Only
now, in her room, did she smell the groundpine.

Only now did the conscious part of her brain begin to make words
of the whispering.

'*Amarantha,*' she remembered, '*Amarantha sweet and fair.*' That
was as far as she could go for the moment, except that the rhyme
with 'fair' was 'hair.' But then a puzzle, held in abeyance, brought
other words. She wondered what 'ravel Ed' could mean. '*Most excellently ravelléd.*' It was left to her mother to bring the end.

They gave up trying to keep her mother out at last. The poor
woman's prostration took the form of fussiness.

'Good gracious, daughter, you look a sight. Them new shoes, half
ruined; ain't your feet *dead?* And look at your hair, all tangled like
a wild one!'

She got a comb.

'Be quiet, daughter; what's ailin' you. Don't shake your head!'

'"*But shake your head and scatter day.*"'

'What you say, Amarantha?' Mrs. Doggett held an ear down.

'Go away! Lea' me be!'

Her mother was hurt and left. And Mare ran, as she stared at the
wallpaper.

'*Christ, that my love were in my arms. . . .*'

Mare ran. She ran through a wind white with moonlight and wet with 'the small rain.' And the wind she ran through, it ran through her, and made her shiver as she ran. And the man beside her leaped high over the waves of the dead grasses and gathered the wind in his arms, and her hair was heavy and his was tossing, and a little fox ran before them across the top of the world. And the world spread down around in waves of black and silver, more immense than she had ever known the world could be, and more beautiful.

'God Almighty beautiful, to take your breath away!'

Mare wondered, and she was not used to wondering. 'Is it only crazy folks ever run like that and talk that way?'

She no longer ran; she walked; for her breath was gone. And there was some other reason, some other reason. Oh, yes, it was because her feet were hurting her. So, at last, and roundabout, her shoes had made contact with her brain.

Bending over the side of her bed, she loosened one of them mechanically. She pulled it half off. But then she looked down at it sharply, and she pulled it on again.

'How beautiful . . .'

Color overspread her face in a slow wave.

'How beautiful are thy feet with shoes. . . .'

'Is it only crazy folks ever say such things?'

'O prince's daughter!'

'Or call you that?'

By and by there was a knock at the door. It opened, and Ruby Herter came in.

'Hello, Mare old girl!' His face was red. He scowled and kicked at the floor. 'I'd 'a' been over sooner, except we got a mule down sick.' He looked at his dumb betrothed. 'Come on, cheer up, forget it! He won't scare you no more, not that boy, not what's left o' him. What you lookin' at, sourface? Ain't you glad to see me?'

Mare quit looking at the wallpaper and looked at the floor. 'Yeh,' she said.

'That's more like it, babe.' He came and sat beside her; reached down behind her and gave her a spank. 'Come on, give us a kiss, babe!' He wiped his mouth on his jumper sleeve, a good farmer's sleeve, spotted with milking. He put his hands on her; he was used to handling animals. 'Hey, you, warm up a little; reckon I'm goin' to do all the lovin'?'

'Ruby, lea' me be!'

'What!'

She was up, twisting. He was up, purple.

'What's ailin' of you, Mare? What you bawlin' about?'

'Nothin'—only go 'way!'

She pushed him to the door and through it with all her strength, and closed it in his face, and stood with her weight against it, crying, 'Go 'way! Go 'way! Lea' me be!'

William Faulkner

William Faulkner's world, disclosed in several novels and many short stories about the region of his native Oxford, Mississippi, is strange and disturbing to the Northerner's imagination, and to that of many a Southerner. His characters often move in a phantasmagoria of violence and terror, and his vision of the world's evil has been likened to that of the poet, Robinson Jeffers.

He is a stylist, interested in experimental expression, and his phrases are sensuous and evocative. It is significant that as a college student he was completely absorbed in Swinburne, and later in the Elizabethan poets whom Swinburne also loved. His range in craftsmanship is wide. In fact he is one of the few writers who on the one hand can turn out immediately popular tales for the magazines and on the other produce prose which is baffling to his most sympathetic readers. He is a writer at least partly by inheritance, the namesake of a great grandfather who published a best seller, The White Rose of Memphis.

Faulkner was born in 1897, served with the British Royal Air Force in the World War, and did odd jobs in his native University town while he experimented with writing. His career now soundly established, he lives in his plantation house in Oxford. Among his best books are The Sound and the Fury (1929), These Thirteen (short stories, 1931), Light in August (1932), and The Unvanquished (short stories, 1938).

THAT EVENING SUN *

William Faulkner

Monday is no different from any other week day in Jefferson now. The streets are paved now, and the telephone and electric companies are cutting down more and more of the shade trees—the water oaks, the maples and locusts and elms—to make room for iron poles bearing clusters of bloated and ghostly and bloodless grapes, and we have a city laundry which makes the rounds on Monday morning, gathering the bundles of clothes into bright-colored, specially made motor-cars: the soiled wearing of a whole week now flees apparition-like behind alert and irritable electric horns, with a long diminishing noise of rubber and asphalt like a tearing of silk, and even the Negro women who still take in white peoples' washing after the old custom, fetch and deliver it in automobiles.

But fifteen years ago, on Monday morning the quiet, dusty, shady streets would be full of Negro women with, balanced on their steady turbaned heads, bundles of clothes tied up in sheets, almost as large as cotton bales, carried so without touch of hand between the kitchen door of the white house and the blackened wash-pot beside a cabin door in Negro Hollow.

Nancy would set her bundle on the top of her head, then upon the bundle in turn she would set the black straw sailor hat which she wore Winter and Summer. She was tall, with a high, sad face sunken a little where her teeth were missing. Sometimes we would go a part of the way down the lane and across the pasture with her, to watch the balanced bundle and the hat that never bobbed nor wavered, even when she walked down into the ditch and climbed out again and stooped through the fence. She would go down on her hands and knees and crawl through the gap, her head rigid, up-tilted, the bundle steady as a rock or a balloon, and rise to her feet and go on.

Sometimes the husbands of the washing women would fetch and deliver the clothes, but Jubah never did that for Nancy, even before father told him to stay away from our house, even when Dilsey was sick and Nancy would come to cook for us.

And then about half the time we'd have to go down the lane to Nancy's house and tell her to come on and get breakfast. We would

* From *These Thirteen* by William Faulkner, 1931. Reprinted by permission of Random House, Inc.

stop at the ditch, because father told us not to have anything to do with Jubah—he was a short black man, with a razor scar down his face—and we would throw rocks at Nancy's house until she came to the door, leaning her head around it without any clothes on.

"What yawl mean, chunking my house?" Nancy said. "What you little devils mean?"

"Father says for you to come and get breakfast," Caddy said. "Father says it's over a half an hour now, and you've got to come this minute."

"I ain't studying no breakfast," Nancy said. "I going to get my sleep out."

"I bet you're drunk," Jason said. "Father says you're drunk. Are you drunk, Nancy?"

"Who says I is?" Nancy said. "I got to get my sleep out. I ain't studying no breakfast."

So after a while we quit chunking the house and went back home. When she finally came, it was too late for me to go to school. So we thought it was whisky until that day when they arrested her again and they were taking her to jail and they passed Mr. Stovall. He was the cashier in the bank and a deacon in the Baptist Church, and Nancy began to say:

"When you going to pay me, white man? When you going to pay me, white man? It's been three times now since you paid me a cent—" Mr. Stovall knocked her down, but she kept on saying, "When you going to pay me, white man? It's been three times now since—" until Mr. Stovall kicked her in the mouth with his heel and the marshal caught Mr. Stovall back, and Nancy lying in the street, laughing. She turned her head and spat out some blood and teeth and said, "It's been three times now since he paid me a cent."

That was how she lost her teeth, and all that day they told about Nancy and Mr. Stovall, and all that night the ones that passed the jail could hear Nancy singing and yelling. They could see her hands holding to the window bars, and a lot of them stopped along the fence, listening to her and to the jailer trying to make her shut up. She didn't shut up until just before daylight, when the jailer began to hear a bumping and scraping upstairs and he went up there and found Nancy hanging from the window bar. He said it was cocaine and not whisky, because no nigger would try to commit suicide unless he was full of cocaine, because a nigger full of cocaine was not a nigger any longer.

The jailer cut her down and revived her; then he beat her, whipped her. She had hung herself with her dress. She had fixed it all right, but when they arrested her she didn't have on anything except a dress and so she didn't have anything to tie her hands with and she couldn't make her hands let go of the window ledge. So the jailer heard the noise and ran up there and found Nancy hanging from the window, stark naked.

When Dilsey was sick in her cabin and Nancy was cooking for us, we could see her apron swelling out; that was before father told Jubah to stay away from the house. Jubah was in the kitchen, sitting behind the stove, with his razor scar on his black face like a piece of dirty string. He said it was a watermelon that Nancy had under her dress. And it was Winter, too.

"Where did you get a watermelon in the Winter?" Caddy said.

"I didn't," Jubah said. "It wasn't me that give it to her. But I can cut it down, same as if it was."

"What makes you want to talk that way before these chillen?" Nancy said. "Whyn't you go on to work? You done et. You want Mr. Jason to catch you hanging around his kitchen, talking that way before these chillen?"

"Talking what way, Nancy?" Caddy said.

"I can't hang around white man's kitchen," Jubah said. "But white man can hang around mine. White man can come in my house, but I can't stop him. When white man want to come in my house, I ain't got no house. I can't stop him, but he can't kick me outen it. He can't do that."

Dilsey was still sick in her cabin. Father told Jubah to stay off our place. Dilsey was still sick. It was a long time. We were in the library after supper.

"Isn't Nancy through yet?" mother said. "It seems to me she has had plenty of time to have finished the dishes."

"Let Quentin go and see," father said. "Go and see if Nancy is through, Quentin. Tell her she can go on home."

I went to the kitchen. Nancy was through. The dishes were put away and the fire was out. Nancy was sitting in a chair, close to the cold stove. She looked at me.

"Mother wants to know if you are through," I said.

"Yes," Nancy said. She looked at me. "I done finished." She looked at me.

"What is it?" I said. "What is it?"

"I ain't nothing but a nigger," Nancy said. "It ain't none of my fault."

She looked at me, sitting in the chair before the cold stove, the sailor hat on her head. I went back to the library. It was the cold stove and all, when you think of a kitchen being warm and busy and cheerful. And with a cold stove and the dishes all put away, and nobody wanting to eat at that hour.

"Is she through?" mother said.

"Yessum," I said.

"What is she doing?" mother said.

"She's not doing anything. She's through."

"I'll go and see," father said.

"Maybe she's waiting for Jubah to come and take her home," Caddy said.

"Jubah is gone," I said. Nancy told us how one morning she woke up and Jubah was gone.

"He quit me," Nancy said. "Done gone to Memphis, I reckon. Dodging them city *po*-lice for a while, I reckon."

"And a good riddance," father said. "I hope he stays there."

"Nancy's scaired of the dark," Jason said.

"So are you," Caddy said.

"I'm not," Jason said.

"Scairy cat," Caddy said.

"I'm not," Jason said.

"You, Candace!" mother said. Father came back.

"I am going to walk down the lane with Nancy," he said. "She says Jubah is back."

"Has she seen him?" mother said.

"No. Some Negro sent her word that he was back in town. I won't be long."

"You'll leave me alone, to take Nancy home?" mother said. "Is her safety more precious to you than mine?"

"I won't be long," father said.

"You'll leave these children unprotected, with that Negro about?"

"I'm going too," Caddy said. "Let me go, father."

"What would he do with them, if he were unfortunate enough to have them?" father said.

"I want to go, too," Jason said.

"Jason!" mother said. She was speaking to father. You could tell that by the way she said it. Like she believed that all day father had been trying to think of doing the thing that she wouldn't like the most, and that she knew all the time that after a while he would think of it. I stayed quiet, because father and I both knew that mother would want him to make me stay with her, if she just thought of it in time. So father didn't look at me. I was the oldest. I was nine and Caddy was seven and Jason was five.

"Nonsense," father said. "We won't be long."

Nancy had her hat on. We came to the lane. "Jubah always been good to me," Nancy said. "Whenever he had two dollars, one of them was mine." We walked in the lane. "If I can just get through the lane," Nancy said, "I be all right then."

The lane was always dark. "This is where Jason got scared on Hallowe'en," Caddy said.

"I didn't," Jason said.

"Can't Aunt Rachel do anything with him?" father said. Aunt Rachel was old. She lived in a cabin beyond Nancy's, by herself. She had white hair and she smoked a pipe in the door, all day long; she didn't work any more. They said she was Jubah's mother. Sometimes she said she was and sometimes she said she wasn't any kin to Jubah.

"Yes you did," Caddy said. "You were scairder than Frony. You were scairder than T. P. even. Scairder than niggers."

"Can't nobody do nothing with him," Nancy said. "He say I done woke up the devil in him, and ain't but one thing going to lay it again."

"Well, he's gone now," father said. "There's nothing for you to be afraid of now. And if you'd just let white men alone."

"Let what white men alone?" Caddy said, "How let them alone?"

"He ain't gone nowhere," Nancy said. "I can feel him. I can feel him now, in this lane. He hearing us talk, every word, hid somewhere, waiting. I ain't seen him, and I ain't going to see him again but once more, with that razor. That razor on that string down his back, inside his shirt. And then I ain't going to be even surprised."

"I wasn't scaired," Jason said.

"If you'd behave yourself, you'd have kept out of this," father said. "But it's all right now. He's probably in St. Louis now. Probably got another wife by now and forgot all about you."

"If he has, I better not find out about it," Nancy said. "I'd stand there and every time he wropped her, I'd cut that arm off. I'd cut his head off and I'd slit her belly and I'd shove—"

"Hush," father said.

"Slit whose belly, Nancy?" Caddy said.

"I wasn't scared," Jason said. "I'd walk right down this lane by myself."

"Yah," Caddy said. "You wouldn't dare to put your foot in it if we were not with you."

II

Dilsey was still sick, and so we took Nancy home every night until mother said, "How much longer is this going to go on? I to be left alone in this big house while you take home a frightened Negro?"

We fixed a pallet in the kitchen for Nancy. One night we waked up, hearing the sound. It was not singing and it was not crying, coming up the dark stairs. There was a light in mother's room and we heard father going down the hall, down the back stairs, and Caddy and I went into the hall. The floor was cold. Our toes curled away from the floor while we listened to the sound. It was like singing and it wasn't like singing, like the sounds that Negroes make.

Then it stopped and we heard father going down the back stairs, and we went to the head of the stairs. Then the sound began again, in the stairway, not loud, and we could see Nancy's eyes half way up the stairs, against the wall. They looked like cat's eyes do, like a big cat against the wall, watching us. When we came down the steps to where she was she quit making the sound again, and we stood there until father came back up from the kitchen, with his pistol in his hand. He went back down with Nancy and they came back with Nancy's pallet.

We spread the pallet in our room. After the light in mother's room went off, we could see Nancy's eyes again. "Nancy," Caddy whispered, "are you asleep, Nancy?"

Nancy whispered something. It was oh or no, I don't know which. Like nobody had made it, like it came from nowhere and went nowhere, until it was like Nancy was not there at all; that I had looked so hard at her eyes on the stair that they had got printed on my eyelids, like the sun does when you have closed your eyes and there is no sun. "Jesus," Nancy whispered. "Jesus."

"Was it Jubah?" Caddy whispered. "Did he try to come into the kitchen?"

"Jesus," Nancy said. Like this: Jeeeeeeeeeeeeeeesus, until the sound went out like a match or a candle does.

"Can you see us, Nancy?" Caddy whispered. "Can you see our eyes too?"

"I ain't nothing but a nigger," Nancy said. "God knows. God knows."

"What did you see down there in the kitchen?" Caddy whispered. "What tried to get in?"

"God knows," Nancy said. We could see her eyes. "God knows."

Dilsey got well. She cooked dinner. "You'd better stay in bed a day or two longer," father said.

"What for?" Dilsey said. "If I had been a day later, this place would be to rack and ruin. Get on out of here, now, and let me get my kitchen straight again."

Dilsey cooked supper, too. And that night, just before dark, Nancy came into the kitchen.

"How do you know he's back?" Dilsey said. "You ain't seen him."

"Jubah is a nigger," Jason said.

"I can feel him," Nancy said. "I can feel him laying yonder in the ditch."

"Tonight?" Dilsey said. "Is he there tonight?"

"Dilsey's a nigger too," Jason said.

"You try to eat something," Dilsey said.

"I don't want nothing," Nancy said.

"I ain't a nigger," Jason said.

"Drink some coffee," Dilsey said. She poured a cup of coffee for Nancy. "Do you know he's out there tonight? How come you know it's tonight?"

"I know," Nancy said. "He's there, waiting. I know. I done lived with him too long. I know what he's fixing to do fore he knows it himself."

"Drink some coffee," Dilsey said. Nancy held the cup to her mouth and blew into the cup. Her mouth pursed out like a spreading adder's, like a rubber mouth, like she had blown all the color out of her lips with blowing the coffee.

"I ain't a nigger," Jason said. "Are you a nigger, Nancy?"

"I hell-born, child," Nancy said. "I won't be nothing soon. I going back where I come from soon."

III

She began to drink the coffee. While she was drinking, holding the cup in both hands, she began to make the sound again. She made the sound into the cup and the coffee sploshed out on to her hands and her dress. Her eyes looked at us and she sat there, her elbows on her knees, holding the cup in both hands, looking at us across the wet cup, making the sound.

"Look at Nancy," Jason said. "Nancy can't cook for us now. Dilsey's got well now."

"You hush up," Dilsey said. Nancy held the cup in both hands, looking at us, making the sound, like there were two of them: one looking at us and the other making the sound. "Whyn't you let Mr. Jason telefoam the marshal?" Disley said. Nancy stopped then, holding the cup in her long brown hands. She tried to drink some coffee again, but it sploshed out of the cup, on to her hands and her dress, and she put the cup down. Jason watched her.

"I can't swallow it," Nancy said. "I swallows but it won't go down me."

"You go down to the cabin," Dilsey said. "Frony will fix you a pallet and I'll be there soon."

"Won't no nigger stop him," Nancy said.

"I ain't a nigger," Jason said. "Am I, Dilsey?"

"I reckon not," Dilsey said. She looked at Nancy. "I don't reckon so. What you going to do, then?"

Nancy looked at us. Her eyes went fast, like she was afraid there wasn't time to look, without hardly moving at all. She looked at us, at all three of us at one time. "You member that night I stayed in yawls' room?" she said. She told about how we waked up early the next morning, and played. We had to play quiet, on her pallet, until father woke and it was time for her to go down and get breakfast. "Go and ask you maw to let me stay here tonight," Nancy said. "I won't need no pallet. We can play some more," she said.

Caddy asked mother. Jason went too. "I can't have Negroes sleeping in the house," mother said. Jason cried. He cried until mother said he couldn't have any dessert for three days if he didn't stop. Then Jason said he would stop if Dilsey would make a chocolate cake. Father was there.

"Why don't you do something about it?" mother said. "What do we have officers for?"

"Why is Nancy afraid of Jubah?" Caddy said. "Are you afraid of father, mother?"

"What could they do?" father said. "If Nancy hasn't seen him, how could the officers find him?"

"Then why is she afraid?" mother said.

"She says he is there. She says she knows he is there tonight."

"Yet we pay taxes," mother said. "I must wait here alone in this big house while you take a Negro woman home."

"You know that I am not lying outside with a razor," father said.

"I'll stop if Dilsey will make a chocolate cake," Jason said. Mother told us to go out and father said he didn't know if Jason would get a chocolate cake or not, but he knew what Jason was going to get in about a minute. We went back to the kitchen and told Nancy.

"Father said for you to go home and lock the door, and you'll be all right," Caddy said. "All right from what, Nancy? Is Jubah mad at you?" Nancy was holding the coffee cup in her hands, her elbow on her knees and her hands holding the cup between her knees. She was looking into the cup. "What have you done that made Jubah mad?" Caddy said. Nancy let the cup go. It didn't break on the floor, but the coffee spilled out, and Nancy sat there with her hands making the shape of the cup. She began to make the sound again, not loud. Not singing and not un-singing. We watched her.

"Here," Dilsey said. "You quit that, now. You get a-holt of yourself. You wait here. I going to get Versh to walk home with you." Dilsey went out.

We looked at Nancy. Her shoulders kept shaking, but she had quit making the sound. We watched her. "What's Jubah going to do to you?" Caddy said. "He went away."

Nancy looked at us. "We had fun that night I stayed in yawls' room, didn't we?"

"I didn't," Jason said. "I didn't have any fun."

"You were asleep," Caddy said. "You were not there."

"Let's go down to my house and have some more fun," Nancy said.

"Mother won't let us," I said. "It's too late now."

"Don't bother her," Nancy said. "We can tell her in the morning. She won't mind."

"She wouldn't let us," I said.

"Don't ask her now," Nancy said. "Don't bother her now."

"They didn't say we couldn't go," Caddy said.

"We didn't ask," I said.

"If you go, I'll tell," Jason said.

"We'll have fun," Nancy said. "They won't mind, just to my house. I been working for yawl a long time. They won't mind."

"I'm not afraid to go," Caddy said. "Jason is the one that's afraid. He'll tell."

"I'm not," Jason said.

"Yes you are," Caddy said. "You'll tell."

"I won't tell," Jason said. "I'm not afraid."

"Jason ain't afraid to go with me," Nancy said. "Is you, Jason?"

"Jason is going to tell," Caddy said. The lane was dark. We passed the pasture gate. "I bet if something was to jump out from behind that gate, Jason would holler."

"I wouldn't," Jason said. We walked down the lane. Nancy was talking loud.

"What are you talking so loud for, Nancy?" Caddy said.

"Who; me?" Nancy said. "Listen at Quentin and Caddy and Jason saying I'm talking loud."

"You talk like there was four of us here," Caddy said. "You talk like father was here too."

"Who; me talking loud, Mr. Jason?" Nancy said.

"Nancy called Jason 'Mister,'" Caddy said.

"Listen how Caddy and Quentin and Jason talk," Nancy said.

"We're not talking loud," Caddy said. "You're the one that's talking like father—"

"Hush," Nancy said; "hush, Mr. Jason."

"Nancy called Jason 'Mister' aguh—"

"Hush," Nancy said. She was talking loud when we crossed the ditch and stooped through the fence where she used to stoop through with the clothes on her head. Then we came to her house. We were going fast then. She opened the door. The smell of the house was like the lamp and the smell of Nancy was like the wick, like they were waiting for one another to smell. She lit the lamp and closed the door and put the bar up. Then she quit talking loud, looking at us.

"What're we going to do?" Caddy said.

"What you all want to do?" Nancy said.

"You said we would have some fun," Caddy said.

There was something about Nancy's house; something you could smell. Jason smelled it, even. "I don't want to stay here," he said. "I want to go home."

"Go home, then," Caddy said.

"I don't want to go by myself," Jason said.

"We're going to have some fun," Nancy said.

"How?" Caddy said.

Nancy stood by the door. She was looking at us, only it was

like she had emptied her eyes, like she had quit using them.

"What do you want to do?" she said.

"Tell us a story," Caddy said. "Can you tell a story?"

"Yes," Nancy said.

"Tell it," Caddy said. We looked at Nancy. "You don't know any stories," Caddy said.

"Yes," Nancy said. "Yes I do."

She came and sat down in a chair before the hearth. There was some fire there; she built it up; it was already hot. You didn't need a fire. She built a good blaze. She told a story. She talked like her eyes looked, like her eyes watching us and her voice talking to us did not belong to her. Like she was living somewhere else, waiting somewhere else. She was outside the house. Her voice was there and the shape of her, the Nancy that could stoop under the fence with the bundle of clothes balanced as though without weight, like a balloon, on her head, was there. But that was all. "And so this here queen come walking up to the ditch, where that bad man was hiding. She was walking up the ditch, and she say, 'If I can just get past this here ditch,' was what she say. . . ."

"What ditch?" Caddy said. "A ditch like that one out there? Why did the queen go into the ditch?"

"To get to her house," Nancy said. She looked at us. "She had to cross that ditch to get home."

"Why did she want to go home?" Caddy said.

IV

Nancy looked at us. She quit talking. She looked at us. Jason's legs stuck straight out of his pants, because he was little. "I don't think that's a good story," he said. "I want to go home."

"Maybe we had better," Caddy said. She got up from the floor. "I bet they are looking for us right now." She went toward the door.

"No," Nancy said. "Don't open it." She got up quick and passed Caddy. She didn't touch the door, the wooden bar.

"Why not?" Caddy said.

"Come back to the lamp," Nancy said. "We'll have fun. You don't have to go."

"We ought to go," Caddy said. "Unless we have a lot of fun." She and Nancy came back to the fire, the lamp.

"I want to go home," Jason said. "I'm going to tell."

"I know another story," Nancy said. She stood close to the

lamp. She looked at Caddy, like when your eyes look up at a stick balanced on your nose. She had to look down to see Caddy, but her eyes looked like that, like when you are balancing a stick.

"I won't listen to it," Jason said. "I'll bang on the floor."

"It's a good one," Nancy said. "It's better than the other one."

"What's it about?" Caddy said. Nancy was standing by the lamp. Her hand was on the lamp, against the light, long and brown.

"Your hand is on that hot globe," Caddy said. "Don't it feel hot to your hand?"

Nancy looked at her hand on the lamp chimney. She took her hand away, slow. She stood there, looking at Caddy, wringing her long hand as though it were tied to her wrist with a string.

"Let's do something else," Caddy said.

"I want to go home," Jason said.

"I got some popcorn," Nancy said. She looked at Caddy and then at Jason and then at me and then at Caddy again. "I got some popcorn."

"I don't like popcorn," Jason said. "I'd rather have candy."

Nancy looked at Jason. "You can hold the popper." She was still wringing her hand; it was long and limp and brown.

"All right," Jason said. "I'll stay a while if I can do that. Caddy can't hold it. I'll want to go home, if Caddy holds the popper."

Nancy built up the fire. "Look at Nancy putting her hands in the fire," Caddy said. "What's the matter with you, Nancy?"

"I got popcorn," Nancy said. "I got some." She took the popper from under the bed. It was broken. Jason began to cry.

"We can't have any popcorn," he said.

"We ought to go home, anyway," Caddy said. "Come on, Quentin."

"Wait," Nancy said; "wait. I can fix it. Don't you want to help me fix it?"

"I don't think I want any," Caddy said. "It's too late now."

"You help me, Jason," Nancy said. "Don't you want to help me?"

"No," Jason said. "I want to go home."

"Hush," Nancy said; "hush. Watch. Watch me. I can fix it so Jason can hold it and pop the corn." She got a piece of wire and fixed the popper.

"It won't hold good," Caddy said.

"Yes it will," Nancy said. "Yawl watch. Yawl help me shell the corn."

The corn was under the bed too. We shelled it into the popper and Nancy helped Jason hold the popper over the fire.

"It's not popping," Jason said. "I want to go home."

"You wait," Nancy said. "It'll begin to pop. We'll have fun then." She was sitting close to the fire. The lamp was turned up so high it was beginning to smoke.

"Why don't you turn it down some?" I said.

"It's all right," Nancy said. "I'll clean it. Yawl wait. The popcorn will start in a minute."

"I don't believe it's going to start," Caddy said. "We ought to go home, anyway. They'll be worried."

"No," Nancy said. "It's going to pop. Dilsey will tell um yawl with me. I been working for yawl long time. They won't mind if you at my house. You wait, now. It'll start popping in a minute."

Then Jason got some smoke in his eyes and he began to cry. He dropped the popper into the fire. Nancy got a wet rag and wiped Jason's face, but he didn't stop crying.

"Hush," she said. "Hush." He didn't hush. Caddy took the popper out of the fire.

"It's burned up," she said. "You'll have to get some more popcorn, Nancy."

"Did you put all of it in?" Nancy said.

"Yes," Caddy said. Nancy looked at Caddy. Then she took the popper and opened it and poured the blackened popcorn into her apron and began to sort the grains, her hands long and brown, and we watching her.

"Haven't you got any more?" Caddy said.

"Yes," Nancy said; "yes. Look. This here ain't burnt. All we need to do is—"

"I want to go home," Jason said. "I'm going to tell."

"Hush," Caddy said. We all listened. Nancy's head was already turned toward the barred door, her eyes filled with red lamplight. "Somebody is coming," Caddy said.

Then Nancy began to make that sound again, not loud, sitting there above the fire, her long hands dangling between her knees; all of a sudden water began to come out on her face in big drops, running down her face, carrying in each one a little turning ball of firelight until it dropped off her chin.

"She's not crying," I said.

"I ain't crying," Nancy said. Her eyes were closed. "I ain't crying. Who is it?"

"I don't know," Caddy said. She went to the door and looked

out. "We've got to go home now," she said. "Here comes father."

"I'm going to tell," Jason said. "You all made me come."

The water still ran down Nancy's face. She turned in her chair. "Listen. Tell him. Tell him we going to have fun. Tell him I take good care of yawl until in the morning. Tell him to let me come home with yawl and sleep on the floor. Tell him I won't need no pallet. We'll have fun. You remember last time how we had so much fun?"

"I didn't have any fun," Jason said. "You hurt me. You put smoke in my eyes."

V

Father came in. He looked at us. Nancy did not get up.

"Tell him," she said.

"Caddy made us come down here," Jason said. "I didn't want to."

Father came to the fire. Nancy looked up at him. "Can't you go to Aunt Rachel's and stay?" he said. Nancy looked up at father, her hands between her knees. "He's not here," father said. "I would have seen. There wasn't a soul in sight."

"He in the ditch," Nancy said. "He waiting in the ditch yonder."

"Nonsense," father said. He looked at Nancy. "Do you know he's there?"

"I got the sign," Nancy said.

"What sign?"

"I got it. It was on the table when I come in. It was a hog bone, with blood meat still on it, laying by the lamp. He's out there. When yawl walk out that door, I gone.

"Who's gone, Nancy?" Caddy said.

"I'm not a tattletale," Jason said.

"Nonsense," father said.

"He out there," Nancy said. "He looking through that window this minute, waiting for yawl to go. Then I gone."

"Nonsense," father said. "Lock up your house and we'll take you on to Aunt Rachel's."

" 'Twon't do no good," Nancy said. She didn't look at father now, but he looked down at her, at her long, limp, moving hands. "Putting it off won't do no good."

"Then what do you want to do?" father said.

"I don't know," Nancy said. "I can't do nothing. Just put it off. And that don't do no good. I reckon it belong to me. I reckon what I going to get ain't no more than mine."

"Get what?" Caddy said. "What's yours?"

"Nothing," father said. "You all must get to bed."

"Caddy made me come," Jason said.

"Go on to Aunt Rachel's," father said.

"It won't do no good," Nancy said. She sat before the fire, her elbows on her knees, her long hands between her knees. "When even your own kitchen wouldn't do no good. When even if I was sleeping on the floor in the room with your own children, and the next morning there I am, and blood all—"

"Hush," father said. "Lock the door and put the lamp out and go to bed."

"I scared of the dark," Nancy said. "I scared for it to happen in the dark."

"You mean you're going to sit right here, with the lamp lighted?" father said. Then Nancy began to make the sound again, sitting before the fire, her long hands between her knees. "Ah, damnation," father said. "Come along, chillen. It's bedtime."

"When yawl go, I gone," Nancy said. "I be dead tomorrow. I done had saved up the coffin money with Mr. Lovelady—"

Mr. Lovelady was a short, dirty man who collected the Negro insurance, coming around to the cabins and the kitchens every Saturday morning, to collect fifteen cents. He and his wife lived in the hotel. One morning his wife committed suicide. They had a child, a little girl. After his wife committed suicide Mr. Lovelady and the child went away. After a while Mr. Lovelady came back. We would see him going down the lanes on Saturday morning. He went to the Baptist church.

Father carried Jason on his back. We went out Nancy's door; she was sitting before the fire. "Come and put the bar up," father said. Nancy didn't move. She didn't look at us again. We left her there, sitting before the fire with the door opened, so that it wouldn't happen in the dark.

"What, father?" Caddy said. "Why is Nancy scared of Jubah? What is Jubah going to do to her?"

"Jubah wasn't there," Jason said.

"No," father said. "He's not there. He's gone away."

"Who is it that's waiting in the ditch?" Caddy said. We looked at the ditch. We came to it, where the path went down into the thick vines and went up again.

"Nobody," father said.

There was just enough moon to see by. The ditch was vague, thick, quiet. "If he's there, he can see us, can't he?" Caddy said.

"You made me come," Jason said on father's back. "I didn't want to."

The ditch was quite still, quite empty, massed with honeysuckle. We couldn't see Jubah, any more than we could see Nancy sitting there in her house, with the door open and the lamp burning, because she didn't want it to happen in the dark. "I just done got tired," Nancy said. "I just a nigger. It ain't no fault of mine."

But we could still hear her. She began as soon as we were out of the house, sitting there above the fire, her long brown hands between her knees. We could still hear her when we had crossed the ditch, Jason high and close and little about father's head.

Then we had crossed the ditch, walking out of Nancy's life. Then her life was sitting there with the door open and the lamp lit, waiting, and the ditch between us and us going on, the white people going on, dividing the impinged lives of us and Nancy.

"Who will do our washing now, father?" I said.

"I'm not a nigger," Jason said on father's shoulders.

"You're worse," Caddy said, "you are a tattletale. If something was to jump out, you'd be scairder than a nigger."

"I wouldn't," Jason said.

"You'd cry," Caddy said.

"Caddy!" father said.

"I wouldn't," Jason said.

"Scairy cat," Caddy said.

"Candace!" father said.

Walter D. Edmonds

WALTER D. EDMONDS was born in 1903 at Boonville, New York, the region out of whose colorful past he summons the legend of Perry Joslin and Blind Eve. As a writer of historical fiction he is both scrupulous and imaginative, true to his background and able to create characters and action which express it. At Harvard he was a student in the class of C. T. Copeland (the famous "Copey"), and when he graduated in 1926 he had already seen some of his stories in print.

His first book Rome Haul (1929) dealt with the Erie Canal days of the Fifties of the last century. Two more novels The Big Barn (1930) and Erie Water (1933) followed before the publication of a group of short stories Mostly Canallers (1934). The most popular of his historical novels Drums Along the Mohawk appeared in 1936.

Modest and hardworking in his attempt to bring to life the reality of other days, he is not given to theorizing. "Of writing as an art," he comments, "I think authors have the least to say."

BLIND EVE *

Walter D. Edmonds

1

AT THE BLAST of a horn, Perry Joslin came out of his house and looked away down the canal. That way was south. The evening sun still showed over the western lip of the gorge, sending the shadows of the hills to his very feet; but he himself stood in the light of the sun.

Canallers said that Perry was the craziest lock-tender in the Kill

---

* From *Mostly Canallers,* by Walter D. Edmonds, an Atlantic Monthly Press Publication. Reprinted by permission of Little, Brown & Company.

Gorge. All lock-tenders were crazy. A man had to be crazy or religious to stand the winds that went down the valley in the early spring or the late fall. And where Perry's lock was, the canal was turning the shoulder of a hill, halfway up from the Lansing Kill; and Perry's shanty stood outside the lock on a spot that made it seem to overhang the valley, and he could see from his window the whole curve of the canal to the next hill, and hear the top leaves of the big elms in the valley rustling underneath the sill. It was a wild, lonely place in the late sixties, when only the mules and the boats and the boaters went up and down the everlasting locks—with the shadows of the clouds.

The plank road followed the canal, but in this place it was high above, hidden by trees, and when a wagon did go past, Perry could not see it. It came with a rumble of wheels like thunder; and on a still day even the sound was swallowed by the echoes. In his first years there Perry had been used to look up for a sight of the wagon; but by this time his ears seemed to have lost the trick of hearing.

He did look crazy, standing there, tall and gawky as a heron, with his red undershirt flashing in the sunlight and his floppy hat shading the white hair that blew upon his shoulders.

His hands were chapped with the cold winds of March, and his thin face was red. The wind brought water to his pale eyes. He had fine small features; but they were weak, as if good blood somewhere in his forebears dared show itself only in a surreptitious fashion.

But the sound of the horn from southward had wakened gladness in his small face. He shaded his eyes and peered for the boat. He could just make it out in the shadow of the far end of the curve. It was the first boat coming upstream.

The canal had been opened for three days; but so far trade was slack, and the only traffic had been down. Perry used to say that for him the spring did not really come until he saw the first boat rising from the south.

The feeling of spring had not yet entered the gorge. What wind it had still came from the north; and the snow showed under the hemlocks on the upper part of the hills and along the Lansing Kill in the valley bottom. The Kill had not yet reached highwater mark; nor had it shown the thick brown turbulence of meadows laid bare at the head of the gorge. It flowed sullenly, its roar still hushed by snow banks, a yellow untossed stream.

The boat was coming on at a crawl, the horses bent low over

crooked knees. The towpath was slushy under foot; there had not been teams enough yet to churn through the frozen mud. The driver leaned into the wind, his heavy boots slipping, his hands in his pockets, and the long whip under his arm trailing its lash behind him.

Perry moved leisurely to the upper gates and closed them. The lock was at high level—he had filled it again, against regulations, hoping that at last a boat might come up from the south and put him in the wrong. If he took a chance of wasting a lockful the boat might come, he thought, and he had been right. But he had time enough to bring the level down before the laboring team could reach the gates.

He heaved up the sluice lever in the nearest gate and watched the water boiling out with a yellow froth. Then he went across the plank and opened the other. The water went down quickly, revealing inch by inch the blocks of which the walls were built. Wet moss and green slime grew in the cracks between and trailed water down with sleepy echoes in the pit of the lock.

The sound of the overflow stopped. Gazing over, Perry watched his reflection sinking until at last it was broken into bits in the nearest whirlpool and sucked out through the sluice. He often wondered where it went to, away down south to the Erie perhaps, to Utica, to Albany; from what he had heard it might ride all the way to New York City and the ocean. People bathing in June, on the beaches canallers had told him of, might see it rocking on the ocean waves. It never went north.

He threw his weight on the balance beam and marched it round to open the gate, and closed the sluice. He recrossed the lock to the other gate and opened it. When he looked up then, he saw the team close upon him, stretched against the boat's weight by the taut line. He could hear them panting as they scrabbled up the slope to the head of the lock.

The driver cried, "Hello, Perry! How be you this year?"

Perry smiled. "Good, good. How be you?"

"Are we the first boat up?"

"Yes."

"I thought we was."

He held out his hand and shook.

"You'd ought to wear mittens," he said.

Perry looked down at the cracks over his knuckles.

"Maybe I'd ought to," he admitted.

The team seemed to hang on their legs, racked by their panting. Their heads dropped. One showed a new sore coming under his collar.

"They're soft yet," said the driver, as Perry stroked them. "It's hard hauling. How's your lock? We had to drag it over mud on Five, below here."

"I guess it's all right. I been stirring it up and the mud's about gone."

The driver spat. He was a tough-built Irishman who thought Perry was soft-hearted as well as soft-headed.

"Well," he said, "the brutes ought to be grateful to you."

The boat came sliding in on its own momentum. The boater steered it through without lifting a splinter. Esau Brown was a rank hand at steering a boat. If there were any scars on the *Young Lion,* they were put on by other boaters shaving it. He was a little man with a sheepskin jacket on and skin breeches, and he wore a cap with the ear muffles down. You could see only his red nose till he tilted his head back and showed you two burning black eyes under the visor. He and his driver, John, made the toughest boat to fight with on the Black River Canal.

"Tie her by," he said to John, and jumped on the edge of the lock the minute the boat's deck reached the level. "How are you, Perry?" He shook hands. "Come aboard," he invited. "The missus wants for you to have a cup of tea."

Perry looked up the canal doubtfully and then down. "No one's in back of me," said Esau; "and if anybody comes along, why me and John will swill them through. Come in."

"I'm glad to see you," said Perry slowly, in reply to the greeting; "real glad. Thanks."

2

The *Young Lion* was an old bullhead boat painted a yellow green. The very color of it suggested the first turn of the leaves into green. It made Perry's thin nose almost snuff for grass. John had put the gang out and tied-by to the snubbing posts above the lock. He was throwing blankets over the horses—they were glad of a rest.

Perry had to bend his long body nearly double going down the cramped steps through the door into the bright warmth of the cabin. Missus Brown was sitting on a rocker in front of the stove, of which she had opened all four leaves of the oven door. Perry looked round him appreciatively. He wished his house had pretty yellow curtains.

Missus Brown was a big woman, fat and blowsy, with stringy dust-colored hair and a broad red face.

" 'Ullo, Perry!" She held out a hand which had a mammoth emerald ring on it; the peddler had said it was emerald.

Perry took his hat off.

"Hello, Missus Brown!"

" 'Ow are you vis spring?"

"Fine," he said.

Missus Brown had come over from London, England, as a lady's maid. There was a charitable lady in Utica who went abroad every few years and brought back servants with her. When they got to Utica they decided six dollars a month and an unheated attic room were not so comfortable as joining on with Lucy Cashdollar, who ran the Agency for Bachellor Boaters in Bentley's Bar. Celia had struck on with Esau and now she was married.

"I'm reel sorry, Perry, to 'ear 'ow your muvver is dead."

Perry pressed his hat between his hands and looked round and round above the heads of the three boaters.

"It makes me sad," he said.

"Well," said the lady, "there's the pot boiling. Esau, 'and it to me. Drink some tea, Perry?"

"No, thanks."

"Just a little warm wet," she coaxed him. He consented. They all had it and a cruller apiece, the men drinking gulpily and Missus Brown sipping from her saucer in the proper way. She took plenty of brown sugar, keeping a little supply on the edge of her saucer and washing the tea up against it. She smacked her lips gently.

"Well," said Missus Brown, " 'ere we are again. Every week, abaht, I says to Esau, won't it be good, I says, to get back up the Kill Gorge and 'ave a wet of tea wiv Perry? 'E's such a nice man. It always seems we're boating again when we 'ave a wet of tea wiv Perry. Ain't it a fact, Esau?"

She poured a second cup.

"How many years have you been here, Perry?" Esau asked.

"Ten years, odd. I come here five years after the canal was open." He looked around him again with his restless vague gaze.

"It's lonely. The old lady must've been a trile to you, Perry. But you must miss 'er."

He did. He could think once how glad he would be to have her go away. She had adopted him. She had been trailing gypsies and had come down off the plank road one day and called herself his mother and adopted him, house and lock and wages. She took the last for monthly trips to Westernville to drink it up. She used to beat Perry sometimes. Now he missed her. She had died in the middle of February. He still owed eighty-five cents for the headstone.

"You ought to get married, Perry," said Missus Brown. "That's what you ought."

Married—he ought to get married, that's what he ought. Perry did not know how to go about it; but he wondered if it was true as he watched the *Young Lion* hauling north into the dusk. He did not care about it very much.

He was a queer fellow; everyone said so. "There's Perry," a boater would say. "He's the queerest coot on the whole canawl." And Perry would nod his head and say "That's right, I guess." And lock them through. He did not know what it would be like to be in love. People talked about it. Would it be like Missus Brown? He had seen a shanty-boat once hauled by a rusty mule, and an old man on the deck kissing a young girl. The man had a beard as white as Perry's hair, and the girl had loose brown eyes.

He did not know what it was to be loved. He had just come upon himself in the world. He voted the ticket of the party in at Albany each fall and drew his pay from the pay wagon every month but one, which went for the party's war chest. At least no lock-tender ever saw the pay wagon in October. They did not ask.

Perry's neighbor, a wild Irishman, had asked and lost his job. He had licked the tar out of the pay wagon the next time it came. He had drunk for a day waiting for it, and he had jumped on and taken off the guns and thrown them in the lock, and thrown the men in too when he had done some things to them, and taken the harness off the horses and thrown rocks at them till they ran away clean crazy, and then he had spent an hour with an axe taking the wagon to pieces. Perry lived alone and did as he was told. He always had. He had no mother, no father. He was just in the world, appearing with his white hair out of nowhere, like a thistle seed in August. He could not even say that he had been born. He did not know. He was queer.

The queerest thing about him was that he could read. He did not understand that either. He liked reading. A minister had given him a Bible and he had *The Old Curiosity Shop*. He read that book over and over.

3

He got him his supper alone. No more boats had passed, but he did not feel lonely any more. When the Browns went up it meant that spring had come, for him.

He baked himself some beans and sat by the window eating them off a plate he held in his hand close under his chin. The stove purred and ticked with the dry wood. The lantern hung from the ceiling put the shadows in the corners. Now and then he would glance up at a picture, on the wall, of a lady in long gloves. It was in bright colors—purple, pink, and green. He had seen it in the leaf of a lady's book and cut it out. It was the most beautiful woman he had ever looked at. She was young, with a clean, hard, cold face.

That was all the decoration he had. And he had put that up only after the woman who called herself his mother had died. She would have torn it off.

He had three chairs and a table and a bunk in the corner which the state had built in for him. He used to sleep in the loft room. But now his blankets were there on the straw he begged from boaters. . . .

Perry looked out of the window. The sun was gone. All the cup of the valley was full of darkness. It was still. So still that he got up at last and went outdoors.

The wind had died with the sun. It was warm. Warm, moist stars had appeared in the black sky. It would not freeze to-night. Even as he stood there he heard the tinkle of water running into the rain barrel. A cloud was coming out of the south and drops were falling. The note of the overflow round the lock, falling down the wooden stairs, was thick and soft.

He stood breathing great breaths until he felt the wet seeping through on his shoulders. Then he went inside again. He stretched himself on his bunk and took the Bible in his hand. He could not read. He could only think of Missus Brown; she had said he ought to get married.

The rain drove harder and harder against the shanty walls. It was washing the cold out of the air. Rolling and rolling. Spring was coming for a fact, even up the gorge.

4

Perry had the weather warm through the opening two weeks in April. He went about his work with a kind of joyousness, swinging back and forth across his lock and throwing off talk like any happy man. But odd moments by himself found him moody. It was nicer without the old woman round the shanty; but it was lonely, too. He kept thinking of Missus Brown's advice, that he ought to get married, that was what he ought.

Perry would sit by himself in the afternoon before the lock, with the clouds drifting overhead in the wet gray April skies, and watch the silent muster of the spring. The gorge was a small route for birds.

Squirrels and rabbits were tracking the last snow with crazy dancing patterns; the branches on the spruce trees lifted with the oozing out of frost; if a man got away from the roar of the Kill, he could hear a ticking in the woods, like a small clock marking time out of sight.

Perry had planted a lilac in front of his shanty when he first came there. A boater had given him a little plant out of a shipment from Carthage. It was a French lilac tree, and it bloomed a vivid purple red. Perry used to watch the buds every morning in the spring; but now he could see no change.

April closed that year with cold weather. The birds disappeared— no more were going north.

The men on the pay wagon the last day of the month had themselves wrapped up. They stopped in on Perry for a cup of tea; and they told him the canal would shut down for three days in the next two weeks while a culvert below the Five Combines was patched and new planking was put into the aqueduct at Stringer Brook.

"You might as well take the time off for your sparking," said the bigger one, which made the little one laugh.

Two weeks—that would make it fall on Monday. There would not be heavy traffic Sunday.

Sparking. So he would. Perry's face flushed and he went inside out of the cold and combed his long white hair. He had often wondered how it was a man could have such long white hair and no beard on his face. He darned his socks that night before the stove and thought about it.

Perry rose that Monday morning with a sparkle of excitement in his pale eyes. He had pressed his pants with the old iron the night before and greased his shoes. He had heard the water dying out of the waste weir, and this morning when he stepped outside it had the barest trickle tinkling down.

But Perry did not stop to look. The sky was deep blue and filled with golden sunlight; the clouds floating so still were warm and soft. Trees at last showed color. The maples were pink and violet and the birches and the poplars yellow-green.

Perry stood still on the end of his long morning shadow. He had a little leather-back satchel full of food, bread, cheese, tea, and a tart a boater's cook had given him the day before. His pants looked clean and his boots were soft with grease. He wore a blue flannel shirt under his old black coat with the swallow-fork lapels. With a deep breath he set out upon his sparking.

He had not thought of where he was to go; but he took the path down into the Kill. There was a footbridge there and a trail that led up onto Potato Hill. Before he looked round he would get up on Potato Hill and get a good look at all the world. That was the idea.

He walked with long easy strides.

All the spring had come at once. Pin-point blades of grass had pierced the old sod with green. Wild onion was flung in banners through the woods. There were pools still at the boles of trees, full cups in the root fingers, that showed blue at one's feet, and a man could search the limits of the sky by looking down. Perry went down to the Kill and stepped out on the bridge. The muddy water came within an inch of his feet and slopped little driblets against his boot soles. He looked down the straight wild-tossing stretch, while the roar sang in his head, and he found that he could hear the wind—the winter wind, and the sough of summer breathings, and the blasts of fall, all in the water's passage from the land.

Then he went on. The trail toiled up a slope so steep he had to use his hands to climb. The mud in the track had come up brown and thick. Ferns were unfurling, dogtooth violet leaves were stealing out. A little stream coming down gushed out suddenly from under a rock. He listened, and inside the hill face he could hear it falling.

He climbed swiftly until he was tired, and he thought he must rest when he came suddenly over the edge, and there he found the stream again falling into a hole in the ground, and a blue jay drinking at the edge of it.

It was warmer in the woods at the top of the slope, and Perry sweated with his walking. There were old trees there, and the ground was level, and far ahead he saw a color on the leaves, like snow with shadows of blue and rose, that had just fallen; and in a minute he came among the anemones. To walk over them made him feel dizzy. It was the first color of the year, and it was the purest and the sweetest.

Perry ceased to feel tired. His long legs swung him steadily on when the ground rose again, his hair swayed with his stride.

He was quite blinded when he stepped suddenly onto the shoulder of a hillock where the grass was short and showing green, and the sun came down full upon his shoulders. Over the edge of the hill he saw a house roof with a barn roof to keep it company. They rose up to his strides until he came to the barnyard and saw the road. It was a muddy track, stopping at the farm.

There was no paint on the buildings; they looked poor and ill cared for. Hens were scratching and picking in a garden patch. A black and white dog barked and fell silent. Some ducks marched round and round among the puddles slandering one another. Only a lone gray goose seemed really disturbed at his arrival. She screamed and screamed, and ran into the barn, and then looked out of the door at him and hissed. A cat was sleeping on the porch. A woman was hanging wash out. Two children in short pants played with sticks at being Indians. One was being scalped.

Perry stopped before the woman, panting slightly. She had a worn face and dull brown hair and tired eyes. Her age was what the world had made it. She said her husband was trading in Boonville, but that she had no objection to Perry's stopping in the barn to eat his luncheon.

Perry entered the barn doors and walked along the board run between the wooden stanchions to a pile of hay. It was a poor farm. He could see in the gutters the broken brakes the farmer had been using for bedding instead of straw. But the cattle were out and only the herd smell was left.

5

Perry sat on the hay and took out his lunch before he heard the girl. She was sitting in the shadow just beside him.

"Hello," said Perry.

"Hello, mister."

She spoke oddly, blurring the words in her throat so that they were hard to hear.

Perry offered her a bit of his cheese. She came out of the shadow slowly then, walking straight for him until he thought she was going to walk over him. She stopped, though, and held her hands out.

"What's your name?"

"Perry Joslin."

He put the cheese in her hands and she hunkered down like an animal in front of him. She had the most beautiful dark brown eyes Perry had ever seen and long black hair that came below her hips. She wore only a dress of faded gingham. Her bare legs were round and hard and her brown fingers quick and supple as she broke the cheese. Her mouth had red lips, moist, with a kind of wild look, but her eyes were very steady.

"What do you look like, mister?"

Perry drew back.

"Why?"

He saw then that her eyes were looking a little past him; but whenever he spoke they would turn to his lips.

She said, "I'm blind."

"Oh!"

"Can I feel you over, mister?" she asked timidly.

"Surely."

She moved forward onto her knees and he felt the balls of her fingers on his face. She was like a curious young animal—almost as if she used her nose; but when he looked for it he could not be sure. She was the most beautiful thing his eyes had ever noticed; her hair was so black, dull black, with blue shadows that moved. Her fingers were like light, quick-hovering moths. They had a faint sweet smell of earth and woods. As they touched him he could feel the coolness of the wind, the peace of grass, the tender swaying of the barley; he could smell violets by springs, the Mayflowers in the swamps; he could see the golden spots of marigolds, and old red trilliums all alone.

"What color are your eyes?"

"Blue."

"You've no beard. How old are you, mister?"

"I don't know."

"I'm seventeen."

"You're a tall, big girl for seventeen."

"Pa says I am. You're tall, too."

Her hands were shy, but had no bashfulness. Perry sat still under their touch. His heart was cool and peaceful. He felt gladness deep down almost out of touch.

"My, you've got long hair."

"Yes. But not like yours."

"No. Mine is long. Ma tells me so."

"It's beautiful hair."

He wanted to touch it.

"Is it? What color's yours? It's so fine to feel."

"Gold," said Perry.

"Pure gold?"

Perry stiffened. He had not meant to say so. But he had seen the admiration in her face. She was looking at him hard with her sightless eyes. He saw shadows there, like stirring depths. He would not unsay himself.

She was making a little pucker between her brows. "I can't remember gold."

"It's like yellow."

"Is it like buttercups?"

"A little."

"Blue eyes."

He felt so sorry for her.

"I'm glad you don't cut your hair, mister."

"Were you born blind?"

"No. I can remember seeing. I was sick."

"Oh! what do you do here?"

"I can't help ma so good, so I get the cows. I can milk. I take care of the ducks and hens. I can talk to animals and call them."

"Don't you get lost ever, going for the cows?"

"I call them."

"How do you call them?"

She made a noise through her lips. The old goose came with hurrying, web feet patting the floor.

"Like that, only that's goose talk."

The old goose came up to her and rubbed its head against her arm and looked wisely at Perry.

"What's your name?"

"Eve. Eve Winslow. They call me Blind Eve."

She looked up at him and her hand came out to touch his hair.

"Are you happy, Eve?"

"Sometimes." And her lips said to herself, though Perry could read, "Gold."

"Where are you going to, mister?" she asked after a time.

He said uneasily, "I'm sparking."

"What's that?"

"Looking for a girl to live with me."

"Oh! Where do you live?"

"I live by the canal and mind a lock. I have a house with two rooms, one above and one below."

"Have you found the girl?"

"No. I ain't yet."

"Can you hear the wind?"

"Yes. There's wind. The house stands high on the edge of the valley."

"Down there?" She pointed.

"Down there. Then up the other side."

"What's the canal?"

"It's water people go on in their boats."

"Can you hear them?"

"Yes. They blow a horn for the lock and they can't get through until I come out to let them. I let the water out below and the boat goes down and you can hear the water running."

"Oh! mister!"

Her eyes were shining.

"I'd like to live there."

"Would you?"

He told her all about the shanty; and then, as they sat in the moted air of the barn, she told him how she had always stayed on the farm. No one ever came to visit except when a child was born; it was the end of the road, with the forest just beyond. She could not talk with wild animals. It was hard sometimes talking with people. Some could not understand what she said.

From time to time in silences she touched his hair.

They shared the tart.

"Would you come and live with me?"

"Oh, yes," she said.

Perry was not conscious that the house he offered her was splendid —that he had found a poorer being than he. She was the most beautiful thing he had ever seen. He forgot that he had not gone up Potato Hill at first to take a look at all the world as he had planned.

"I'll ask your pa."

"He'll soon be back."

"We'll get married."

"Like ma and pa?"

"Yes, like them."

"Ma's told me how she got wedded in a city, with a gown and dresses. I haven't any dresses."

"I'll bring one. Stand up."

She rose easily.

Her legs were straight, her back just curved to the proper hollow. She looked, as she stood, what Perry had never been—free. He saw then that her chin was strong and her neck round. It was like the wind to see her. He measured himself against her to know her height. She was as tall as he was, but broader in the shoulders, with hips and breast like a full-grown woman's.

He thought suddenly he ought to kiss her, and he put his arms about her shoulders. He had never kissed a girl. She was stiff at his touch. He felt her lips moist and cool and tight, and then they loosened, and suddenly she was shivering and shivering. He let go stiffly and felt cold; but the blood leaped up and sang in his ears. His voice shook; he took her hand; and they walked out like children and told her mother.

The woman was bent over her ironing board.

"Yeah. I didn't think it would happen, mister. You'll have to ask my husband. But I guess he'll be real glad."

They went out and sat on the porch.

Winslow was a short-spoken bearded fellow who was glad to see his daughter off his hands. She was no real help. But he spoke kindly of her and said she would learn to make a good wife, he made no doubt. They set the wedding time for two weeks. The mother wanted it at the house, but the father said it would cost too much to bring a preacher all the way from Boonville. It had been a bad year. And he was proud. Perry said he could come for Eve and take her to Boonville to be married.

6

He kissed her again and left her shining-eyed at the pasture bars in the dusk. As he went back to the gorge he heard the cows coming out of pasture. He did not look back. When he was in the woods he ran. He laughed to see an old buck rabbit jump and scurry ahead of him. He could hear in his ears Eve's low voice saying, "Oh, yes." His lips still felt her awkward kiss. He shouted out aloud.

He slept that night unconscious of the roaring of the Kill; he had done his sparking, done it proud; the blood sang.

He counted up his money the next morning. He saw that he must keep so much for food. He would have to buy some new blankets.

Missus Brown would get them for him, he thought. He must get a
license, as he had heard tell. He would have five dollars left.

Boaters coming by when the canal opened again two days later asked
him where he had been.

"Sparking," he said, and they burst into laughter.

"What's she look like, Perry?"

"She's seventeen, but as tall as me."

"Cripus! A big girl! Is she pretty?"

"She's got black hair to her hips. She's the most beautiful girl you
ever see."

They laughed and laughed.

"How'd you come to find her?"

"I went sparking."

"How'd she come to have you?"

"I don't know that. She said she liked my hair maybe."

They laughed again.

It made him uneasy. He gave up telling how she liked his hair. They
made such a joke of it. They might tell her his hair was white, he was
afraid.

But when the *Young Lion* came Missus Brown only smiled, and
Esau swore he would show up, haul or no haul, to mind the lock for
Perry for two days when the wedding day came round. John grinned
and shook his hand, and said if he had trouble with the boaters just to
let him know.

He gave Missus Brown the money for the blankets and they went in
and looked at the shanty. It was bright enough outside where the state
painted it salmon pink and white, but for the first time the inside
disturbed his comfort. "No matter, Perry," said the woman. "She won't
see. Even if she had sight she wouldn't see."

"She's the most beautifulest thing there is," he said huskily.

And standing in the door, his bow-legged shadow sprawled across
the floor, Esau nodded. "Sure."

Perry saw he wasn't smiling, and looked at Missus Brown. It puzzled
him to see her flushed and nervous, and her eyes shining.

Perry made time to get the license as Esau told him he should do.
May slept drowsily along. The hot days of June were just coming into
the gorge, and the trees and grass were rank with green. The Kill was
a blue-green thread in the bottom of the valley. Horses went slowly
with the boats. Men chaffed Perry for his wedding day. One brought
an umbrella for a wedding gift to shield his golden hair, and it made

a joke, canallers say, that went all the way to New York City.

Then at last the *Young Lion* hauled up with cement on the way to Boonville and tied by. Next morning Perry had his breakfast in the cabin and Missus Brown kissed him good-bye. Another crew, seeing him start off, began to cheer until John hopped aboard and offered to disconnect their heads.

Perry did not hear them. His thin face was bent seriously toward the ground. He felt afraid and glad. His knees did not seem to belong to him.

A hawk cut circles in the sunlight over his head and red-winged blackbirds jarred the air with song. It was warm, dusty; the land was ripe and ready for the harvests soon to come.

He came to Boonville in the afternoon and bought a suit for three dollars secondhand. He got a ring for fifty cents and strung it on a red ribbon round his neck. He took all his nerves in his dry hands and went into a dry-goods store and got a dress for two more dollars because it had a tear which a pitying saleswoman mended while he waited. He had fifty cents for the minister. He went to speak to him. The minister was a tall man, too, thin and sad. But Perry seemed to make him smile.

When it was all done Perry started out for Potato Hill. It was dark by now. The birds beside the road were twittering sleepily. Only the whippoorwills called clear and loud. He would walk onto the singing, and the bird would hush, and when he had gone a way it would break out again behind him, but he never saw the bird.

He came to the farm in the dark and stole into the barn. The goose remembered him and barely hissed from her nest under the stairs. He lay down close to it in his new clothes and slept.

When he awoke, Eve was stroking his hair. The cows had come in for milking and a row of their bony heads looked on him quietly as they switched tails and breathed softly over their cuds.

He undid his package and gave Eve her dress. She felt it all over; then ran into the house to put it on. He followed in a while. The two small boys gazed at him wonderingly and went round the house. The mother had dressed Eve. She had bound her hair with a piece of ribbon. She had no hat; and her shoes were a pair her mother had worn years before. But these she was to carry in her hand until she reached Boonville.

The mother was tearful now; but the farmer joked as they ate breakfast.

7

They walked away quite peacefully before the dew had risen. "Forever and ever, amen."

Perry could hear the words as he and Eve walked down the towpath with the afterglow still on the hills.

Here and there they passed a boat tied by, its lantern a firefly spot in the dusk. But people did not see them. Only a child or two watched them pass, with big eyes. They walked hand in hand, Perry telling the road for her bare feet.

Eve said nothing. From time to time she raised the hand that had the ring to her mouth and touched it with her tongue. Her black hair swayed as she walked.

They had eaten supper out of Perry's leather-back satchel in a corner of a pasture lot, sharing the grass with an old cow and some hornets drowsy-winged with dew.

Now they were coming home.

Once she asked the color of the ring, and when he said "Gold" she put her fingers on his hair.

He saw the bow-lantern of the *Young Lion* at last.

He saw a bright light in the shanty window.

As they stood hand in hand in the door, he could smell the lilac tree in bloom.

Missus Brown was inside. There was a rocking chair, a supper set of crockery upon the table, curtains at the window in bright blue, and a real oil lamp, wedding presents from the three.

Missus Brown said no word, but took Eve's hand and kissed her. But she looked round Eve's shoulder, and, seeing her eyes shine, Perry was made proud.

Esau and John came in laughing and took off their caps.

Perry saw then that they, too, thought that Eve was the beautifulest thing in the world, as he had said.

He wanted to thank them, but Missus Brown said to Eve, "Perry is a good man, dearie. And your house is the pleasantest one in the world. I know. I've been 'ere two days now."

They went out. Eve sat down, shading her eyes against the light. Perry stood still after he had closed the door. The bunk was made up; the room was clean and sweet. His heart came high.

He could hear the Kill muttering. He could hear the peepers singing. Outside the door he heard the lock sluices running as Esau and John locked the *Young Lion* through. They went north with the word of Blind Eve. Later they would go south; but they would find that the word of Blind Eve had gone before them, as had the joke of Perry's golden hair, all the way to New York City, till men talked about her all the way along the whole canal.

They lived together many years. Boaters tried to tell her that Perry's hair was not gold, but to such she showed the ring for an answer. He had said they were the same. Others tried to make love to her, but she had a fine indignation and was strong, and neither she nor Perry ever called on Esau or John.

Horses came to know her. No matter how worn they were she got them through the lock without a lash. She learned the house by touch. She learned to cook. Her feet on the plank across the lock were as sure as Perry's. Children loved to look at her and listen to her husky singing in the evening as Perry locked their boats through. Some of those children are men in middle life to-day, but they remember her story, and some will tell it to you.

For she never changed from Perry, and when he died she cut off a lock of his golden hair to remember him by.

ℒois 𝒮eyster ℳontross

IN THE EARLY Twenties, Lois Montross, just out of college, wrote a
series of stories in collaboration with her husband, Lynn Montross,
which explored, with humor, audacity, and satiric candor, the college
world of undergraduates, administrators, and professors. The subject
had long been waiting for competent treatment, and Town and
Gown (1923) was discussed on every American campus. The stories
initiated a vogue, and a second collection, Fraternity Row, was published by the Montrosses in 1926.

Lois Montross was born in Kempton, Illinois, and educated at the
University of Illinois. In recent years her interest has turned chiefly
to novels, but she continues to publish short stories of expert craftsmanship in many magazines. "A Day in New York" won a prize of
$1,000 in a story contest conducted by the Pictorial Review.

Among Mrs. Montross's other books are The Crimson Cloak
(1924), a volume of poetry; Among Those Present (1927), a collection of short stories; and the novels Wind Before Dawn (1932) and
The Perfect Pair (1934).

A DAY IN NEW YORK *

Lois Seyster Montross

THERE IS a belief that woman's beauty is a power which captures
man unfailingly. And certain it is that beauty is a net for ensnaring
his eyes. But there are other invisible qualities which catch and hold a
man's heart. One of these is gallantry in women.

Dan Byrd knew nothing about gallantry. If he had thought about it
at all he would have called it "being a good sport." Dan Byrd knew

---

* From *The Pictorial Review*, September, 1930. Reprinted by permission of the
author and *The Pictorial Review*.

everything about carburetors and vacuum tanks and hydraulic brakes and pistons. He worked at the Paramount Garage and Filling Station, and he never went anywhere without a pair of pliers in his hip pocket —just as another man will carry a microscope or a camera or a flask against a time of need.

Rosy saw him slipping the pliers into his blue-serge pocket this exciting Friday morning. "Oh, Dan! You won't need to take them to New York! Did you think the train would break down and you might have to fix it?"

He grinned sheepishly and put the pliers back into the overalls hanging behind the kitchen door. With the black wire hairbrush he attacked his thick blond hair, which stood up in two stubborn wings on each side of a central parting. His face was ruddy, honest, large, freshly scrubbed and shaven above the semisoft collar which held his chin uncomfortably thrust upward.

"All ready, Rosy? The train leaves at 5:10; don't you forget it."

"Oh, but I've got to tell Lorna some more things about the kids." Rosy, usually so calm and plumply stolid, was curiously trembling, and her round, freckled cheeks were very nearly pale from excitement. She swallowed her hot coffee hastily, bit a large mouthful from a cruller, and cried, "Lorna! Lorna!"

Her sister appeared from the bedroom off the kitchen. She was a larger edition of Rosy, a bit stouter, a bit sandier, with bolder freckles and redder hair. "Francis and Arline got to get to school at nine, don't they?"

"Yes, and be sure Arly wears her sweater. And the baby has orange juice at ten. Oh, and could you wash this pair of stockings here for Joey? They'll be dry before he wakes up—the only pair. Lorna, how does my new hat look? I sat up till two last night to finish it."

Rosy was pulling it on over her curly copper head. She dabbed her nose with a matronly powder puff, which she wrapped in a white handkerchief and returned to her new $2.98 purse. She was thirty, and she looked thirty-five, with the frank air of not expecting to look younger. With four children you worry about their ages, not yours.

But there was something appealingly childish about her sudden exclamation, "Ooh, gosh! I'm so excited!"

Lorna looked at her with admiration. "You look swell. Don't worry about anything!"

Dan had stood waiting impatiently all this time in his overcoat and hat, with the small brown satchel in one large hand. "Come on, for Pete's sake! That train leaves at—"

"If you say that again I'll yell. Oh, where are my gloves? My new gloves?"

"Whaddye want gloves for?"

"You big dummy, a lady has to have gloves to ride on the train. Thanks, Lorna." She pulled on the gloves with an attempt at calm dignity. "And they don't put them on in the street, either; do they, Lorna?"

The sisters laughed, pecked each other on the cheek, and Rosy followed Dan through the doorway.

"Don't take any wooden nickels!" shouted Lorna.

They stood on the platform of the village station and gazed up the tracks. There were still twenty minutes before the train came. The sun was rising above the low Pennsylvania hills with sleepy deliberation, casting aside gauzy gray walls of mist and silken coverlets of rose and gold. The blue sky was shot with arrows of light.

Dan looked at the sun and wondered if there were any way to harness its force.

Rosy looked at the sun and wished she had a dress—one of those new long dresses made of tulle flounces in that delicate violet and primrose and sea shell.

They were going to have one day in New York.

Many things had happened to make this vacation possible. First there had been the eloping young couple. They had paid Dan fifty dollars to drive them to Pittsburgh. His car was old and secondhand, but he kept the engine in smooth perfection. Then there was the chance for him to get Friday off from working at the filling station because Harry Mintz came to town and hadn't found a job yet.

Next was the astonishing coincidence that the people Lorna worked for as second maid had to go to a funeral, and she was able to look after Rosy's children.

"Honestly, it's just like some story you might see in the movies, isn't it?" said Rosy, squeezing Dan's arm.

"Yeah," said Dan, "Only you'd hardly believe it in the movies. You'd say it couldn't happen."

It was the first time that either of them had gone to New York City. People in Upson, Pennsylvania, went to Pittsburgh instead.

Thursday evening Dan had worked late on a radio he was repairing for Mr. Marshall, the owner of the Paramount Garage. Rosy's preparations for the trip had been so elaborate that she had not gone to bed until two this morning, and they had both risen at four. Dan's best blue suit had to be cleaned and pressed, Rosy's silk underwear and stockings washed, the new hat finished, school clothes for the children mended. But the Byrds were too excited yet to be sleepy and tired, and even in the train they were self-conscious beyond drowsiness.

They had taken seats in the parlor car because Dan wanted every detail to be luxurious. He sat stiffly upright, talking in stilted mono-syllables. Rosy affected a languid elegance for the benefit of a marcelled lady across the aisle whose moleskin coat dripped carelessly from her shoulders. Rosy wished Dan had not said loudly just as the train stopped, "Of course a mechanic like me could 'a' told him right away it was the ignition—"

Then she hated herself for being ashamed. He was a darn good mechanic, anyway. Funny big Dan. Anybody could see he was a country boy—his red face, his big hands with square-cut, battered nails. City men had such pale faces. And something different about their clothes. Perhaps they were tailored. It would be nice if Dan could have a tailored suit sometime. When Joey grew up she meant him to wear tailored suits always and go to Yale and play wonderful football and wear a gardenia in his buttonhole and bow over women's hands— a composite of John Barrymore and Red Grange. Would he be ashamed of her and Dan? Oh, no, he couldn't! Joey couldn't!

They walked through the Pennsylvania Station, not looking at each other or speaking. They didn't want anybody to suspect that they found it breath-taking. A redcap reached for the brown valise. Dan clung to it obstinately. Rosy whispered, "Oh, have him carry it, honey. Everybody does." Dan relinquished it and strode along looking em-barrassed as if he were thinking, "A big guy like me letting somebody carry that little bag!" But Rosy swayed grandly in the wake of the porter to the cab. She got in with the airs of a duchess. It was easy for her, a woman, to assume effete mannerisms. It was impossible for Dan to be anybody but Dan.

They drove to one of the biggest hotels in the heart of the city. Dan had remembered the name of this hotel because Harry Mintz had once sent him a post-card picture of it. The post card had said, Two thou-sand rooms with baths, and Harry had written beneath, "And I'm not in a darn one of them."

As the bell boy left their room Dan gave him a quarter. "Here, son," he said kindly, "buy some cigarettes for yourself."

The bell boy's blank expression did not change. "Thank you, sir," he said crisply, and the door slammed.

Dan grinned at Rosy. "I bet he feels pretty good. I bet he doesn't often get more than a dime."

"I bet he doesn't!" said Rosy.

She ran all around the large room, exultantly examining the blankets, the closet, the bathroom. "Dan, look! There's running ice water in here!"

He stood in the doorway of the gleaming bathroom. "Say, I'd like a shower like that. Do you suppose we could? I could put it in myself."

"And I could make a curtain. I've seen pictures of shower curtains made out of rubberized chintz."

"Yeah! Say, for Pete's sake what's this?" It was a silver contrivance on the wall with a little arm like a corkscrew. He poked it, thumbed it, looked at it from all angles. "Well, that beats me, Rosy. I can't figure that out." After a while he examined all the electric-light fixtures, the valet service in the door, and the dial telephone. He described a complete change of lighting that should be effective, and felt for his pliers with an absent gesture.

There was something wrong with the socket to the floor lamp, and Dan took out a screw driver which had lurked, unsuspected by Rosy, in his overcoat pocket. He cured the socket's illness with quick, deft movements of his blunt fingers.

Rosy had unpacked the little bag and put out the talcum powder, wash cloths, and tooth brushes. She wished there were more things to put away, but they hadn't brought much, for it was necessary to return on the midnight train to-night. Both Lorna and Dan must be back at work Saturday morning at eight o'clock.

It was eleven in the morning now. They planned to walk up Broadway and Fifth Avenue, and Rosy was going to buy some little things for the children and a pretty chemise for Lorna. At noon they would eat dinner and after that they wanted to go to the movies to see "The Cock-eyed World."

Dan said wickedly that after that he would like to go to a speakeasy.

Rosy laughed and said "Oh, Dan!" There had never been any drinking in her family, but she thought a little beer was all right.

"It'll be the most wonderful day!" cried Rosy. She hung her fuchsia crepe with the uneven hem line carefully in the closet. "Do you suppose I could afford a new dress if I saw something awfully pretty?"

"Sky's the limit," said Dan magnificently. "We'll shoot the works. That fifty was so much velvet anyhow."

They studied the menu spread under the glass top of the bureau. "Alligator pears—one-sixty. What are they, Dan?"

"Great big pears," Dan explained. "But isn't it a little bit steep here for us to eat?"

"Oh, sure," said Rosy. "I'd rather go somewhere, anyhow, I wish we could go to an automat. Lorna went to one in Pittsburgh, and she said she nearly died laughing."

"Well, you're the doctor, old woman," said Dan. He yawned, crushed out his cigarette. "Gosh my feet hurt in these shoes!"

"Mine, too!" They took off their shoes with domestic sighs of relief. Rosy lay down on the bed. "Listen, Dan, couldn't we take a little bit of a nap? I think we'll enjoy ourselves more if we're not so sleepy."

"That's a fine idea. I was just going to say I was sleepy, but I was afraid you'd be mad."

They climbed into the soft, luxurious bed. "Half an hour sleep be enough? If we're going to buy those things before the show—"

"Yes, I'll wake you in half an hour. If I say it over and over in my mind I'll be sure to wake up."

They didn't know about putting in a call at the desk. And if they had known it they would have been timid about the procedure.

Dan awoke first, and stared, puzzled, around the dark room. Through the window the lights of Seventh Avenue blinked like impish eyes. He felt wonderfully rested, relaxed, and contented. But the strange darkness confused him. Had there been an eclipse of the sun? None of the papers had mentioned it. He looked at his watch. It was ten forty-five.

Ten forty-five in the morning?

He tried to make himself believe that, but with a terrible sinking of the heart he knew that it was really ten forty-five at night. Just time to eat something quickly and catch the midnight train for Upson. Their day in New York . . .

Rosy lay with one plump arm twisted about her curly red head. There was a little smile on her mouth.

Ah, poor kid! She had been so tired.

It would break her heart when she found out it was night now.

He shook her gently. "Hey, Rosy! Listen. I guess we're the double-dyed idiots. Know what time it is?" He tried to grin. "Say, we got a good sleep for once, didn't we?"

When she understood, Rosy got up slowly, put on her shoes, and packed the clothes into the small bag. Then she laughed and laughed and laughed.

"Why, listen, hon, do you realize we not only got a good sleep but we saved at least twenty-five dollars? Or maybe a lot more if I'd found a nice dress in one of those Broadway shops!"

When Dan realized that she didn't care he didn't mind so much either.

"We won't tell Harry Mintz or Lorna," he said, tying his Oxfords. "We'll tell them all about how the movies were grand and we liked Grant's Tomb and Riverside Drive."

Just before they left the room Rosy went into the bathroom and sat on the edge of the bathtub. Looking up at the beautiful shower, she cried and cried and cried, with a ludicrous puckering of her mouth and chin. But she put on some powder before she came out, and Dan didn't notice the tear stains about her eyes.

Before leaving she carefully turned out all the lights.

"You're a good sport," said Dan.

"Applesauce!" said Rosy.

There are invisible qualities which catch and hold a man's heart. One of these is gallantry in women.

Ernest Hemingway

ERNEST HEMINGWAY *is the most influential writer of his generation in America. That generation was dubbed "lost" by Gertrude Stein, and Hemingway has memorably recorded its attitude—its disillusionment, its impatience with mere words, its fatalistic acceptance of life's treachery, its profound scorn of hypocrisy. "Nothing ever happens to the brave"—play and work and take the breaks. So impatient are Hemingway's characters with reflection that hostile critics accuse them of being athletic animals who don't think, but simply react.*

He is more than the voice of a generation. He is an artist seriously trying to extend the possibilities of prose expression. At its best his writing, terse, clipped, and unabashed, is extraordinary in conveying the effect of firsthand experience—whether it is the feel of a trout to the hand or the appearance of the dead on a battlefield. He has brought a new freshness to the language.

Ernest Hemingway was born in Illinois in 1898. He was a newspaper man before the War, served on the Italian front where he was wounded, and after the war acted as correspondent in Paris, the Near East, and, more recently, Spain. His books of short stories, In Our Time *(1924),* Men Without Women *(1927) and* Winner Take Nothing *(1933), have now been collected, together with a play, in the volume* The Fifth Column and the First Forty-nine Stories *(1938). His novels are* The Sun Also Rises *(1926),* A Farewell to Arms *(1928), and* To Have and Have Not *(1937).*

AFTER THE STORM *

Ernest Hemingway

IT WASN'T about anything, something about making punch, and then
we started fighting and I slipped and he had me down kneeling on
my chest and choking me with both hands like he was trying to kill
me and all the time I was trying to get the knife out of my pocket to
cut him loose. Everybody was too drunk to pull him off me. He was
choking me and hammering my head on the floor and I got the knife
out and opened it up; and I cut the muscle right across his arm and he
let go of me. He couldn't have held on if he wanted to. Then he rolled
and hung on to his arm and started to cry and I said:

"What the hell you want to choke me for?"

I'd have killed him. I couldn't swallow for a week. He hurt my
throat bad.

Well, I went out of there and there were plenty of them with him
and some come out after me and I made a turn and was down by the
docks and I met a fellow and he said somebody killed a man up the
street. I said "Who killed him?" and he said "I don't know who killed
him but he's dead all right," and it was dark and there was water
standing in the street and no lights and windows broke and boats all
up in the town and trees blown down and everything all blown and I
got a skiff and went out and found my boat where I had her inside of
Mango Key and she was all right only she was full of water. So I bailed
her out and pumped her out and there was a moon but plenty of clouds
and still plenty rough and I took it down along; and when it was
daylight I was off Eastern Harbor.

Brother, that was some storm. I was the first boat out and you never
saw water like that was. It was just as white as a lye barrel and coming
from Eastern Harbor to Sou'west Key you couldn't recognize the
shore. There was a big channel blown right out through the middle of
the beach. Trees and all blown out and a channel cut through and all
the water white as chalk and everything on it; branches and whole
trees and dead birds, and all floating. Inside the keys were all the
pelicans in the world and all kinds of birds flying. They must have
gone inside there when they knew it was coming.

I lay at Sou'west Key a day and nobody came after me. I was the

* From *Winner Take Nothing* by Ernest Hemingway. Charles Scribner's Sons, 1933.
Reprinted by permission of Charles Scribner's Sons.

first boat out and I seen a spar floating and I knew there must be a wreck and I started out to look for her. I found her. She was a three-masted schooner and I could just see the stumps of her spars out of water. She was in too deep water and I didn't get anything off of her. So I went on looking for something else. I had the start on all of them and I knew I ought to get whatever there was. I went on down over the sand-bars from where I left that three-masted schooner and I didn't find anything and I went on a long way. I was way out toward the quicksands and I didn't find anything so I went on. Then when I was in sight of the Rebecca Light I saw all kinds of birds making over something and I headed over for them to see what it was and there was a cloud of birds all right.

I could see something looked like a spar up out of water and when I got over close the birds all went up in the air and stayed all around me. The water was clear out there and there was a spar of some kind sticking out just above the water and when I come up close to it I saw it was all dark under water like a long shadow and I came right over it and there under water was a liner; just lying there all under the water as big as the whole world. I drifted over her in the boat. She lay on her side and the stern was deep down. The port holes were all shut tight and I could see the glass shine in the water and the whole of her; the biggest boat I ever saw in my life laying there and I went along the whole length of her and then I went over and anchored and I had the skiff on the deck forward and I shoved it down into the water and sculled over with the birds all around me.

I had a water glass like we use sponging and my hand shook so I could hardly hold it. All the port holes were shut that you could see going along over her but way down below near the bottom something must have been open because there were pieces of things floating out all the time. You couldn't tell what they were. Just pieces. That's what the birds were after. You never saw so many birds. They were all around me; crazy yelling.

I could see everything sharp and clear. I could see her rounded over and she looked a mile long under the water. She was lying on a clear white bank of sand and the spar was a sort of foremast or some sort of tackle that slanted out of water the way she was laying on her side. Her bow wasn't very far under. I could stand on the letters of her name on her bow and my head was just out of water. But the nearest port hole was twelve feet down. I could just reach it with the grains pole and I tried to break it with that but I couldn't. The glass was too stout.

So I sculled back to the boat and got a wrench and lashed it to the end of the grains pole and I couldn't break it. There I was looking down through the glass at that liner with everything in her and I was the first one to her and I couldn't get into her. She must have had five million dollars worth in her.

It made me shaky to think how much she must have in her. Inside the port hole that was closest I could see something but I couldn't make it out through the water glass. I couldn't do any good with the grains pole and I took off my clothes and stood and took a couple of deep breaths and dove over off the stern with the wrench in my hand and swam down. I could hold on for a second to the edge of the port hole and I could see in and there was a woman inside with her hair floating all out. I could see her floating plain and I hit the glass twice with the wrench hard and I heard the noise clink in my ears but it wouldn't break and I had to come up.

I hung onto the dinghy and got my breath and then I climbed in and took a couple of breaths and dove again. I swam down and took hold of the edge of the port hole with my fingers and held it and hit the glass as hard as I could with the wrench. I could see the woman floated in the water through the glass. Her hair was tied once close to her head and it floated all out in the water. I could see the rings on one of her hands. She was right up close to the port hole and I hit the glass twice and I didn't even crack it. When I came up I thought I wouldn't make it to the top before I'd have to breathe.

I went down once more and I cracked the glass, only cracked it, and when I came up my nose was bleeding and I stood on the bow of the liner with my bare feet on the letters of her name and my head just out and rested there and then I swam over to the skiff and pulled up into it and sat there waiting for my head to stop aching and looking down into the water glass, but I bled so I had to wash out the water glass. Then I lay back in the skiff and held my hand under my nose to stop it and I lay there with my head back looking up and there was a million birds above and all around.

When I quit bleeding I took another look through the glass and then I sculled over to the boat to try and find something heavier than the wrench but I couldn't find a thing; not even a sponge hook. I went back and the water was clearer all the time and you could see everything that floated out over that white bank of sand. I looked for sharks but there weren't any. You could have seen a shark a long way away. The water was so clear and the sand white. There was a grapple for an anchor on the skiff and I cut it off and went overboard and down with it. It carried me right down and past the port hole and I grabbed and couldn't hold anything and went on down and down, sliding along the curved side of her. I had to let go of the grapple. I heard it bump once and it seemed like a year before I came up through to the top of the water. The skiff was floated away with the tide and I swam over to her with my nose bleeding in the water while I swam and I was plenty glad there weren't sharks; but I was tired.

My head felt cracked open and I lay in the skiff and rested and then I sculled back. It was getting along in the afternoon. I went down once more with the wrench and it didn't do any good. That wrench was too light. It wasn't any good diving unless you had a big hammer or something heavy enough to do good. Then I lashed the wrench to the grains pole again and I watched through the water glass and pounded on the glass and hammered until the wrench came off and I saw it in the glass, clear and sharp, go sliding down along her and then off and down into the quicksand and go in. Then I couldn't do a thing. The wrench was gone and I'd lost the grapple so I sculled back to the boat. I was too tired to get the skiff aboard and the sun was pretty low. The birds were all pulling out and leaving her and I headed for Sou'west Key towing the skiff and the birds going on ahead of me and behind me. I was plenty tired.

That night it came on to blow and it blew for a week. You couldn't get out to her. They come out from town and told me the fellow I'd had to cut was all right except for his arm and I went back to town and they put me under five hundred dollar bond. It came out all right because some of them, friends of mine, swore he was after me with an ax, but by the time we got back out to her the Greeks had blown her open and cleaned her out. They got the safe out with dynamite. Nobody ever knows how much they got. She carried gold and they got it all. They stripped her clean. I found her and I never got a nickel out of her.

It was a hell of a thing all right. They say she was just outside of Havana harbor when the hurricane hit and she couldn't get in or the owners wouldn't let the captain chance coming in; they say he wanted to try; so she had to go with it and in the dark they were running with it trying to go through the gulf between Rebecca and Tortugas when she struck on the quicksands. Maybe her rudder was carried away. Maybe they weren't even steering. But anyway they couldn't have known they were quicksands and when she struck the captain must have ordered them to open up the ballast tanks so she'd lay solid. But it was quicksand she'd hit and when they opened the tanks she went in stern first and then over on her beam ends. There were four hundred and fifty passengers and the crew on board of her and they must all have been aboard of her when I found her. They must have opened the tanks as soon as she struck and the minute she settled on it the quicksands took her down. Then her boilers must have burst and that must have been what made those pieces that came out. It was funny there weren't any sharks though. There wasn't a fish. I could have seen them on that clear white sand.

Plenty of fish now though; jewfish, the biggest kind. The biggest part of her 's under the sand now but they live inside of her; the biggest kind of jewfish. Some weigh three to four hundred pounds. Sometime we'll go out and get some. You can see the Rebecca light from where she is. They've got a buoy on her now. She's right at the end of the quicksand right at the edge of the gulf. She only missed going through by about a hundred yards. In the dark in the storm they just missed it; raining the way it was they couldn't have seen the Rebecca. Then they're not used to that sort of thing. The captain of a liner isn't used to scudding that way. They have a course and they tell me they set some sort of a compass and it steers itself. They probably didn't know where they were when they ran with that blow but they come close to making it. Maybe they'd lost the rudder though. Anyway there wasn't another thing for them to hit till they'd get to Mexico once they were in that gulf. Must have been something though when they struck in that rain and wind and he told them to open her tanks. Nobody could have been on deck in that blow and rain. Everybody must have been below. They couldn't have lived on deck. There must have been some scenes inside all right because you know she settled fast. I saw that wrench go into the sand. The captain couldn't have known it was quicksand when she struck unless he knew these waters. He just knew it wasn't rock. He must have seen it all up in the bridge. He must have known what it was about when she settled. I wonder how fast she made it. I wonder if the mate was there with him. Do you think they stayed inside the bridge or do you think they took it outside? They never found any bodies. Not a one. Nobody floating. They float a long way with life belts too. They must have took it inside. Well, the Greeks got it all. Everything. They must have come fast all right. They picked her clean. First there was the birds, then me, then the Greeks, and even the birds got more out of her than I did.

Ruth Suckow

WHEN RUTH SUCKOW began to publish her first short stories twenty years ago, discerning readers at once recognized a fresh, independent, and vigorous talent. Her unaffected, closely-observed interpretations of midwestern people were both an affirmation of the vitality of the short story and a rejection of the slick formula-making that too many magazine editors had come to foster. She, like Sherwood Anderson, became a pioneering figure in the history of the American story, and if now her gifts seem less extraordinary than they did when H. L. Mencken first praised her work, it is because others have tried to follow the path she made. No short story writer in this country has done more to release the story from dulling "requirements of the trade." No writer has been more scrupulous in maintaining a high level of accomplishment.

Miss Suckow was born in Hawarden, Iowa, in 1892, and was educated at Grinnell College and the University of Iowa. Her first stories were printed in Mencken's Smart Set, and in 1924 she published her first book, Country People, a novel. After writing a second novel The Odyssey of a Nice Girl (1925), she collected some of her short stories for the book Iowa Interiors (1928). Among later novels The Folks (1934) was regarded by many readers as the greatest study of an American family ever made by a modern writer. Another collection of short stories, Children and Older People, appeared in 1931; and in 1937 Miss Suckow published Carry-over, an omnibus volume containing two novels Country People and The Bonney Family (1928) together with sixteen short stories.

GOLDEN WEDDING *

Ruth Suckow

"You ought to change your clothes, pa."

"What you in such a hurry to get my clothes changed for?"

"Well, you want to be ready when George comes in, don't you?"

"Aw, he won't get in today. How can he get the car through all this snow?"

"He will, too. Didn't they invite us out there?"

"Yeah, but they didn't know it was goin' tuh snow like this."

"You go now and put your other clothes on."

He grumbled, but finally obeyed—which was just like him.

Yes, but why did he always have to act this way? He had been doing it ever since they were married. He went through just so much grumbling first before he would do anything that he knew he must. It was the same thing over again every time they went anywhere; and all her prodding hadn't done any good that she could see.

"Won't get in today." That was just like him, too. If he knew that she was counting on anything, he had to hold out and belittle it, raise objections. He never wanted to admit that anything was going to turn out right. He always had good arguments to oppose to her faith, which he declared didn't take any account of the facts. But she still held to this blind faith of hers, and he to his objections. Sometimes things worked out her way; sometimes his. She pulling ahead, he pulling back. But the pulling had amounted to this much in fifty years—that he usually gave in in the end; and that she was a little worried in spite of her hopeful assertions that things were going to justify her belief.

So that now she did have to admit to herself that it was snowing hard. She was sure that George would come . . . but her eyes screwed up anxiously as she looked out over the plants at air thick with misty flakes. It looked as if it wasn't going to stop all day. The covered plants and peony bushes just outside were big clumps of whiteness. Fine dark twigs stuck out from the snow humped over the bending raspberry bushes. When she peered down the street, she could barely see the willow trees at the farther end, bluish and dim. Few passers-by came down this little side street where the old Willeys lived. The glimmery softness of the white road showed only two crooked tracks from a

---

morning milk-wagon that were already nearly filled, and as white as all the rest of the world.

Just the same, she believed that George was going to get in somehow. Mr. Willey came back into the room.

She looked up sharply, and cried in despair, "Oh, pa, why did you have to go put on that old necktie?"

"What old necktie?"

"Oh, you know what I mean! That old thing that I should think you'd be ashamed to wear around the place any more, let alone where we're going today. Go and put on your nice one—the one Jenny sent you for Christmas."

"Whatta I wanta put thet on fur! To ride out in this snow?"

"Snow!" she scoffed. "How's the snow going to hurt it? Can't you cover it up? Now you go and put that on. Try and look decent for once, today. You don't know who may be there to see us."

"Yes, you keep talkin' about that. Who do you think's goin' to be there?"

"Well, pa, you know the dinner's for us."

"Oh, I guess they aint such a whole grist of folks comin' out in all this snow jest to eat dinner with *us*."

"You go and put that other tie on."

He went. But her small frail hands, bluish and veined, shook a little at the crocheting with which she was trying to fill in the time. Her eyes moistened, and her mouth tightened into a childish grimace of weeping. Why did pa have to be so mean—and just today? They knew each other with such terrible intimacy that each had an uncanny perception of just what tiny things could hurt the other. Pretending this dinner wasn't going to amount to anything; depreciating her proud glory as a bride of fifty years; bringing up the sense of all the intimate, dingy happenings to tarnish the splendor of this occasion. Putting on that old tie today was a blow at her importance as his wife, at their marriage. He was always insisting upon their age and insignificance . . . and the silent, ghost-white street, the meagerness of their little yard with the few bushes, the bleak lines of the storm entry, those half-filled wheel tracks—all bore him out. Two old people, out of things, living in a little house off the main road. Denying the significance of their one achievement of continuity.

It made her bitter, too. What did it amount to that they had been married fifty years? Pa was so mean. Sentimental thoughts with which she had begun the day—unconsciously framing themselves in her mind in the grandiloquent terms of the town paper—were stringently checked by the terrible familiarity of his attitude. Just then, she didn't see why she *had* been such a fool as to have lived with him fifty years, why anyone should celebrate it.

Oh, well—but then, that was pa. After all, she knew how much the grumbling amounted to. Why did she let herself be so riled by it every time? Her best dress of dark gray silk, shimmering so nicely in the light from the window, raised the occasion, would not let her feel harsh. She knew that all those objections were partly a defense against the ill fortune of which they had had enough—he was not going to admit that things might turn out well, so that he wouldn't be disappointed again. He had had to make an assertion with that old tie to conceal a sneaking hope that this dinner might be a big affair, with people met to celebrate. Their long years together stretched out before her inner vision. . . . He'd been a pretty good husband after all, had worked hard, hadn't spent his money for drink or run after other women. She supposed you couldn't have everything.

She cried excitedly, "Pa! Here comes George! Now you hurry up and get yourself ready."

But she was the one after all, who had to scurry to the dresser for a last hair-pin to stick into her neat little knob of hair, to refasten her brooch in her lace collar, search for another handkerchief. He was ready, tie and all, and she was still in the bedroom when George, their son-in-law, came stamping in, scuffing the thick soft snow off his big overshoes.

"Aint you ready, folks?"

"Ma! Hurry up! Well, what in thunder's she doing?—thought she was ready an hour ago."

II

"I didn't know as you'd get here, George."

"Yep—oh, there's lots of ways of gettin' in."

"The old bobs still come in pretty handy, I'll tell ye," Mr. Willey said.

"Wrapped up good, grandma?"

"Oh, yes, I know how to bundle." Her voice came muffled through the fascinator that she had wound around her head over a knitted hood. She stepped along blindly behind George, down the covered walk, squinting against the misty flakes, trying to keep hold of the coarse brown hair of George's fur coat . . . feet making soft cavernous

dents in the thick snow. . . . "Why, there's Reverend and Mrs. Baxter
in the bob, aint it?"

"Yeah, they're going along with us. Can yuh get in, grandma?"

George lifted her over the side of the bob, and with a little scramble
she managed to get in. The Methodist minister and his wife were
tucked snugly into a corner. Mr. Baxter shouted jovial greetings. Mrs.
Baxter smiled and nodded, only glints of eyes showing between squinted
eyelids, two little hard red cheeks and a ruddy blob of nose let out
of the big scarf tied over her head.

"Get in. Lots of room."

Four ministerial feet in heavy, shining rubbers were hitched awkwardly over the thick robe covering the floor of the bob, through little
holes of which stuck bent yellow straws. The old people squatted down
stiffly, and Mr. Baxter drew the fur robe over them.

"Well, how's the wedding party?"

"Oh . . . I guess they're all right," Mrs. Willey said with shy
pleasure.

"Looks more like a silver wedding than golden wedding today."

"Yes, aint the snow bad!"

"All fixed back there?" George called.

"All fixed! Let'er go!"

"*Gid*-dap!"

The two big horses gave a plunge forward, the bob rocked, tilted
up on the edge of the road. . . . They passed the snowy willows and
got out on the main road, where there were already silvery-smooth
bob tracks above the gravel, no ruts to make the women give little
shrieks and put out hands blindly. The horses settled into an even trot.

"Isn't this nice, though?" Mrs. Baxter exulted.

All felt the exhilaration. The strangeness of the snow made the day
a festival.

They stopped trying to shout things at one another, getting the wet
small flakes in their mouths. They snuggled down on the straw under
the fur robe. The bob went softly through the new, pure whiteness.
Snow kept falling, falling, gentle as mist—tiny flakes, and big tufted
splotches. The road ahead and the road behind were lost—there was
only a place of dim white silence, and they moving in it.

"Are we there?"

"Why, I guess we are!"

"I didn't hardly know where we're getting."

The bob trundled over the wooden planks across the ditch and into the drive between willow trees that were blue-brown through the snow . . . misty, dreamlike, strange. The place had a festive air, too, because of the magic difference the snow made—the big barn roof white against the shrouded sky; the old wagon standing out there softly covered, rounded, all its stark angles gone.

"Well, I guess I didn't spill anybody out," George said.

They plodded to the house. George had let them out near the back door. They went up the steps, with a great stamping and scuffing— Clara in the doorway urging them in, they protesting that they must "sweep themselves off."

"Aw, it's just the kitchen—won't hurt this floor—come on in."

They went in, brushing and shaking. At once they were enveloped in warmth from the big range, with scents of chicken browning, biscuits, coffee, that their nostrils breathed in with a sharp delicious-ness . . . snow melting on their wraps, shaking off in a fine chill spray, making pools on the linoleum. They had a glimpse of Darlene, the youngest girl, at the stove, her face flushed a deep hot rose under the brown hair. Many dishes about. . . .

"Oh, don't stay in here!" Clara was urging. "No, your things won't hurt anything. Aint the first time there's been snow in this house today."

Mrs. Baxter and Mrs. Willey found themselves pushed into the chilly downstairs bedroom, where they unwrapped scarfs and fas-cinators; and where Mrs. Baxter—with apology and an alert glance at the door—yanked up her skirt and revealed black woolen tights which she tugged off her portly legs.

"Didn't know but what the snow might get in," she panted. "So I thought I'd come prepared. I guess I won't shock you ladies getting these off—hope none of the men'll look in here—might see a sight—"

"They aint around," Clara said comfortingly. "That's just all right— just the thing to wear."

Clara stood until the wraps were off. She was heated so that her grayish-brown hair looked dry and sheeny above her flushed face. She wore a large bungalow apron. And yet she looked festive, too. Extra clean, her mother thought, with her fat arms bare to the elbow, her perspiring neck.

"Well, if you've got everything you want—"

"Oh, yes! Don't pay any attention to us, Clara. I'll come out and help you just as soon as I get my things off."

"No, now ma. You go in the parlor and visit with Mrs. Baxter. I don't want either of you in the kitchen. Minnie'll help me."

"Oh, is Minnie and John here?"

"Yes, they're here. Minnie's here and the rest are coming."

"Well, I guess we'll have to obey," Mrs. Willey said with a pleased, flattered laugh.

They went into the parlor and seated themselves nicely. Mrs. Willey bent down to pick off a tiny straw clinging to her gray silk dress. Then she folded her hands and rocked.

She had half expected all along to find people here. And she saw no one but Clara and Darlene, and her daughter-in-law Minnie, who peeped in a moment. But the minister's family being here made it all right to have worn the gray silk—justified her in having ordered the necktie. Mrs. Baxter had on a dark blue taffeta that rustled as she rocked.

All the same, the old lady could sense an air of preparation. The odors in the kitchen, that quick, half-realized glimpse of dishes. . . . Even the bedroom had been specially clean; a glossy white scarf on the dresser, and the tatting-edged pillow shams. Clara had her best things out. The dining-room door was closed. Yes, and in the parlor too the chairs were set so neatly. The perfect order of the mission table suggested something beyond the every-day. As they rocked, Mrs. Willey was alert for every sound. There was a shrill excited tone in the noise and laughter in the kitchen, abruptly stilled, and then breaking out again; a tramping, a going back and forth that suggested more people in the house than were apparent; children's voices in some upstairs room.

The realization of the occasion brought back heightened memories. As she looked about the parlor, with its new Victrola and davenport and miscellaneous chairs, Mrs. Willey was on the point of saying to Mrs. Baxter, "This don't look much the way the place did when Mister and I first came here!" But she could not communicate that poignant memory of the old rooms, that was somewhere deep in her mind . . . small, bare, a few walnut furnishings, the feeling of raw openness all around. . . . She rocked. Her eyes had a distant look.

She was excited by the scents from the kitchen, the subdued bustle there.

Shouts came from outside. Mrs. Willey turned quickly to the window —the shouts an answer to her expectation.

A great bob load was coming up to the house, rocking as it turned into the drive—people shouting, waving. Mrs. Willey's hands felt trembling, her heart beat sharply, as she rose. The two old people stood blinking, she gratified, he sheepish, as a confused lot of people came tramping in, and crying:

"Where's the bridal couple? Look at the blushing groom! Well, well, well,—many happy returns of the day!"

III

The dining-room door opened—

"Go in, ma."

"Yes, the bridal couple must lead the way."

The old people protested, as a matter of duty, but inwardly pleased to be pushed in ahead of the others, to sit at the head of the long table. Old Mr. Willey looked sheepish—all this splendor for an old couple like them. But Mrs. Willey was exalted. She saw the room in a heightened dazzle of bright confusion—glitter of tumblers, plates and silver, shine of white and yellow. Laughing, calling appreciative murmurs . . . and then all of them standing there, suddenly and uncomfortably grave, Mrs. Willey still tremulous with excitement, while the minister gave the blessing, appropriately solemn and loud-toned . . . only one high, unconscious piping from the children's table in the corner.

The company seated themselves. The laughter, the murmurs broke out again.

"My, isn't this lovely!"

"Well, grandma, what do you think of it?"

"Well, I . . . I don't hardly know *what* to say," the old lady quavered.

The others laughed delightedly.

But as she sat at the head of the table, waited upon, getting served first, gradually things began to emerge out of that first shining confusion. She had known that this would happen, marvelous as it was. She recognized her daughter-in-law Minnie's best table cloth, pieced out at the farther end (where George sat) with one of Clara's—that table cloth with a crocheted border, that had been laid away in a chiffonier drawer to be peeped at by admiring women, that had been used only at the weddings of Minnie's daughters. The granddaughters must have brought their best wedding silver in carefully packed baskets. Clara and George had never accumulated any silver. But even more thrilling than this was the festive look of the room, with its decorations—the yellow crêpe paper drawn from the center piece and tied in bows at the four corners, the yellow tissue paper flowers (Gertrude was the one who had made those) at every place . . . and all the decorations converging significantly toward the center of the table where a huge cake frosted in yellow, frilled about with paper and flowers, stood under a hanging, ruffly, yellow wedding bell.

She looked about the long, crowded table. They were all there—all the people whose lives were bound up with hers and pa's. Clara and George, Minnie and John, grandsons, and grandsons-in-law, "connections" from Prospect and the country around; even Nels Olson, a prosperous merchant in town now, but years ago the Willey's hired man. The children at the square table were gleeful, and in their best.

And it was for them—for her and pa. She felt that exalted swelling in her breast, and tears stayed just behind the surface glisten of her eyes. Let pa say again that they were old and left behind, that no one thought of them, their day was over! No, this occasion was as glorious as she had been imagining it, in spite of his pessimistic objections. After all these work-filled years—fifty years—that had seemed at times to be petering out into a small meager loneliness, to sit here, honored, receiving again the delicious food and wine of personal recognition. All her people met to do her honor, to show that her life work had counted. . . . There was just one little twinge of disappointment. Robert had not come from Seattle. She had thought against all reason that when she opened this door, she would miraculously find Robert. She was glad she had mentioned it to no one. Pa's scoffing would have been justified.

It showed the grandeur of the occasion that Clara was "sitting down to table" beside George; although she gave hasty uneasy glances toward the kitchen. She had changed her apron, at the last minute, for her best dark green taffeta, above which her fat neck and face were flushed hotly. The granddaughters were waiting on the table, squeezing in between the chairs and the wall with their great platters of fowl, and bowls of gravy, and shining coffee pot. The meal was like an old-time harvest dinner in abundance—beside the chicken, two big platters of goose that Minnie had cooked at home and brought over warm, and covered, to be heated in Clara's oven; potatoes, baked beans, escalloped corn and peas, three kinds of bread and biscuits, relishes and jellies and pickles. But there were, beside, the special dishes that marked the importance of wedding and reunion dinners in Prospect and the country around—perfection salad, made the day before by the married granddaughters, great biscuit pans full of it; mayonnaise; and the women guests at the table had already discerned that the huge, yellow-frosted cake was Golden Companion, for which Lottie Disbrow had the community recipe.

The first absorption in food was giving way to a chatter. The children at the small table were yielding pieces of chicken that they had snatched, consenting to wait for "something *awful* good" promised by mothers in a deep whisper. Faces shone and glistened with warmth and food . . . and past the window panes drifted the last aimless flakes of the big snowfall.

There were satisfied, admiring comments on the food . . . "Aint these biscuits just fine! You make these, Clara?" "Yes, I was afraid they wasn't going to come out good." "Oh, they're lovely!" . . . "More chicken? Well sir, I've had a good deal already. Do you let folks have their third piece?" A worried, "Oh, now, Henry, you want to be careful. You've had enough." "Aw, go on and take it, Reverend. You need that drum stick."

John said expansively, "Don't pay any attention to the women folks! This is the time when a fellow can eat all he pleases. Can't have a golden wedding dinner every day."

"Yes, but then you'll expect your wives to run around for you maybe half the night because you eat too much again," Minnie put in smartly.

All the wives murmured, "I guess so!" And laughed significantly.

But the men said, "Time enough to worry about that afterwards. Anyway, I can't see but you're eatin' plenty yourself."

Talk, clatter of dishes, shrill voices of children, babies waking and wailing in the bedroom. Mrs. Baxter said, "It seems a shame to eat, and spoil this lovely table." But it was spoiled now—littered—the hand-painted jelly dishes messy, the salad bowls nearly empty, some of the crêpe paper torn and pushed askew. The dinner was ending. The girls brought heaping dishes of home-made ice cream with chocolate sauce.

"Oh, my! Look at this! I don't know where the room for it's coming from, but I'll have to find some."

Mr. Willey muttered, "What's this stuff on here?"

Mrs. Willey nudged him. "Pa! That's choc'late."

"Huh! Well, I dunno—"

"You rather have yours without, grandpa?"

"No, no!" Mrs. Willey protested, shocked. "He'll eat it this way. It looks lovely." She gave him a look.

The women perceived—felt in the air—what was about to come. But some of the men took up their spoons, began to eat, were reprimanded by their wives, and looked about, belligerent and then subdued. Mrs. Willey knew what it meant. Her small, faded mouth quivered. Clara was getting ready, half apologetic, to make the people listen. Gertrude stood behind her grandmother's chair, smiling.

"Sh! Sh!"

Clara got up with difficulty, squeezed between the table and her chair. Her voice had the toneless quavering of one unaccustomed and half ashamed to speak before others.

"Friends . . . and—a . . . As long as this is our mother's and father's golden wedding day, maybe now we better ask mother to cut the wedding cake."

Mr. Baxter relieved the silent moment that followed by a loud, cheerful, "That's right—let the bride do it." There were repetitions of "bride"; and they all laughed and murmured. Gertrude handed her grandmother the large knife; and the old lady, her hands trembling slightly, cut through the Golden Companion. The first wedge came out, moist, rich and yellow. They applauded. There were shouts of laughter when Mr. Baxter found the old maid's thimble in his piece. Lottie Disbrow had marked the location of the ring, and Gertrude gave that piece to her grandmother.

"I'm gona be rich—look mama, I'm gona be rich!" one of the children cried, holding up the coin.

The wedding cake was passed about the table. The groom's cake— a dark, spicy fruit cake—was brought in already cut. Plates of angel food were passed about—"Better eat this, girls," the women told the unmarried girls, "and save your wedding cake to sleep on!" Now all the table relaxed into a warm, easy, chattering exhilaration. Even old Mr. Willey had dropped his defenses, carried along by the spirit of the hour.

How did everyone feel it now? But those still talking relapsed into startled silence. Throat-clearings. The men looked down, rigid, embarrassed. The children turned with round, bright, fascinated eyes. Mrs. Willey's heart pounded. Clara's eyes began to water.

The Rev. Mr. Baxter rose, tapped on his glass with his knife.

"Sh—sh!" to the children.

Silence.

Mr. Baxter began to speak, while the old couple sat expectant, tremulous and abashed. Although he spoke in the slow, portentous voice that he used for the texts of his sermons, only significant phrases stood out, echoed and diminished in the minds of the listeners . . . "met together today . . . do honor to these two people . . . long journey together . . . achievement . . . God's blessing on this couple. . . ." Words irradiated by the winter sunshine that came through the windows now, sparkling off the snow, and striking iridescence from the silver and glass, the glossy table cloth, the warm shining heads of the listening children. The old couple at the head of the table took on a deep significance into which a lifetime of meaning was compressed, brought to a sudden realization. . . . "And now I have been asked by all these good people to present this token of the occasion. And may it always bring to your minds, Mr. and Mrs. Willey, the memory of the affection of your children and neighbors, and their appreciation of your having reached this day."

He took the package that Gertrude handed him. Old Mr. Willey had to receive it—unwrap it—show to everyone the silver loving-cup. There were applause, hand-clappings, nose-blowings. A telegram from Robert was read. The sun shone warmly on the silver cup with its gilt lining, flashed off the two handles. The old lady could only murmur that she "thanked her dear children and neighbors." But the old man was flushed, carried beyond himself. He saw everything heightened . . . and his vision, like his wife's, stretched back and back to scenes so long ago that he scarcely knew how to communicate his sense of them. But he had to say something if she didn't.

He remembered when he first came out to Ioway, he said. The bob ride had brought back old times. Things that the children had thought old stuff, the tales that old men tell sitting on benches in front of the hotel—they listened to now with a sense of drama and event, of time passing. When he talked about the wedding day fifty years ago, the children heard him with delighted appreciation.

"In them days, we didn't go to all this fuss we do now for weddings. When folks wanted to git married, they just hitched up and drove into town, and that ended it. Well, sir, I was thinking what kind of a day that was. Not snowy—one of them real muddy days—and I tell ye, there *was* mud in those times! You fellers talk about roads, but you don't know what roads can be. Well sir, we'd fixed on that day—and I was willing to put it off—but *she'd* got her mind set on it and of course it had to be." "Asa!" (Applause from the men, protests from the women.) "We took my brother Luke's team, and him and me and her and Luke's girl—girl he had then, name of Tressy Bowers, she went

out to Dakoty later—we started, with the horses all slicked up and
their manes combed out, to drive into Prospect. Well, good enough
goin' for a ways—and then jest out here beyond where Ted Bloom-
quist's place is now, we run into one of them mud holes about three
foot deep. Mud splashes up—girls screeches—and them two horses gits
stuck so they can't pull out. Well, then the womenfolks has a time!
They don't want us to git out in the mud because it'll spoil our wedding
clothes, and they aint nothing else for us to do but set there until
somebody comes along. Well, a fellow did, and he helped us, and we
got out.

"But then me and Luke's about as muddy as the team, and the
women thought it was awful to go into town to the preacher's that
way. So before we reached town—right down there by the crick, in
what's Hibbert's pasture now—they made us fellers git out; and the
girls they took sticks and whatever they could find handy, and tore
a big chunk out o' their underskirts—women wore plenty o' clothes
them days—and they made us fellers stand up and hev the mud scraped
off our pants—and then when we's cleaned up a little, we went along
to the preacher's and got married."

"And it's lasted quite a while!"

"Yes sir. He done a good job of it."

Mrs. Willey was flustered, protesting—"You know it wasn't near
as bad as that! What do you want to go and tell such things for?"—
blushing when the underskirts were mentioned. In the warm relieved,
easy glow that followed, the loving cup was passed about the table
and admired. The names of all the givers were engraved upon it; and
beneath the names of Asa Willey and Angie Pilgrim Willey, the two
dates:

1874–1924

Finally it was time to leave the table. The granddaughters would
not let the older women into the kitchen. Carrie Gustafson had been
called to help out with the dish-washing. The others went into the
parlor, all the women urging one another to take the best rockers;
looking out of the windows and commenting that the day had "turned
out nice" after all. They were moving still in that warm, easy exhilaration that came from food and coffee and that high moment at the
table. "Tired, grandma?" "Oh, no, I aint tired." The sun glistened
on the snow. Mrs. Willey sat in an ease in which it seemed that she
could never know what fatigue was—strangely free, her spirit exulting,

doing what it pleased with her body. The great dinner was over, but the day was not ended yet. There were things to come. And then there would be the afterglow lingering for a long, long time.

"Guess we'll have a little music, folks," George said.

They listened, sentimentally gratified, when a mellifluous baritone with an over-done accent sang "Silver Threads Among the Gold." But the murmuring and chatter, the pleas and shouts of children, sounded above the music—George's few "good" records, conscientiously played: "Il Trovatore," "A Perfect Day," "The Last Rose of Summer." George began to yield to the children's pleas for "This one, grandpa," "Play this one, Uncle George"—"Morning in the Barnyard" and the "Uncle Josh" monologue. The room was filled with a high noise of chatter, laughter, resolute music, sounds from the kitchen . . . and outside, the sun sparkling off the great, untouched spread of snow across the yard and the fields.

Shouts from the road, and then a running to the windows. Charlie, one of George's boys, came tramping into the house, ruddy-faced, in his sheepskin coat . . . from somewhere a jingle of sleighbells. The girls followed him from the kitchen, dish towels in their hands.

"Well, grandma and grandpa, do you want a sleigh-ride? Team's out here ready."

The others urged, laughing, excited, pushing toward the dining-room windows from which—through a blinding sparkle—they could see the sleigh. The young men were out there, patting the horses. They had got the Tomlinsons' old two-seated sleigh, that had been packed away in a musty, cluttered barn corner for years. It was furbished, decked with sleigh-bells the boys had found somewhere. John's big horses stamping, shaking and turning their heads to see where the jingling came from, letting out clouds of silvery vapor.

"It ain't cold—just grand! Better go, grandma."

"Take your wedding journey!"

The bedroom was full of women laughing, encouraging, helping to bundle her into heavy wraps—shouting to George to get his fur coat for grandpa. There was discussion as to who should have the place beside Charlie. "You go, Clara." "Oh no—some of the rest of you." "Mr. and Mrs. Baxter—" "Oh no, no! Let some of these little people." "Me, mama! I want a sleigh-ride!" "No, you children can have lots of fun here." "I think Clara'd ought to go. She's the only one aint had a ride today." Clara would not go without Minnie. The two plump women were packed into the front seat, with Charlie squeezed between them. The old Willeys had the place of honor in the back of the sleigh.

All the company flung on wraps, shawls, whatever they could pick up, and hurried out to the back steps to watch the sleighing party leave. The women hugged their arms in their shawls, squinted against the sharp flash of sun from the drive and the glistening shed roofs.

"Look-a there! Ain't that great?"

They pointed to the placard that the boys had fastened with a white streamer to the back of the sleigh—

JUST MARRIED.

"Get back—get those kids back. These horses are rarin' to go."

The clustered company waved, shouted, as the sleigh started with a jerk and frosty jangle of bells; watched it out of sight around the turn; then went back to the house, away from the white emptiness in which the new sleigh tracks had left steely marks.

Bobs had been along this road since it had stopped snowing, making the going easier. The jingling bells, the sky a dazzle of blue after the snow fall. . . . The world they were passing through was as shining, remote, as those ethereal, silvery hills and thickets drawn on frosty window panes. The sunlight glittered on the horses' smooth-curving backs. The sleigh runners left narrow, hard, flashing tracks. The low rounded hills were crusted deep with sparkling white. Corn stalks, humped with snow, shone stiff and pale gold. They had to close their eyes against that blinding radiance.

They drove into Prospect—not down that little street where the old people lived, but "right through the main part of town." People halted at the sound of bells, laughed at the placard, waved and called out greetings. The sleighing party, warmed still by the happy intoxication of the wedding dinner, responded hilariously.

"What's this—an elopement?" Judge Brubaker shouted.

"We've got to stop for you to have your pictures taken," Clara turned to say.

"Oh, no!" Mrs. Willey protested.

But she liked it—even grandpa liked it. They climbed the sloping wooden stairs to the gallery, covered with thick soft snow. The photograph would be in the Des Moines paper. "Prospect Couple Celebrate Golden Wedding." It would have their names—tell about the loving-cup, and Robert's telegram. The long room of the gallery, filled with snowy light, had the same dazzle as the street today.

The old man was lifted above his gloom and forebodings. He raised his wife's hand clasped in his, and shouted back at people. A crowd of little boys swarmed out into the road, making for the sleigh with ludicrous determination. "Hop on, boys!" he called jovially. They clung until a jerk at the corner threw them off the runners; and they stilled trailed the sleigh for a block or two.

IV

"Well, was the ride nice, grandma?"

"Oh, it was fine!"

"Get cold?"

"Not a bit cold. . . . I guess I am a little chilly now, though."

And as she trudged up through the heavy snow to the farm house again, she realized that the afternoon was late, the best of the sunshine over. When she went into the house, too, there was a different feeling. The big bob-load of people had left during the sleigh-ride. Now there were only the family themselves—the granddaughters sitting wearily in the parlor after their long siege in the kitchen. "Oh, children, be still a while. You make such a racket." Carrie Gustafson was plodding about in the kitchen doing the last of the cleaning up.

Standing in the bedroom, taking off many wraps, Mrs. Willey realized that the chill of the winter day had sunk into her. Her eyes were reddened, her small faded lips were blue. Her thin frail hands felt stiff and chilled.

"I guess you did get kind o' cold, grandma."

"Oh, not so very. It was awful nice."

They sat about in the parlor, where the grandchildren were playing with undiminished liveliness, even wilder than at noon. The older people were tired. The men talked, and the women, in two camps. Then some of the women went out to the kitchen to "set out a few things for supper."

"Now, don't go to a lot of trouble. We don't really need a thing after all we've et."

"Oh, the men'll want something. We'll just put on what's left."

But when they went to the table, the cold goose and chicken, the warmed-over potatoes, the different bits of salad, tasted good after all. There was a revived cheer, an intimacy in gathering around the remnants of the great meal after the outsiders had left. The glossy table-cloth had spots of jelly. The yellow bell still hung there; but the flowers and crêpe paper and wedding cake were gone. Plates of angel food and fruit cake, a little crumbled, were put on. The coffee tasted better than anything else.

Under the old woman's smile lay tremulous fatigue. She could scarcely sit at the table. As soon as the meal was over, George hitched up the bob to take the old people and some of the grandchildren home.

"Well, sir, it's been quite a day."

Now they had seen too much to notice the whiteness of the fields that they passed, the willows dim and motionless. The straw was warm under the robe on the floor of the bob. The plop-plop-plop of the big horses' hoofs was magically soothing . . . and the slight jolt and sway of the bob, going over rough places in the road, turning corners. . . .

They were all surprised when the bob stopped.

"Are we here?"

"Sure. Where'd you think we was?"

"Why, I didn't hardly know."

"Wait a minute, grandma, I'll lift you out."

George lifted her over the side of the bob. When he put her down, her legs felt stiff and queer, and she could scarcely make her feet move. She looked with a kind of wonder at the house standing bleak, silent, no shine from the windows, no smoke from the chimney. She entered it with the feeling of a traveler from splendid scenes who still carries a trace of their radiance with him to shed upon the familiar home. The little entry was cold.

"Wait a minute," George said. "I'll get your fire going for you."

"Oh, you needn't to bother, George."

"Sure. Only take a minute."

The sound of his heavy boots, the crackle of wood and rattle of coal, made a cheerful bustle. "There! I guess she'll warm up now." Then he was gone. Shouts of good-bye from the bob—it trundled off down the snowy street, around a corner.

It seemed as if the day could not be over. But they were in the house together. There was nothing for them to do, after all, but go to bed.

V

Their bedroom was chilly.

It took the old woman longer to put away all her cherished best things—her silk dress and lace collar and brooch. He was in bed long before she was, and impatient. She wanted to linger. The silk dress kept the feeling of the occasion. There was still a sense of exaltation—a jumbled memory of the dinner, the shining table, the jangle of bells and the sparkling snow; the greetings along the street.

But the old pieces of furniture, set with a meager exactness in the chilly room, exerted the long-known influence of the every-day. After all—it was this that they must come back to. The day had been fine, but the day was over and would not come again. Now, when they were alone, they had so little to say. Their room was too close, too familiar. Their knowledge of each other was too intimate for their speech to go outside its daily boundaries—they were afraid of that. They fell so quickly into the old ways with each other. She struggled against admitting this.

"The cake was nice, wa'ant it?"

"Hm?"

"The cake. It was nice."

"Um. Yeah. Ain't you nearly ready?"

"It was nice of the children to plan it for us that way, a surprise like that."

. . . But it was no use. He would never talk about things. He was pulling her down to the old level again. She folded away the lace collar, put the brooch in the small jeweler's box with her watch chain and an old ring. She would have liked to go over the whole day, picking out and holding up the intimate and significant details—but he wanted the light out, wanted to get to sleep. She was softened toward him, thinking of that moment on the snowy street when he had lifted their two hands. She was not ready to let the day go. Why couldn't pa ever talk things over with her? He'd talk more to anybody than to her.

She felt the still, frosty wonder of the night, as she stood a moment at the small window. And because she could not share this—felt so helpless—a little old, thin bitterness seeped through her proud exaltation, tincturing it with the familiar quality of every-day. . . .

He turned over restlessly. "Well, ma! Aint ye ever comin' to bed?"

"Well, can't you give me time to put away my things?"

"Hmp . . . 'time!'" And other mutterings, half intelligible.

But when she put out the light and climbed into the creaking bed beside him, he was at ease. He soon went to sleep. She lay beside him, awake for a long time. The irritation died away into calm, and she lay holding in the solitude of her own mind deeply felt, wordless things . . . as she had done in countless other nights; holding quiet both the beauty and the bitterness, encompassing them in the tranquillity of her comprehension . . . not so ill content, after all, that he should drop off childlike to sleep, and leave her and those incommunicable thoughts alone.

$\mathcal{O}$wen $\mathcal{F}$rancis

BORN IN 1898 in a small Pennsylvania town, Owen Francis began to work in the steel mills after his third year of high school. He enlisted for the World War, was gassed, and while in the hospital read the masters of story telling and determined to become a writer. After his discharge from the army he roamed the country as an itinerant worker: "I picked cantaloupe in Imperial Valley, washed dishes in San Francisco, labored over an open hearth furnace in Johnstown, swung a pick for hours-on-end into the roads of three states, stood behind a lunch counter in Syracuse, was a bus boy in Los Angeles, and sold spark plugs in Oregon and life insurance in Pittsburgh."

The interval of three years' study at the University of California and five years in Hollywood as press agent for movie stars were unrewarding for his purpose, and he turned once more to the steel mills of Pennsylvania. He told of this experience in the story "A Prodigal Returns," published in The American Mercury for November, 1929. A year later he wrote for Scribner's Magazine the first of a series of vivid stories about the steel workers whom he knew and understood so well. Besides the story here reprinted he wrote "Steel Mill Lullaby," "Hunkie Wedding," "Men Who Make Steel," "Record Month," and "The Saga of Joe Magarac."

THE LADIES CALL ON MR. PUSSICK *

Owen Francis

IN STEEL-MILL towns there is invariably a section called Hunkietown. Here live the major portion of the Hungarians, Poles, Czech and Jugo-Slavs, and the few Russians and Negroes who have come to work in the mills.

---

* From *Life in the United States.* Charles Scribner's Sons, 1933. Reprinted by permission of Charles Scribner's Sons.

Always near the mill, Hunkietowns are a jumble of unpainted, frame houses blackened by mill grime, crooked streets usually unpaved, and numerous children.

By day there is an incessant din from the children playing at steel making; by night there are louder shouts from the elders, a wailing of violins and accordions. And always there is the aroma of cooking cabbage mingling with the pungent smell of wine, fermenting malt, and the stench of defective sewerage systems.

To the Hunkie, Hunkietown is a highly desirable place to live. For one thing, he is grouped with people who have the same ideas of work and recreation as he has; for another, his rent is cheap, enabling him to tuck away in the mattress more money from his pay or send a larger amount each month to the old country, where what money he sends enables his parents to live without worry and pay the passage of a cousin who has ambitions to come to America—"land of the free." If left alone the Hunkie will go about his work in the mill cheerfully, become an American citizen as soon as possible, raise a family of future steel makers, and live at peace with the world. Try to change his mode of living and there will be a misunderstanding, as was the case of Peter Pussick when it came to the attention of the Excelsior Club.

Pete Pussick was a typical Hunkie steel worker. He had come to America six years before and had been given a job in the 18-inch mill shovelling scale from beneath the rolls. The pay was $4.40 a day. Pete considered himself a fortunate man. He worked hard, repaid the passage fare to a friend who had sent it to him in the old country, and, when he realized his ambition by being given a job pushing billets out of the furnace, an important position indeed and one that paid tonnage rates, like "American mans," he married a wide-hipped, red-cheeked Slavish maiden and settled down in Hunkietown to the business of raising a family. Pete did well: his work was satisfactory to his boss, his wife made good prune-jack, Young Pete and Johnnie had been born, and another child was soon to come. With the exception of an occasional billet falling off the furnace trough and delaying the rolling of steel, Pete had nothing to worry him.

One evening he sat on the porch of his company-rented house looking down at the mill. He had just come from work and was tired. His bare feet were propped on the porch rail, where his toes could cool comfortably. It had been a hard turn: steel orders had been small, the day had been warm. What breeze there had been had come down the river, blowing the heat of the furnaces toward him, and the end of his pusher bar had been stuck in the furnace for a half-hour. But the small orders were finished now, it was cool on the porch, a bottle of beer was on the floor beside him, and from the kitchen came the smell of *chicken paprikas* with noodles. Pete sighed with contentment. He was at peace with the world.

There came a brisk knocking at the front door. Anna, his wife, yelled at him to see who was there. Pete went slowly to the door.

Before him stood five women: there were Mrs. Walker, whom he recognized, having seen her with Henry Walker, his boss in the mill, and four others.

"How do you do," said one of the ladies. "You are Mr. Peter Pussick, I believe."

"Sure," Pete answered. "Pete Pussick, dat's me."

"Mr. Pussick," continued the spokesman, "we are a delegation from the Excelsior Club. Do you mind if we step inside?"

"Ya damn right, you comit inside. Maybe you liket bottle beer what my old lady makit," answered Peter, leading the ladies into the combination dining-room and bedroom.

"I don't believe so, Mr. Pussick, thank you," was the answer as the other ladies seated themselves, two on the bed, two at the table. "We have come to be of service to you and your family. Each year we have done our missions of charity and I will say we have done good work. And this year we girls have a new plan which I know, with your co-operation, will be successful. I have talked with Mr. Andrews, who is in favor of the plan, and he has given us the house rent free for our experiment. We have made the house into a model home and want you and your family to move in. Is that agreeable to you, Mr. Pussick?"

"Sure, ya betcha," answered Pete, not understanding half of what was said, but recognizing the name of Mr. Andrews, who was general superintendent of the mill.

Mrs. Pussick came into the room to stand twisting her apron in her hands embarrassedly. As usual she was barefooted and as usual she utilized the spare moment to quiet Johnnie, who screamed lustily, by nursing him at her breast. The ladies looked from one to the other trying to avoid seeing Anna Pussick's bare feet and breast, the beer bottles stacked in the corner, and the dirty bed linen.

"I was just telling your husband, Mrs. Pussick," the spokesman said hurriedly, "of our plan. We have a model home which will be a godsend to you, as busy as you are with the children. Just think, Mrs. Pussick, you will live in a home that has convertible tubs in the basement, carpets on the floor, a vacuum cleaner, chintz curtains, a tile bath. In fact, it has every modern convenience and is a home that any of us would be pleased to have. Isn't that just splendid, Mrs. Pussick?"

"Me no speak good English," Mrs. Pussick answered, looking hopefully toward Pete. "If Pete say all right—all right."

Pete turned to his wife, speaking in Slavish:

"Go back to the kitchen! What the hell you want come monkey around here for anyway? I fix this business."

Pete then turned to the ladies apologetically.

"Old lady never learn nothing. She just knowit how to cook, how to have kids, how to makit prune-jack, dat's all. You tell me and I fix everything."

"Then everything is arranged," continued the woman, glad that her work was done and she would have the opportunity of getting out into the air again. "We will have a van here early in the morning to move your personal belongings to your new home in New Plan Extension. And we thank you, Mr. Pussick, for your co-operation. We just know that our plan will work beautifully. Remember, we are relying upon you to set an example for the others and you won't mind if we bring the other Hunk—that is, the other Polish and Slavish matrons, to see just how a family should live, will you, Mr. Pussick?"

"Sure, bring everybody, dat's all right," agreed Pete heartily, as he shoved Young Pete out of their way with his foot.

The ladies left; Pete went back to his porch, where he sat with his brow wrinkled in deep thought. When supper was ready he gave up the perplexing problem until he could talk it over with his boss at the mill, but told Anna that in the morning the ladies would return, and for her to do as they said or he would clout her ears.

At the mill, the next day, Pete told Henry Walker, the heater, what had happened. Henry listened, trying hard to keep from laughing. He had often argued with his wife about her activities with the Ladies' Club, with the result that she never mentioned their plans until they were put into action. He now saw the opportunity of proving to her for once and for all that the members of the Excelsior Club would be of more value to the community if they stayed in their own kitchens, where, as he often told her, they belonged.

"That's good business," Henry told Pete. "Why, you will get a house for nothing. You won't have the fifteen bucks taken out of your pay each month. Go ahead, Pete, take the house."

Later on, to a group of us gathered in the shearman's shanty, he said laughingly:

"Jesus! but this is good. The Excelsior Club is on a rampage again, and what do you suppose they're up to now? They're moving Pete Pussick and his family into a model home to show the other Hunkies how they ought to live. Holy cats! What a shock they're going to get! I wouldn't miss this chance of razzing the missus for the world, so I told Pete to go ahead. All I got to do now is wait."

That night Pete went to his new home. Anna, her hair pulled in curls about her ears and dressed in a new gingham dress, sat stiffly on the sofa in the parlor, with Young Pete and Johnnie, scrubbed until they shone and too scared even to cry, beside her. In the kitchen three of the members of the Excelsior Club worked busily preparing supper while others straightened the curtains, moved the furniture, and rearranged the house to their liking. Pete moved about like a stranger. There was no beer in the cellar; Anna told him that the ladies had refused to bring it along, and there was no railing on the back porch for him to prop his feet against.

Mrs. Walker served them with supper, the other ladies sitting at the table with Pete and Anna. Pete ate the flat-tasting food, to be polite, in silence.

It was after eight o'clock when the ladies left, and Pete had a chance of going down to his old home for the beer. When he came back Anna had a pot of cabbage ready, Young Pete was lying contentedly naked upon the floor, and Johnnie was sticking the butcher knife in the table top.

On the next Wednesday afternoon, at the regular weekly meeting of the Excelsior Club, there were an even dozen Hunkie women brought in cars by the regular members. They were dressed in the finest for the occasion and all had the look of wonderment on their broad faces. Mrs. Walker spoke briefly:

"Ladies, we have invited you here today as our guests for a purpose. It has always been our aim to better the conditions of the foreigners in our midst and today you will see the result of what can be done with a home when the proper efforts have been made. We are going to take you to the home of Mr. Pussick. Last week Mr. Pussick lived as you are living now. Today Mr. Pussick is the proud occupant of a home equipped with modern appliances and lives under sanitary conditions. We will visit his home today, and I hope all of you welcome the opportunity of seeing what you too can do in your own homes. Mrs. Finney, will you take charge of the guests, please?"

Followed by the Hunkie women the members of the Excelsior Club drove to the home of Pete Pussick in New Plan Extension.

After they had knocked several times the door opened, and Pete, in undershirt and pants and with a sleepy grin on his face, greeted them.

"I workit night turn dis week and was sleeping," he explained.

They followed him into the house. During the week the home had undergone a change: the curtains were missing and the blinds were pulled down over the windows; the carpets were rolled into a corner (Pete explained with a laugh that they stuck Anna's bare feet); the furnishings were moved from the parlor, and two beds, now occupied by boarders, moved in; a half-fermented batch of beer filled the tubs in the basement; the remnants of breakfast were still on the table; a pot of cabbage boiled on the stove, and Mrs. Pussick, barefooted and with hair pulled tight in a knot at the back of her head, had her waist front opened for the convenience of Young Pete, who was noisily taking advantage of the opportunity.

The Hunkie women greeted Mrs. Pussick loudly and enthusiastically, while Pete offered them beer and cakes, telling them he liked the new home fine and that it didn't cost anything.

After an impromptu meeting, the members of the Excelsior Club departed hastily, leaving the Hunkie women with their former neighbors.

Pete is back at his old home in Hunkietown. He still has his job at the mill and on warm evenings sits on his porch with his bare feet on the rail and a bottle of beer on the floor beside him. To this day he cannot understand why he was given a house to live in for nothing one week and had it taken away the next.

We had a lot of fun with Pete at the mill after that. Asking him "How do you like your new home, Pete?" became a regular greeting.

When we would ask him he would make a sour face, and sometimes stick out his tongue in disgust.

When the Red Cross had their regular drive that year the Excelsior Club members did the soliciting as usual. The ladies stood at the mill gate on pay day and, knowing what was coming, we had our five dollars ready. One of them stopped Pete.

"I am a member of the Excelsior Club," she said, "designated to collect funds for the Red Cross. Now, I want you to contribute as much as you can, for remember it is in a good cause. Will you give five dollars, as most of the men are doing?"

Pete looked at her for a moment and then started laughing.

"Lak hell!" he answered. "You get 'nother mans, dis time. By God, nobody gone to play joke on me again."

$\mathcal{B}$urges $\mathcal{J}$ohnson

As a writer and a teacher of college classes in the art of writing, Burges Johnson has long been interested in the craftsmanship of the story. An ingenious reflection of this interest is his "Three Bites at a Story," which may be regarded both as a good yarn in itself and as a kind of "finger exercise" in plot manipulation. Although his favorite forms are the essay and light verse, he has contributed a number of short stories to Scribner's, Harper's, Century, and other magazines.

Burges Johnson was born in Vermont in 1877, graduated from Amherst, and held various editorial posts in New York City before accepting a professorship of English at Vassar College. He has also taught at Syracuse University and at Union College where he is now chairman of the Field of English. Among his books are Essaying an Essay (1927), A Little Book of Necessary Nonsense (1929), Sonnets from the Pekinese (1935), and Professor at Bay (1937).

THREE BITES AT A STORY *

Burges Johnson

HARKNESS walked softly as he passed the door marked "Manag. Ed." and then stepped out more briskly toward the long stairway leading to the street. He had half intended to knock, but he knew so well what the result would be. A voice would have barked "Come in!" followed by an irascible "Well, what is it now, Harkness? Don't you know I'm working on my leader and can't be disturbed? By the way, I'll need a half column for my lawlessness editorial. See you save it for me."

Old Man Popham certainly belonged in a story, thought Harkness.

* Published by permission of the author.

His pompousness and his finality of utterance were reflected in those editorial leaders which made the city-room grin and curse, and all the staid old subscribers nod their heads in grave satisfaction. Personally Harkness rather liked the old fellow despite his Jovian paragraphs; though he thought any managing editor showed bad judgment as well as bad taste who bullyragged his city editor in the presence of reporters. "You're soft" the Old Man would complain; "too much humor and too little of the drill sergeant. You're letting 'em loll around. You've got too damn much salt and too little iron in your system." Popham was proud of his metaphors. Pity he never laughed at himself.

Half-way down the stair Harkness lingered. The ancient hand-rail was ink-stained and greasy. Habitually his fingertips had beaten a light tattoo upon it as he hurried to the street on an assignment, or his hand had gripped it as he hauled his weary body up the long stairs on his return. Today was an anniversary. Ten years ago he had left footwork for the assistant city-desk. The promotion had flattered him, but he had often regretted it. Now as city editor he was more of a slave, body and mind, than in those care-free days. Then he was sure, like every other reporter, that he would soon write his short stories and begin his novel. Now he knew he never would. All the legacy left him of that boyish certainty was the habit of seeing himself moving through the successive incidents that might have shaped into a plot.

All today this whimsy had possessed him like a nostalgia. *"The city editor opened the street door and paused a moment listening to the jumbled voices of the city. He often felt, as he stood in this battered doorway, a rush of regret for the old days when he had gone out to sift those voices. There was one adventure of his reportorial past . . ."* Harkness grinned sheepishly at his own fancy. He stepped into the street, turned north, passed half-a-dozen doorways and entered Jerre's crowded little bar-room and grill. There he swung himself onto a high stool that was hurriedly vacated by one of the young men in the place. It was Landon, he noticed; a likeable young cub, half impudent, half respectful. Typical reporter; might fit well into a story as a bit of color, or even as the central figure.

"I'm through, Chief," grinned the lad; "take my seat. I was just composin' a great lead."

"Save it," said Harkness; "so am I through, upstairs. Mac is putting the final to bed, and I'll go back and look in on him, after a beer and a swiss. Been a quiet day." Jerre had been hovering behind the counter, alert for an order, and now instant with service thudded plate and mug upon the bar.

"Thanks, Jerre"; Harkness pulled a respectable roll of bills from his pocket to feel for silver further down, while young Landon joined acquaintances at a near-by table.

A man on the next high stool turned and spoke. Harkness noted first of all the thread-bare coat, the soiled shirt collar, the unshaven chin, and then the heavy-lidded eyes half meeting his from under a shapeless hat-brim. "Kin I see ya a minute alone? Got a story."

Harkness was unsurprised, unhurried. He quaffed deeply, took a large bite of the sandwich. Presently he said, "Sure. Go ahead."

The dull eyes included half the room in a shifting glance. "Alone, I says. I gotter have quiet."

Harkness finished his beer, munched the rest of the sandwich. "Jerre's got a room he calls his office. We'll take a look." He slid off his stool, pushed his way along the length of the bar and around the end, opened a door and led the way into a small room,—dingy, unfurnished, except for a table and two chairs. One window lighted it. He turned to see the man closing the door and locking it. Then the hand which pocketed the key was raised suddenly and he stared at a steadily pointed gun, its graceful shape marred by a bulky silencer.

"What the hell is all this?" Harkness whipt out the words.

"Gimme that roll," said the man; "make it snappy. It's in yer pants pocket."

"Why you crazy fool! You haven't any get-away. That room out there is full of my friends."

"I aint waitin' for 'em. I knows my business. Fork out!"

Harkness lounged against the table and stared his wonder. "Look here, man, that alley outside the window goes just one way—toward police headquarters. Only a perfect shot would prevent at least half a yell. I might be yelling now instead of talking. Jerre'll try the door any minute to see if we want beer. It's a thousand to one. Is this a joke, or are you practicing dramatics, or"—he studied the man's eyes—"are you really a desperate fool?"

The man heard him through, finger still steady on the trigger. "Shut up and fork out. I aint afraid to shoot and then take what I get."

Harkness grinned. "You know," he said, "you're phoney. You're not in character. Even your dialect isn't authentic. You can't get away with this. Why not come across, yourself? I'm no cop."

"Authentic enough" growled the man. "I got away with it once today in a tighter spot than this."

Harkness laughed outright. "Authentic!" he jibed. "Fine word for a tough guy! What are you—an author?"

The man hesitated a moment, then spoke and the crude dialect had disappeared, but the weapon still pointed. "Newspaper man—Minneapolis; quit like a damn fool for a job further east, and I've reached bottom. No jobs—no food—kicked out of the last place I tried. Chanced on this gun in a ditch when I got bounced off a freight: some poor devil must have thrown it there when he found the cops closing in on him. I kept it and I've used it once today. This is again."

"You couldn't see it through," said Harkness with cool conviction. "Tell me about that other hold-up. Come across! I'll buy your story, and I don't need names."

The man eyed him somberly for a moment. "There was nothing to it," he said. "I had the gun; I could pawn it or use it. If I pawned it they'd be after me for some other fellow's crime. So I used it. Half an hour ago. Not much of a haul—so I figured I could do it twice if I could do it once, and then pull my freight. So fork over that roll."

Harkness's thoughts were racing. He might make his move and not be quick enough. The man might be just crazy enough to shoot, and the shot would take him between the eyes. The man would bend over his body where it lay, half under the table, find the money, step quickly to the window, lower himself out and run down the alley. He would be caught half a block away, perhaps killed as he ran, or in course of time hanged. But he would spoil a good story by his perfect shot. True, there would be a front-page story in the *Gazette* with generous editorial space. Old Popham would spread himself. But it wouldn't be the real story. Obviously Harkness couldn't tell it, and there would be so much good stuff left over. Popham ought to be in it; and that accusation of too much humor and too little of the drill sergeant was sharp characterization. This hold-up man himself—not an ordinary type.

"—Figured I could do it twice if I could do it once," the man was saying; "so fork it over!"

Harkness grinned a friendly grin. "It's not often I offer space rates and a bonus to a reporter out of a job, and then have to repeat the offer. Here's your pay in advance"—he took out the roll and laid it on the table. "Where was this other hold-up? How did you feel when you were at it? Did the other fellow show fight?"

The man stepped forward, not lowering his gun. Harkness's eyes narrowed. Now was the moment when he might leap and grab. "That's what I thought—gun's not loaded! Jerre! Pete! Landon!" But there would be no fight in the man. He would allow himself to be disarmed and hand over the key of the door. He'd get five years; and there would be space on the police blotter, and many pages of court record, and a half-column or so in the papers. But Harkness could neither play himself up nor spread the story of a newspaper man in hard luck who had turned crook. There'd be no real story; just an attempted hold-up that failed.

—The man stepped forward and laid his gun on the table. "Guess I'm a damn fool" he said, "but I never was paid yet for a story and didn't deliver." He too grinned a little. "My other victim was a pompous guy, but when he saw my gun the wind went out of him like a pricked balloon. It was in another bar and grill like this one, only bigger and cleaner, up this street beyond the *Gazette* building—"

"Bordoni's," nodded Harkness.

"I'd been thrown out of the *News-Express*. So desperate by that time I guess I demanded a job, and they didn't like my lack of tact. I drifted into that Bordoni place to think, and maybe pick up a bit of left-overs," he flushed. "I was hungry and mean, and I had this gun. I saw a fat old guy at a table, and he flashed bills, just like you. Somebody spoke to him, passing his table, and I learned he was a newspaper man. There was a side room with two doors, and no one in it. I looked in, and both doors had keys. I got the roller towel from the wash-room and chucked it in there under a chair. Then I went back and pulled my stuff about a story. He fell for it like a lamb. All excitement, like he was a kid reporter; didn't want anyone else to notice us, so it would be *his* story. When I got him in there and pulled the gun he just folded up, like I said. I gagged him with the towel, took his bill-fold, locked him in, and came here. Figured I could do it twice and then leave town. Here's what I lifted off him. It wasn't worth the risk. When I get a job I'll mail it back to him."

Harkness glanced at the leather fold,—then glanced again. Seized it, explored it, then began upon such a fit of laughter he had to sit down. "Man, man," he choked, "what you've done!" He sat there a moment or two in thought, punctuated by guffaws. Suddenly he seized the gun, grasping it as a hefty little bludgeon. "Hand over that key!"

The man started, hesitated, cursed, but tossed the key to the table.

"Sit down" said Harkness sharply, "and stay there!" He unlocked the door, without letting his eyes leave the man for more than a second. "Pete!" he called; "Landon!"

There was a scramble in the bar-room. "Yes sir," said a voice. It was young Landon. Here was a way to use that young man again.

"Beat it up to the Old Man's room. Tell him I've got to see him—right here—I'll apologize for bringing him down. Hustle!"

Harkness was at the table again. "What's your name?"

"Smith." The answer was sullen.

"Don't be a fool" said Harkness. "I'm not double-crossing. You're a made man. What's your real name?"

"Keyser,—Peter B.—one time Minneapolis *Globe*—" the answer was grudging.

"All right, Keyser, I'll do the talking; you play up."

There was a mild commotion outside and the door was pushed open. A heavy querulous voice said "What's all this, Harkness?"

Harkness blocked the doorway a moment. "Thanks, Landon; run along. Important conference. Come in, Mr. Popham. Meet my old friend, Peter B. Keyser, late of the Minneapolis *Globe*. He wants a job."

Popham ought to be described at this point, but one must hurry now with the action. Harkness had missed an opportunity to picture him back there in the first paragraph.

The managing editor was breathing heavily. Amazement and annoyance were in his eyes and voice, but he stepped in, and Harkness closed the door. Then the face became apoplectic. "Thief!" he burst out—"Gun-man! Harkness, do you know who you've got here? Call the police!"

"Just a moment, Mr. Popham. My little joke. Once a week for the past eight weeks you've been giving us one of those editorial leaders about lawlessness,—playing up your theory that if citizens had the guts to resist any man with a gun in his hand there'd be no more hold-ups. We were fed up with them in the city-room. When this old police reporter friend of mine turned up I took advantage of the fact, and persuaded him to try you out. Here's your bill-fold; better count the money. The gun wasn't loaded."

But Mr. Popham was loaded, and he blew up. "Harkness, damn your sense of humor; you're fired! As for this man, loaded gun or not, he committed a crime, and you'll both suffer for it. Let me out!"

"Certainly, Mr. Popham, certainly. But you can't expect me to keep quiet about this if I'm fired and move across to the *News-Express*. Have to serve my new employer unreservedly. And you can't keep the towel out of court. Wouldn't go well with all those editorials."

Popham sank into a chair, and his head drooped. He was thinking, but not much thought was needed. Harkness was sorry for him. The Old Man had his points, and only a very little too much fat covered them.

"Don't take it so hard, Mr. Popham. You're sure of my loyalty. And now that you've taken this man Keyser on,"—Popham blinked once—"you couldn't get a word out of him that would hurt the paper or you."

Popham blinked again, stood up, laughed with surprising heartiness on such short notice, and put out his hand. "You've got too damn much humor, Harkness, but I'd hate to lose you. All right, Keyser, report tomorrow morning. And Harkness—forgot to tell you—I want top of second column for my lawlessness ed. tomorrow. Little longer than usual—most of the column—but it's a damn good one" he added as he bustled out, "a damn good one, if I do say it."

Harkness paid his reckoning and swung to his feet. Then he paused and grinned at the seedy-looking fellow on the next stool: "And take the price of yours out of this, Keyser" he said, slapping a coin on the bar. The man looked around at him startled and suspicious. "Thanks," he said. "My name's Smith."

"O well" sighed Harkness, "let it ride. Come on, Landon, back to the mines."

Marjorie Kinnan Rawlings

MARJORIE KINNAN RAWLINGS *has not always belonged to the region
about which she writes with the fresh perception and the intimate
sympathy which made the readers of South Moon Under (1933) feel
that they had discovered a new country. She herself found this country—the hammock country in the region of the Oklawaha and St.
Johns rivers, Florida—after a childhood in Washington, D.C., an education at the University of Wisconsin, and an interval of several
years' work in newspaper feature writing. Now she lives near Hawthorn, taking care of her orange grove and writing with the conscience
of an artist about the people and the land she has come to know. To
the Northerner such a novel as The Yearling (1938) with its story
of the boy Jody and the fawn Flag may have almost the quality of
pure idyll, but Mrs. Rawlings never forgets that nature is uncaring
and man is sometimes brutal. Her tenderness is unsentimental.*

*Mrs. Rawlings' other novels are Jacob's Ladder, published in Scrib-
ner's Magazine in 1931, and South Moon Under (1933). She has also
published several short stories in various magazines, one of them "Gal
Young Un" winning the O. Henry Memorial Award for the best
short story of 1933. The story here printed was called by James Boyd
"a practically perfect story."*

THE PARDON *

Marjorie Kinnan Rawlings

A DRIFT of small hard leaves clicked from the live oak at the main
gate of the penitentiary. The man Adams looked at the sky
and turned up the collar of his misfit coat. Then he turned it down

---

* From *Scribner's Magazine,* August, 1934. Reprinted by permission of the author
and *Scribner's Magazine.*

again, with the uncertainty of a man for whom decisions have been made too long. The sky was gray, mottled with the harsh blue of November.

A guard at the gate said, "Don't forget anything. It's unlucky to turn back."

The trusties clustered at the gate-house made a clatter of thin laughter.

A man serving a life sentence said, "It's more unlucky, turning in—" and they laughed again, with the sound of men applauding from a distance.

Adams put his hand inside his coat and touched the sharp edge of parchment paper that was the pardon. He wanted to show it. His fumbling was ignored and he let his hand drop at his side.

He said, "Well, so long."

The guard answered indifferently, "So long," and spat into the sand. The group was silent; immobile; understanding the futility of speech or movement.

Adams shuffled into the roadway and searched the line of parked cars of visitors. A woman fluttered toward him and retreated to the protection of an open Ford. She lifted a hand, entrenched on the far side of the high hood.

He called "Emma!" and moved his feet faster, his pulse thick in his throat. He saw that it was Joe Porter at the wheel of the Ford.

He said, "Hey, Joe."

Joe said, "Hey," and absorbed himself with the gears.

Adams turned to the woman.

He said, "Hey, wife."

She looked at him. He thought that he had never before noticed how much she looked like a rabbit. When he had worked on the penitentiary farm they had killed dozens of rabbits. They sat staring with frightened eyes and trembling noses, pretending not to be seen.

He asked, "Where's the two young uns?"

She said, belligerently, "I didn't see fitten to carry 'em. I ain't never yet carried 'em here."

"No," he said.

He hesitated between the front seat and the back, and climbed stiffly into the back. The woman licked her lips.

She said, "I reckon you'll be glad of the room," and stepped into the front seat beside Joe Porter.

Joe said, "First chance in seven years to spread hisself eh, Emma?"

Adams stared at the back of his wife's neck. It was plump, with the hair dark and low-growing.

The Ford lurched in the deep ruts of the sand road leading away from the penitentiary. Adams bounced on the worn springs, holding his black felt hat with one hand against the wind that whipped through the rear of the car. It seemed to him that he was moving with incredible speed. The prison farm trailed out of sight; the nursery telescoping into the dairy farm; the dairy farm into the hog pasture; the hog pasture into the open fields; the fields, at last, beyond the bridge, into pine woods.

Nine miles beyond the penitentiary the Ford left the dirt road and ran smoothly along a paved highway. The pine forest appeared to march, closing its ranks, filling in its shadowy spaces with its own dark members. He abandoned himself to the motion. He felt as he had once done under the influence of gas in the prison hospital. He was conscious of a rush of blood in his body, of wind in his ears, of an increasing numbness; conscious of a darkness on either side of him through which he passed, hour after hour, without effort or volition of his own.

Joe said to Emma, "It'll be dusk dark, time we get him home."

Adams stirred uneasily. He felt like a sack of mule feed, or a hog's carcass. He wanted to call to Joe above the wind, to apologize, to transform himself into a sentient being. He hunched forward, gripping the front seat with his fingers. No one noticed him and he could not think of anything to say. He leaned back and the pardon creaked inside his pocket. His heart jumped with relief, as though he were a child, forgetting its recitation on the school platform, who had been prompted.

He shouted, "I didn't some way never figure I'd get a pardon."

There was no answer. He thought he had not been heard. Then he wondered in a panic whether he had actually spoken. He may only, as he had so often, have imagined his voice in loud clear speech.

Joe said, "Didn't nobody else figure so, neither."

The car began to pass through towns he knew. Near Busby marsh, turtle doves in a flock hurled themselves toward the night's watering place. Their under-bodies were rosy, facing the west. Then they passed into the sunset and were at once black, as though charred to crisp by its heatless fire. The doves wheeled and could be seen plunging to the marsh edge.

Adams called out, "We been having them things by the hundreds in the chufa fields. You got chufas this year, Emma?"

She turned her head half-way across her shoulder and shook it briefly.

Joe said, "She can't raise nothing hardly, for other folks' hogs. Rooting and rambling. Them fences you left wasn't none too good when you left 'em. I've mended parts of 'em."

She added, "Joe put new brick to the old chimney for me. I couldn't scarcely have managed."

The Ford left the highway for the sand road that led through Busby flat woods to the farm. The wind was high. It lashed the flexible boughs of the pine trees and they flailed the car top. Adams recognized landmarks; an abandoned cattle pen; a sinkhole; the pond where his hogs had always watered. Yet the house moved unexpectedly into sight around the familiar bend, standing suddenly small and smoke-gray in the November twilight.

The Ford stopped outside the gate. The chinaberry tree in the yard had grown higher than the house, and in the silence of the car's halting, its gaunt branches scraped the bricks of the chimney. Adams passed through the gate and took a few steps up the path. The place seemed uninhabited; not his home, but merely a place he had remembered. He waited for Joe and Emma, lagging behind when the woman lifted the shoestring latch and pushed open the door.

At first the large kitchen appeared empty. He blinked. An oak fire glowed dull in the range. He searched the darkness. There was a stirring in the dusk in the far corner. The faces of two children took shape, their eyes wide and glinting.

Adams called across the room, "It ain't Quincie and Lila, is it?"

Joe said, "Ain't either of you girls big enough to get the lamp going without somebody should come home and light it for you?"

Emma said, "Hush up, Joe. I'll light it. Go fetch me an armful of wood. You girls come speak to your father."

The girls moved woodenly into the light of the swinging kerosene lamp. They too, he thought, looked like rabbits, small-mouthed and frightened. They had grown tall and thin.

He questioned, "Quincie, that you with them longest legs? Let's see—I been away seven years—you must be thirteen. Lila? You about ten—"

He held out one hand toward them. They did not move.

Emma called, "Start the bacon, Quincie. We'll never be done."

Adams stood in the middle of the floor. The bustle of supper-making stirred about him. Joe returned by the back door, dropping wood in the box with a clatter. He washed his hands in the basin on the water shelf and combed his thick hair with a comb he took from behind the mirror.

He called to Adams, "Set down, man."

Emma said sharply, "Let him come wash first. He's got that jail house smell."

Adams flushed.

"We all kept mighty clean up there," he said. "We had running water. My clothes is all clean."

Joe dilated his nostrils, testing the air with relish.

"It's the disinfectant they use in them places," he said.

Adams moved to the water shelf and washed his face and hands carefully. He dampened an end of the towel and rubbed it inside his collar. He smoothed his hair with his hands and edged into a chair at the long table against the wall. His wife leaned over him to place a plate of cold biscuits. He caught at a fold of her skirt as she moved away.

He said playfully, "Don't make company of me in my own house, Emma."

The thin girls gaped at him. He was uncomfortable, as though he had tried to make a joke in church. Emma brought hot dishes from the stove. She stood looking at the table, and pushed back a forelock of hair. The gesture made her in an instant his wife again. He remembered teasing her about it, telling her she would wear herself baldheaded. He had seen her lie in bed beside him, her hair braided neatly for the night, and lift her hand to brush back that very soft dark forelock. A sharp sweetness struck through him.

A rap sounded on the door. Voices lifted, and the near neighbors, Mr. and Mrs. Mobbley, came noisily into the kitchen. Adams jerked from his chair to shake hands. He was pleased and proud that they had come to see him on his first night at home.

Emma said in a low voice, "Fetch Jackie," and in the confusion the older girl went out of the room, returning with a child of four, rubbing his eyes from sleep. Adams glanced at him vaguely, turning back to Mobbley with a delight in the visit. The Mobbleys were obese and florid. Insisting that they had already eaten, they sat at the table and joined heartily in the food.

Mobbley said between mouthfuls, "I ain't one to hold his trouble against a man. I've always said, you didn't do no more than ary other man in a quarrel, and the argument going against him. If you hadn't of pushed that sorry Wilbur out of the rowboat into the lake, he'd of pitched you out and it would of been you drowned and him in the penitentiary."

Adams said eagerly, "That's what the new superintendent said, getting me the pardon. He said it was self-defense, like, and I shouldn't never of been allowed to plead guilty to second-degree murder. It was manslaughter at the very worst, he said, and that ain't serious. Not twenty years sentence, no-how."

Mobbley frowned.

He said, "Course, it ain't every neighbor would come to you right off, like me. There's folks figure the jail is the jail."

Adams said humbly, "It's mighty good of you, coming." He hitched himself about on his chair. He asked eagerly, "You want to see the pardon?"

They leaned forward in their chairs.

"I've always wanted to see one," Mrs. Mobbley said.

The kitchen became vitalized with the pardon. He drew it out slowly from his inside coat pocket and unrolled it. The large seal shone in the lamp-light. The parchment paper was thick and white, like a magnolia petal. Mrs. Mobbley trailed her fingers over its smoothness.

Mobbley asked, "Do the governor hisself sign them?"

Adams pointed to the scrawled name.

"I'll be blest." Mobbley studied the signature. "He don't write no better than no other man."

Adams apologized, "I reckon he gets to writing careless, with all them state documents to sign."

The four-year-old boy whimpered.

The girl Quincie whispered, "Lila, give him some gravy for his grits. You know he don't like 'em dry."

Mrs. Mobbley said, "I reckon home cooking tastes mighty good after jail-house rations."

He brought himself back with a start from the pardon to the table. The food was inferior to the penitentiary fare.

He said reluctantly, "Well, we had mighty good rations. Not much change—If you got tired of beans, why, nobody felt bad about it— you had to eat beans, or go hungry, right on."

Mobbley and Joe Porter laughed with him. His numbness dissolved.

He was aware of the warmth of the room and the crackling of wood in the stove. He stretched his legs under the table, feeling the pine boards of the floor rough under his feet.

He said, "Dogged if the floor don't feel peculiar. The floor up yonder was cement."

The penitentiary loomed before his sight; immensely white; modern and bright and handsome. It was a cross between heaven and hell, he thought hazily, a fabulous place where doomed men moved in a silent torment in the midst of electric-lit, immaculate surroundings. The gray unpainted room about him, fire-lit and intimate in the November darkness, was the world, and he had come back to it. His toes and fingers tingled, as though life had begun to prick through a disembodied spirit.

The two girls and the small boy sat stiffly in the pain of young sleepiness, their eyelids fluttering. The Mobbleys took up the talk and chattered of county news, correcting each other. Emma said, "I'd ought to clear up the table," but she sat still, moving only her hands, now along the edge of the oilcloth table-cover, now up and back across her hair. Joe Porter filled his pipe and teetered in his chair. The Mobbleys rose to take their leave. Mrs. Mobbley looked quickly from Emma to Adams, and then to Joe.

She asked with an excited sucking of breath, "Joe, you coming with us tonight?"

He teetered a moment. He moved slowly to the stove and knocked out his pipe against it.

"I reckon," he said and joined the Mobbleys at the door.

Emma called after him, "You studying on digging the sweet potatoes tomorrow?"

He hesitated.

"I'll let you know about it."

Adams left them talking in the doorway and walked to the larger of the two bedrooms. On the bed was a quilt he recognized. His heart raced. The door closed after Joe and the Mobbleys and the front gate clicked. Emma walked past into the bedroom and knelt down to draw extra quilts from a box under the double bed. He followed her and crouched beside her. He put an arm around her waist. It felt rounder than he had remembered it. Her flesh was soft and pliable.

"Emma—"

She did not answer. Her eyes focused without attention on the box of quilts.

"No need to be so rabbity with me, Honey," he said.

She dropped a quilt on the floor, handling it absently.

"I been thinking the past hour," he said, "about sleeping with you."

She said desperately, "You got the right. The law gives you the right."

He stood up.

"I hate you should talk about the law for such as that." He pondered, "I reckon I feel strange to you."

She straightened, standing with her back to the wall, the quilt bundled in front of her. Her mouth quivered. Her eyes were like a mare's in panic. He looked out into the kitchen. The two girls were putting away the last of the dishes. The four-year-old boy lay curled on the floor in front of the stove, sleeping like a puppy. Adams stared at him. A sick fear paralyzed him.

"Emma—" He seemed to hear his own voice coming from a great distance. "Who's the little feller?" The woman did not speak. He faltered, "I figured he come with Mobbleys—"

The older girl bent protectively over the child, arranging his clothes. The younger girl called shrilly, "He's ours."

His head thickened. He shook it to lighten the weight. His mouth jumped at one corner. He turned toward the woman. She stood with the back of her head pressed hard against the wall, rolling it from side to side. Her eyes were closed. The quilt slid from her arms and she lifted one hand and crammed it against her mouth. She opened her eyes and looked at him.

She cried out in a loud voice, "I had to have help on the place. A woman can't farm it alone. The fences was near about rotted to the ground."

He opened and closed his fingers. Fire moved in tongues across his numbness, as though life and death competed for his body.

The woman whimpered, "Nobody didn't figure on no pardon."

The wind in the chinaberry was blowing from an alien world and passing to another. The room lay inside it, lost in stillness. The fire died away through his limbs and the numbness possessed him. He moved to the door of the smaller bedroom.

"Where must I sleep?" he asked.

"I just don't know—"

He looked from one bedroom toward the other.

She offered hurriedly, "The girls is mighty big to be sleeping in the bed with a man—but the little bed is awful small."

The girl Quincie carried the child toward them. She looked questioningly from the man to the woman.

Emma said, moistening her lips, "You'll have to let your father say, about the sleeping."

He said dully, "You and the two girls keep the big bed."

The girl went into the smaller room with the child; fumbled with its garments and left it and went away. The door of the large bedroom closed behind her.

The man felt chilled. He undressed by the kitchen range, hanging his clothes on the wooden pegs on the wall. He turned out the kerosene lamp. Darkness closed in on him. Where he had been cold, he was suffocated. He shuffled across the boards in his bare feet, careless of splinters, and threw open the front door. The wind bit like cold teeth into his body. He shivered and closed the door, standing uncertainly with his hands against it.

It seemed to him that he had forgotten something. He rubbed his forehead. He had forgotten the pardon. He had left it lying on the table, where something might happen to it in the night. A gust of wind might blow it near the stove and a spark ignite it. He groped his way across the kitchen and laid his hands on the parchment. An ember glowed in the range and the seal shone briefly in the blackness. He rolled up the paper and went to his bedroom.

The boy lay sleeping. Adams could not bring himself to lie down beside him. He sat on the edge of the narrow bed, warming his feet one with the other. He twisted the roll of parchment aimlessly in his hands. The room was a black box over him. He crossed his arms over his stomach, bending his upper body, swaying.

He pictured the penitentiary at this moment. It would be not quite dark, for a light would be glinting at the far end of the corridor. It would be not quite silent, for the guard would walk along the cement floor. It would be not quite lonely, for every man had a cell-mate. A wave of desolation washed over him, so that he thought he should never swim to the top of it.

Beside him, the child mumbled. Adams drew a deep breath. He reached out his hand and touched the fine hair of the head. He trembled. He moved his hand slowly over the small hump of body under the quilt.

"Pore little bastard," he said, "I reckon you wasn't much wanted."

The boy cried out sharply in a nightmare. His legs convulsed. Adams drew the quilt closer about the thin neck.

"Running from the booger-man, sonny?" he asked. "Don't you fret—I've got a-holt of you."

He slipped under the covers and pushed the pardon carefully beneath his pillow.

Josephine Johnson

WHEN JOSEPHINE JOHNSON won the Pulitzer Prize with her first novel
Now in November (1934), it seemed remarkable to many critics that
so distinguished a story was the work of a young woman of twenty-
four. It was youthful in its sustained intensity and its poetic realization of life's cruelty and beauty, assured and mature in its command
over style. Now in November dealt with farm life in the Middle
West, a life of bitter struggle against drought, poverty, and incipient
madness, and in her later work Miss Johnson has even more strongly
sounded a protest against the social injustice which increases the odds
against man's chances of living decently and well. Her book of short
stories Winter Orchard was published in 1935, and Jordanstown, a
novel of industrial strife under the depression, appeared in 1937.

Miss Johnson has a poet's love for the beauty of every-day things,
a poet's hatred for the destructive standardization of the present social order. Her story "Arcadia Recalled" revives a memory of happiness; and all her writing looks to the possibility of restoring serenity
in American living.

She was born in Missouri in 1910, educated at Washington University in St. Louis, and has lived most of her life on a farm in St. Louis
county.

ARCADIA RECALLED *

Josephine Johnson

THE TRAIN moved like a caterpillar. It would be supper time when
they got there, and Aunt Elizabeth was probably making the
biscuits already. Millie and Mary Josephine discussed the possibility

* From *Winter Orchard and Other Stories* by Josephine Johnson. Simon and Schuster,
New York, 1935. Reprinted by permission of the author and of Simon and Schuster.

of there being fried chicken the first night, and decided it was more likely to come the next day. If not tonight, next day, certain as life is. Aunt Effie was putting on her hat already, and letting the porter sweep her shoes. So was Katy, but Mary Josephine and Millie were embarrassed and shook their heads when he wanted to whisk them off. When he was gone, they wished he had.

There were only three of them, but they felt like a whole herd because they were sisters and everybody remarked on how much they looked alike, although they didn't at all. Millie was nine, and Mary Josephine ten, and Katy was twelve. They all had navy blue straw hats with velvet streamers down the back, and a big steamer-trunk had to be sent along with them every summer when they visited the aunts—a trunk full of pant-waists and button-drawers and hot, perspiry undershirts that always rolled up from the bottom and showed out at the neck. Millie and Mary Josephine worried about these shirts sometimes, but Katy never did. If she didn't like shirts, she took them off. Any old time she felt like it. She had big eyelashes, too, long as whisk-brooms, only curlier, and heavy hair. Mary Josephine's was thin. Very soft and exasperating. Very straight. They told her she was terribly homely right after she was born.—One eye slightly popped, and a kind of furry face. This was a consolation sometimes, because she looked so normal now.

It was after six o'clock when they reached the farm. They could see the purple clematis and the rambler roses, fist-big and red as fire. Everything was cool and quiet, and the smell of new-cut grass came from the lawn. It was so clean they felt almost alien and out of place, train-soiled and smeary. There was a sizzling sound—a warm, delicious sound. Aunt Elizabeth came out in her apron with the white braid edge, starched and beautifully clean just as always.—Everything was just as always. The good-smelling fir trees, the striped awnings and the croquet set waiting to be put out on the grass—just as always. Mary Josephine sighed with ecstasy. Nothing had changed.

Inside were the cool white beds, the extra cot, the pitchers full of cistern water, and the clean towels on the rack—the beautiful white towels embroidered in satin stitch with roses. The aunts always gave them the best of everything they had. Always. That they were only children made no difference. It was wonderful.

They ate fried ham with soft fat edges crumbling with brown

sugar and cloves. Big cold tomatoes, firm and hugely sliced. And biscuits with butter drooling out the sides. And mounds of mashed potatoes with the wonderful, indefinable, mysterious taste that nobody else could ever make. And there were ripe strawberries, with powdered sugar mounds to put them in, and a white iced cake full of soft fudge filling in between its layers. It was heaven to be hungry and eat great piles of food.

Then, when even the icing crumbles had no tempting look, Aunt Elizabeth stacked the dishes up for tomorrow and they went outside where it was still washed light, though the sun was gone. They sat a long time sprawled in the hammock, pushing with their feet, and then turned somersaults on the ground so that the cut grass clung in myriad places to their clothes. When it grew darker they watched the moon-flowers open, slow as the hour-hand of a clock. So slow they could run around the house and back before the blossoms came out wide and white in the shadow. They were deliciously sweet, but if you smelled them too long or often the fragrance went away.— Millie nearly smothered herself by sticking her nose in deep and then drawing breath to make the petals shut around it, the way petunia-trumpets did.

There were fireflies by now, turning off and on in the grass and making candle-stars above their heads in the fir-needles. They chased the lights with cupped hands, and saw how they swarmed thick like burning gnats over the clover field, beyond the garden where the red phlox were. Then Aunt Effie walked with Katy over across the road where Aunt Edna lived and Katy always stayed, because Ruth (who was their cousin and belonged to Aunt Edna) lived there.—Millie and Mary Josephine hardly ever played with Katy the rest of the summer. They sat on the porch now and watched the lantern flicker down the path, like a huge and steadfast lightning bug, and turn down the road and in at Aunt Edna's gate. Then they knew Aunt Elizabeth was going to say it was time for bed, and so commenced to talk very fast and trundle each other about for wheel-barrows, but all the time knowing she was going to say it just the same.

Still it was nice to squeeze into the wash-tub, scarcely big enough to stretch out legs, and slop here and there with the rag, not scrubbing raw nor seriously, since the lamp was high up in the room and there was a pleasant gloominess down near the floor. When they were dry and in clean nightgowns carefully shaken from the trunk, they sat out on the porch again with bottles of cold soda-pop, waiting for the lantern and Aunt Effie to come back along the road. They felt safe and confidential in the dark, and told each other things no inquisition could have squeezed by day.

Afterward Mary Josephine lay awake in bed, just to enjoy it longer. There was the loud sound of frog voices, and once the faint whine of a mosquito. She pulled the sheet over her head, and he got discouraged after a while and went away. A little screech-owl came near in the moonlight. She could see its round head moving on the shoulders. . . . It was nice to be alive.

It was cool in the mornings, and the cut grass soaking wet. It clung all over their bare feet and in between the toes. The shirts felt good, after all, though they thought best to complain some so as not to set a precedent. The morning-glories were open, with the sun coming through their purple skins, and kept jumping nervously on thin stems. Aunt Effie was always out where the garden was, pulling crab-grass in the strawberry-bed, by the time they were dressed; and they went out to help, because crab-grass was easy to pull and left big bare places when its roots came out.

Then they drank each a glass of pump-water, because it was supposed to be good for you, and then ran down to the woodshed and back to hear its splosh inside. They could smell the coffee coming out the window, and another smell like sausage, and they looked at each other furtively, edging near the window but ashamed to peer directly in. Then Aunt Effie pulled up the last green octopus-like clump and said she'd better help Aunt Elizabeth put things on; and they thought perhaps there was something they could do to help, and rushed in the back door, not certain what this thing was going to be, but full of good intentions.

"You can pour the water now," Aunt Elizabeth would say: and that meant everything was ready—even the napkins, separately ringed, in place.

Millie always wanted coffee because she couldn't have it at home; and Aunt Effie poured her a tablespoon in a cup. It looked sort of like brown cream when she got through, but had a coffee-smell and made her feel old and individual. The sausages were really there— not link ones, but in neat dark pats—and plate-size pancakes wallowing in syrup. Mary Josephine ate four, and felt mild and generous toward the world. Millie's cover-alls were tight and smooth where her breakfast was.

They didn't even need to wipe the dishes afterward, so they did, acting as though it were a great task, and spent much time in the china-closet counting all the ginger-ale glasses. They were pale brown, with blue enameled flowers around the top, and Katy had already asked to have them when she got married. Mary Josephine hadn't asked for anything because she couldn't decide what she wanted. There were thin, translucent cups like sea-shells, and a dark turquoise one, gold-rimmed, and a baby egg-cup; but then, too, there was a holder for pot-handles, made of velvet and in the shape of a gray cockatoo with a pink crest and each feather round and cut out on the sides. He had a soft feeling. Then there was the coffee-cozy, very large and fat, made of reddish-black cloth and quilted on the inside with red satin. They used to put it on their heads sometimes. If she hadn't hated coffee so much Mary Josephine might have asked for that. But she never could decide on any of the things definitely, and so came after a time to feel she owned them all.

Later in the morning, after Aunt Effie brought them back from marketing, Mary Josephine and Millie always went down and played around the barns, or shut each other in the grain-shed where the wheat was piled. There were stones sunk in the grass to make a path to the barn, and near them a mock-orange tree with great bad-smelling balls of fruit, green and small-poxed on their rinds. They stopped to watch a tumblebug rolling up his ball of sheep manure, struggling with it in the dust. Pretty soon another tumblebug came along to help, but pushed the wrong way so that they got nowhere. There were no tumblebugs at home. They belonged to the country dust and all the long and lazy summers, so that to see one gave a pleasant feeling of leisure and excitement.

The path ended at the water trough where the calves came thirsty and fighting in the evenings, and there was always something drowning to scoop out with a leaf. Mary Josephine got a burdock and began to fish out the beetles. Most were black and stupid, but sometimes they had bright green wings like polished tin; or there were wasps with bodies of blue steel. There were always ants too, alive and swimming desperately. It seemed hopeless to try and rescue all of them, but she put leaves to float so they could climb aboard and breathe a while. It worried her a few minutes, but one couldn't stand all day in the sun fishing bugs out of a trough, and more kept falling in with gross stupidity. The grasshoppers were worst because they were big and it was hard not to notice how they struggled. You could pretend the ants were dead by not looking close, but the grasshoppers were too insistent and unsubtle in their desire to stay alive.

After a while they both gave up and wandered inside the barn, half-afraid there might be something in the empty stalls. It was quiet inside and hung with chaff-filled cobwebs. The stalls had a nice smell of old dung and straw, and there were bins of grain along the wall. The barn was shoebox-shaped and partitioned off in separate sections, each with a door that opened only on the outside, so that you had to go out and come in again each time. Rabbits burrowed in the dirt floor, and there were rows of phoebe nests in gradual stages of decay, their moss linings gray and dry. It was dark, and only one window opened in the wall near where a ladder went up to the loft. It was only a short way up, on account of the low ceiling, but Mary Josephine was afraid. She was afraid of falling off the ladder or having the loft floor crumble underfoot, so she never got courage to go beyond the second rung.

Millie went all the way to the top and walked around. She reported nothing but bales of straw and loose hay. Still Mary Josephine wished she could get up there, without going up. She felt there must be something else, and hated herself for being such a coward. However, there was some consolation in creeping outside and slipping the door bolt while Millie's seat and legs were all you could see through the trap-door and she couldn't get down in time to put her feet in the crack. After a while Millie got tired of pretending to jump out of the high loft opening, and decided it was time to have the jailer go off and forget to lock up the prisoner. So Mary Josephine pulled open the bolt with great secrecy, and ran around the barn.

She hid herself in the harness-room where there was a big mud home of wasps up under the rafter, and long brown excrescences on all the logs. They looked like the scabs on jungle natives in the geographic magazine—the lumpy places where they cut themselves and rubbed dirt in. The wasps went in and out a knothole and paid her no attention. She thought it would be fearful and exciting to be stung, and remembered how Katy had looked once, her face all bloated out and swollen like a monstrous pear. It had given her eyes a sphinx-like and oriental look, and her expression never changed for a whole day. It was worse almost than the time they had the mumps, only then they were all swelled together and had to keep from looking at each other because it hurt to laugh. They'd looked horrible—like frogs getting ready to sing.

Millie was a long time coming near the harness-room. Mary Josephine could hear her poking around in all the stalls and talking to herself. Sometimes she would say silly things in hopes to make her laugh, but Mary Josephine would think about the Armenians in the war and about the time she stood up to answer Miss Howey's question out loud when they were supposed to be doing a written examination, and Miss Howey said, "Well, wasn't that nice?—you told everybody!" so she didn't feel like laughing in the least.

It was comfortable and dark. Something kept moving around in the corner, and she hoped it was a mouse, because there was no telling what a skunk might do if it was a skunk; but after a while it went away. She couldn't hear the rustling of Millie any more, and wondered if she had been abandoned. Pleasant mournful thoughts took the place of listening to be found, and she felt comfortably as though the rest of the world had vanished some place and left only herself and a foot or two of warm blackness, with wasps sizzing in and out the hole.

Millie was cooling herself outside in the barn-shadow. She lay flat on her stomach and sorted little piles of gravel according to degrees of gold. If Mary Josephine got tired of waiting, or too suffocated, she would just come out of wherever she was at. She was sure to come out, anyway, when Aunt Effie called for dinner, because she knew there was going to be sweet potatoes with brown-sugar goo. Millie saved an especially glittering stone to mollify her in case she was very mad.

She only had four piles when she heard Katy and Ruth bellowing together. "Milleeeee!" they bellowed. "—Milleeeee! Mary Josepheeeen!" They sounded mad. Millie scrambled up, the gold ore scattering every which way, and started to run. Then she remembered Mary Josephine. Maybe she hadn't heard, or maybe she was smothered some place, or had run her hand on a rusty nail and gotten tetanus already. There were lots of rusty nails about everywhere—

"Mary Josephine!" she screamed. Loud and needle-shrill. Tears started to come out of her eyes. Then the harness-room door opened with a burst, and Mary Josephine stumbled out, still half-asleep. She blinked like an old toad, and looked all red and puffy. Millie wiped her eyes, mad because she'd cried for nothing. "Hurry up!" she shouted. "They called us. They called us almost an hour ago, I guess!"

"I went to sleep," Mary Josephine said. "It was so dark I went to sleep."

"I bet they're mad at us for being late. I bet Katy and Ruth are mad, anyway. They sounded mad. They sounded mad as hops."

—Katy looked at them with a glare. She was all red and cross from shouting in the sun. "What made you kids so late? Haven't you kids any sense at *all?*" She stuck her hands on her hips and sneered.

"None of your business," said Millie. She marched right by Katy and sat down where her napkin-ring was. There was a big pile of something wrapped up in a towel next to her plate. "I bet they're raisin rolls," she whispered to Mary Josephine. "I bet Aunt Effie made them for us especially."

"I see some sweet potatoes, too. . . ." They talked with their hands fixed so that Katy and Ruth couldn't hear across the table. ". . . They've got bubbles coming up around the edges still. They're cooking still, even in the dish."

"We'll get the drum-sticks, because we always did last year, and Katy'll get the wish-bone—you watch!"

"I don't care. It's too greasy to pull, anyway, and I always forget what to wish." Mary Josephine opened a roll, and shoved her whole pat of butter inside. She squashed it hard so the butter would ooze out and look like yellow blood. Then she and Millie tried to see how much would go inside their mouths at once. Millie got all her roll except one corner in, but she had to pull it out again. Mary Josephine took another roll—there were two kinds, one with raisins and one without: this time she took one without, and put her chicken leg inside. The skin was so crisp you could hear it crinkle, but was lush and soft.

Katy and Ruth drank Welch's grape-juice. It was sort of exotic to do that, Millie thought—drinking with your meals. But it was better to have more room for other things than just liquid.—Katy and Ruth could hold a lot inside, though. Once they ate a thirty-pound watermelon all by themselves. They always did exciting things like that. Once they stayed up all night in the haystack. Aunt Edna let them.— She let them do 'most anything. "Didn't you get cold?" Mary Josephine said. She was sort of awed. "Oh, along toward morning it was icy."—Katy looked nonchalant. "Our clothes got wet with dew, but pooh! My heavens! you act like you thought it was something dangerous!" She hoped everybody did.

"I bet you went to sleep," Millie announced. She could always punch a pin in anybody's romantics.

"No, we didn't—Not more than an hour or two, anyway."

"Blah!" said Millie.

Mary Josephine scooped up a big piece of sweet potato. The juice was dark and slimy. Just right. She wondered what the kids would do this summer. Katy and Ruth were "the kids" to her and Millie, and she and Millie were "the kids" to Ruth and Katy. . . . It was nice to have somebody to do exciting things for your benefit. One summer Ruth and Katy tried to see how long they could wear their shirts without washing. They went two whole weeks, and it was awful to be near them at the table. Aunt Edna made them wash the old things outside in tubs. Millie and Mary Josephine snickered at them, but that was just because they were jealous Ruth and Katy said.

A hot wind came in the window. It smelled of hay and honeysuckle. Everything was just as it used and ought to be. Millie stretched. "I hope there's ice-cream for dessert," she said. She said this because she knew it was sitting in the cellar right now.

"Well, for goodness' sake! You rude thing!" Mary Josephine said, but her mouth was full of mashed potatoes (there were two kinds of potatoes, mashed and sweet) so Millie didn't have her feelings hurt, because she pretended it was probably something else that was said. The kids looked disgusted, but they liked looking that way. It was older.

Everybody felt sleepy when dinner was over. Millie and Mary Josephine wished they could fall down and sleep right away. They were stuffed. They felt comfortable and good-natured, not inclined to quarrel or get mad at anything. They put the dishes away and shut each other in the china-closet. Mary Josephine sat down on the table-cloths.

Then Millie opened the door and made her get up. "Aunt Effie is going to read out of Wilkie Collins," she said. Her dress was off, and there was nothing but pants and waist on. You could see her skinny shoulder-blades sticking out.

Mary Josephine had a hard time pulling off her dress. It was damp, and clung to her all over. The difference when she took it off was so wonderful she wanted to put it on again so she could take it off again. Millie jumped on the bed and put her feet in the air. "What happened last time?" she wanted to know. She never remembered from one time to the next, because she hardly ever listened anyway.

Mary Josephine lay down on the cot. It felt good; her feet were tired from carrying her dinner around. The awning was down, and a breeze came in the door. She could see the pond from where she was, and the cows standing up to their knees in it, switching at the flies. Ruth and Katy had gone off some place. They never took naps. Sometimes they even worked after lunch, cutting grass. And when there was haying, Ruth was water-boy and drove back and forth from the fields in a peaked straw hat.

After a while they went to sleep. Aunt Effie read on, flapping cautiously at flies and at the wasps that came down from the attic. She was afraid they might wake up if she should stop, and so went on with dark intrigue and coming calamity, heard only by bluebottle ears. Aunt Elizabeth slept a while, too, on the sofa, her hands still in a knitting way, and the collie's tail thumped gently on the porch. Wagon-wheels rumbled a long way off and faint. . . .

After a while Katy and Ruth gave a big whoop outside and started running toward the gate. They were always rushing off. Suddenly and with furious speed. Mary Josephine and Millie sat up, used as they were to these mysterious fleeings. They thought perhaps a neighbor bull was loose again. Pawing and rampaging up and down the fence, horns locked with old Red Flag, the big herd-bull. Once one had gotten loose, and all night they heard the ominous bellowing up and down the pasture fence, and in the morning men had come on horses, with lassoes. Aunt Effie never left the road-gate open after that, and they always looked carefully each way up and down the road as far as they could see before they loosed the chain.

It wasn't anything this time, though. Not even a stray mule cluttering up the lawn. "They forgot about the milking, I bet," Millie said. She planked herself down again on the bed. Katy could milk pretty well, but she and Mary Josephine couldn't ever get more than a skinny drizzle, and the cows always got so nervous. Aunt Edna said they must be pinching, so after a while they didn't try any more.

Mary Josephine got up, though. "Let's go over and watch them anyway," she yawned. "Maybe a calf will get born or something."

Millie stuck her feet up in the air, and looked at the pleasant film of dust between her toes. "We'll have to get some more clothes on if we do, because Uncle Davis is over there," she objected.

Mary Josephine considered this a while. "There's swallows' nests over in the barn. . . . Maybe Aunt Edna will let us garbage Agamemnon," she said.

Millie got up and wiped her face. "If we go for a drive tonight, let's be the first, so we can get the outside places or else in front," she said. Mary Josephine had been thinking this too, off and on. She was glad Millie had suggested it first, though. She pretended to be shocked. "Blah!" said Millie. She wasn't fooled in the least. "—You just about knock everybody down getting there first, yourself!" She picked her nose defiantly.

Mary Josephine didn't deny this. It was probably true, she thought. Besides, there wasn't much use trying to deny anything Millie said. You only got all red and lumpy in the face trying to explain the way things seemed. And explanations to Millie always sounded like excuses, anyway.—There was, for instance, taking the biggest hermit on the plate when Aunt Elizabeth passed them to her: not because she was a pig, but she thought confusedly that Aunt Elizabeth might think she didn't appreciate them enough, or something. But how make Millie understand this opportune confusion of the moment?—especially as the hermit was clear over on the far side of the plate.

The cows were all milked by the time they got there. Old Red Flag stood ruminating in the lane, and they both stopped and looked at each other. "We've got to go on!" Mary Josephine said. She stared at his heavy head and ox-big horns.

"I'm not!" Millie stood firm with terror.

"He never hurt anybody yet," Mary Josephine said. She got behind Millie and tried to shove her on. It looked silly.—It looked as though she wanted Millie to get punched the first, but she really didn't. They heard Uncle Davis laughing. Old Red Flag turned his back and walked away. It was terribly humiliating.

Aunt Edna came out with the dishpan full of potato-peelings and old bread. They followed her to the pig-pasture where Agamemnon was. Agamemnon was enormous. Twice as big as other people's pigs. Some people's pigs looked like dirigibles, and walked as though they had on high-heeled boots. But Agamemnon was barrel-like and tightly fat. Low-slung, with lordly eyes. He was already there and waiting at the trough. No frantic shoat-like galloping across the pasture. He did not come to get his food: they brought it to him. The field beyond was dotted with pig-houses, but Agamemnon had a lot unto himself. The houses were wood with pointed tops. They looked the way roofs would look if you put them down on the ground without any walls: green triangles sitting upright in the grass.

When Agamemnon had finished—he ate stuffingly and with speed, but not with one eye on the next peeling for fear it would be gone (in the nervous manner of those whose troughs are shared with other snouts)—Millie climbed up on the gate and swung her foot above his head. Above the trough, too. She might have fallen in any minute. Agamemnon would have eaten her if she had—that is, if she kept still enough and pretended to be part of the slop. Mary Josephine was in a panic. She was always afraid for other people when they did things, though not for herself when she did them. She wondered if she would have courage to go in and pull Millie out of Agamemnon's mouth—provided there was something to catch a hold of—decided she might, and wondered what Aunt Elizabeth would say.

She was glad when the wind stopped and it was quiet. Glad because the wind always stopped about six o'clock, and so it must be time for supper, and if it was time for supper Millie would have to get down off the fence. She ran around the barn corner and looked across the road. If she could see Aunt Elizabeth's white apron come out on the porch and move around looking for them, Millie might be saved.

"Where're you going?" Millie shrieked after her. She thought Mary Josephine was running away—the old blob—she'd catch her quick enough! She slid down off the gate, almost kicking Agamemnon on the nose.

"No place," said Mary Josephine. She got all red for fear Millie would understand—Millie had a way of finding out these things. "I thought maybe Aunt Elizabeth called us." ("Might be going to have called us," she amended to her conscience.)

"Agamemnon," said Millie.

Mary Josephine didn't mind. She never minded when Millie made fun of her because Millie was nice and had a kindly way about doing things.

They went down the lane fast, not stopping even to watch tumble-bugs. Frogs were singing in the left-over pool along the road, but no matter how high or softly you stepped they would hear and stop. Mary Josephine felt thwarted. All her life she had wanted to see one puffed and singing, and never had. Only in pictures. She wished she could see one and then show it to Millie who would be all excited, too, and it would feel like being double—being excited herself, and Millie's on top of that. She wanted it so much sometimes she couldn't understand why it didn't happen. It didn't seem reasonable that a thing you wanted terribly enough never happened. But the frogs had always shut up as though they thought *that* was what she wanted, instead.

It was quiet, though, and that was pleasant. They could hear the doves a long way off, cooing up by Jim's house. They were sad and sweet enough to make you cry. There was another sound, too—a better one—coming out the front door. It was of the oven-door, and sauce-pans scraped across the stove. They stopped and tried to separate the smells that mingled out. There was one, a fresh and subtle smell that might be—surely must be—*was*—OYSTERS! Four big bowls of them! You could see their gray backs wallowing in the milk, like little whales, and round pools of butter spreading out on top.

It was light still when they finished—the clean light from a sun gone down, no longer visible in body. Aunt Elizabeth took down her gray knit shawl, and three old sweaters, on account of the chill along the lower road even before dark came. Millie climbed into the Ford and started to steer the wheel all around. Mary Josephine shrieked for Aunt Effie to come stop her because she was making the wheels move underneath. "Oh, pew!" Millie shouted recklessly, and twisted them every which way in contempt. The engine wasn't on, but Mary Josephine was afraid to get in for fear the car might go bounding off with only Millie at the wheel to steer. She was glad when Aunt Effie came and they started off, only it was a wonder they didn't run up on the front porch—the way Millie had the wheels all switched around.

They went down Bethel lane past the Rockford place, overgrown and choked with jimson weed, and the porch not level any more. North of the Rockford place was a field of corn, and pastures full of white-oak trees that flowered silvery in the spring, and beyond a pale oat-field with malty smells. Later on, when they passed it coming home, it looked like an acre-wide of moonlight lying in the darkness. . . . Mary Josephine liked to lean out the side and see the bouncing-betties, if they were there where they grew each year with horsetails and wild lettuce plants. They were exciting, in the way they looked so much like garden phlox and yet were here and nonchalant along the road with weeds. . . . There were rail-fences everywhere, broken down and held together with the arms of moonseed and carrion-vines. They looked like deep and secret places to find bird-nests in. It was the month for elder bushes to be white, and the wild roses grew in monstrous bush-like clumps along the road. They were petal-scattering and lightly sweet.

Once in a while they would pass farmers, tired and driving slow, or a stray calf wandering in the ditch. Millie spent a lot of time practicing faces to make at people when they passed, and if it was dark enough would blow out her cheeks in a horrible grimace when carts went rattling by. Most of the time it was quiet, though, without even a barreled pig snuffling at the fence. The hay-ricks looked like pointed muffins set upon a hill, and there were fields deep-sifted with the daisies blooming. Down some of the roads the owlet-butterflies were thick as gnats, brown flickerings from root to bark. They would have liked to drive all night until next morning came, and after a while stopped the clatter of their voices to hear the owls and whip-poor-wills crying and calling in the woods. A damp, good smell came up from clover plants along the road.

Katy and Ruth didn't usually come with them. Instead they rode the horses till 'way late. Sometimes till moonlight. And were always having "experiences"—like finding stones in Nadine's shoe, or seeing Mr. Perry drunk along the roadside. Things like that never happened to Millie or Mary Josephine. Either their imaginations weren't as good, or their consciences were better; but anyway the most they ever saw was a skunk loping across the pasture, right out in the open, and a whole herd of baby-pigs gotten loose and trundling down the middle of the road without sense enough to move aside when the horn began to honk. This was enough, though—it was enough to talk about for a long time.

The coming back was rather sad; but still there was the soda-pop to look forward to, and the moonflower smell back of the wood-house. Mary Josephine and Aunt Elizabeth always got out near the door, but Millie and Aunt Effie rode down to the car-shed and locked the Ford inside. Mary Josephine suspected Millie of guiding the wheel these times, but couldn't prove it.

They sat on the porch-edge after, and rubbed their feet around in the dew. The ramblers made moving shadows up and down the pillar-sides. . . . They thought they could never again be so happy in life. All the summer was still to come.—All the afternoons when they could put on Aunt Edna's wedding-dress with the thousand fine accordion-pleats, and squeeze into the high-necked waist, satin-topped and heavy with its lace; none of them could fasten it without getting purple in the face, but once inside there was a dignity about being squeezed upright and stately. . . . And there was the square brown-velvet box almost big as a chest, with trays of old jewelry inside, beautiful and thick.

—The fireflies swarmed bright in the hayfield, and some kill-deers cried. The night air smelled of flowering grapes. Mary Josephine and Millie got into the hammock and pushed themselves slowly back and forth. The moon was so near you could see the crater-wrinkles on its face. . . . There didn't seem any end or beginning to this happiness. It was themselves, and big as all the world.

William Saroyan

WHEN THE magazine Story accepted "The Daring Young Man on the Flying Trapeze" for its issue of February, 1934, it made American story history. It lent a hand to a young man who was to need no more helping. William Saroyan astonished his discoverers by sending in a story or two every day for a month. Presently he began to appear in other magazines, and in the same year appeared his first book of stories under the title with which he began. Other volumes followed: Inhale and Exhale (1936), Little Children (1937), Three Times Three (1937), Love, here is my Hat (1938), and The Trouble with Tigers (1938). He was born in California in 1908, the son of an Armenian immigrant; and his education, a good one for a writer, was acquired through public schools, public libraries, and odd jobs.

Criticism has been in turn amused, indignant, bewildered, and excited by the stories of Saroyan. At his worst he attitudinizes and makes verbiage. At his best his stories do what he wants them to do: "restore man to his natural dignity and gentleness." His good stories are ardent and alive and, spurning traditional pattern, achieve a form of their own. His influence has been healthful for story writing, but his imitators should beware. Good stories, including Saroyan's, are more than deep-breathing exercises.

A COLD DAY *

William Saroyan

Dear M—,

I want you to know that it is very cold in San Francisco today, and that I am freezing. It is so cold in my room that every time I start to write a short story the cold stops me and I have to get up and do bending exercises. It means, I think, that something's got to be done about keeping short story writers warm. Sometimes when it is very cold I am able to do very good writing, but at other times I am not. It is the same when the weather is excessively pleasant. I very much dislike letting a day go by without writing a short story and that is why I am writing this letter: to let you know that I am very angry about the weather. Do not think that I am sitting in a nice warm room in sunny California, as they call it, and making up all this stuff about the cold. I am sitting in a very cold room and there is no sun anywhere, and the only thing I can talk about is the cold because it is the only thing going on today. I am freezing and my teeth are chattering. I would like to know what the Democratic party ever did for freezing short story writers. Everybody else gets heat. We've got to depend on the sun and in the winter the sun is undependable. That's the fix I am in: wanting to write and not being able to, because of the cold.

One winter day last year the sun came out and its light came into my room and fell across my table, warming my table and my room and warming me. So I did some brisk bending exercises and then sat down and began to write a short story. But it was a winter day and before I had written the first paragraph of the story the sun had fallen back behind clouds and there I was in my room, sitting in the cold, writing a story. It was such a good story that even though I knew it would never be printed I had to go on writing it, and as a result I was frozen stiff by the time I finished writing it. My face was blue and I could barely move my limbs, they were so cold and stiff. And my room was full of the smoke of a package of Chesterfield cigarettes, but even the smoke was frozen. There were clouds of it in my room, but my room was very cold just the same. Once, while I was writing, I thought of getting a tub and making a fire in it. What I intended to do was to burn a half dozen of my books and keep warm, so that I could write my story.

* From *The Daring Young Man on the Flying Trapeze,* 1934. Reprinted by permission of Random House, Inc.

I found an old tub and I brought it to my room, but when I looked around for books to burn I couldn't find any. All of my books are old and cheap. I have about five hundred of them and I paid a nickel each for most of them, but when I looked around for titles to burn, I couldn't find any. There was a large heavy book in German on anatomy that would have made a swell fire, but when I opened it and read a line of that beautiful language, *sie bestehen aus zwei Hüft-gelenkbeugemuskeln des Oberschenkels, von denen der eine breitere,* and so on, I couldn't do it. It was asking too much. I couldn't understand the language, I couldn't understand a word in the whole book, but it was somehow too eloquent to use for a fire. The book had cost me five cents two or three years ago, and it weighed about six pounds, so you see that even as fire wood it had been a bargain and I should have been able to tear out its pages and make a fire.

But I couldn't do it. There were over a thousand pages in the book and I planned to burn one page at a time and see the fire of each page, but when I thought of all that print being effaced by fire and all that accurate language being removed from my library, I couldn't do it, and I still have the book. When I get tired of reading great writers, I go to this book and read language that I cannot understand, *während der Kindheit ist sie von birnförmiger Gestalt und liegt vorzugsweise in der Bauchhöhle.* It is simply blasphemous to think of burning a thousand pages of such language. And of course I haven't so much as mentioned the marvelous illustrations.

Then I began to look around for cheap fiction.

And you know the world is chock full of such stuff. Nine books out of ten are cheap worthless fiction, inorganic stuff. I thought, well, there are at least a half dozen of those books in my library and I can burn them and be warm and write my story. So I picked out six books and together they weighed about as much as the German anatomy book. The first was *Tom Brown At Oxford: A Sequel to School Days At Rugby,* Two Volumes in One. The first book had 378 pages, and second 430, and all these pages would have made a small fire that would have lasted a pretty long time, but I had never read the book and it seemed to me that I had no right to burn a book I hadn't even read. It looked as if it ought to be a book of cheap prose, one worthy of being burned, but I couldn't do it. I read, *The belfry-tower rocked and reeled as that peal rang out, now merry, now scornful, now plaintive, from those narrow belfry windows, into the bosom of the soft south-west wind, which was playing round the old gray tower of Englebourn church.* Now that isn't exactly tremendous prose, but it isn't such very bad prose either. So I put the book back on the shelf.

The next book was *Inez: A Tale of the Alamo,* and it was dedicated to The Texan Patriots. It was by the author of another book called *Beulah,* and yet another called *St. Elmo.* The only thing I knew about this writer or her books was that one day a girl at school had been severely reprimanded for bringing to class a book called *St. Elmo.* It was said to be the sort of book that would corrupt the morals of a young girl. Well, I opened the book and read, *I am dying; and, feeling as I do, that few hours are allotted me, I shall not hesitate to speak freely and candidly. Some might think me deviating from the delicacy of my sex; but, under the circumstances, I feel that I am not. I have loved you long, and to know that my love is returned, is a source of deep and unutterable joy to me.* And so on.

This was such bad writing that it was good, and I decided to read the whole book at my first opportunity. There is much for a young writer to learn from our poorest writers. It is very destructive to burn bad books, almost more destructive than to burn good ones.

The next book was *Ten Nights In A Bar Room, and What I Saw There* by T. S. Arthur. Well, even this book was too good to burn. The other three books were by Hall Caine, Brander Matthews, and Upton Sinclair. I had read only Mr. Sinclair's book, and while I didn't like it a lot as a piece of writing, I couldn't burn it because the print was so fine and the binding so good. Typographically it was one of my best books.

Anyway, I didn't burn a single page of a single book, and I went on freezing and writing. Every now and then I burned a match just to remind myself what a flame looked like, just to keep in touch with the idea of heat and warmth. It would be when I wanted to light another cigarette and instead of blowing out the flame I would let it burn all the way down to my fingers.

It is simply this: that if you have any respect for the mere idea of books, what they stand for in life, if you believe in paper and print, you cannot burn any page of any book. Even if you are freezing. Even if you are trying to do a bit of writing yourself. You can't do it. It is asking too much.

Today it is as cold in my room as the day I wanted to make a fire of books. I am sitting in the cold, smoking cigarettes, and trying to get this coldness onto paper so that when it becomes warm again in San Francisco I won't forget how it was on the cold days.

I have a small phonograph in my room and I play it when I want to exercise in order to keep warm. Well, when it gets to be very cold in my room this phonograph won't work. Something goes wrong inside, the grease freezes and the wheels won't turn, and I can't have music while I am bending and swinging my arms. I've got to do it without music. It is much more pleasant to exercise with jazz, but when it is very cold the phonograph won't work and I am in a hell of a fix. I have been in here since eight o'clock this morning and it is now a quarter to five, and I am in a hell of a mess. I hate to let a day go by without doing something about it, without saying something, and all day I have been in here with my books that I never read, trying to get started and I haven't gotten anywhere. Most of the time I have been walking up and down the room (two steps in any direction brings you to a wall) and bending and kicking and swinging my arms. That's practically all I have been doing. I tried the phonograph a half dozen times to see if the temperature hadn't gone up a little but it hadn't, and the phonograph wouldn't play music.

I thought I ought to tell you about this. It's nothing important. It's sort of silly, making so much of a little cold weather, but at the same time the cold is a fact today and it is the big thing right now and I am speaking of it. The thing that amazes and pleases me is that my typewriter hasn't once clogged today. Around Christmas when we had a very cold spell out here it was always clogging, and the more I oiled it the more it clogged. I couldn't do a thing with it. The reason was that I had been using the wrong kind of oil. But all this time that I have been writing about the cold my typewriter has been doing its work excellently, and this amazes and pleases me. To think that in spite of the cold this machine can go right on making the language I use is very fine. It encourages me to stick with it, whatever happens. If the machine will work, I tell myself, then you've got to work with it. That's what it amounts to. If you can't write a decent short story because of the cold, write something else. Write anything. Write a long letter to somebody. Tell them how cold you are. By the time the letter is received the sun will be out again and you will be warm again, but the letter will be there mentioning the cold. If it is so cold that you can't make up a little ordinary Tuesday prose, why, what the hell, say anything that comes along, just so it's the truth. Talk about your toes freezing, about the time you actually wanted to burn books to keep warm but couldn't do it, about the phonograph. Speak of the little unimportant things on a cold day, when your mind is numb and your feet and hands frozen. Mention the things you wanted to write but couldn't. This is what I have been telling myself.

After coffee this morning, I came here to write an important story. I was warm with the coffee and I didn't realize how really cold it was. I brought out paper and started to line up what I was going to say in this important story that will never be written because once I lose a thing I lose it forever, this story that is forever lost because of the cold that got into me and silenced me and made me jump up from my chair and do bending exercises. Well, I can tell you about it. I can give you an idea what it was to have been like. I remember that much about it, but I didn't write it and it is lost. It will give you something of an idea as to how I write.

I will tell you the things I was telling myself this morning while I was getting this story lined up in my mind:

Think of America, I told myself this morning. The whole thing. The cities, all the houses, all the people, the coming and going, the coming of children, the going of them, the coming and going of men and death, and life, the movement, the talk, the sound of machinery, the oratory, think of the pain in America and the fear and the deep inward longing of all things alive in America. Remember the great machines, wheels turning, smoke and fire, the mines and the men working them, the noise, the confusion. Remember the newspapers and the moving picture theatres and everything that is a part of this life. Let this be your purpose: to suggest this great country.

Then turn to the specific. Go out to some single person and dwell with him, within him, lovingly, seeking to understand the miracle of his being, and utter the truth of his existence and reveal the splendor of the mere fact of his being alive, and say it in great prose, simply, show that he is of the time, of the machines and the fire and smoke, the newspapers and the noise. Go with him to his secret and speak of it gently, showing that it is the secret of man. Do not deceive. Do not make up lies for the sake of pleasing anyone. No one need be killed in your story. Simply relate what is the great event of all history, of all time, the humble, artless truth of mere being. There is no greater theme: No one need be violent to help you with your art. There *is* violence. Mention it of course when it is time to mention it. Mention the war. Mention all ugliness, all waste. Do even this lovingly. But emphasize the glorious truth of mere being. It is the major theme. You do not have to create a triumphant climax. The man you write of need not perform some heroic or monstrous deed in order to make your prose great. Let him do what he has always done, day in and day out, continuing to live. Let him walk and talk and think and sleep and dream and awaken and walk again and talk again and move and be alive. It is enough. There is nothing else to write about. You have never seen a short story in life. The events of life have never fallen into the form of the short story or the form of the poem, or into any other form. Your own consciousness is the only form you need. Your own awareness is the only action you need. Speak of this man, recognize his existence. Speak of man.

Well, this is a poor idea of what the story was to have been like. I was warm with coffee when I was telling myself what and how to write, but now I am freezing, and this is the closest I can come to what I had in mind. It was to have been something fine, but now all that I have is this vague remembrance of the story. The least I can do is put into words this remembrance. Tomorrow I will write another story, a different story. I will look at the picture from a different viewpoint. I don't know for sure, but I may feel cocky and I may mock this country and the life that is lived here. It is possible. I can do it. I have done it before, and sometimes when I get mad about political parties and political graft I sit down and mock this great country of ours. I get mean and I make man out to be a rotten, worthless, unclean thing. It isn't man, but I make out as if it is. It's something else, something less tangible, but for mockery it is more convenient to make out that it is man. It's my business to get at the truth, but when you start to mock, you say to hell with the truth. Nobody's telling the truth, why should I? Everybody's telling nice lies, writing nice stories and novels, why should I worry about the truth. There is no truth. Only grammar, punctuation, and all that rot. But I know better. I can get mad at things and start to mock, but I know better. At its best, the whole business is pretty sad, pretty pathetic.

All day I have been in this room freezing, wanting to say something solid and clean about all of us who are alive. But it was so cold I couldn't do it. All I could do was swing my arms and smoke cigarettes and feel rotten.

Early this morning when I was warm with coffee I had this great story in my mind, ready to get into print, but it got away from me.

The most I can say now is that it is very cold in San Francisco today, and I am freezing.

Kathleen Morehouse

"WITH THE FOG" was one of the stories early accepted by Whit Burnett and Martha Foley for their magazine Story which has done so much to encourage fresh and honest expression. It tells of a region and of a people that Kathleen Morehouse has known intimately since 1929 when she left New England to help her husband manage a fruit orchard in the Brushy Mountain country of western North Carolina.

In 1936 Mrs. Morehouse published her first novel about the Carolina mountain folk, Rain on the Just. The story of a young girl, Least Dolly Allen, it is, with no self-conscious picturesqueness, soundly and beautifully imagined. For her next book Mrs. Morehouse has turned to a study of the whaling days of New Bedford. She was born in Oak Bluffs, Massachusetts, and graduated from Mount Holyoke College in 1924.

WITH THE FOG *

Kathleen Morehouse

THE SERVICE trees were blowing white over the mountain sides. Against the grayness of the winter woods, their early April flowering stood out pure and fresh in the spring sunlight. Poplar buds were beginning to swell, and dogwoods were giving earnest of future glory. The air smelled warm, and clean, and the ground felt live and eager. Violets were pushing through, arbutus was almost pink, and bees and yellow-jackets flashed back and forth, droning loudly. Rising far across the valley below, the Blue Ridge, clear and harsh across the sky, ended the known world of the average Brushy Mountain family.

A pair of mourning doves, tail feathers fanwise, fluttered down in

---

* From Story, February, 1933. The story was first printed under the name Kathleen Salisbury. Reprinted by permission of the author and of Story.

the clearing before the tenant house where Edgar Gentle and his family lived. It was strangely still. Only the thick smoke curling up from the rough pointed chimney indicated any life within the slab-sided cabin, and the doves, as they waddled around, pecking hopefully at the stony soil, were as unaware of Jettie Gentle and her cares as she of them.

Jettie Gentle was thirteen, a pale little bit of a thing, with great blue eyes, and a shock of rough black hair. Too young and tender for the hard unending toil of a mountain woman, too frail and small for the tasks already bending her childish shoulders.

"Jettie," a low, rather pleasant voice spoke a little breathlessly. "Jettie, better be sending up the mountain for old Miss Tevie soon now. Where's your pappy and the boys?"

"Plowing up the bottom, all but Rufe—"

Over in the rickety wooden bed, which occupied nearly a quarter of the low, roughly sealed cabin room, Edgar Gentle's old woman, Jettie's mammy, pulled herself up. She was barely forty, but work in the fields, and ten living children had pinched and aged her sorely. But her eyes, unfaded, and bluer even than Jettie's own, were still brilliant and youthful in the withered setting of her face.

"Where's Rufe at?" demanded Medey Gentle. "Where's he at, you Jettie?"

Jettie backed off defensively. Mammy had a sting in her tongue as sharp as the feel of a hickory switch.

"I forget, Mammy. Around somewhere. Helping spray most likely, up at the Preacher's Place." Jettie turned to the fire. It would never do to let Mammy know that Rufe had drawn his time from the Preacher, and gone off with a gang of boys loafering to Hunting Creek. And she had almost told. With her tongue between her teeth, she picked up the least baby—Fraily, his name was—from the cold floor where he was sitting, staring impassively at the fire, and jumped him a little. If Mammy knew that Rufe, her eldest born, was drinking with those low-down Hunting Creek folks, she'd get off her death bed to hound him home—and Jettie had promised to keep Mammy down.

Medey Gentle sank back on her stale hot bed, lay almost motionless, barely groaning from time to time. Her blue eyes stared at the girl and the baby. Only her flickering fingers as she smoothed the Rose of Sharon spread she saved for bornings, and her lips, as she chewed on a twig of black gum, kept busy.

Jettie stopped to fix another log in the fireplace, brushed up the hot ashes over a dish of corn pone, and swung the kettle of water over the flames.

"Holler to one of the boys to go fetch Miss Tevie. And when she comes, Jettie, you go on down, and help your pappy till Miss Tevie calls you. And don't let your pappy go off a-drinking. Mind, Jettie." The voice lost its pleasant warmth suddenly. "Get along, Jettie. Put the baby up here by me."

"Let me tote Fraily along with me, Mammy," begged Jettie in a sudden agony. "I'll wrop him up a-plenty."

"Git along, Jettie. I done told you, Jettie. He'd catch his never-get-overs in this blowing weather. Git." Mammy Gentle's voice rose in a scream. Fraily, his thin face puckered, began to whimper. He was just by his first year.

Before Jettie had time either to soothe the baby, or argue, a tiny, bent woman, carrying an overflowing paper poke, fumbled her way in through the always open doorway.

"Howdy, Medey. I guessed you'd be wanting of me, and Roxie Chatham does sure, so I followed down the branch from up yonder, 'stid o' waitin' to hear."

Old Miss Tevepaugh was eighty and upwards, and had birthed all the young uns on the mountain, as well as the most part of their mammies and pappies. Fair weather and foul, Miss Tevie kept busy. "Lord's Work" she called it, and through the coves and the hollers, along the creeks and the branches, wherever a mountain family had raised a roof, Miss Tevie was known and honored.

"You, Jettie," she ordered in her thin cracked voice, "git water b'ilin', and scorch me some clean rags. And take this here young un off'n the bed. Tain't no time since I was here, Medey. Right peart little feller, he is, too. What you havin' for me this time, Medey?"

All the time old Miss Tevie's tongue was clacking, she was bustling about, arranging things to suit herself.

"You, Jettie, take this young un, and go 'long now, I'll holler when I need ye."

Jettie, only too glad to disregard her mammy's orders, and obey Miss Tevie whose word was always law, snatched up the baby, and bundled him so securely in a big black shawl, that he was to all intents and purposes completely insulated from the air and sunlight.

"You said I could name hit, Mammy," urged Jettie, gingerly approaching the bedside. Poor Mammy, she was surely took worse each time, though of course, Jettie couldn't remember any of the bornings but Kenor, who was five, and Fraily. And the twins, betwixt Kenor and little Fraily, little girls, hardly born before they died.

Mighty funny about children, Jettie thought, as she lugged Fraily down the steep little path that plunged to the bottom. You don't have enough food for the children you have, so you make more crops, and then you got to have more children—boys, if so be—to work them. Oh, yes, Jettie knew how endless was the more children, more crops, more children business.

Down in the bottom it was warm, and sunny, and Jettie really considered taking Fraily out of his bundle.

"Kenor," she called. "Kenor."

Kenor, who in name and appearance, might have been either boy or girl, was a little girl. She had passed far beyond the bundling stage. Kenor was already barefoot, and through the holes in her cut-down apron it was easy to see that underwear was an inessential. Her rough short hair would have curled a bit, with any encouragement, in a really girlish fashion but there was little enough time and opportunity for keeping Kenor covered or clean, let alone frilled up, Jettie thought, as Kenor, barefooted, came leaping carelessly over brambles and boulders alike.

"Watch Fraily while I go see Pappy," said Jettie.

Kenor nodded. Kenor was almost as inarticulate as Fraily. Mountain children are slow to talk, besides being shy.

Pappy and Theed, who at sixteen, was next above Jettie, and Cic'ro, who at eleven, was next below her, were stacking up the fall-stripped fodder. Alverda, who looked exactly like Kenor, except a size larger at nine, was helping tie.

"Miss Tevie come down Cub Creek?" asked Edgar Gentle calmly.

"No, down the Wildcat," said Jettie. "And did Rufe come back? He better be here afore Miss Tevie's through, or Mammy will be out and after him."

Edgar Gentle was silent. Inwardly he yearned to do just what Rufe was doing. Get a jug of corn licker, or even sweet mash, and enjoy hisself. Forget about shares to the Preacher, and a new mouth to feed. And just be drunk. Sunday drunk. Meetin' for women folks on Sunday, and stillin' for men folks. Spiritual comfort for women folks, drink for men folks.

Jettie knew the signs. Saturday nights and bornings always made Pappy restless and yearning.

"Pappy," said Jettie. "Pappy, will hit be raining this evening?" If she could only get Pappy started on studying out the weather, he might stand around long enough so that Miss Tevie would call, and then he couldn't get to go off anywhere.

"I told you, Jettie. I done told you April borrowed ten days from March. Wind's a-coming powerful, and shouldn't wonder to see fog afore wind."

Edgar Gentle was a tall, mild-looking man, stout and husky for all his name and bearing, and like all the mountain men of family, hard-working on week-days, and hard drinking over Sundays.

He stood now, lazily at ease, sniffing the wind. Edgar Gentle had worked hard all his life, but the years had not told so harsh a tale, and his lean muscularity showed none of the wrack that Medey's maternity-worn frame exhibited. Fathering a family was plumb easy, Jettie thought as she looked at her pappy. It was easier to be a boy, Jettie was sure. Look at Rufe, and Theed, and Cic'ro, Click, and even little Fraily. Look at Mayhew, Jettie's oldest sister, just nineteen, and already with three young uns. Mayhew had been right pretty before she was married, and before babies and crop-tending had aged and withered her. Look at Angie, just sixteen, and almost in trouble all the time.

"Look yonder, Jettie. Fog's a-droppin' now. Stack up, you Theed, and Cic'ro. Git that under cover afore hit's damped off again." Pappy himself set to work with a sudden burst of zeal. "Hit'll be mighty thick afore Angie and Click gits home."

Angie, who was sixteen, and Click, who was seven, both went down mountain to the lower school which kept longer than the Crest school where all the rest of the young Gentles went. The Crest school ran from November to March, and the lower school usually a week or two more. Crops had to be tended to, and young uns were cheap hands. And schoolin' wasn't much account nohow. However, Angie and Click said they liked the teaching down at the lower school, and so day after day they walked the six miles down and back quite faithfully. People did say Angie liked the teacher better than common. She'd been highest in the fifth grade for three years now—and that meant the biggest, not the smartest. Click went along because he was Angie's pet. Angie'd raised Click, the same as Jettie was raising Fraily.

Way off to the East, Jettie could see cottony wisps of cloud, not quite in the sky, and yet not low enough for ground mist. Just hanging in mid-air. And somehow the April sun was losing its warmth. North, the Blue Ridge was slowly hazing over.

"Best wrop Fraily up again," said Jettie. "Will there be rain, Pappy?"

But Pappy was really working. For a time at least, Pappy had for-gotten the borning, and Rufe's flight.

Jettie went back to Fraily and Kenor, playing solemnly with a handful of dogwood berries, some galax leaves and a burnished snail shell. Alverda, tieing up bundles awkwardly, whispered as Jettie went by. Alverda didn't know the rights of new babies yet.

"Miss Tevie bring hit with her, Jet?" Alverda had learned that what Rufe said wasn't so—'Mammy finds 'em under cabbage leaves'—but in spite of plenty of calves, and unending families of kittens, Alverda was still a little questioning.

"Jettie, Jettie." High and shrill, Miss Tevie's voice rang out.

"I'm a-coming," shouted Jettie, her pale face suddenly flushed. She snatched the reluctant Fraily, almost stumbling over Kenor, and raced up the path to the cabin.

"Jettie, has your pappy a drop o' whiskey about? Your mammy needs some, and needs it real bad. Ef you kin find it, I druther you did than rouse up your pappy."

Old Miss Tevie turned slightly from the bedside where she was wiping up not one baby but two.

Jettie put Fraily down before the fire where he sat as impassively as before, staring into the flames.

"Reckon I can find some, Miss Tevie," she said, dragging a chair over to the cupboard that filled nearly one wall of the cabin. "Is she bad?" Jettie's voice hardly changed its even tone. Mountain children did not cry, did not laugh easily.

"A hurtin' in her side," said old Miss Tevie, wrapping up the second of the red mites in a swaddling of blankets.

"These yere are sure man size babies, Jettie. Hev ye two namin's ready? Man namin's?"

Jettie, an old quart jar in her hand, came over to Miss Tevie.

"Peach brandy, 'tis," she said. "I been hidin' it for sickness."

She peered at the babies, whose squinty little faces were hardly visible in the dusk of the room. "I like Fraily better," she said. "Whar'll we put 'em, Miss Tevie?"

Medey Gentle opened her eyes, moved slightly.

"Whar but with me, Jettie Gentle? I never let a young un sleep its first year anywhere but on my arm, and I hev two arms for two young uns. Hand 'em here, Miss Tevie."

"Take this first, Medey. It'll cure your hurtin', and help you strengthen quicker." Miss Tevie licked her testing finger meditatively.

"Now, open your mouth, Medey. Open your mouth."

Medey Gentle blinked and swallowed. Her eyes that had been dull and sleepy sparkled slightly.

"Your pappy, what is he at, Jettie?"

"Gettin' in fodder afore fog, Mammy," said Jettie. "And the boys."

Medey Gentle pulled the two babies, still whimpering in their tiny voices, up to her:

"Useter get right up and cook a meal for you, didn't I, Miss Tevie? I'm getting poor and puny, seems like. Angie'll be home afore long, and she'll get up some dinner."

Jettie glanced out the open doorway. Slowly, steadily, the fog was rolling in. Pretty soon the Preacher's orchard would be swallowed up, and before long, the corn crib at the end of the clearing, and the mule stalls would be covered over.

"Won't wait for a meal, Medey. I better get along to Roxie Chatham's whilst I can. Jettie can see to you, till Angie comes. And maybe better than Angie, from all talk has about Angie," she added, just a little maliciously.

Angie was prettier even than Mayhew had been. Angie and Rufe and Mayhew all took after the Gentle generations—tall, and colorful. Medey had given her blue eyes to Jettie, and Click, and Fraily, but Kenor, and Alverda, and Cic'ro, and Theed were all plain to ugly like Medey's generation, the Joinses. Angie was pretty, and so people talked more.

Jettie knew people were saying Angie Gentle'd do better to marry in the Bumgarners than keep her eyes on the Teacher down to the Lower School. Folks knew how Angie'd acted Protracted Meeting week last August up to the New Hope church. Angie'd spent a sight more time out under the trees than getting spiritual grace—and Angie of all the Gentles should have been right up front on the Mourners' Bench.

"Well, Medey, next year again about this time?" Miss Tevie laughed, poking at Fraily with her soft slippered toe as she started for the door. "Send word to the Chathams if you need me," and Miss Tevie disappeared in the fog.

The old dominicker crowed shrilly. In the stall, Kate and Dock, the mules, whinnied wildly. The peaceful silence of the early morning had gone. With the coming of the fog, thick and troubled as it rose and fell, beating up against the cabin only to fade away, there was a general disquiet.

"Angie'll not be liking it," said Jettie softly, more to herself than to her Mammy, who, with a baby in each arm, was lying almost relaxed in the old wooden bed.

Gerald Warner Brace

GERALD WARNER BRACE's first novel The Islands (1936), the story of young Edgar Thurlow, the son of a Maine fisherman, revealed a fine talent for fresh, clear description of the natural world, and for the interpretation of characters worth knowing. His second novel The Wayward Pilgrims (1938) is unusual in theme and treatment, being both the narration of a Vermont walking trip and a causerie between a man and a woman who make conversation a vital and memorable experience. In both his novels Mr. Brace shows a craftsman's regard for integrity of character portrayal and for distinction in expression. He has written a number of short stories, and is now at work upon a third novel.

Gerald Warner Brace was born in 1901 at Islip, New York, and has spent most of his life in New England. He graduated from Amherst in 1922, received his doctor's degree from Harvard in 1930, and taught literature at Williams, Radcliffe, and Dartmouth. He is now teaching at Mount Holyoke College where he has been a member of the Department of English since 1934.

DEEP WATER MAN*

Gerald Warner Brace

HE REMINDED me of a rabbit when I first saw him. There was something hoppity about him, and his head stuck straight up above his thin shoulders. I had seen him pottering about his tidy yard, carrying sticks from one place to another; often he bobbed his head at me as I went by along the road.

One day I found out that he wasn't so much like a rabbit as I had

---

* Published by permission of the author.

thought. He was far stranger than that; more like a remote bird, perhaps, with steely eyes that don't look quite at you. I was strolling past his place in the late afternoon, enjoying the March smell of emerging earth and wet fields, when he poked his sudden head out of an upper window in the barn and beckoned. No sound—just a peremptory beckon. He didn't even wait to see if I were coming.

I went, of course. Through a side door, round the end of—well, I may as well explain right here that it was one of those old steam cars, standing there like a large baby carriage with brass headlamps. It startled me, naturally; steam cars used to count ten, white horses nine, and ordinary cars only one, when we played games out of train windows—and that was a long time ago. This one had hard rubber tires, a hood about the size and shape of an inverted washtub—and this year's license plates. That's more than you can say for the one in the Smithsonian Institute (if there is one). I continued on up some dark stairs, came out in a low-roofed small loft, and was welcomed by the rabbit—only now that I could see his metal-sharp, crossed eyes I began to change my mind. He waved a hand and spoke—a sharp voice. "I thought you'd like to see my boats."

Boats. The little loft seemed to be full of them. Skiffs tucked away under the rafters, a mustard-colored dory, a punt or two, and a round-bottomed dinghy blocked up in the middle of the floor—a sweet look-ing little boat, so far as I could tell. I'm not competent to judge boats, but it turned out that I was right about the dinghy—as we'll see. And I had a feeling too that the dory would have been more at ease in Gloucester than here by an inland river a hundred miles from the sea. It was unexpected, that loft almost salty; you began to look round for lobster pots and pieces of dried codfish on the work bench and coils of tarred line.

"I didn't know you were a boat builder," I said vaguely.

He straightened up to his full five feet four and bobbed his head sharply. "Certainly I'm a boat builder."

I felt that somehow I hadn't been tactful. I tried again. "Do you use these boats on the river here? They say there's good fishing—"

This time he added a full inch to his stature. His blue eyes flashed. "I'm a deep water man," he said. "I'm Captain Tuttle. I don't build river boats." He readjusted his teeth with a sudden click.

"Oh." I had been here in Somerfield only a week, but I thought someone should have told me about Captain Tuttle. "You're quite a way from deep water," I added, giving what I hoped was the right sort of lead. It was.

It seemed that his wife had suffered from the sea dampness. They had lived inland for four years in this place her grandfather had left her beside the Connecticut. "I gave up my career," he said with dignity, clicking his teeth again. "We were happy here even so." He waved a hand and focussed his eyes on me as best he could. "This is an ignorant community, you know. Ignorant and provincial. But we—we managed."

I felt that a question had been suggested. "Your—er—wife?"

"Dead," he nodded. "Infection here"—tapping his sinus. "We should have gone out west of course. Arizona—somewhere like that." He shrugged. "You can't stay alive without money."

It was strange how his eyes could gleam. He stood there like an elderly scarecrow in overalls, a crumpled hat tilted back above his narrow cranium, but you wouldn't have smiled at him.

"I've never wanted money—more than you need to live. I haven't asked for fame"—he stood as straight as a steel rule when he said that. "I've been contented to do my work. But it's another thing to be cheated and then denied in time of need."

It occurred to me that I didn't know what he was talking about—not that it seriously mattered; he was the kind of person you couldn't expect to understand all the time. But he was eyeing me closely, and I ventured a remark—something about the difficulty of making a living on the sea these days.

He dismissed the idea with one of his lofty gestures. "I retired from the sea in nineteen ten," he said.

"Oh? And what did you do then?"

A smile touched his thin lips, and his head went back a notch. "I became an inventor," he said.

I found myself nodding as though I might have expected it all along.

He waved a hand at the boats. "I built vessels," he went on. "I made sails—I'm a sailmaker, you know." I nodded again without undue surprise. "But I'm really an inventor. That's my business."

I'm not apt at the literary allusion, being a student of engineering, but as I looked at the little man I could almost hear the accents of my Mother's voice as she quoted the White Knight's song:

> *I cried 'Come, tell me how you live!'*
> *And thumped him on the head.*

But I wasn't tempted to thump him on the head. Nothing that he said seemed unreasonable: he might have gone on to explain that he hunted haddocks' eyes in the heather bright or searched the grassy knolls for wheels of Hansom-cabs—and I should have acknowledged the high seriousness of his pursuit.

"What do you invent?"

"Anything."

He challenged me with those cross-angled eyes. I nodded soberly.

"I built the first single-step hydroplane," he snapped out. "Do you know that for fifteen years American boats couldn't be beaten? I taught 'em how to do it. They used to try to drive a hull through the water—but you can't do that, I don't care how much power you use. I built a twenty-foot hydroplane, put a forty horse engine in it, and beat everything on the coast. Nothing to it."

Once more he challenged me. "You've read about the America's Cup races back in nineteen one?" He didn't wait for my vague response, but kept right on: "Well, I saved the cup that year. They couldn't make the *Columbia's* mainsail set right; the more they tried the worse it got. Two days before the race it bulged out right along the luff like a balloon—she wouldn't sail six points to the wind." Again he fixed me with his eye. "They sent for me. They said, 'Tuttle, we're stuck.' They were, too."

He paused to observe my response, and once more a smile flickered across his lips as he relished the memory. Then he waved a hand and spoke casually.

"I fixed it," he said. "I recut the head and put in a wire luff rope. They said you couldn't use wire—but I showed 'em how: I showed 'em how to make it flexible so you could tie bow knots in it. They've been using it ever since."

"And the *Columbia* won?"

"Of course she won. Three straight races. She was a sweet boat, you know—and the only defender ever to win two series." Again he watched for my response, still speaking: "I helped design her. Nat Herreshoff showed me the first model he made for her—asked me how I liked it. I told him to give her a finer run. He did." His teeth clicked as he snapped his mouth shut.

I felt that Captain Tuttle was exaggerating, but there was something spacious about the way he did it. I had been in Somerfield only a week or so, surveying my uncle James McAusland's estate, and it seemed a still, small sort of place. The river rippled past day and night unchanging: the little green—now brown and snow-heaped—with the store and half dozen houses, seemed forever fixed in quietness. But here in this loft, with the smell of new-cut wood and copper paint, with the hull forms of salt-water boats under your hand, you could almost taste the winds of a far-flung coast. "I sailed out of Gloucester when I was a boy," he was saying. "Five years on the Banks . . ." I tried to picture the frail body handling a dory in winter weather. "I was mate aboard the *Atlantic* when she made her twelve day westward passage, Sandy Hook to the Lizard, in 1903—a record that'll never be beaten, though it was just bad luck we didn't cut half a day off that. I told Charlie Barr to fetch in close to the Scillies and catch the flood off Land's End, with a breeze drawing up through there—but he thought he knew better." Captain Tuttle chuckled, but his keen eye was on me to see how I took it. I tried to take it well. There was no doubt in my mind that he actually trod the *Atlantic's* decks—though as to what he said to Charlie Barr off the Scillies. . . .

"I worked out the principle of what they called the Diesel engine in nineteen eleven," he went on. "That's when I had a shop in East Boston. You couldn't get anybody to touch it then, though." He spoke with contempt. "That's the way it is with everything. I built one of these auto trailers twenty years ago and camped out in it all the way to California and back—my wife and I. They thought we were crazy, but now look at 'em. I invented the reduction gear for marine engines—" He broke off and looked at me sharply. "Do you know McAusland up the road here in the brick house?"

"He's my uncle."

There was an odd pause then. Captain Tuttle had opened his mouth to speak, but nothing came out. His eyes narrowed and seemed to flicker. Abruptly he turned to his bench, squirted some oil on a stone, and began whetting the edge of a plane blade. His face had tightened and his back was stiff.

"Tuttle's Gears," I exclaimed aloud. It came to me in a flash: the old man had actually been telling the truth. The Tuttle Reduction Gear and V-Drive, manufactured exclusively by the McAusland Corporation—and here was Tuttle himself in a pair of patched overalls, a forgotten and indignant scarecrow. My uncle had recently retired from active business and was raising Morgan horses on this farm of his that took in a good part of the Somerfield township.

There wasn't much I could think of to say.

But before I turned to go he spoke again, drawing himself up with a gesture that was by now familiar. "I haven't asked for money for myself," he said. "If some people live for nothing but money, that's their business. All I've asked for is a chance to do my work." He waved at the surrounding boats. "You wanted to know what I do with them. Well, I could sell them down along shore—I could make a few dollars on each one. I've done it often enough. But I don't care about that now—I don't need to any more. Your uncle saw to that." He stood in silence a moment, thinking, then went on: "I'm a man with a strong temper, you know. Many's the time I've wanted to settle with McAusland, and after what happened last winter—after I even went to see him, I come pretty close to doing it. I could if I wanted to." I heard his loose teeth click faintly. One eye was fixed on me, the other seemed to be staring far away. "She was a peaceable woman, though— she said all she wanted was to rest easy. . . ."

As I started down the stairs he called sharply to me: "Tell McAusland to turn his horses loose tonight."

I stopped. "Why?"

The loft had grown shadowy by then, but his thin face seemed to be lit from within. "No'theaster," he said simply. He tapped the aneroid barometer above the bench, and nodded with bird-like intensity. "Rain tonight—flood tomorrow. The river's up to the bridge right now."

I laughed, glad of the opening. "Well, you've got the boats for it. You needn't worry."

As I passed the old steam car again it seemed less surprising, now that I knew its owner.

My uncle's interest in horses might have been explained by the fact that he looked like one himself. It was almost a consanguine relationship. He had a long bony face that bobbed up and down on a loose neck; there was something about his fleshless arms and legs that made you think of a horse. I remember how his sorrel hair slanting down over his knobby forehead and his long sorrel mustache had given me a horsey feeling even when I was a kid, when he had first appeared as the man who was to marry my Aunt Susan. I had been willing then to think well of my fellow men, even such a long-nosed, long-chinned one as that; but when I found that he never smiled, never regarded me with a benevolent eye, never responded to tentative remarks about receiving sets or Babe Ruth, I abandoned him. He may not have noticed. The others said that he was a capable man and made lots of money.

This spring he had offered me twenty-five dollars to come up and re-survey his farm, and Aunt Susan added in a postscript that they'd be very glad to see me. And I had been enjoying those long days on the hills, even the deep old snow of the woods. There was a faint scent of woodsmoke in the air from the sugarhouse fires, occasionally a whiff of rare sweetness from the boiling sap itself.

The farm covered all sorts of terrain. Its eastern boundary was the river bank, where the land was flat and fertile; its western boundary was a wild hill ridge nearly a thousand feet higher and four miles straight back from the river. The brick house stood on a small knoll on the edge of the flat land, about three-quarters of a mile below Somerfield village. The barns and stables were in a little dip between the house and the higher land farther west.

I spoke to Uncle James at supper about a flood; he nodded glumly, and said the flat land would probably be washed out.

"What about the stables?"

They'd be all right, he thought. In bad floods the water covered the road in front of the house and flowed round into the wagon shed under the cowbarn. "It makes a devil of a mess," he muttered.

"Captain Tuttle says you'd better turn your horses out to pasture," I said.

No change of expression flickered on Uncle James's face. He went on chewing for three seconds. "Who's Captain Tuttle?" he said.

I explained in a general sort of way, thinking to approach the subject tactfully. But Uncle James seemed indifferent. He may have snorted faintly.

Aunt Susan remarked in her weary, well-bred voice that she thought he was considered rather—er—queer.

"Just plain cracked," Uncle James snapped out.

"He calls himself an inventor," I said.

Uncle James lifted his narrow eyes for an instant. "I suppose he told you about Tuttle's Gears?"

"Yes."

Again he snorted. "He came round to me with that story last fall— told me a long tale about inventing an automatic pancake machine besides. You'd think he was Thomas Edison, the way he talks."

"So he didn't invent Tuttle's Gears?"

"God knows." Uncle James gave his snort a mirthful interpretation. "It's his own hard luck if he did."

"Yes," I said. "He looked like a poor man."

"I offered him fifty dollars. He said his wife was sick or something."

"Did he take it?"

This time the snort contained contempt. "I went into the study, got the money, came back—and he'd gone. I didn't chase after him."

"His wife died, you know."

He nodded shortly. "I feel sorry for the poor devil. Slightly off his nut, of course. But what can you do—with the world full of incompetents—"

"Such a shame," Aunt Susan was saying. "I've spoken to the minister about him. It was the Auxiliary that sent Mrs. Tuttle to the hospital last winter, you know. We've tried to do something for the poor man since then—at Easter time we sent him quite a nice basket of things. But he hasn't seemed—er—grateful. I really do think he's a little bit—well, a little bit queer."

The White Knight's song occurred to me again. I wondered if Aunt Susan remembered reading it to me:

> *"I sell them unto men," he said,*
> *"Who sail on stormy seas;*
> *And that's the way I get my bread—*
> *A trifle, if you please."*

She looked at me politely when I spoke the lines, with an uncertain smile as though she were all ready to see the point but hadn't quite.

Uncle James grumbled impatiently, "What the devil has all that got to do with it?" and pushed his chair back.

"Mutton pies, weren't they?" I said.

He scowled at me. Ordinarily his disapproval left me uncomfortable, but tonight I felt released, and I looked at him as though he were a stranger. I could even feel sorry for him: there was no relief in that long, grim face, no light in the narrow eyes.

He said nothing more, but reached into the sideboard for a new bottle of Black and White and stalked off to his "study."

The northeaster blew up stronger through the night, with pelting, steady rain. In the morning when we looked out the water lay across the flat land, across the road, and made a dark pool in the wagon shed under the cow barn. By the time we had finished breakfast it was touching the cement foundations of the stables and licking in across the corrals. The rain held steady.

Henry Judd, Uncle James's superintendent, came in then and said we had better drive the horses and cattle up into the higher pastures. He had sent his wife and four children off to West Somerfield on the ridge; the water had already surrounded his own house. He advised us to get out too. Uncle James snorted again, and said his house had been standing on that knoll for a century and a half—there wasn't any sense in getting excited. But Aunt Susan was frankly scared, and the cook walked in with a suitcase in her hand and her hat on backwards and said she was going to start right then. When I offered to take them in the car they agreed enthusiastically: Aunt Susan dashed off to get her coat and hat and shouted upstairs for the other girl, who was dutifully making beds. Uncle James went out still grumbling and Henry Judd followed with muttered forebodings.

I got them through in the car safely, though the dirt road up to West Somerfield was a muddy torrent. Coming back I stopped a minute in front of Captain Tuttle's house and tooted the horn. The whole place was a lake by then: the car was standing in six inches of water in the middle of the main road, and the grey, wind-brushed sheet stretched off into the mist in all directions. I tooted again, watching the house. Suddenly I saw him peering at me from his upper barn door, just as he was yesterday, with a glittery little smile on his face.

"Come on," I shouted. "I'll take you up the hill."

His voice cut sharply through the storm as though he were speaking in his natural tones. "I've got more work to do on my dinghy here. I'm going to rig her with a wishbone boom, you know—that's what they call the thing, though I built one back in nineteen—" A roar of new wind and pelting rain swept his voice away then. He waved me on, still smiling within himself, and shut the hinged door.

I didn't make it with the car. The road dipped just where the drive turned in to the brick house; there had been about a foot of water when I came out, and now there must have been nearly three. I shouldn't have tried it, but by then I felt as though a little more water wouldn't do any harm: the whole affair was crazy anyway. It wasn't so amusing, though, when I had to step off hip deep into that liquid ice and wallow up to the house a hundred yards away.

Uncle James was building a fire in the study, muttering to himself. The furnace was out—five feet of water in the cellar. Telephone and electricity cut off. He felt personally injured at the thoughtlessness of nature, and finished off the bottle of Black and White in deference to his feelings.

By noon we had begun to move things upstairs. It was eery to see that water ooze up through the floors—the fine waxed floors that Aunt Susan took pride in. You felt at first like getting a mop and pail—but after an hour it was deep and real. We got the last of the moveable furniture up the stairs, and Uncle James opened a new bottle. There was nothing else to do except to keep the fire going in one of the front rooms and watch the rising waters. We could see the wind-driven ripples break over the roof of the car as though it were a submerged ledge.

The rain grew thinner by mid-afternoon, and the wind seemed to be blowing from the north, straight down the valley. Before dusk the flat cloud-ceiling began to break, and presently the sky was full of flying masses and tatters with glimpses of blue between. The wind backed into the northwest and hardened into a dark cold squall. There was snow in the air then, and the unearthly light of sunset smouldered darkly among the broken cloud ranks and gleamed crimson on the strange far-flung waters. Now and then the curtain of a snow squall cut it all off, leaving us only the hollow-throated booming sound of the wind.

Uncle James had been sitting a long time by the fire with a cold pipe in his hand, drowsy with whiskey. When twilight fell in the room, I fixed up two candles on the table and read *War and Peace*. And I remember how much more real and close the battles of that book seemed than the fantastic flood we were in the middle of. It must have been several seconds before I became aware of someone knocking, a sound distinct from all other sounds. Uncle James was asleep. I took a candle into the hall, feeling a trifle creepy, and was starting for the back of the house when the knocking came again lightly right behind me.

I turned, and saw Captain Tuttle's face close to the hall window. He seemed very pale there, and his smile had that mysterious look I had noticed before. But when he climbed in and was standing beside me he seemed as poised and certain as ever.

"I got my dinghy overboard," he said calmly. "She's tied up to your porch roof there."

I peered out, and there she was riding quietly in the lee of the front porch, her fore deck about three feet below the edge of the roof.

"Is McAusland here?" he asked.

I nodded toward the bedroom.

"Tell him to come along. I'll set you ashore."

"Well, we're all right—"

"You won't be when the Millerton Dam goes out."

"You'd better talk to him," I began, but he stopped me.

"I'm not here to talk. Get him and come along."

In the end I did, but it wasn't easy. He was in a state of supreme mulishness. And he didn't fully appreciate that it was Tuttle until he had plunked down into the dinghy and turned round. It seemed to make him angry.

"Look here, Tom," he shouted, "I'm not going off with this lunatic—"

But even as he sputtered Tuttle had got the sail up and was calmly coiling the halyard while we drifted out of the shelter of the house. I guess he knew what was coming, but we didn't. Uncle James had actually begun to shake a fist, and half stood up to express his mind better, when a squall whistled round the corner of the house. It might have been sheer lightning, by the way the dinghy behaved. Uncle James hit the bilge first, and I caromed across the centerboard box and brought up with both knees in his stomach. A bucket or so of icy water sloshed over us.

By then the boat was streaking along like a jackrabbit. We climbed back to the upper side and looked around. The purple twilight seemed to be screaming past us, the whole angry, dim-lit evening all going one way. The rolling clouds were still edged with faint daylight, up above where our pointed sail quivered and dipped; the waters still flickered with ruddy color.

Captain Tuttle was leaning at ease in the stern, holding sheet and tiller, watching the water churn along the lower rail, glancing up at the mast or off into the unsteady wind. He smiled a little, but he seemed remote from us, concerned with more elemental affairs. An inner light seemed to be shining in his face as he eased his boat through the explosive squalls; he nodded sharply sometimes when she came out of a particularly vicious one. I knew enough about handling sails to recognize that he was a master at it, and that I couldn't have kept the dinghy right side up for two minutes.

We had swung away from the front of the house, had crossed the road, and were now far out over the flat land with the wind about on our beam. Gradually we seemed to be paying off before the wind and heading for the open river. The water stretched away in every direction into the vast windy shadow.

Uncle James had been silent since the first taste of wind, but now he leaned toward me and spoke hoarsely. "Ask him where the devil he thinks he's going." There was a nervous intensity in his voice that at first made me smile, but as I glanced at Tuttle it occurred to me suddenly that our situation might be precarious. We had squared off pretty well before the wind, and were boiling along at the boat's maximum speed with two great rolls of foam spreading from the bow. And the captain was smiling with that glittery tight smile of his.

"Where away, skipper?" I shouted.

He didn't answer.

I shouted again. He glanced aloft at the hard-bellied sail and let three inches of sheet slip through his fingers.

We cut past a big river-bank elm and felt a sudden eddy grip and release the keel. The current was sweeping hard out there, with cakes of white ice and half invisible timbers riding downward on the flood. We streaked past everything.

Uncle James nudged me. "For God's sake, Tom, ask him what he's doing."

I leaned aft and tapped his knee. "Hey, skipper! Where bound?"

This time he looked at me and nodded faintly. "That rig," he said. "Works nice. The sail don't wrap round the mast the way it would if you had a regular boom on it."

Uncle James jumped up then and bellowed at him himself. "Listen, Tuttle, we'll be down the falls if you don't watch what you're doing. What's the idea?"

But Tuttle was fighting the eddies just then. The boat slewed and whirled. One jibe would have snapped the mast out of her.

Uncle James and I looked at each other. His long face had slackened and his mouth was a little bit open—not like a horse any more, but rather like a hopelessly anxious fish. He stammered something about a raving maniac, then grabbed my arm and whispered with sudden ferocity, "Hit him in the jaw, Tom. Paste him one. It's the only thing to do." His eyes darted up and down the length of the boat, searching for a weapon.

I tried to point out what would happen if Tuttle let go of the tiller even for a second. "We've got to go where he takes us," I explained in what I hoped was a reasonable tone of voice, expecting meanwhile to see the mast go overboard any moment.

Uncle James sank back muttering to himself, then started up suddenly again, leaning in front of me. "Look here, Tuttle, let's be sensible about this." He had to shout at the top of his voice, and somehow it sounded odd. But he kept on. "If you feel that we owe you something, why that's fair enough. I'll see to it myself—I give you my word right now—"

Tuttle's face was almost joyous as he stared straight ahead into the gloom. The sail shone white in the last of the westerly light, and beyond it was a great range of night-blue cloud lifting above the dark flood. We seemed to be racing down wind and down stream with fantastic speed, as though we too were part of that wild flying night. And ahead somewhere at the base of that cloud range was the black slick lip of a waterfall—even then I could hear the sustained roar of it sounding up against the wind.

"Do you hear, Tuttle?" Uncle James shouted again. "Just let me know what it is you want—"

It was as though he were screaming at the sky. Tuttle smiled and nodded again. The dinghy was slewing in the eddies, rolling down sometimes till the water foamed over the side. "You couldn't handle her with a gaff rig," he said. "You can see how clean she runs, too. No drag under the counter at all—"

It was probably true, but just then I had my mind on other things. I was, in fact, scared; I could feel my heart hammering up close to my throat. But I tried to speak rationally. "Why not try her to windward?" I suggested. "That would be a real test in this wind."

He glanced at me keenly. "Don't worry, son. I know what I'm doing."

I think those simple words destroyed whatever hopes I had grasped at. It was true; he knew exactly what he was doing. There was nothing more to be said.

We drove on down the river; the noise of the falls rose louder, like the sound of many trains. And Uncle James seemed to collapse little by little, as though his whole bodily structure were changing. That guarded, self-contained face slackened, drooped into a feeble caricature of itself in the same manner that sculptured ice gives way and distorts under a warm sun. His chin was trembling loosely and his eyes flickered from one thing to another without seeing anything; I wondered what images were fixed inside his brain—whether the image of the smooth, solid pour of the falls was there, and the engulfing tumult below them where life would end. He said nothing, though I think he tried several times to speak.

I remember how I felt no longer related to my own body. I was still aware of the enormity of the night—the great wind and torn clouds and the flood all rushing southward down the valley, and we seeming to rush faster, to ride the very crest itself of all that fury. A part of me was still clinging to the rail of the boat in half-senseless fright; somewhere inside me was the extreme nausea, the ultimate, annihilating dread of death; but above all that was a separate sort of consciousness, watching the dark fires of sunset far and low in the west, watching the white-flecked water, the hissing waves and the black flaws of wind streaking on ahead, watching Captain Tuttle's erect figure, his thin, joyous face peering off over our heads and commanding us. I remember thinking that as far as a human being could triumph under the conditions of life, he had done so; and I thought too that as far as one could suffer defeat and come to complete annihilation before the fact of death itself, Uncle James had done so.

It may have been that Captain Tuttle understood it too. He acted all through with superb certainty, as though each move had been perfectly arranged in advance, as though he had known exactly the point where he would ease the helm, gather in the sheet, and slant across to the slack water on the east shore. It was just when we could see clearly the white mist shrouding the falls, when the roar had risen high above the wind, and the river seemed to gather for the last, straight rush to the edge.

I don't think Uncle James realized when we cut out of the current. I had observed it in a detached sort of way, as though I were looking down on the manoeuvre from the top of the mast. It didn't surprise me, I think, or at the moment relieve my feelings. One probably counts on life even up to the moment of extinction, and is surprised only after it is too late.

But Uncle James was hardly aware of anything. When the captain with a last brilliant play of the helm had shot us to windward, dropped sail, and swung off to ground against a grassy hillside, Uncle James was still crouching against the rail, one hand gripping it with white-knuckled fingers. He got to land stupidly, with quivering limbs, and sat abruptly on the grass, staring down at it.

Captain Tuttle stood erect in his boat and bobbed his head at me, resetting his crumpled hat.

"You can tell your uncle," he said with dignity, "that he needn't worry about me anymore." He smiled faintly. "I expect you'll find a dry resting place."

I noticed that the boat's nose had swung off away from the bank; water was widening between.

"Throw me a line," I called.

He reached forward and hauled up his sail in one swift motion. There was some shelter here by the bank, but it snapped like a flag as he neatly coiled the halyard. Then he lowered the centerboard, took in the sheet. His smile was cheerful as he waved to me, and suddenly the boat quickened and leaped out into the twilight.

"I thought I'd try her to windward," his voice cut back clearly.

I saw the dark sail lean far over, then straighten again as the boat swept down the relentless torrent of the river.

James Still

THE STORIES and poems of James Still, appearing only within the last two or three years, have already given him a distinguished reputation as the interpreter of a region. One feels in his writing a deep-rooted love for his heritage, and a natural, intimate art which gives a full-flavored recording of Kentucky people and the Cumberland country. His characters, tenacious and individualistic, move against a background exactly and vividly observed by the eye of a poet.

Besides writing, James Still acts as librarian of the Hindman Settlement in Hindman, Kentucky. Among the stories which he has contributed to The Atlantic Monthly, The Yale Review, Story, and other magazines are "All Their Ways Are Dark," "The Egg Tree," "So Large a Thing as Seven," and "Brother to Methuselum." A book of poems Hounds on the Mountain was published recently.

JOB'S TEARS *

James Still

I

THE FALL HAD been dry and the giant milkweed pods broke early in September. Lean Neck Creek dried to a thread, and all the springs under the moss were damp pockets without a sound of water. Father had sent me over from Little Carr in April to help Grandma with the crop while Uncle Jolly laid out a spell in the county jail for dynamiting a mill dam. I was seven and Grandma was eighty-four, and we patched out two acres of corn. Even with the crows, the crab grass, and the dwarfed stalks we made enough bread to feed us until spring, but when the grass was gone there would be nothing for the mare. The hayloft was empty and the corncrib a nest of shucks.

* From The Atlantic Monthly, March, 1937. Copyright, 1937, by The Atlantic Monthly. Reprinted by permission of The Atlantic Monthly and the author.

Uncle Luce sent word from Pigeon Roost that he would come to help gather the crop early in September. Grandma's bones ached with rheumatism and she was not able to go again in the fields. She sat in the cool of the dogtrot, dreading the sun. We waited through the parching days, pricking our ears to every nag's heel against a stone in the valley, to the creak of harness and dry-wheel groan of wagons in the creek bed. Field mice fattened in the patches. Heavy orange cups of the trumpet vine bloomed in the cornstalks, and field larks blew dustily from row to row, feeding well where the mice had scattered their greedy harvesting. We waited impatiently for Uncle Luce, knowing that when he came we should hear from Uncle Jolly, and that Uncle Luce would take the mare home for the winter.

'It's Rilla that's keeping him away,' Grandma said. 'Luce's woman was always sot agin' him doing for his ol' Mommy. I reckon Luce fotched her off too young. She wasn't nigh sixteen when they married.'

We waited for Uncle Luce until the moon was full in October. The leaves ripened, and the air was bloated with the smell of pawpaws where the black fruit lay rotting upon the ground. Possums came to feed there in the night, and two got into a box trap I set above the barn. We ate one, steeped in gravy with sweet potatoes. I shut the other up in a pen, Grandma saying we would eat it when Uncle Jolly got home. She was lonesome for him, and spoke of him through the days. 'I reckon he's a grain wild and hardheaded,' Grandma said, 'but he tuk care of his ol' Mommy.'

One morning Grandma said we could wait no longer for Uncle Luce. She took her grapevine walking stick and we went into the cornfield. We worked two days pulling corn from the small, hoe-tended stalks. When all the runted ears were gathered she measured them out in pokes, pulling her bonnet down over her face to hide the rheumatic pain twisting her face. There were sixteen bushels. 'We won't be needin' the barn this time,' she said. 'We'll just sack up the puny nubbins and put them in the shedroom.'

With the corn in we waited a few days until Grandma's rheumatism had been doctored with herbs and bitter cherry-bark tea. Then there were the heavy-leaved cabbages, the cushaws and sweet potatoes to be gathered. The potatoes had grown large that year. Grandma crawled along the rows on her knees, digging in the baked earth with her hands. It was good to see such fine potatoes. 'When Jolly comes home he'll shore eat a bellyful,' she said.

I ran along the rows with a willow basket, piling it full and spreading the potatoes in the sun to sweeten. Once I ran into a bull nettle, and it was like fire burning my bare legs. I scratched and whimpered. Grandma took a twist of tobacco out of her apron, chewed a piece for a few minutes, and rubbed the juice on the fiery flesh. 'You ain't big as a tick,' she said, 'but you're a right smart help to your ol' Granny.'

The days shortened. There was a hint of frost in the air. The nights were loud with honking geese, and suddenly the leaves were down before gusts of wind. The days were noisy with blowing, and the house filled with the sound of crickets' thighs. There were no birds in the bare orchard, not even the small note of a chewink through the days.

Before frost fell we went into Grandma's flower bed in a corner of the garden and picked the dry seeds before they scattered. We broke off the brown heads of old maids and the smooth buttons of Job's tears hanging on withered stalks. 'There's enough tears for a pretty string of beads,' Grandma said, 'and enough seed left for planting.'

Later we pulled and bundled the fodder in the field, stripping the patches for the mare in her dark stall. 'If Luce don't come, Poppet is going to starve afore the winter goes out,' Grandma said. 'It's Rilla hating me that keeps him from coming. Oh, she'll larn all her children to grow up hating their ol' Granny.'

Uncle Luce came after the first frost. He came whistling up the path from Dry Neck with the icy stones crackling under his feet. Since the gathering, Grandma had been in bed with rheumatism in her back, getting up only to cook. Uncle Luce was filled with excuses. Rilla was sick, and it was getting near her time. His four daughters had had chicken pox. 'I'm hoping and praying the next one will be a boy-child,' Luce said. 'A day's coming when I'll need help with my crap. Girls ain't fitten to grub stumps and hold a plough in the ground.'

Grandma noticed Uncle Luce's hands were blackened with resin, and asked if he'd been logging. 'I had to scratch up a little something to buy medicine for Rilla,' he said. 'My crap never done nothing this year. It never got the proper seasoning. I reckon I'll be buying bread afore spring.'

'I was reckoning you'd take the mare home for the winter,' Grandma said. 'I was thinking you could ride her back to Pigeon Roost.'

'I hain't got feed for my own mare,' Luce said. 'I'll be buying corn for my nag afore another month. I reckon Poppet has already eat up more than she's worth. She must be twelve years old. The day's com-

ing you'll need another nag to crap with. It would be right proper
to take ol' Poppet out and end her misery.'

Grandma raised up in anger. 'Luce Baldridge, if you was in reach
I'd pop your mouth,' she said. Then she lay back and cried a little.
Uncle Luce went over and shook her, saying he never meant a word
about old Poppet. He wouldn't shoot her for a war pension.

Uncle Luce didn't say a word about Uncle Jolly until Grandma
asked him. She waited a long time, giving him a chance to tell her
without asking. 'You hain't said a word yet about your own brother,'
Grandma said. 'It's about time you told.' Then we learned that Uncle
Jolly's trial had come up the last of September, and he had been
sentenced to the state penitentiary for two years. 'I'll get one of the
boys to move in with you next March,' Uncle Luce said. 'Toll would
be right glad to come. He's renting land, anyway. And his wife
would be a sight o' company.'

'No,' Grandma said. 'We'll make out. My children I've worked and
slaved for have thrown their ol' Mommy away. Now that I can't
fetch and carry for them, they never give me a grain o' thought. I've
been patient and long-suffering. The Lord knows that.'

She was crying again now, thinking how Uncle Luce had waited
until the crop was gathered to come, thinking how Rilla hadn't come
to see her in three years, and how Uncle Jolly was shut up in jail.

'I figure you'd fare better with Toll than Jolly,' Luce said. 'Toll is
solid as rock and never give you a minute's trouble. Jolly is a puore
devil. He jumps in and out of trouble like a cricket. I hope the pen
will make him pull his horns in a little.'

Grandma's voice trembled a little as she spoke. 'Jolly is young,' she
said. 'He just turned grown last year. He ain't mean to the bone, and
he's the only one of my boys that looks after their ol' Mommy. I'm
afeared I won't live till he gets back. I pray the Lord to keep me
breathing till he comes.'

Grandma was quiet again when Uncle Luce got ready to go. She
brought out a string of Job's tears she had been threading. 'It might
pleasure Rilla to have them,' she said. 'It might help with her time
coming.'

II

During the short winter days the sun was feeble and pale, shining
without heat. Frost lay thick in the mornings, and crusts of hard earth
rose in the night on little toadstools of ice. Footsteps upon the ground

rang metal-clear, and there was a pattern of furred feet where the rabbits came down out of the barren fields into the yard. My possum rolled himself into a gray ball in his pen, refusing to eat the potatoes I brought him, and then one morning I found him dead. His rusty, hairless tail was frozen as stiff as a stickweed. The mare grew gaunt in her stall, and there was not a wisp of straw left underfoot. I gleaned the loft of every fodder blade, and the crib of shucks. I filled the manger with cobs, but she did not gnaw upon them, choosing instead to nibble the rotting poplar logs of the wall. I led her down to Lean Neck every day, breaking a hole in the ice near the bank. After a few days she would not drink, and I began to take a bucket of water to the barn. I fed her a little corn—as much as I dared—out of our nubbin pile in the shedroom.

The cold increased and the whole valley was drawn as tight as a drum. The breaking of a bough in the wood shattered the air, the sound dropping like a plummet down the hills, striking against the icy ridges. In the evenings I took an old quilt out to the barn and covered Poppet. I dug frozen chunks of coal out of a pile beside the smokehouse for the fire, and when it seemed there was not going to be enough to last the winter through I went out on the mountain beyond the beech grove and picked up small lumps where the coal bloomed darkly under the ledge. The fire was fed from my pickings until snow fell, covering all traces of the brittle veins.

There were days when Grandma was too sick to get out of bed. I baked potatoes, fried thick slices of side meat, and cooked a corn pone in a skillet on the fire. We used the coffee grounds until there was no strength in them. When the meal gave out I shelled off some corn and ran it through the coffee grinder. It came out coarse and lumpy, but it made good bread.

As Grandma got better she would sit up in bed with a pile of pillows at her back. She slept only at night. During the day she was busy listening and counting. She knew how many knots there were in the ceiling planks. She could look at a knot a long time, and then tell you a man who had a face like it. Most of them were old folks, dead before my time, but there they were. There was one knot that looked like Uncle Jolly. Grandma used to look at it by the hour. 'I'm afeared I'll have to piddle my days out looking at this knot,' she would say.

One day she counted the stitches in the piece-quilt on her bed. They ran to a count I had never heard. 'I learnt to figure,' Grandma said, 'but I never learnt to read writing. My man could read afore he died, and he done all the reading and I done the figuring. We always worked our learning like a team of horses.' We had no calendar, but Grandma worked the number of days until Uncle Jolly would get out of the penitentiary. 'It's nigh on to six hundred and fifty-five,' she said when the counting was done. The time had not seemed so long before. Now it stretched along an endless road of days.

There were hours of talk about Uncle Jolly. Grandma said he had held no old grudge against Pate Horn. Grandpa used to log with Pate before he died. Uncle Toll had married one of Pate's daughters. It had been the dam he built across Troublesome Creek that Uncle Jolly hadn't liked. The fish couldn't jump it, and none could get up into Lean Neck to spawn. He sent Pate word to open up one end of the dam until the spawning season was over. Pate didn't move a peg. Uncle Jolly went down one day and set off two sticks of dynamite under the left bank, blowing out three logs. He went down, with daylight burning, to blow that dam up.

'Jolly ought not to done it,' Grandma said. 'It looks like the Lord is trying my patience in my last days when I'm weak and porely.'

Sometimes she would tell about the things Uncle Jolly had done as a boy. 'Once he got a hollow log and tied a strip o' dried bull's hide over it,' she said. 'Then he got a hickory limb and sawed on it. It sounded like a passel o' wildcats tearing each other's eyeballs out. Cattle all over the country jumped the rails and tuk down the hollows. The horses and mules kicked barn doors down and lit out. Oh, he never meant no harm. It was just boy-mischief.'

Near the middle of December the mare stopped eating the nubbins of corn I took her. She would mull her nose in the bucket of water without drinking, and roll her moist eyes at me.

I opened her stall door and let her wander into the midday sunlight. She did not go far, lifting her leaden hoofs through the snow, and turning from the wind. Presently she went back into the stall and stayed there with her head drooped and her eyes half closed. One morning I went out and found her stretched upon the ground. Her nose was thinly sheeted with ice. She was dead. I latched the stall door and did not go back into the barn again that winter.

III

January was a bell in Lean Neck Valley. The ring of the axe was a mile wide, and all passage over the spewed-up earth was lifted on the frosty air and sounded against fields of ice. Icicles as large as a man's body hung from limestone cliffs. Grandma listened to the little sounds when her work was done. She was better now. At times when the wind was not so keen she cooked on the stove instead of the fireplace, but it was hard to keep warm in the drafty kitchen.

One Sunday Grandma heard a nag's hoofs on the path to the house. It was Uncle Toll from Troublesome Creek. He brought us a letter from Uncle Jolly and he read it to us. His face was dull with worry. Uncle Jolly was coming home. There had been a fire in the prison. 'Mommy, do you reckon he broke jail during that fire?' he asked. 'He ain't nigh started his spell.'

'Jolly is liable to do anything he sets his mind to,' Grandma said. 'He always had his mind sot on looking after his ol' Mommy. I reckon he'd do anything to get out.' And now there was no joy in his coming. There was nothing to do but wait, and those three days before he came seemed longer than any count Grandma ever made.

Suddenly he was there one morning, hollering to us from the yard. There was Uncle Jolly. He had slipped up on us, and even Grandma had not heard him come. He stood there before the door, his eyes bright as a thrush's. He had on a black suit, and a black hat with the crown pinched up sitting at an angle on his head. We sat looking at him, awed and not moving. He jumped into the room and grabbed me up in his arms, pitching me headlong toward the ceiling and bumping my head against the rafters. It hurt a little. He jerked Grandma out of her chair and swung her over the floor. She was laughing and crying together. 'For God's sake, Jolly,' she said, 'don't crack your ol' Mommy's ribs.'

Then he was all over the house, prying and looking. He opened up the meat box and sniffed into it. He thumped the pork shoulder we had been saving. 'Ripe as a melon,' he said. 'It smells like kingdom come.' He reached elbow-deep into his pocket and drew out a knife. It was a big one. With a single blade open, it was nearly a foot long. There was a blue racer carved on one side with a forked tongue. 'I made it in the workshop,' he said. 'They never knowed I was making it.' He swung it through the air, striking toward me. *Plunk* it went into the pork shoulder. Uncle Jolly was devilish like that. Grandma was already sifting out meal, and he cut off a half-dozen slices of meat to fry.

Uncle Jolly found the corn in the shedroom. He picked up one of the runted ears and pinched a grain. 'Is this all you raised?' he asked.

'We got some might pretty cushaws,' Grandma said. 'The sweet taters done right well, too.'

'The mare will starve on this corn,' Jolly said. 'You know what I'm going to do? I'm going to buy ol' Poppet a sack of sweet feed mixed with molasses and bran. I reckon her teeth is wore down to the gum.'

He began to gather up some ears to take to the barn.

'Just you wait, son,' Grandma called. 'Just you wait till we get dinner over.' Grandma looked hard at me. I didn't say a word.

When we sat down to the table, Uncle Jolly began to eat with both hands. 'I ain't had a fitten meal since I left Lean Neck,' he said. He loaded his plate with shucky beans and a slice of meat, talking as he ate. 'I stayed at Luce's house last night,' he said. 'Luce and Rilla's got another girl-child born three weeks ago.'

Grandma laid her fork down and stirred in her chair. 'Is Rilla getting along tolerable?' she asked.

'Rilla is up and doing,' Uncle Jolly said. 'They named the baby after you, Mommy. They named it Lonie.'

Grandma blinked and made a little clicking noise with her teeth. 'It's good to have grandchildren growing up honoring and respecting their ol' folks,' she said.

'Oh, Uncle Jolly,' I begged, 'tell us about the jail fire and how you got out.' Uncle Jolly swallowed, the raw lump of his Adam's apple jumping in his throat. 'It was the biggest fire ever was,' he said. 'It caught the woodshop and tool sheds, and it was eating fast. It might o' got the jailhouse if I hadn't stayed there and fit it with a waterspout. Everybody else run around like a chicken with its head pinched off. Then the Governor heard how I fit the fire and never run, and he give me a pardon. He sent me word to go home.'

Grandma settled in her chair. 'It was dangerous, son,' she said. 'It might o' burned up the jail. Whoever sot that fire ought to be whipped with oxhide. Some folks is everly destroying and putting nothing back. Who lit that fire, son?'

Uncle Jolly's mouth was too full to answer. He dropped his eyes and swallowed. 'I sot it, Mommy,' he said. He took another slice of meat, and heaped more beans on his plate. Grandma sat quiet and watching, her blue-veined hands clasped in her lap. Her face was sad, but her eyes were bright with wonder.

'You know what I done coming up Troublesome Creek this morning?' Uncle Jolly asked suddenly. 'I pulled another log out of Pate Horn's mill dam. There's a good-sized hole now. The perch will be swarming into Lean Neck this spring.'

Sherwood Anderson

THE FIRST stories of Sherwood Anderson, appearing in experimental magazines a generation ago, were extraordinarily fresh and exciting. Like D. H. Lawrence, whose work he came to admire after his own position was established, he was preoccupied with the inner drama of the soul, and he sought to express his faith in instinct, in the groping impulse which moved his characters toward something finer than they knew. In his rejection of the "plot" story, his scorn of contrived fiction, he became a powerful influence upon American story telling. His style, owing much to Gertrude Stein, is artful in its naiveté. At the worst his stories are confused and soft; at their best they show a beautiful understanding and compassion for the troubles of ordinary people. No American writer has surpassed him in the sympathetic portrayal of "grotesques" in character and situation.

Sherwood Anderson was born in Ohio in 1876, the third child of a poverty-stricken, nomadic family. His father, he tells us, was himself a born story-teller. After many odd jobs, Anderson was successful in a business career which he deliberately abandoned to follow his desire for creative expression. He began writing in Chicago. His most interesting books are Winesburg, Ohio (1919); The Triumph of the Egg (1921); Horses and Men (1923); A Story-teller's Story (1924); Dark Laughter (1925); and Death in the Woods (1933). He now lives in Marion, Virginia, the country editor of two newspapers.

SOPHISTICATION *

Sherwood Anderson

IT WAS EARLY evening of a day in the late fall and the Winesburg County Fair had brought crowds of country people into town. The day had been clear and the night came on warm and pleasant. On the Trunion Pike, where the road after it left town stretched away between berry fields now covered with dry brown leaves, the dust from passing wagons arose in clouds. Children, curled into little balls, slept on the straw scattered on wagon beds. Their hair was full of dust and their fingers black and sticky. The dust rolled away over the fields and the departing sun set it ablaze with colors.

In the main street of Winesburg crowds filled the stores and the sidewalks. Night came on, horses whinnied, the clerks in the stores ran madly about, children became lost and cried lustily, an American town worked terribly at the task of amusing itself.

Pushing his way through the crowds in Main Street, young George Willard concealed himself in the stairway leading to Doctor Reefy's office and looked at the people. With feverish eyes he watched the faces drifting past under the store lights. Thoughts kept coming into his head and he did not want to think. He stamped impatiently on the wooden steps and looked sharply about. "Well, is she going to stay with him all day? Have I done all this waiting for nothing?" he muttered.

George Willard, the Ohio village boy, was fast growing into manhood and new thoughts had been coming into his mind. All that day, amid the jam of people at the Fair, he had gone about feeling lonely. He was about to leave Winesburg to go away to some city where he hoped to get work on a city newpaper and he felt grown up. The mood that had taken possession of him was a thing known to men and unknown to boys. He felt old and a little tired. Memories awoke in him. To his mind his new sense of maturity set him apart, made of him a half-tragic figure. He wanted someone to understand the feeling that had taken possession of him after his mother's death.

There is a time in the life of every boy when he for the first time takes the backward view of life. Perhaps that is the moment when

* From *Winesburg, Ohio* by Sherwood Anderson. Copyright, 1919. Published by The Viking Press, Inc., New York.

he crosses the line into manhood. The boy is walking through the street of his town. He is thinking of the future and of the figure he will cut in the world. Ambitions and regrets awake within him. Suddenly something happens; he stops under a tree and waits as for a voice calling his name. Ghosts of old things creep into his consciousness; the voices outside of himself whisper a message concerning the limitations of life. From being quite sure of himself and his future he becomes not at all sure. If he be an imaginative boy a door is torn open and for the first time he looks out upon the world, seeing, as though they marched in procession before him, the countless figures of men who before his time have come out of nothingness into the world, lived their lives and again disappeared into nothingness. The sadness of sophistication has come to the boy. With a little gasp he sees himself as merely a leaf blown by the wind through the streets of his village. He knows that in spite of all the stout talk of his fellows he must live and die in uncertainty, a thing blown by the winds, a thing destined like corn to wilt in the sun. He shivers and looks eagerly about. The eighteen years he has lived seem but a moment, a breathing space in the long march of humanity. Already he hears death calling. With all his heart he wants to come close to some other human, touch someone with his hands, be touched by the hand of another. If he prefers that the other be a woman, that is because he believes that a woman will be gentle, that she will understand. He wants, most of all, understanding.

When the moment of sophistication came to George Willard his mind turned to Helen White, the Winesburg banker's daughter. Always he had been conscious of the girl growing into womanhood as he grew into manhood. Once on a summer night when he was eighteen, he had walked with her on a country road and in her presence had given way to an impulse to boast, to make himself appear big and significant in her eyes. Now he wanted to see her for another purpose. He wanted to tell her of the new impulses that had come to him. He had tried to make her think of him as a man when he knew nothing of manhood and now he wanted to be with her and to try to make her feel the change he believed had taken place in his nature.

As for Helen White, she also had come to a period of change. What George felt, she in her young woman's way felt also. She was no longer a girl and hungered to reach into the grace and beauty of womanhood. She had come home from Cleveland, where she was attending college, to spend a day at the Fair. She also had begun to have memories. During the day she sat in the grandstand with a young man, one of the instructors from the college, who was a guest of her mother's. The young man was of a pedantic turn of mind and she felt at once he would not do for her purpose. At the Fair she was glad to be seen in his company as he was well dressed and a stranger. She knew that the fact of his presence would create an impression. During the day she was happy, but when night came on she began to grow restless. She wanted to drive the instructor away, to get out of his presence. While they sat together in the grand-stand and while the eyes of former schoolmates were upon them, she paid so much attention to her escort that he grew interested. "A scholar needs money. I should marry a woman with money," he mused.

Helen White was thinking of George Willard even as he wandered gloomily through the crowds thinking of her. She remembered the summer evening when they had walked together and wanted to walk with him again. She thought that the months she had spent in the city, the going to theatres and the seeing of great crowds wandering in lighted thoroughfares, had changed her profoundly. She wanted him to feel and be conscious of the change in her nature.

The summer evening together that had left its mark on the memory of both the young man and woman had, when looked at quite sensibly, been rather stupidly spent. They had walked out of town along a country road. Then they had stopped by a fence near a field of young corn and George had taken off his coat and let it hang on his arm. "Well, I've stayed here in Winesburg—yes— I've not yet gone away but I'm growing up," he had said. "I've been reading books and I've been thinking. I'm going to try to amount to something in life."

"Well," he explained, "that isn't the point. Perhaps I'd better quit talking."

The confused boy put his hand on the girl's arm. His voice trembled. The two started to walk back along the road toward town. In his desperation George boasted, "I'm going to be a big man, the biggest that ever lived here in Winesburg," he declared. "I want you to do something, I don't know what. Perhaps it is none of my business. I want you to try to be different from other women. You see the point. It's none of my business I tell you. I want you to be a beautiful woman. You see what I want."

The boy's voice failed and in silence the two came back into town and went along the street to Helen White's house. At the gate he tried to say something impressive. Speeches he had thought out came into his head, but they seemed utterly pointless. "I thought —I used to think—I had it in my mind you would marry Seth Richmond. Now I know you won't," was all he could find to say as she went through the gate and toward the door of her house.

On the warm fall evening as he stood in the stairway and looked at the crowd drifting through Main Street, George thought of the talk beside the field of young corn and was ashamed of the figure he had made of himself. In the street the people surged up and down like cattle confined in a pen. Buggies and wagons almost filled the narrow thoroughfare. A band played and small boys raced along the sidewalk, diving between the legs of men. Young men with shining red faces walked awkwardly about with girls on their arms. In a room above one of the stores, where a dance was to be held, the fiddlers tuned their instruments. The broken sounds floated down through an open window and out across the murmur of voices and the loud blare of the horns of the band. The medley of sounds got on young Willard's nerves. Everywhere, on all sides, the sense of crowding, moving life closed in about him. He wanted to run away by himself and think. "If she wants to stay with that fellow she may. Why should I care? What difference does it make to me?" he growled and went along Main Street and through Hern's grocery into a side street.

George felt so utterly lonely and dejected that he wanted to weep but pride made him walk rapidly along, swinging his arms. He came to Westley Moyer's livery barn and stopped in the shadows to listen to a group of men who talked of a race Westley's stallion, Tony Tip, had won at the Fair during the afternoon. A crowd had gathered in front of the barn and before the crowd walked Westley, prancing up and down and boasting. He held a whip in his hand and kept tapping the ground. Little puffs of dust arose in the lamplight. "Hell, quit your talking," Westley exclaimed. "I wasn't afraid, I knew I had 'em beat all the time. I wasn't afraid."

Ordinarily George Willard would have been intensely interested in the boasting of Moyer, the horseman. Now it made him angry. He turned and hurried away along the street. "Old windbag," he sputtered. "Why does he want to be bragging? Why don't he shut up?"

George went into a vacant lot and as he hurried along, fell over a pile of rubbish. A nail protruding from an empty barrel tore his trousers. He sat down on the ground and swore. With a pin he mended the torn place and then arose and went on. "I'll go to Helen White's house, that's what I'll do. I'll walk right in. I'll say that I want to see her. I'll walk right in and sit down, that's what I'll do," he declared, climbing over a fence and beginning to run.

On the veranda of Banker White's house Helen was restless and distraught. The instructor sat between the mother and daughter. His talk wearied the girl. Although he had also been raised in an Ohio town, the instructor began to put on the airs of the city. He wanted to appear cosmopolitan. "I like the chance you have given me to study the background out of which most of our girls come," he declared. "It was good of you, Mrs. White, to have me down for the day." He turned to Helen and laughed. "Your life is still bound up with the life of this town?" he asked. "There are people here in whom you are interested?" To the girl his voice sounded pompous and heavy.

Helen arose and went into the house. At the door leading to a garden at the back she stopped and stood listening. Her mother began to talk. "There is no one here fit to associate with a girl of Helen's breeding," she said.

Helen ran down a flight of stairs at the back of the house and into the garden. In the darkness she stopped and stood trembling. It seemed to her that the world was full of meaningless people saying words. Afire with eagerness she ran through a garden gate and turning a corner by the banker's barn, went into a little side street. "George! Where are you, George?" she cried, filled with nervous excitement. She stopped running, and leaned against a tree to laugh hysterically. Along the dark little street came George Willard, still saying words. "I'm going to walk right into her house. I'll go right in and sit down," he declared as he came up to her. He stopped and stared stupidly. "Come on," he said and took hold of her hand. With hanging heads they walked away along the street under the trees. Dry leaves rustled under foot. Now that he had found her George wondered what he had better do and say.

At the upper end of the fair ground, in Winesburg, there is a half decayed old grand-stand. It has never been painted and the

boards are all warped out of shape. The fair ground stands on top
of a low hill rising out of the valley of Wine Creek and from the
grand-stand one can see at night, over a cornfield, the lights of the
town reflected against the sky.

George and Helen climbed the hill to the fair ground, coming
by the path past Waterworks Pond. The feeling of loneliness and
isolation that had come to the young man in the crowded streets
of his town was both broken and intensified by the presence of
Helen. What he felt was reflected in her.

In youth there are always two forces fighting in people. The
warm unthinking little animal struggles against the thing that reflects
and remembers, and the older, the more sophisticated thing had
possession of George Willard. Sensing his mood, Helen walked beside
him filled with respect. When they got to the grand-stand they
climbed up under the roof and sat down on one of the long bench-
like seats.

There is something memorable in the experience to be had by
going into a fair ground that stands at the edge of a Middle
Western town on a night after the annual fair has been held. The
sensation is one never to be forgotten. On all sides are ghosts, not
of the dead, but of living people. Here, during the day just passed,
have come the people pouring in from the town and the country
around. Farmers with their wives and children and all the people
from the hundreds of little frame houses have gathered within these
board walls. Young girls have laughed and men with beards have
talked of the affairs of their lives. The place has been filled to overflowing with life. It has itched and squirmed with life and now it
is night and the life has all gone away. The silence is almost terrifying. One conceals oneself standing silently beside the trunk of
a tree and what there is of a reflective tendency in his nature is
intensified. One shudders at the thought of the meaninglessness of
life while at the same instant, and if the people of the town are his
people, one loves life so intensely that tears come into the eyes.

In the darkness under the roof of the grandstand, George Willard
sat beside Helen White and felt very keenly his own insignificance
in the scheme of existence. Now that he had come out of town where
the presence of the people stirring about, busy with a multitude of
affairs, had been so irritating the irritation was all gone. The presence
of Helen renewed and refreshed him. It was as though her woman's
hand was assisting him to make some minute readjustment of the

machinery of his life. He began to think of the people in the town where he had always lived with something like reverence. He had reverence for Helen. He wanted to love and to be loved by her, but he did not at the moment want to be confused by her womanhood. In the darkness he took hold of her hand and when she crept close put a hand on her shoulder. A wind began to blow and he shivered. With all his strength he tried to hold and to understand the mood that had come upon him. In that high place in the darkness the two oddly sensitive human atoms held each other tightly and waited. In the mind of each was the same thought. "I have come to this lonely place and here is this other," was the substance of the thing felt.

In Winesburg the crowded day had run itself out into the long night of the late fall. Farm horses jogged away along lonely country roads pulling their portion of weary people. Clerks began to bring samples of goods in off the sidewalks and lock the doors of stores. In the Opera House a crowd had gathered to see a show and further down Main Street the fiddlers, their instruments tuned, sweated and worked to keep the feet of youth flying over a dance floor.

In the darkness in the grand-stand Helen White and George Willard remained silent. Now and then the spell that held them was broken and they turned and tried in the dim light to see into each others eyes. They kissed but that impulse did not last. At the upper end of the fair ground a half dozen men worked over horses that had raced during the afternoon. The men had built a fire and were heating kettles of water. Only their legs could be seen as they passed back and forth in the light. When the wind blew the little flames of the fire danced crazily about.

George and Helen arose and walked away into the darkness. They went along a path past a field of corn that had not yet been cut. The wind whispered among the dry corn blades. For a moment during the walk back into town the spell that held them was broken. When they had come to the crest of Waterworks Hill they stopped by a tree and George again put his hands on the girl's shoulders. She embraced him eagerly and then again they drew quickly back from that impulse. They stopped kissing and stood a little apart. Mutual respect grew big in them. They were both embarrassed and to relieve their embarrassment dropped into the animalism of youth. They laughed and began to pull and haul at each other. In some way chastened and purified by the mood they had been in they became, not man and woman, not boy and girl, but excited little animals.

It was so they went down the hill. In the darkness they played like two splendid young things in a young world. Once, running swiftly forward, Helen tripped George and he fell. He squirmed and shouted. Shaking with laughter, he rolled down the hill. Helen ran after him. For just a moment she stopped in the darkness. There is no way of knowing what woman's thoughts went through her mind but, when the bottom of the hill was reached and she came up to the boy, she took his arm and walked beside him in dignified silence. For some reason they could not have explained they had both got from their silent evening together the thing needed. Man or boy, woman or girl, they had for a moment taken hold of the thing that makes the mature life of men and women in the modern world possible.

$\mathcal{F}erner \ \mathcal{N}uhn$

FERNER NUHN's stories are not many, but they are distinguished because they are the expression of an imagination which goes directly to its specific experience, enjoys it, and records it naturally with no literary pretense. Mr. Nuhn is a writer who likes, more than most, to know what the writer is up to, and in his essay "Art and Identity," published in American Caravan IV, he has made an absorbing comment upon the province and privilege of the artist.

Three of his stories "Ten," "Millennium," and "The Old Ladies' Man" appeared in The American Mercury when that magazine, under H. L. Mencken's editorship, was publishing some of the best writing in the country. He has written a number of articles on Iowa affairs for The Nation and The New Republic; and has been at work in recent years upon a critical book The Wind Blows from the East, dealing with the aristocratic tradition in American letters.

Ferner Nuhn was born in Cedar Falls, Iowa, in 1903, graduated from North Central College in Illinois, taught English at the University of Illinois, and for a while was "some time student" at the Columbia Graduate School. He is married to Ruth Suckow.

TEN *

Ferner Nuhn

I

SUPPER WAS over in the cottage and Eric must go ·after the milk. But he liked to go after the milk. He jumped off the back porch and sidled through the posts in the fence, fixed in a triangle to keep

---

* From *The American Mercury*, December, 1927. Reprinted by permission of Ferner Nuhn and revised by him for this book.

out cows. He raced along the black damp path that cut the low brush-land till you got to Sunfish Creek. That was Eric's name for it. At the creek, scorning the safe bridge made of two logs and cross-boards—which was all right for cowardly adults and skittish young girls—he balanced precariously over the old single log, moss-covered and water-soaked now, and holding back a mass of weeds and drift-wood on the up-stream side. He climbed the bluff on the other side and set out across what he called The Plateau.

The sun was still high in the west, with the long June evening ahead. A light wind had come up to break the still heat of the afternoon. At the far side of The Plateau, Eric's two giant cotton-woods lifted their great branches, and their glossy leaves flashed like spangles where they caught the sun.

Eric liked to go after the milk. He was proud that he go after it alone, the mile through the woods to Christiansen's farmhouse. Last summer, his father had always gone with him—or rather, he had gone with his father. This summer he could do it alone. It was one of the reasons he had looked forward especially to the time when his father had his two-weeks vacation, and the family took the cottage up the river.

The cottage was made of barn-siding, painted white, perched on piles three feet above the ground—that was because of the spring floods. Eric thought it was splendid. The river was splendid, too, flowing big and deep and cool in front of the cottage. But even more wonderful was what lay in back of the cottage: woods, and ravines, and creeks, and ponds—a regular wilderness. Of course, if you went far enough, you came out on the farms again, like Christiansen's farm, where he was going. But then, if you stuck to the creeks and ponds you could go a long way—any distance, as far as Eric knew—without running into houses or civilized things.

Frogs jumped in front of you from the banks of the ponds, plopping into the water with a sound like pulling a cork. You could throw a pebble and see whether the little black knob on the surface of the water was the head of a turtle or only the top of a snag. There were deep pools in the creeks containing unknown great fish, only waiting for the right kind of bait to be caught. Some of the mounds you came across in the woods were undoubtedly Indian Mounds, with old bones and weapons in them, if you knew where to dig. Eric's father had found a tomahawk head once, right on The Plateau! It was in the relic room of the Public Library: "Indian

Tomahawk Head, Probably Sioux, Found on the Banks of the Manetka River by Thorvald Morgenson, 1910." Eric had never ceased looking for tomahawk and arrow heads.

Eric took the path on the other side of The Plateau. He looked longingly at the Grapevine Swing, the great, snaky cable dropping from the sky-branches of an elm. No time to climb it now, maybe tomorrow, tomorrow morning, early. He raced along the path, where it dipped through the gloom of a dense little wild-plum thicket, then emerged in a flat meadow of rag weed and wild grasses. He stopped to examine an Indian Tobacco plant. The tobacco was still green. It would be cured later in the summer—brown and crisp—so that you could shell it off with your fingers.

He walked on, but suddenly stopped short, then moved back three paces, his eyes fixed on the edge of The Sand Pit, thirty yards ahead. His face hardened with resolution; he took two or three deep breaths, shifted the milk pail to a firm hold in his right hand, and sprinted with all his might. He leapt into empty space, twelve feet out and four feet down, and his bare heels pounded deep into the soft sand. The force of landing sent him sprawling on his side; and the milk pail rolled away, losing its cover. He got up quickly, leaving the pail where it was, and knelt down to examine his jump. "Nope," he muttered, sighting across to a peg on the edge of the pit, "missed her by about four inches." The peg told what his best jump was, and he shook his head at not having beat his record.

Then he rose up, making a few chance strokes at his knickerbockers with a general view to brushing them, and recovered the milk pail. This he knocked upside down against his knee to shake the sand out. He climbed out of the pit.

II

Presently he heard laughter and voices. They came from the direction of Second Bayou, a backwater of the Manetka River, and a favorite picnic spot. Eric crept silently toward the voices. Soon through the trees he made out a party of young people, "spooners" Eric called them, with a lot of baskets and cushions. Their canoes were pulled up on the shore; Second Bayou behind them was a brown mirror with the green trees opposite glimmering vertically in it. Eric stalked the party from the side of a tree.

One of the fellows was fumbling at a pile of sticks and papers, and a girl was laughing at him. She said, "Carl has just used up the last match! Isn't he a fine boy scout!"

The fellow stood up and ran his hand through his hair. "Anybody got some more matches?" he asked.

The others dropped what they were doing and looked at Carl. "Good Lord, did you use all those I gave you?" somebody said.

"Damn wood is wet," said Carl.

"What's a weenie roast without a fire?" pouted the girl.

Eric by his tree hesitated, trembled, then stepped forward. "I can get you some matches," he said. He surprised himself as much as he did the others.

One girl gave a little yelp and they all swung around. "Huck Finn to the rescue," said one.

"Fine," said Carl. "How soon?"

Eric said, "I'll borrow some at Christiansen's. I'll be back this way in ten minutes."

"Great stuff!" said Carl.

Eric turned about and ran, clutching the milk pail against his side. "Run the whole way," he muttered through set teeth. Soon he was bounding over the little grassy hummocks in Christiansen's pasture. He banked around the curve of Christiansen's pond, clambered over the wooden gate of the farm yard. Panting at the back door he asked, "Morgenson's milk, please. And . . . could you lend me . . . some matches? There are some . . . people who . . . can't start a fire."

Fat Mrs. Christiansen said, "My, such a hurry we're in! Winifred! Bring Eric some matches." She took the milk pail and waddled out to the milk shed.

Eric hurried back with the matches, holding the pail of milk carefully away from him, so that it wouldn't spill.

The party greeted him hilariously.

"Real service, I'll say," said Carl. He was going to take the matches from Eric, but Eric held on to them, looking down at the pile of sticks that had been meant for a fire.

"Say!" said Eric, "That's no way to build a fire." He set the milk pail next a tree and knelt down by the sticks. "Let me show you."

"Now Carl!" said the girl. "Take a lesson from a real woodsman."

All the fellows and girls gathered around to watch, jollying Carl and making up to Eric. Eric blushed and was embarrassed, but proud. He scattered Carl's pile with a lordly gesture, wrinkled up a bit of paper, and built a pyramid of small sticks over it, putting the smallest and driest next to the paper. Some of the sticks he tossed aside, grumbling, "Too green!" He stuck a finger in his mouth and held it scientifically in the air. "Wind's from the south," he announced. One of the boys turned to the others as if relaying a message. "Wind's from the south!" he sang out.

They all laughed.

Eric carefully lit the paper at the windward side. When it began to catch he added larger sticks, and when it was blazing strongly he got up and handed the rest of the matches to Carl. "Here," he said. "I didn't need 'em."

The party laughed loudly. Carl took the matches. Eric was stooping to pick up his milk when Carl said, "I lose, and I ought to pay for it. Here, Mr. Dan Beard. Accept this little gift as a token of your victory and my high esteem!"

He handed Eric a fifty cent piece. Eric's jaw dropped. Slowly he reached for it. "Gee," he said. "Thanks!"

The happening had turned from something quite interesting, something to tell the folks, to something terrific, inconceivable! Eric hurried home, balancing the milk pail in one hand, clutching the fifty cent piece in the other. He would not risk putting it in a pocket. It grew hot and moist inside his fist.

He didn't even see The Sand Pit when he went by, nor The Grapevine Swing, nor his two giant cotton-woods withdrawing themselves grand and mysterious in the twilight. All he could think of was the miracle. He had never owned a fifty cent piece before: never outright, like this. His Christmas and birthday money Dad always put away, to save it for him when he grew up. He had never had more than a dime, to do with as he pleased. It seemed impossible to own a fifty cent piece, got by himself, hard and real in his hand. What should he do with it? Well, he would keep it for awhile, anyway, in his personal possession, while he decided what to do with it. At Sunfish Creek he took the double-log. This was no time to be running risks on the single log.

III

Back in the cottage he put the milk in the ice-box, and hurried into the big screened-in front porch where the lamp was lit. Father was smoking his pipe in the large wicker chair, his heavy, blond brows fixed in the permanent thoughtful scowl, the creases in his forehead shadowed in the lamplight. Mother was reading; Thorvald,

Eric's little brother, was pushing a cast-iron locomotive around the edge of the rag carpet.

"Shut the ice-box tight?" asked his mother, without looking up.

Eric said, "Yes," energetically, brimming with his stupendous adventure.

"What took you so long to-night?"

Then it all tumbled out. Eric's blue eyes were big with excitement as he told it. Father turned his head, holding his pipe in his hand. Mother's generous, double-chinned face was friendly with interest. Tow-headed Thorvald, sitting on one leg, drank it all in with wide eyes and open mouth. At the end Eric held up the fifty cent piece triumphantly, the real, solid proof of the miracle.

Thorvald got onto his feet and stood looking at the piece of silver as if mesmerized. Father said, "You better give it to me and let me take it to the bank. Next thing you know you'll lose it if you leave it around here."

The glow died out of Eric's face; his hand dropped slowly to his side. Everything went very still inside of him and he heard a June-bug thumping against the screen trying to get in. He said, "No! I want to keep it!"

"What do you want to keep it for?" said his father.

That was hard to say. What does one want to keep anything for, except just to have it? Eric stammered, "I just want to keep it!"

"The bank will keep it for you," said his father. "Keep it safer than you can."

"I'll keep it safe!" cried Eric eagerly. Of course he would keep it safe! As if he would lose it!

"*Naa* but what good will it do you here?" asked his father, frowning hard. "You can't buy anything with it here."

Eric's eyes fell away from his father's, went to his mother's, then to the floor. "I know it," he said. "But I just wanted to *keep* it a while." He was almost ready to give it up. He hated disagreements with his father.

His father puffed his pipe and looked solemn. Eric waited, trying not to cry.

Presently Mrs. Morgenson said, "Oh Thorvald, let him keep it a while if he wants to."

Mr. Morgenson went on puffing his pipe. The June-bug was still blundering against the screen. At last he took his pipe out of his mouth. "*Ja,* and lose it likely as not," he said, and went on puffing.

So Eric knew he could keep it. But much of his high joy was gone. He went to bed feeling ugly and uncomfortable.

He awoke with the sunshine blinding him from a square on the floor. He rolled over on his back and looked up at the rafters, where the white-wash was scaled off in places. There was one blackish spot that looked like a man riding a horse. . . . Then suddenly he thought of yesterday, and the fifty cent piece. He hopped out of bed, jerked open the top bureau drawer. Yes, there it was. It was real. It all had happened. He decided to wear his overalls today. He would put the fifty cent piece in the deep watch pocket on the front of them.

During breakfast, Donald Berger's whistle sounded in the distance and then nearer and nearer. Eric answered it. Soon Donald came bashfully in and half sat on a chair while Eric was finishing his oatmeal and coffee-cake. But Eric couldn't finish before he had to jump up, work the fifty cent piece out of the watch pocket, and show it to Donald.

"Where do you suppose I got it?"

Donald couldn't guess. Eric told him all about it, emphasizing especially, with great scorn, how those fellows didn't know anything about building a fire. Donald's black eyes glowed appreciatively.

After Eric had gulped down the last milky spoonful of oatmeal they went outside. Immediately came an astonishing change over Donald. His bashfulness was gone. Donald whooped, he ran, he leapt high in the air and caught the small bole of a sapling elm tree, spiralling around it as he gradually slipped back to the ground. His black eyes sparkled. He dashed for the river, hurtling to a certain and watery grave. But at the last moment he collapsed and rolled on the ground, bringing up on his stomach at the very brink of disaster. Eric ran after him.

They sat on the boat landing, swinging brown, toughened feet above the water. A brisk breeze stirred the river; chips of sunlight rocked and glinted all over it. They discussed what they should do that day. Donald was full of suggestions, which Eric turned down one after another. At last they agreed on a fishing trip: "An all day fishing trip, 'way up Snag Creek, further than we've ever been before."

There was permission to be got, lunches to be packed, worms to be dug. They set about immediately. Donald rushed away after the necessary things from *his* home base, galloping down the shore path at a terrific rate, whirling one arm in circles like a windmill.

IV

By nine o'clock they were on their way to Snag Creek. The lunches were in a haversack, borrowed from Donald's older brother. Each carried a bamboo fish pole, the lines wrapped around them, the hooks stuck into the corks. Eric carried an old salmon can in which were the worms, and a canteen slung at his side. A spirited wind whipped the little trees with sudden gusts, and rattled the hard leaves of big cotton-woods. White clouds raced across the blue sky, getting in the way of the sun some times, and making everything dark for a minute.

They crossed The Plateau, heading for the neck of land between Bull-head Lake and Mirror Lake. On the banks of Bull-head they stopped at the Chinning Limb. Donald slipped off his accouterments, caught the limb, and chinned himself nine times, grunting hard on the last, and fell in an exhausted heap. Eric chinned himself eleven times, taking them more slowly, and was not exhausted. In the meantime Donald had wholly recovered, and as soon as he saw Eric had beaten him, dashed toward Mirror Lake. When Eric caught up with him, he was studying intently some marks on the wet sand.

"I think," said Donald, "it's muskrat, but it may be skunk." He sniffed. "Don't you smell just a teeny smell of skunk in the air?"

Eric sniffed. "No!" he said scornfully, "What's eatin' you! Skunks don't go into the water!"

"I guess it's muskrat," Donald conceded. Then he philosophized, "You know, a real forester—or 'n Indian—can read the woods like a book. Everything means something. Why, for instance, the way that stick is lying there would mean something to a real forester."

The stick, perfectly innocent and unnoticed a second ago, suddenly took on a mysterious individuality. There *was* something about it, the way it lay crookedly on its side. "Or a broken weed, like this one," said Donald. Eric looked at the weed. Then he looked all around him, at the trees, the bushes, the water, the sand—the little ridges left in the wet sand where the water had washed it. He saw it all in a new light. Everything, waving in the wind, was suddenly mysterious with a hidden meaning. He was impressed.

Donald, however, was through reading the forest. "Come on!" he shouted. "We're almost to Snag Creek!" They ran single file where the path dipped through a damp muddy hollow and the weeds pushed up higher than their heads. Hairy, rank, you could smell them like some bad, unclean form of life. They were glad to climb out onto the high bank over Snag Creek, where they stopped to look over the edge at the water flowing slowly below. Donald spied a fish, a big carp, gliding like a shadow three feet below the surface. Then Eric saw two more. What a cool, lazy life a fish leads! The wind swooped down and sent a flurry of ripples over the surface, screening the lazy carp from view. Donald was all for settling right there and starting fishing. But Eric said, "Naw, we've fished here before. Lots of times. And never caught anything either! These carp are too old and smart. We want to go 'way up the Creek where we've never been before."

Donald was easily converted. The thought of fishing where they'd never been before, where maybe nobody had ever fished before. . . .

They followed the winding creek, sometimes on one side, sometimes on the other. They used the low, wet sandbars when convenient, and then again climbed the bank and followed brown cow-paths as they wound between the oaks and maples and red cedars. The sun, climbing to noon, grew hotter, and Donald stopped suddenly. "Let's eat," he said.

They dropped in the shade of a gnarly oak tree. Donald dug the lunches out of the haversack. The sandwiches of cold meat, jelly, and peanut butter were squashed and twisted—and very delicious as the teeth bit into them. The water from the canteen was luke-warm, but it was water.

About an hour later Eric caught the first fish, a sunfish. He had dropped his line into a pool just above a tree that had fallen into the creek, its branches trailing in the stream, its brown roots rearing up out of the broken earth. Eric had got many tantalizing nibbles, and some false alarms when the cork sailed away pulled by a fish too small to take it under. At last came a sunfish big enough to do business. The cork went under and away at a downward slant. Eric let him have it. Down, down went the cork, rocking a little from side to side as it disappeared. Eric pulled slowly, then gave a jerk that brought the sunfish flashing out in a silver arc through the air. It landed safe and helpless on the dry grass above. Donald came running. There was consternation when it was discovered neither had brought along a stringer. Eric finally had to make one of a yard of line off his pole and a couple of sticks. Through gill and mouth he threaded the sunfish, and moored it in the shallows.

More sunfish came, and some bull-heads: slimy brown fellows with beady eyes, and ugly feelers drooping like a Chinaman's mustache. Donald raised a hue and cry when a monster of some sort dashed away with his line, making him hold on with all his might to save the pole. Eric dropped his own and ran over, encouraging Donald with much noisy advice. At last the fellow was captured and lay gasping on the bank, but he turned out to be a vile dogfish, black and leathery, and leering with all his teeth. Donald's proud excitement turned to anger; he killed the dogfish with a stone and hurled him into the bushes.

In the middle of the afternoon the fish stopped biting, and Eric suddenly drew a deep breath and realized how hot it was. The wind had died down; the creek lay glassy and inert under the sun's rays. Donald came with his pole over his shoulder. He sat down on the edge of the bank and looked up the creek with a far-away look. Then he stiffened suddenly and life came back into his eyes. "Eric!" he cried.

Eric looked at Donald, then upstream where Donald was pointing. "See that sandbar?" said Donald. "Wouldn't that be a peach of a place to go swimming! Golly!"

Donald jumped up and started for the sandbar, ripping off his shirt on the way. "Come on!" he cried. Eric caught Donald's excitement. He started to pull in his line. Then vague thoughts came into his mind: "holes"—the bug-a-boo of swimmers; and his father's warnings; and his promises to his mother not to go in swimming unless Father was along. Dang it all!

He stood undecided, watching Donald, who had stopped just long enough on the sandbar to fling off his shirt and let his knickerbockers slip to the sand. He was capering in the shallows yelling, "Come on!" "Gee, this is great!" He scooted along the edge of the water, kicking glistening sheets of it in front of him.

Eric pulled in his line decisively. He would go wading at least. He ran along the bank and jumped off onto the sandbar. Donald dashed toward him, kicking water at him. "Get off your clothes! Get off your clothes!"

Eric drew back laughing, and found himself slipping off his clothes. He raced along the sandbar and jumped off the end of it where the water was a couple feet deep. He hit the water with a spank; it curled up around him, cooling, glorious! Then he had a water fight with Donald that began with jetting water from cupped hands and ended in a tussle in the shallows. They ran a race, but Eric protested his defeat by claiming that he had to run where the water was deeper. They shifted lanes, and Donald won anyway. Then they began to look about them, and to venture out into the middle of the stream. Eric struck a step-off and drew back, scared. Gingerly he tested the depth of the step-off, sliding his toes down the crumbling sides. He found it was only waist deep at the bottom.

Here you could swim! He thrashed about, dog-stroke, thrusting his chin up out of the water. He was not a natural swimmer. But now he was the admitted leader, Donald the follower. Donald ventured only where Eric went.

At last they grew tired of swimming, came out of the water, and lay on the white, hot sand. They rolled about and covered themselves with sliding, tickling sand. Before they could put on their clothes again, they had to dash back into the water to wash themselves. The water felt colder than before. They felt, all of a sudden, a little lonely.

They decided to go back home. They couldn't risk being late for supper! They gathered up their gear, pulled the string of fish out of the water, and set off. One side of the creek was enough for them, going back.

V

Eric was undressing for bed. He was very tired. He had begged hard not to have to wash his feet, but his mother had made him. The light from the lamp on the front porch slanted through the doorway of his bedroom, making a yellow streak on the wall. Eric undressed mechanically.

As he dropped his overalls on the chair suddenly he remembered the fifty cent piece. He had forgot all about it up to this minute. He fumbled the overalls to find the watch pocket. He found it. The fifty cents wasn't in it. He was electrified, he was suddenly wide-awake. He couldn't believe it wasn't there. He felt again. Gone. Rapidly his thoughts went back over the day. He wondered if he had put it somewhere else. There was just a chance. . . . He went over to the bureau and opened the top drawer. It wasn't there; of course not. He went back to the overalls, fumbled the other pockets, but without hope of finding it. He turned once about in the middle of the room, feeling helpless. Without deliberating about it, he finished undressing, got into bed. Instinctively he did not want his folks to know that anything out of the ordinary had happened.

He stared up at the roof, lit dimly by light from the porch lamp, and shadowed grotesquely. A moment ago he was going to bed, just as on any other night; now this thing had happened. It absorbed his whole consciousness, giving him an unreal feeling, as if he were some-one else. Try as he would, he could not make himself feel calm, natural. It was one of those times when the world grew unstable, when one lost confidence in it entirely, and in oneself.

His mind began racing back over his movements during the day. He tried to determine when he had handled the fifty cent piece last. Did he have it with him going up Snag Creek? He must have. With distress he recalled all the stunts they had done on the way. He might have lost it any of half a dozen places along the creek . . . or in the creek! The whole trip took on an evil cast. Then with a shock he remembered going in swimming, taking off his overalls. Of course! It had fallen out then. Fallen out in the sand.

He reproduced in his mind the place where they had gone in swimming. Only now he saw it as in the dark: Snag Creek flowing blackly by in the night. A vague feeling grew in him, took shape, and suddenly he saw it all in a flash: *he was being punished for going in swimming.* The waters of Snag Creek grew darker and more swirling as he thought about it. That step-off! He felt as if he had escaped from the brink of a precipice. Escaped with his life, but now he was being punished for it.

He was being punished by having lost the fifty cent piece. With sharp clearness he remembered how his father had wanted to save it for him. And he had been so sure he would not lose it. Yes, he saw what he had got himself into. His father would ask him soon about the fifty cent piece, what had happened to it. He wouldn't be able to tell. They would question him; he wouldn't be able to answer. It would come out about the swimming . . . he was trapped. What *could* he . . .?

Suddenly the ceiling went black; his father had put out the lamp. He heard his father and mother getting ready for bed in the next room, heard them talking quietly together. They must not know about this. They were enemies. But they didn't know it,—yet. Presently he heard his father's deep, regular breathing. His father was asleep and he was awake. He alone in the world was awake. The steady sing-song of night noises: the croaking of frogs, the chirping of crickets and kady-dids, made him all the more alone.

He went over and over it again, till the back of his neck ached. There was just the slimmest chance that he might find the fifty cent piece, somewhere,—perhaps in the sand where he had taken off his overalls. But he hardly dared hope for that; indeed it was impossible to conceive of such a thing actually happening: to imagine finding it there, shiny and real in the sand. It couldn't be. The fifty cent piece had become a mythical thing, a dream. In the bottom of his stomach he felt he would never see it again. This time he was up against something beyond ordinary happenings, beyond ordinary luck. Working against him he felt strong, dark forces—God, and his parents.

But gradually he began to see what it was he would have to do. He formed a plan. Next morning he would get his mother to let him go fishing again. He would go alone. He would take his pole and his lunch, as usual. But more than that he would make up a little camping kit, a frying pan, knife, and things. He would go 'way up Snag Creek, past where they had gone in swimming. If he found the fifty cent piece, well and good. He would come back. If not, there was no coming back. Not for a long time. Not for weeks and months. He must be prepared to live in the woods, alone. Others had done it. There was the story of Juan and Juanita. *They* didn't have any equipment to begin with even, not even fish hooks. He would take along plenty of fishing tackle. There would be berries to eat; perhaps roots to be dug. Perhaps he could find some farmer with whom he could trade fish for vegetables, and milk. Some farmer who didn't know him. Or he could steal the vegetables. . . . He was an outcast. . . . He must take along a blanket, and a piece of canvas to build a shelter. He would hide the blanket and the canvas in the woods first, then pick them up later. A hand axe. . . . He would have to find a spring. . . . A piece of rope. . . .

VI

He awoke next morning with a heavy, dull feeling. Then he remembered. It wasn't a dream. It was like an awful dream, but it was real. Life was black. He got up wearily, feeling like an old man. Half-heartedly he dipped his hands into the cold water from the kitchen pump, barely dabbing his face with it. He didn't feel up to the harsh facts of life at all. He went outside, looked at the river, looked at the woods. The woods were green and bright in the morning sun. But they were not inviting.

His mother called him to breakfast. He came dragging by. She asked him what was the matter. He said, "Nothing!" and feigned an appetite. She was very solicitous,—asked him if he didn't want another piece of banana to slice on his oatmeal.

Thorvald came to him with his engine,—"broke!" Eric looked at it. Simple matter! He twisted a casting back into place, tightened the nut that held it, returned the engine to Thorvald. Thorvald tried it on the floor. It worked! Thorvald turned a radiant face to Eric, full of adoring gratitude for one so wonderful as Eric! Eric felt sad.

Eric stood on the front porch, looking out over the river. His brows were tightened into a young frown which promised, some day, to stiffen into his father's permanent scowl. He was coming to a decision. He would postpone until to-morrow going away for good. To-day he would simply go on a fishing trip, and look for the fifty cent piece. Yes, that would be the thing to do. No use hurrying matters. If he didn't find the fifty cent piece he would come back to-night, and to-morrow morning leave for good. He went back to the kitchen to ask his mother if he could go fishing again to-day.

"To-day again!"

"Yes!" He grew talkative about a wonderful deep pool they had come across yesterday, but hadn't had time to fish. Oh yes, he must go right away again. His mother shrugged her shoulders, smiled, and told him to go along.

He dug worms, gathered his fishing tackle, and got his mother to fix a lunch. Then off through the woods he trudged, by himself.

VII

Mr. and Mrs. Morgenson sat under the maple at the side of the cottage. It was very hot. After the noon meal they had taken their chairs outdoors, trying to find what shade they could, and maybe a little breeze.

Probably Thorvald had the coolest place—under the cottage itself, on the damp sandy soil. He was constructing something with small sticks and a clam shell. But even he was slowed down by the heat; he mostly squatted, studying his mysterious structure in a dreamy sort of way.

"Do you think he'll have sense enough to keep out of the direct sun?" said Mrs. Morgenson. She looked up at the blazing sky, her face anxious.

"They don't feel it so much, at that age." Mr. Morgenson knocked his pipe against his chair. "You let him go, though."

"I didn't know it would turn out such a burning day."

"He'll be all right."

Mrs. Morgenson selected a small limp stocking from her basket, explored its ravages with spread fingers. "He seemed kind of funny when he went off."

"He ain't a baby any more," Mr. Morgenson said easily. You had to keep women from worrying. Still, he was a little puzzled himself. He had a distinct feeling the boy had been avoiding him the last couple days. This going off alone was new, too. But then, that was what this camping up here was for, give the youngsters a little free-dom, chance to learn things on their own. Morgenson was rather proud of his being able to do this every year for his family. Wasn't that the advantage of this country, the elbow-room there was in it yet? His people had come from the land. He'd got into the factory, but he loved this idle time, away from the town and the pavements, where they could all do as they pleased. The boy too. Morgenson's head slowly dropped. His pipe slipped from his fingers.

Mr. Morgenson was startled by his wife's cry.

"Why Eric! Are you back already!"

Little Thorvald had jumped too. There was no question about it, here was Eric, spilling his fishing gear on the grass and throwing himself down beside it in the shade. His face was fiery red, perfectly blazing.

"Heavens!" said Mrs. Morgenson. "You didn't get a sun stroke back there!"

Eric grinned easily. "Nope! Feel fine." He twitted his mother. "If I had a sun stroke back there, how did I get here? Maybe flew on a magic carpet!"

His mother didn't seem to appreciate the joke. "You seem to have flown all right, and a silly thing too, at the hottest time."

Mr. Morgenson had retrieved his pipe and was filling it. He sat looking at his elder son. "Where are the fish?"

"Where are the fish?" echoed Thorvald.

"The fish?" Eric was quite superior about it. "Oh they aren't biting to-day. Saw it was too hot. They don't bite on real hot days."

"You ate your lunch?" asked Mrs. Morgenson anxiously.

"Oh sure."

Mr. Morgenson struck his match under the seat of the chair and pulled the flame into the bowl. He puffed, scowling his blond bushy scowl that didn't really mean much—it was only a sort of frosty northern feature of his face. Eric understood this, and at the moment wasn't even bothering to look at his father.

The father studied his son, and was puzzled. Funny, unaccountable youngster. Watching him as he lay stretched on the grass, the slim chest still lifting from his exertion, but a self-possessed look on his face for all its fiery color, the father had a feeling that had never come to him before: that the lad was a person in his own right.

Something of this feeling was in his tone when he said, after a time, "By the way, how do you like being a man of means, by now? I imagine you've got it all figured out, what you want to do with that half dollar."

Eric lay as he was. "Oh, that!" he said as if just remembering. He laughed carelessly. "That's all right."

But now he sat up deliberately. "I suppose you want to put it in the bank again for me. Well—" he tugged at the pocket of his overalls, making as casual a matter as one could of bringing out the coin, considering that it was not only squeezed in the small pocket, but tied up tightly in a dirty handkerchief. "Well, you can as far as I'm concerned. Doesn't make any difference to me!"

Mr. Morgenson took it, as Eric negligently handed it over. "You certainly had it stowed away, at that!" said Mr. Morgenson.

Eric only smiled. "Gee, I'm thirsty!" he said, jumping up.

Frances Newman

FRANCES NEWMAN'S all too brief contribution to American literature is not as likely to be utterly forgotten as some of the more pretentious works of the 1920's. Her genuine distinction will always be freshly rediscovered by readers who like to deviate from paths too plainly marked. Lawrence Sterne is in her literary ancestry, and so is Thomas Love Peacock. She had a remarkable style, precise and mannered, which she turned with equal effectiveness to intransigent criticism, to two novels of dismaying originality, and to "Rachel and Her Children," her single published story, the winner of an O. Henry Memorial prize in 1924. All of her prose—even when it becomes perverse in its artifice—is informed by an imposing erudition and a ready wit. Voltaire, she said, was her standard of perfection.

Miss Newman's first book was The Short Story's Mutations (1924), a brilliant study and anthology beginning with Petronius and ending with Paul Morand. In 1926 she published The Hard-boiled Virgin, which James Branch Cabell called a "shining minor masterpiece." Her second novel Dead Lovers are Faithful Lovers was published in the year of her death, 1928. Her last work Six Moral Tales by Jules Laforgue, a translation, and her Letters were published posthumously.

She was born in Atlanta, Georgia, educated in Agnes Scott College and other schools, travelled widely, and held the position of librarian in the Carnegie Library, Atlanta. Her writing first came to attention when she began to contribute reviews to the Atlanta Sunday Constitution, and to Emily Clark's The Reviewer in Richmond, Virginia.

RACHEL AND HER CHILDREN *

Frances Newman

EVERYONE agreed that a perfect stranger could not have seen Mrs. Foster's funeral without realizing that Mrs. Foster had lived a well-rounded life. There was her husband in the front pew, vainly struggling to conceal his grief so that he could console Mrs. Foster's mother, old Mrs. Overton. There were her two sons, vainly struggling to conceal their grief so that they could console Mrs. Foster's daughters-in-law, their wives. There were her four little grandchildren, as downcast as anyone could ask. There were her six faithful servants, as heartbroken as her daughters-in-law. The society of Colonial Dames was there, in a body, and the Daughters of the Confederacy were there, in a body. The Woman's Club was there, in a body, and even the Chamber of Commerce was there, in a body. There was all of the Social Register which did not happen to be on its yachts, or in sanitoria, or abroad. And there were the wreaths, and the harps, and the crescents, and the sheaves of all those bodies and of all those personages.

The hearts of the community went out to every member of Mrs. Foster's stricken family, so the rector told his audience and his God. But in particular it went out to Mrs. Foster's mother, for not a month before she had stood by her only son's open grave, and now she was about to stand beside her only daughter's open grave. She sat among them in the church—as the rector said, like Rachel weeping for her children. But she was veiled in English crêpe of excellent quality and so the most acute eyes of the community could not count the number of her tears. It was fortunate indeed, that Mr. Foster could afford that excellent quality of crêpe, for old Mrs. Overton was not actually weeping like Rachel—in fact, she was not weeping at all.

Old Mrs. Overton had dreamed indirectly of Mrs. Foster's funeral on at least a hundred different nights. Thus, she had now no difficulty in realizing that her brilliant daughter's mortal remains were reposing in that gray coffin which was so magnificently concealed by its blanket of lilies and pink roses. Old Mrs. Overton was seventy-four years old; she belonged to a generation which believed that dreaming of a funeral was a sign of a wedding, and that dreaming of a wedding

* From *The American Mercury,* May, 1924. Reprinted by permission of the heirs of Frances Newman.

was a sign of a funeral. She had never read the works of Dr. Siegmund Freud—she had, in fact, never heard of Dr. Freud—and so she had no idea what Dr. Freud's disciples would have entered on the card describing her case. Old Mrs. Overton sat comfortably in the best corner of the cushioned pew and, in the pleasant shelter of her well-draped veil, thought about things.

She thought of the time when she was sixteen, back in 1864. She thought of Captain Ashby, with his black plume and his black horse. They had stood in the box garden, and she had fairly ached with adoration of his six feet, his black hair, his black eyes, of the wound in some vaguely invisible spot that no Southern lady could even think about, of his gallant war record, not yet embalmed in the Confederate Museum. She was familiar with the works of Mr. Dickens and Mr. Thackeray and Sir Walter Scott, but she had never been allowed to read the story of Jane Eyre and Mr. Rochester. She flutteringly expected . . . she flutteringly hoped . . . that one night soon, perhaps that very night, Captain Ashby would drop on his grey-trousered knees, and implore her to do him the great honor of becoming his wife. She would accept the great honor, she would beg him not to kneel before one so unworthy, and Captain Ashby would rise. He would timidly bend down and kiss her respectfully on the forehead. And then Captain Ashby and his betrothed would walk in to his betrothed's father, and Captain Ashby would ask her hand in marriage. That was what Mr. Dickens and Mr. Thackeray led one to expect, and that was what her mother, who had been twice married and therefore twice engaged, led her to expect.

But that was not what happened. Captain Ashby stopped talking. Even eager questions about his recent heroic deeds were barely answered. The moment might be approaching. Sally had no desire to postpone it, and so she stopped asking the eager questions. Captain Ashby seized her in a passionate embrace, he covered her face with passionate kisses, he kissed her under her soft chin, and just below the brown curls on her neck. It was instantly obvious to Sally that Captain Ashby did not love her. Ivanhoe would never have kissed the fair Rowena like that; David Copperfield would never have kissed the angelic Agnes like that, or even Dora who could not keep her accounts straight. Sally's heart was broken. She tore herself from the embrace of this man who had proved that he did not love her by kissing her, she rushed into her father's house, and up the stairs to her own four-poster. She wept there until her mother came to find her, and to hear the tragic tale. And her mother, though she had been twice married and twice engaged, confirmed Sally's belief that she had been insulted. And Captain Ashby rode away on his black horse.

Mrs. Overton sighed a little under the crêpe veil. She had waited six months for the black horse to gallop back up the avenue between the magnolias, but it had been years before she discovered that a kiss before proposal did not necessarily insult a great love. Meanwhile, her mother had decided to marry her to a certain Colonel Overton, and had had no great difficulty in overcoming Colonel Overton's intention of being legally faithful to the memory of his Julia. Sally's heart, of course, was broken, but that was no reason for being a forlorn old maid, and she thought it would be rather pleasant to decide for herself what frock she would wear, and whether she would go to the Springs in the Summer, and how she would do her hair. Elderly husbands were said to be tractable, and Sally had been very tired of talking only when mama didn't want to talk, or only to people mama didn't want to talk to, and of always sitting with her back to the horses like an inconsequential Prince Consort. She had been convinced that the dignity of marriage would offset its disadvantages, and, besides, she had no very clear idea of marriage except that it meant a change of name and of residence, and sitting at the head of one's own table, behind one's own silver tea-service. People hardly talked then of the boredom of sitting at the other end of the table from the wrong man every morning; certainly they never talked of the occasions when there wasn't a table between one and the wrong man.

The choir was singing "Lead, Kindly Light," which had been Mrs. Foster's favorite hymn, and which, she always mentioned, was written by the late Cardinal Newman before he became a Catholic, much less a Cardinal. Old Mrs. Overton shivered a little under her veil when they came to

> And with the morn those angel faces smile
> That I have loved long since and lost awhile.

Mrs. Overton had no doubt that mama, tule cap, black bombazine, and all, and Colonel Overton, beard, temper and all, would be smiling among those angels, and the idea was not cheering. She had been an old man's darling, but she had also been an old man's slave, a carefully treasured harem of one. Colonel Overton had been fond of saying, of declaiming, that he did not believe in the honor of any man, or the virtue of any woman. Sally had never thought of deceiving him even about the price of a new gown, but even if she had been the most abandoned creature she would have been saved in spite of herself. When she went to a dentist, Colonel Overton was beside her. When she bought a new hat, Colonel Overton was there to protect her from the shop's manager and also from an unbecoming bonnet. Sally had never danced even the Virginia Reel or the Lancers after the morning when Colonel Overton had confirmed her idea of respectful proposals by asking the honor of her hand in marriage and then kissing her chastely on the brow.

Now she looked at the lilies and pink roses that concealed Mrs. Foster's coffin under their expensive fragrance. She was thinking of the day Mrs. Foster was born—something less than a year after the respectful proposal. It was not a coincidence that the baby, now a corpse, had been christened Cornelia for the maternal grandmother whose capacity for being obeyed she had inherited. Mrs. Overton's mother had not waited to receive a namesake with that pleased surprise which ordinarily greets namesakes and proposals and legacies. She had taken the name for granted, quite audibly, on the day when a granddaughter's probable advent was announced to her. The younger Cornelia had justified her grandmother. She allowed her mother to sit in her own carriage facing her own horses, and she allowed her to continue filling her own cups with tea and coffee from her own silver urn. That was the correct thing, and Cornelia always did the correct thing, in all matters from sleeves and shoes to husbands and religions. But after Cornelia was four years old, her mother was never allowed to talk to the people she wanted to talk to about the things she wanted to talk about—not even when her husband permitted her the luxury of an unchaperoned feminine visit. And when Colonel Overton very unwillingly died, Cornelia had seen that her mother was faithful to his memory.

Cornelia was nineteen when that event took place, and just in the process of marrying herself to a rising young lawyer named Henry Foster. The marriage took place shortly afterward, with a simple elegance which the newspaper notices attributed to the recent bereavement in the bride's family. But the simplicity of the elegance at Cornelia's marriage was really due to the disappearance of the late colonel's prosperity rather than to the disappearance of the late colonel himself. His wife and his daughter and his son knew that their acquaintances attributed part of this disappearance to the colonel's extraordinary gratitude to a prepossessing colored—just barely colored—nurse, who had been the comfort of his declining years. But Mrs. Overton had never been so indiscreet as to mention this theory to her daughter, even on the most tempting occasions.

Mrs. Overton had been as faithful to her husband as her sex required in the days when a good woman had no history except that recorded in the parish register. Her husband, she supposed, had been no more faithful to her than his sex will continue to require until nature changes her ways. But her daughter was inexpressibly shocked when she began to show signs of considering a second alliance.

Mrs. Overton, at that time, was still sufficiently under forty not to have begun comparing the corners of her eyes and the line under her chin with those of her contemporaries. The aspiring Mr. Robinson was not an Overton, but the war had been over long enough for prosperous Robinsons and impoverished Overtons to marry each other without scandal. Mrs. Overton would have liked to sit behind her own silver tea service again, and in her own drawing-room, and Mr. Robinson would have been so honored by the gift of her hand in marriage that she would at last have been able to talk to the people she wanted to talk to about the things she wanted to talk about. But Cornelia disapproved of second marriages so positively that people who did not know her might well have thought she was sorry that she had been born. Cornelia was then expecting the birth of that son who was now trying to conceal his own grief so that he could console her first daughter-in-law. And Cornelia had been thrown into such a state by her mother's announcement that Mrs. Overton had felt obliged to give up the idea.

So she had continued to sit on the side of her daughter's table for nine months of every year, and on the side of her son William's table for three months of every year. Even when tea-services on breakfast tables went out, and round tables came in, tables continued to have a head and a side, and Mrs. Overton had continued to grieve for her own tea-service and her own table. She had never ceased to long for a house where a ringing telephone would mean that someone in the world wanted to talk with her badly enough to go through the trouble of getting a telephone number; where a ringing door bell would mean that someone wanted to see her, if it were only a book-agent, or the laundry man.

For thirty-four years, Mrs. Overton had spoken to Daughters of the American Revolution and Daughters of the Confederacy and newspaper reporters and officers of those clubs which seem to exist chiefly to elect officers. But she had spoken only to tell them that Mrs. Foster was lunching or dining or presiding at some house or some club where she either could or could not be called to the telephone. She had talked to a great many callers, but she had talked to callers of no consequence while Mrs. Foster talked to callers of great consequence—local, if not international. And then Mrs. Foster had fallen ill. And William Overton had fallen ill. And old Mrs. Overton began to be Rachel weeping for her children.

Mrs. Foster was ill, desperately ill, for six months. For their convenience, if not for hers, the doctors decreed that Mrs. Foster must be in a hospital, and that she must receive no visitors. Old Mrs. Overton suffered with her daughter, but she revived the pleasant old custom of pouring the breakfast coffee from her own silver urn, and Mr. Foster was delighted. She carried the pantry keys, and the silver closet keys, and the linen room keys; she went to market alone; she went shopping alone. All the ladies of high position, and all the officers of all Mrs. Foster's clubs came to call on Mrs. Overton—to ask about Mrs. Foster, of course, but even on such occasions other subjects are discussed, and Mrs. Overton must be cheered and strengthened for the ordeal she was undergoing. Then William Overton was mercifully released from his sufferings. And then Mrs. Foster was mercifully released from her longer sufferings.

Old Mrs. Overton had received hundreds of notes. She had scores of callers, and she had felt herself able to receive them all—decorously, in her own bedroom, one or two at a time. Her fortitude was considered remarkable. She had ordered delicate lunches for the faithful friends who were downstairs receiving the wreaths and the sheaves of Mrs. Overton's other friends and of all her societies. And she had ordered her own veil of the best English crêpe.

The choir was singing "Asleep in Jesus," and Mrs. Foster's funeral was nearly over. Mrs. Overton began to look about a little, under the shadow of her veil. She was thinking of all the visitors she would have the next day and the next week; of the days the granddaughters-in-law and the great-grandchildren would spend with her, of the birthday party she would give for little Cornelia in the Spring—Mrs. Foster would want her namesake to have the party she had promised her. She was thinking of all the people who would beg her and Mr. Foster to come and have dinner with them, very quietly—since they, too, had loved Mrs. Foster.

And then Mrs. Overton happened to look across the aisle at Mrs. Turner and Mrs. Turner was looking beyond her at Mr. Foster. Mrs. Turner's look was only a decorous look of heartfelt sympathy, but Mrs. Overton suddenly felt cold and forlorn. She remembered how attentive Mrs. Turner had been to her and to Mr. Foster. And she remembered that Mrs. Turner had lost Mr. Turner three years before. And she remembered how many of the kind women who had come to cheer her for her great ordeal, who had received the flowers that were banked about the chancel, had lost their husbands three or four or five years before. She remembered the statistics of the number of widows in the State that she had read for one of Mrs. Foster's erudite club papers. The whole church, the whole world, seemed to be filled with widows—widows whose daughters would not discourage their mothers from taking names different from their own.

Mrs. Overton had no doubt that in a year she would go back to the side of another Mrs. Foster's table, that she would receive telephone messages for another Mrs. Foster—and that this Mrs. Foster would not even be her daughter.

The last prayer was over. The eight eminent pallbearers were gathering. Mr. Foster rose and offered his arm to his mother-in-law. Mrs. Overton stood up, shaking with bitter sobs, and took the offered arm. She walked up the aisle behind the blanket of lilies and pink roses that covered Mrs. Foster's coffin. All the hearts of the community went out to old Mrs. Overton, weeping like Rachel for her children.

$\mathcal{E}dwin$ $\mathcal{G}ranberry$

IN THREE novels The Ancient Hunger (1927), Strangers and Lovers (1928), The Erl King (1930), and in a number of short stories appearing in The Forum, The London Mercury, Colliers, and other magazines, Edwin Granberry has expressed in sensitive prose the implications, often tragic, of experiences usually set against an exotic Florida background. To call his writing "stark realism"—a phrase which has been applied to "A Trip to Czardis"—is to confess the helplessness of labels. His work is not harsh, although it is undeterred from seizing the full significance of its theme. It is rich in connotation, and quick to perceive the mind's plight when confronted by things beyond understanding. It can evoke illusion—the final power of the artist.

Edwin Granberry was born in Mississippi and educated at the University of Florida, Columbia University, and at Harvard, where he studied the drama under Professor Baker. He now has charge of creative writing courses at Rollins College. "A Trip to Czardis" won the O. Henry Memorial Award as the best short story of the year, 1932.

A TRIP TO CZARDIS *

Edwin Granberry

IT WAS STILL dark in the pine woods when the two brothers awoke. But it was plain that day had come, and in a little while there would be no more stars. Day itself would be in the sky and they would be getting along the road. Jim waked first, coming quickly out of sleep and sitting up in the bed to take fresh hold of the things in his head, starting them up again out of the corners of his mind

---

* From The Forum, April, 1932. Copyright, 1932, by Forum Magazine. Reprinted by permission of Forum Magazine and the author.

where sleep had tucked them. Then he waked Daniel and they sat up together in the bed. Jim put his arm around his young brother, for the night had been dewy and cool with the swamp wind. Daniel shivered a little and whimpered, it being dark in the room and his baby concerns still on him somewhat, making sleep heavy on his mind and slow to give understanding its way.

"Hit's the day, Dan'l. This day that's right here now, we are goen. You'll recollect it all in a minute."

"I recollect. We are goen in the wagon to see papa—"

"Then hush and don't whine."

"I were dreamen, Jim."

"What dreamen did you have?"

"I can't tell. But it were fearful what I dreamt."

"All the way we are goen this time. We won't stop at any places, but we will go all the way to Czardis to see papa. I never see such a place as Czardis."

"I recollect the water tower—"

"Not in your own right, Dan'l. Hit's by my tellen it you see it in your mind."

"And lemonade with ice in it I saw—"

"That too I seen and told to you."

"Then I never seen it at all?"

"Hit's me were there, Dan'l. I let you play like, but hit's me who went to Czardis. Yet I never till this day told half how much I see. There's sights I never told."

They stopped talking, listening for their mother's stir in the kitchen. But the night stillness was unlifted. Daniel began to shiver again.

"Hit's dark," he said.

"Hit's your eyes stuck," Jim said. "Would you want me to drip a little water on your eyes?"

"Oh!" cried the young one, pressing his face into his brother's side, "don't douse me, Jim, no more. The cold aches me."

The other soothed him, holding him around the body.

"You won't have e're chill or malarie ache today, Dan'l. Hit's a fair day—"

"I won't be cold?"

"Hit's a bright day. I hear mournen doves starten a'ready. The sun will bake you warm. . . . Uncle Holly might buy us somethen new to eat in Czardis."

"What would it be?"

"Hit ain't decided yet. . . . He hasn't spoke. Hit might be some-then sweet. Maybe a candy ball fixed on to a rubber string."

"A candy ball!" Daniel showed a stir of happiness. "Oh, Jim!" But it was deceit of the imagination, making his eyes shine wistfully; the grain of his flesh was against it. He settled into a stillness by himself.

"My stomach would retch it up, Jim. . . . I guess I couldn't eat it."

"You might could keep a little down."

"No. . . . I would bring it home and keep it. . . ."

Their mother when they went to bed had laid a clean pair of pants and a waist for each on the chair. Jim crept out of bed and put on his clothes, then aided his brother on with his. They could not hear any noise in the kitchen, but hickory firewood burning in the kitchen stove worked a smell through the house, and in the forest guinea fowls were sailing down from the trees and poking their way along the half-dark ground toward the kitchen steps, making it known the door was open and that within someone was stirring about at the getting of food.

Jim led his brother by the hand down the dark way of yellow-pine stairs that went narrowly and without banisters to the rooms below. The young brother went huddling in his clothes, ague-like, knowing warmth was near, hungering for his place by the stove, to sit in peace on the bricks in the floor by the stove's side and watch the eating, it being his nature to have a sickness against food.

They came in silence to the kitchen, Jim leading and holding his brother by the hand. The floor was lately strewn with fresh bright sand and that would sparkle when the day-break got above the forest, though now it lay dull as hoarfrost and cold to the unshod feet of the brothers. The door to the firebox of the stove was open and in front of it their mother sat in a chair speaking low as they entered, muttering under her breath. The two boys went near and stood still, thinking she was blessing the food, there being mush dipped up and steaming in two bowls. And they stood cast down until she lifted her eyes to them and spoke.

"Your clothes on already," she said. "You look right neat." She did not rise, but kept her chair, looking cold and stiff, with the cloth of her black dress sagging between her knees. The sons stood in front of her and she laid her hand on first one head and then the other and spoke a little about the day, charging them to be sober and of few words, as she had raised them.

Jim sat on the bench by the table and began to eat, mixing dark molasses sugar through his bowl of mush. But a nausea began in Daniel's stomach at the sight of the sweet and he lagged by the stove, gazing at the food as it passed into his brother's mouth.

Suddenly a shadow filled the back doorway and Holly, their uncle, stood there looking in. He was lean and big and dark from wind and weather, working in the timber as their father had done. He had no wife and children and would roam far off with the timber gangs in the Everglades. This latter year he did not go far, but stayed near them. Their mother stopped and looked at the man and he looked at her in silence. Then he looked at Jim and Daniel.

"You're goen to take them after all?"

She waited a minute, seeming to get the words straight in her mind before bringing them out, making them say what was set there.

"He asked to see them. Nobody but God-Almighty ought to tell a soul hit can or can't have."

Having delivered her mind, she went out into the yard with the man and they spoke more words in an undertone, pausing in their speech.

In the silence of the kitchen, Daniel began to speak out and name what thing among his possessions he would take to Czardis to give his father. But the older boy belittled this and that and everything that was called up, saying one thing was of too little consequence for a man, and that another was of no account because it was food. But when the older boy had abolished the idea and silence had regained, he worked back to the thought, coming to it roundabout and making it new and as his own, letting it be decided that each of them would take their father a pomegranate from the tree in the yard.

They went to the kitchen door. The swamp fog had risen suddenly. They saw their mother standing in the lot while their uncle hitched the horse to the wagon. Leaving the steps, Jim climbed to the first crotch of the pomegranate tree. The reddest fruits were on the top branches. He worked his way higher. The fog was now curling up out of the swamp, making gray mountains and rivers in the air and strange ghost shapes. Landmarks disappeared in the billows, or half-seen, they bewildered the sight and an eye could so little mark the known or strange that a befuddlement took hold of the mind, like the visitations sailors beheld in the fogs of Okeechobee. Jim could not find the ground. He seemed to have climbed into the mountains. The light was unnatural and dark and the pines were blue and dark over the mountains.

A voice cried out of the fog:

"Are worms gnawen you that you skin up a pomegranate tree at this hour? Don't I feed you enough?"

The boy worked his way down. At the foot of the tree he met his mother. She squatted and put her arm around him, her voice tight and quivering, and he felt tears on her face.

"We ain't come to the shame yet of you and Dan'l hunten your food off trees and grass. People seein' you gnawen on the road will say Jim Cameron's sons are starved, foragen like cattle of the field."

"I were getten the pomegranates for papa," said the boy, resigned to his mother's concern. She stood up when he said this, holding him in front of her skirts. In a while she said:

"I guess we won't take any, Jim. . . . But I'm proud it come to you to take your papa somethen."

And after a silence, the boy said:

"Hit were Dan'l it come to, Mamma."

Then she took his hand, not looking down, and in her throat, as if in her bosom, she repeated:

"Hit were a fine thought and I'm right proud . . . though to-day we won't take anything. . . ."

"I guess there's better pomegranates in Czardis where we are goen—"

"There's no better pomegranates in Czardis than right here over your head," she said grimly. "If pomegranates were needed, we would take him his own. . . . You are older'n Dan'l, Jim. When we get to the place we are goen', you won't know your papa after so long. He will be pale and he won't be as bright as you recollect. So don't labor him with questions but speak when it behooves you and let him see you are upright."

When the horse was harnessed and all was ready for the departure, the sons were seated on the shallow bed of hay in the back of the wagon and the mother took the driver's seat alone. The uncle had argued for having the top up over the seat, but she refused the shelter, remarking that she had always driven under the sky and would still do it today. He gave in silently and got upon the seat of his own wagon, which took the road first, their wagon following. This was strange and the sons asked:

"Why don't we all ride in Uncle Holly's wagon?"

But their mother made no reply.

For several miles they traveled in silence through their own part of the woods, meeting no one. The boys whispered a little to themselves, but their mother and their uncle sat without speaking, nor did they turn their heads to look back. At last the narrow road they were following left the woods and came out to the highway and it was seen that other wagons besides their own were going to Czardis. And as they got farther along, they began to meet many other people going to town, and the boys asked their mother what day it was. It was Wednesday. And then they asked her why so many wagons were going along the road if it wasn't Saturday and a market day. When she told them to be quiet, they settled down to watching the people go by. Some of them were faces that were strange and some of them were neighbors who lived in other parts of the woods. Some who passed them stared in silence and some went by looking straight to the front. But there were none of them who spoke, for their mother turned her eyes neither right nor left, but drove the horse on like a woman in her sleep. All was silent as the wagons passed, except the squeaking of the wheels and the thud of the horses' hoofs on the dry, packed sand.

At the edge of the town, the crowds increased and their wagon got lost in the press of people. All were moving in one direction.

Finally they were going along by a high brick wall on top of which ran a barbed-wire fence. Farther along the way in the middle of the wall was a tall, stone building with many people in front. There were trees along the outside of the wall and in the branches of one of the trees Daniel saw a man. He was looking over the brick wall down into the courtyard. All the wagons were stopping here and hitching through the grove in front of the building. But their Uncle Holly's wagon and their own drove on, making way slowly as through a crowd at a fair, for under the trees knots of men were gathered, talking in undertone. Daniel pulled at his mother's skirts and whispered:

"What made that man climb up that tree?"

Again she told him to be quiet.

"We're not to talk today," said Jim. "Papa is sick and we're not to make him worse." But his high, thin voice made his mother turn cold. She looked back and saw he had grown pale and still, staring at the iron-barred windows of the building. When he caught her gaze, his chin began to quiver and she turned back front to dodge the knowledge of his eyes.

For the two wagons had stopped now and the uncle gotten down and left them sitting alone while he went to the door of the building and talked with a man standing there. The crowd fell silent, staring at their mother.

"See, Jim, all the men up the trees!" Daniel whispered once more, leaning close in to his brother's side.

"Hush, Dan'l. Be still."

The young boy obeyed this time, falling into a bewildered stare at all the things about him he did not understand, for in all the trees along the brick wall men began to appear perched high in the branches, and on the roof of a building across the way stood other men, all gaping at something in the yard back of the wall.

Their uncle returned and hitched his horse to a ring in one of the trees. Then he hitched their mother's horse and all of them got out and stood on the ground in a huddle. The walls of the building rose before them. Strange faces at the barred windows laughed aloud and called down curses at the men below.

Now they were moving, with a wall of faces on either side of them, their uncle going first, followed by their mother who held to each of them by a hand. They went up the steps of the building. The door opened and their uncle stepped inside. He came back in a moment and all of them went in and followed a man down a corridor and into a bare room with two chairs and a wooden bench. A man in a black robe sat on one of the chairs, and in front of him on the bench, leaning forward looking down between his arms, sat their father. His face was lean and gray, which made him look very tall. But his hair was black, and his eyes were blue and mild and strange as he stood up and held his two sons against his body while he stooped his head to kiss their mother. The man in black left the room and walked up and down outside in the corridor. A second stranger stood in the doorway with his back to the room. The father picked up one of the sons and then the other in his arms and looked at them and leaned their faces on his own. Then he sat down on the bench and held them against him. Their mother sat down beside them and they were all together.

A few low words were spoken and then a silence fell over them all. And in a little while the parents spoke a little more and touched one another. But the bare stone floor and the stone walls and the unaccustomed arms of their father hushed the sons with the new and strange. And when the time had passed, the father took his watch from his pocket:

"I'm goen to give you my watch, Jim. You are the oldest. I want you to keep it till you are a grown man. . . . And I want you to always do what mamma tells you. . . . I'm goen to give you the chain, Dan'l. . . ."

The young brother took the chain, slipped out of his father's arms, and went to his mother with it. He spread it out on her knee and began to talk to her in a whisper. She bent over him, and again all of them in the room grew silent.

A sudden sound of marching was heard in the corridor. The man rose up and took his sons in his arms, holding them abruptly. But their uncle, who had been standing with the man in the doorway, came suddenly and took them and went out and down through the big doorway by which they had entered the building. As the doors opened to let them pass, the crowd gathered round the steps pressed forward to look inside. The older boy cringed in his uncle's arms. His uncle turned and stood with his back to the crowd. Their mother came through the doors. The crowd fell back. Again through a passageway of gazing eyes, they reached the wagons. This time they sat on the seat beside their mother. Leaving their uncle and his wagon behind, they started off on the road that led out of town.

"Is papa coming home with Uncle Holly?" Jim asked in a still voice. His mother nodded her head.

Reaching the woods once more and the silence he knew, Daniel whispered to his brother:

"We got a watch and chain instead, Jim."

But Jim neither answered nor turned his eyes.

Nancy Hale

Some of Nancy Hale's first published stories were brief dialogues between two people—like casually overheard conversations—but when you had read them, you understood a human relationship and its dramatic implications. In later stories Miss Hale employed other forms—especially the monologue—but her purpose remained the same: to catch and hold in discerning, warmly-textured prose the mind's involvement with its passions, with memory and desire. She has a poet's distinction of phrase.

Nancy Hale (Mrs. Charles Wertenbaker) was born in Boston, the daughter of Philip Hale, the artist, and the granddaughter of Edward Everett Hale. Her first novel The Young Die Good (1932) was written while she held an editorial post in New York. A second novel Never Any More appeared two years later. Her short stories, appearing in Scribner's Magazine, The American Mercury, Vanity Fair, and The New Yorker, were collected in the volume The Earliest Dreams in 1936.

NO ONE MY GRIEF CAN TELL *

Nancy Hale

I

AMANDA LAY inert and burning hot in the sand on the little beach, under a huge red July sun like a fat zinnia in the blue sky. The sky made the sun look redder and the sun made the sky look bluer. She stared at the sun through slitted eyes and watched it get smaller, contract, and then burst open redder than ever, so hot that she could imagine that it sang, a sizzling, piercing hum of heat.

She turned herself over in the lazy yellow sift of sand and felt her

---

* From *The Earliest Dreams* by Nancy Hale. Charles Scribner's Sons, 1936. Reprinted by permission of Charles Scribner's Sons.

backbone burn and melt, her limbs slide sensuously against the dry warmth under. Her pale green bathing suit was still wet, hot wet, and she imagined herself lying there with a drift of condensing steam rising up from her into the sun, all damp darkness and vicious liquids leaving her and rising, leaving her as clean and hard and chalky dry as a piece of coral. Her head lay resistlessly on her hand, sidewise, and in her upper ear she heard the hissing song of the sun and in her under ear the interminable whisper and shift of grains of sand.

Ten feet away from her, her child played with fearful concentration, leaning over a big log of driftwood, his little yellow jersey backside making a small hummock along the beach, while his carroty head bent lower and lower and lower over the sea-shells, or whatever objects gripped him with this absorption. He could stand there for hours in this position, legs straight and fat, trunk suddenly tipped downward from baby loins, his head nearly as low as his feet. His lips were tightly compressed, his face red, and he breathed violently through his nose, so that Amanda could just hear the loud whiffling sound of his concentration. He was four years old.

Part of me, she thought vaguely, playing with sea-shells. The loosened cell growing to be itself. The sun bakes him to a dry coral baby, dry and clean and well; the sun dries him from the pervading dampness of his beginning. He is being dried and cleared and healed from the wet wound of me, and lightened from the deep darkness of me, and he is becoming his wound-healed and complete self. As I am healed of him. O loop cut from my skein and once an undifferentiated strand within my skein, flap of my flesh cut away and healed again! He has no rawness where the knife once was, he is round and finished and without seam. And I am healed, but there is scar-tissue that will not whiten, and a seam that is wrinkled and pursed. I cannot forget that something was a bubble of me that now is round and seamless and floats alone.

She pushed herself up on her elbow and held one hand flat shelved above her eyes and called.

"Baby! Are your feet wet?"

The yellow jersey hummock caved in slowly and reluctantly; the baby stood up, scowling furiously.

"Unh-*unh.*" He stared at her with infant resentment for a minute and then jerked himself around, expressively, back to the log and again addressed himself with ferocity to his sea-shells.

Let him alone. Let him swell and bubble. Let the sun dry away the primordial dampness and make him coral. What in the world did I call him for? How would his feet possibly get wet? The old scar itches, the flesh presses uselessly against that which once it owned, pressing and pressing, but they are two flesh. You are of me, but I am not of you. How is that, and how and why?

The sun got small again before her eyes, a far off point of light, and she watched it spring back near and huge and red, with a humming and a clash of brass. She lay on her back again so that the sun burned at all that was within the round trench of her bones, as though the top had been lifted and she lay broiling, the damp meat within the spiny carcass. Dry those damp and intricate darknesses within me, wither those dark and caverned sources of hate and revulsion and cunning, of furious possession and the corruption that it is to be a woman.

After a while she stood up and slapped at the crust of sand along her thighs.

II

She began to run along the beach, first through the soft deep sand, then down across the sharp mesh of dry seaweed, and then along the dark hard sand nearest the sea, marked with a Chinese tracery of the little waves that had now receded with the tide.

She raced near the edge of the water, running as fast as she had ever been able to run, and as neatly, taking long clean bounds and feeling her toes and the balls of her feet jab into the damp grittiness in sharp even rhythm. She could run as fast, her neck was as straight and firm, as ever. But she could not feel the same, or as free, or as ruthlessly young. It was no use. She put her head down into the light sea-wind and sprinted, running away.

At the end of the beach she came to a mounting pile of brown rocks, spattered with white barnacles and netted with sea-weed. She sat on the wet slippery summit. She slid her eyes back and forth along the knife-edge of the horizon where two blues met.

I love a beach and I love the sea. And a pirate ship came galloping straight over the horizon, bound for the beach, bulging with buccaneers hanging out both sides, and on top a fat square white sail and the black flag. Maxfield Parrish, with the sea the color of an alcohol flame. No ocean looks its best without a sail showing somewhere. What the well-dressed ocean will wear. Steam-ships—bad ocean fashions, the sea would do well to sink them all.

And the beaches. The yellow sands of the New World, and the chalk cliffs of Dover, the pink beaches of the far Bermudas, the dark and sinister dunes where up climbed the pirates carrying hooped chests under the tropical sun that gave them fever. Where stood Miranda all alone, staring out to sea—come unto these yellow sands. The marooned and the exiled. (My child? Don't look, you must try to become whole, that he can become whole. Don't look, think your own thoughts about yourself, or your thoughts about him will kill him.) Drake in the Pacific, Westward Ho, Salvation Yeo. He said, Sail On, Sail On! Sir Richard Grenville lay. In Flores in the Azores. While the hollow oak our fortress is, our heritage the sea. We—something something, balked the eternal sea. To hell with it!

She had to stand up to see where her child was. Way up the beach a small yellow dot, bright against the straw-yellow of the sand, walked next to white trousers and a blue coat. That was Oliver, his father. The afternoon train was in. The family man had come home and had joined his litt-le femily on th' beach and was taking his litt-le son for a walk, so sweet. We, meant to founder, something something, balked the eternal sea.

Should I never go back now, should I swim out into the gargantuan deeps, into the deep indigo darkness, what? Should I never return now, never walk back across the beach into the hot buzzing little box where live I, but with one paroxysm of desire, throw myself into depth and darkness and majestic oblivion, what? Home is where the heart is, ha ha! And the heart lies deep in beaded wells of forgetfulness and in the august and oblivious sea. The heart is drowned in yesterday, in fathoms deep of accumulated years and talking too much and always getting a little farther and a little farther from the early and fragile truth. Where is the truth, and where is the heart? Dropped into the shifting strata of the sea, and floating downward through interminable fathoms. Far, far away, and never to be regained.

Since life can never be brought back to beauty, and since the way has led off and away from faith or the slightest knowledge of what it is all about, why try to mend the way, why try to love what is intolerable? And all the things that life was going to be have dissolved, somehow, into the rest of impractical youth, like all good things. Now there is only existing and taking care of things and looking at faces and listening to people and talking and talking and talking.

All but my child. He is young and whole and an unseamed bubble and as pure and hard of heart as coral; he is beauty and he is mine, but I want him too much. Because, in the end, there is nothing left but dust and talk, all that I gave to myself and to ineffable and impossible dreaming and to the core of the world in me, all this must go somewhere. And there is nowhere for it to go but to him. It will possess him. He will become mine and the receptacle of my love. And the receptacle of my hate.

Is it fair? It is not fair. No one can contain more than he is himself, for if there is more than that given to him, he must throw away his own dreams and himself, for there is no room for them. He will become utterly the violin of me, and he will be utterly mine, for I will fill him with more passion than he can understand, and it will possess him.

All the time she had been walking back along the beach, lifting her feet and setting them into the sand delicately and disdainfully. She looked up, and saw the sun upon its downward course, drifting, still hot and quivering, down the sky. I hate to see—that evening sun go down. It takes away the heat, and when the heat is gone I become all damp again, dark with liquid corruption which is possessive love. The sea was a little mauve now, and gulls flew along in scalloped lines.

"Hi!" Oliver called when she was within calling distance.

"Hi!" she called back. "Isn't it a swell day?"

He began to laugh as she got near him.

"You ought to see yourself," he said. "You've got a burn like a house afire. You're a beet. Did you know it?"

"I lay out here all day," she said. "It doesn't hurt."

"It doesn't?" He threw back his arm and gave her a terrific slap between the shoulder blades. "I bet that hurt."

"Sure it hurt," she said, laughing.

"The kid's burned too. For God's sake, why didn't you put a hat on him?"

"It's supposed to be good for him. He likes it."

The baby, released, had gone back to his sea-shells, and was singing, an interminable, noteless wail, in the late afternoon quiet. Oliver lay down in the sand and closed his eyes. He took a long breath.

"Nice, darling?" Amanda dropped down beside him and put her hand in his. He took his away and scratched his nose.

"By the way," he said, and then closed his mouth as if he had finished a sentence.

"What?"

"I'll be out to dinner."

"Who? Beatrice?"

"I don't know why you say it in that tone of voice."

"No reason."

"I'll be home early."

"All right."

"Well, I *will* be home early."

"All *right,* I said."

III

The evening sun kept going down. Amanda got up and put a sweater on the baby. He was so fat his arms had to be squeezed into the stretchy knitted sleeves.

The baby was sleepy and pushed his head back comfortably into her breast. He was a nice fat size, and felt warm and delicious in her arms. She felt at last relaxed and untormented. She dug her chin gently into the top of his head and looked out to sea, feeling healed and well with her child against her. He stopped all pain, closed all wounds. It was as easy as that. He rolled his head around luxuriously.

"Mmmmmmh," he murmured, half asleep. His response and unconscious love were so agonizingly right to her that she could not help drawing her arms tighter around him, with a stabbing knot tied inside her. He smelt so good. Everything in her ached to be given to him, to pour love and love upon his round head. There was so much pent inside her and so much that beat to get out.

Oliver got up.

"I've got to dress sometime," he said. "Coming?"

"I guess so. I hate to put the baby down, you know," she grinned up at him.

He burst out laughing again.

"God, you look like hell. Your nose is glittering, it's so shiny."

"Darling," she said, "I wish you'd stick around tonight."

He looked at her and gave another of his laughs.

"Well, baby, so that's the way you feel? We got the rest of our lives for seeing each other. Got to live, you know, get around, do things before we're old."

He gave her a little cheerful kick with his foot, and started up the beach.

The baby stirred again and threw one arm violently around her. She tightened her arms wildly about him. The old scar aches, the tissue is not healed. This flesh that was mine, returns to me, but closer, closer.

All that I have so long, so much, take it; let the ancient blood flow back between us once more. I love you, my own flesh, and I love nothing else in the world. I can give to nobody else.

He lay perfectly still against her, swelling with his baby breathing. He was so warm, so terribly alive and new. She let her eyes seek the indefinite horizon, thinking of nothing, wanting nothing, letting her love and her need and her beating want flow into him, as though no knife had ever cut them, as if there had been no wound and no scar. She held him a little tighter for a minute before she got up to go, for it was turning a little chill; the sun bobbed like a bubble above the horizon.

English Stories

Wilkie Collins

WILKIE COLLINS was once a greatly popular writer, enjoying the friendship of Charles Dickens, and contributing, like him, to the entertainment of the common reader. His works did not possess the rich humanity which is apparent in even the most careless of Dickens' pages, but they will not be utterly forgotten so long as people enjoy clever and ingenious situations. For Collins could plot superbly, and his two novels The Woman in White (1860) and The Moonstone (1868) are classics in the literature of mystery and adventure. The short stories in his book After Dark (1856) are old fashioned in their "framework" construction, but they never falter in narrative suspense, and one of them, the story here printed, is worthy of Poe.

Collins was born in London in 1824, the son of a well-known landscape painter. He began a career in business, abandoned it for the law, and in turn abandoned the law for literature. He published many novels and tales, some of them appearing serially. He died in London in 1889.

A TERRIBLY STRANGE BED *
Wilkie Collins

SHORTLY AFTER my education at college was finished, I happened to be staying at Paris with an English friend. We were both young men then, and lived, I am afraid, rather a wild life, in the delightful city of our sojourn. One night we were idling about the neighborhood of the Palais Royal, doubtful to what amusement we should next betake ourselves. My friend proposed a visit to Frascati's; but his suggestion was not to my taste. I knew Frascati's, as the French saying is, by

---

* From *After Dark* by Wilkie Collins, 1856.

heart; had lost and won plenty of five-franc pieces there, merely for amusement's sake, until it was amusement no longer, and was thoroughly tired, in fact, of all the ghastly respectabilities of such a social anomaly as a respectable gambling-house.

"For Heaven's sake," said I to my friend, "let us go somewhere where we can see a little genuine, blackguard, poverty-stricken gaming, with no false gingerbread glitter thrown over it at all. Let us get away from fashionable Frascati's, to a house where they don't mind letting in a man with a ragged coat, or a man with no coat, ragged or otherwise."

"Very well," said my friend, "we needn't go out of the Palais Royal to find the sort of company you want. Here's the place just before us; as blackguard a place, by all report, as you could possibly wish to see."

In another minute we arrived at the door, and entered the house.

When we got upstairs, and had left our hats and sticks with the doorkeeper, we were admitted into the chief gambling-room. We did not find many people assembled there. But, few as the men were who looked up at us on our entrance, they were all types—lamentably true types—of their respective classes.

We had come to see blackguards; but these men were something worse. There is a comic side, more or less appreciable, in all blackguardism: here there was nothing but tragedy—mute, weird tragedy. The quiet in the room was horrible. The thin, haggard, long-haired young man, whose sunken eyes fiercely watched the turning up of the cards, never spoke; the flabby, fat-faced, pimply player, who pricked his piece of pasteboard perseveringly, to register how often black won, and how often red, never spoke; the dirty, wrinkled old man, with the vulture eyes and the darned great-coat, who had lost his last *sou,* and still looked on desperately after he could play no longer, never spoke. Even the voice of the croupier sounded as if it were strangely dulled and thickened in the atmosphere of the room. I had entered the place to laugh, but the spectacle before me was something to weep over. I soon found it necessary to take refuge in excitement from the depression of spirits which was fast stealing on me. Unfortunately I sought the nearest excitement, by going to the table and beginning to play. Still more unfortunately, as the event will show, I won—won prodigiously; won incredibly; won at such a rate that the regular players at the table crowded round me; and staring at my stakes with hungry, superstitious eyes, whispered to one another that the English stranger was going to break the bank.

The game was *Rouge et Noir*. I had played at it in every city in Europe, without, however, the care or the wish to study the Theory of Chances—that philosopher's stone of all gamblers! And a gambler, in the strict sense of the word, I had never been. I was heart-whole from the corroding passion for play. My gaming was a mere idle amusement. I never resorted to it by necessity, because I never knew what it was to want money. I never practised it so incessantly as to lose more than I could afford, or to gain more than I could coolly pocket without being thrown off my balance by my good luck. In short, I had hitherto frequented gambling-tables—just as I frequented ball-rooms and opera-houses—because they amused me, and because I had nothing better to do with my leisure hours.

But on this occasion it was very different—now, for the first time in my life, I felt what the passion for play really was. My successes first bewildered, and then, in the most literal meaning of the word, intoxicated me. Incredible as it may appear, it is nevertheless true, that I only lost when I attempted to estimate chances, and played according to previous calculation. If I left everything to luck, and staked without any care or consideration, I was sure to win—to win in the face of every recognized probability in favor of the bank. At first some of the men present ventured their money safely enough on my color; but I speedily increased my stakes to sums which they dared not risk. One after another they left off playing, and breathlessly looked on at my game.

Still, time after time, I staked higher and higher, and still won. The excitement in the room rose to fever pitch. The silence was interrupted by a deep-muttered chorus of oaths and exclamations in different languages, every time the gold was shoveled across to my side of the table—even the imperturbable croupier dashed his rake on the floor in a (French) fury of astonishment at my success. But one man present preserved his self-possession, and that man was my friend. He came to my side, and whispering in English, begged me to leave the place, satisfied with what I had already gained. I must do him the justice to say that he repeated his warnings and entreaties several times, and only left me and went away, after I had rejected his advice (I was to all intents and purposes gambling-drunk) in terms which rendered it impossible for him to address me again that night.

Shortly after he had gone, a hoarse voice behind me cried, "Permit me, my dear sir—permit me to restore to their proper place, two napoleons which you have dropped. Wonderful luck, sir! I pledge you my word of honor, as an old soldier, in the course of my long experience in this sort of thing, I never saw such luck as yours—never! Go on, sir—*Sacré mille bombes!* Go on boldly, and break the bank!"

I turned round and saw, nodding and smiling at me with inveterate civility, a tall man, dressed in a frogged and braided surtout.

If I had been in my senses, I should have considered him, personally, as being rather a suspicious specimen of an old soldier. He had goggling, bloodshot eyes, mangy mustaches, and a broken nose. His voice betrayed a barrack-room intonation of the worst order, and he had the dirtiest pair of hands I ever saw—even in France. These little personal peculiarities exercised, however, no repelling influence on me. In the mad excitement, the reckless triumph of that moment, I was ready to "fraternize" with anybody who encouraged me in my game. I accepted the old soldier's offered pinch of snuff; clapped him on the back, and swore he was the honestest fellow in the world—the most glorious relic of the Grand Army that I had ever met with. "Go on!" cried my military friend, snapping his fingers in ecstasy—"Go on, and win! Break the bank—*Mille tonnerres!* my gallant English comrade, break the bank!"

And I *did* go on—went on at such a rate, that in another quarter of an hour the croupier called out, "Gentlemen, the bank has discontinued for to-night." All the notes, and all the gold in that "bank," now lay in a heap under my hands; the whole floating capital of the gambling-house was waiting to pour into my pockets!

"Tie up the money in your pocket-handkerchief, my worthy sir," said the old soldier, as I wildly plunged my hands into my heap of gold. "Tie it up as we used to tie up a bit of dinner in the Grand Army; your winnings are too heavy for any breeches-pockets that ever were sewed. There! that's it—shovel them in, notes and all! *Credié!* what luck! Stop! another napoleon on the floor! *Ah! sacré petit polisson de Napoleon!* have I found thee at last? Now then, sir—two tight double knots each way with your honorable permission, and the money's safe. Feel it! feel it, fortunate sir! hard and round as a cannon-ball—*À bas* if they had only fired such cannon-balls at us at Austerlitz —*nom d'une pipe!* if they only had! And now, as an ancient grenadier, as an ex-brave of the French army, what remains for me to do? I ask what? Simply this, to entreat my valued English friend to drink a bottle of champagne with me, and toast the goddess Fortune in foaming goblets before we part!"

"Excellent ex-brave! Convivial ancient grenadier! Champagne by all means! An English cheer for an old soldier! Hurrah! hurrah! Another English cheer for the goddess Fortune! Hurrah! hurrah! hurrah!"

"Bravo! the Englishman; the amiable, gracious Englishman, in whose veins circulates the vivacious blood of France! Another glass? *A bas!*—the bottle is empty! Never mind! *Vive le vin!* I, the old soldier, order another bottle, and half a pound of *bonbons* with it!"

"No, no, ex-brave; never—ancient grenadier! *Your* bottle last time; *my* bottle this! Behold it! Toast away! The French Army! the great Napoleon! the present company! the croupier! the honest croupier's wife and daughters—if he has any! the ladies generally! everybody in the world!"

By the time the second bottle of champagne was emptied, I felt as if I had been drinking liquid fire—my brain seemed all aflame. No excess in wine had ever had this effect on me before in my life. Was it the result of a stimulant acting upon my system when I was in a highly excited state? Was my stomach in a particularly disordered condition? Or was the champagne amazingly strong?

"Ex-brave of the French Army!" cried I, in a mad state of exhilaration, "*I* am on fire! how are *you?* You have set me on fire! Do you hear, my hero of Austerlitz? Let us have a third bottle of champagne to put the flame out!"

The old soldier wagged his head, rolled his goggle-eyes, until I expected to see them slip out of their sockets; placed his dirty forefinger by the side of his broken nose; solemnly ejaculated "Coffee!" and immediately ran off into an inner room.

The word pronounced by the eccentric veteran seemed to have a magical effect on the rest of the company present. With one accord they all rose to depart. Probably they had expected to profit by my intoxication; but finding that my new friend was benevolently bent on preventing me from getting dead drunk, had now abandoned all hope of thriving pleasantly on my winnings. Whatever their motive might be, at any rate they went away in a body. When the old soldier returned and sat down again opposite to me at the table, we had the room to ourselves. I could see the croupier, in a sort of vestibule which opened out of it, eating his supper in solitude. The silence was now deeper than ever.

A sudden change, too, had come over the "ex-brave." He assumed a portentously solemn look; and when he spoke to me again, his speech was ornamented by no oaths, enforced by no finger-snapping, enlivened by no apostrophes or exclamations.

"Listen, my dear sir," said he, in mysteriously confidential tones—
"listen to an old soldier's advice. I have been to the mistress of the
house (a very charming woman, with a genius for cookery!) to impress
on her the necessity of making us some particularly strong and good
coffee. You must drink this coffee in order to get rid of your little
amiable exaltation of spirits before you think of going home—*you
must,* my good and gracious friend! With all that money to take home
to-night, it is a sacred duty to yourself to have your wits about you.
You are known to be a winner to an enormous extent by several gentlemen present to-night, who, in a certain point of view, are very worthy
and excellent fellows; but they are mortal men, my dear sir, and they
have their amiable weaknesses! Need I say more? Ah, no, no! you
understand me! Now, this is what you must do—send for a cabriolet
when you feel quite well again—draw up all the windows when you
get into it—and tell the driver to take you home only through the large
and well-lighted thoroughfares. Do this; and you and your money will
be safe. Do this; and to-morrow you will thank an old soldier for
giving you a word of honest advice."

Just as the ex-brave ended his oration in very lachrymose tones, the
coffee came in, ready poured out in two cups. My attentive friend
handed me one of the cups with a bow. I was parched with thirst, and
drank it off at a draft. Almost instantly afterward I was seized with a
fit of giddiness, and felt more completely intoxicated than ever. The
room whirled round and round furiously; the old soldier seemed to be
regularly bobbing up and down before me like the piston of a steam-
engine. I was half deafened by a violent singing in my ears; a feeling of
utter bewilderment, helplessness, idiocy, overcame me. I rose from my
chair, holding on by the table to keep my balance; and stammered out
that I felt dreadfully unwell—so unwell that I did not know how I was
to get home.

"My dear friend," answered the old soldier—and even his voice
seemed to be bobbing up and down as he spoke—"my dear friend, it
would be madness to go home in *your* state; you would be sure to lose
your money; you might be robbed and murdered with the greatest
ease. *I* am going to sleep here: do *you* sleep here, too—they make up
capital beds in this house—take one; sleep off the effects of the wine,
and go home safely with your winnings to-morrow—to-morrow, in
broad daylight."

I had but two ideas left: one, that I must never let go hold of my
handkerchief full of money; the other, that I must lie down some-

where immediately, and fall off into a comfortable sleep. So I agreed to the proposal about the bed, and took the offered arm of the old soldier, carrying my money with my disengaged hand. Preceded by the croupier, we passed along some passages and up a flight of stairs into the bedroom which I was to occupy. The ex-brave shook me warmly by the hand, proposed that we should breakfast together, and then, followed by the croupier, left me for the night.

I ran to the wash-hand stand; drank some of the water in my jug; poured the rest out, and plunged my face into it; then sat down in a chair and tried to compose myself. I soon felt better. The change for my lungs, from the fetid atmosphere of the gambling-house to the cool air of the apartment I now occupied; the almost equally refreshing change for my eyes, from the glaring gaslights of the "salon" to the dim, quiet flicker of one bedroom-candle, aided wonderfully the restorative effects of cold water. The giddiness left me, and I began to feel a little like a reasonable being again. My first thought was of the risk of sleeping all night in a gambling-house; my second, of the still greater risk of trying to get out after the house was closed, and of going home alone at night through the streets of Paris with a large sum of money about me. I had slept in worse places than this on my travels; so I determined to lock, bolt, and barricade my door, and take my chance till the next morning.

Accordingly, I secured myself against all intrusion; looked under the bed, and into the cupboard; tried the fastening of the window; and then, satisfied that I had taken every proper precaution, pulled off my upper clothing, put my light, which was a dim one, on the hearth among a feathery litter of wood-ashes, and got into bed, with the handkerchief full of money under my pillow.

I soon felt not only that I could not go to sleep, but that I could not even close my eyes. I was wide awake, and in a high fever. Every nerve in my body trembled—every one of my senses seemed to be preternaturally sharpened. I tossed and rolled, and tried every kind of position and perseveringly sought out the cold corners of the bed, and all to no purpose. Now I thrust my arms over the clothes; now I poked them under the clothes; now I violently shot my legs straight out down to the bottom of the bed; now I convulsively coiled them up as near my chin as they would go; now I shook out my crumpled pillow, changed it to the cool side, patted it flat, and lay down quietly on my back; now I fiercely doubled it in two, set it up on end, thrust it against the board of the bed, and tried a sitting posture. Every effort was in vain; I groaned with vexation as I felt that I was in for a sleepless night.

What could I do? I had no book to read. And yet, unless I found out some method of diverting my mind, I felt certain that I was in the condition to imagine all sorts of horrors; to rack my brain with forebodings of every possible and impossible danger; in short, to pass the night in suffering all conceivable varieties of nervous terror.

I raised myself on my elbow, and looked about the room—which was brightened by a lovely moonlight pouring straight through the window—to see if it contained any pictures or ornaments that I could at all clearly distinguish. While my eyes wandered from wall to wall, a remembrance of Le Maistre's delightful little book, *Voyage autour de ma Chambre*, occurred to me. I resolved to imitate the French author, and find occupation and amusement enough to relieve the tedium of my wakefulness, by making a mental inventory of every article of furniture I could see, and by following up to their sources the multitude of associations which even a chair, a table, or a wash-hand stand may be made to call forth.

In the nervous, unsettled state of my mind at that moment, I found it much easier to make my inventory than to make my reflections, and thereupon soon gave up all hope of thinking in Le Maistre's fanciful track—or, indeed, of thinking at all. I looked about the room at the different articles of furniture, and did nothing more.

There was, first, the bed I was lying in; a four-post bed, of all things in the world to meet with in Paris!—yes, a thorough clumsy British four-poster, with a regular top lined with chintz—the regular fringed valance all round—the regular stifling, unwholesome curtains, which I remembered having mechanically drawn back against the posts without particularly noticing the bed when I first got into the room. Then there was the marble-topped wash-hand stand, from which the water I had spilled, in my hurry to pour it out, was still dripping, slowly and more slowly, on to the brick floor. Then two small chairs, with my coat, waistcoat, and trousers flung on them. Then a large elbow-chair covered with dirty white dimity, with my cravat and shirt collar thrown over the back. Then a chest of drawers with two of the brass handles off, and a tawdry, broken china inkstand placed on it by way of ornament for the top. Then the dressing-table, adorned by a very small looking-glass, and a very large pincushion. Then the window— an unusually large window. Then a dark old picture, which the feeble candle dimly showed me. It was the picture of a fellow in a high Spanish hat, crowned with a plume of towering feathers. A swarthy, sinister ruffian, looking upward, shading his eyes with his hand, and looking intently upward—it might be at some tall gallows on which he was going to be hanged. At any rate, he had the appearance of thoroughly deserving it.

This picture put a kind of constraint upon me to look upward too—at the top of the bed. It was a gloomy and not an interesting object, and I looked back at the picture. I counted the feathers in the man's hat—they stood out in relief—three white, two green. I observed the crown of his hat, which was of conical shape, according to the fashion supposed to have been favored by Guido Fawkes. I wondered what he was looking up at. It couldn't be at the stars; such a desperado was neither astrologer nor astronomer. It must be at the high gallows, and he was going to be hanged presently. Would the executioner come into possession of his conical-crowned hat and plume of feathers? I counted the feathers again—three white, two green.

While I still lingered over this very improving and intellectual employment, my thoughts insensibly began to wander. The moonlight shining into the room reminded me of a certain moonlight night in England—the night after a picnic party in a Welsh valley. Every incident of the drive homeward, through lovely scenery, which the moonlight made lovelier than ever, came back to my remembrance, though I had never given the picnic a thought for years; though, if I had *tried* to recollect it, I could certainly have recalled little or nothing of that scene long past. Of all the wonderful faculties that help to tell us we are immortal, which speaks the sublime truth more eloquently than memory? Here was I, in a strange house of the most suspicious character, in a situation of uncertainty, and even of peril, which might seem to make the cool exercise of my recollection almost out of the question; nevertheless, remembering, quite involuntarily, places, people, conversations, minute circumstances of every kind, which I had thought forgotten forever; which I could not possibly have recalled at will, even under the most favorable auspices. And what cause had produced in a moment the whole of this strange, complicated, mysterious effect? Nothing but some rays of moonlight shining in at my bedroom window.

I was still thinking of the picnic—of our merriment on the drive home—of the sentimental young lady who *would* quote *Childe Harold* because it was moonlight. I was absorbed by these past scenes and past amusements, when, in an instant, the thread on which my memories hung snapped asunder; my attention immediately came back to present things more vividly than ever, and I found myself, I neither knew why nor wherefore, looking hard at the picture again.

Looking for what?

Good God! the man had pulled his hat down on his brows! No! the hat itself was gone! Where was the conical crown? Where the feathers—three white, two green? Not there! In place of the hat and feathers, what dusky object was it that now hid his forehead, his eyes, his shading hand?

Was the bed moving?

I turned on my back and looked up. Was I mad? drunk? dreaming? giddy again? or was the top of the bed really moving down—sinking slowly, regularly, silently, horribly, right down throughout the whole of its length and breadth—right down upon me, as I lay underneath?

My blood seemed to stand still. A deadly, paralyzing coldness stole all over me as I turned my head round on the pillow and determined to test whether the bed-top was really moving or not, by keeping my eye on the man in the picture.

The next look at the picture was enough. The dull, black, frowsy outline of the valance above me was within an inch of being parallel with his waist. I still looked breathlessly. And steadily, and slowly—very slowly—I saw the figure, and the line of frame below the figure, vanish, as the valance moved down before it.

I am, constitutionally, anything but timid. I have been on more than one occasion in peril of my life, and have not lost my self-possession for an instant; but when the conviction first settled on my mind that the bed-top was really moving, was steadily and continuously sinking down upon me, I looked up shuddering, helpless, panic-stricken, beneath the hideous machinery for murder, which was advancing closer and closer to suffocate me where I lay.

I looked up, motionless, speechless, breathless. The candle, fully spent, went out; but the moonlight still brightened the room. Down and down, without pausing and without sounding, came the bed-top, and still my panic terror seemed to bind me faster and faster to the mattress on which I lay—down and down it sank, till the dusty odor from the lining of the canopy came stealing into my nostrils.

At that final moment the instinct of self-preservation startled me out of my trance, and I moved at last. There was just room for me to roll myself sidewise off the bed. As I dropped noiselessly to the floor, the edge of the murderous canopy touched me on the shoulder.

Without stopping to draw my breath, without wiping the cold

sweat from my face, I rose instantly on my knees to watch the bed-top. I was literally spellbound by it. If I had heard footsteps behind me, I could not have turned round; if a means of escape had been miraculously provided for me, I could not have moved to take advantage of it. The whole life in me was, at that moment, concentrated in my eyes.

It descended—the whole canopy, with the fringe round it, came down—down—close down; so close that there was not room now to squeeze my finger between the bed-top and the bed. I felt at the sides, and discovered that what had appeared to me from beneath to be the ordinary light canopy of a four-post bed was in reality a thick, broad mattress, the substance of which was concealed by the valance and its fringe. I looked up and saw the four posts rising hideously bare. In the middle of the bed-top was a huge wooden screw that had evidently worked it down through a hole in the ceiling, just as ordinary presses are worked down on the substance selected for compression. The frightful apparatus moved without making the faintest noise. There had been no creaking as it came down; there was now not the faintest sound from the room above. Amidst a dead and awful silence I beheld before me—in the Nineteenth Century, and in the civilized capital of France—such a machine for secret murder by suffocation as might have existed in the worst days of the Inquisition, in the lonely inns among the Hartz Mountains, in the mysterious tribunals of Westphalia! Still, as I looked on it, I could not move, I could hardly breathe, but I began to recover the power of thinking, and in a moment I discovered the murderous conspiracy framed against me in all its horror.

My cup of coffee had been drugged, and drugged too strongly. I had been saved from being smothered by having taken an overdose of some narcotic. How I had chafed and fretted at the fever fit which had preserved my life by keeping me awake! How recklessly I had confided myself to the two wretches who led me into this room, determined, for the sake of my winnings, to kill me in my sleep by the surest and most horrible contrivance for secretly accomplishing my destruction! How many men, winners like me, had slept, as I had proposed to sleep, in that bed, and had never been seen or heard of more! I shuddered at the bare idea of it.

But ere long all thought was again suspended by the sight of the murderous canopy moving once more. After it had remained on the bed—as nearly as I could guess—about ten minutes, it began to move up again. The villains who worked it from above evidently believed that their purpose was now accomplished. Slowly and silently, as it had descended, that horrible bed-top rose toward its former place. When it reached the upper extremities of the four posts, it reached the ceiling too. Neither hole nor screw could be seen; the bed became in appearance an ordinary bed again—the canopy an ordinary canopy—even to the most suspicious eyes.

Now, for the first time, I was able to move—to rise from my knees—to dress myself in my upper clothing—and to consider of how I should escape. If I betrayed by the smallest noise that the attempt to suffocate me had failed, I was certain to be murdered. Had I made any noise already? I listened intently, looking toward the door.

No! No footsteps in the passage outside—no sound of a tread, light or heavy, in the room above—absolute silence everywhere. Besides locking and bolting my door, I had moved an old wooden chest against it, which I had found under the bed. To remove this chest (my blood ran cold as I thought of what its contents *might* be!) without making some disturbance was impossible; and, moreover, to think of escaping through the house, now barred up for the night, was sheer insanity. Only one chance was left me—the window. I stole to it on tiptoe.

My bedroom was on the first floor, above an *entresol,* and looked into the back street. I raised my hand to open the window, knowing that on that action hung, by the merest hair-breadth, my chance of safety. They keep vigilant watch in a House of Murder. If any part of the frame cracked, if the hinge creaked, I was a lost man! It must have occupied me at least five minutes, reckoning by time—five *hours* reckoning by suspense—to open that window. I succeeded in doing it silently—in doing it with all the dexterity of a house-breaker—and then looked down into the street. To leap the distance beneath me would be almost certain destruction! Next, I looked round at the sides of the house. Down the left side ran a thick water-pipe—it passed close by the outer edge of the window. The moment I saw the pipe, I knew I was saved. My breath came and went freely for the first time since I had seen the canopy of the bed moving down upon me!

To some men the means of escape which I had discovered might have seemed difficult and dangerous enough—to *me* the prospect of slipping down the pipe into the street did not suggest even a thought of peril. I had always been accustomed, by the practise of gymnastics, to keep up my school-boy powers as a daring and expert climber;

and knew that my head, hands, and feet would serve me faithfully in any hazards of ascent or descent. I had already got one leg over the window-sill, when I remembered the handkerchief filled with money under my pillow. I could well have afforded to leave it behind me, but I was revengefully determined that the miscreants of the gambling-house should miss their plunder as well as their victim. So I went back to the bed and tied the heavy handkerchief at my back by my cravat.

Just as I had made it tight and fixed it in a comfortable place, I thought I heard a sound of breathing outside the door. The chill feeling of horror ran through me again as I listened. No! Dead silence still in the passage—I had only heard the night air blowing softly into the room. The next moment I was on the window-sill—and the next I had a firm grip on the water-pipe with my hands and knees.

I slid down into the street easily and quietly, as I thought I should, and immediately set off at the top of my speed to a branch "Prefecture" of Police, which I knew was situated in the immediate neighborhood. A "Sub-prefect," and several picked men among his subordinates, happened to be up, maturing, I believe, some scheme for discovering the perpetrator of a mysterious murder which all Paris was talking of just then. When I began my story, in a breathless hurry and in very bad French, I could see that the Sub-prefect suspected me of being a drunken Englishman who had robbed somebody; but he soon altered his opinion as I went on, and before I had anything like concluded, he shoved all the papers before him into a drawer, put on his hat, supplied me with another (for I was bareheaded), ordered a file of soldiers, desired his expert followers to get ready all sorts of tools for breaking open doors and ripping up brick flooring, and took my arm, in the most friendly and familiar manner possible, to lead me with him out of the house. I will venture to say that when the Sub-prefect was a little boy, and was taken for the first time to the play, he was not half as much pleased as he was now at the job in prospect for him at the gambling-house!

Away we went through the streets, the Sub-prefect cross-examining and congratulating me in the same breath as we marched at the head of our formidable *posse comitatus*. Sentinels were placed at the back and front of the house the moment we got to it; a tremendous battery of knocks was directed against the door; a light appeared at a window; I was told to conceal myself behind the police—then came more knocks, and a cry of "Open in the name of the law!" At that terrible

summons bolts and locks gave way before an invisible hand, and the
moment after the Sub-prefect was in the passage, confronting a waiter
half dressed and ghastly pale. This was the short dialogue which
immediately took place:

"We want to see the Englishman who is sleeping in this house?"

"He went away hours ago."

"He did no such thing. His friend went away; *he* remained. Show
us to his bedroom!"

"I swear to you, Monsieur le Sous-prefect, he is not here! He—"

"I swear to you, Monsieur le Garçon, he is. He slept here—he didn't
find your bed comfortable—he came to us to complain of it—here he
is among my men—and here am I ready to look for a flea or two in
his bedstead. Renaudin!" (calling to one of the subordinates, and
pointing to the waiter), collar that man, and tie his hands behind
him. Now, then, gentlemen, let us walk upstairs!"

Every man and woman in the house was secured—the "Old Soldier"
the first. Then I identified the bed in which I had slept, and then
we went into the room above.

No object that was at all extraordinary appeared in any part of it.
The Sub-prefect looked round the place, commanded everybody to be
silent, stamped twice on the floor, called for a candle, looked attentively at the spot he had stamped on, and ordered the flooring there
to be carefully taken up. This was done in no time. Lights were
produced, and we saw a deep raftered cavity between the floor of this
room and the ceiling of the room beneath. Through this cavity there
ran perpendicularly a sort of case of iron thickly greased; and inside
the case appeared the screw, which communicated with the bed-top
below. Extra lengths of screw, freshly oiled; levers covered with felt;
all the complete upper works of a heavy press—constructed with
infernal ingenuity so as to join the fixtures below, and when taken
to pieces again to go into the smallest possible compass—were next
discovered and pulled out on the floor. After some little difficulty the
Sub-prefect succeeded in putting the machinery together, and, leaving
his men to work it, descended with me to the bedroom. The smother-
ing canopy was then lowered, but not so noiselessly as I had seen it
lowered. When I mentioned this to the Sub-prefect, his answer, simple
as it was, had a terrible significance, "My men," said he, "are working
down the bed-top for the first time—the men whose money you won
were in better practise."

We left the house in the sole possession of two police agents—every one of the inmates being removed to prison on the spot. The Sub-prefect, after taking down my *"procès verbal"* in his office, returned with me to my hotel to get my passport. "Do you think," I asked, as I gave it to him, "that any men have really been smothered in that bed, as they tried to smother *me?"*

"I have seen dozens of drowned men laid out at the Morgue," answered the Sub-prefect, "in whose pocketbooks were found letters stating that they had committed suicide in the Seine, because they had lost everything at the gaming-table. Do I know how many of those men entered the same gambling-house that *you* entered? won as *you* won? took that bed as *you* took it? slept in it? were smothered in it? and were privately thrown into the river, with a letter of explanation written by the murderers and placed in their pocketbooks? No man can say how many or how few have suffered the fate from which you have escaped. The people of the gambling-house kept their bedstead machinery a secret from *us*—even from the police! The dead kept the rest of the secret for them. Good-night, or rather good-morning, Monsieur Faulkner! Be at my office again at nine o'clock—in the meantime, *au revoir!"*

The rest of my story is soon told. I was examined and re-examined; the gambling-house was strictly searched all through from top to bottom; the prisoners were separately interrogated; and two of the less guilty among them made a confession. I discovered that the Old Soldier was the master of the gambling-house—*justice* discovered that he had been drummed out of the army as a vagabond years ago; that he had been guilty of all sorts of villainies since; that he was in possession of stolen property, which the owners identified; and that he, the croupier, another accomplice, and the woman who had made my cup of coffee, were all in the secret of the bedstead. There appeared some reason to doubt whether the inferior persons attached to the house knew anything of the suffocating machinery; and they received the benefit of the doubt, by being treated simply as thieves and vagabonds. As for the Old Soldier and his two head myrmidons, they went to the galleys; the woman who had drugged my coffee was imprisoned for I forget how many years; the regular attendants at the gambling-house were considered "suspicious," and placed under "surveillance"; and I became, for one whole week (which is a long time), the head "lion" in Parisian society. My adventure was dramatized by three illustrious play-makers, but never saw theatrical daylight; for the censorship forbade the introduction on the stage of a correct copy of the gambling-house bedstead.

One good result was produced by my adventure, which any censorship must have approved: it cured me of ever again trying *Rouge et Noir* as an amusement. The sight of a green cloth, with packs of cards and heaps of money on it, will henceforth be forever associated in my mind with the sight of a bed canopy descending to suffocate me in the silence and darkness of the night.

Charles Dickens

THE MOST popular of all English novelists, Charles Dickens wrote short stories as an exuberant by-product of a prodigal genius occupied with revealing the whole panorama of British middle-class life in rich, digressive narratives charged with pathos and humor. Even his short stories are for the most part novels in little. He was quite untouched by the innovating technique of Hawthorne or Poe, but belonged, rather, to the leisurely tradition of Scott or Irving. His first short narratives Sketches by Boz (1836) are descriptive pieces and exercises in personality.

This is not to say that he could not have mastered the newer technique, had he wished. Several of his Christmas stories, compressed within a narrow space by journalistic necessity, look toward the story of the future, and "The Signal Man" in particular has been hailed as a swift, impressionistic tale worthy of all that Poe could teach of craftsmanship. Another of his brief stories much praised in its day, "A Child's Dream of a Star," (1850) is more a prose poem, a sentimental fantasy, than a story.

The life of Charles Dickens is familiar history. Born in 1812, the son of a government clerk, his early London days were bitter with poverty. Beginning his career as a journalist, he won national acclaim in 1836 with the Pickwick Papers, and by middle life commanded through his series of great novels the widest and most loyal literary following of the Victorian era. He died in 1870.

THE SIGNAL-MAN *

Charles Dickens

"HALLOA! Below there!"

When he heard a voice thus calling to him, he was standing at the door of his box, with a flag in his hand, furled around its short pole. One would have thought, considering the nature of the ground, that he could not have doubted from what quarter the voice came; but, instead of looking up to where I stood on the top of the steep cutting nearly over his head, he turned himself about, and looked down the Line. There was something remarkable in his manner of doing so, though I could not have said for my life what. But I know it was remarkable enough to attract my notice, even though his figure was foreshortened and shadowed, down in the deep trench, and mine was high above him, so steeped in the glow of an angry sunset, that I had shaded my eyes with my hand before I saw him at all.

"Halloa! Below!"

From looking down the Line, he turned himself about again, and, raising his eyes, saw my figure high above him.

He looked up at me without replying, and I looked down at him without pressing him too soon with a repetition of my idle question. Just then there came a vague vibration in the earth and air, quickly changing into a violent pulsation, and an oncoming rush that caused me to start back, as though it had force to draw me down. When such vapor as rose to my height from this rapid train had passed me, and was skimming away over the landscape, I looked down again, and saw him refurling the flag he had shown while the train went by.

I repeated my inquiry. After a pause, during which he seemed to regard me with fixed attention, he motioned with his rolled-up flag towards a point on my level, some two or three hundred yards distant. I called down to him, "All right!" and made for that point. There, by dint of looking closely about me, I found a rough zigzag descending path notched out, which I followed.

The cutting was extremely deep, and unusually precipitate. It was made through a clammy stone that became oozier and wetter as I went down. For these reasons, I found the way long enough to recall a singular air of reluctance or compulsion with which he had pointed out the path.

* From *Christmas Stories* by Charles Dickens, 1866.

When I came down low enough upon the zigzag descent to see him again, I saw that he was standing between the rails on the way by which the train had lately passed, in an attitude as if he were waiting for me to appear. He had his left hand at his chin, and that left elbow rested on his right hand, crossed over his breast. His attitude was one of such expectation and watchfulness, that I stopped a moment, wondering at it.

I resumed my downward way, and stepping out upon the level of the railroad, and drawing nearer to him, saw that he was a dark, sallow man, with a dark beard and rather heavy eyebrows. His post was in as solitary and dismal a place as ever I saw. On either side a dripping-wet wall of jagged stone, excluding all view but a strip of sky: the perspective one way only a crooked prolongation of this great dungeon; the shorter perspective in the other direction terminating in a gloomy red light, and the gloomier entrance to a black tunnel, in whose massive architecture there was a barbarous, depressing, and forbidding air. So little sunlight ever found its way to this spot that it had an earthy, deadly smell; and so much cold wind rushed through it, that it struck chill to me, as if I had left the natural world.

Before he stirred, I was near enough to him to have touched him. Not even then removing his eyes from mine, he stepped back one step, and lifted his hand.

This was a lonesome post to occupy (I said), and it had riveted my attention when I looked down from up yonder. A visitor was a rarity, I should suppose; not an unwelcome rarity, I hoped? In me, he merely saw a man who had been shut up within narrow limits all his life, and who being at last set free, had a newly awakened interest in these great works. To such purpose I spoke to him; but I am far from sure of the terms I used; for, besides that I am not happy in opening any conversation, there was something in the man that daunted me.

He directed a most curious look towards the red light near the tunnel's mouth, and looked all about it, as if something were missing from it, and then looked at me.

That light was part of his charge,—was it not?

He answered in a low voice,—"Don't you know it is?"

The monstrous thought came into my mind, as I perused the fixed eyes and the saturnine face, that this was a spirit, not a man. I have speculated, since, whether there may have been infection in his mind.

In my turn I stepped back. But, in making the action, I detected in his eyes some latent fear of me. This put the monstrous thought to flight.

"You look at me," I said, forcing a smile, "as if you had a dread of me."

"I was doubtful," he returned, "whether I had seen you before."

"Where?"

He pointed to the red light he had looked at.

"There?" I said.

Intently watchful of me, he replied (but without sound), "Yes."

"My good fellow, what should I do there? However, be that as it may, I never was there, you may swear."

"I think I may," he rejoined. "Yes. I am sure I may."

His manner cleared, like my own. He replied to my remarks with readiness, and in well-chosen words. Had he much to do there? Yes; that was to say, he had enough responsibility to bear; but exactness and watchfulness were what was required of him, and of actual work—manual labor—he had next to none. To change that signal, to trim those lights, and to turn this iron handle now and then, was all he had to do under that head. Regarding those many long and lonely hours of which I seemed to make so much, he could only say that the routine of his life had shaped itself into that form, and he had grown used to it. He had taught himself a language down here,—if only to know it by sight, and to have formed his own crude ideas of its pronunciation, could be called learning it. He had also worked at fractions and decimals, and tried a little algebra; but he was, and had been as a boy, a poor hand at figures. Was it necessary for him when on duty always to remain in that channel of damp air, and could he never rise into the sunshine from between those high stone walls? Why, that depended upon times and circumstances. Under some conditions there would be less upon the Line than under others, and the same held good as to certain hours of the day and night. In bright weather, he did choose occasions for getting a little above these lower shadows; but, being at all times liable to be called by his electric bell, and at such times listening for it with redoubled anxiety, the relief was less than I would suppose.

He took me into his box, where there was a fire, a desk for an official book in which he had to make certain entries, a telegraphic instrument with its dial, face, and needles, and the little bell of which he had spoken. On my trusting that he would excuse the remark that he had been well educated, and (I hoped I might say without offence) perhaps

educated above that station, he observed that instances of slight in-
congruity in such wise would rarely be found wanting among large
bodies of men; that he had heard it was so in workhouses, in the police
force, even in that last desperate resource, the army; and that he knew
it was so, more or less, in any great railway staff. He had been, when
young (if I could believe it, sitting in that hut,—he scarcely could), a
student of natural philosophy, and had attended lectures; but he had
run wild, misused his opportunities, gone down, and never risen again.
He had no complaint to offer about that. He had made his bed, and
he lay upon it. It was far too late to make another.

All that I have here condensed he said in a quiet manner, with his
grave dark regards divided between me and the fire. He threw in the
word, "Sir," from time to time, and especially when he referred to his
youth,—as though to request me to understand that he claimed to be
nothing but what I found him. He was several times interrupted by
the little bell, and had to read off messages, and send replies. Once he
had to stand without the door, and display a flag as a train passed, and
make some verbal communication to the driver. In the discharge of
his duties, I observed him to be remarkably exact and vigilant, breaking off his discourse at a syllable, and remaining silent until what he
had to do was done.

In a word, I should have set this man down as one of the safest of
men to be employed in that capacity, but for the circumstance that
while he was speaking to me he twice broke off with a fallen color,
turned his face towards the little bell when it did NOT ring, opened
the door of the hut (which was kept shut to exclude the unhealthy
damp), and looked out towards the red light near the mouth of the
tunnel. On both of those occasions he came back to the fire with the
inexplicable air upon him which I had remarked, without being able
to define, when we were so far asunder.

Said I, when I rose to leave him, "You almost make me think that
I have met with a contented man."

(I am afraid I must acknowledge that I said it to lead him on.)

"I believe I used to be so," he rejoined, in the low voice in which
he had first spoken; "but I am troubled, sir, I am troubled."

He would have recalled the words if he could. He had said them,
however, and I took them up quickly.

"With what? What is your trouble?"

"It is very difficult to impart, sir. It is very, very difficult to speak of.
If ever you make me another visit, I will try to tell you."

"But I expressly intend to make you another visit. Say, when shall it be?"

"I go off early in the morning, and I shall be on again at ten to-morrow night, sir."

"I will come at eleven."

He thanked me, and went out at the door with me. "I'll show my white light, sir," he said, in his peculiar low voice, "till you have found the way up. When you have found it, don't call out! And when you are at the top, don't call out!"

His manner seemed to make the place strike colder to me, but I said no more than, "Very well."

"And when you come down to-morrow night, don't call out! Let me ask you a parting question. What made you cry, 'Halloa! Below there!' tonight?"

"Heaven knows," said I. "I cried something to that effect—"

"Not to that effect, sir. Those were the very words. I know them well."

"Admit those were the very words. I said them, no doubt, because I saw you below."

"For no other reason?"

"What other reason could I possibly have?"

"You had no feeling that they were conveyed to you in any super-natural way?"

"No."

He wished me good-night, and held up his light. I walked by the side of the down Line of rails (with a very disagreeable sensation of a train coming behind me) until I found the path. It was easier to mount than to descend, and I got back to my inn without any adventure.

Punctual to my appointment, I placed my foot on the first notch of the zigzag next night as the distant clocks were striking eleven. He was waiting for me at the bottom, with his white light on. "I have not called out," I said, when we came close together; "may I speak now?" "By all means, sir." "Good-night, then, and here's my hand." "Good-night, sir, and here's mine." With that we walked side by side to his box, entered it, closed the door, and sat down by the fire.

"I have made up my mind, sir," he began, bending forward as soon as we were seated, and speaking in a tone but a little above a whisper, "that you shall not have to ask me twice what troubles me. I took you for some one else yesterday evening. That troubles me."

"That mistake?"

"No. That some one else."

"Who is it?"

"I don't know."

"Like me?"

"I don't know. I never saw the face. The left arm is across the face, and the right arm is waved,—violently waved. This way."

I followed his action with my eyes, and it was the action of an arm gesticulating with the utmost passion and vehemence,—"For God's sake clear the way!"

"One moonlight night," said the man, "I was sitting here, when I heard a voice cry, 'Halloa! Below there!' I started up, looked from that door, and saw this Some one else standing by the red light near the tunnel, waving as I just now showed you. The voice seemed hoarse with shouting, and it cried, 'Look out! Look out!' And then again, 'Halloa! Below there! Look out!' I caught up my lamp, turned it on red, and ran towards the figure, calling, 'What's wrong? What has happened? Where?' It stood just outside the blackness of the tunnel. I advanced so close upon it that I wondered at its keeping the sleeve across its eyes. I ran right up at it, and had my hand stretched out to pull the sleeve away, when it was gone."

"Into the tunnel," said I.

"No. I ran on into the tunnel, five hundred yards. I stopped, and held my lamp above my head, and saw the figures of the measured distance, and saw the wet stains stealing down the walls and trickling through the arch. I ran out again faster than I had run in (for I had a mortal abhorrence of the place upon me), and I looked all round the red light, with my own red light, and I went up the iron ladder to the gallery atop of it, and I came down again, and ran back here. I telegraphed both ways, 'An alarm has been given. Is anything wrong?' The answer came back, both ways, 'All well.' "

Resisting the slow touch of a frozen finger tracing out my spine, I showed him how that this figure must be a deception of his sense of sight; and how that figures, originating in disease of the delicate nerves that minister to the functions of the eye, were known to have often troubled patients, some of whom had become conscious of the nature of their affliction, and had even proved it by experiments upon themselves. "As to an imaginary cry," said I, "do but listen for a moment to the wind in this unnatural valley while we speak so low, and to the wild harp it makes of the telegraph wires!"

That was all very well, he returned, after we had sat listening for a while, and he ought to know something of the wind and wires,—he who so often passed long winter nights there, alone and watching. But he would beg to remark that he had not finished.

I asked his pardon, and he slowly added these words, touching my arm:—

"Within six hours after the Appearance, the memorable accident on this Line happened, and within ten hours the dead and wounded were brought along through the tunnel over the spot where the figure had stood."

A disagreeable shudder crept over me, but I did my best against it. It was not to be denied, I rejoined, that this was a remarkable coincidence, calculated deeply to impress his mind. But it was unquestionable that remarkable coincidences did continually occur, and they must be taken into account in dealing with such a subject. Though to be sure I must admit, I added (for I thought I saw that he was going to bring the objection to bear upon me), men of common sense did not allow much for coincidence in making the ordinary calculations of life.

He again begged to remark that he had not finished.

I again begged his pardon for being betrayed into interruptions.

"This," he said, again laying his hand upon my arm, and glancing over his shoulder with hollow eyes, "was just a year ago. Six or seven months passed, and I had recovered from the surprise and shock, when one morning, as the day was breaking, I, standing at that door, looked towards the red light, and saw the spectre again." He stopped, with a fixed look at me.

"Did it cry out?"

"No. It was silent."

"Did it wave its arm?"

"No. It leaned against the shaft of the light, with both hands before the face. Like this."

Once more I followed his action with my eyes. It was an action of mourning. I have seen such an attitude in stone figures on tombs.

"Did you go up to it?"

"I came in and sat down, partly to collect my thoughts, partly because it had turned me faint. When I went to the door again, daylight was above me, and the ghost was gone."

"But nothing followed? Nothing came of this?"

He touched me on the arm with his forefinger twice or thrice, giving a ghastly nod each time.

"That very day, as the train came out of the tunnel, I noticed, at a carriage window on my side, what looked like a confusion of hands and heads, and something waved. I saw it just in time to signal the driver, stop! He shut off, and put his brake on, but the train drifted past here a hundred and fifty yards or more. I ran after it, and, as I went along, heard terrible screams and cries. A beautiful young lady had died instantaneously in one of the compartments, and was brought in here, and laid down on this floor between us."

Involuntarily I pushed my chair back, as I looked from the boards at which he pointed to himself.

"True, sir. True. Precisely as it happened, so I tell it you."

I could think of nothing to say, to any purpose, and my mouth was very dry. The wind and the wires took up the story with a long lamenting wail.

He resumed. "Now, sir, mark this, and judge how my mind is troubled. The spectre came back a week ago. Ever since it has been there, now and again, by fits and starts."

"At the light?"

"At the Danger-light."

"What does it seem to do?"

He repeated, if possible with increased passion and vehemence, that former gesticulation of, "For God's sake, clear the way!"

Then he went on. "I have no peace or rest for it. It calls to me, for many minutes together, in an agonized manner, 'Below there! Look out! Look out!' It stands waving to me. It rings my little bell—"

I caught at that. "Did it ring your bell yesterday evening when I was here, and you went to the door?"

"Twice."

"Why see," said I, "how your imagination misleads you. My eyes were on the bell, and my ears were open to the bell, and if I am a living man, it did NOT ring at those times. No, nor at any other time, except when it was rung in the natural course of physical things by the station communicating with you."

He shook his head. "I have never made a mistake as to that yet, sir. I have never confused the spectre's ring with the man's. The ghost's ring is a strange vibration in the bell that it derives from nothing else, and I have not asserted that the bell stirs to the eye. I don't wonder that you failed to hear it. But I heard it."

"And did the spectre seem to be there, when you looked out?"

"It WAS there."

"Both times?"

He repeated firmly: "Both times."

"Will you come to the door with me and look for it now?"

He bit his under lip as though he were somewhat unwilling, but arose. I opened the door, and stood on the step, while he stood in the doorway. There was the Danger-light. There was the dismal mouth of the tunnel. There were the stars above them.

"Do you see it?" I asked him, taking particular note of his face. His eyes were prominent and strained, but not very much more so, perhaps, than my own had been when I had directed them earnestly towards the same spot.

"No," he answered. "It is not there."

"Agreed," said I.

We went in again, shut the door, and resumed our seats. I was thinking how best to improve this advantage, if it might be called one, when he took up the conversation in such a matter-of-course way, so assuming that there could be no serious question of fact between us, that I felt myself placed in the weakest of positions.

"By this time, you will fully understand, sir," he said, "that what troubles me so dreadfully is the question, What does the spectre mean?"

I was not sure, I told him, that I did fully understand.

"What is its warning against?" he said, ruminating, with his eyes on the fire, and only by times turning them on me. "What is the danger? Where is the danger? There is danger overhanging somewhere on the Line. Some dreadful calamity will happen. It is not to be doubted this third time, after what has gone before. But surely this is a cruel haunting of *me*. What can *I* do?"

He pulled out his handkerchief, and wiped the drops from his heated forehead.

"If I telegraph Danger, on either side of me, or on both, I can give no reason for it," he went on, wiping the palms of his hands. "I should get into trouble, and do no good. They would think I was mad. This is the way it would work,—Message: 'Danger! Take care!' Answered: 'What Danger? Where?' Message: 'Don't know. But for God's sake, take care!' They would displace me. What else could they do?"

His pain of mind was most pitiable to see. It was the mental torture of a conscientious man, oppressed beyond endurance by an unintelligible responsibility involving life.

"When it first stood under the Danger-light," he went on, putting his dark hair back from his head, and drawing his hands outward across and across his temples in an extremity of feverish distress, "why not tell me where that accident was to happen,—if it must happen? Why not tell me how it could be averted,—if it could have been averted? When on its second coming it hid its face, why not tell me, instead, 'She is going to die. Let them keep her at home?' If it came, on those two occasions, only to show me that its warnings were true, and so to prepare me for the third, why not warn me plainly now? And I, Lord help me! A mere poor signal-man on this solitary station! Why not go to somebody with credit to be believed, and power to act?"

When I saw him in this state, I saw that for the poor man's sake, as well as for the public safety, what I had to do for the time was to compose his mind. Therefore, setting aside all question of reality or unreality between us, I represented to him that whoever thoroughly discharged his duty must do well, and that at least it was his comfort that he understood his duty, though he did not understand these confounding Appearances. In this effort I succeeded far better than in the attempt to reason him out of his conviction. He became calm; the occupations incidental to his post as the night advanced began to make larger demands on his attention; and I left him at two in the morning. I had offered to stay through the night, but he would not hear of it.

That I more than once looked back at the red light as I ascended the pathway; that I did not like the red light, and that I should have slept but poorly if my bed had been under it, I see no reason to conceal. Nor did I like the two sequences of the accident and the dead girl. I see no reason to conceal that, either.

But what ran most in my thoughts was the consideration, how ought I to act, having become the recipient of this disclosure? I had proved the man to be intelligent, vigilant, painstaking, and exact; but how long might he remain so, in his state of mind? Though in a subordinate position, still he held a most important trust, and would I (for instance) like to stake my own life on the chances of his continuing to execute it with precision?

Unable to overcome a feeling that there would be something treacherous in my communicating what he had told me to his superiors in the Company, without first being plain with himself and proposing a middle course to him, I ultimately resolved to offer to accompany him (otherwise keeping his secret for the present) to the wisest medical practitioner we could hear of in those parts, and to take his opinion. A change in his time of duty would come round next night, he had apprised me, and he would be off an hour or two after sunrise, and on again soon after sunset. I had appointed to return accordingly.

Next evening was a lovely evening, and I walked out early to enjoy it. The sun was not yet quite down when I traversed the field-path near the top of the deep cutting. I would extend my walk for an hour, I said to myself, half an hour on and half an hour back, and it would then be time to go to my signal-man's box.

Before pursuing my stroll, I stepped to the brink, and mechanically looked down, from the point from which I had first seen him. I cannot describe the thrill that seized upon me, when, close at the mouth of the tunnel, I saw the appearance of a man, with his left sleeve across his eyes, passionately waving his right arm.

The nameless horror that oppressed me passed in a moment, for in a moment I saw that this appearance of a man was a man indeed, and that there was a little group of other men, standing at a short distance, to whom he seemed to be rehearsing the gesture he made. The Danger-light was not yet lighted. Against its shaft, a little low hut, entirely new to me, had been made of some wooden supports and tarpaulin. It looked no bigger than a bed.

With an irresistible sense that something was wrong,—with a flashing self-reproachful fear that fatal mischief had come of my leaving the man there, and causing no one to be sent to overlook or correct what he did,—I descended the notched path with all the speed I could make.

"What is the matter?" I asked the men.

"Signal-man killed this morning, sir."

"Not the man belonging to that box?"

"Yes, sir."

"Not the man I know?"

"You will recognize him, sir, if you knew him," said the man who spoke for the others, solemnly uncovering his own head and raising an end of the tarpaulin, "for his face is quite composed."

"O, how did this happen, how did this happen?" I asked, turning from one to another as the hut closed in again.

"He was cut down by an engine, sir. No man in England knew his work better, but somehow he was not clear of the outer rail. It was just at broad day. He had struck the light, and had the lamp in his hand. As the engine came out of the tunnel, his back was towards her, and she cut him down. That man drove her, and was showing how it happened. Show the gentleman, Tom."

The man, who wore a rough dark dress, stepped back to his former place at the mouth of the tunnel:—

"Coming round the curve in the tunnel, sir," he said, "I saw him at the end, like as if I saw him down a perspective-glass. There was no time to check speed, and I knew him to be very careful. As he didn't seem to take heed of the whistle, I shut it off when we were running down upon him, and called to him as loud as I could call."

"What did you say?"

"I said, 'Below there! Look out! Look out! For God's sake, clear the way!'"

I started.

"Ah! it was a dreadful time, sir. I never left off calling to him. I put this arm before my eyes not to see, and I waved this arm to the last; but it was no use."

Without prolonging the narrative to dwell on any one of its curious circumstances more than any other, I may, in closing it, point out the coincidence that the warning of the Engine-Driver included, not only the words which the unfortunate Signal-man had repeated to me as haunting him, but also the words which I myself—not he—had attached, and that only in my own mind, to the gesticulation he had imitated.

Robert Louis Stevenson

In "A Gossip on Romance," an essay published in 1882, Robert Louis Stevenson complained that "English people of the present day are apt, I know not why, to look somewhat down on incident, and reserve their admiration for the clink of teaspoons and the accents of the curate." He himself strove to create romance—"the poetry of circumstance"—and it was a great day in the history of the English story when, five years earlier, he had published his first narrative "A Lodging for the Night" in Temple Bar for October, 1877. The accents of the curate are not in it, but it contains all the reader could desire of swift incident, romantic atmosphere, and vivid characterization.

"A Lodging for the Night" was the first of many brilliant, impressionistic stories which carried the craftsmanship of the tale beyond all that such predecessors as Dickens or Wilkie Collins or Kingsley had done for it. Stevenson was a great artificer with a French sense for form and style, and an English sense for moral values. His stories, no matter how romantic, are sound and shrewd in their comment on life's meaning.

Essayist, poet, and novelist as well as story-teller, Stevenson lived a career too well known to be detailed here. Born at Edinburgh in 1850, he first studied the law and then turned to writing. Always the victim of frail health, he travelled much, both in Europe and the United States, and in 1888 settled in the South Sea Islands, dying at Samoa in 1894. His short stories appear in such volumes as New Arabian Nights (1882), The Merry Men (1887), and Tales and Fantasies (1905).

A LODGING FOR THE NIGHT *

Robert Louis Stevenson

IT WAS LATE in November, 1456. The snow fell over Paris with rigorous, relentless persistence; sometimes the wind made a sally and scattered it in flying vortices; sometimes there was a lull, and flake after flake descended out of the black night air, silent, circuitous, interminable. To poor people, looking up under moist eyebrows, it seemed a wonder where it all came from. Master Francis Villon had propounded an alternative that afternoon, at a tavern window: was it only Pagan Jupiter plucking geese upon Olympus, or were the holy angels moulting? He was only a poor Master of Arts, he went on; and as the question somewhat touched upon divinity, he durst not venture to conclude. A silly old priest from Montargis, who was among the company, treated the young rascal to a bottle of wine in honor of the jest and grimaces with which it was accompanied, and swore on his own white beard that he had been just such another irreverent dog when he was Villon's age.

The air was raw and pointed, but not far below freezing; and the flakes were large, damp, and adhesive. The whole city was sheeted up. An army might have marched from end to end and not a footfall given the alarm. If there were any belated birds in heaven, they saw the island like a large white patch, and the bridges like slim white spars, on the black ground of the river. High up overhead the snow settled among the tracery of the cathedral towers. Many a niche was drifted full; many a statue wore a long white bonnet on its grotesque or sainted head. The gargoyles had been transformed into great false noses, drooping toward the point. The crockets were like upright pillows swollen on one side. In the intervals of the wind there was a dull sound of dripping about the precincts of the church.

The cemetery of St. John had taken its own share of the snow. All the graves were decently covered; tall, white housetops stood around in grave array; worthy burghers were long ago in bed, benightcapped like their domiciles; there was no light in all the neighborhood but a little peep from a lamp that hung swinging in the church choir, and tossed the shadows to and fro in time to its oscillations. The clock was hard on ten when the patrol went by with halberds and a lantern, beating

* From *New Arabian Nights* by Robert Louis Stevenson. Charles Scribner's Sons, 1882. Reprinted by permission of Charles Scribner's Sons.

their hands; and they saw nothing suspicious about the cemetery of St. John.

Yet there was a small house, backed up against the cemetery wall, which was still awake, and awake to evil purpose, in that snoring district. There was not much to betray it from without; only a stream of warm vapor from the chimney top, a patch where the snow melted on the roof, and a few half-obliterated footprints at the door. But within, behind the shuttered windows, Master Francis Villon, the poet, and some of the thieving crew with whom he consorted, were keeping the night alive and passing around the bottle.

A great pile of living embers diffused a strong and ruddy glow from the arched chimney. Before this straddled Dom Nicolas, the Picardy monk, with his skirts picked up and his fat legs bared to the comfortable warmth. His dilated shadow cut the room in half; and the firelight only escaped on either side of his broad person, and in a little pool between his outspread feet. His face had the beery, bruised appearance of the continual drinker's; it was covered with a network of congested veins, purple in ordinary circumstances, but now pale violet, for even with his back to the fire the cold pinched him on the other side. His cowl had half fallen back, and made a strange excrescence on either side of his bull neck. So he straddled, grumbling, and cut the room in half with the shadow of his portly frame.

On the right, Villon and Guy Tabary were huddled together over a scrap of parchment; Villon making a ballade which he was to call the *Ballade of Roast Fish,* and Tabary spluttering admiration at his shoulder. The poet was a rag of a man, dark, little, and lean, with hollow cheeks and thin black locks. He carried his four-and-twenty years with feverish animation. Greed had made folds about his eyes, evil smiles had puckered his mouth. The wolf and pig struggled together in his face. It was an eloquent, sharp, ugly, earthly countenance. His hands were small and prehensile, with fingers knotted like a cord; and they were continually flickering in front of him in violent and expressive pantomime. As for Tabary, a broad, complacent, admiring imbecility breathed from his squash nose and slobbering lips: he had become a thief, just as he might have become the most decent of burgesses, by the imperious chance that rules the lives of human geese and human donkeys.

At the monk's other hand, Montigny and Thevenin Pensete played a game of chance. About the first there clung some flavor of good birth and training, as about a fallen angel; something long, lithe, and courtly in the person; something aquiline and darkling in the face. Thevenin, poor soul, was in great feather: he had done a good stroke of knavery that afternoon in the Faubourg St. Jacques, and all night he had been gaining from Montigny. A flat smile illuminated his face; his bald head shone rosily in a garland of red curls; his little protuberant stomach shook with silent chucklings as he swept in his gains.

"Doubles or quits?" said Thevenin.

Montigny nodded grimly.

"Some may prefer to dine in state," wrote Villon, *"On bread and cheese on silver plate.* Or—or—help me out, Guido!"

Tabary giggled.

"Or parsley on a golden dish," scribbled the poet.

The wind was freshening without; it drove the snow before it, and sometimes raised its voice in a victorious whoop, and made sepulchral grumblings in the chimney. The cold was growing sharper as the night went on. Villon, protruding his lips, imitated the gust with something between a whistle and a groan. It was an eerie, uncomfortable talent of the poet's, much detested by the Picardy monk.

"Can't you hear it rattle in the gibbet?" said Villon. "They are all dancing the devil's jig on nothing, up there. You may dance, my gallants, you'll be none the warmer! Whew, what a gust! Down went somebody just now! A medlar the fewer on the three-legged medlar-tree!—I say, Dom Nicolas, it'll be cold tonight on the St. Denis Road?" he asked.

Dom Nicolas winked both his big eyes, and seemed to choke upon his Adam's apple. Montfaucon, the great grisly Paris gibbet, stood hard by the St. Denis Road, and the pleasantry touched him on the raw. As for Tabary, he laughed immoderately over the medlars; he had never heard anything more light-hearted; and he held his sides and crowed. Villon fetched him a fillip on the nose, which turned his mirth into an attack of coughing.

"Oh, stop that row," said Villon, "and think of rhymes to 'fish.'"

"Doubles or quits," said Montigny doggedly.

"With all my heart," quoth Thevenin.

"Is there any more in that bottle?" asked the monk.

"Open another," said Villon. "How do you ever hope to fill that big hogshead, your body, with little things like bottles? And how do you expect to get to heaven? How many angels, do you fancy, can be spared to carry up a single monk from Picardy? Or do you think yourself another Elias—and they'll send the coach for you?"

"Hominibus impossibile," replied the monk, as he filled his glass.
Tabary was in ecstasies.

Villon filliped his nose again.

"Laugh at my jokes, if you like," he said.

"It was very good," objected Tabary.

Villon made a face at him. "Think of rhymes to 'fish,'" he said.
"What have you to do with Latin? You'll wish you knew none of it
at the great assizes, when the devil calls for Guido Tabary, clericus—
the devil with the hump-back and red-hot finger-nails. Talking of the
devil," he added in a whisper, "look at Montigny!"

All three peered covertly at the gamester. He did not seem to be
enjoying his luck. His mouth was a little to a side; one nostril nearly
shut, and the other much inflated. The black dog was on his back,
as people say, in terrifying nursery metaphor; and he breathed hard
under the gruesome burden.

"He looks as if he could knife him," whispered Tabary, with round
eyes.

The monk shuddered, and turned his face and spread his open hands
to the red embers. It was the cold that thus affected Dom Nicolas, and
not any excess of moral sensibility.

"Come now," said Villon—"about this ballade. How does it run so
far?" And beating time with one hand, he read it aloud to Tabary.

They were interrupted at the fourth rhyme by a brief and fatal
movement among the gamesters. The round was completed, and
Thevenin was just opening his mouth to claim another victory, when
Montigny leaped up, swift as an adder, and stabbed him to the heart.
The blow took effect before he had time to utter a cry, before he had
time to move. A tremor or two convulsed his frame; his hands opened
and shut, his heels rattled on the floor; then his head rolled backward
over one shoulder with the eyes open, and Thevenin Pensete's spirit
had returned to Him who made it.

Every one sprang to his feet; but the business was over in two twos.
The four living fellows looked at each other in rather a ghastly
fashion; the dead man contemplating a corner of the roof with a
singular and ugly leer.

"My God!" said Tabary, and he began to pray in Latin.

Villon broke out into hysterical laughter. He came a step forward
and ducked a ridiculous bow at Thevenin, and laughed still louder.
Then he sat down suddenly, all of a heap, upon a stool, and continued
laughing bitterly as though he would shake himself to pieces.

Montigny recovered his composure first.

"Let's see what he has about him," he remarked; and he picked the dead man's pockets with a practised hand, and divided the money into four equal portions on the table. "There's for you," he said.

The monk received his share with a deep sigh, and a single stealthy glance at the dead Thevenin, who was beginning to sink into himself and topple sideways off the chair.

"We're all in for it," cried Villon, swallowing his mirth. "It's a hanging job for every man jack of us that's here—not to speak of those who aren't." He made a shocking gesture in the air with his raised right hand, and put out his tongue and threw his head on one side, so as to counterfeit the appearance of one who has been hanged. Then he pocketed his share of the spoil, and executed a shuffle with his feet as if to restore the circulation.

Tabary was the last to help himself; he made a dash at the money, and retired to the other end of the apartment.

Montigny stuck Thevenin upright in the chair, and drew out the dagger, which was followed by a jet of blood.

"You fellows had better be moving," he said, as he wiped the blade on the victim's doublet.

"I think we had," returned Villon with a gulp. "Damn his fat head!" he broke out. "It sticks in my throat like phlegm. What right has a man to have red hair when he is dead?" And he fell all of a heap again upon the stool, and fairly covered his face with his hands.

Montigny and Dom Nicolas laughed aloud, even Tabary feebly chiming in.

"Cry baby," said the monk.

"I always said he was a woman," added Montigny with a sneer. "Sit up, can't you?" he went on, giving another shake to the murdered body. "Tread out that fire, Nick."

But Nick was better employed; he was quietly taking Villon's purse, as the poet sat, limp and trembling, on the stool where he had been making a ballade not three minutes before. Montigny and Tabary dumbly demanded a share of the booty, which the monk silently promised as he passed the little bag into the bosom of his gown. In many ways an artistic nature unfits a man for practical existence.

No sooner had the theft been accomplished than Villon shook himself, jumped to himself, and began helping to scatter and extinguish the embers. Meanwhile Montigny opened the door and cautiously peered into the street. The coast was clear; there was no meddlesome patrol in sight. Still it was judged wiser to slip out severally; and as Villon was himself in a hurry to escape from the neighborhood of the dead Thevenin, and the rest were in a still greater hurry to get rid of him before he should discover the loss of his money, he was the first by general consent to issue forth into the street.

The wind had triumphed and swept all the clouds from heaven. Only a few vapors, as thin as moonlight, fleeted rapidly across the stars. It was bitter cold; and by a common optical effect, things seemed almost more definite than in the broadest daylight. The sleeping city was absolutely still: a company of white hoods, a field full of little Alps, below the twinkling stars. Villon cursed his fortune. Would it were still snowing! Now, wherever he went he left an indelible trail behind him on the glittering streets; wherever he went he was still tethered to the house by the cemetery of St. John; wherever he went he must weave, with his own plodding feet, the rope that bound him to the crime and would bind him to the gallows. The leer of the dead man came back to him with a new significance. He snapped his fingers as if to pluck up his own spirits, and choosing a street at random, stepped boldly forward in the snow.

Two things preoccupied him as he went: the aspect of the gallows at Montfaucon in this bright windy phase of the night's existence, for one; and for another, the look of the dead man with his bald head and garland of red curls. Both struck cold upon his heart, and he kept quickening his pace as if he could escape from unpleasant thoughts by mere fleetness of foot. Sometimes he looked back over his shoulder with a sudden nervous jerk; but he was the only moving thing in the white streets, except when the wind swept around a corner and threw up the snow, which was beginning to freeze, in spouts of glittering dust.

Suddenly he saw, a long way before him, a black clump and a couple of lanterns. The clump was in motion, and the lanterns swung as though carried by men walking. It was a patrol. And though it was merely crossing his line of march, he judged it wiser to get out of eyeshot as speedily as he could. He was not in the humor to be challenged, and he was conscious of making a very conspicuous mark upon the snow. Just on his left hand there stood a great hotel, with some turrets and a large porch before the door; it was half-ruinous, he remembered, and had stood long empty; and so he made three steps of it and jumped inside the shelter of the porch. It was pretty dark inside, after the glimmer of the snowy streets, and he was groping forward with outspread hands, when he stumbled over some substance which offered an indescribable mixture of resistances, hard and soft, firm and loose. His heart gave a leap, and he sprang two steps back and stared dreadfully at the object. Then he gave a little laugh of relief. It was only a woman, and she dead. He knelt beside her to make sure upon this latter point. She was freezing cold, and rigid like a stick. A little ragged finery fluttered in the wind about her hair, and her cheeks had been heavily rouged that same afternoon. Her pockets were quite empty; but in her stocking, underneath the garter, Villon found two small coins that went by the name of whites. It was little enough; but it was always something; and the poet was moved with a deep sense of pathos that she should have died before she had spent her money. That seemed to him a dark and pitiable mystery; and he looked from the coins in his hand to the dead woman, and back again to the coins, shaking his head over the riddle of man's life. Henry V of England, dying at Vincennes just after he had conquered France, and this poor jade cut off by a cold draught in a great man's doorway, before she had time to spend her couple of whites—it seemed a cruel way to carry on the world. Two whites would have taken such a little while to squander; and yet it would have been one more good taste in the mouth, one more smack of the lips, before the devil got the soul, and the body was left to birds and vermin. He would like to use all his tallow before the light was blown out and the lantern broken.

While these thoughts were passing through his mind, he was feeling, half-mechanically, for his purse. Suddenly his heart stopped beating; a feeling of cold scales passed up the back of his legs, and a cold blow seemed to fall upon his scalp. He stood petrified for a moment; then he felt again with one feverish motion; and then his loss burst upon him, and he was covered with perspiration. To spendthrifts money is so living and actual—it is such a thin veil between them and their pleasures! There is only one limit to their fortune—that of time; and a spendthrift with only a few crowns is the Emperor of Rome until they are spent. For such a person to lose his money is to suffer the most shocking reverse, and fall from heaven to hell, from all to nothing, in a breath. And all the more if he has put his head in the halter for it; if he may be hanged to-morrow for that same purse, so dearly earned, so foolishly departed. Villon stood and cursed; he threw the two whites into the street; he shook his fist at heaven; he stamped, and was not horrified to find himself trampling the poor corpse. Then he began rapidly to retrace his steps toward the house beside the cemetery. He had forgotten all fear of the patrol, which was long gone by at any rate, and he had no idea but that of his lost purse. It was in vain that he looked right and left upon the snow; nothing was to be seen. He had not dropped it in the streets. Had it fallen in the house? He would have liked dearly to go in and see; but the idea of the grisly occupant unmanned him. And he saw besides, as he drew near, that their efforts to put out the fire had been unsuccessful; on the contrary, it had broken into a blaze, and a changeful light played in the chinks of the door and window, and revived his terror for the authorities and Paris gibbet.

He returned to the hotel with the porch, and groped about in the snow for the money he had thrown away in his childish passion. But he could only find one white; the other had probably struck sideways and sunk deeply in. With a single white in his pocket, all his projects for a rousing night in some wild tavern vanished utterly away. And it was not only pleasure that fled laughing from his grasp; positive discomfort, positive pain, attacked him as he stood ruefully before the porch. His perspiration had dried upon him; and though the wind had now fallen, a binding frost was setting in stronger with every hour, and he felt benumbed and sick at heart. What was to be done? Late as was the hour, improbable as was success, he would try the house of his adopted father, the chaplain of St. Benoît.

He ran there all the way, and knocked timidly. There was no answer. He knocked again and again, taking heart with every stroke; and at last steps were heard approaching from within. A barred wicket fell open in the iron-studded door, and emitted a gush of yellow light.

"Hold up your face to the wicket," said the chaplain from within.

"It's only me," whimpered Villon.

"Oh, it's only you, is it?" returned the chaplain; and he cursed him with foul unpriestly oaths for disturbing him at such an hour, and bade him be off to hell, where he came from.

"My hands are blue to the wrists," pleaded Villon; "my feet are dead and full of twinges; my nose aches with the sharp air; the cold lies at my heart. I may be dead before morning. Only this once, father, and before God I will never ask again!"

"You should have come earlier," said the ecclesiastic, coolly. "Young men require a lesson now and then." He shut the wicket and retired deliberately into the interior of the house.

Villon was beside himself; he beat upon the door with his hands and feet, and shouted hoarsely after the chaplain.

"Wormy old fox!" he cried. "If I had my hand under your twist, I would send you flying into the bottomless pit."

A door shut in the interior, faintly audible to the poet down long passages. He passed his hand over his mouth with an oath. And then the humor of the situation struck him, and he laughed and looked lightly up to heaven, where the stars seemed to be winking over his discomfiture.

What was to be done? It looked very like a night in the frosty streets. The idea of the dead woman popped into his imagination, and gave him a hearty fright; what had happened to her in the early night might very well happen to him before morning. And he so young! and with such immense possibilities of disorderly amusement before him! He felt quite pathetic over the notion of his own fate, as if it had been some one else's, and made a little imaginative vignette of the scene in the morning when they should find his body.

He passed all his chances under review, turning the white between his thumb and forefinger. Unfortunately he was on bad terms with some old friends who would once have taken pity on him in such a plight. He had lampooned them in verses, he had beaten and cheated them; and yet now, when he was in so close a pinch, he thought there was at least one who might perhaps relent. It was a chance. It was worth trying at least, and he would go and see.

On the way, two little accidents happened to him which colored his musings in a very different manner. For, first, he fell in with the track of a patrol, and walked in it for some hundred yards, although it lay out of his direction. And this spirited him up; at least he had confused his trail; for he was still possessed with the idea of people tracking him all about Paris over the snow, and collaring him next morning before he was awake. The other matter affected him quite differently. He passed a street corner, where, not so long before, a woman and her child had been devoured by wolves. This was just the kind of weather, he reflected, when wolves might take it into their heads to enter Paris again; and a lone man in these deserted streets would run the chance of something worse than a mere scare. He stopped and looked upon the place with an unpleasant interest— it was a centre where several lanes intersected each other; and he looked down them all one after another, and held his breath to listen, lest he should detect some galloping black things on the snow or hear the sound of howling between him and the river. He remembered his mother telling him the story and pointing out the spot, while he was yet a child. His mother! If he only knew where she lived, he might make sure at least of shelter. He determined he would inquire upon the morrow; nay, he would go and see her, too, poor old girl! So thinking, he arrived at his destination—his last hope for the night.

The house was quite dark, like its neighbors; and yet after a few taps, he heard a movement overhead, a door opening, and a cautious voice asking who was there. The poet named himself in a loud whisper, and waited, not without some trepidation, the result. Nor had he to wait long. A window was suddenly opened, and a pailful of slops splashed down upon the doorstep. Villon had not been unprepared for something of the sort, and had put himself as much in shelter as the nature of the porch admitted; but for all that, he was deplorably drenched below the waist. His hose began to freeze almost at once. Death from cold and exposure stared him in the face; he remembered he was of phthisical tendency, and began coughing tentatively. But the gravity of the danger steadied his nerves. He stopped a few hundred yards from the door where he had been so rudely used, and reflected with his finger to his nose. He could only see one way of getting a lodging, and that was to take it. He had noticed a house not far away which looked as if it might be easily broken into, and thither he betook himself promptly, entertaining himself on the way with the idea of a room still hot, with a table still loaded with the remains of a supper, where he might pass the rest of the black hours, and whence he should issue, on the morrow, with an armful of valuable plate. He even considered on what viands and wines he should prefer; and as he was calling the roll of his favorite dainties, roast fish presented itself with an odd mixture of amusement and horror.

"I shall never finish that ballade," he thought to himself; and then, with another shudder at the recollection, "Oh, damn his fat head!" he repeated fervently, and spat upon the snow.

The house in question looked dark at first sight; but as Villon made a preliminary inspection in search of the handiest point of attack, a little twinkle of light caught his eye from behind a curtained window.

"The devil!" he thought. "People awake! Some student or some saint, confound the crew! Can't they get drunk and lie in bed snoring like their neighbors! What's the good of a curfew, and poor devils of bell-ringers jumping at a rope's-end in bell-towers? What's the use of day, if people sit up all night? The gripes to them!" He grinned as he saw where his logic was leading him. "Every man to his business, after all," added he, "and if they're awake, by the Lord, I may come by a supper honestly for once, and cheat the devil."

He went boldly to the door, and knocked with an assured hand. On both previous occasions he had knocked timidly and with some dread of attracting notice; but now, when he had just discarded the thought of a burglarious entry, knocking at a door seemed a mighty simple and innocent proceeding. The sound of his blows echoed through the house with thin, phantasmal reverberations, as though it were quite empty; but these had scarcely died away before a measured tread drew near, a couple of bolts were withdrawn, and one wing was opened broadly, as though no guile or fear of guile were known to those within. A tall figure of a man, muscular and spare, but a little bent, confronted Villon. The head was massive in bulk, but finely sculptured; the nose blunt at the bottom but refining upward to where it joined a pair of strong and honest eyebrows; the mouth and eyes surrounded with delicate markings, and the whole face based upon a thick white beard, boldly and squarely trimmed. Seen as it was by the light of a flickering hand-lamp, it looked perhaps nobler than it had a right to do; but it was a fine face, honorable rather than intelligent, strong, simple, and righteous.

"You knock late, sir," said the old man in resonant, courteous tones.

Villon cringed, and brought up many servile words of apology; at a crisis of this sort, the beggar was uppermost in him, and the man of genius hid his head with confusion.

"You are cold," repeated the old man, "and hungry? Well, step in." And he ordered him into the house with a noble enough gesture.

"Some great seigneur," thought Villon, as his host, setting down the lamp on the flagged pavement of the entry, shot the bolts once more into their places.

"You will pardon me if I go in front," he said, when this was done; and he preceded the poet up-stairs into a large apartment, warmed with a pan of charcoal and lit by a great lamp hanging from the roof. It was very bare of furniture; only some gold plate on a sideboard; some folios; and a stand of armor between the windows. Some smart tapestry hung upon the walls, representing the crucifixion of our Lord in one piece, and in another a scene of shepherds and shepherdesses by a running stream. Over the chimney was a shield of arms.

"Will you seat yourself," said the old man, "and forgive me if I leave you? I am alone in my house tonight, and if you are to eat I must forage for you myself."

No sooner was his host gone than Villon leaped from the chair on which he had just seated himself, and began examining the room, with the stealth and passion of a cat. He weighed the gold flagons in his hand, opened all the folios, and investigated the arms upon the shield, and the stuff with which the seats were lined. He raised the window-curtains, and saw that the windows were set with rich stained glass in figures, so far as he could see, of martial import. Then he stood in the middle of the room, drew a long breath, and retaining it with puffed cheeks, looked round and round him, turning on his heels, as if to impress every feature of the apartment on his memory.

"Seven pieces of plate," he said. "If there had been ten I would have risked it. A fine old house, and a fine old master, so help me all the saints!"

And just then, hearing the old man's tread returning along the corridor, he stole back to his chair, and began toasting his wet legs before the charcoal pan.

His entertainer had a plate of meat in one hand and a jug of wine in the other. He set down the plate upon the table, motioning Villon to draw in his chair, and going to the sideboard, brought back two goblets, which he filled.

"I drink to your better fortune," he said, gravely touching Villon's cup with his own.

"To our better acquaintance," said the poet, growing bold. A mere man of the people would have been awed by the courtesy of the old seigneur, but Villon was hardened in that matter; he had made mirth for great lords before now, and found them as black rascals as himself. And so he devoted himself to the viands with a ravenous gusto, while the old man, leaning backward, watched him with steady, curious eyes.

"You have blood on your shoulder, my man," he said.

Montigny must have laid his wet right hand upon his shoulder as he left the house. He cursed Montigny in his heart.

"It was none of my shedding," he stammered.

"I had not supposed so," returned his host quietly. "A brawl?"

"Well, something of that sort," Villon admitted with a quaver. "Perhaps a fellow murdered?"

"Oh, no, not murdered," said the poet more and more confused. "It was all fair play—murdered by accident. I had no hand in it, God strike me dead!" he added fervently.

"One rogue the fewer, I dare say," observed the master of the house.

"You may dare to say that," agreed Villon, infinitely relieved. "As big a rogue as there is between here and Jerusalem. He turned up his toes like a lamb. But it was a nasty thing to look at. I dare say you've seen dead men in your time, my lord?" he added, glancing at the armor.

"Many," said the old man. "I have followed the wars, as you imagine."

Villon laid down his knife and fork, which he had just taken up again.

"Were any of them bald?" he asked.

"Oh yes, and with hair as white as mine."

"I don't think I would mind the white so much," said Villon. "His was red." And he had a return of his shuddering and tendency to laughter, which he drowned with a great draught of wine. "I'm a little put out when I think of it," he went on. "I knew him—damn him! And the cold gives a man fancies—or the fancies give a man cold, I don't know which."

"Have you any money?" asked the old man.

"I have one white," returned the poet laughing. "I got it out of a dead jade's stocking in a porch. She was as dead as Caesar, poor wench, and as cold as a church, with bits of ribbon sticking in her hair. This is a hard world in winter for wolves and wenches and poor rogues like me."

"I," said the old man, "am Enguerrand de la Feuillée, seigneur de Brisetout, bailly du Patatrac. Who and what may you be?"

Villon rose and made a suitable reverence. "I am called Francis Villon," he said, "a poor Master of Arts of this university. I know some Latin, and a deal of vice. I can make chansons, ballades, lais, virelais, and roundels, and I am very fond of wine. I was born in a garret, and I shall not improbably die upon the gallows. I may add, my lord, that from this night forward I am your lordship's very obsequious servant to command."

"No servant of mine," said the knight; "my guest for this evening, and no more."

"A very grateful guest," said Villon politely; and he drank in dumb show to his entertainer.

"You are shrewd," began the old man, tapping his forehead, "very shrewd; you have learning; you are a clerk; and yet you take a small piece of money off a dead woman in the street. Is it not a kind of theft?"

"It is a kind of a theft much practiced in the wars, my lord."

"The wars are the field of honor," returned the old man proudly. "There a man plays his life upon the cast; he fights in the name of his lord, the king, his Lord God, and all their lordships the holy saints and angels."

"Put it," said Villon, "that I were really a thief, should I not play my life also, and against heavier odds?"

"For gain, and not for honor."

"Gain?" repeated Villon with a shrug. "Gain! The poor fellow wants supper, and takes it. So does the soldier in a campaign. Why, what are all these requisitions we hear so much about? If they are not gain to those who take them, they are loss enough to others. The men-at-arms drink by a good fire, while the burgher bites his nails to buy them wine and wood. I have seen a good many ploughmen swinging on trees about the country; ay, I have seen thirty on one elm, and a very poor figure they made; and when I asked some one how all these came to be hanged, I was told it was because they could not scrape together enough crowns to satisfy the men-at-arms."

"These things are a necessity of war, which the low-born must endure with constancy. It is true that some captains drive overhard; there are spirits in every rank not easily moved by pity; and, indeed, many follow arms who are no better than brigands."

"You see," said the poet, "you cannot separate the soldier from the brigand; and what is a thief but an isolated brigand with circumspect manners? I steal a couple of mutton chops, without so much as disturbing the farmer's sheep; the farmer grumbles a bit, but sups none the less wholesomely on what remains. You come up blowing gloriously on a trumpet, take away the whole sheep, and beat the farmer pitifully into the bargain. I have no trumpet; I am only Tom, Dick, or Harry; I am a rogue and a dog, and hanging's too good for me—with all my heart—but just you ask the farmer which of us he prefers, just find out which of us he lies awake to curse on cold nights."

"Look at us two," said his lordship. "I am old, strong, and honored. If I were turned from my house tomorrow, hundreds would be proud to shelter me. Poor people would go out and pass the night in the streets with their children, if I merely hinted that I wished to be alone. And I find you up, wandering homeless, and picking farthings off dead women by the wayside! I fear no man and nothing; I have seen you tremble and lose countenance at a word. I wait God's summons contentedly in my own house, or, if it please the king to call me out again, upon the field of battle. You look for the gallows; a rough, swift death, without hope or honor. Is there no difference between these two?"

"As far as to the moon," Villon acquiesced. "But if I had been born lord of Brisetout, and you had been the poor scholar Francis, would the difference have been any less? Should not I have been warming my knees at this charcoal pan, and would not you have been groping for farthings in the snow? Should not I have been the soldier, and you the thief?"

"A thief!" cried the old man. "I a thief! If you understood your words, you would repent them."

Villon turned out his hands with a gesture of inimitable impudence. "If your lordship had done me the honor to follow my argument!" he said.

"I do you too much honor in submitting to your presence," said the knight. "Learn to curb your tongue when you speak with old and honorable men, or some one hastier than I may reprove you in a sharper fashion." And he rose and paced the lower end of the apartment, struggling with anger and antipathy. Villon surreptitiously filled his cup, and settled himself more comfortably in his chair, crossing his knees and leaning his head upon one hand and the elbow against the back of the chair. He was now replete and warm; and he was in nowise frightened for his host, having gauged him as justly as was possible between two such different characters. The night was far spent, and in very comfortable fashion after all; and he felt morally certain of a safe departure on the morrow.

"Tell me one thing," said the old man, pausing in his walk. "Are you really a thief?"

"I claim the sacred rights of hospitality," returned the poet. "My lord, I am."

"You are very young," the knight continued.

"I should never have been so old," replied Villon, showing his fingers, "if I had not helped myself with these ten talents. They have been my nursing mothers and my nursing fathers."

"You may still repent and change."

"I repent daily," said the poet. "There are few people more given to repentance than poor Francis. As for change, let somebody change my circumstances. A man must continue to eat, if it were only that he may continue to repent."

"The change must begin in the heart," returned the old man solemnly.

"My dear lord," answered Villon, "do you really fancy that I steal for pleasure? I hate stealing, like any other piece of work or danger. My teeth chatter when I see the gallows. But I must eat, I must drink, I must mix in society of some sort. What the devil! Man is not a solitary animal—*Cui Deus foeminam tradit.* Make me king's pantler— make me abbot of St. Denis; make me bailly of the Patatrac; and then I shall be changed indeed. But as long as you leave me the poor scholar Francis Villon, without a farthing, why, of course, I remain the same."

"The grace of God is all-powerful."

"I should be a heretic to question it," said Francis. "It has made you lord of Brisetout, and bailly of the Patatrac; it has given me nothing but the quick wits under my hat and these ten toes upon my hands. May I help myself to wine? I thank you respectfully. By God's grace, you have a very superior vintage."

The lord of Brisetout walked to and fro with his hands behind his back. Perhaps he was not quite settled in his mind about the parallel between thieves and soldiers; perhaps Villon had interested him by some cross-thread of sympathy; perhaps his wits were simply muddled by so much unfamiliar reasoning; but whatever the cause, he somehow yearned to convert the young man to a better way of thinking, and could not make up his mind to drive him forth again into the street.

"There is something more than I can understand in this," he said, at length. "Your mouth is full of subtleties, and the devil has led you far astray; but the devil is only a very weak spirit before God's truth, and all his subtleties vanish at a word of true honor, like darkness at morning. Listen to me once more. I learned long ago that a gentleman should live chivalrously and lovingly to God, and the king, and his lady; and though I have seen many strange things done, I have still striven to command my ways upon that rule. It is not only written in all noble histories, but in every man's heart, if he will take care to read. You speak of food and wine, and I know very well that hunger is a difficult trial to endure; but you do not speak of other wants; you say nothing of honor, of faith to God and other men, of courtesy, of love without reproach. It may be that I am not very wise— and yet I think I am—but you seem to me like one who has lost his way and made a great error in life. You are attending to the little wants, and you have totally forgotten the great and only real ones, like a man who should be doctoring a toothache on the Judgment Day. For such things as honor and love and faith are not only nobler than food and drink, but, indeed, I think that we desire them more, and suffer more sharply for their absence. I speak to you as I think you will most easily understand me. Are you not, while careful to fill your belly, disregarding another appetite in your heart, which spoils the pleasure of your life and keeps you continually wretched?"

Villon was sensibly nettled under all this sermonizing. "You think I have no sense of honor!" he cried. "I'm poor enough, God knows! It's hard to see rich people with their gloves, and you blowing in your hands. An empty belly is a bitter thing, although you speak so lightly of it. If you had had as many as I, perhaps you would change your tune. Anyway, I'm a thief—make the most of that—but I'm not a devil from hell, God strike me dead. I would have you to know that I've an honor of my own, as good as yours, though I don't prate about it all day long, as if it were a God's miracle to have any. It seems quite natural to me; I keep it in its box till it's wanted. Why now, look you here, how long have I been in this room with you? Did you not tell me you were alone in this house? Look at your gold plate! You're strong, if you like, but you're old and unarmed, and I have my knife. What did I want but a jerk of the elbow, and here would have been you with the cold steel in your bowels, and there would have been me, linking in the streets, with an armful of gold cups! Did you suppose I hadn't wit enough to see that? And I scorned the action. There are your damned goblets, as safe as in a church; there are you, with your heart ticking as good as new; and here am I, ready to go out again as poor as I came in, with my one white that you threw in my teeth! And you think I have no sense of honor—God strike me dead!"

The old man stretched out his right arm. "I will tell you what you are," he said. "You are a rogue, my man, an impudent and black-

hearted rogue and vagabond. I have passed an hour with you. Oh!
believe me, I feel myself disgraced! And you have eaten and drunk
at my table. But now I am sick at your presence; the day has come,
and the night-bird should be off to his roost. Will you go before,
or after?"

"Which you please," returned the poet, rising. "I believe you to be
strictly honorable." He thoughtfully emptied his cup. "I wish I could
add you were intelligent," he went on, knocking on his head with
his knuckles. "Age, age, the brains stiff and rheumatic."

The old man preceded him from a point of self-respect; Villon
followed, whistling, with his thumbs in his girdle.

"God pity you," said the lord of Brisetout at the door.

"Good-bye, papa," returned Villon, with a yawn. "Many thanks
for the cold mutton."

The door closed behind him. The dawn was breaking over the
white roofs. A chill, uncomfortable morning ushered in the day.
Villon stood and heartily stretched himself in the middle of the road.

"A very dull old gentleman," he thought. "I wonder what his
goblets may be worth."

Thomas Hardy

THOMAS HARDY told the stories which are deeply rooted in the life of a people who stay at home for generation after generation—stories of family history, of local legend and lore as authentic as the patina of an antique cabinet. With him character, environment, and incident are one commentary, one fusion in which man, nature, and circumstance form a harmony for the artist. The harmony is often sombre, but in "Tony Kytes, the Arch-Deceiver," Hardy displays the racy country humor which so often relieves the grimness of such great, tragic novels as The Return of the Native or The Mayor of Casterbridge.

Thomas Hardy was born in Dorsetshire in 1840, studied architecture in his youth, and turned to literature with a short story published in 1865. His first novel Desperate Remedies (1871), read and criticized by the great George Meredith, introduced a long series of novels which powerfully interpreted the workings of fate in his own beloved "Wessex." After the publication of Jude, the Obscure in 1895, a story whose stark tragedy dismayed the public, Hardy returned to his first love in literature—the writing of lyric verse. His greatest single work is The Dynasts (1908), a vast epic-drama of the Napoleonic Wars. His best short tales are collected in the two volumes Wessex Tales (1888) and Life's Little Ironies (1894). Hardy died in 1928.

TONY KYTES, THE ARCH-DECEIVER *

Thomas Hardy

"I SHALL NEVER forget Tony's face. 'Twas a little, round, firm, tight face, with a seam here and there left by the smallpox, but not enough to hurt his looks in a woman's eye, though he'd had it badish when

---

* From *Life's Little Ironies* by Thomas Hardy. Harper & Brothers. Reprinted by permission of Harper & Brothers.

he was a little boy. So very serious looking and unsmiling 'a was, that young man, that it really seemed as if he couldn't laugh at all without great pain to his conscience. He looked very hard at a small speck in your eye when talking to 'ee. And there was no more sign of a whisker or beard on Tony Kytes's face than on the palm of my hand. He used to sing "The Tailor's Breeches" with a religious manner, as if it were a hymn:

' *"O the petticoats went off, and the breeches they went on!"* and all the rest of the scandalous stuff. He was quite the women's favourite, and in return for their likings he loved 'em in shoals.

'But in course of time Tony got fixed down to one in particular, Milly Richards, a nice, light, tender little thing; and it was soon said that they were engaged to be married. One Saturday he had been to market to do business for his father, and was driving home the waggon in the afternoon. When he reached the foot of the very hill we shall be going over in ten minutes who should he see waiting for him at the top but Unity Sallet, a handsome girl, one of the young women he'd been very tender toward before he'd got engaged to Milly.

'As soon as Tony came up to her she said, "My dear Tony, will you give me a lift home?"

' "That I will, darling," said Tony. "You don't suppose I could refuse 'ee?"

'She smiled a smile, and up she hopped, and on drove Tony.

' "Tony," she says, in a sort of tender chide, "why did ye desert me for that other one? In what is she better than I? I should have made 'ee a finer wife, and a more loving one too. 'Tisn't girls that are so easily won at first that are the best. Think how long we've known each other—ever since we were children almost—now haven't we, Tony?"

' "Yes, that we have," says Tony, a-struck with the truth o't.

' "And you've never seen anything in me to complain of, have ye, Tony? Now tell the truth to me?"

' "I never have, upon my life," says Tony.

' "And—can you say I'm not pretty, Tony? Now look at me!"

'He let his eyes light upon her for a long while. "I really can't," says he. "In fact, I never knowed you was so pretty before!"

' "Prettier than she?"

'What Tony would have said to that nobody knows, for before he could speak, what should he see ahead, over the hedge past the turning, but a feather he knew well—the feather in Milly's hat—she to whom he had been thinking of putting the question as to giving out the banns that very week.

'"Unity," says he, as mild as he could, "here's Milly coming. Now I shall catch it mightily if she sees 'ee riding here with me; and if you get down she'll be turning the corner in a moment, and, seeing 'ee in the road, she'll know we've been coming on together. Now, dearest Unity, will ye, to avoid all unpleasantness, which I know ye can't bear any more than I, will ye lie down in the back part of the waggon, and let me cover you over with the tarpaulin till Milly has passed? It will all be done in a minute. Do!—and I'll think over what we've said; and perhaps I shall put a loving question to you, after all, instead of to Milly. 'Tisn't true that it is all settled between her and me."

'Well, Unity Sallet agreed, and lay down at the back end of the waggon, and Tony covered her over, so that the waggon seemed to be empty but for the loose tarpaulin; and then he drove on to meet Milly.

'"My dear Tony!" cries Milly, looking up with a pout at him as he came near. "How long you've been coming home! Just as if I didn't live at Upper Longpuddle at all! And I've come to meet you as you asked me to do, and to ride back with you, and talk over our future home—since you asked me, and I promised. But I shouldn't have come else, Mr. Tony!"

'"Ay, my dear, I did ask ye—to be sure I did, now I think of it—but I had quite forgot it. To ride back with me, did you say, dear Milly?"

'"Well of course! What can I do else? Surely you don't want me to walk, now I've come all this way?"

'"O no, no! I was thinking you might be going on to town to meet your mother. I saw her there—and she looked as if she might be expecting 'ee."

'"O no; she's just home. She came across the fields, and so got back before you."

'"Ah! I didn't know that," says Tony. And there was no help for it but to take her up beside him.

'They talked on very pleasantly, and looked at the trees, and beasts, and birds, and insects, and at the ploughmen at work in the fields, till presently who should they see looking out of the upper window of a house that stood beside the road they were following, but Hannah Jolliver, another young beauty of the place at that time,

and the very first woman that Tony had fallen in love with—before
Milly and before Unity, in fact—the one that he had almost arranged
to marry instead of Milly. She was a much more dashing girl than
Milly Richards, though he'd not thought much of her of late. The
house Hannah was looking from was her aunt's.

' "My dear Milly—my coming wife, as I may call 'ee," says Tony in
his modest way, and not so loud that Unity could overhear, "I see a
young woman alooking out of window, who I think may accost me.
The fact is, Milly, she had a notion that I was wishing to marry her,
and since she's discovered I've promised another, and a prettier than
she, I'm rather afeared of her temper if she sees us together. Now,
Milly, would you do me a favour—my coming wife, as I may say?"

' "Certainly, dearest Tony," says she.

' "Then would ye creep under the empty sacks just here in front
of the waggon, and hide there out of sight till we've passed the
house? She hasn't seen us yet. You see, we ought to live in peace
and good-will since 'tis almost Christmas, and 'twill prevent angry
passions rising, which we always should do."

' "I don't mind, to oblige you, Tony," Milly said; and though she
didn't care much about doing it, she crept under, and crouched down
just behind the seat, Unity being snug at the other end. So they drove
on till they got near the road-side cottage. Hannah had soon seen
him coming, and waited at the window, looking down upon him.
She tossed her head a little disdainful and smiled off-hand.

' "Well, aren't you going to be civil enough to ask me to ride home
with you!" she says, seeing that he was for driving past with a nod and
a smile.

' "Ah, to be sure! What was I thinking of?" said Tony, in a flutter.
"But you seem as if you was staying at your aunt's?"

' "No, I am not," she said. "Don't you see I have my bonnet and
jacket on? I have only called to see her on my way home. How can
you be so stupid, Tony?"

' "In that case—ah—of course you must come along wi' me," says
Tony, feeling a dim sort of sweat rising up inside his clothes. And he
reined in the horse, and waited till she'd come downstairs, and then
helped her up beside him. He drove on again, his face as long as a
face that was a round one by nature well could be.

'Hannah looked round sideways into his eyes. "This is nice, isn't
it, Tony?" she says. "I like riding with you."

'Tony looked back into her eyes. "And I with you," he said after

a while. In short, having considered her, he warmed up, and the more
he looked at her the more he liked her, till he couldn't for the life of
him think why he had ever said a word about marriage to Milly or
Unity while Hannah Jolliver was in question. So they sat a little
closer and closer, their feet upon the footboard and their shoulders
touching, and Tony thought over and over again how handsome
Hannah was. He spoke tenderer and tenderer, and called her "dear
Hannah" in a whisper at last.

' "You've settled it with Milly by this time, I suppose," said she.

' "N—no, not exactly."

' "What? How low you talk, Tony."

' "Yes—I've a kind of hoarseness. I said, not exactly."

' "I suppose you mean to?"

' "Well, as to that—" His eyes rested on her face, and hers on his.
He wondered how he could have been such a fool as not to follow
up Hannah. "My sweet Hannah!" he burst out, taking her hand,
not being really able to help it, and forgetting Milly and Unity, and
all the world besides. "Settled it? I don't think I have!"

' "Hark!" says Hannah.

' "What?" says Tony, letting go her hand.

' "Surely I heard a little sort of screaming squeak under those sacks?
Why, you've been carrying corn, and there's mice in this waggon,
I declare'!" She began to haul up the tails of her gown.

' "Oh no; 'tis the axle," said Tony in an assuring way. "It do go
like that sometimes in dry weather."

' "Perhaps it was. . . . Well now, to be quite honest, dear Tony,
do you like her better than me? Because—because, although I've held
off so independent, I'll own at last that I do like 'ee, Tony, to tell the
truth; and I wouldn't say no if you asked me—you know what."

'Tony was so won over by this pretty offering mood of a girl who
had been quite the reverse (Hannah had a backward way with her
at times, if you can mind) that he just glanced behind, and then
whispered very soft, "I haven't quite promised her, and I think I
can get out of it, and ask you that question you speak of."

' "Throw over Milly?—all to marry me! How delightful!" broke out
Hannah, quite loud, clapping her hands.

'At this time there was a real squeak—an angry, spiteful squeak,
and afterward a long moan, as if something had broke its heart, and
a movement of the empty sacks.

' "Something's there!" said Hannah, starting up.

' "It's nothing, really," says Tony in a soothing voice, and praying inwardly for a way out of this. "I wouldn't tell 'ee at first, because I wouldn't frighten 'ee. But, Hannah, I've really a couple of ferrets in a bag under there, for rabbiting, and they quarrel sometimes. I don't wish it knowed, as 'twould be called poaching. Oh, they can't get out, bless ye—you are quite safe! And—and—what a fine day it is, isn't it, Hannah, for this time of year? Be you going to market next Saturday? How is your aunt now?" And so on, says Tony, to keep her from talking any more about love in Milly's hearing.

'But he found his work cut out for him, and wondering again how he should get out of this ticklish business, he looked about for a chance. Nearing home he saw his father in a field not far off, holding up his hand as if he wished to speak to Tony.

' "Would you mind taking the reins for a moment, Hannah," he said, much relieved, "while I go and find out what father wants?"

'She consented, and away he hastened into the field, only too glad to get breathing time. He found that his father was looking at him with rather a stern eye.

' "Come, come, Tony," says old Mr. Kytes, as soon as his son was alongside him, "this won't do, you know."

' "What?" says Tony.

' "Why, if you mean to marry Milly Richards, do it, and there's an end o't. But don't go driving about the country with Jolliver's daughter and making a scandal. I won't have such things done."

' "I only asked her—that is, she asked me, to ride home."

' "She? Why, now, if it had been Milly, 'twould have been quite proper; but you and Hannah Jolliver going about by yourselves—"

' "Milly's there too, father."

' "Milly? Where?"

' "Under the corn-sacks! Yes, the truth is, father, I've got rather into a nunny-watch, I'm afeared! Unity Sallet is there too—yes, at the other end, under the tarpaulin. All three are in that waggon, and what to do with 'em I know no more than the dead! The best plan is, as I'm thinking, to speak out loud and plain to one of 'em before the rest, and that will settle it; not but what 'twill cause 'em to kick up a bit of a miff, for certain. Now which would you marry, father, if you was in my place?"

' "Whichever of 'em did *not* ask to ride with thee."

' "That was Milly, I'm bound to say, as she only mounted by my invitation. But Milly—"

' "Then stick to Milly, she's the best. . . . But look at that!"
'His father pointed toward the waggon. "She can't hold that horse
in. You shouldn't have left the reins in her hands. Run on and take
the horse's head, or there'll be some accident to them maids!"

'Tony's horse, in fact, in spite of Hannah's tugging at the reins, had
started on his way at a brisk walking pace, being very anxious to
get back to the stable, for he had had a long day out. Without another
word Tony rushed away from his father to overtake the horse.

'Now of all things that could have happened to wean him from
Milly there was nothing so powerful as his father's recommending
her. No; it could not be Milly, after all. Hannah must be the one,
since he could not marry all three. This he thought while running
after the waggon. But queer things were happening inside it.

'It was, of course, Milly who had screamed under the sack-bags,
being obliged to let off her bitter rage and shame in that way at what
Tony was saying, and never daring to show, for very pride and dread
o' being laughed at, that she was in hiding. She became more and more
restless, and in twisting herself about, what did she see but another
woman's foot and white stocking close to her head. It quite frightened
her, not knowing that Unity Sallet was in the waggon likewise. But
after the fright was over she determined to get to the bottom of all
this, and she crept and crept along the bed of the waggon, under the
tarpaulin, like a snake, when lo and behold she came face to face
with Unity.

' "Well, if this isn't disgraceful!" says Milly in a raging whisper
to Unity.

' " 'Tis," says Unity, "to see you hiding in a young man's waggon
like this, and no great character belonging to either of ye!"

' "Mind what you are saying!" replied Milly, getting louder. "I am
engaged to be married to him, and haven't I a right to be here? What
right have you, I should like to know? What has he been promising
you? A pretty lot of nonsense, I expect! But what Tony says to other
women is mere wind, and no concern to me!"

' "Don't you be too sure!" says Unity. "He's going to have Hannah,
and not you, nor me either; I could hear that."

'Now at these strange voices sounding from under the cloth Hannah
was thunderstruck a'most into a swound; and it was just at this time
that the horse moved on. Hannah tugged away wildly, not knowing
what she was doing; and as the quarrel rose louder and louder
Hannah got so horrified that she let go the reins altogether. The horse

went on at his own pace, and coming to the corner where we turn round to drop down the hill to Lower Longpuddle he turned too quick, the off wheels went up the bank, the waggon rose sideways till it was quite on edge upon the near axles, and out rolled the three maidens into the road in a heap.

'When Tony came up, frightened and breathless, he was relieved to see that neither of his darlings was hurt, beyond a few scratches from the brambles of the hedge. But he was rather alarmed when he heard how they were going on at one another.

' "Don't ye quarrel, my dears—don't ye!" says he, taking off his hat out of respect to 'em. And then he would have kissed them all round, as fair and square as a man could, but they were in too much of a taking to let him, and screeched and sobbed till they was quite spent.

' "Now I'll speak out honest, because I ought to," says Tony, as soon as he could get heard. "And this is the truth," says he. "I've asked Hannah to be mine, and she is willing, and we are going to put up the banns next—"

'Tony had not noticed that Hannah's father was coming up behind, nor had he noticed that Hannah's face was beginning to bleed from the scratch of a bramble. Hannah had seen her father, and had run to him, crying worse than ever.

' "My daughter is *not* willing, sir!" says Mr. Jolliver hot and strong. "Be you willing, Hannah? I ask ye to have spirit enough to refuse him, if yer virtue is left to 'ee and you run no risk?"

' "She's as sound as a bell for me, that I'll swear!" says Tony, flaring up. "And so's the others, come to that, though you may think it an onusual thing in me!"

' "I have spirit, and I do refuse him!" says Hannah, partly because her father was there, and partly, too, in a tantrum because of the discovery, and the scratch on her face. "Little did I think when I was so soft with him just now that I was talking to such a false deceiver!"

' "What, you won't have me, Hannah?" says Tony, his jaw hanging down like a dead man's.

' "Never—I would sooner marry no—nobody at all!" she gasped out, though with her heart in her throat, for she would not have refused Tony if he had asked her quietly, and her father had not been there, and her face had not been scratched by the bramble. And having said that, away she walked upon her father's arm, thinking and hoping he would ask her again.

'Tony didn't know what to say next. Milly was sobbing her heart out; but as father had strongly recommended her he couldn't feel inclined that way. So he turned to Unity.

' "Well, will you, Unity dear, be mine?" he says.

' "Take her leavings? Not I!" says Unity. "I'd scorn it!" And away walks Unity Sallet likewise, though she looked back when she'd gone some way, to see if he was following her.

'So there at last were left Milly and Tony by themselves, she crying in watery streams, and Tony looking like a tree struck by lightning.

' "Well, Milly," he says at last, going up to her, "it do seem as if fate had ordained that it should be you and I, or nobody. And what must be must be, I suppose. Hey, Milly?"

' "If you like, Tony. You didn't really mean what you said to them?"

' "Not a word of it!" declares Tony, bringing down his fist upon his palm.

'And then he kissed her, and put the waggon to rights, and they mounted together; and their banns were put up the very next Sunday. I was not able to go to their wedding, but it was a rare party they had, by all account.'

George Gissing

In America the reputation of George Gissing has made its way with unhurried persistence. Those who like him want others to share their liking, and no author has a more faithful following. Gissing's name is not writ large on the list of English masters of the short story, but while he was writing his novels of London streets, he found time for two collections of stories Human Odds and Ends (1898) and The House of Cobwebs (1906) which effectively present his special qualities. These stories do not depend upon surprise of plot or brilliance of expression, but they are distinctive in their sturdy honesty of style, their wry acceptance of life's slings and arrows, their patient understanding of people. No better corrective for the smooth unrealities of "slick" fiction could be found.

Gissing's forty-six years were not easy; his victories came late and hard-won. He was born at Wakefield in 1857, educated at Owens College, Manchester, and lived a life of bitter privation while he was trying to get a foot-hold in the world of literature. For a brief time he wandered, lonely and unemployed, in the United States. He returned to London and began doggedly to turn out the careful, realistic novels which critics began slowly to recognize, and which the public at large ignored. Gissing had a cultivated taste for the classics, and many of his books reflect his interest in the ancient world. His best known works are his Charles Dickens (1898), a critical study; the autobiographical Private Papers of Henry Ryecroft (1903); and the novel, New Grub Street (1891).

THE PIG AND WHISTLE *

George Gissing

'I POSSESS a capital of thirty thousand pounds. One-third of this is invested in railway shares, which bear interest at three and a half per cent.; another third is in Government stock, and produces two and three-quarters per cent.; the rest is lent on mortgages, at three per cent. Calculate my income for the present year.'

This kind of problem was constantly being given out by Mr. Ruddiman, assistant master at Longmeadows School. Mr. Ruddiman, who had reached the age of five-and-forty, and who never in his life had possessed five-and-forty pounds, used his arithmetic lesson as an opportunity for flight of imagination. When dictating a sum in which he attributed to himself enormous wealth, his eyes twinkled, his slender body struck a dignified attitude, and he smiled over the class with a certain genial condescension. When the calculation proposed did not refer to personal income it generally illustrated the wealth of the nation, in which Mr. Ruddiman had a proud delight. He would bid his youngsters compute the proceeds of some familiar tax, and the vast sum it represented rolled from his lips on a note of extraordinary satisfaction, as if he gloried in this evidence of national prosperity. His salary at Longmeadows just sufficed to keep him decently clad and to support him during the holidays. He had been a master here for seven years, and earnestly hoped that his services might be retained for at least seven more; there was very little chance of his ever obtaining a better position, and the thought of being cast adrift, of having to betake himself to the school agencies and enter upon new engagements, gave Mr. Ruddiman a very unpleasant sensation. In his time he had gone through hardships such as naturally befall a teacher without diplomas and possessed of no remarkable gifts; that he had never broken down in health was the result of an admirable constitution and of much native cheerfulness. Only at such an establishment as Longmeadows—an old-fashioned commercial 'academy,' recommended to parents by the healthiness of its rural situation—could he have hoped to hold his ground against modern educational tendencies, which aim at obliterating Mr. Ruddiman and all his kind. Every one liked him; impossible not to like a man so abounding in kindliness and good humour; but his knowledge was anything but extensive, and his

---

* From *The House of Cobwebs, and other Stories* by George Gissing, 1906.

methods in instruction had a fine flavour of antiquity. Now and then Mr. Ruddiman asked himself what was to become of him when sickness or old age forbade his earning even the modest income upon which he could at present count, but his happy temper dismissed the troublesome reflection. One thing, however, he had decided; in future he would find some more economical way of spending his holidays. Hitherto he had been guilty of the extravagance of taking long journeys to see members of his scattered family, or of going to the seaside, or of amusing himself (oh, how innocently!) in London. This kind of thing must really stop. In the coming summer vacation he had determined to save at least five sovereigns, and he fancied he had discovered a simple way of doing it.

On pleasant afternoons, when he was 'off duty,' Mr. Ruddiman liked to have a long ramble by himself about the fields and lanes. In solitude he was never dull; had you met him during one of these afternoon walks, more likely than not you would have seen a gentle smile on his visage as he walked with head bent. Not that his thoughts were definitely of agreeable things; consciously he thought perhaps of nothing at all; but he liked the sunshine and country quiet, and the sense of momentary independence. Every one would have known him for what he was. His dress, his gait, his countenance, declared the under-master. Mr. Ruddiman never carried a walking-stick; that would have seemed to him to be arrogating a social position to which he had no claim. Generally he held his hands together behind him; if not so, one of them would dip its fingers into a waistcoat pocket and the other grasp the lapel of his coat. If anything he looked rather less than his age, a result, perhaps, of having always lived with the young. His features were agreeably insignificant; his body, though slight of build, had something of athletic outline, due to long practice at cricket, football, and hockey.

If he had rather more time than usual at his disposal he walked as far as the Pig and Whistle, a picturesque little wayside inn, which stood alone, at more than a mile from the nearest village. To reach the Pig and Whistle one climbed a long, slow ascent, and in warm weather few pedestrians, or, for the matter of that, folks driving or riding, could resist the suggestion of the ivy-shadowed porch which admitted to the quaint parlour. So long was it since the swinging sign had been painted that neither of Pig nor of Whistle was any trace now discoverable; but over the porch one read clearly enough the landlord's name: William Fouracres. Only three years ago had Mr. Fouracres established himself here; Ruddiman remembered his predecessor, with whom he had often chatted whilst drinking his modest bottle of ginger beer. The present landlord was a very different sort of man, less affable, not disposed to show himself to every comer. Customers were generally served by the landlord's daughter, and with her Mr. Ruddiman had come to be on very pleasant terms.

But as this remark may easily convey a false impression, it must be added that Miss Fouracres was a very discreet, well-spoken, deliberate person, of at least two-and-thirty. Mr. Ruddiman had known her for more than a year before anything save brief civilities passed between them. In the second twelvemonth of their acquaintance they reached the point of exchanging reminiscences as to the weather; discussing the agricultural prospects of the county, and remarking on the advantage to rural innkeepers of the fashion of bicycling. In the third year they were quite intimate; so intimate, indeed, that when Mr. Fouracres chanced to be absent they spoke of his remarkable history. For the landlord of the Pig and Whistle had a history worth talking about, and Mr. Ruddiman had learnt it from the landlord's own lips. Miss Fouracres would never have touched upon the subject with any one in whom she did not feel confidence; to her it was far from agreeable, and Mr. Ruddiman established himself in her esteem by taking the same view of the matter.

Well, one July afternoon, when the summer vacation drew near, the under-master perspired up the sunny road with another object than that of refreshing himself at the familiar little inn. He entered by the ivied porch, and within, as usual, found Miss Fouracres, who sat behind the bar sewing. Miss Fouracres wore a long white apron, which protected her dress from neck to feet, and gave her an appearance of great neatness and coolness. She had a fresh complexion, and features which made no disagreeable impression. At sight of the visitor she rose, and, as her habit was, stood with one hand touching her chin, whilst she smiled the discreetest of modest welcomes.

'Good day, Miss Fouracres,' said the under-master, after his usual little cough.

'Good day, sir,' was the reply, in a country voice which had a peculiar note of honesty. Miss Fouracres had never yet learnt her acquaintance's name.

'Splendid weather for the crops. I'll take a ginger beer, if you please.'

'Indeed, that it is, sir. Ginger beer; yes, sir.'

Then followed two or three minutes of silence. Miss Fouracres had resumed her sewing, though not her seat. Mr. Ruddiman sipped his beverage more gravely than usual.

'How is Mr. Fouracres?' he asked at length.

'I'm sorry to say, sir,' was the subdued reply, 'that he's thinking about the Prince.'

'Oh, dear!' sighed Mr. Ruddiman, as one for whom this mysterious answer had distressing significance. 'That's a great pity.'

'Yes, sir. And I'm sorry to say,' went on Miss Fouracres, in the same confidential tone, 'that the Prince is coming here. I don't mean *here*, sir, to the Pig and Whistle, but to Woodbury Manor. Father saw it in the newspaper, and since then he's had no rest, day or night. He's sitting out in the garden. I don't know whether you'd like to go and speak to him, sir?'

'I will. Yes, I certainly will. But there's something I should like to ask you about first, Miss Fouracres. I'm thinking of staying in this part of the country through the holidays'—long ago he had made known his position—'and it has struck me that perhaps I could lodge here. Could you let me have a room? Just a bedroom will be enough.'

'Why, yes, sir,' replied the landlord's daughter. 'We have two bedrooms, you know, and I've no doubt my father would be willing to arrange with you.'

'Ah, then I'll mention it to him. Is he in very low spirits?'

'He's unusual low to-day, sir. I shouldn't wonder if it did him good to see you, and talk a bit.'

Having finished his ginger beer, Mr. Ruddiman walked through the house and passed out into the garden, where he at once became aware of Mr. Fouracres. The landlord, a man of sixty, with grizzled hair and large, heavy countenance, sat in a rustic chair under an apple-tree; beside him was a little table, on which stood a bottle of whisky and a glass. Approaching, Mr. Ruddiman saw reason to suspect that the landlord had partaken too freely of the refreshment ready to his hand. Mr. Fouracres' person was in a limp state; his cheeks were very highly coloured, and his head kept nodding as he muttered to himself. At the visitor's greeting he looked up with a sudden surprise, as though he resented an intrusion on his privacy.

'It's very hot, Mr. Fouracres,' the under-master went on to remark with cordiality.

'Hot? I dare say it is,' replied the landlord severely. 'And what else do you expect at this time of the year, sir?'

'Just so, Mr. Fouracres, just so!' said the other, as good-humouredly as possible. 'You don't find it unpleasant?'

'Why should I, sir? It was a good deal hotter day than this when His Royal Highness called upon me; a good deal hotter. The Prince didn't complain; not he. He said to me—I'm speaking of His Royal Highness, you understand; I hope you understand that, sir?'

'Oh, perfectly!'

'His words were—"Very seasonable weather, Mr. Fouracres." I'm not likely to forget what he said; so it's no use you or any one else trying to make out that he didn't say that. I tell you he *did!* "Very seasonable weather, Mr. Fouracres"—calling me by name, just like that. And it's no good you nor anybody else——'

The effort of repeating the Prince's utterance with what was meant to be a princely accent proved so exhausting to Mr. Fouracres that he sank together in his chair and lost all power of coherent speech. In a moment he seemed to be sleeping. Having watched him a little while, Mr. Ruddiman spoke his name, and tried to attract his attention; finding it useless he went back into the inn.

'I'm afraid I shall have to put it off to another day,' was his remark to the landlord's daughter. 'Mr. Fouracres is—rather drowsy.'

'Ah, sir!' sighed the young woman. 'I'm sorry to say he's often been like that lately.'

Their eyes met, but only for an instant. Mr. Ruddiman looked and felt uncomfortable.

'I'll come again very soon, Miss Fouracres,' he said. 'You might just speak to your father about the room.'

'Thank you, sir. I will, sir.'

And, with another uneasy glance, which was not returned, the under-master went his way. Descending towards Longmeadows, he thought over the innkeeper's history, which may be briefly related. Some ten years before this Mr. Fouracres occupied a very comfortable position; he was landlord of a flourishing inn—called an hotel—in a little town of some importance as an agricultural centre, and seemed perfectly content with the life and the society natural to a man so circumstanced. His manners were marked by a certain touch of pompousness, and he liked to dwell upon the excellence of the entertainment which his house afforded, but these were innocent characteristics which did not interfere with his reputation as a sensible and sound man of business. It happened one day that two gentlemen on horseback, evidently riding for their pleasure, stopped at the inn door, and, after a few inquiries, announced that they would alight and have lunch. Mr. Fouracres—who himself received these gentlemen—regarded one of them with much curiosity, and presently came to the startling conclusion that he was about to entertain no less a person than the Heir Apparent. He knew that the Prince was then staying at a great house some ten miles away, and there could be no doubt that one of his guests had a strong resemblance to the familiar portraits of His Royal Highness. In his excitement at the supposed discovery, Mr. Fouracres at once communicated it to those about him, and in a very few minutes half the town had heard the news. Of course the host would allow no one but himself to wait at the royal table—which was spread in the inn's best room, guarded against all intrusion. In vain, however, did he listen for a word from either of the gentlemen which might confirm his belief; in their conversation no name or title was used, and no mention made of anything significant. They remained for an hour. When their horses were brought round for them a considerable crowd had gathered before the hotel, and the visitors departed amid a demonstration of exuberant loyalty. On the following day, one or two persons who had been present at this scene declared that the two gentlemen showed surprise, and that, though both raised their hats in acknowledgment of the attention they received, they rode away laughing.

For the morrow brought doubts. People began to say that the Prince had never been near the town at all, and that evidence could be produced of his having passed the whole day at the house where he was a visitor. Mr. Fouracres smiled disdainfully; no assertion or argument availed to shake his proud assurance that he had entertained the Heir to the Throne. From that day he knew no peace. Fired with an extraordinary arrogance, he viewed as his enemy every one who refused to believe in the Prince's visit; he quarrelled violently with many of his best friends; he brought insulting accusations against all manner of persons. Before long the man was honestly convinced that there existed a conspiracy to rob him of a distinction that was his due. Political animus had, perhaps, something to do with it, for the Liberal newspaper (Mr. Fouracres was a stout Conservative) made more than one malicious joke on the subject. A few townsmen stood by the landlord's side and used their ingenuity in discovering plausible reasons why the Prince did not care to have it publicly proclaimed that he had visited the town and lunched at the hotel. These partisans scorned the suggestion that Mr. Fouracres had made a mistake, but they were unable to deny that a letter, addressed to the Prince himself, with a view to putting an end to the debate, had elicited (in a secretarial hand) a brief denial of the landlord's story. Evidently something very mysterious underlay the whole affair, and there was much shaking of heads for a long time.

To Mr. Fouracres the result of the honour he so strenuously vindicated was serious indeed. By way of defiance to all mockers he wished to change the time-honoured sign of the inn, and to substitute for it the Prince of Wales's Feathers. On this point he came into conflict with the owner of the property, and, having behaved very violently, received notice that his lease, just expiring, would not be renewed. Whereupon what should Mr. Fouracres do but purchase land and begin to build for himself an hotel twice as large as that he must shortly quit. On this venture he used all, and more than all, his means, and, as every one had prophesied, he was soon a ruined man. In less than three years from the fatal day he turned his back upon the town where he had known respect and prosperity, and went forth to earn his living as best he could. After troublous wanderings, on which he was accompanied by his daughter, faithful and devoted, though she had her doubts on a certain subject, the decayed publican at length found a place of rest. A small legacy from a relative had put it in his power to make a new, though humble, beginning in business; he established himself at the Pig and Whistle.

The condition in which he had to-day been discovered by Mr. Ruddiman was not habitual with him. Once a month, perhaps, his melancholy thoughts drove him to the bottle; for the most part he led a sullen, brooding life, indifferent to the state of his affairs, and only animated when he found a new and appreciative listener to the story of his wrongs. That he had been grievously wronged was Mr. Fouracres' immutable conviction. Not by His Royal Highness; the Prince knew nothing of the strange conspiracy which had resulted in Fouracres' ruin; letters addressed to His Royal Highness were evidently intercepted by underlings, and never came before the royal eyes. Again and again had Mr. Fouracres written long statements of his case, and petitioned for an audience. He was now resolved to adopt other methods; he would use the first opportunity of approaching the Prince's person, and lifting up his voice where he could not but be heard. He sought no vulgar gain; his only desire was to have this fact recognised, that he had, indeed, entertained the Prince, and so put to shame all his scornful enemies. And now the desired occasion offered itself. In the

month of September His Royal Highness would be a guest at Wood-
bury Manor, distant only some couple of miles from the Pig and
Whistle. It was the excitement of such a prospect which had led Mr.
Fouracres to undue indulgence under the apple-tree this afternoon.

A week later Mr. Ruddiman again ascended the hill, and, after
listening patiently to the narrative which he had heard fifty times,
came to an arrangement with Mr. Fouracres about the room he wished
to rent for the holidays. The terms were very moderate, and the under-
master congratulated himself on this prudent step. He felt sure that a
couple of months at the Pig and Whistle would be anything but disagreeable. The situation was high and healthy; the surroundings were
picturesque. And for society, well, there was Miss Fouracres, whom
Mr. Ruddiman regarded as a very sensible and pleasant person.

Of course, no one at Longmeadows had an inkling of the under-
master's intention. On the day of 'breaking up' he sent his luggage, as
usual, to the nearest railway station, and that same evening had it
conveyed by carrier to the little wayside inn, where, much at ease in
mind and body, he passed his first night.

He had a few books with him, but Mr. Ruddiman was not much of
a reader. In the garden of the inn, or somewhere near by, he found a
spot of shade, and there, pipe in mouth, was content to fleet the hours
as they did in the golden age. Now and then he tried to awaken his
host's interest in questions of national finance. It was one of Mr.
Ruddiman's favourite amusements to sketch Budgets in anticipation of
that to be presented by the Chancellor of the Exchequer, and he always
convinced himself that his own financial expedients were much superior to those laid before Parliament. All sorts of ingenious little
imposts were constantly occurring to him, and his mouth watered with
delight at the sound of millions which might thus be added to the
national wealth. But to Mr. Fouracres such matters seemed trivial. A
churchwarden between his lips, he appeared to listen, sometimes giving
a nod or a grunt; in reality his thoughts were wandering amid bygone
glories, or picturing a day of brilliant revenge.

Much more satisfactory were the conversations between Mr. Ruddiman and his host's daughter; they were generally concerned with the
budget, not of the nation, but of the Pig and Whistle. Miss Fouracres
was a woman of much domestic ability; she knew how to get the
maximum of comfort out of small resources. But for her the inn would
have been a wretched little place—as, indeed, it was before her time.
Miss Fouracres worked hard and prudently. She had no help; the

garden, the poultry, all the cares of house and inn were looked after by her alone—except, indeed, a few tasks beyond her physical strength, which were disdainfully performed by the landlord. A pony and cart served chiefly to give Mr. Fouracres an airing when his life of sedentary dignity grew burdensome. One afternoon, when he had driven to the market town, his daughter and her guest were in the garden together, gathering broad beans and gossiping with much contentment.

'I wish I could always live here!' exclaimed Mr. Ruddiman, after standing for a moment with eyes fixed meditatively upon a very large pod which he had just picked.

Miss Fouracres looked at him as if in surprise, her left hand clasping her chin.

'Ah, you'd soon get tired of it, sir.'

'I shouldn't! No, I'm sure I shouldn't. I like this life. It suits me. I like it a thousand times better than teaching in a school.'

'That's your fancy, sir.'

As Miss Fouracres spoke a sound from the house drew her attention; some one had entered the inn.

'A customer?' said Mr. Ruddiman. 'Let me go and serve him—do let me!'

'But you wouldn't know how, sir.'

'If it's beer, and that's most likely, I know well enough. I've watched you so often. I'll go and see.'

With the face of a schoolboy he ran into the house, and was absent about ten minutes. Then he reappeared, chinking coppers in his hand and laughing gleefully.

'A cyclist! Pint of half-and-half! I served him as if I'd done nothing else all my life.'

Miss Fouracres looked at him with wonder and admiration. She did not laugh; demonstrative mirth was not one of her characteristics; but for a long time there dwelt upon her good, plain countenance a half-smile of placid contentment. When they went in together, Mr. Ruddiman begged her to teach him all the mysteries of the bar, and his request was willingly granted. In this way they amused themselves until the return of the landlord, who, as soon as he had stabled his pony, called Mr. Ruddiman aside, and said in a hoarse whisper—

'The Prince comes to-morrow!'

'Ha! does he?' was the answer, in a tone of feigned interest.

'I shall see him. It's all settled. I've made friends with one of the gardeners at Woodbury Manor, and he's promised to put me in the way of meeting His Royal Highness. I shall have to go over there for a day or two, and stay in Woodbury, to be on the spot when the chance offers.'

Mr. Fouracres had evidently been making his compact with the aid of strong liquor; he walked unsteadily, and in other ways betrayed imperfect command of himself. Presently, at the tea-table, he revealed to his daughter the great opportunity which lay before him, and spoke of the absence from home it would necessitate.

'Of course you'll do as you like, father,' replied Miss Fouracres, with her usual deliberation, and quite good-humouredly, 'but I think you're going on a fool's errand, and that I tell you plain. If you'd just forget all about the Prince, and settle down quiet at the Pig and Whistle, it'ud be a good deal better for you.'

The landlord regarded her with surprise and scorn. It was the first time that his daughter had ventured to express herself so unmistakably.

'The Pig and Whistle!' he exclaimed. 'A pothouse! I who have kept an hotel and entertained His Royal Highness. You speak like an ignorant woman. Hold your tongue, and don't dare to let me hear your voice again until to-morrow morning!'

Miss Fouracres obeyed him. She was absolutely mute for the rest of the evening, save when obliged to exchange a word or two with rustic company or in the taproom. Her features expressed uneasiness rather than mortification.

The next day, after an early breakfast, Mr. Fouracres set forth to the town of Woodbury. He had the face of a man with a fixed idea, and looked more obstinate, more unintelligent than ever. To his daughter he had spoken only a few cold words, and his last bidding to her was 'Take care of the pothouse!' This treatment gave Miss Fouracres much pain, for she was a soft-hearted woman, and had never been anything but loyal and affectionate to her father all through his disastrous years. Moreover, she liked the Pig and Whistle, and could not bear to hear it spoken of disdainfully. Before the sound of the cart had died away she had to wipe moisture from her eyes, and at the moment when she was doing so Mr. Ruddiman came into the parlour.

'Has Mr. Fouracres gone?' asked the guest, with embarrassment.

'Just gone, sir,' replied the young woman, half turned away, and nervously fingering her chin.

'I shouldn't trouble about it if I were you, Miss Fouracres,' said Mr. Ruddiman in a tone of friendly encouragement. 'He'll soon be back, he'll soon be back, and you may depend upon it there'll be no harm done.'

'I hope so, sir, but I've an uneasy sort of feeling; I have indeed.'

'Don't you worry, Miss Fouracres. When the Prince has gone away he'll be better.'

Miss Fouracres stood for a moment with eyes cast down, then, looking gravely at Mr. Ruddiman, said in a sorrowful voice—

'He calls the Pig and Whistle a pothouse.'

'Ah, that was wrong of him!' protested the other, no less earnestly. 'A pothouse, indeed! Why, it's one of the nicest little inns you could find anywhere. I'm getting fond of the Pig and Whistle. A pothouse, indeed! No, I call that shameful.'

The listener's eyes shone with gratification.

'Of course we've got to remember,' she said more softly, 'that father has known very different things.'

'I don't care what he has known!' cried Mr. Ruddiman. 'I hope I may never have a worse home than the Pig and Whistle. And I only wish I could live here all the rest of my life, instead of going back to that beastly school!'

'Don't you like the school, Mr. Ruddiman?'

'Oh, I can't say I *dis*like it. But since I've been living here—well, it's no use thinking of impossibilities.'

Towards midday the pony and trap came back, driven by a lad from Woodbury, who had business in this direction. Miss Fouracres asked him to unharness and stable the pony, and whilst this was being done Mr. Ruddiman stood by, studiously observant. He had pleasure in every detail of the inn life. To-day he several times waited upon passing guests, and laughed exultantly at the perfection he was attaining. Miss Fouracres seemed hardly less pleased, but when alone she still wore an anxious look, and occasionally heaved a sigh of trouble.

Mr. Ruddiman, as usual, took an early supper, and soon after went up to his room. By ten o'clock the house was closed, and all through the night no sound disturbed the peace of the Pig and Whistle.

The morrow passed without news of Mr. Fouracres. On the morning after, just as Mr. Ruddiman was finishing his breakfast, alone in the parlour, he heard a loud cry of distress from the front part of the inn. Rushing out to see what was the matter, he found Miss Fouracres in agitated talk with a man on horseback.

'Ah, what did I say!' she cried at sight of the guest. 'Didn't I *know* something was going to happen? I must go at once—I must put in the pony— —'

'I'll do that for you,' said Mr. Ruddiman. 'But what has happened?'

The horseman, a messenger from Woodbury, told a strange tale. Very early this morning, a gardener walking through the grounds at Woodbury Manor, and passing by a little lake or fishpond, saw the body of a man lying in the water, which at this point was not three feet in depth. He drew the corpse to the bank, and, in so doing, recognized his acquaintance, Mr. Fouracres, with whom he had spent an hour or two at a public-house in Woodbury on the evening before. How the landlord of the Pig and Whistle had come to this tragic end neither the gardener nor any one else in the neighbourhood could conjecture.

Mr. Ruddiman set to work at once on harnessing the pony, while Miss Fouracres, now quietly weeping, went to prepare herself for the journey. In a very few minutes the vehicle was ready at the door. The messenger had already ridden away.

'Can you drive yourself, Miss Fouracres?' asked Ruddiman, looking and speaking with genuine sympathy.

'Oh yes, sir. But I don't know what to do about the house. I may be away all day. And what about you, sir?'

'Leave me to look after myself, Miss Fouracres. And trust me to look after the house too, will you? You know I can do it. Will you trust me?'

'It's only that I'm ashamed, sir— —'

'Not a bit of it. I'm very glad, indeed, to be useful; I assure you I am.'

'But your dinner, sir?'

'Why, there's cold meat. Don't you worry, Miss Fouracres. I'll look after myself, and the house too; see if I don't. Go at once, and keep your mind at ease on my account, pray do!'

'It's very good of you, sir, I'm sure it is. Oh, I *knew* something was going to happen! Didn't I *say* so?'

Mr. Ruddiman helped her into the trap; they shook hands silently, and Miss Fouracres drove away. Before the turn of the road she looked back. Ruddiman was still watching her; he waved his hand, and the young woman waved to him in reply.

Left alone, the under-master took off his coat and put on an apron, then addressed himself to the task of washing up his breakfast things. Afterwards he put his bedroom in order. About ten o'clock the first customer came in, and, as luck had it, the day proved a busier one than usual. No less than four cyclists stopped to make a meal. Mr. Ruddiman was able to supply them with cold beef and ham; moreover, he cooked eggs, he made tea—and all this with a skill and expedition which could hardly have been expected of him. None the less did he think constantly of Miss Fouracres. About five in the afternoon wheels sounded; aproned and in his shirt-sleeves, he ran to the door—as he had already done several times at the sound of a vehicle—and with great satisfaction saw the face of his hostess. She, too, though her eyes showed she had been weeping long, smiled with gladness; the next moment she exclaimed distressfully.

'Oh, sir! To think you've been here alone all day! And in an apron!'

'Don't think about me, Miss Fouracres. You look worn out, and no wonder. I'll get you some tea at once. Let the pony stand here a little; he's not so tired as you are. Come in and have some tea, Miss Fouracres.'

Mr. Ruddiman would not be denied; he waited upon his hostess, got her a very comfortable tea, and sat near her whilst she was enjoying it. Miss Fouracres' story of the day's events still left her father's death most mysterious. All that could be certainly known was that the landlord of the Pig and Whistle had drunk rather freely with his friend the gardener at an inn at Woodbury, and towards nine o'clock in the evening had gone out, as he said, for a stroll before bedtime. Why he entered the grounds of Woodbury Manor, and how he got into the pond there, no one could say. People talked of suicide, but Miss Fouracres would not entertain that suggestion. Of course there was to be an inquest, and one could only await the result of such evidence as might be forthcoming. During the day Miss Fouracres had telegraphed to the only relatives of whom she knew anything, two sisters of her father, who kept a shop in London. Possibly one of them might come to the funeral.

'Well,' said Mr. Ruddiman, in a comforting tone, 'all you have to do is to keep quiet. Don't trouble about anything. I'll look after the business.'

Miss Fouracres smiled at him through her tears.

'It's very good of you, sir, but you make me feel ashamed. What sort of a day have you had?'

'Splendid! Look here!'

He exhibited the day's receipts, a handful of cash, and, with delight decently subdued, gave an account of all that had happened.

'I like this business!' he exclaimed. 'Don't you trouble about anything. Leave it all to me, Miss Fouracres.'

One of the London aunts came down, and passed several days at the Pig and Whistle. She was a dry, keen, elderly woman, chiefly interested in the question of her deceased brother's property, which proved to be insignificant enough. Meanwhile the inquest was held, and all the countryside talked of Mr. Fouracres, whose story, of course, was published in full detail by the newspapers. Once more opinions were divided as to whether the hapless landlord really had or had not entertained His Royal Highness. Plainly, Mr. Fouracres' presence in the grounds of Woodbury Manor was due to the fact that the Prince happened to be staying there. In a state of irresponsibility, partly to be explained by intoxication, partly by the impulse of his fixed idea, he must have gone rambling in the dark round the Manor, and there, by accident, have fallen into the water. No clearer hypothesis resulted from the legal inquiry, and with this all concerned had perforce to be satisfied. Mr. Fouracres was buried, and, on the day after the funeral, his sister returned to London. She showed no interest whatever in her niece, who, equally independent, asked neither counsel nor help.

Mr. Ruddiman and his hostess were alone together at the Pig and Whistle. The situation had a certain awkwardness. Familiars of the inn—country-folk of the immediate neighbourhood—of course began to comment on the state of things, joking among themselves about Mr. Ruddiman's activity behind the bar. The under-master himself was in an uneasy frame of mind. When Miss Fouracres' aunt had gone, he paced for an hour or two about the garden; the hostess was serving cyclists. At length the familiar voice called to him.

'Will you have your dinner, Mr. Ruddiman?'

He went in, and, before entering the parlour, stood looking at a cask of ale which had been tilted forward.

'We must tap the new cask,' he remarked.

'Yes, sir, I suppose we must,' replied his hostess, half absently.

'I'll do it at once. Some more cyclists might come.' For the rest of the day they saw very little of each other. Mr. Ruddiman rambled musing. When he came at the usual hour to supper, guests were occupying the hostess. Having eaten, he went out to smoke his pipe in the garden, and lingered there—it being a fine, warm night—till after ten o'clock. Miss Fouracres' voice aroused him from a fit of abstraction.

'I've just locked up, sir.'

'Ah! Yes. It's late.'

They stood a few paces apart. Mr. Ruddiman had one hand in his waistcoat pocket, the other behind his back; Miss Fouracres was fingering her chin.

'I've been wondering,' said the under-master in a diffident voice, 'how you'll manage all alone, Miss Fouracres.'

'Well, sir,' was the equally diffident reply, 'I've been wondering too.'

'It won't be easy to manage the Pig and Whistle all alone.'

'I'm afraid not, sir.'

'Besides you couldn't live here in absolute solitude. It wouldn't be safe.'

'I shouldn't quite like it, sir.'

'But I'm sure you wouldn't like to leave the Pig and Whistle, Miss Fouracres?'

'I'd much rather stay, sir, if I could any way manage it.'

Mr. Ruddiman drew a step nearer.

'Do you know, Miss Fouracres, I've been thinking just the same. The fact is, I don't like the thought of leaving the Pig and Whistle; I don't like it at all. This life suits me. Could you'—he gave a little laugh 'engage me as your assistant, Miss Fouracres?'

'Oh, sir!'

'You couldn't?'

'How can you think of such a thing, sir.'

'Well, then, there's only one way out of the difficulty that I can see. Do you think— —'

Had it not been dark Mr. Ruddiman would hardly have ventured to make the suggestion which fell from him in a whisper. Had it not been dark Miss Fouracres would assuredly have hesitated much longer before giving her definite reply. As it was, five minutes of conversation solved what had seemed a harder problem than any the under-master set to his class at Longmeadows, and when these two turned to enter the Pig and Whistle, they went hand in hand.

John Galsworthy

Born near London in 1867, John Galsworthy took an honor degree in law at Oxford and set out, without enthusiasm, to practice his profession. *His wide reading in literature, his natural instincts, and perhaps his early friendship with Joseph Conrad whom he encouraged to write turned his own career to writing. "In two years," he said, "I wrote nine tales. They had every fault." But he persisted, and just before his death in 1933, he had won the greatest recognition in the world of letters—the Nobel Prize for literature.*

Galsworthy will always be known best for his great series of novels The Forsyte Saga *(1906–1929) which chronicles the rise and decline of a Victorian family in its conflict between the sense for property and the sense for beauty. He was a distinguished playwright, essayist, and short story writer as well; and in all of his work he exercised a fastidious regard for the ideals of his profession.*

While his variation "Salta Pro Nobis" has nothing to do with his usual subject, English family life, it is characteristic of him in its dramatic conflict between discipline and the life-releasing power of beauty. Galsworthy's best stories appear in the two collections Caravan *(1925) and* On Forsyte 'Change *(1930).*

SALTA PRO NOBIS *

A VARIATION

John Galsworthy

"THE DANCER, my Mother, is very sad. She sits with her head on her hands. She looks into the emptiness. It is frightful to watch. I have tried to make her pray, my Mother, but the poor girl—she does not

* From *Caravan* by John Galsworthy. Charles Scribner's Sons, 1925. Reprinted by permission of Charles Scribner's Sons.

know how; she has no belief. She refuses even to confess herself. She is pagan—but quite pagan. What could one do for her, my Mother—to cheer her a little during these hours? I have tried to make her tell me of her life. She does not answer. She sits and looks always into the emptiness. It does me harm in the heart to see her. Is there nothing one can do to comfort her a little before she dies? To die so young—so full of life; for her who has no faith! To be shot—so young, so beautiful; but it is frightful, my Mother!"

When she had finished speaking thus, the little elderly Sister raised her hands, and crossed them quietly on her grey-clothed breast. Her eyes, brown and mild, looked up, questioning the face before her, wax pale under its coif and smooth grey hair. Straight, thin, as it were bodiless beneath the grey and white of her garb, the Mother Superior stood pondering. The spy-woman in her charge, a dancer with gypsy blood they said—or was it Moorish?—who had wormed secrets from her French naval lover, and sold them to the Germans in Spain. At the trial they said there was no doubt. And they had brought her to the Convent saying, "Keep her for us till the fifteenth. She will be better with you than in prison." To be shot—a woman! It made one shiver! And yet—it was war! It was for France!

Looking down at the little Sister with the soft brown eyes, the Mother Superior answered:

"One must see, my daughter. Take me to her cell."

Along the corridor they passed, and went in gently. The dancer was sitting on her bed, with legs crossed under her. There was no colour in her skin, save the saffron sprinkled into it by Eastern blood. The face was oval, the eyebrows slanted a little up; black hair formed on her forehead a V reversed; her lips, sensuous but fine, showed a gleam of teeth. Her arms were crossed, as though compressing the fire within her supple body. Her eyes, colour of Malaga wine, looked through and beyond the whitened walls, through and beyond her visitors, like the eyes of a caged leopard.

The Mother Superior spoke:

"What can we do for you, my daughter?"

The daughter shrugged her body from the waist; one could see its supple shivering beneath her silk garment.

"You suffer, my daughter. They tell me you do not pray. It is a pity."

The dancer smiled—that quickly passing smile had sweetness, as of something tasted, of a rich tune, of a long kiss; she shook her head.

"One would not say anything to trouble you, my daughter; one feels pity for your suffering. One comprehends. Is there a book you would read; some wine you would like; in a word, anything which could distract you a little?"

The dancer untwined her arms, and clasped them behind her neck. The movement was beautiful, sinuous—all her body beautiful; and into the Mother Superior's waxen cheeks a faint colour came.

"Will you dance for us, my daughter?"

Again the smile, like the taste of a sweet wine, came on the dancer's face, and this time did not pass.

"Yes," she said, "I will dance for you—willingly. It will give me pleasure, Madame!"

"That is good. Your dresses shall be brought. This evening in the refectory, after the meal. If you wish music—one can place a piano. Sister Mathilde is a good musician."

"Yes, music—some simple dances. Madame, could I smoke?"

"Certainly, my daughter. I will have cigarettes brought to you."

The dancer stretched out her hand. Between her own, fragile with thin blue veins, the Mother Superior felt its supple warmth, and shivered. To-morrow it would be cold and stiff!

"*Au revoir!* then, my daughter. . . ."

"The dancer will dance for us!" This was the word. One waited, expectant, as for a marvel. One placed the piano; procured music; sat eating the evening meal—whispering. The strangeness of it! The intrusion! The little gay ghosts of memories! Ah! the dramatic, the strange event! Soon the meal was finished; the tables cleared, removed; against the wall, on the long benches sixty grey figures with white coifs waited—in the centre the Mother Superior, at the piano Sister Mathilde.

The little elderly Sister came first; then, down the long whitened refectory, the dancer walking slowly over the dark oak floor. Every head was turned—alone the Mother Superior sat motionless, thinking: 'If only it does not put notions into some light heads!'

The dancer wore a full skirt of black silk, she had silvery shoes and stockings, round her waist was a broad tight network of gold, over her bust tight silvery tissue, with black lace draped; her arms were bare; a red flower was set to one side of her black hair; she held a black and ivory fan. Her lips were just touched with red, her eyes just touched with black; her face was like a mask. She stood in the very centre, with eyes cast down. Sister Mathilde began to play. The dancer lifted her fan. In that dance of Spain she hardly moved from where she stood, swaying, shivering, spinning, poised; only the eyes of her face seemed alive, resting on this face and on that of the long row of faces, where so many feelings were expressed—curiosity and doubt, pleasure, timidity, horror, curiosity. Sister Mathilde ceased playing, the dancer stood still; a little murmur broke along the line of nuns, and the dancer smiled. Then Sister Mathilde began again to play, a Polish dance; for a moment the dancer listened as if to catch the rhythm of music strange to her; then her feet moved, her lips parted, she was sweet and gay, like a butterfly, without a care; and on the lips of the watching faces smiles came, and little murmurs of pleasure escaped.

The Mother Superior sat without moving, her thin lips pressed together, her thin fingers interlaced. Images from the past kept starting out, and falling back, like figures from some curious old musical box. That long-ago time—she was remembering—when her lover was killed in the Franco-Prussian war, and she entered religion. This supple figure from the heathen world, the red flower in the black hair, the whitened face, the sweetened eyes, stirred up remembrance, sweet and yearning, of her own gay pulses, before they had seemed to die, and she brought them to the Church to bury them.

The music ceased; began again a Habañera, reviving memories of the pulses after they were buried—secret, throbbing, dark. The Mother Superior turned her face to left and right. Had she been wise? So many light heads, so many young hearts! And yet, why not soothe the last dark hours of this poor heathen girl? She was happy, dancing. Yes, she was happy! What power! And what abandonment! It was frightening. She was holding every eye—the eyes even of Sister Louise—holding them as a snake holds a rabbit's eyes. The Mother Superior nearly smiled. That poor Sister Louise! And then, just beyond that face of fascinated horror, the Mother Superior saw young Sister Marie. How the child was staring—what eyes, what lips! Sister Marie—so young— just twenty—her lover dead in the war—but one year dead! Sister Marie—prettiest in all the Convent! Her hands—how tightly they seemed pressed together on her lap! And—but yes—it was at Sister Marie that the dancer looked; at Sister Marie she twirled and writhed those supple fiery limbs! For Sister Marie the strange sweet smile came and went on those enticing reddened lips. In dance after dance—like a bee on a favorite flower—to Sister Marie the dancer seemed to cling. And the Mother Superior thought: 'Is this the Blessed Virgin's work I have done, or—the Devil's?'

Close along the line of nuns the dancer was sweeping now; her eyes glowed, her face was proud, her body supreme. Sister Marie! What was it? A look, a touch with the fan! The music ceased! The dancer blew a kiss. It lighted—where? *"Gracias, Senoras! Adios!"*

Slowly, swaying, as she had come, she walked away over the dark floor; and the little old Sister followed.

A sighing sound from the long row of nuns; and—yes—one sob! "Go to your rooms, my daughters! Sister Marie!"

The young nun came forward; tears were in her eyes.

"Sister Marie, pray that the sins of that poor soul be forgiven. But yes, my child, it is sad. Go to your room. Pray!"

With what grace the child walked! She, too, had the limbs of beauty. The Mother Superior sighed. . . .

Morning, cold, grey, a sprinkle of snow on the ground; they came for the dancer during Mass. A sound of firing! With trembling lips, the Mother Superior prayed for the soul dancing before her God. . . .

That evening they searched for Sister Marie, but could not find her. After two days a letter came:

"Forgive me, my Mother. I have gone back to life."

"Marie."

The Mother Superior sat quite still. Life in death! Figures starting out from that old musical box of memory; the dancer's face, red flower in the hair, dark sweetened eyes, lips, touched with flying finger, parted in a kiss!

James Joyce

THE GENERAL reader associates the name of James Joyce with literary productions which are as impenetrable as they are prodigious. His great Ulysses, first published in Paris in 1922, has been called the most influential work of the twentieth century, a vast innovating experiment to which many writers have turned for creative incitement. His Work in Progress, from which two baffling excerpts were published in 1930 and 1932, goes beyond Ulysses in its revolutionary technique, its amazing verbal manipulations.

But the general reader should not forget that James Joyce who has broken the bounds of conventional expression has also demonstrated his mastery of traditional forms. His first published work, Chamber Music (1907), was a group of delicate lyrics which have often been set to melody. His Dubliners is a collection of short stories which report the life of his native city with clarity, detachment, and an ultimate impression of pathos, like music heard remotely. It was remarkable writing for a young man in his early twenties; remarkable, too, in that Dublin would not publish it. The stories were first printed in London in 1914. His autobiographical novel, A Portrait of the Artist as a Young Man, (1916) contains some of the most beautiful, the most subtly cadenced prose of our time.

James Joyce was born in Dublin in 1882 and received his degree from University College. He now lives in Paris, occupied with his Work in Progress which, says Eugene Jolas, "reveals literary and intellectual possibilities that have never previously been envisaged."

A LITTLE CLOUD *

James Joyce

EIGHT YEARS before he had seen his friend off at the North Wall and wished him godspeed. Gallaher had got on. You could tell that at once by his travelled air, his well-cut tweed suit, and fearless accent. Few fellows had talents like his and fewer still could remain unspoiled by such success. Gallaher's heart was in the right place and he had deserved to win. It was something to have a friend like that.

Little Chandler's thoughts ever since lunch-time had been of his meeting with Gallaher, of Gallaher's invitation and of the great city London where Gallaher lived. He was called Little Chandler because, though he was but slightly under the average stature, he gave one the idea of being a little man. His hands were white and small, his frame was fragile, his voice was quiet and his manners were refined. He took the greatest care of his fair silken hair and moustache and used perfume discreetly on his handkerchief. The half-moons of his nails were perfect and when he smiled you caught a glimpse of a row of childish white teeth.

As he sat at his desk in the King's Inns he thought what changes those eight years had brought. The friend whom he had known under a shabby and necessitous guise had become a brilliant figure on the London Press. He turned often from his tiresome writing to gaze out of the office window. The glow of a late autumn sunset covered the grass plots and walks. It cast a shower of kindly golden dust on the untidy nurses and decrepit old men who drowsed on the benches; it flickered upon all the moving figures—on the children who ran scream-ing along the gravel paths and on everyone who passed through the gardens. He watched the scene and thought of life; and (as always happened when he thought of life) he became sad. A gentle melan-choly took possession of him. He felt how useless it was to struggle against fortune, this being the burden of wisdom which the ages had bequeathed to him.

He remembered the books of poetry upon his shelves at home. He had bought them in his bachelor days and many an evening, as he sat in the little room off the hall, he had been tempted to take one down from the bookshelf and read out something to his wife. But shyness had always held him back; and so the books had remained on their

---

* From *Dubliners* by James Joyce. Published by The Viking Press, Inc. New York.

shelves. At times he repeated lines to himself and this consoled him.

When his hour had struck he stood up and took leave of his desk and of his fellow-clerks punctiliously. He emerged from under the feudal arch of the King's Inns, a neat modest figure, and walked swiftly down Henrietta Street. The golden sunset was waning and the air had grown sharp. A horde of grimy children populated the street. They stood or ran in the roadway or crawled up the steps before the gaping doors or squatted like mice upon the thresholds. Little Chandler gave them no thought. He picked his way deftly through all that minute vermin-like life and under the shadow of the gaunt spectral mansions in which the old nobility of Dublin had roystered. No memory of the past touched him, for his mind was full of a present joy.

He had never been in Corless's but he knew the value of the name. He knew that people went there after the theatre to eat oysters and drink liqueurs; and he had heard that the waiters there spoke French and German. Walking swiftly by at night he had seen cabs drawn up before the door and richly dressed ladies, escorted by cavaliers, alight and enter quickly. They wore noisy dresses and many wraps. Their faces were powdered and they caught up their dresses, when they touched earth, like alarmed Atalantas. He had always passed without turning his head to look. It was his habit to walk swiftly in the street even by day and whenever he found himself in the city late at night he hurried on his way apprehensively and excitedly. Sometimes, however, he courted the causes of his fear. He chose the darkest and narrowest streets and, as he walked boldly forward, the silence that was spread about his footsteps troubled him, the wandering, silent figures troubled him; and at times a sound of low fugitive laughter made him tremble like a leaf.

He turned to the right towards Capel Street. Ignatius Gallaher on the London Press! Who would have thought it possible eight years before? Still, now that he reviewed the past, Little Chandler could remember many signs of future greatness in his friend. People used to say that Ignatius Gallaher was wild. Of course, he did mix with a rakish set of fellows at that time, drank freely and borrowed money on all sides. In the end he had got mixed up in some shady affair, some money transaction: at least, that was one version of his flight. But nobody denied him talent. There was always a certain . . . something in Ignatius Gallaher that impressed you in spite of yourself. Even when he was out at elbows and at his wits' end for money he

kept up a bold face. Little Chandler remembered (and the remembrance brought a slight flush of pride to his cheek) one of Ignatius
Gallaher's sayings when he was in a tight corner:

"Half time now, boys," he used to say light-heartedly. "Where's my
considering cap?"

That was Ignatius Gallaher all out; and, damn it, you couldn't but
admire him for it.

Little Chandler quickened his pace. For the first time in his life he
felt himself superior to the people he passed. For the first time his soul
revolted against the dull inelegance of Capel Street. There was no
doubt about it: if you wanted to succeed you had to go away. You
could do nothing in Dublin. As he crossed Grattan Bridge he looked
down the river towards the lower quays and pitied the poor stunted
houses. They seemed to him a band of tramps, huddled together along
the river-banks, their old coats covered with dust and soot, stupefied by
the panorama of sunset and waiting for the first chill of night to bid
them arise, shake themselves and be gone. He wondered whether he
could write a poem to express his idea. Perhaps Gallaher might be
able to get it into some London paper for him. Could he write something original? He was not sure what idea he wished to express but the
thought that a poetic moment had touched him took life within him
like an infant hope. He stepped onward bravely.

Every step brought him nearer to London, farther from his own
sober inartistic life. A light began to tremble on the horizon of his
mind. He was not so old—thirty-two. His temperament might be said
to be just at the point of maturity. There were so many different moods
and impressions that he wished to express in verse. He felt them
within him. He tried to weigh his soul to see if it was a poet's soul.
Melancholy was the dominant note of his temperament, he thought,
but it was a melancholy tempered by recurrences of faith and resigna-
tion and simple joy. If he could give expression to it in a book of poems
perhaps men would listen. He would never be popular: he saw that.
He could not sway the crowd but he might appeal to a little circle of
kindred minds. The English critics, perhaps, would recognise him as
one of the Celtic school by reason of the melancholy tone of his poems;
besides that, he would put in allusions. He began to invent sentences
and phrases from the notice which his book would get. *"Mr. Chandler
has the gift of easy and graceful verse."* . . . *"A wistful sadness per-
vades these poems."* . . . *"The Celtic note."* It was a pity his name was
not more Irish-looking. Perhaps it would be better to insert his mother's

name before the surname: Thomas Malone Chandler, or better still: T. Malone Chandler. He would speak to Gallaher about it.

He pursued his revery so ardently that he passed his street and had to turn back. As he came near Corless's his former agitation began to overmaster him and he halted before the door in indecision. Finally he opened the door and entered.

The light and noise of the bar held him at the doorways for a few moments. He looked about him, but his sight was confused by the shining of many red and green wine-glasses. The bar seemed to him to be full of people and he felt that the people were observing him curiously. He glanced quickly to the right and left (frowning slightly to make his errand appear serious), but when his sight cleared a little he saw that nobody had turned to look at him: and there, sure enough, was Ignatius Gallaher leaning with his back against the counter and his feet planted far apart.

"Hallo, Tommy, old hero, here you are! What is it to be? What will you have? I'm taking whisky: better stuff than we get across the water. Soda? Lithia? No mineral? I'm the same. Spoils the flavour. . . . Here, *garçon,* bring us two halves of malt whisky, like a good fellow. . . . Well, and how have you been pulling along since I saw you last? Dear God, how old we're getting! Do you see any signs of aging in me—eh, what? A little grey and thin on the top—what?"

Ignatius Gallaher took off his hat and displayed a large closely cropped head. His face was heavy, pale and clean-shaven. His eyes, which were of bluish slate-colour, relieved his unhealthy pallor and shone out plainly above the vivid orange tie he wore. Between these rival features the lips appeared very long and shapeless and colourless. He bent his head and felt with two sympathetic fingers the thin hair at the crown. Little Chandler shook his head as a denial. Ignatius Gallaher put on his hat again.

"It pulls you down," he said, "Press life. Always hurry and scurry, looking for copy and sometimes not finding it: and then, always to have something new in your stuff. Damn proofs and printers, I say, for a few days. I'm deuced glad, I can tell you, to get back to the old country. Does a fellow good, a bit of a holiday. I feel a ton better since I landed again in dear dirty Dublin. . . . Here you are, Tommy. Water? Say when."

Little Chandler allowed his whisky to be very much diluted.

"You don't know what's good for you, my boy," said Ignatius Gallaher. "I drink mine neat."

"I drink very little as a rule," said Little Chandler modestly. "An odd half-one or so when I meet any of the old crowd: that's all."

"Ah, well," said Ignatius Gallaher, cheerfully, "here's to us and to old times and old acquaintance."

They clinked glasses and drank the toast.

"I met some of the old gang to-day," said Ignatius Gallaher. "O'Hara seems to be in a bad way. What's he doing?"

"Nothing," said Little Chandler. "He's gone to the dogs."

"But Hogan has a good sit, hasn't he?"

"Yes; he's in the Land Commission."

"I met him one night in London and he seemed to be very flush. . . . Poor O'Hara! Booze, I suppose?"

"Other things, too," said Little Chandler shortly.

Ignatius Gallaher laughed.

"Tommy," he said, "I see you haven't changed an atom. You're the very same serious person that used to lecture me on Sunday mornings when I had a sore head and a fur on my tongue. You'd want to knock about a bit in the world. Have you never been anywhere even for a trip?"

"I've been to the Isle of Man," said Little Chandler.

Ignatius Gallaher laughed.

"The Isle of Man!" he said. "Go to London or Paris: Paris, for choice. That'd do you good."

"Have you seen Paris?"

"I should think I have! I've knocked about there a little."

"And is it really so beautiful as they say?" asked Little Chandler.

He sipped a little of his drink while Ignatius Gallaher finished his boldly.

"Beautiful?" said Ignatius Gallaher, pausing on the word and on the flavour of his drink. "It's not so beautiful, you know. Of course, it is beautiful. . . . But it's the life of Paris; that's the thing. Ah, there's no city like Paris for gaiety, movement, excitement. . . ."

Little Chandler finished his whisky and, after some trouble, succeeded in catching the barman's eye. He ordered the same again.

"I've been to the Moulin Rouge," Ignatius Gallaher continued when the barman had removed their glasses, "and I've been to all the Bohemian Cafés. Hot stuff! Not for a pious chap like you, Tommy."

Little Chandler said nothing until the barman returned with two glasses: then he touched his friend's glass lightly and reciprocated the former toast. He was beginning to feel somewhat disillusioned. Galla-

her's accent and way of expressing himself did not please him. There
was something vulgar in his friend which he had not observed before.
But perhaps it was only the result of living in London amid the bustle
and competition of the Press. The old personal charm was still there
under this new gaudy manner. And, after all, Gallaher had lived, he
had seen the world. Little Chandler looked at his friend enviously.

"Everything in Paris is gay," said Ignatius Gallaher. "They believe
in enjoying life—and don't you think they're right? If you want to
enjoy yourself properly you must go to Paris. And, mind you, they've
a great feeling for the Irish there. When they heard I was from Ireland
they were ready to eat me, man."

Little Chandler took four or five sips from his glass.

"Tell me," he said, "is it true that Paris is so . . . immoral as they
say?"

Ignatius Gallaher made a catholic gesture with his right arm.

"Every place is immoral," he said. "Of course you do find spicy bits
in Paris. Go to one of the student's balls, for instance. That's lively,
if you like, when the *cocottes* begin to let themselves loose. You know
what they are, I suppose?"

"I've heard of them," said Little Chandler.

Ignatius Gallaher drank off his whisky and shook his head.

"Ah," he said, "you may say what you like. There's no woman like
the Parisienne—for style, for go."

"Then it is an immoral city," said Little Chandler, with timid
insistence—"I mean, compared with London or Dublin?"

"London!" said Ignatius Gallaher. "It's six of one and half-a-dozen
of the other. You ask Hogan, my boy. I showed him a bit about
London when he was over there. He'd open your eye. . . . I say,
Tommy, don't make punch of that whisky: liquor up."

"No, really. . . ."

"O, come on, another one won't do you any harm. What is it?
The same again, I suppose?"

"Well . . . all right."

"*François,* the same again. . . . Will you smoke, Tommy?"

Ignatius Gallaher produced his cigar-case. The two friends lit their
cigars and puffed at them in silence until their drinks were served.

"I'll tell you my opinion," said Ignatius Gallaher, emerging after
some time from the clouds of smoke in which he had taken refuge,
"it's a rum world. Talk of immorality! I've heard of cases—what am I
saying?—I've known them: cases of . . . immorality. . . ."

Ignatius Gallaher puffed thoughtfully at his cigar and then, in a calm historian's tone, he proceeded to sketch for his friend some pictures of the corruption that was rife abroad. He summarised the vices of many capitals and seemed inclined to award the palm to Berlin. Some things he could not vouch for (his friends had told him), but of others he had had personal experience. He spared neither rank nor caste. He revealed many of the secrets of religious houses on the Continent and described some of the practices which were fashionable in high society and ended by telling, with details, a story about an English duchess—a story which he knew to be true. Little Chandler was astonished.

"Ah, well," said Ignatius Gallaher, "here we are in old jog-along Dublin where nothing is known of such things."

"How dull you must find it," said Little Chandler, "after all the other places you've seen!"

"Well," said Ignatius Gallaher, "it's a relaxation to come over here, you know. And, after all, it's the old country, as they say, isn't it? You can't help having a certain feeling for it. That's human nature. . . . But tell me something about yourself. Hogan told me you had . . . tasted the joys of connubial bliss. Two years ago, wasn't it?"

Little Chandler blushed and smiled.

"Yes," he said. "I was married last May twelve months."

"I hope it's not too late in the day to offer my best wishes," said Ignatius Gallaher. "I didn't know your address or I'd have done so at the time."

He extended his hand, which Little Chandler took.

"Well, Tommy," he said, "I wish you and yours every joy in life, old chap, and tons of money, and may you never die till I shoot you. And that's the wish of a sincere friend, an old friend. You know that?"

"I know that," said Little Chandler.

"Any youngsters?" said Ignatius Gallaher.

Little Chandler blushed again.

"We have one child," he said.

"Son or daughter?"

"A little boy."

Ignatius Gallaher slapped his friend sonorously on the back.

"Bravo," he said, "I wouldn't doubt you, Tommy."

Little Chandler smiled, looked confusedly at his glass and bit his lower lip with three childishly white front teeth.

"I hope you'll spend an evening with us," he said, "before you go back. My wife will be delighted to meet you. We can have a little music and—"

"Thanks awfully, old chap," said Ignatius Gallaher, "I'm sorry we didn't meet earlier. But I must leave to-morrow night."

"To-night, perhaps . . . ?"

"I'm awfully sorry, old man. You see I'm over here with another fellow, clever young chap he is too, and we arranged to go to a little card-party. Only for that . . ."

"O, in that case. . . ."

"But who knows?" said Ignatius Gallaher considerately. "Next year I may take a little skip over here now that I've broken the ice. It's only a pleasure deferred."

"Very well," said Little Chandler, "the next time you come we must have an evening together. That's agreed now, isn't it?"

"Yes, that's agreed," said Ignatius Gallaher. "Next year if I come, *parole d'honneur.*"

"And to clinch the bargain," said Little Chandler, "we'll just have one more now."

Ignatius Gallaher took out a large gold watch and looked at it.

"Is it to be the last?" he said. "Because you know, I have an a. p."

"O, yes, positively," said Little Chandler.

"Very well, then," said Ignatius Gallaher, "let us have another one as a *deoc an doruis*—that's good vernacular for a small whisky, I believe."

Little Chandler ordered the drinks. The blush which had risen to his face a few moments before was establishing itself. A trifle made him blush at any time: and now he felt warm and excited. Three small whiskies had gone to his head and Gallaher's strong cigar had confused his mind, for he was a delicate and abstinent person. The adventure of meeting Gallaher after eight years, of finding himself with Gallaher in Corless's surrounded by lights and noise, of listening to Gallaher's stories and of sharing for a brief space Gallaher's vagrant and tri-umphant life, upset the equipoise of his sensitive nature. He felt acutely the contrast between his own life and his friend's, and it seemed to him unjust. Gallaher was his inferior in birth and education. He was sure that he could do something better than his friend had ever done, or could ever do, something higher than mere tawdry journalism if he only got the chance. What was it that stood in his way? His un-fortunate timidity! He wished to vindicate himself in some way, to assert his manhood. He saw behind Gallaher's refusal of his invitation. Gallaher was only patronising him by his friendliness just as he was patronising Ireland by his visit.

The barman brought their drinks. Little Chandler pushed one glass towards his friend and took up the other boldly.

"Who knows?" he said, as they lifted their glasses. "When you come next year I may have the pleasure of wishing long life and happiness to Mr. and Mrs. Ignatius Gallaher."

Ignatius Gallaher in the act of drinking closed one eye expressively over the rim of his glass. When he had drunk he smacked his lips decisively, set down his glass and said:

"No blooming fear of that, my boy. I'm going to have my fling first and see a bit of life and the world before I put my head in the sack—if I ever do."

"Some day you will," said Little Chandler calmly.

Ignatius Gallaher turned his orange tie and slate-blue eyes full upon his friend.

"You think so?" he said.

"You'll put your head in the sack," repeated Little Chandler stoutly, "like everyone else if you can find the girl."

He had slightly emphasised his tone and he was aware that he had betrayed himself; but, though the colour had heightened in his cheek, he did not flinch from his friend's gaze. Ignatius Gallaher watched him for a few moments and then said:

"If ever it occurs, you may bet your bottom dollar there'll be no mooning and spooning about it. I mean to marry money. She'll have a good fat account at the bank or she won't do for me."

Little Chandler shook his head.

"Why, man alive," said Ignatius Gallaher, vehemently, "do you know what it is? I've only to say the word and to-morrow I can have the woman and the cash. You don't believe it? Well, I know it. There are hundreds—what am I saying?—thousands of rich Germans and Jews, rotten with money, that'd only be too glad. . . . You wait a while, my boy. See if I don't play my cards properly. When I go about a thing I mean business, I tell you. You just wait."

He tossed his glass to his mouth, finished his drink and laughed loudly. Then he looked thoughtfully before him and said in a calmer tone:

"But I'm in no hurry. They can wait. I don't fancy tying myself up to one woman, you know."

He imitated with his mouth the act of tasting and made a wry face. "Must get a bit stale, I should think," he said.

Little Chandler sat in the room off the hall, holding a child in his arms. To save money they kept no servant but Annie's young sister Monica came for an hour or so in the morning and an hour or so in the evening to help. But Monica had gone home long ago. It was a quarter to nine. Little Chandler had come home late for tea and, moreover, he had forgotten to bring Annie home the parcel of coffee from Bewley's. Of course she was in a bad humour and gave him short answers. She said she would do without any tea but when it came near the time at which the shop at the corner closed she decided to go out herself for a quarter of a pound of tea and two pounds of sugar. She put the sleeping child deftly in his arms and said:

"Here. Don't waken him."

A little lamp with a white china shade stood upon the table and its light fell over a photograph which was enclosed in a frame of crumpled horn. It was Annie's photograph. Little Chandler looked at it, pausing at the thin tight lips. She wore the pale blue summer blouse which he had brought her home as a present one Saturday. It had cost him ten and elevenpence; but what an agony of nervousness it had cost him! How he had suffered that day, waiting at the shop door until the shop was empty, standing at the counter and trying to appear at his ease while the girl piled ladies' blouses before him, paying at the desk and forgetting to take up the odd penny of his change, being called back by the cashier, and finally, striving to hide his blushes as he left the shop by examining the parcel to see if it was securely tied. When he brought the blouse home Annie kissed him and said it was very pretty and stylish; but when she heard the price she threw the blouse on the table and said it was a regular swindle to charge ten and elevenpence for it. At first she wanted to take it back but when she tried it on she was delighted with it, especially with the make of the sleeves, and kissed him and said he was very good to think of her.

Hm! . . .

He looked coldly into the eyes of the photograph and they answered coldly. Certainly they were pretty and the face itself was pretty. But he found something mean in it. Why was it so unconscious and ladylike? The composure of the eyes irritated him. They repelled him and defied him: there was no passion in them, no rapture. He thought of what Gallaher had said about rich Jewesses. Those dark Oriental eyes, he thought, how full they are of passion, of voluptuous long-ing! . . . Why had he married the eyes in the photograph?

He caught himself up at the question and glanced nervously round the room. He found something mean in the pretty furniture which he had bought for his house on the hire system. Annie had chosen it herself and it reminded him of her. It too was prim and pretty. A dull resentment against his life awoke within him. Could he not escape from his little house? Was it too late for him to try to live bravely like Gallaher? Could he go to London? There was the furni-ture still to be paid for. If he could only write a book and get it published, that might open the way for him.

A volume of Byron's poems lay before him on the table. He opened it cautiously with his left hand lest he should waken the child and began to read the first poem in the book:

> *"Hushed are the winds and still the evening gloom,*
> *Not e'en a Zephyr wanders through the grove,*
> *Whilst I return to view my Margaret's tomb*
> *And scatter flowers on the dust I love."*

He paused. He felt the rhythm of the verse about him in the room. How melancholy it was! Could he, too, write like that, express the melancholy of his soul in verse? There were so many things he wanted to describe: his sensation of a few hours before on Grattan Bridge, for example. If he could get back again into that mood. . . .

The child awoke and began to cry. He turned from the page and tried to hush it: but it would not be hushed. He began to rock it to and fro in his arms but its wailing cry grew keener. He rocked it faster while his eyes began to read the second stanza:

> *"Within this narrow cell reclines her clay,*
> *That clay where once . . ."*

It was useless. He couldn't read. He couldn't do anything. The wailing of the child pierced the drum of his ear. It was useless, useless! He was a prisoner for life. His arms trembled with anger and suddenly bending to the child's face he shouted:

"Stop!"

The child stopped for an instant, had a spasm of fright and began to scream. He jumped up from his chair and walked hastily up and down the room with the child in his arms. It began to sob piteously, losing its breath for four or five seconds, and then bursting out anew.

The thin walls of the room echoed the sound. He tried to soothe it but it sobbed more convulsively. He looked at the contracted and quivering face of the child and began to be alarmed. He counted seven sobs without a break between them and caught the child to his breast in fright. If it died! . . .

The door was burst open and a young woman ran in, panting.

"What is it? What is it?" she cried.

The child, hearing its mother's voice, broke out into a paroxysm of sobbing.

"It's nothing, Annie . . . it's nothing. . . . He began to cry. . . ."

She flung her parcels on the floor and snatched the child from him.

"What have you done to him?" she cried, glaring into his face.

Little Chandler sustained for one moment the gaze of her eyes and his heart closed together as he met the hatred in them. He began to stammer:

"It's nothing. . . . He . . . he began to cry. . . . I couldn't . . . I didn't do anything. . . . What?"

Giving no heed to him she began to walk up and down the room, clasping the child tightly in her arms and murmuring:

"My little man! My little mannie! Was 'ou frightened, love? . . . There now, love! There now! . . . Lambabaun! Mamma's little lamb of the world! . . . There now!"

Little Chandler felt his cheeks suffused with shame and he stood back out of the lamplight. He listened while the paroxysm of the child's sobbing grew less and less; and tears of remorse started to his eyes.

D. H. Lawrence

For D. H. Lawrence the instinct was wiser than the intellect. A man of hyper-sensitive intuition and of profound conviction that life can be rejuvenated by powers beyond the conscious mind, he wrote from an impulse to make men over. His stories do not "entertain" in the popular sense; they explore the deep-hidden, often unspoken impulses that flow like electricity between his highly-charged characters. He was himself a thwarted personality, and his interpretation is sometimes too dark for understanding, but at its best his art was wonderfully vital and spontaneous.

Lawrence was born in 1885, the son of a Nottinghamshire miner and of a gifted mother who greatly influenced him. His career was brilliant and restless—a constant travelling and a constant pouring forth of novels, stories, poetry, essays, and sketches. He died of tuberculosis in Italy in 1930. Many biographical studies of him have been presented by his friends. His books of short stories are The Prussian Officer (1914); England, My England (1922); The Captain's Doll (1923); and The Woman Who Rode Away (1928).

THE BLIND MAN *

D. H. Lawrence

Isabel Pervin was listening for two sounds—for the sound of wheels on the drive outside and for the noise of her husband's footsteps in the hall. Her dearest and oldest friend, a man who seemed almost indispensable to her living, would drive up in the rainy dusk of the closing November day. The trap had gone to fetch him from the station. And her husband, who had been blinded in Flanders, and

---

who had a disfiguring mark on his brow, would be coming in from the out-houses.

He had been home for a year now. He was totally blind. Yet they had been very happy. The Grange was Maurice's own place. The back was a farmstead, and the Wernhams, who occupied the rear premises, acted as farmers. Isabel lived with her husband in the handsome rooms in front. She and he had been almost entirely alone together since he was wounded. They talked and sang and read together in a wonderful and unspeakable intimacy. Then she reviewed books for a Scottish newspaper, carrying on her old interest, and he occupied himself a good deal with the farm. Sightless, he could still discuss everything with Wernham, and he could also do a good deal of work about the place—menial work, it is true, but it gave him satisfaction. He milked the cows, carried in the pails, turned the separator, attended to the pigs and horses. Life was still very 'ull and strangely serene for the blind man, peaceful with the almost incomprehensible peace of immediate contact in darkness. With his wife he had a whole world, rich and real and invisible.

They were newly and remotely happy. He did not even regret the loss of his sight in these times of dark, palpable joy. A certain exultance swelled his soul.

But as time wore on, sometimes the rich glamour would leave them. Sometimes, after months of this intensity, a sense of burden overcame Isabel, a weariness, a terrible *ennui,* in that silent house approached between a colonnade of tall-shafted pines. Then she felt she would go mad, for she could not bear it. And sometimes he had devastating fits of depression, which seemed to lay waste his whole being. It was worse than depression—a black misery, when his own life was a torture to him, and when his presence was unbearable to his wife. The dread went down to the roots of her soul as these black days recurred. In a kind of panic she tried to wrap herself up still further in her husband. She forced the old spontaneous cheerfulness and joy to continue. But the effort it cost her was almost too much. She knew she could not keep it up. She felt she would scream with the strain, and would give anything, anything, to escape. She longed to possess her husband utterly; it gave her inordinate joy to have him entirely to herself. And yet, when again he was gone in a black and massive misery, she could not bear him, she could not bear herself; she wished she could be snatched away off the earth altogether, anything rather than live at this cost.

Dazed, she schemed for a way out. She invited friends, she tried to give him some further connection with the outer world. But it was no good. After all their joy and suffering, after their dark, great year of blindness and solitude and unspeakable nearness, other people seemed to them both shallow, prattling, rather impertinent. Shallow prattle seemed presumptuous. He became impatient and irritated, she was wearied. And so they lapsed into their solitude again. For they preferred it.

But now, in a few weeks' time, her second baby would be born. The first had died, an infant, when her husband first went out to France. She looked with joy and relief to the coming of the second. It would be her salvation. But also she felt some anxiety. She was thirty years old, her husband was a year younger. They both wanted the child very much. Yet she could not help feeling afraid. She had her husband on her hands, a terrible joy to her, and a terrifying burden. The child would occupy her love and attention. And then, what of Maurice? What would he do? If only she could feel that he, too, would be at peace and happy when the child came! She did so want to luxuriate in a rich, physical satisfaction of maternity. But the man, what would he do? How could she provide for him, how avert those shattering black moods of his, which destroyed them both?

She sighed with fear. But at this time Bertie Reid wrote to Isabel. He was her old friend, a second or third cousin, a Scotchman, as she was a Scotchwoman. They had been brought up near to one another, and all her life he had been her friend, like a brother, but better than her own brothers. She loved him—though not in the marrying sense. There was a sort of kinship between them, an affinity. They understood one another instinctively. But Isabel would never have thought of marrying Bertie. It would have seemed like marrying in her own family.

Bertie was a barrister and a man of letters, a Scotchman of the intellectual type, quick, ironical, sentimental, and on his knees before the woman he adored but did not want to marry. Maurice Pervin was different. He came of a good old country family—the Grange was not a very great distance from Oxford. He was passionate, sensitive, perhaps over-sensitive, wincing—a big fellow with heavy limbs and a forehead that flushed painfully. For his mind was slow, as if drugged by the strong provincial blood that beat in his veins. He was very sensitive to his own mental slowness, his feelings being quick and acute. So that he was just the opposite to Bertie, whose mind was much quicker than his emotions, which were not so very fine.

From the first the two men did not like each other. Isabel felt that they *ought* to get on together. But they did not. She felt that if only each could have the clue to the other there would be such a rare understanding between them. It did not come off, however. Bertie adopted a slightly ironical attitude, very offensive to Maurice, who returned the Scotch irony with English resentment, a resentment which deepened sometimes into stupid hatred.

This was a little puzzling to Isabel. However, she accepted it in the course of things. Men were made freakish and unreasonable. Therefore, when Maurice was going out to France for the second time, she felt that, for her husband's sake, she must discontinue her friendship with Bertie. She wrote to the barrister to this effect. Bertram Reid simply replied that in this, as in all other matters, he must obey her wishes, if these were indeed her wishes.

For nearly two years nothing had passed between the two friends. Isabel rather gloried in the fact; she had no compunction. She had one great article of faith, which was, that husband and wife should be so important to one another, that the rest of the world simply did not count. She and Maurice were husband and wife. They loved one another. They would have children. Then let everybody and everything else fade into insignificance outside this connubial felicity. She professed herself quite happy and ready to receive Maurice's friends. She was happy and ready: the happy wife, the ready woman in possession. Without knowing why, the friends retired abashed, and came no more. Maurice, of course, took as much satisfaction in this connubial absorption as Isabel did.

He shared in Isabel's literary activities, she cultivated a real interest in agriculture and cattle-raising. For she, being at heart perhaps an emotional enthusiast, always cultivated the practical side of life, and prided herself on her mastery of practical affairs. Thus the husband and wife had spent the five years of their married life. The last had been one of blindness and unspeakable intimacy. And now Isabel felt a great indifference coming over her, a sort of lethargy. She wanted to be allowed to bear her child in peace, to nod by the fire and drift vaguely physically, from day to day. Maurice was like an ominous thunder cloud. She had to keep waking up to remember him.

When a little note came from Bertie, asking if he were to put up a tombstone to their dead friendship, and speaking of the real pain he felt on account of her husband's loss of sight, she felt a pang, a fluttering agitation of re-awakening. And she read the letter to Maurice.

"Ask him to come down," he said.

"Ask Bertie to come here!" she re-echoed.

"Yes—if he wants to."

Isabel paused for a few moments.

"I know he wants to—he'd only be too glad," she replied. "But what about you, Maurice? How would you like it?"

"I should like it."

"Well—in that case— But I thought you didn't care for him—"

"Oh, I don't know. I might think differently of him now," the blind man replied. It was rather abstruse to Isabel.

"Well, dear," she said, "if you're quite sure—"

"I'm sure enough. Let him come," said Maurice.

So Bertie was coming, coming this evening, in the November rain and darkness. Isabel was agitated, racked with her old restlessness and indecision. She had always suffered from this pain of doubt, just an agonising sense of uncertainty. It had begun to pass off, in the lethargy of maternity. Now it returned, and she resented it. She struggled as usual to maintain her calm, composed, friendly bearing, a sort of mask she wore over all her body.

A woman had lighted a tall lamp beside the table, and spread the cloth. The long dining-room was dim, with its elegant but rather severe pieces of old furniture. Only the round table glowed softly under the light. It had a rich, beautiful effect. The white cloth glistened and dropped its heavy, pointed lace corners almost to the carpet, the china was old and handsome, creamy-yellow, with a blotched pattern of harsh red and deep blue, the cups large and bell-shaped, the teapot gallant. Isabel looked at it with superficial appreciation.

Her nerves were hurting her. She looked automatically again at the high, uncurtained windows. In the last dusk she could just perceive outside a huge fir-tree swaying its boughs: it was as if she thought it rather than saw it. The rain came flying on the window panes. Ah, why had she no peace? These two men, why did they tear at her? Why did they not come—why was there this suspense?

She sat in a lassitude that was really suspense and irritation. Maurice, at least, might come in—there was nothing to keep him out. She rose to her feet. Catching sight of her reflection in a mirror, she glanced at herself with a slight smile of recognition, as if she were an old friend to herself. Her face was oval and calm, her nose a little arched. Her neck made a beautiful line down to her shoulder. With hair knotted loosely behind, she had something of a warm, maternal look. Thinking this of herself, she arched her eyebrows and her rather heavy eyelids, with a little flicker of a smile, and for a moment her grey eyes looked amused and wicked, a little sardonic, out of her transfigured Madonna face.

Then, resuming her air of womanly patience—she was really fatally self-determined—she went with a little jerk towards the door. Her eyes were slightly reddened.

She passed down the wide hall, and through a door at the end. Then she was in the farm premises. The scent of dairy, and of farm-kitchen, and of farm-yard and of leather almost overcame her: but particularly the scent of dairy. They had been scalding out the pans. The flagged passage in front of her was dark, puddled and wet. Light came out from the open kitchen door. She went forward and stood in the doorway. The farm-people were at tea, seated at a little distance from her, round a long, narrow table, in the centre of which stood a white lamp. Ruddy faces, ruddy hands holding food, red mouths working, heads bent over the tea-cups: men, land-girls, boys: it was tea-time, feeding-time. Some faces caught sight of her. Mrs. Wernham, going round behind the chairs with a large black teapot, halting slightly in her walk, was not aware of her for a moment. Then she turned suddenly.

"Oh, is it Madam!" she exclaimed. "Come in, then, come in! We're at tea." And she dragged forward a chair.

"No, I won't come in," said Isabel. "I'm afraid I'll interrupt your meal."

"No—no—not likely, Madam, not likely."

"Hasn't Mr. Pervin come in, do you know?"

"I'm sure I couldn't say! Missed him, have you, Madam?"

"No, I only wanted him to come in," laughed Isabel, as if shyly.

"Wanted him, did ye? Get up, boy—get up, now—"

Mrs. Wernham knocked one of the boys on the shoulder. He began to scrape to his feet, chewing largely.

"I believe he's in top stable," said another face from the table.

"Ah! No, don't get up. I'm going myself," said Isabel.

"Don't you go out of a dirty night like this. Let the lad go. Get along wi' ye, boy," said Mrs. Wernham.

"No, no," said Isabel, with a decision that was always obeyed. "Go on with your tea, Tom. I'd like to go across to the stable, Mrs. Wernham."

"Did ever you hear tell!" exclaimed the woman.

"Isn't the trap late?" asked Isabel.

"Why, no," said Mrs. Wernham, peering into the distance at the tall, dim clock. "No, Madam—we can give it another quarter or twenty minutes yet, good—yes, every bit of a quarter."

"Ah! It seems late when darkness falls so early," said Isabel.

"It do, that it do. Bother the days, that they draw in so," answered Mrs. Wernham. "Proper miserable!"

"They are," said Isabel, withdrawing.

She pulled on her overshoes, wrapped a large tartan shawl around her, put on a man's felt hat, and ventured out along the causeways of the first yard. It was very dark. The wind was roaring in the great elms behind the outhouses. When she came to the second yard the darkness seemed deeper. She was unsure of her footing. She wished she had brought a lantern. Rain blew against her. Half she liked it, half she felt unwilling to battle.

She reached at last the just visible door of the stable. There was no sign of a light anywhere. Opening the upper half, she looked in: into a simple well of darkness. The smell of horses, and ammonia, and of warmth was startling to her, in that full night. She listened with all her ears, but could hear nothing save the night, and the stirring of a horse.

"Maurice!" she called, softly and musically, though she was afraid. "Maurice—are you there?"

Nothing came from the darkness. She knew the rain and wind blew in upon the horses, the hot animal life. Feeling it wrong, she entered the stable, and drew the lower half of the door shut, holding the upper part close. She did not stir, because she was aware of the presence of the dark hind-quarters of the horses, though she could not see them, and she was afraid. Something wild stirred in her heart.

She listened intensely. Then she heard a small noise in the distance —far away, it seemed—the chink of a pan, and a man's voice speaking a brief word. It would be Maurice, in the other part of the stable. She stood motionless, waiting for him to come through the partition door. The horses were so terrifyingly near to her, in the invisible.

The loud jarring of the inner door-latch made her start; the door was opened. She could hear and feel her husband entering and invisibly passing among the horses near to her, in darkness as they were.

actively intermingled. The rather low sound of his voice as he spoke to the horses came velvety to her nerves. How near he was, and how invisible! The darkness seemed to be in a strange swirl of violent life, just upon her. She turned giddy.

Her presence of mind made her call, quietly and musically:

"Maurice! Maurice—dea-ar!"

"Yes," he answered. "Isabel?"

She saw nothing, and the sound of his voice seemed to touch her.

"Hello!" she answered cheerfully, straining her eyes to see him. He was still busy, attending to the horses near her, but she saw only darkness. It made her almost desperate.

"Won't you come in, dear?" she said.

"Yes, I'm coming. Just half a minute. *Stand over—now!* Trap's not come, has it?"

"Not yet," said Isabel.

His voice was pleasant and ordinary, but it had a slight suggestion of the stable to her. She wished he would come away. Whilst he was so utterly invisible she was afraid of him.

"How's the time?" he asked.

"Not yet six," she replied. She disliked to answer into the dark. Presently he came very near to her, and she retreated out of doors.

"The weather blows in here," he said, coming steadily forward, feeling for the doors. She shrank away. At last she could dimly see him.

"Bertie won't have much of a drive," he said, as he closed the doors.

"He won't indeed!" said Isabel calmly, watching the dark shape at the door.

"Give me your arm, dear," she said.

She pressed his arm close to her, as she went. But she longed to see him, to look at him. She was nervous. He walked erect, with face rather lifted, but with a curious tentative movement of his powerful, muscular legs. She could feel the clever, careful, strong contact of his feet with the earth, as she balanced against him. For a moment he was a tower of darkness to her, as if he rose out of the earth.

In the house-passage he wavered, and went cautiously, with a curious look of silence about him as he felt for the bench. Then he sat down heavily. He was a man with rather sloping shoulders, but with heavy limbs, powerful legs that seemed to know the earth. His head was small, usually carried high and light. As he bent down to unfasten his gaiters and boots he did not look blind. His hair was brown and crisp, his hands were large, reddish, intelligent, the veins stood out in the wrists; and his thighs and knees seemed massive. When he stood up his face and neck were surcharged with blood, the veins stood out on his temples. She did not look at his blindness.

Isabel was always glad when they had passed through the dividing door into their own regions of repose and beauty. She was a little afraid of him, out there in the animal grossness of the back. His bearing also changed, as he smelt the familiar, indefinable odour that pervaded his wife's surroundings, a delicate, refined scent, very faintly spicy. Perhaps it came from the pot-pourri bowls.

He stood at the foot of the stairs, arrested, listening. She watched him, and her heart sickened. He seemed to be listening to fate.

"He's not here yet," he said. "I'll go up and change."

"Maurice," she said, "you're not wishing he wouldn't come, are you?"

"I couldn't quite say," he answered. "I feel myself rather on the *qui vive.*"

"I can see you are," she answered. And she reached up and kissed his cheek. She saw his mouth relax into a slow smile.

"What are you laughing at?" she said roguishly.

"You consoling me," he answered.

"Nay," she answered. "Why should I console you? You know we love each other—you know *how* married we are! What does anything else matter?"

"Nothing at all, my dear."

He felt for her face, and touched it, smiling.

"You're all right, aren't you?" he asked, anxiously.

"I'm wonderfully all right, love," she answered. "It's you I am a little troubled about, at times."

"Why me?" he said, touching her cheeks delicately with the tips of his fingers. The touch had an almost hypnotising effect on her.

He went away upstairs. She saw him mount into the darkness, unseeing and unchanging. He did not know that the lamps on the upper corridor were unlighted. He went on into the darkness with unchanging step. She heard him in the bath-room.

Pervin moved about almost unconsciously in his familiar surroundings, dark though everything was. He seemed to know the presence of objects before he touched them. It was a pleasure to him to rock thus through a world of things, carried on the flood in a sort of blood-prescience. He did not think much or trouble much. So long as he kept this sheer immediacy of blood-contact with the substantial world he was happy, he wanted no intervention of visual consciousness. In this state there was a certain rich positivity, bordering sometimes on rapture. Life seemed to move in him like a tide lapping, lapping and advancing, enveloping all things darkly. It was a pleasure to stretch forth the hand and meet the unseen object, clasp it, and possess it in pure contact. He did not try to remember, to visualise. He did not want to. The new way of consciousness substituted itself in him.

The rich suffusion of this state generally kept him happy, reaching its culmination in the consuming passion for his wife. But at times the flow would seem to be checked and thrown back. Then it would beat inside him like a tangled sea, and he was tortured in the shattered chaos of his own blood. He grew to dread this arrest, this throw-back, this chaos inside himself, when he seemed merely at the mercy of his own powerful and conflicting elements. How to get some measure of control or surety, this was the question. And when the question rose maddening in him, he would clench his fists as if he would *compel* the whole universe to submit to him. But it was in vain. He could not even compel himself.

To-night, however, he was still serene, though little tremors of unreasonable exasperation ran through him. He had to handle the razor very carefully, as he shaved, for it was not at one with him, he was afraid of it. His hearing also was too much sharpened. He heard the woman lighting the lamps on the corridor, and attending to the fire in the visitor's room. And then, as he went to his room he heard the trap arrive. Then came Isabel's voice, lifted and calling, like a bell ringing:

"Is it you, Bertie? Have you come?"

And a man's voice answered out of the wind:

"Hello, Isabel! There you are."

"Have you had a miserable drive? I'm so sorry we couldn't send a closed carriage. I can't see you at all, you know."

"I'm coming. No, I liked the drive—it was like Perthshire. Well, how are you? You're looking fit as ever, as far as I can see."

"Oh, yes," said Isabel. "I'm wonderfully well. How are you? Rather thin, I think—"

"Worked to death—everybody's old cry. But I'm all right, Ciss. How's Pervin?—isn't he here?"

"Oh, yes, he's upstairs changing. Yes, he's awfully well. Take off your wet things; I'll send them to be dried."

"And how are you both, in spirits? He doesn't fret?"

"No—no, not at all. No, on the contrary, really. We've been wonderfully happy, incredibly. It's more than I can understand—so wonderful: the nearness, and the peace—"

"Ah! Well, that's awfully good news—"

They moved away. Pervin heard no more. But a childish sense of desolation had come over him, as he heard their brisk voices. He seemed shut out—like a child that is left out. He was aimless and excluded, he did not know what to do with himself. The helpless desolation came over him. He fumbled nervously as he dressed himself, in a state almost of childishness. He disliked the Scotch accent in Bertie's speech, and the slight response it found on Isabel's tongue. He disliked the slight purr of complacency in the Scottish speech. He disliked intensely the glib way in which Isabel spoke of their happiness and nearness. It made him recoil. He was fretful and beside himself like a child, he had almost a childish nostalgia to be included in the life circle. And at the same time he was a man, dark and powerful and infuriated by his own weakness. By some fatal flaw, he could not be by himself, he had to depend on the support of another. And this very dependence enraged him. He hated Bertie Reid, and at the same time he knew the hatred was nonsense, he knew it was the outcome of his own weakness.

He went downstairs. Isabel was alone in the dining-room. She watched him enter, head erect, his feet tentative. He looked so strong-blooded and healthy, and, at the same time, cancelled. Cancelled—that was the word that flew across her mind. Perhaps it was his scars suggested it.

"You heard Bertie come, Maurice?" she said.

"Yes—isn't he here?"

"He's in his room. He looks very thin and worn."

"I suppose he works himself to death."

A woman came in with a tray—and after a few minutes Bertie came down. He was a little dark man, with a very big forehead, thin, wispy hair, and sad, large eyes. His expression was inordinately sad—almost funny. He had odd, short legs.

Isabel watched him hesitate under the door, and glance nervously at her husband. Pervin heard him and turned.

"Here you are, now," said Isabel. "Come, let us eat."

Bertie went across to Maurice.

"How are you, Pervin," he said as he advanced.

The blind man stuck his hand out into space, and Bertie took it.

"Very fit. Glad you've come," said Maurice.

Isabel glanced at them, and glanced away, as if she could not bear to see them.

"Come," she said. "Come to table. Aren't you both awfully hungry? I am, tremendously."

"I'm afraid you waited for me," said Bertie, as they sat down.

Maurice had a curious monolithic way of sitting in a chair, erect and distant. Isabel's heart always beat when she caught sight of him thus.

"No," she replied to Bertie. "We're very little later than usual. We're having a sort of high tea, not dinner. Do you mind? It gives us such a nice long evening, uninterrupted."

"I like it," said Bertie.

Maurice was feeling, with curious little movements, almost like a cat kneading her bed, for his place, his knife and fork, his napkin. He was getting the whole geography of his cover into his consciousness. He sat erect and inscrutable, remote-seeming. Bertie watched the static figure of the blind man, the delicate tactile discernment of the large, ruddy hands, and the curious mindless silence of the brow, above the scar. With difficulty he looked away, and without knowing what he did, picked up a little crystal bowl of violets from the table, and held them to his nose.

"They are sweet-scented," he said. "Where do they come from?"

"From the garden—under the windows," said Isabel.

"So late in the year—and so fragrant! Do you remember the violets under Aunt Bell's south wall?"

The two friends looked at each other and exchanged a smile, Isabel's eyes lighting up.

"Don't I?" she replied. *"Wasn't* she queer!"

"A curious old girl," laughed Bertie. "There's a streak of freakishness in the family, Isabel."

"Ah—but not in you and me, Bertie," said Isabel. "Give them to Maurice, will you?" she added, as Bertie was putting down the flowers. "Have you smelled the violets, dear? Do!—they are so scented."

Maurice held out his hand, and Bertie placed the tiny bowl against his large, warm-looking fingers. Maurice's hand closed over the thin white fingers of the barrister. Bertie carefully extricated himself. Then the two watched the blind man smelling the violets. He bent his head and seemed to be thinking. Isabel waited.

"Aren't they sweet, Maurice?" she said at last, anxiously.

"Very," he said. And he held out the bowl. Bertie took it. Both he and Isabel were a little afraid, and deeply disturbed.

The meal continued. Isabel and Bertie chatted spasmodically. The blind man was silent. He touched his food repeatedly, with quick, delicate touches of his knife-point, then cut irregular bits. He could not bear to be helped. Both Isabel and Bertie suffered: Isabel wondered why. She did not suffer when she was alone with Maurice. Bertie made her conscious of a strangeness.

After the meal the three drew their chairs to the fire, and sat down to talk. The decanters were put on a table near at hand. Isabel knocked the logs on the fire, and clouds of brilliant sparks went up the chimney. Bertie noticed a slight weariness in her bearing.

"You will be glad when your child comes now, Isabel?" he said. She looked up to him with a quick wan smile.

"Yes, I shall be glad," she answered. "It begins to seem long. Yes, I shall be very glad. So will you, Maurice, won't you?" she added.

"Yes, I shall," replied her husband.

"We are both looking forward so much to having it," she said.

"Yes, of course," said Bertie.

He was a bachelor, three or four years older than Isabel. He lived in beautiful rooms overlooking the river, guarded by a faithful Scottish man-servant. And he had his friends among the fair sex—not lovers, friends. So long as he could avoid any danger of courtship or marriage, he adored a few good women with constant and unfailing homage, and he was chivalrously fond of quite a number. But if they seemed to encroach on him, he withdrew and detested them.

Isabel knew him very well, knew his beautiful constancy, and kindness, also his incurable weakness, which made him unable ever to enter into close contact of any sort. He was ashamed of himself, because he could not marry, could not approach women physically. He wanted to do so. But he could not. At the centre of him he was afraid, helplessly and even brutally afraid. He had given up hope, had ceased to expect any more that he could escape his own weakness. Hence he was a brilliant and successful barrister, also *littérateur* of high repute, a rich man, and a great social success. At the centre he felt himself neuter, nothing.

Isabel knew him well. She despised him even while she admired him. She looked at his sad face, his little short legs, and felt contempt of him. She looked at his dark grey eyes, with their almost childlike intuition, and she loved him. He understood amazingly—but she had no fear of his understanding. As a man she patronised him.

And she turned to the impassive, silent figure of her husband. He sat leaning back, with folded arms, and face a little uptilted. His knees were straight and massive. She sighed, picked up the poker, and again began to prod the fire, to rouse the clouds of soft, brilliant sparks.

"Isabel tells me," Bertie began suddenly, "that you have not suffered unbearably from the loss of sight."

Maurice straightened himself to attend, but kept his arms folded.

"No," he said, "not unbearably. Now and again one struggles against it, you know. But there are compensations."

"They say it is much worse to be stone deaf," said Isabel.

"I believe it is," said Bertie. "Are there compensations?" he added, to Maurice.

"Yes. You cease to bother about a great many things." Again Maurice stretched his figure, stretched the strong muscles of his back, and leaned backwards, with uplifted face.

"And that is a relief," said Bertie. "But what is there in place of the bothering? What replaces the activity?"

There was a pause. At length the blind man replied, as out of a negligent, unattentive thinking:

"Oh, I don't know. There's a good deal when you're not active."

"Is there?" said Bertie. "What, exactly? It always seems to me that when there is no thought and no action, there is nothing."

Again Maurice was slow in replying.

"There is something," he replied. "I couldn't tell you what it is."

And the talk lapsed once more, Isabel and Bertie chatting gossip and reminiscence, the blind man silent.

At length Maurice rose restlessly, a big, obtrusive figure. He felt tight and hampered. He wanted to go away.

"Do you mind," he said, "if I go and speak to Wernham?"

"No—go along, dear," said Isabel.

And he went out. A silence came over the two friends. At length Bertie said:

"Nevertheless, it is a great deprivation, Cissie."

"It is, Bertie. I know it is."

"Something lacking all the time," said Bertie.

"Yes, I know. And yet—and yet—Maurice is right. There is something else, something *there,* which you never knew was there, and which you can't express."

"What is there?" asked Bertie.

"I don't know—it's awfully hard to define it—but something strong and immediate. There's something strange in Maurice's presence—indefinable—but I couldn't do without it. I agree that it seems to put one's mind to sleep. But when we're alone I miss nothing; it seems awfully rich, almost splendid, you know."

"I'm afraid I don't follow," said Bertie.

They talked desultorily. The wind blew loudly outside, rain chattered on the window-panes, making a sharp, drum-sound, because of the closed, mellow-golden shutters inside. The logs burned slowly, with hot, almost invisible small flames. Bertie seemed uneasy, there were dark circles round his eyes. Isabel, rich with her approaching maternity, leaned looking into the fire. Her hair curled in odd, loose strands, very pleasing to the man. But she had a curious feeling of old woe in her heart, old, timeless night-woe.

"I suppose we're all deficient somewhere," said Bertie.

"I suppose so," said Isabel wearily.

"Damned, sooner or later."

"I don't know," she said, rousing herself. "I feel quite all right, you know. The child coming seems to make me indifferent to everything, just placid. I can't feel that there's anything to trouble about, you know."

"A good thing, I should say," he replied slowly.

"Well, there it is. I suppose it's just Nature. If only I felt I needn't trouble about Maurice, I should be perfectly content—"

"But you feel you must trouble about him?"

"Well—I don't know—" She even resented this much effort.

The evening passed slowly. Isabel looked at the clock. "I say," she said. "It's nearly ten o'clock. Where can Maurice be? I'm sure they're all in bed at the back. Excuse me a moment."

She went out, returning almost immediately.

"It's all shut up and in darkness," she said. "I wonder where he is. He must have gone out to the farm—"

Bertie looked at her.

"I suppose he'll come in," he said.

"I suppose so," she said. "But it's unusual for him to be out now."

"Would you like me to go out and see?"

"Well—if you wouldn't mind. I'd go, but—" She did not want to make the physical effort.

Bertie put on an old overcoat and took a lantern. He went out from the side door. He shrank from the wet and roaring night. Such weather had a nervous effect on him: too much moisture everywhere made him feel almost imbecile. Unwilling, he went through it all. A dog barked violently at him. He peered in all the buildings. At last, as he opened the upper door of a sort of intermediate barn, he heard a grinding noise, and looking in, holding up his lantern, saw Maurice, in his shirtsleeves, standing listening, holding the handle of a turnip-pulper. He had been pulping sweet roots, a pile of which lay dimly heaped in a corner behind him.

"That you, Wernham?" said Maurice, listening.

"No, it's me," said Bertie.

A large, half-wild grey cat was rubbing at Maurice's leg. The blind man stooped to rub its sides. Bertie watched the scene, then unconsciously entered and shut the door behind him. He was in a high sort of barn-place, from which, right and left, ran off the corridors in front of the stalled cattle. He watched the slow, stooping motion of the other man, as he caressed the great cat.

Maurice straightened himself.

"You came to look for me?" he said.

"Isabel was a little uneasy," said Bertie.

"I'll come in. I like messing about doing these jobs."

The cat reared her sinister, feline length against his leg, clawing at his thigh affectionately. He lifted her claws out of his flesh.

"I hope I'm not in your way at all at the Grange here," said Bertie, rather shy and stiff.

"My way? No, not a bit. I'm glad Isabel has somebody to talk to. I'm afraid it's I who am in the way. I know I'm not very lively company. Isabel's all right, don't you think? She's not unhappy, is she?"

"I don't think so."

"What does she say?"

"She says she's very content—only a little troubled about you."

"Why me?"

"Perhaps afraid that you might brood," said Bertie, cautiously.

"She needn't be afraid of that." He continued to caress the flattened grey head of the cat with his fingers.

"What I am a bit afraid of," he resumed, "is that she'll find me a dead weight, always alone with me down here."

"I don't think you need think that," said Bertie, though this was what he feared himself.

"I don't know," said Maurice. "Sometimes I feel it isn't fair that she's saddled with me." Then he dropped his voice curiously. "I say," he asked, secretly struggling, "is my face much disfigured? Do you mind telling me?"

"There is the scar," said Bertie, wondering. "Yes, it is a disfigurement. But more pitiable than shocking."

"A pretty bad scar, though," said Maurice.

"Oh, yes."

There was a pause.

"Sometimes I feel I am horrible," said Maurice, in a low voice, talking as if to himself. And Bertie actually felt a quiver of horror.

"That's nonsense," he said.

Maurice again straightened himself, leaving the cat.

"There's no telling," he said. Then again, in an odd tone, he added: "I don't really know you, do I?"

"Probably not," said Bertie.

"Do you mind if I touch you?"

The lawyer shrank away instinctively. And yet out of very philanthropy, he said, in a small voice: "Not at all."

But he suffered as the blind man stretched out a strong, naked hand to him. Maurice accidentally knocked off Bertie's hat.

"I thought you were taller," he said, starting. Then he laid his hand on Bertie Reid's head, closing the dome of the skull in a soft, firm grasp, gathering it, as it were; then, shifting his grasp and softly closing again, with a fine, close pressure, till he had covered the skull and the face of the smaller man, tracing the brows, and touching the full, closed eyes, touching the small nose and the nostrils, the rough, short moustache, the mouth, the rather strong chin. The hand of the blind man grasped the shoulder, the arm, the hand of the other man. He seemed to take him, in the soft, travelling grasp.

"You seem young," he said quietly, at last.

The lawyer stood almost annihilated, unable to answer.

"Your head seems tender, as if you were young," Maurice repeated. "So do your hands. Touch my eyes, will you?—touch my scar."

Now Bertie quivered with revulsion. Yet he was under the power of the blind man, as if hypnotised. He lifted his hand, and laid the fingers on the scar, on the scarred eyes. Maurice suddenly covered them with his own hand, pressed the fingers of the other man upon his disfigured eye-sockets, trembling in every fibre, and rocking slightly, slowly, from side to side. He remained thus for a minute or more, whilst Bertie stood as if in a swoon, unconscious, imprisoned.

Then suddenly Maurice removed the hand of the other man from his brow, and stood holding it in his own.

"Oh, my God," he said, "we shall know each other now, shan't we? We shall know each other now."

Bertie could not answer. He gazed mute and terror-struck, overcome by his own weakness. He knew he could not answer. He had an unreasonable fear, lest the other man should suddenly destroy him. Whereas Maurice was actually filled with hot, poignant love, the passion of friendship. Perhaps it was this very passion of friendship which Bertie shrank from most.

"We're all right together now, aren't we?" said Maurice. "It's all right now, as long as we live, so far as we're concerned?"

"Yes," said Bertie, trying by any means to escape.

Maurice stood with head lifted, as if listening. The new delicate fulfilment of mortal friendship had come as a revelation and surprise to him, something exquisite and unhoped-for. He seemed to be listening to hear if it were real.

Then he turned for his coat.

"Come," he said, "we'll go to Isabel."

Bertie took the lantern and opened the door. The cat disappeared. The two men went in silence along the causeways. Isabel, as they came, thought their footsteps sounded strange. She looked up pathetically and anxiously for their entrance. There seemed a curious elation about Maurice. Bertie was haggard, with sunken eyes.

"What is it?" she asked.

"We've become friends," said Maurice, standing with his feet apart, like a strange colossus.

"Friends!" re-echoed Isabel. And she looked again at Bertie. He met her eyes with a furtive, haggard look; his eyes were as if glazed with misery.

"I'm so glad," she said, in sheer perplexity.

"Yes," said Maurice.

He was indeed so glad. Isabel took his hand with both hers, and held it fast.

"You'll be happier now, dear," she said.

But she was watching Bertie. She knew that he had one desire—
to escape from this intimacy, this friendship, which had been thrust
upon him. He could not bear it that he had been touched by the
blind man, his insane reserve broken in. He was like a mollusc whose
shell is broken.

James Stephens

A REMARKABLE character who seems to have stepped from the pages of his own books, James Stephens was born in 1882 in Dublin where he spent a boyhood of poverty. George Russell (AE) discovered him working as a clerk in a lawyer's office, and encouraged him in the writing of his highly original poems and stories. The first book to win wide recognition was The Crock of Gold (1912), and since then his works have delighted an ever-increasing audience. On the occasion of his first lecture tour to America in 1925, Burton Rascoe wrote a vivid impression of his exciting personality: "Never have I seen a man who impressed me as being so easy, free and natural, so un-tamed. . . ."

The imagination of James Stephens is wild, but unerring. There is deep understanding in his whimsicality, and what may at first seem a sportive fancy will suddenly expose stupidity and cruelty with sardonic suddenness. Of his poetry Louis Untermyer has written "No fresher or more brightly vigorous imagination has come out of Ireland since J. M. Synge." The tribute applies as well to his stories, which include Here Are Ladies (1913), Irish Fairy Tales (1920), and Etched in Moonlight (1928).

James Stephens is an ardent lover of Irish literature and of the Gaelic tongue. He wants, he says, to contribute to Ireland "a new mythology to take the place of the threadbare mythology of Greece and Rome."

THE HORSES *

James Stephens

HE WAS TALL and she was short. He was bulky, promising to be fat. She was thin, and, with a paring here and there, would have been skinny. His face was sternly resolute, solemn indeed, hers was prim, and primness is the most everlasting, indestructible trait of humanity. It can outface the Sphinx. It is destructible only by death. Whoever has married a prim woman must hand over his breeches and his purse, he will collect postage stamps in his old age, he will twiddle his thumbs and smile when the visitor asks him a question, he will grow to dislike beer, and will admit and assert that a man's place is the home—these things come to pass as surely as the procession of the seasons.

It may be asked why he had married her, and it would be difficult to find an answer to that question. The same query might be put to almost any couple, for (and it is possibly right that it should be so) we do not marry by mathematics, but by some extraordinary attraction which is neither entirely sexual nor mental. Something other than these, something as yet uncharted by psychology, is the determining factor. It may be that the universal, strange chemistry of nature, planning granite and twig, ant and onion, is also ordering us more imperatively and more secretly than we are aware.

He had always been a hasty creature. He never had any brains, and had never felt the lack of them. He was one of those men who are called "strong," because of their imperfect control over themselves. His appetites and mental states ruled him. He was impatient of any restraint; whatever he wanted to do he wanted urgently to do and would touch no alternatives. He had the robust good humour which will cheerfully forgive you to-morrow for the wrongs he has done you to-day. He bore no malice to any one on earth except those who took their medicine badly. Meek people got on very well with him because they behaved themselves, but he did not like them to believe they would inherit the earth.

Some people marry because other people have done so. It is in the air, like clothing and art and not eating with a knife. He, of course, got married because he wanted to, and the singular part of it was that he did not mate with a meek woman. Perhaps he thought she was

* From *Here Are Ladies* by James Stephens. The Macmillan Company, 1913. Reprinted by permission of The Macmillan Company, publishers.

meek, for before marriage there is a habit of deference on both sides which is misleading and sometimes troublesome.

From the beginning of their marriage he had fought against his wife with steadiness and even ferocity. Scarcely had they been wed when her gently-repressive hand was laid upon him, and, like a startled horse, he bounded at the touch into freedom—that is, as far as the limits of the matrimonial rope would permit. Of course he came back again—there was the rope, and the unfailing, untiring hand easing him to the way he was wanted to go.

There was no fighting against that. Or, at least, it did not seem that fighting was any use. One may punch a bag, but the bag does not mind, and at last one grows weary of unproductive quarrelling. One shrugs one's shoulders, settles to the collar, and accepts whatever destiny the gods, in their wisdom, have ordained. Is life the anvil upon which the gods beat out their will? It is not so. The anvil is matter, the will of the gods is life itself, urging through whatever torment to some identity which it can only surmise or hope for; and the one order to life is that it shall not cease to rebel until it has ceased to live; when, perhaps, it can take up the shaping struggle in some other form or some other place.

But he had almost given in. Practically he had bowed to the new order. Domestic habits were settling about him thick as cobwebs, and as clinging. His feet were wiped on the mat when he came in. His hat was hung on the orthodox projection. His kiss was given at the stated time, and lasted for the regulation period. The chimney-corner claimed him and got him. The window was his outlook on life. Beyond the hall door were foreign lands inhabited by people who were no longer of his kind. The cat and the canary, these were his familiars, and his wife was rapidly becoming his friend.

Once a day he trod solemnly forth on the designated walk—

"Be back before one o'clock," said the voice of kind authority, "lunch will be ready."

"Won't you be back before two?" said that voice, "the lawn has to be rolled."

"Don't stay out after three," the voice entreated, "we are going to visit Aunt Kate."

And at one and two and three o'clock he paced urgently wifeward. He ate the lunch that was punctually ready. He rolled the inevitable lawn. He trod sturdily to meet the Aunt Kate and did not quail, and then he went home again. One climbed to bed at ten o'clock, one was gently spoken to until eleven o'clock, and then one went to sleep.

On a day she entrusted him with a sum of money, and requested that he should go down to the town and pay at certain shops certain bills, the details whereof she furnished to him on paper.

"Be back before three o'clock," said the good lady, "for the Fegans are coming to tea. You need not take your umbrella, it won't rain, and you ought to leave your pipe behind, it doesn't look nice. Bring some cigarettes instead, and your walking-stick if you like, and be sure to be back before three."

He pressed his pipe into a thing on the wall which was meant for pipes, put his cigarette-case into his pocket, and took his walking-stick in his hand.

"You did not kiss me good-bye," said she gently.

So he returned and did that, and then he went out.

It was a delicious day. The sun was shining with all its might. One could see that it liked shining, and hoped everybody enjoyed its art. If there were birds about anywhere it is certain they were singing. In this suburb, however, there were only sparrows, but they hopped and flew, and flew and hopped, and cocked their heads sideways and chirped something cheerful, but possibly rude, as one passed. They were busy to the full extent of their beings, playing innocent games with happy little flies, and there was not one worry among a thousand of them.

There was a cat lying on a hot window-ledge. She was looking drowsily at the sparrows, and any one could see that she loved them and wished them well.

There was a dog stretched across a doorway. He was very quiet, but he was not in the least bored. He was taking a sun bath, and he was watching the cat. So steadily did he observe her that one discerned at a glance he was her friend, and would protect her at any cost.

There was a small boy who held in his left hand a tin can and a piece of string. With his right hand he was making affectionate gestures to the dog. He loved playing with animals, and he always rewarded their trust in him.

Our traveller paced slowly onwards, looking at his feet as he went. He noticed with a little dismay that he could not see as much of his legs as he thought he should see. There was a slight but nicely-shaped curve between him and his past—

"I am getting fat," said he to himself, and the reflection carried him back to the morning mirror—

"I am getting a bit bald, too," said he, and a quiet sadness took possession of him.

But he reassured himself. One does get fat. "Everyone gets fat," said he, "after he gets married." He reviewed his friends and acquaintances, and found that this was true, and he bowed before an immutable decree.

"One does get bald," quoth he. "Everybody gets bald. The wisest people in the world lose their hair. Kings and generals, rich people and poor people, they are all bald! It is not a disgrace," said he; and he trod soberly forward in the sunshine.

A young man caught up on him from behind, and strode past. He was whistling. His coat-tails were lifted and his hands were thrust in his pockets. His elbows jerked to left and right as he marched.

"A fellow oughtn't to swagger about like that," said our traveller. "What does he want to tuck up his coat for, anyhow? It's not decent," said he in a low voice. "It makes people laugh," said he.

A girl came out of a shop near by and paced down in their direction. She looked at the young man as they passed, and then she turned again, a glance, no more, and looked after him without stopping her pace. She came on. She had no pockets to stick her hands in, but she also was swaggering. There was a left and right movement of her shoulders, an impetus and retreat of her hips. Something very strong and yet reticent about her surging body. She passed the traveller and went down the road.

"She did not look at me," said he, and his mind folded its hands across its stomach, and sat down, while he went forward in the sunlight to do his errands.

He stopped to light a cigarette, and stood for a few minutes watching the blue smoke drifting and thinning away on the air. While he stood a man drove up with a horse and car. The car was laden with groceries—packets of somebody's tea, boxes of somebody's chocolate, bottles of beer and of mineral water, tins of boot blacking, and parcels of soap; confectionery, and tinned fish, cheese, macaroni, and jam.

The man was beating the horse as he approached, and the traveller looked at them both through a wreath of smoke.

"I wonder," said he, "why that man beats his horse?"

The driver was sitting at ease. He was not angry. He was not impatient. There was nothing the matter with him at all. But he was steadily beating the horse; not harshly, gently in truth. He beat the horse without ill-will, almost without knowing he was doing it. It was a sort of wrist exercise. A quick, delicate twitch of the whip that caught the animal under the belly, always in the same place. It was very skilful, but the driver was so proficient in his art that one wondered why he had to practice at it any longer. And the horse did not make any objection! Not even with his ears; they lay back to his mane as he jogged steadily forward in the sunlight. His hooves were shod with iron, but they moved with an unfaltering, humble regularity. His mouth was filled with great, yellow teeth, but he kept his mouth shut, and one could not see them. He did not increase or diminish his pace under the lash; he jogged onwards, and did not seem to mind it.

The reins were jerked suddenly, and the horse turned into the path and stopped, and when he stood he was not any quieter than when he had been moving. He did not raise his head or whisk his tail. He did not move his ears to the sounds behind and on either side of him. He did not paw and fumble with his feet. There was a swarm of flies about his head; they moved along from the point of his nose to the top of his forehead, but mostly they clustered in black, obscene patches about his eyes, and through these patches his eyes looked out with a strange patience, a strange mildness. He was stating a fact over and over to himself, and he could not think of anything else—

"There are no longer any meadows in the world," said he. "They came in the night and took away the green meadows, and the horses do not know what to do." . . . Horse! Horse! Little horse! . . . You do not believe me. There are those who have no whips. There are children who would love to lift you in their arms and stroke your head. . . .

The driver came again, he mounted to his seat, and the horse turned carefully and trotted away.

The man with the cigarette looked after them for a few minutes, and then he also turned carefully to do his errands.

He reached the Railway Station and peered in at the clock. There were some men in uniform striding busily about. Three or four people were moving up the steps towards the ticket office. A raggedy man shook a newspaper in his face, paused for half a second, and fled away bawling his news. A red-faced woman pushed hastily past him. She was carrying a big basket and a big baby. She was terribly engrossed by both, and he wondered if she had to drop one which of them it would be. A short, stout, elderly man was hoisting himself and a great leather portmanteau by easy stages up the steps. He was very determined. He bristled at everybody as at an enemy. He regarded inanimate nature as if he was daring it to move. It would not be easy to make that man miss a train. A young lady trod softly up the steps. She draped snowy garments about her, but her ankles rebelled: whoever looked quickly saw them once, and then she spoke very severely to them, and they hid themselves. It was plain that she could scarcely control them, and that they would escape again when she wasn't looking. A young man bounded up the steps; he was too late to see them, and he looked as if he knew it. He stared angrily at the girl, but she lifted her chin slightly and refused to admit that he was alive. A very small boy was trying to push a large india-rubber ball into his mouth, but his mouth was not big enough to hold it, and he wept because of his limitations. He was towed along by his sister, a girl so tall that one might say her legs reached to heaven, and maybe they did.

He looked again at the hour. It was one minute to two o'clock; and then something happened. The whole white world became red. The oldest seas in the world went suddenly lashing into storm. An ocean of blood thundered into his head, and the noise of that primitive flood, roaring from what prehistoric gulfs, deafened him at an instant. The waves whirled his feet from under him. He went foaming up the steps, was swept violently into the ticket office, and was swirled away like a bobbing cork into the train. A guard tried to stop him, for the train was already taking its pace, but one cannot keep out the tide with a ticket-puncher. The guard was overwhelmed, caught in the backwash, and swirled somewhere, anywhere, out of sight and knowledge. The train gathered speed, went flying out of the station into the blazing sunlight, picked up its heels and ran, and ran, and ran; the wind leaped by the carriage window, shrieking with laughter; the wide fields danced with each other, shouting aloud.

"The horses are coming again to the green meadows. Make way, make way for the great, wild horses!"

And the trees went leaping from horizon to horizon shrieking and shrieking the news.

A. E. Coppard

"THE MOST original and provocative English writer of short stories at the present moment" says a critic of A. E. Coppard in the last edition of the Encyclopedia Britannica, and there is no reason to qualify the estimate. His stories are full-bodied and tenacious, holding long in the memory. His love for the English countryside, and his unpretentious, sure understanding of its people is like Thomas Hardy's, but his manner, high-spirited and diverting, suggests nothing of Hardy's heavy fatalism. Ford Madox Ford has remarked: "Mr. Coppard is almost the first English writer to get into English prose the peculiar quality of English lyric poetry." His statement is discerning, and inevitably recalls another name in Coppard's literary kinship —George Meredith. But comparisons can not convey his qualities; only his stories can.

A. E. Coppard came to writing with a talent matured and disciplined. He published his first book, Adam and Eve and Pinch Me (1921) at the age of forty-one. The first production of the Golden Cockerel Press, a communal society of craftsmen, this collection of stories found a quick response. The next year Coppard published his first volume of verse, Hips and Haws. Since then many other poems and stories have followed—among them, Collected Poems (1928); The Black Dog (1923); Fishmonger's Fiddle (1925); Silver Circus (1928); and Nixey's Harlequin (1931).

A. E. Coppard was born at Folkstone, England, in 1878. He now lives at Walberswick in Suffolk.

THE HANDSOME LADY *

A. E. Coppard

Towards the close of the Nineteenth century the parish of Tull was a genial but angular hamlet hung out on the north side of a midland hill, with scarcely renown enough to get itself marked on a map. Its felicities, whatever they might be, lay some miles distant from a railway station, and so were seldom regarded, being neither boasted of by the inhabitants nor visited by strangers.

But here as elsewhere people were born and, as unusual, inconspicuously born. John Pettigrove made a note of them then, and when people came in their turns to die Pettigrove made a note of that too, for he was the district registrar. In between whiles, like fish in a pond, they were immersed in labour until the Divine Angler hooked them to the bank, and then, as is the custom, they were conspicuously buried and laboured presumably no more.

The registrar was perhaps the one person who had love and praise for the simple place. He was born and bred in Tull, he had never left Tull, and at forty years of age was as firmly attached to it as the black clock to the tower of Tull Church, which never recorded anything but twenty minutes past four. His wife Carrie, a delicate woman, was also satisfied with Tull, but as she owned two or three small pieces of house property there her fancy may not have been entirely beyond suspicion; possession, as you might say, being nine points of the prejudice just as it is of the law. A year or two after their marriage Carrie began to suffer from a complication of ailments that turned her into a permanent invalid; she was seldom seen out of the house and under her misfortunes she peaked and pined, she was troublesome, there was no pleasing her. If Pettigrove went about unshaven she was vexed; it was unclean, it was lazy, disgusting; but when he once appeared with his moustache shaven off she was exceedingly angry; it was scandalous, it was shameful, maddening. There is no pleasing some women—what is a man to do? When he began to let it grow again and encouraged a beard she was more tyrannical than ever.

The grey church was small and looked shrunken, as if it had sagged; it seemed to stoop down upon the green yard, but the stones and mounds, the cypress and holly, the strangely faded blue of a door

* From *The Black Dog and Other Stories* by A. E. Coppard. Alfred A. Knopf, Inc., 1923. Reprinted by permission of the author.

that led through the churchyard wall to the mansion of the vicar, were beautiful without pretence, and though as often as not the parson's goats used to graze among the graves and had been known to follow him into the nave, there was about the ground, the indulgent dimness under the trees, and the tower with its unmoving clock, the very delicacy of solitude. It inspired compassion and not cynicism as, peering as it were through the glass of antiquity, the stranger gazed upon its mortal register. In its peace, its beauty, and its age, all those pious records and hopes inscribed upon its stones seemed not uttered in pride nor all in vain. But to speak truth the church's grace was partly the achievement of its lofty situation. A road climbing up from sloping fields turned abruptly and traversed the village, sidling up to the church; there, having apparently satisfied some itch of curiosity, it turned abruptly again and trundled back another way into that northern prospect of farms and forest that lay in the direction of Whitewater Copse, Hangman's Corner and One O'clock.

It was that prospect which most delighted Pettigrove, for he was a simple-minded countryman full of ambling content. Not even the church allured him so much, for though it pleased him and was just at his own threshold, he never entered it at all. Once upon a time there had been talk of him joining the church choir, for he had a pleasant singing voice, but he would not go.

"It's flying in the face of Providence," cried his exasperated wife— her mind, too, was a falsetto one: "You've as strong a voice as anyone in Tull, in fact stronger, not that that is saying much, for Tull air don't seem good for songsters if you may judge by that choir. The air is too thick maybe, I can't say, it certainly oppresses my own chest, or perhaps it's too thin, I don't thrive on it myself; but you've the strength and it would do you credit; you'd be a credit to yourself and it would be a credit to me. But that won't move you! I can't tell what you'd be at; a drunken man 'ull get sober again, but a fool . . . well, there!"

John, unwilling to be a credit, would mumble an objection to being tied down to that sort of thing. That was just like him, no spontaneity, no tidiness in his mind. Whenever he addressed himself to any discussion he had, as you might say, to tuck up his intellectual sleeves, give a hitch to his argumentative trousers. So he went on singing, just when he had a mind to it, old country songs, for he disliked what he called "gimcrack ballads about buzzums and roses."

Pettigrove's occupation dealt with the extreme features of existence, but he himself had no extreme notions. He was a good medium type of man mentally and something more than that physically, but nevertheless he was a disappointment to his wife—he never gave her any opportunity to shine by his reflected light. She had nurtured foolish ideas of him first as a figure of romance, then of some social importance; he ought to be a parish councillor or develop eminence somehow in their way of life. But John was nothing like this, he did not develop, or shine, or offer counsel, he was just a big, solid, happy man. There were times when his childless wife hated every ounce and sign of him, when his fair clipped beard and hair, which she declared were the colour of jute, and his stolidity, sickened her.

"I do my duty by him and, please God, I'll continue to do it. I'm a humble woman and easily satisfied. An afflicted woman has no chance, no chance at all," she said. After twelve years of wedded life Pettigrove sometimes vaguely wondered what it would have been like not to have married anybody.

One Michaelmas a small house belonging to Mrs. Pettigrove was let to a widow from Eastbourne. Mrs. Cronshaw was a fine upstanding woman, gracefully grave and, as the neighbours said, clean as a pink. For several evenings after she had taken possession of the house Pettigrove, who was a very handy sort of man, worked upon some alterations to her garden, and at the end of the third or fourth evening she had invited him into her bower to sip a glass of some cordial, and she thanked him for his labours.

"Not at all, Mrs. Cronshaw." And he drank to her very good fortune. Just that and no more.

The next evening she did the same, and the very next evening to that again. And so it was not long before they spoke of themselves to each other, turn and turn about as you might say. She was the widow of an ironmonger who had died two years before, and the ironmonger's very astute brother had given her an annuity in exchange for her interest in the business. Without family and with few friends she had been lonely.

"But Tull is such a hearty place," she said. "It's beautiful. One might forget to be lonely."

"Be sure of that," commented Pettigrove. They had the light of two candles and a blazing fire. She grew kind and more communicative to him; a strangely, disturbingly attractive woman, dark, with an abundance of well-dressed hair and a figure of charm. She had carpet all over her floor; nobody else in Tull dreamed of such a thing. She did not cover her old dark table with a cloth as everybody else habitually did. The pictures on the wall were real, and the black-lined sofa had cushions on it of violet silk which she sometimes actually sat upon. There was a dainty dresser with china and things, a bureau, and a tall clock that told the exact time. But there was no music, music made her melancholy. In Pettigrove's home there were things like these but they were not the same. His bureau was jammed in a corner with flowerpots upon its top; his pictures comprised two photo prints of a public park in Swansea—his wife had bought them at an auction sale. Their dresser was a cumbersome thing with knobs and hooks and jars and bottles, and the tall clock never chimed the hours. The very armchairs at Mrs. Cronshaw's were wells of such solid comfort that it made him feel uncomfortable to use them.

"Ah, I should like to be sure of it!" she continued. "I have not found kindly people in the cities—they do not even seem to notice a fine day!—I have not found them anywhere, so why should they be in Tull? You are a wise man, tell me, is Tull the exception?"

"Yes, Mrs. Cronshaw. You must come and visit us whenever you've a mind to; have no fear of loneliness."

"Yes, I will come and visit you," she declared, "soon, I will."

"That's right, you must visit us."

"Yes, soon, I must."

But weeks passed over and the widow did not keep her promise although she only lived a furlong from his door. Pettigrove made no further invitation for he found excuses on many evenings to visit her. It was easy to see that she did not care for his wife, and he did not mind this for neither did he care for her now. The old wish that he had never been married crept back into his mind, a sly, unsavoury visitant; it was complicated by a thought that his wife might not live long, a dark, shameful thought that nevertheless trembled into hope. So on many of the long winter evenings, while his wife dozed in her bed, he sat in the widow's room talking of things that were strange and agreeable. She could neither understand nor quite forgive his parochialism; this was sweet flattery to him. He had scarcely ever set foot outside a ten-mile radius of Tull, but he was an intelligent man, and all her discourse was of things he could perfectly understand! For the first time in his life Pettigrove found himself lamenting the dullness of existence. He tried to suppress this tendency, but words would come and he was distressed. He had always been in love with things that lasted, that had stability, that gave him a recognition and guidance, but now his feelings were flickering like grass in a gale.

"How strange that is," she said, when he told her this, "we seem to have exchanged our feelings. I am happy here, but I know that dark thought, yes, that life is a dull journey on which the mind searches for variety, unvarying variety."

"But what for?" he cried.

"It is constantly seeking change."

"But for why? It seems like treachery to life."

"It may be so, but if you seek, you find."

"What?"

"Whatever you are seeking."

"What am I seeking?"

"Not to know that is the blackest treachery to life. We are growing old," she added inconsequently, stretching her hands to the fire. She wore black silk mittens.

"Perhaps that's it," he allowed, with a laugh. "Childhood's best."

"Surely not," she protested.

"Ah, but I was gay enough then. I'm not a religious man, you know —and perhaps that's the reason—but however—I can remember things of great joy and pleasure then."

And it seemed from his recollections that not the least pleasant and persistent was his memory of the chapel, a Baptist hall long since closed and decayed, to which his mother had sent him on Sunday afternoons. It was a plain, tough, little tabernacle, with benches of deal, plain deal, very hard, covered with a clear varnish that smelled pleasant. The platform and its railing, the teacher's desk, the pulpit were all of deal, the plainest deal, very hard and all covered with the clear varnish that smelled very pleasant. And somehow the creed and the teacher and the attendants were like that too, all plain and hard, covered with a varnish that was pleasant. But there was a way in which the afternoon sun beamed through the cheap windows that lit up for young Pettigrove an everlasting light. There were hymns with tunes that he hoped would be sung in Paradise. The texts, the stories, the admonitions of the teachers, were vivid and evidently beautiful in his memory. Best of all was the privilege of borrowing a book at the end of school time—*Pilgrim's Progress* or *Uncle Tom's Cabin*.

For a while his recollections restored him to cheerfulness, but his dullness soon overcame him again.

"I have been content all my life. Never was a man more content. And now! It's treachery if you like. My faith's gone, content gone, for why?"

He rose to go, and as he paused at the door to bid her good-night she took his hand and softly and tenderly said: "Why are you depressed? Don't be so. Life is not dull, it is only momentarily unkind."

"Ah, I'll get used to it."

"John Pettigrove, you must never get used to dullness, I forbid you."

"But I thought Tull was beautiful," he said as he paused upon the doorsill. "I thought Tull was beautiful. . . ."

"Until I came?" It was so softly uttered and she closed the door so quickly upon him. They called "Good-night, good-night" to each other through the door.

He went away through the village, his mind streaming with strange emotions. He exulted, and yet he feared for himself and for the widow, but he could not summon from the depths of his mind what it was he feared. He passed a woman in the darkness who, perhaps mistaking him for another, said "Good-night, my love."

The next morning he sat in the kitchen after breakfast. It wanted but a few days to Christmas. There was no frost in the air; the wind roared, but the day, though grey, was not gloomy; only the man was gloomy.

"Nothing ever happens," he murmured. "True, but what would you want to happen?"

Out in the scullery a village girl was washing dishes; as she rattled the ware she hummed a song. From his back window Pettigrove could see a barn in a field, two broken gates, a pile of logs, faggots, and a single pollarded willow whose head was strangled under a hat of ivy. Beside a barley stack was a goose with a crooked neck; it stood sulking. High aloft in the sky thousands of blown rooks wrangled like lost men. And Pettigrove vowed he would go no more to the widow—not for a while. Something inside him kept asking, Why not? And he as quickly replied to himself: "You know, you know. You'll find it all in God-a-mighty's own commandments. Stick to them, you can't do more—at least, you might, but what would be the good?"

So that evening he went along to the Christmas lottery held in a vast barn, dimly lit and smelling of vermin. A rope hung over each of its two giant beams, dangling smoky lanterns. There was a crowd of men and boys inspecting the prizes in the gloomy corners, a pig sulking in a pen of hurdles, sacks of wheat, live hens in coops, a row of dead hares hung on the rail of a wagon. Amid silence a man plunged his hand into a corn measure and drew forth a numbered ticket; another man drew from a similar measure a blank ticket or a prize ticket. Each time a prize was drawn a hum of interest spread through the onlookers, but when the chief prize, the fat pig, was drawn against number seventy-nine there was agitation, excitement even.

"Who be it?" cried several. "Who be number seventy-nine for the fat pig?"

A man consulted a list and said doubtfully: "Miss Subey Jones— who be she?"

No one seemed to know until a husky alto voice from a corner piped: "I know her. She's from Shottsford way, over by Squire Marchand's."

"Oh," murmured the disappointed men; the husky voice continued: "Day afore yesterday she hung herself."

For a few seconds there was a pained silence, until a powerful voice cried: "It's a mortal shame, chaps."

The ceremony proceeded until all the tickets were drawn and all the prizes won and distributed. The cackling hens were seized from the pens by their legs and handed upside down to their new owners. The pig was bundled squealing into a sack. Bags of wheat were shouldered and the white-bellied hares were held up to the light. Everybody was animated and chattered loudly.

"I had number thirty in the big chance and I won nothing. And I had number thirty-one in the little chance and I won a duck. Number thirty-one was my number, and number thirty in the big draw; I won nothing in that, but in the little draw I won a duck. Well, there's flesh for you."

Some of those who had won hens held them out to a white-faced youth who smoked a large rank pipe; he took each fowl quietly by the neck and twisted it till it died. A few small feathers stuck to his hands or wavered to the floor, and even after the bird was dead and carried away it continued slowly and vaguely to flap its big wings and scatter its lorn feathers.

Pettigrove spent most of the next day in the forest plantation south of Tull Great Wood, where a few chains of soil had been cultivated and reserved for seedlings, trees of larch and pine no bigger than potted geraniums, groves of oaks with stems slender as a cockerel's leg and most of the stiff brown leaves still clinging to the famished twigs; or sycamores, thin but tall, flourishing in a mat of their own dropped foliage that was the colour of butter fringed with blood and stained with black gouts like a child's copy-book. It was a toy forest, dense enough for the lair of a beast, and dim enough for an anchorite's meditations, but a dog could leap over it, and a boy could stand amid its growth and look like Gulliver in Lilliput.

"May I go into the wood?" a voice called to Pettigrove. Looking sharply up he saw Mrs. Cronshaw, clad in a long dark blue cloak with a fur necklet, a grey velvet hat trimmed with a pigeon's wing confining her luxuriant hair.

"Ah, you may," he said, stalking to her side, "but you'd best not, 'tis a heavy marshy soil within and the ways are stabbled by the hunters' horses. Better keep out till summer comes, then 'tis dry and pleasant-like."

She sat down awkwardly on a heap of faggots, her feet turned slightly inwards, but her cheeks were dainty pink in the cold air. What a smart lady! He stood telling her things about the wood, its birds and foxes; deep in the heart of it all was a lovely open space covered with the greenest grass and a hawthorn tree in the middle of that. It bloomed in spring with heavy creamy blossom. No, he had never seen any fairies there. Come to that, he did not expect to, he had never thought of it.

"But there are fairies, you know," cried the widow. "O yes, in old times, I mean very old times, before the Romans, in fact before Abraham, Isaac, and Jacob then, the Mother of the earth had a big family, thousands, something like the old woman who lived in a shoe she was. And one day God sent word to say he was coming to visit her. Well, then! She was so excited—the Mother of the earth—that she made a great to do, you may be sure, and after she had made her house sparkle with cleanliness and had baked a great big pie she began to wash her children. All of a sudden she heard the trumpets blow—God was just a-coming! So as she hadn't got time to finish them all, she hid those unwashed ones away out of sight, and bade them to remain there and make no noise or she would be angry and punish them. But you can't conceal anything from the King of All and He knew of those hidden children, and he caused them to be hidden from mortal eyes for ever, and they are the fairies, O yes!"

"No, nothing can be concealed," Pettigrove admitted in his slow grave fashion, "murder will out, as they say, but that's a tough morsel if you're going to swallow it all."

"But I like to believe in those things I wish were true."

"Ah, so, yes," said Pettigrove.

It was an afternoon of damp squally blusters, uncheering, with slaty sky; the air itself seemed slaty, and though it had every opportunity and invitation to fall, the rain, with strange perversity, held off. In the oddest corners of the sky, north and east, a miraculous glow could be seen, as if the sun in a moment of aberration had determined to set just then and just there. The wind made a long noise in the sky, the smell of earth rose about them, of timber and of dead leaves; except for rooks, or a wren cockering itself in a bush, no birds were to be seen.

Letting his spade fall Pettigrove sat down beside the widow and kissed her. She blushed red as a cherry and he got up quickly.

"I ought not to ha' done it, I ought not to ha' done that, Mrs. Cronshaw!"

"Caroline!" said she, smiling the correction at him.

"Is that your name?" He sat down by her again. "Why, it is the same as my wife's."

And Caroline said "Humph! You're a strange man, but you are wise and good. Tell me, does she understand you?"

"What is there to understand? We are wed and we are faithful to each other, I can take my oath on that to God or man."

"Yes, yes, but what is faith—without love between you? You see? You have long since broken your vows to love and cherish, understand that, you have broken them in half."

She had picked up a stick and was drawing patterns of cubes and stars in the soil.

"But what is to be done, Caroline? Life is good, but there is good living and there is bad living, there is fire and there is water. It is strange what the Almighty permits to happen."

A slow-speaking man; scrupulous of thought and speech he weighed each idea before its delivery as carefully as a tobacconist weighs an ounce of tobacco.

"Have some cake?" said Caroline, drawing a package from a pocket. "Will you have a piece . . . John?"

She seemed to be on the point of laughing aloud at him. He took the fragment of cake but he did not eat it as she did. He held it between finger and thumb and stared at it.

"It's strange how a man lets his tongue wag now and again as if he'd got the universe stuck on the end of a common fork."

"Or at the end of a knitting needle, yes, I know," laughed Caroline, brushing the crumbs from her lap. Then she bent her head, patted her lips, and regurgitated with a gesture of apology—just like a lady. "But what are you saying? If there is love between you there is faithfulness, if there is no love there is no fidelity."

He bit a mouthful off the cake at last.

"Maybe true, but you must have respect for the beliefs of others. . . ."

"How can you if they don't fit in with your own?"

"Or there is sorrow." He bolted the rest of his cake. "O you are right, I daresay, Caroline, no doubt; it's right, I know, but is it reasonable?"

"There are afflictions," she said, "which time will cure, so they don't matter; but there are others which time only aggravates, so what can we do? I daresay it's different with a man, but a woman, you know, grasps at what she wants. That sounds reasonable, but you don't think it's right?"

In the cold whistling sky a patch of sunset had now begun to settle in its proper quarter, but as frigid and unconvincing as a stage fireplace. Pettigrove sat with his great hands clasped between his knees. Perhaps she grew tired of watching the back of him; she rose to go, but she said gently enough: "Come in to-night, I want to tell you something."

"I will, Caroline."

Later, when he reached home, he found two little nieces had arrived, children of some relatives who lived a dozen miles away. A passing farmer had dropped them at Tull; their parents were coming a day later to spend Christmas with the Pettigroves.

They sat up in his wife's room after tea, for Carrie left her bed only for an hour or two at noon. She dozed against her pillows, a brown shawl covering her shoulders, while the two children played by the hearth. Pettigrove sat silent, gazing in the fire.

"What a racket you are making, Polly and Jane!" quavered Carrie.

The little girls thereupon ceased their sporting and took a picture book to the hearthrug where they examined it in awed silence by the firelight. After some minutes the invalid called out: "Don't make such a noise turning over all them leaves."

Polly made a grimace and little Jane said: "We are looking at the pictures."

"Well," snapped Mrs. Pettigrove, "why can't you keep to the one page!"

John sat by the fire vowing to himself that he would not go along to the widow, and in the very act of vowing he got up and began putting on his coat.

"Are you going out, John?"

"There's a window catch to put right along at Mrs. Cronshaw's," he said. At other times it had been a pump to mend, a door latch to adjust, or a jamb to ease.

"I never knew things to go like it before—I can't understand it," his wife commented. "What with windows and doors and pumps and bannisters anyone would think the house had got the rot. It's done for the purpose, or my name's not what it is."

"It won't take long," he said as he went.

The wind had fallen away, but the sky, though clearer, had a dull opaque mean appearance, and the risen moon, without glow, without refulgence, was like a brass-headed nail stuck in a kitchen wall.

The yellow blind at the widow's cot was drawn down and the candles within cast upon the blind a slanting image of the birdcage hanging at the window; a fat dapper bird appeared to be snoozing upon its rod; a tiny square was probably a lump of sugar; the glass well must have been half full of water, it glistened and twinkled on the blind. The shadowy bird shifted one foot, then the other, and just opened its beak as Pettigrove tapped at the door.

They did not converse very easily, there was constraint between them, Pettigrove's simple mind had a twinge of guilt.

"Will you take lime juice or cocoa?" asked the widow, and he said: "Cocoa."

"Little or large?"

And he said: "Large."

While they sat sipping the cocoa Caroline began: "Well, I am going away, you know. No, not for good, just a short while, for Christmas only, or very little longer. I must go."

She nestled her blue shawl more snugly round her shoulders. A cough seemed to trouble her. "There are things you can't put on one side for ever. . . ."

"Even if they don't fit in with your own ideas!" he said slyly.

"Yes, even then."

He put down his cup and took both her hands in his own. "How long?"

"Not long, not very long, not long enough. . . ."

"Enough for what?" He broke up her hesitation. "For me to forget you? No, no, not in the fifty-two weeks of the whole world of time."

"I did want to stay here," she said, "and see all the funny things country people do now." She was rather vague about those funny things. "Carols, mumming, visiting; go to church on Christmas morning, though how I should get past those dreadful goats, I don't know; why are they always in the churchyard?"

"Teasy creatures they are! Followed parson into service one Sunday, indeed, ah! one of 'em did. Jumped up in his pulpit, too, so 'tis said. But when are you coming back?"

She told him it was a little uncertain, she was not sure, she could not say, it was a little uncertain.

"In a week, maybe?"

Yes, a week; but perhaps it would be longer, she could not say, it was uncertain.

"So. Well, all right then, I shall watch for you."

"Yes, watch for me."

They gave each other good wishes and said good-bye in the little dark porch. The shadowy bird on the blind stood up and shrugged itself. Pettigrove's stay had scarcely lasted an hour, but in that time the moon had gone, the sky had cleared, and in its ravishing darkness the stars almost crackled, so fierce was their mysterious perturbation. The village man felt Caroline's arms about him and her lips against his mouth as she whispered a "God bless you." He turned away home, dazed, entranced, he did not heed the stars. In the darkness a knacker's cart trotted past him with a dim lantern swinging at its tail and the driver bawling a song. In the keen air the odour from the dead horse sickened him.

Pettigrove passed Christmas gaily enough with his kindred, and even his wife indulged in brief gaieties. Her cousin was one of those men full of affable disagreements; an attitude rather than an activity of mind. He had a curious face resembling an owl's except in its colour (which was pink) and in its tiny black moustache curling downwards like a dark ring under his nose. If Pettigrove remarked upon a fine sunset the cousin scoffed, scoffed benignantly; there was a sunset every day, wasn't there?—common as grass, weren't they? As for the farming hereabouts, nothing particular in it was there? The scenery was, well, it was just scenery, a few hills, a few woods, plenty of grass fields. No special suitability of soil for any crop; corn would be just average, wasn't that so? And the roots, well, on his farm at home he could show mangolds as big as young porkers, forty to the cartload, or thereabouts. There weren't no farmers round here making a fortune, he'd be bound, and as for their birds, he should think they lived on rook pie.

Pettigrove submitted that none of the Tull farmers looked much the worse for farming.

"Well, come," said the other, "I hear your workhouses be middling full. Now an old neighbor of mine, old Frank Stinsgrove, was a man as *could* farm, any mortal thing. He wouldn't have looked at this land, not at a crown an acre, and he was a man as *could* farm, any mortal thing, oranges and lemons if he'd a mind to it. What a head that man had, God bless, his brain was stuffed! Full!! He'd declare black was white, and what's more he could prove it. I like a man like that."

The cousin's wife was a vast woman, shaped like a cottage loaf. For some reason she clung to her stays: it could not be to disguise or curb her bulk, for they merely put a gloss upon it. You could only view her as a dimension, think of her as a circumference, and wonder grimly what she looked like when she prepared for the bath. She devoured turkey and pig griskin with such audible voracity that her husband declared that he would soon be compelled to wear corks in his earholes at meal times, yes, the same as they did in the artillery. She was quite unperturbed by this even when little Jane giggled, and she avowed that good food was a great enjoyment to her.

"O 'tis a good thing and a grand thing, but take that child now," said her father. Resting his elbow on the table he indicated with his fork the diminutive Jane; upon the fork hung a portion of meat large enough to half-sole a lady's shoe. "She's just the reverse, she eats as soft as a fly, a spillikin a day, and not a mite more; no, very dainty is our Jane." Here he swallowed the meat and treated four promising potatoes with very great savagery. "Do you know our Jane is going to marry a house-painter, yah, a house painter, or is it a coach-painter? 'Tis smooth and gentle work, she says, not like rough farmers or chaps that knock things pretty hard, smiths and carpenters, you know. O Lord! eight years old, would you believe it? The spillikin! John, this griskin's a lovely bit of meat."

"Beautiful meat," chanted his wife, "like a pig we killed a month ago. That was a nice pig, fat and contented as you'd find any pig, 'twould have been a shame to keep him alive any longer. It dressed so well, a picture it was, the kidneys shun like gold."

"That reminds me of poor old Frank Stinsgrove," said her husband. "He'd a mint of money, a very wealthy man, but he didn't like parting with it. He'd got oldish and afraid of his death, must have a doctor calling to examine him every so often. Didn't mind spending a fortune on doctors, but every other way he'd skin a flint. And there was nought wrong with him, 'cept age. So his daughter ups and says to him one day—You are wasting your money on all these doctors, father, they do you no good, what you must have is nice, dainty, nourishing food. Now what about some of these new laid eggs? How much are they fetching now? old Frank says. A penny farthing, says she. A penny farthing! I cannot afford it. And there was that man with a mint of money, a mint, could have bought Buckingham Palace— you understand me—and yet he must go on with his porridge and his mustard plasters and his syrup of squills, until at last a smartish doctor really did find something the matter with him, in his kidneys. They operated, mark you, and they say—but I never quite had the rights of it—they say they gave him a new kidney made of wax; a new wax kidney, ah, and I believe it was successful, only he had not to get himself into any kind of a heat, of course, nor sit too close to the fire. 'Stonishing what them doctors can do with your innards. But of course he was too old, soon died. Left a fortune, a mint of money, could have bought the crown of England. Staunch old chap, you know."

Throughout the holidays John sang his customary ballads, "The Bicester Ram," "The Unquiet Grave," and dozens of others. After songs there would be things to eat. Then a game of cards, and after that things to eat. Then a walk to the inn, to the church, to a farm, or to a friend's where, in all jollity, there would be things to eat and drink. They went to a meet of the hounds, a most successful outing for it gave them ravening appetites. In short, as the cousin's wife said when bidding farewell, it was a time of great enjoyment.

And Pettigrove said so too. He believed it, and yet was glad to be quit of his friends in order to contemplate the serene dawn that was to come at any hour now. By New Year's Day Mrs. Cronshaw had not returned, but the big countryman was patient, his mind, though not at rest, was confident. The days passed as invisibly as warriors in a hostile country, and almost before he had begun to despair February came, a haggard month to follow a frosty January. Mist clung to the earth as tightly as the dense grey fur on the back of a cat, ice began to uncongeal, adjacent lands became indistinct, and distant fields could not be seen at all. The banks of the roads and the squat hedges were heavily dewed. The cries of invisible rooks, the bleat of unseen sheep,

made yet more gloomy the contours of motionless trees wherefrom
the slightest movement of a bird fetched a splatter of drops to the
road, cold and uncheering.

All this inclemency crowded into the heart of the waiting man, a
distress without a gleam of anger or doubt, but only a fond anxiety.
Other anxieties came upon him which, without lessening his melancholy, somewhat diverted it: his wife suffered a sudden grave decline
in health, and on calling in the doctor Pettigrove was made aware of
her approaching end. Torn between a strange recovered fondness
for his sinking wife and the romantic adventure with the widow,
which, to his mind at such a juncture, wore the sourest aspect of
infidelity, Pettigrove dwelt in remorse and grief until the night of
St. Valentine's Day, when he received a letter. It came from a coast
town in Norfolk, from a hospital; Caroline, too, was ill. She made
light of her illness, but it was clear to him now that this and this alone
was the urgent reason of her retreat from Tull at Christmas. It was
old tubercular trouble (that was consumption, wasn't it?) which had
driven her into sanatoriums on several occasions in recent years. She
was getting better now, she wrote, but it would be months before she
would be allowed to return. It had been rather a bad attack, so sudden.
Now she had no other thought or desire in the world but to be back
at Tull with her friend, and in time to see that fairy may-tree at
bloom in the wood—he had promised to show it to her—they would
often go together, wouldn't they—and she signed herself his, "with
the deepest affection."

He did not remember any promise to show her the tree, but he sat
down straightway and wrote her a letter of love, incoherently disclosed
and obscurely worded for any eyes but hers. He did not mention his
wife; he had suddenly forgotten her. He sealed the letter and put it
aside to be posted on the morrow. Then he crept back to his wife's
room and continued his sick vigil.

But in that dim room, lit by one small candle, he did not heed the
invalid. His mind, feverishly alert, was devoted to thoughts of that
other who also lay sick, and who had intimidated him. He had feared
her, feared for himself. He had behaved like a lost wanderer who at
night, deep in a forest, had come upon the embers of a fire left
mysteriously glowing, and had crept up to it frightened, without
stick or stone: if only he had conquered his fear he might have lain
down and rested by its strange comfort. But now he was sure of her
love, sure of his own, he was secure, he would lay down and rest.

She would come with all the sweetness of her passion and the valour of her frailty, stretching smooth, quiet wings over his lost soul.

Then he began to be aware of a soft, insistent noise, tapping, tapping, tapping, that seemed to come from the front door below. To assure himself he listened intently, and soon it became almost the only sound in the world, clear but soft, sharp and thin, as if struck with the fingernails only, tap, tap, tap, quickly on the door. When the noise ceased he got up and groped stealthily down his narrow crooked staircase. At the bottom he waited in an uncanny pause until just beyond him he heard the gentle urgency again, tap, tap, and he flung open the door. There was enough gloomy light to reveal the emptiness of the porch; there was nothing there, nothing to be seen, but he could distinctly hear the sound of feet being vigorously shuffled on the doormat below him, as if the shoes of some light-foot visitor were being carefully cleaned before entry. Then it stopped. Beyond that—nothing. Pettigrove was afraid, he dared not cross the startling threshold, he shot back the door, bolted it in a fluster, and blundered away up the stairs.

And there was now darkness, the candle in his wife's room having spent itself, but as a glow from the fire embers remained he did not hasten to light another candle. Instead, he fastened the bedroom door also, and stood filled with wondering uneasiness, dreading to hear the tap, tap, tap come again, just there, behind him. He listened for it with stopped breath, but he could hear nothing, not the faintest scruple of sound, not the beat of his own heart, not a flutter from the fire, not a rustle of feet, not a breath—no! not even a breathing! He rushed to the bed and struck a match: that was a dead face. . . . Under the violence of his sharpening shock he sank upon the bed beside dead Carrie and a faint crepuscular agony began to gleam over the pensive darkness of his mind, with a promise of mad moonlight to follow.

Two days later a stranger came to the Pettigrove's door, a short brusque, sharp-talking man with iron-grey hair and iron-rimmed spectacles. He was an ironmonger.

"Mr. Pettigrove? My name is Cronshaw, of Eastbourne, rather painful errand, my sister-in-law, Mrs. Cronshaw, tenant of yours, I believe."

Pettigrove stiffened into antagonism: what the devil was all this? "Come in," he remarked grimly.

"Thank you," said Cronshaw, following Pettigrove into the parlour where, with many sighs and much circumstance, he doffed his overcoat and stood his umbrella in a corner. "Had to walk from the station, no conveyances; that's pretty stiff, miles and miles."

"Have a drop of wine?" invited Pettigrove.

"Thank you," said the visitor.

"It's dandelion."

"Very kind of you, I'm sure." Cronshaw drew a chair up to the fireplace, though the fire had not been lit, and the grate was full of ashes, and asked if he might smoke. Pettigrove did not mind; he poured out a glass of the yellow wine while Cronshaw lit his pipe. The room smelled stuffy, heavy noises came from overhead as if men were moving furniture. The stranger swallowed a few drops of the wine, coughed, and said: "My sister-in-law is dead, I'm sorry to say. You had not heard, I suppose?"

"Dead!" whispered Pettigrove. "Mrs. Cronshaw! No, no, I had not, I had not heard that, I did not know. Mrs. Cronshaw dead—is it true?"

"Ah," said the stranger with a laboured sigh. "Two nights ago in a hospital at Mundesley. I've just come on from there. It was very sudden, O, frightfully sudden, but it was not unexpected, poor woman, it's been off and on with her for years. She was very much attached to this village, I suppose, and we're going to bury her here, it was her last request. That's what I want to do now. I want to arrange about the burial and the disposal of her things and to give up possession of your house. I'm very sorry for that."

"I'm uncommon grieved to hear this," said Pettigrove. "She was a handsome lady."

"O yes," the ironmonger took out his pocket-book and prepared to write in it.

"A handsome lady," continued the countryman tremulously, "handsome, handsome."

At that moment someone came heavily down the stairs and knocked at the parlour door.

"Come in," cried Pettigrove. A man with red face and white hair shuffled into the room; he was dressed in a black suit that had been made for a man not only bigger, but probably different in other ways.

"We shall have to shift her down here now," he began. "I was sure we should, the coffin's too big to get round that awkward crook in these stairs when it's loaded. In fact, 'tis impossible. Better have her down now afore we put her in, or there'll be an accident on the day as sure as judgment." The man, then noticing Cronshaw, said: "Good-morning, sir, you'll excuse me."

The ironmonger stared at him with horror, and then put his note-book away.

"Yes, yes, then," mumbled Pettigrove. "I'll come up in a few minutes."

The man went out and Cronshaw jumped up and said: "You'll pardon me, Mr. Pettigrove, I had no idea that you had had a be-reavement too."

"My wife," said Pettigrove dully, "two nights ago."

"Two nights ago! I am very sorry, most sorry," stammered the other, picking up his umbrella and hat. "I'll go away. What a sad coincidence!"

"There's no call to do that; what's got to be done must be done."

"I'll not detain you long then, just a few details: I am most sorry, very sorry, it's extraordinary."

He took out his notebook again—it had red edges and a fat elastic band—and after conferring with Pettigrove for some time the stranger went off to see the vicar, saying, as he shook hands: "I shall of course see you again when it is all over. How bewildering it is, and what a shock it is; from one day to another and then nothing; and the day after to-morrow they'll be buried beside one another. I am very sorry, most sorry. I shall of course come and see you again when it is all over."

After he had gone Pettigrove walked about the room murmuring: "She was a lady, a handsome lady," and then, still murmuring, he stumbled up the stairs to the undertakers. His wife lay on the bed in a white gown. He enveloped her stiff thin body in a blanket and carried it downstairs to the parlour; the others, with much difficulty, carried down the coffin and when they had fixed it upon some trestles they unwrapped Carrie from the blankets and laid her in it.

Caroline and Carrie were buried on the same day in adjoining graves, buried by the same men, and as the ironmonger was prevented by some other misfortune from attending the obsequies there were no other mourners than Pettigrove. The workshop sign of the Tull carpenter bore the following notice:

		Small
☞	COMPLETE UNDERTAKER	Hearse
		Kept

and therefore it was he who ushered the handsome lady from the station on that bitter day. Frost was so heavy that the umbrage of pine and fir looked woolly, thick grey swabs. Horses stood miserably in the frozen fields, breathing into any friendly bush. Rooks pecked industriously at the tough pastures, but wiser fowls, unlike the fabulous good child, could be neither seen nor heard. And all day someone was grinding corn at the millhouse; the engine was old and kept on emitting explosions that shook the neighbourhood like a dreadful bomb. Pettigrove, who had not provided himself with a black overcoat and therefore wore none at all, shivered so intensely during the ceremony that the keen edge of his grief was dulled, and indeed from that time onwards his grief, whatever its source, seemed deprived of all keenness: it just dulled him with a permanent dullness.

He caused to be placed on his wife's grave a headstone, quite small, not a yard high, inscribed to

CAROLINE
The beloved wife
of
John Pettigrove

Some days after its erection he was astonished to find the headstone had fallen flat on its face. It was very strange, but after all it was a small matter, a simple affair, so in the dusk he himself took a spade and set it up again. A day or two later it had fallen once more. He was now inclined to some suspicion, he fancied that mischievous boys had done it; he would complain to the vicar. But Pettigrove was an easy-going man, he did not complain; he replaced the stone, setting it more deeply in the earth and padding the turf more firmly around it.

When it fell the third time he was astonished and deeply moved, but he was no longer in doubt, and as he once more made a good upheaval by the grave in the dusk he said in his mind, and he felt too in his heart, that he understood.

"It will not fall again," he said, and he was right: it did not.

Pettigrove himself lived for another score of years, during which the monotony of his life was but mildly varied; he just went on registering births and deaths and rearing little oaks and pines, firs and sycamores. Sentimental deference to the oft-repeated wish of his wife led him to join the church choir and sing its anthems and hymns with a secular blitheness that was at least mellifluous. Moreover, after a year or two, he *did* become a parish councillor and in a modest way was something of a "shining light."

"If I were you," observed an old countryman to him, "and I had my way, I know what I would do: I would live in a little house and have a quiet life, and I wouldn't care the toss of a ha'penny for nothing and nobody!"

In the time of May, always, Pettigrove would wander in Tull Great Wood as far as the hidden pleasaunce where the hawthorn so whitely bloomed. None but he knew of that, or remembered it, and when its dying petals were heaped upon the grass he gathered handfuls to keep in his pocket till they rotted. Sometimes he thought he would leave Tull and see something of the world; he often thought of that, but it seemed as if time had stabilized and contracted round his heart and he did not go. At last, after twenty years of widowhood, he died and was buried, and this was the manner of that.

Two men were digging his grave on the morning of the interment, a summer's day so everlasting beautiful that it was incredible anyone should be dead. The two men, an ancient named Jethro and a younger whom he called Mark, went to sit in the cool porch for a brief rest. The work on the grave had been very much delayed, but now the old headstone was laid on one side, and most of the earth that had covered his wife's body was heaped in untidy mounds upon the turf close by. Otherwise there was no change in the yard or the trees that grew so high, the grass that grew so greenly, the dark brick wall, or the door of fugitive blue; there was even a dappled goat quietly cropping. A woman came into the porch, remarked upon the grand day, and then passed into the church to her task of tidying up for the ceremony. Jethro took a swig of drink from a bottle and handed it to his mate.

"You don't remember old Fan as used to clean the church, do you? No, 'twas 'fore you come about these parts. She was a smartish old gal. Bother me if one of them goats didn't follow her into the darn church one day, ah, and wouldn't be drove out on it, neither, no, and she chasing of it from here to there and one place and another but out it would not go, that goat. And at last it act-u-ally marched up into the pulpit and put its two forelegs on the holy book and said 'Baa-a-a!'" Here Jethro gave a prolonged imitation of a goat's cry. "Well, old Fan had been a bit skeered but she was so overcome by that bit of piety that, darn me, if she didn't sit down and play the organ for it!"

Mark received this narration with a lack-lustre air and at once the two men resumed their work. Meanwhile a man ascended the church tower; other men had gone into the home of the dead man. Soon the vicar came hurrying through the blue door in the wall and the bell gave forth its first solemn toll.

"Hey, Jethro," called Mark from the grave. "What d'you say's the name of this chap?"

"Pettigrove. Hurry up, now."

Mark, after bending down, whispered from the grave: "What was his wife's name?"

"Why, man alive, that 'ud be Pettigrove, too." The bell in the tower gave another profoundly solemn beat.

"What's the name on that headstone?" asked Mark.

"Caroline Pettigrove. What be you thinking on?"

"We're in the wrong hole, Jethro; come and see for yourself, the plate on this old coffin says Caroline Cronshaw, see for yourself, we're in the wrong hole."

Again the bell voiced its melancholy admonition.

Jethro descended the short ladder and stood in the grave with Mark just as the cortège entered the church by the door on the opposite side of the yard. He knelt down and rubbed with his own fingers the dulled inscription on the mouldering coffin; there was no doubt about it, Caroline Cronshaw lay there.

"Well, may I go to glory," slowly said the old man. It may have occurred to Mark that this was an extravagantly remote destination to prescribe; at any rate he said: "There ain't no time, now, come on."

"Who the devil be she? However come that wrong headstone to be put on this wrong grave?" quavered the kneeling man.

"Are you coming out?" growled Mark, standing with one foot on the ladder, "or ain't you? They'll be chucking him on top of you in a couple o'minutes. There's no time, I tell you."

" 'Tis a strange come-up as ever I see," said the old man; striking one wall of the grave with his hand: "that's where we should be, Mark, next door, but there's no time to change it and it must go as it is, Mark. Well, it's fate; what is to be must be whether it's good or right and you can't odds it, you darn't go against it, or you be wrong." They stood in the grave muttering together. "Not a word, Mark, mind you!" At last they shovelled some earth back upon the tell-tale name-plate, climbed out of the grave, drew up the ladder, and stood with bent heads as the coffin was borne from the church towards them. It was lowered into the grave, and at the "earth to earth" Jethro, with a flirt of his spade dropped in a handful of sticky marl, another at "ashes to ashes," and again at the "dust to dust." Finally, when they were alone together again, they covered in the old lovers, dumping the earth tightly and everlastingly about them, and reset the headstone, Jethro remarking as they did so: "That headstone, well, 'tis a mystery, Mark! And I can't bottom it, I can't bottom it at all, 'tis a mystery."

And indeed, how should it not be, for the secret had long since been forgotten by its originator.

Walter de la Mare

THE AMERICAN reader is likely first to meet Walter de la Mare in the pages of anthologies through such haunting and delicate lyrics as "The Listeners" or "Old Susan," poems which convey a magic such as, in an earlier day, only Coleridge knew how to summon. He began as a poet, and to the distinguished novels and short stories which followed, he brought a poet's candid and gentle understanding of human nature. Sometimes his stories lie on the margin between the known and the unknown; that area he explores with the quiet tread of one to whom mystery is familiar. Sometimes, as in "The Nap," he explores the essential mystery of life's ordinary routine, and we behold the unconscious heroism of the stalwart householder, Mr. Thripp.

Walter de la Mare was born in 1873 at Charleston, a village in Kent, England. For eighteen years he acted as bookkeeper in the London office of the Anglo-American Oil Company, but poetry was his real career, and in 1902 his first volume Songs of Childhood was published under the pseudonym "Walter Ramal." Two years later he published the novel Henry Brocken under his own name. A grant from the Privy Purse enabled him to turn more fully to his chosen career, and since 1904 he has written more than twenty-five books, among which the story collections include The Riddle (1924); Broomsticks (1925); The Connoisseur (1926); and On the Edge (1930). He now lives at Taplow in Buckinghamshire, England.

THE NAP *

Walter de la Mare

THE AUTUMNAL afternoon was creeping steadily on towards night; the sun after the morning's rain was now—from behind thinning clouds—glinting down on the chimney-pots and slate roofs of Mr. Thripp's suburb. And the day being a Saturday, across Europe, across England, an immense multitudinous stirring of humanity was in progress. It had begun in remote Australia and would presently sweep across the Atlantic into vast America, resembling the rustling of an ant-heap in a pine wood in sunny June. The Christian world, that is, was preparing for its weekly half-holiday; and Mr. Thripp was taking his share.

As if time were of unusual importance to him, two clocks stood on his kitchen mantelpiece: one, gay as a peepshow in the middle, in a stained wood case with red and blue flowers on the glass front; the other an "alarum"—which though it was made of tin had a voice and an appearance little short of the brazen. Above them, as if entirely oblivious of their ranting, a glazed King Edward VII stared stolidly out of a Christmas lithograph, with his Orders on his royal breast.

Mr. Thripp's kitchen table was at this moment disordered with the remains of a meal, straggling over a tablecloth that had now gallantly completed its full week's service. Like all Saturday dinners in his household, this has been a hugger-mugger dinner—one of vehement relays. Mr. Thripp himself had returned home from his office at a quarter to two—five minutes after his daughter Millie and Mrs. Thripp had already begun. Charlie Thripp had made his appearance a little before the hour; and James—who somehow had never become Jim or Jimmie—arrived soon afterwards. To each his due, kept warm.

But the hasty feeding was now over. Mr. Thripp in his shirt-sleeves, and with his silver watch-chain disposed upon his front, had returned once more from the scullery with his empty tray. He was breathing heavily, for he inclined nowadays, as he would sometimes confess, to the *ongbongpong*. He had remarkably muscular arms for a man of his sedentary profession, that of ledger-clerk in Messrs. Bailey, Bailey and Company's counting house. His small eyes, usually half-hidden by their plump lids, were of a bright, clear blue. His round

* From *The Connoisseur and Other Stories* by Walter de la Mare. Alfred A. Knopf, Inc., 1926. Reprinted by permission of the author.

head was covered with close-cut hair; he had fullish lips, and his ample jowl always appeared as if it had been freshly shaved—even on Saturday afternoons.

Mr. Thripp delighted in Saturday afternoons. He delighted in housework. Though he never confessed it to a living soul (and even though it annoyed Tilda to hear him) he delighted too in imitating the waitresses in the tea-shops, and rattled the plates and dishes together as if they were made of a material unshatterable and everlasting. When alone at the sink he would hiss like a groom currying a full-grown mare. He packed the tray full of dirty dishes once more, and returned into the steam of the scullery.

"You get along now, Tilda," he said to his wife who was drying up. "We shall have that Mrs. Brown knocking every minute, and that only flusters you."

Mrs. Thripp looked more ill-tempered than she really was—with her angular face and chin, pitch-dark eyes, and dark straight hair. With long damp fingers she drew back a limp strand of hair that had straggled over her forehead.

"What beats me is, you never take a bit of enjoyment yourself," she replied. "It isn't fair to *us*. I slave away, morning, noon and night; but that's just as things are. But other husbands get out and about; why not you? *Let* her knock! She's got too much money to waste; that's what's the matter with *her*. I don't know what you wouldn't take her for in that new get-up she's got."

Then what the devil do you go about with her for? were the words that entered Mr. Thripp's mind; and as for slaving, haven't I just *asked* you to give over? Have reason, woman! But he didn't utter them. "That'll be all right," he said instead, in his absurd genial way. "You get on along off, Tilda; I'll see to all this. I enjoy myself my own way, don't you fear. Did you never hear of the selfish sex? Well, that's me!"

"Oh yes, I know all about that," said his wife sententiously: "a pinch of salt on a bird's tail! But there's no need for sarcasms. Now do be careful with that dish, there. It don't belong to us, but to next door. She gave me one of her pancakes on it—and nothing better than a shapeless bit of leather, either. Just to show she was once in service as a cook-general, I suppose; though she never owns to it."

A spiteful old mischief-maker, if you asked me, was Mr. Thripp's inward comment. But "Oh well, Tilda, she means all right," he said soothingly. "Don't you worry. Now get along off with you; it's a hard day, Saturday, but you won't know yourself when you come down again." As if forced into a line of conduct she deprecated and despised, Tilda flung her wet tea-cloth over a chair, and, with heart beating gaily beneath her shrunken breast, hastened away.

Mr. Thripp began to whistle under his breath as he turned on the hot water tap again. It was the one thing he insisted on—a lavish supply of hot water. He was no musician and only himself knew the tune he was in search of; but it kept him going as vigorously as a company of grenadiers on the march, and he invariably did his household jobs against time. It indulged a sort of gambling instinct in him; and the more he hated his job the louder he whistled. So as a small boy he had met the challenge of the terrors of the dark. "Keep going," he would say. "Don't let things mess over. That's waste!"

At that moment, his elder son, James, appeared in the scullery doorway. James took after his mother's side of the family. In his navy blue serge suit, light-brown shoes, mauve socks and spotted tie, he showed what careful dressing can do for a man. A cigarette sagged from his lower lip. His head was oblong, and flat-sided, and his eyes had a damp and vacant look. He thrust his face an inch or two into the succulent steam beyond the door-way.

"Well, dad, I'm off," he said.

Oh, my God! thought his father; if only you'd drop those infernal fags. Smoke, smoke, smoke, morning to night; and you that pasty-looking I can't imagine what the girl sees in you, with your nice superior ways. "Right you are, my son," he said aloud, "I won't ask you to take a hand! Enjoy yourself while you're young, I say. But slow and steady does it. Where might *you* be bound for this afternoon?"

"Oh, tea with Ivy's people," said James magnanimously. "Pretty dull going, I can tell you."

"But it won't be tea all the evening, I suppose?" said his father, pushing a steaming plate into the plate-rack.

"Oh, I dare say we shall loaf off to a Revoo or something," said James. He tossed his cigarette end into the sink, but missed the refuse strainer. Mr. Thripp picked it up with a fork and put it into the receptacle it was intended for, while James "lit up" again.

"Well, so long," said his father, "don't spoil that Sunday-go-to-Meeting suit of yours with all this steam. And by the way, James, I owe you five shillings for that little carpentering job you did for me. It's on the sitting-room shelf."

"Right ho. Thanks, dad," said James. "I thought it was six. But never mind."

His father flashed a glance at his son—a glance like the smouldering of a coal. "That so? Well, make it six, then," he said. "And I'm much obliged."

"Oh, that's nothing," replied James graciously. "Cheerio; don't overdo it, dad."

Mr. Thripp returned to his washing-up. He was thinking rapidly with an extraordinary medley of feeling—as if he were not one Mr. Thripp, but many. None the less, his whistling broke out anew, as though, like a canary, in rivalry with the gushing of the tap. After loading up his tray with crockery for the last time, he put its contents away in the cupboard, and on the kitchen dresser; cleansed the drain, swabbed up the sink, swabbed up the cracked cement floor, hung up his dish-clout, rinsed his hands, and returned into the kitchen.

Millie in a neat, tailor-made costume which had that week marvellously survived dyeing, was now posed before the little cracked square of kitchen looking-glass. She was a pale, slim thing. Her smooth hair, of a lightish brown streaked with gold and parted in the middle, resembled a gilded form surrounding her mild angelic face—a face such as the mediaeval sculptors in France delighted to carve on their altar-pieces. Whatever she wore became her—even her skimpy old pale-blue flannel dressing-gown.

She turned her narrow pretty face sidelong under her hat and looked at her father. She looked at every human being like that—even at her own reflection in a shop window, even at a flower in a glass. She spent her whole life subtly, instinctively, wordlessly courting. She had as many young men as the White Queen has pawns: though not all of them remained long in her service.

It's all very well to be preening yourself in that mirror, my girl, her father was thinking, but you'd be far better off in the long run if you did a bit more to help your mother, even though you do earn a fraction of your living. More thinking and less face, I say. And all that—! But "Why, I never see such a girl as you, Millie," he greeted her incredulously, "for looking your best! And such a best, too, my dear. Which young spark is it to be this afternoon? Eh?"

"Sparks! dad; how you do talk. Why, I don't hardly know, dad. Sparks!" Millie's voice almost invariably ran down the scale like the notes of a dulcimer muted with velvet. "I wasn't thinking of anybody in particular," she went on, continuing to watch her moving mouth in the glass, "but I promised Nellie Gibbs I . . . One thing, I am not going to stay out long on a day like this!"

"What's the matter with the day?" Mr. Thripp enquired.

"The matter! Why, look at it! It's a fair filthy mug of a day." The words slipped off her pretty curved lips like pearls over satin. A delicious anguish seemed to have arched the corners of her eyelids.

"Well, ain't there such a thing as a mackingtosh in the house, then?" enquired her father briskly.

"Mackingtosh! Over this! Oh, isn't that just like a man! I should look a perfect guy." She stood gazing at him, like a gazelle startled by the flurry of a breeze across the placid surface of its drinking-pool.

Now see you here, my girl, that see-saw voice inside her father was expostulating once more, what's the good of them fine silly airs? I take you for an honest man's daughter with not a ha'penny to spare on fal-lals and monkey-traps. *That* won't get you a husband. But Mr. Thripp once more ignored its interruption. He smiled almost roguishly out of his bright blue eyes at his daughter. "Ask *me* what I take you for, my dear? Why, I take you for a nice, well-meaning, though remarkably plain young woman. Eh? But there, there, don't worry. What I say is, make sure of the best (and the best that's *inside*) and let the other young fellows go."

He swept the last clean fork on the table into the drawer and folded up the tablecloth.

"Oh, dad, how you do go on!" breathed Millie. "It's always fellows you're thinking of. As if fellows made any difference." Her glance roamed a little startledly around the room. "What *I* can't understand," she added quickly, "is why we never have a clean tablecloth. How can anybody ask a friend home to their own place if that's the kind of thing they are going to eat off of?" The faint nuance of discontent in her voice only made it the more enchanting and seductive. She might be Sleeping Beauty babbling out of her dreams.

A cataract of invective coursed through the channels of Mr. Thripp's mind. He paused an instant to give the soiled tablecloth another twist and the table another prolonged sweep of that formidable right arm which for twenty-three years had never once been lifted in chastisement of a single one of his three offspring. Then he turned and glanced at the fire.

"I wouldn't," he said, seizing the shovel, "I wouldn't let mother hear that, my dear. We all have a good many things to put up with. And what I say is, all in good time. *You* bring that Mr. Right along! and I can promise him not only a clean tablecloth but something appetising to eat off of it. A bit of a fire in the sitting-room too, for that matter."

"You're a good sort, dad," said Millie, putting up her face to be kissed—in complete confidence that the tiny powder-puff in her vanity-bag would soon adjust any possible mishap to the tip of her small nose. "But I don't believe you ever think *I* think of anything."

"Good-bye, my dear," said Mr. Thripp; "don't kiss me. I am all of a smother with the washing-up."

"Toodle-loo, ma," Millie shrilled, as her father followed her out into the passage. He drew open the front door, secreting his shirt-sleeves well behind it in case of curious passers-by.

"Take care of yourself, my dear," he called after her, "and don't be too late."

"Late!" tossed Millie, "any one would think I had been coddled up in a hot-house."

Out of a seething expense of spirit in Mr. Thripp's mind only a few words made themselves distinct. "Well, never mind, my precious dear. I'm *with* you for ever, whether you know it or not."

He returned into the house, and at once confronted his younger son, Charlie, who was at that moment descending the stairs. As a matter of fact he was descending the stairs like fifteen Charlies, and nothing so much exasperated his father as to feel the whole house rock on its foundations at each fresh impact.

"Off to your Match, my boy?" he cried. "Some day I expect you will be taking a hand in the game yourself. Better share than watch!"

Every single Saturday afternoon during the football season Mr. Thripp ventured to express some such optimistic sentiment as this. But Charlie had no objection; not at all.

"Not me, dad," he assured him good-humouredly. "I'd sooner pay a bob to see other fellows crocked up. You couldn't lend me one, I suppose?"

"Lend you what?"

"Two tanners; four frippenies; a twelfth of a gross of coppers."

Good God! yelled Mr. Thripp's inward monitor, am I *never* to have a minute's rest or relief? But it yelled in vain.

"Right you are, my son," he said instead, and thrusting his fleshy hand into his tight-fitting trouser-pocket he brought out a fistful of silver and pence. "And there," he added, "there's an extra sixpence free, *gratis,* and for nothing, for the *table d'hôte.* All I say is, Charlie, better say 'give' when there isn't much chance of keeping to the 'lend.'

I don't want to preach; but that's always been *my* rule; and kept it too, as well as I could."

Charles counted the coins in his hand, and looked at his father. He grinned companionably. He invariably found his father a little funny to look at. He seemed somehow to be so remote from anything you could mean by things as they are, and things as they are now. He wasn't so much old-fashioned, as just a Gone-by. He was his father, of course, just as a jug is a jug, and now and then Charlie was uncommonly fond of him, longed for his company, and remembered being a little boy walking with him in the Recreation Ground. But he wished he wouldn't be always giving advice, and especially the kind of advice which he had himself assiduously practised.

"Ta, dad," he said; "that's doing me proud. I'll buy you a box of Havanas with what's over from the *table d'hôte*. And now we're square. Good-bye, dad." He paused as he turned to go. "Honour bright," he added, "I hope I shall be earning a bit more soon, and then I shan't have to ask you for anything."

A curious shine came into Mr. Thripp's small lively eyes; it seemed almost to spill over on to his plump cheeks. It looked as if those cheeks had even paled a little.

"Why, that's all right, Charlie, me boy," he mumbled, "I'd give you the skin off me body if it would be of any use. That's all right. Don't stand about too long but just keep going. What I can't abide is these young fellows that swallow down their enjoyments like so much black draught. But we are not that kind of a family, I'm thankful to say."

"Not me!" said Charles, with a grimace like a good-humoured marmoset, and off he went to his soccer match.

Hardly had the sound of his footsteps ceased—and Mr. Thripp stayed there in the passage, as if to listen till they were for ever out of hearing—when there came a muffled secretive tap on the panel of the door. At sound of it the genial podgy face blurred and blackened.

Oh, it's you, you cringing Jezebel, is it?—the thought scurried through his mind like a mangy animal. Mr. Thripp indeed was no lover of the ultra-feminine. He either feared it, or hated it, or both feared *and* hated it. It disturbed his even tenour. It was a thorn in the side of the Mr. Thripp that not only believed second thoughts were best, but systematically refused to give utterance to first. Any sensible person, he would say, ought to know when he's a bit overtaxed, and act according.

The gloved fingers, Delilah-like, had tapped again. Mr. Thripp tip-toed back into the kitchen, put on his coat, and opened the door.

"Oh, it's you, Mrs. Brown," he said. "Tilda won't be a moment. She's upstairs titivating. Come in and take a seat."

His eyes meanwhile were informing that inward censor of his precisely how many inches thick the mauvish face-powder lay on Mrs. Brown's cheek, the liver-coloured lip-stick on her mouth, and the dye on her loaded eye-lashes. Those naturally delicate lashes swept down in a gentle fringe upon her cheek as she smiled in reply. She was a graceful thing, too, but practised; and far more feline, far far more body-conscious than Millie. No longer in the blush of youth either; though still mistress of the gift that never leaves its predestined owner —the impulse and power to fascinate mere man. Still, there were limitations even to Mrs. Brown's orbit of attraction, and Mr. Thripp might have been Neptune itself he kept himself so far out in the cold.

He paused a moment at the entrance to the sitting-room, until his visitor had seated herself. He was eyeing her Frenchified silk scarf, her demure new hat, her smart high-heeled patent-leather shoes, but his eyes dropped like stones when he discovered her own dark languishing ones surveying him from under that hat's beguiling brim.

"Nice afternoon after the rain," he remarked instantly. "Going to the pictures, I suppose? As for meself, these days make me want to be out and in at the same time. It's the musty, fusty, smoky dark of them places *I* can't stand."

Mrs. Brown rarely raised her voice much above a whisper. Indeed it appeared to be a physical effort to her to speak at all. She turned her face a little sidelong, her glance on the carpet. "Why, it's the dark I enjoy, Mr. Thripp," she said. "It"—and she raised her own—"it rests the eyes so."

For an instant Mr. Thripp's memory returned to Millie, but he made no comment.

"Here's Mrs. Brown, Tilda," he called up the stair-case. Good heavens, the woman might as well be the real thing, the voice within was declaring. But the words that immediately followed up this piece of news were merely, "You'll be mighty surprised to hear, Tilda, Mrs. Brown's got a new hat." A faint catcall of merriment descended the stairs.

"Oh, now, Mr. Thripp, listen to that!" whispered the peculiar voice from out of the little airless sitting-room, "you always did make fun of me, Mr. Thripp. Do I deserve it, now?"

A gentle wave of heat coursed over Mr. Thripp as he covertly listened to these accents, but he was out of sight.

"Fun, Mrs. Brown? Never," he retorted gallantly; "It's only my

little way." And then to his immense relief on lifting his eyes, discovered Tilda already descending the stairs.

He saw the pair of them off. Being restored to his coat, he could
watch them clean down the drying street from his gate-post. Astonishing, he thought, what a difference there can be in two women's backs!
Tilda's, straight, angular, and respectable, as you might say; and that
other—sinuous, seductive, as if it were as crafty a means of expression
as the very smile and long-lashed languishments upon its owner's face.
"What can the old woman see in her!" he muttered to himself;
"damned if *I* know!" On this problem Mr. Thripp firmly shut his front
door. Having shut it he stooped to pick up a tiny white feather on the
linoleum; and stooping, sighed.

At last his longed-for hour had come—the hour for which his very
soul pined throughout each workaday week. Not that it was always his
happy fate to be left completely alone like this. At times, indeed, he
had for company far too much housework to leave him any leisure.
But to-day the dinner things were cleared away, the washing-up was
over, the tables fair as a baker's board, the kitchen spick and span, the
house empty. He would just have a look round his own and Tilda's
bed-room (and, maybe, the boys' and Millie's). And then the chair by
the fire; the simmering kettle on the hearth; and the soft tardy autumnal dusk fading quietly into night beyond the window.

It was a curious thing that a man who loved his family so much,
who was as desperately loyal to every member of it as a she-wolf is to
her cubs, should yet find this few minutes' weekly solitude a luxury
such as only Paradise, one would suppose, would ever be able to provide.

Mr. Thripp went upstairs and not only tidied up his own and Tilda's
bedroom, and went on to Millie's and the boys', but even gave a sloosh
to the bath, slid the soap out of the basin where Charles had abandoned
it, and hung up the draggled towels again in the tiny bathroom. What
a place looks like when you come back to it from your little enjoyments—it's *that* makes all the difference to your feelings about a home.
These small chores done, Mr. Thripp put on an old tweed coat with
frayed sleeves, and returned to the kitchen. In a quarter of an hour that
too more than ever resembled a new pin.

Then he glanced up at the clocks; between them the time was a
quarter to four. He was amazed. He laid the tea, took out of his little
old leather bag a pot of jam, which he had bought for a surprise on
his way home, and arranged a bunch of violets in a small jar beside

Tilda's plate. But apart from these family preparations, Mr. Thripp was now depositing a demure little glossy brown teapot all by itself on the kitchen range. This was his Eureka. This was practically the only sensual *secret* luxury Mr. Thripp had ever allowed himself since he became a family man. Tilda's cooking was good enough for him provided that the others had their little dainties now and then. He enjoyed his beer, and could do a bit of supper occasionally with a friend. But the ritual of these solitary Saturday afternoons reached its climax in this small pot of tea. First the nap sweet as nirvana in his easy-chair, then the tea, and then the still, profound quarter of an hour's musing before the door-knocker began again.

Having pulled down the blind a little in order to prevent any chance of draught, Mr. Thripp eased his boot-laces, sat himself in his chair, his cheek turned a little away from the window, his feet on the box that usually lay under the table, and with fingers clasped over his stomach composed himself to sleep. The eyelids closed; the lips set; the thumbs twitched now and again. He breathed deep, and the kettle began a whispered anthem—as if a myriad voices were singing on and on without need of pause or rest, a thousand thousand leagues away.

But now there was none to listen; and beyond, quiet hung thick in the little house. Only the scarce-perceptible hum of the traffic at the end of the narrow side street was audible on the air. Within, the two clocks on the chimney-piece quarrelled furiously over the fleeting moments, attaining unanimity only in one of many ticks. Ever and again a tiny scutter of dying ashes rejoined those that had gone before in the pan beneath the fire. Soon even these faint stirrings became inaudible and in a few moments Mr. Thripp's spirit would have wafted itself completely free awhile from its earthly tenement, if, suddenly, the image of Millie—more vivid than even the actual sight of her a few minutes before—had not floated up into the narrow darkness of her father's tight-shut eyes.

But this was not the image of Millie as her father usually saw her. A pathetic earthly melancholy lay over the fair angelic features. The young cheek was sunken in; the eye was faded, dejected, downcast; and her cheek was stubbornly turned away from her father, as if she resented or was afraid of his scrutiny.

At this vision a headlong anxiety darted across Mr. Thripp's half-slumbering mind. His heart began heavily beating: and then a pulse in his forehead. Where was she now? What forecast, what warning was this? Millie was no fool. Millie knew her way about. And her mother if anything was perhaps a little too censorious of the ways of this wicked world. If you keep on talking at a girl, hinting of things that might otherwise not enter her head—that in itself is dangerous. Love itself even must edge in warily. The tight-shut lids blinked anxiously. But where was Millie now? Somewhere indoors, but where? Who with?

Mr. Thripp saw her first in a teashop, sitting opposite a horrid young man with his hair greased back over his low round head, and a sham pin in his tie. His elbows were on the marble-top table, and he was looking at Millie very much as a young but experienced pig looks at his wash-trough. Perhaps she was at the Pictures? Dulcet accents echoed into the half-dreaming mind—"But I enjoy the dark, Mr. Thripp. . . . It rests the eyes." Why did the woman talk as if she had never more than half a breath to spare? Rest her eyes! She never at any rate wanted to rest the eyes of any fool in trousers who happened to be within glimpse of her own. It was almost unnaturally dark in the cinema of Mr. Thripp's fancy at this moment; yet he could now see his Millie with her pale, harmless, youthful face, as plainly as if she were the "close-up" of some star from Los Angeles on the screen. And now the young man in her company was almost as fair as herself, with a long-chinned sheepish face and bolting eyes; and the two of them were amorously hand in hand.

For a moment Mr. Thripp sat immovable, as if a bugle had sounded in his ear. Then he deliberately opened his eyes and glanced about him. The November daylight was already beginning to fade. Yes, he would have a word with Millie—but not when she came home that evening. It is always wiser to let the actual coming-home be pleasant and welcoming. To-morrow morning, perhaps; that is, if her mother was not goading at her for being late down and lackadaisical when there was so much to be done. Nevertheless, all in good time he would have a little quiet word with her. He would say only what he would not afterwards regret having said. He had meant to do that ages ago; but you mustn't flood a house with water when it's not on fire. She was but a mere slip of a thing—like a flower, not a wild flower, but one of those sweet waxen flowers you see blooming in a florist's window— which you must be careful with and not just expose anywhere.

And yet how his own little place here could be compared with anything in the nature of a hot-house he could not for the life of him understand. Delicate-looking! Everybody said that. God bless me, perhaps her very lackadaisicalness was a symptom of some as yet hidden malady. Good God, supposing! . . . He would take her round to see the doctor as soon as he could. But the worst of it was you had to do these things on your own responsibility. And though Mr. Thripp was now a man close on fifty, sometimes he felt as if he could no longer bear the burden of all these responsibilities. Sometimes he felt as if he couldn't endure to brood over them as he was sometimes wont to do. If he did, he would snap. People *looked* old; but nobody was really old inside; not old at least in the sense that troubles were any the lighter, or forebodings any the more easily puffed away; or tongues easier to keep still; or tempers to control.

And talking of tempers reminded him of Charlie. What on earth was going to be done with Charlie? There was no difficulty in conjuring up, in seeing Charlie—that is if he really did go every Saturday to a football match. But Charlie was now of an age when he might think it a fine manly thing to be loafing about the counter of a pub talking to some flaxen barmaid with a tuppeny cigar between his teeth. Still, Mr. Thripp refused to entertain more than a glimpse of this possibility. He saw him at this moment as clearly as if in a peep-show, packed in with hundreds of other male creatures close as sardines in a tin, with their check caps and their "fags," and their staring eyes revolving in consort as if they were all attached to one wire, while that idiotic ball in the middle of the arena coursed on its helpless way from muddy boot to muddy boot.

Heaven knows, Mr. Thripp himself was nothing much better than a football! You had precious small chance in this life of choosing which boot should give you the next kick. And what about that smug new creeping accountant at the office with his upstart airs and new-fangled book-keeping methods!

Mr. Thripp's mouth opened in a yawn, but managed only to achieve a fraction of it. He rubbed his face; his eyes now shut again. It was not as if any of your children were of much practical help. Why should they be when they could never understand that what you pined for, what you really needed was not only practical help but some inward grace and clearness of mind wherewith they could slip in under your own thoughts and so share your point of view without all that endless terrifying argumentation. He didn't *always* give advice to suit his own ends; and yet whenever he uttered a word to James, tactfully suggesting that in a world like this—however competent a man may be and however sure of himself—you *had* to push your way, you had to make your weight felt, James always looked at him as if he were a superannuated orang-outang in a cage—an orang-outang with queer and not particularly engaging habits.

He wouldn't mind even that so much if only James would take his cigarette out of his mouth when he talked. To see that bit of stained paper attached to his son's lower lip wagging up and down, beneath that complacent smile and those dark helpless-looking eyes, all but sent Mr. Thripp stark staring mad at times. Once, indeed, he had actually given vent to the appalling mass of emotions hoarded up like water in a reservoir in his mind. The remembrance of the scene that followed made him even at this moment tremble in his chair. Thank God, thank God, he hadn't often lost control like that.

Well, James would be married by this time next year, he supposed. And what a nice dainty pickle he was concocting for himself! Mr. Thripp knew that type of young woman, with the compressed lips, and the thin dry hair, and the narrow hips. She'd be a "good manager," right enough, but there's a point in married life where good managing is little short of being in a lunatic asylum between two iron-faced nurses and yourself in a strait waistcoat. The truth of it was, with all his fine airs and neat finish, James hadn't much common-sense. He had a fair share of brains; but brains are no good if you are merely self-opinionated and contemptuous on principle. James was not like anybody in Mr. Thripp's own family. He was a Simpkins.

And then suddenly it was as if some forgotten creature in Mr. Thripp's mind or heart had burst out crying; and the loving look he thereupon cast on his elder son's face in his mind was almost maudlin in its sentimentality. He would do anything for James within reason: anything. But then it would have to be within James's reason—not his own. He knew that. Why he would himself marry the young woman and exult in being a bigamist if only he could keep his son out of her way. And yet, and yet; maybe there were worse women in the world than your stubborn, petulant, niggardly, half-sexed nagger. Mr. Thripp knew a nagger of old. His brother's wife, Fanny, had been a nagger. She was dead now, and George was a free man—but drinking far too much.

Well, as soon as he could get a chance, Mr. Thripp, sitting there in his chair decided, he would have another good think; but that probably wouldn't be until next Saturday, if then. You can't think to much purpose—except in a worried disjointed fashion—when you are in the noise of an office or keeping yourself from saying things you have no

wish to say. The worst of it was it was not much good discussing these
matters with Tilda. Like most women, she always went off at a
tangent. And when you came down to it, and wanted to be reasonable,
there was so little left to discuss. Besides, Tilda had worries enough of
her own.

At this moment Mr. Thripp once more opened his eyes wide. The
small kitchen loomed beatifically rosy and still in the glow of the fire.
Evening had so far edged on its way now that he could hardly see the
hands of his two clocks. He could but just detect the brass pendulum—
imperturbably chopping up eternity into fragments of time. He craned
forward; in five minutes he ought to be brewing his little private pot of
tea. Even if he nodded off now, he would be able to wake in time, but
five minutes doesn't leave *much* margin for dropping off. He shifted a
little on his chair, and once more shut his eyes. And in a moment or
two his mind went completely blank.

He seemed to have been suddenly hauled up helpless with horror
into an enormous vacancy—to be dangling unconfined and motionless
in space. A scene of wild sandy hills and spiky trees—in illimitable
desert, came riding towards him out of nothingness. He hung motionless, and was yet sweeping rapidly forward, but for what purpose and
to what goal there was not the smallest inkling. The wilderness before
him grew ever more desolate and menacing. He began to be deadly
afraid; groaned; stirred—and found himself with fingers clenched on
its arms sitting bolt upright in his chair. And the hands of the clock
looked to be by a hair's breadth precisely in the same position as when
he had started on that ghastly nightmare journey. His face blanched.
He sat appalled, listening to an outrageous wauling of voices. It was as
though a thousand demons lay in wait for him beneath his window
and were summoning him to his doom.

And all this nightmare horror of mind was due solely to a wailing
of cats! And yet even as with flesh still creeping he listened on to this
clamour, it was so human in effect that it might be multitudinous
shades of the unborn that were thronging about the glass of his
window. Mr. Thripp rose from his chair, his face transfigured with
rage and desire for revenge. He went out into the scullery, opened
the back door, and at sound of him the caterwauling instantly ceased.

And almost as instantly his fury died out in him. The cold evening
air fanned his forehead. He smiled quixotically, and looked about him.
There came a furtive rustle in the bushes. "Ah, there you are!" he

sang out gently into the dark. "Have your play while you can, my
fine gentlemen! Take it like your betters, for it's—a sight too soon
over."

Above the one cramped leafless elder-tree in his yard a star was
pricking the sky. A ground mist, too, was rising, already smelling a
little stale. Great London and its suburbs appeared to be in for one
of its autumnal fogs. A few of the upper windows opposite loomed
dim with light. Mr. Thripp's neighbours, it seemed, were also preparing to be off to the pictures or the music-halls. It was very still, and
the air was damp and clammy.

As he stood silent there in the obscurity a deepening melancholy
crept over his mind, though he was unaware into what gloomy folds
and sags his face had fallen. He suddenly remembered that his rates
would have to be paid next week. He remembered that Christmas
would soon be coming, and that he was getting too old to enter into
the fun of the thing as he used to do. His eyes rolled a little in their
sockets. What the . . . ! his old friend within began to suggest. But
Mr. Thripp himself did not even enunciate the missing "hell." Instead,
he vigorously rubbed his face with his stout capable hand. "Well, fog
anyhow don't bring rain," he muttered to himself.

And as if at a signal his own cat and his nextdoor neighbour's cat
and Mrs. Brown's cat and the cat of the painter and decorator whose
back garden abutted his own, together with the ginger-and-white cat
from a news-vendor's beyond, with one consent broke out once more
into their Sabbath eve quintette. The many-stranded strains of it
mounted up into the heavens like the yells of demented worshippers
of Baal.

"And, as I say, I don't blame ye neether," Mr. Thripp retorted, with
a grim smile. "If you knew, my friends, how narrowly you some of
you escaped a bucket of cold water when you couldn't even see out
of your young eyes, you'd sing twice as loud."

He shut the door and returned to his fireside. No more hope of
sleep that afternoon. He laughed to himself for sheer amusement at his
disappointment. What kids men were! He stirred the fire; it leapt
brightly as if intent to please him. He pushed the kettle on; lit the
lamp; warmed his little privy glossy-brown teapot, and fetched out a
small private supply of the richest Ceylon from behind some pots in
the saucepan cupboard.

Puffs of steam were now vapouring out of the spout of the kettle
with majestic pomposity. Mr. Thripp lifted it off the coals and balanced

it over his teapot. And at that very instant the electric bell—which a year or two ago in a moment of the strangest caprice Charles had fixed up in the corner—began jangling like a fire-alarm. Mr. Thripp hesitated. If this was one of the family, he was caught. Caught, that is, unless he was mighty quick in concealing these secret preparations. If it was Tilda—well, valour was the better part of discretion. He poured the water into the pot, replaced the lid, and put it on to the oventop to stew. With a glance of satisfaction at the spinster-like tidiness of the room, he went out, and opened the door.

"Why, it's Millie!" he said, looking out at the slim-shouldered creature standing alone there under the porch; "you don't mean to say it's you, my dear?"

Millie made no reply. Her father couldn't see her face, partly because the lamp-post stationed in front of the house three doors away gave at best a feeble light, and partly because her features were more or less concealed by her hat. She pushed furtively past him without a word, her head still stooping out of the light.

Oh, my God, what's wrong now? yelled her father's inward monstrous monitor, frenziedly clanging the fetters on wrist and ankle. "Come right in, my pretty dear," said Mr. Thripp seductively, "this *is* a pleasant surprise. And what's more, between you and me and the gatepost, I have just been making myself a cup of tea. Not a word to mother; it's *our* little secret. We'll have it together before the others come in."

He followed his daughter into the kitchen.

"Lor, what a glare you are in, pa!" she said in a small muffled voice. She turned the wick of the lamp down so low that in an instant or two the flame flickered and expired, and she seated herself in her father's chair by the fire. But the flamelight showed her face now. It was paler even than usual. A strand of her gilded pale-brown hair had streaked itself over her blue-veined temple. She looked as if she had been crying. Her father, his hands hanging down beside him as uselessly as the front paws of a performing bear, watched her in an appalling trepidation of spirit. This then was the secret of his nightmare; for this the Cats of Fate had chorused!

"What's wrong, Millie love? Are you overtired, my girl? There! Don't say nothing for a minute or two. See, here's my little pot just meant for you and me!"

Millie began to cry again, pushing her ridiculous little handkerchief close to her eyes. Mr. Thripp's hand hovered awkwardly above her dainty hat and then gently fumbled as if to stroke her hair beneath. He knelt down beside her chair.

For heaven's sake! for heaven's sake! for heaven's sake! a secret voice was gabbling frenziedly in his ear. "Tell your old dad, lovey," he murmured out loud, softly as the crooning of a wood-pigeon.

Millie tilted back her pretty hat and dropped her fair head on his shoulder. "It's nothing, dad," she said. "It's only that they are all the same."

"What are all the same?"

"Oh, fellows, dad."

"Which one, precious?" Mr. Thripp lulled wooingly. God strike him dead! muttered his monster.

"Oh, only young Arthur. Like a fool I waited half an hour for him and then saw him with—with that Westcliff girl."

A sigh as voluminous as the suspiration of Niagara swept over Mr. Thripp; but it made no sound. Half a dozen miraculous words of reassurance were storming his mind in a frenzy of relief. He paused an instant, and accepted the seventh.

"What's all that, my precious?" he was murmuring. "Why, when I was courting your mother, I saw just the same thing happen. She was a mighty pretty young thing, too, as a girl, though not quite so trim and neat in the figure as you. I felt I could throttle him where he stood. But no, I just took no notice, trusting in my own charms!"

"That's all very well," sobbed Millie, "but you were a man, and *we* have to fight without seeming to. Not that I care a fig for him: he can go. But—"

"Lord, Millie!" Mr. Thripp interrupted, smoothing her cheek with his squat forefinger, "you'd beat twenty of them Westcliffs, with a cast in both eyes and your hands behind your back. Don't you grieve no more, my dear; he'll come back safe and sound, or he's less of a— of a nice young feller than I take him for."

For a moment Mr. Thripp caught a glimpse of the detestable creature with the goggling eyes and the suède shoes, but he dismissed him sternly from view.

"There now," he said, "give your poor old dad a kiss. What's disappointments, Millie; they soon pass away. And now, just take a sip or two of this extra-strong Bohay! I was hoping I shouldn't have to put up with a lonely cup and not a soul to keep me company. But mind, my precious, not a word to your ma."

So there they sat, father and daughter, comforter and comforted, while Mr. Thripp worked miracles for two out of a teapot for one. And while Millie, with heart comforted, was musing on that other young fellow she had noticed boldly watching her while she was waiting for her Arthur, Mr. Thripp was wondering when it would be safe and discreet to disturb her solacing daydream so that he might be busying himself over the supper.

It's one damn neck-and-neck worry and trouble after another, his voice was assuring him. But meanwhile, his plain square face was serene and gentle as a nestful of halcyons, as he sat sipping his hot water and patting his pensive Millie's hand.

ℋ. ℋ. Munro (Saki)

H. H. Munro (Saki) has been called an English O. Henry, but the comparison is only faintly illuminating. Both story tellers had genius for the odd circumstance, the surprising incident; both were prodigal in invention. But there the likeness ends. Munro eschewed the "slanguage" which often fascinated O. Henry, and his world is more sophisticated, more acquainted with the mockery of well-bred malice than O. Henry's. Both men had the liveliest eye for human frailities and for the jibes of circumstance. Munro's genius found its best expression in the so-called "short-short" of but a few hundred words, but within this limit he compressed an amazingly full and unsolemn comment upon English society.

H. H. Munro was born in Burma of Celtic descent in 1870. He was educated in England, and upon his father's retirement from foreign service, travelled much in Europe. After a brilliant career in London as a journalist, he enlisted immediately upon England's declaration of war against Germany, and was killed in action in 1916 at Beaumont-Hamel. Besides his stort stories, now collected into one volume, The Complete Short Stories of Saki (1930), he wrote several other works, including a novel The Unbearable Bassington (1912), and a number of plays.

MRS. PACKLETIDE'S TIGER *
H. H. Munro

IT WAS Mrs. Packletide's pleasure and intention that she should shoot a tiger. Not that the lust to kill had suddenly descended on her, or that she felt that she would leave India safer and more wholesome than she had found it, with one fraction less of wild beast per million

* From *The Short Stories of Saki* (H. H. Munro). Copyright, 1930, by The Viking Press, Inc., New York.

of inhabitants. The compelling motive for her sudden deviation towards the footsteps of Nimrod was the fact that Loona Bimberton had recently been carried eleven miles in an aeroplane by an Algerian aviator, and talked of nothing else; only a personally procured tiger-skin and a heavy harvest of Press photographers could successfully counter that sort of thing. Mrs. Packletide had already arranged in her mind the lunch she would give at her house in Curzon Street, ostensibly in Loona Bimberton's honour, with a tiger-skin rug occupying most of the foreground and all of the conversation. She had also already designed in her mind the tiger-claw brooch that she was going to give Loona Bimberton on her next birthday. In a world that is supposed to be chiefly swayed by hunger and love Mrs. Packletide was an exception; her movements and motives were largely governed by dislike of Loona Bimberton.

Circumstances proved propitious. Mrs. Packletide had offered a thousand rupees for the opportunity of shooting a tiger without over-much risk or exertion, and it so happened that a neighbouring village could boast of being the favoured rendezvous of an animal of respectable antecedents, which had been driven by the increasing infirmi-ties of age to abandon game-killing and confine its appetite to the smaller domestic animals. The prospect of earning the thousand rupees had stimulated the sporting and commercial instinct of the villagers; children were posted night and day on the outskirts of the local jungle to head the tiger back in the unlikely event of his attempting to roam away to fresh hunting-grounds, and the cheaper kinds of goats were left about with elaborate carelessness to keep him satisfied with his present quarters. The one great anxiety was lest he should die of old age before the date appointed for the memsahib's shoot. Mothers carrying their babies home through the jungle after the day's work in the fields hushed their singing lest they might curtail the restful sleep of the venerable herd-robber.

The great night duly arrived, moonlit and cloudless. A platform had been constructed in a comfortable and conveniently placed tree, and thereon crouched Mrs. Packletide and her paid companion, Miss Mebbin. A goat, gifted with particularly persistent bleat, such as even a partially deaf tiger might be reasonably expected to hear on a still night, was tethered at the correct distance. With an accurately sighted rifle and a thumb-nail pack of patience cards the sportswoman awaited the coming of the quarry.

"I suppose we are in some danger?" said Miss Mebbin.

She was not actually nervous about the wild beast, but she had a morbid dread of performing an atom more service than she had been paid for.

"Nonsense," said Mrs. Packletide; "it's a very old tiger. It couldn't spring up here even if it wanted to."

"If it's an old tiger I think you ought to get it cheaper. A thousand rupees is a lot of money."

Louisa Mebbin adopted a protective elder-sister attitude towards money in general, irrespective of nationality or denomination. Her energetic intervention had saved many a rouble from dissipating itself in tips in some Moscow hotel, and francs and centimes clung to her instinctively under circumstances which would have driven them headlong from less sympathetic hands. Her speculations as to the market depreciation of tiger remnants were cut short by the appearance on the scene of the animal itself. As soon as it caught sight of the tethered goat it lay flat on the earth, seemingly less from a desire to take advantage of all available cover than for the purpose of snatching a short rest before commencing the grand attack.

"I believe it's ill," said Louisa Mebbin, loudly in Hindustani, for the benefit of the village headman, who was in ambush in a neighbouring tree.

"Hush!" said Mrs. Packletide, and at that moment the tiger commenced ambling towards his victim.

"Now, now!" urged Miss Mebbin with some excitement; "if he doesn't touch the goat we needn't pay for it." (The bait was an extra.)

The rifle flashed out with a loud report, and the great tawny beast sprang to one side and then rolled over in the stillness of death. In a moment a crowd of excited natives had swarmed on to the scene, and their shouting speedily carried the glad news to the village, where a thumping of tom-toms took up the chorus of triumph. And their triumph and rejoicing found a ready echo in the heart of Mrs. Packletide; already that luncheon-party in Curzon Street seemed immeasurably nearer.

It was Louisa Mebbin who drew attention to the fact that the goat was in death-throes from a mortal bullet-wound, while no trace of the rifle's deadly work could be found on the tiger. Evidently the wrong animal had been hit, and the beast of prey had succumbed to heart-failure, caused by the sudden report of the rifle, accelerated by senile decay. Mrs. Packletide was pardonably annoyed at the discovery; but, at any rate, she was the possessor of a dead tiger, and the villagers, anxious for their thousand rupees, gladly connived at the fiction that she had shot the beast. And Miss Mebbin was a paid companion.

Therefore did Mrs. Packletide face the cameras with a light heart, and her pictured fame reached from the pages of the *Texas Weekly Snapshot* to the illustrated Monday supplement of the *Novoe Vremya*. As for Loona Bimberton, she refused to look at an illustrated paper for weeks, and her letter of thanks for the gift of a tiger-claw brooch was a model of repressed emotions. The luncheon-party she declined; there are limits beyond which repressed emotions become dangerous.

From Curzon Street the tiger-skin rug travelled down to the Manor House, and was duly inspected and admired by the county, and it seemed a fitting and appropriate thing when Mrs. Packletide went to the County Costume Ball in the character of Diana. She refused to fall in, however, with Clovis's tempting suggestion of a primeval dance party, at which every one should wear the skins of beasts they had recently slain. "I should be in rather a Baby Bunting condition," confessed Clovis, "with a miserable rabbit-skin or two to wrap up in, but then," he added, with a rather malicious glance at Diana's proportions, "my figure is quite as good as that Russian dancing boy's."

"How amused every one would be if they knew what really happened," said Louisa Mebbin a few days after the ball.

"What do you mean?" asked Mrs. Packletide quickly.

"How you shot the goat and frightened the tiger to death," said Miss Mebbin, with her disagreeably pleasant laugh.

"No one would believe it," said Mrs. Packletide, her face changing colour as rapidly as though it were going through a book of patterns before post-time.

"Loona Bimberton would," Miss Mebbin said. Mrs. Packletide's face settled on an unbecoming shade of greenish white.

"You surely wouldn't give me away?" she asked.

"I've seen a week-end cottage near Dorking that I should rather like to buy," said Miss Mebbin with seeming irrelevance. "Six hundred and eighty, freehold. Quite a bargain, only I don't happen to have the money."

Louisa Mebbin's pretty week-end cottage, christened by her "Les Fauves," and gay in summer-time with its garden borders of tiger-lilies, is the wonder and admiration of her friends.

"It is a marvel how Louisa manages to do it," is the general verdict.

Mrs. Packletide indulges in no more big-game shooting.

"The incidental expenses are so heavy," she confides to inquiring friends.

Sheila Kaye-Smith

Miss Sheila Kaye-Smith has written many books since her first stories were introduced to American audiences twenty years ago, and her following here has steadily widened because readers have confidence in her strong and sympathetic interpretation of a people and a countryside which they may never know at first-hand. Like Thomas Hardy she has made a world out of a small province. As Hardy struck his roots deep in the Wessex country, so she has also struck to the foundations of Sussex character, writing of its inhabitants with deeply-felt understanding. Hugh Walpole said of her: "She deals in timeless things, the soil, trees, rivers, corn, food and drink. She has timeless themes, birth, death, love, jealousy, patience, maternity, friendship. . . ." It is interesting to compare her work with that of Mary Webb and Constance Holme.

Miss Kaye-Smith's greatest novels are Sussex Gorse (1916), Joanna Godden (1921), and Susan Spray (1931). In 1926 she published the collection Joanna Godden Married from which "The Mockbeggar" is taken, and in 1938 appeared a second group of stories, Faithful Stranger, dealing with the people of Sussex among whom she was born and with whom she lives today. An autobiography Three Ways Home was published in 1937.

THE MOCKBEGGAR *

Sheila Kaye-Smith

Mr. and Mrs. Reginald Dalrymple were walking along the high-road that leads from Iden to Wittersham across the Isle of Oxney. They were very particular about being given their full name

* From *Joanna Godden Married and Other Stories* by Sheila Kaye-Smith. Harper & Brothers, 1926. Reprinted by permission of the author.

of "Reginald" Dalrymple to distinguish them from Mr. and Mrs. Charley Dalrymple, who were in Northhampton workhouse; from the Peter Dalrymples, who tramped in Wales; from the Stanley Dalrymples, who were in prison; and from Serena Dalrymple, who had put herself outside the pale of decent society on the roads by marrying a "nigger."

Mr. Reginald Dalrymple was about sixty-five years old and his back was bent. Otherwise he looked hale enough, and his face, at least as much as could be seen of it through a thatch of brown whiskers, was as red as an autumn pear. He wore a frock coat, gray-flannel trousers, a pair of brown beach shoes with rather inadequate uppers, and a bowler hat.

Mrs. Reginald Dalrymple was about three years younger than her husband and inclined to stoutness, though she looked an able-bodied woman. She wore a very handsome cape trimmed with jet, a woolen muffler that might have been gray, but to which she referred as "me white scarf," and a man's cap set at a rakish angle. She wheeled a perambulator, which did not, however, contain a baby, but the Reginald Dalrymples' luggage—indeed, it may be said, their complete household equipment, which at first glance would appear to consist entirely of old rags. However, a more sympathetic inspection would reveal a really excellent kettle (the leak was only just below the spout), a suspicious-looking rug, an assortment of cups, a tin plate, a screw driver, an ancient cop of *Tit-Bits,* a photograph of a robust young woman with a hat full of feathers, and another photograph of a sailor.

"I'm beginning to feel me feet," said Mrs. Reginald Dalrymple to her husband.

"And I'm thinking it's coming on to rain," said he, with a look up at the lowering sky.

It was autumn, and the red leaves were shaking against soft clouds of October gray which the wind brought down from Benenden in the west.

"Where's our next chance of a doss?" asked Mrs. Dalrymple.

"There's the Throws up at Potman's Heath," replied her husband, "but I reckon they'll be—damp to-night."

"Reg! Don't use such words," said Mrs. Dalrymple, with dignity. "You forget my mother was a Stanley."

"I'm never likely to forget it, the way you goes on about it. Anyone 'u'd think she'd been Queen Victoria on her throne, to hear you talk!

But what I say is, it's coming on to rain and there ain't no union within fifteen miles. Besides, you're feeling your feet," he added, kindly.

"I've walked twelve miles since dinner, Reg," said Mrs. Dalrymple, with a little plaintive sigh.

"Hook on, then," said he, extending a ragged elbow.

She hooked, and for some moments they walked in silence. Then he said:

"It'll be awkward for you pushing the pram with one hand," and took it from her—though Mr. Reginald Dalrymple had often boasted that he had never come down to wheeling a perambulator, and never would.

"I've been thinking," said she, a few minutes later, by which time the rain was spattering freely in the dust—"I've been thinking we must have come near that mockbeggar place by the Stocks. The house was standing there five year ago when we were on the roads with Sue and her lot, and if it hasn't tumbled down since there's one good room in it, anyway, with the ceiling tight, and there's water in the well at the bottom of the yard."

Mr. Dalrymple reflected. "You're right, Hannah!—I believe you're right this once. We should be coming to that mockbeggar in half an hour. It'll be raining the—skies down by that time, so we might go in and light a fire and not trouble about getting farther to-night. It's a good way from the nearest place and we're not like to be meddled with."

Mrs. Dalrymple was feeling her feet more and more, in spite of the supporting elbow and the removal of the pram. She was also beginning to get wet, though this did not worry her, being of custom. She was far more preoccupied with the thought that she could not walk a twelve-mile stretch without getting tired—and she'd been able to walk twice that as a girl, when she and Reginald had tramped all round the country by Chichester. She had had the children then, as well—one slung at her breast and the other hanging on her skirt when his dad did not carry him. She was glad when she saw three sharp gables suddenly draw themselves against the sky, which sagged low over the fields, squirting rain.

"That's it," she said; "that's the mockbeggar. I knew it was some-where in these parts, though we haven't been here since Sue was on the roads with her man. D'you remember that time we dossed under the stack at Wassal?"

Mr. Dalrymple grunted. He was looking for a gap in the hedge, for it struck him that it would be best to go straight across the fields to shelter instead of walking round by the road. He soon found what he thought was a proper opening, and proceeded to enlarge it to meet the ample requirements of his wife by pushing the perambulator through. He then gallantly offered a hand to Mrs. Dalrymple, and after much gasping and effort and crackling of twigs she was at his side in the paddock which belonged to the mockbeggar.

A "mockbeggar house" in Kent is any large-sized house which stands empty close to a highroad, and seems to mock the beggar who plods along, thinking he will find charity at those doors which, on his close arrival, are found to be either swinging on their hinges or barred on emptiness. The mockbeggar at Wittersham was an especially large house, which, owing to want of repairs, a poor landlord, and a defective water supply, had stood empty for some time. It was probably about fifty years old and was built in comfortable Victorian style, but neglect and the misty weather of the Isle of Oxney—that cone round which steam all the mists of the Rother levels and Shirley brooks—had eaten holes in its solid fabric of roof and wall and made its shelter doubtful even to the Reginald Dalrymples, to whom uncracked walls and fair slated roofs were only the occasional experience of the workhouse.

"A downstairs room 'u'd be best," said Mrs. Reginald.

They went into one next the passage on the ground floor. It was full of dead leaves and bits of glass from a broken window, but there was a grate in it where a fire might possibly burn, and the rain was confined to a small pool under the window sill.

"You unpack here, Hannah, and I'll go and get some water for the kettle."

Mrs. Dalrymple extracted the kettle from the pram, carefully wrapped in a piece of newspaper, and while her husband went off she proceeded to arrange her various belongings. The sinister-looking rug she put in the corner with a nice comfortable bit of sacking; that was the bedroom. The cups, the plate, and a broken knife she put on the remains of a shelf; that was the kitchen. While the two photographs she set proudly among the dust and cobwebs on the mantelpiece; that was the parlor. She was then, according to custom, going on to make herself comfortable by taking off her shoes, when she was startled by a noise overhead.

An empty house is full of noises, and Mrs. Dalrymple had a wide experience of empty houses. Mere scuttlings of rats or hootings of owls or rustlings of crickets or howlings of wind in chimneys could not alarm her, but this sound she knew at once was none of these. It was a footstep, a human footstep, which moved in the room overhead, and she held her breath to listen. The next minute she heard more and worse—that murmur coming to her through the boards was a human voice. She stuck her head out of window (no need to open it first) and made a sign to Reginald, who was coming up the yard with the kettle. The sign urged both silence and attention, also haste. His response was immediate; they had often been together in these emergencies, demanding a quick stealth. He did not speak a word till he was back beside her in the room.

"It's people!" said Mrs. Dalrymple, in a hoarse whisper; "there's people here!"

"How d'you know? where are they?"

"They're up above. Heard them talking. Listen!"

They both listened. The sounds in the upper room continued—voices and footsteps.

"There's two," said Mr. Dalrymple. "I can tell by the feet. Who can it be? It's road people like ourselves, most like; no one else 'u'd come here."

"I wonder if it's anyone we know. It might be the Lovells—you know Lance and Aurelia Lovell are walking in Kent."

"I hope it ain't folk in the house after repairs," said Mr. Dalrymple, struck by a sudden thought. "You never know your luck, and some one may have bought the place."

"I hope it's not that stuck-up Eleanor Ripley and her husband," said Mrs. Dalrymple. "We had enough of their airs when we met them at Maidstone. She's got saucers to all her cups."

"Well, I'd sooner it was her than gaujos," returned Mr. Dalrymple; "it 'u'd never do for us to get found here, and it 'u'd mean a-spoiling of the place for visitors."

"You go and have a look," suggested his wife. "Take off your shoes."

Mr. Dalrymple shuffled them off without undoing the laces, and left the room with extreme caution. His progress upstairs and along the passage was as silent as only his kind know how to make it.

Mrs. Dalrymple strained her ears, which were as quick as they were when she was seventeen. The voices continued, but she detected more than conversation—she thought she heard a sound of sobbing. Time went on. Reginald was evidently maneuvering with his usual discretion, for the flow of talk above remained uninterrupted. Indeed, so velvet-footed was he that he was back at her side before she expected him, and, old stager though she was, nearly made her jump.

"It's gaujos," he said, in a low voice. "There's two of 'em, mighty queer. . . ."

"How queer?"

"Oh, the girl's got short hair like a boy, and the boy he's soft-looking. They're only a boy and girl. Maybe we could scare 'em out."

"I don't want to scare them," said Mrs. Dalrymple. "The night ain't fit for a dog and I'd be sorry to turn 'em out in it. But if they ain't road people, what are they doing here?"

"They're quarreling," said Mr. Dalrymple—"quarreling and crying."

"I thought I heard crying."

"It's the girl's crying, into a handkerchief. She's got a white handkerchief with a blue border."

"Are they gentry?"

"Fine gentry, I should say, by their clothes, but I don't think they're after repairs or taking the house or anything."

"What are they doing, then?"

"Sheltering from the rain, like us, and I don't think they've got much money, for they're talking a lot of words about the price of a ticket to London."

"Is that what the trouble's about?"

"No, I don't know as it is. I can't make out a lot of their foolish words, but it seems as either he wants to marry her and she won't, or else as they are married and she wants to get shut of him and he won't have it."

"I should think not!" said Mrs. Dalrymple. "I'm for sticking to your lawful certificated husband, and that's why I'd never go to the workhouse except just now and again for a rest. You know that Eleanor she says a woman should be able to get rid of her husband if she wants to, and take a new one, which you can't do in a workhouse, but I was always brought up to strict notions as to marriage. My mother was a married woman, and so is my daughter after me."

"Well, maybe they ain't married. I don't rightly know. They had too many words for me to be able to make out the lot of them. But hold your tongue, Hannah; they're coming down."

Steps sounded on the rickety stairs of the mockbeggar—unskillful, gaujo steps that made every stair creak.

Mrs. Dalrymple made a hasty movement as if to gather up her

possessions and thrust them back under the rags in the perambulator, stirred, perhaps, by some dim instinct of far-off ancestors who must not let the stranger look upon their household gods.

Her husband laid hold of her arm. "Don't be scared; they're nothing —hardly cut their teeth yet!"

At the same moment a young man appeared in the doorway. He was tall and loosely knit, with a heavy coltishness about him, as of one not yet fully grown. Behind him a girl's face stood out of the shadows, framed in a queer little stiff mane of cropped hair. Her eyes were bright and resolute, but at the same time frightened.

"Hullo!" said the youth, truculently, to Mr. Dalrymple. "What are you doing here?"

Mr. Dalrymple looked the aggressor up and down. "This place belongs to us as much as you."

"*More* than you," said Mrs. Dalrymple, "seeing as we're road people and you're house people who have no business here!"

"Well, I might ask what your business is?"

"Our business is to have supper and a doss on a wet night, and if you keeps clear and don't come round talking foolishness we won't meddle with you, and there's room enough for the lot of us."

"It's all right, Bob," said the girl. "Let's go back." Her face was flushed, and her eyes were a little swollen under the straight line of her fringe.

Mrs. Dalrymple suddenly became professional.

"I'm not the one to interfere with a real lady and gentleman," she whined, putting on the manner which she kept for well-dressed strangers. "I'm sure you're a real fine lady and gentleman, and if the lady will only cross my palm with silver I'll tell her some gorgeous things about herself, and maybe more about the gentleman, too. I can see a lot of money coming to you, lady—even more than the price of a ticket to London!"

The girl darted a surprised look at her companion.

"Come, lady," wheedled Mrs. Dalrymple. "I'll tell you a high-class tale about husbands."

The girl turned away with a heightening of her flush. "I can't bear this nonsense," she said, in a low voice to the young man. "These people needn't interfere with us, nor we with them. Let's go upstairs."

The youth looked sulky. "It's all very well," he said, "but they've got the only decent room; the rain's coming through all the ceilings above."

"You should have put your traps in here," said Mr. Dalrymple, "then we should have kept out of it; but as we're here we mean to stick. My old woman's wet through, and she's going to have a dry doss, I'm blowed if she ain't."

"Oh, well, come on," said the young man. "It may clear up before night, and then we'll start again."

He turned away, followed by the girl, and the Reginald Dalrymples were left in peace.

"There's queer things you meets on the roads," said Mrs. Dalrymple, "and it isn't so much the people you meet as the places where you meets 'em. Now what are those two doing here? I'm beat."

"You're curious," retorted Mr. Dalrymple, "fair eat up with curiosity, because you're a woman. Now I don't think twice about 'em as long as they leaves me alone, and nor won't you, Hannah, if you've got sense. Here, let's have a fire and get ourselves dry."

He turned to the all-providing pram and from its depths drew forth its last treasures—some blocks of wood and a bundle of sticks. The Dalrymples always carried a supply of dry firewood about with them, for they were getting old and considered themselves entitled to a certain amount of luxury in their old age.

A fire was soon lit and the kettle put on to boil; once it was blazing, the addition of a few damp sticks gathered outside no longer mattered. The room grew warm and Mrs. Dalrymple's clothes began to steam. Her husband took off his coat and put it over her shoulders.

"There you are, Hannah," he said. "I don't want it. This weather makes me sweat, but you've got to take care of your bones."

They made tea, which they drank in great comfort, with half a stale loaf of bread and a lump of lard. Outside, the rain was hissing down, while the wind howled in the chimney.

"It'll be wet upstairs," said Mrs. Dalrymple, pleasantly.

The fire was beginning to die down, and Mr. Dalrymple did not fancy going outside to get in more sticks.

"I'll go and have a look at the banisters," he said, "and maybe there's a bit of a cupboard door."

The banisters looked satisfactory as fuel, and he was in the act of wrenching a couple of them out when he saw the young man on the staircase above him.

"Hi!" said the latter, dejectedly, "we're half flooded out upstairs. I was going to suggest that we come in with you till it stops raining. We'll clear out as soon as the weather lets us."

"We're poor people," said Mr. Dalrymple—"Mrs. Reginald Dalrymple and I are poor people, and we can't afford to take lodgers at our fire without a bit of silver."

"We aren't asking you to take us as lodgers, damn it! I'm just asking you to let the young lady come and sit in a dry place. It's what you wouldn't refuse a dog."

"I would certainly refuse a dog," returned Mr. Dalrymple, with dignity. "My wife and I never allows no dogs to sit with us, it being well-known as dogs have fleas, and my wife being a lady as 'll have nothing to do with fleas!"

The young man surveyed Mr. Dalrymple as if he himself belonged to that species.

"Well, if you want money," he said, "I suppose you must have it. Will a shilling do you?"

"A shilling will do me very well," said Mr. Dalrymple, loftily, "and it includes the fire. We have a very excellent fire!"

"So I gather," said the young man as he coughed in the smoke that was eddying upstairs.

But even the Dalrymple quarters, full of smoke and the smell of ancient rags, were better than the leaking, dripping rooms where he and Meave Anstey had been struggling in vain to keep warm and dry. Meave was shivering now, and her face was no longer flushed, but blue, as she sat down gingerly beside Mrs. Dalrymple's fire.

"Cross my hand with silver, lady," said that good woman, returning unabashed to the attack, "and I'll tell you the prettiest fortune that was ever spoke."

"I don't want your lies," said the girl, angrily, with a sudden gulp.

"Lies, lady! I never tells lies! May I be struck dead if I does."

"My wife is well known as a truth-telling woman," said Mr. Dalrymple, "and I'll thank you not to miscall her!"

For some reason Meave felt rebuked, though she believed neither of them.

"I'm sorry," she said. "Well, you may tell my fortune if you like, but I've only got sixpence."

"Thank you, lady. Thank you kindly, lady. Sixpence will buy me a packet of tea at the next village, lady. And I'll drink your very good health in it, for I never drinks nothing stronger than tea, which is well known."

Meave held out a soft, artistic-looking hand, which by this time was more than a little grimy.

"I likes dirt on the hand," remarked Mrs. Dalrymple; "it helps me to see the lines better. Now what I see is this: I see a railway line, with a train on it going to London, and you and a gentleman are in that train, and when you get to London I sees a church, and a priest, and a great crowd of people, and rice, and slippers. I see all that, and you in the middle of it, beautiful as an angel, and beside you a tall, handsome young gentleman with light hair and brown eyes."

The girl angrily pulled her hand away. "Don't talk such nonsense, please! I can't stand it."

"You don't want to get married?"

"No, I don't. As if I'd—Rice! . . . Slippers! . . . White veil . . . !" The scorn grew in her voice.

"There's a wedding cake," encouraged Mrs. Dalrymple, "with sugar all over it!"

"I don't want to hear any more. Look here, you're a fortune teller, aren't you? I suppose I'm the first girl you've ever met who hasn't wanted to hear about marriage?"

"You would be the first if I believed you," said Mrs. Dalrymple, who had dropped her company manner in the familiarity of the scene.

"Well, you can believe it. I don't want to get married—I don't believe in marriage," and she threw a defiant glance not at Mrs. Dalrymple, but at the young man.

"But a girl can't live by herself. It ain't natural."

"And it ain't safe," said Mr. Dalrymple. "I've known more than one time when my wife here might have got copped off if it hadn't been for having me handy to show her the right trick."

"I don't mean to be alone," said the girl. "I don't believe in that, either. What I hate is the hypocrisy and the slavery of marriage." Her voice rose and warmed; she became a little lecturer. "It's the idea of losing my freedom which I can't bear. If women hadn't been slaves for centuries none of them could bear it. When I choose my mate we shall both of us be free—free to love and free to part. There shall be no keeping of the outer husk when the kernel has rotted."

Mr. and Mrs. Dalrymple stared silently with their mouths open, and the young man looked uneasy.

"You see me and my friend here, now," continued Meave, "and even you, a woman outside the ordinary conventions of society, immediately form the idea that we're going to be married. I tell you you're utterly wrong. If we were going to be married we shouldn't be running away; we should be sitting at home, unpacking wedding presents. We are going to join our lives together, but in freedom, not in bondage. We shall be free to part whenever we choose, free to work, free to go our own ways. . . ." She had almost forgotten that she had not got her debating society before her.

"Well," said Mrs. Dalrymple, "I don't want to part and I don't want to work and I don't want to go any different ways from Mr. Dalrymple, so I can't see the sense of what you're saying. Mr. Dalrymple and me has been married close on forty years, and we've got a daughter Sue who's been married twenty years to a fine feller in the osier trade. She has a caravan with brass rods on the door and lace curtains in the windows, and five of the dearest little children you could think of; leastways, the eldest's nearly grown up now. And we've got a son Jerome who's a sailor and has had two wives one after the other. The wife he's got now lives in a house and has a china tea service. We're proud of our children, but they've gone away from us now and I don't know what we'd do if we hadn't got each other."

"She's uncommon set on her children," said Mr. Dalrymple. "That's their likenesses up there on the shelf, what we carries about with us everywhere. My daughter Sue 'u'd have us stay with her, and once we went and stopped with my son and daughter at Portsmouth and slept in a bed. But we'd just as soon be along of each other here."

"Reckon you wants your husband more when you're old than when you're young," said Mrs. Dalrymple. "I'm getting too old to do most of the things I used, and I don't know what I'd do if it wasn't for Mr. Dalrymple, who does them for me. Our idea is to keep on the roads till we're old enough to go into the married quarters at the workhouse. It 'u'd break our hearts if we was to be separated after all this time. . . . I don't hold with being parted from your certificated husband."

"You gets used to each other like," said Mr. Dalrymple. "If I was to go on the roads with anyone else I'd be so bothered and vexed I shouldn't know what to do."

"If I was ever to see you on the roads with anyone else . . ." said Mrs. Dalrymple, menacingly.

"Not likely, old lady," said he, pushing her cap over one eye in playful affection.

"Now, now," said she, "none of your larks." But she looked pleased and a little proud of him.

The rain had become a storm, with a rush of wind in the chimneys of the mockbeggar. Dead leaves flew rustling round the yard, and the

pool under the window was a little lake. But beside the fire it was
warm and dry, though the smoke, as it eddied and waved under the
low ceiling, made Meave choke a little, and strange tears came into
her eyes—of course that was the smoke. She felt proud and happy.
She had broken free at last . . . and she was saving Bob, who otherwise would have become a slave, having all the instincts of one. . . .

"Ooo-ooo . . . yah!" A loud yawn from Mr. Dalrymple made her
start. "I'm—sleepy," he added, conversationally.

"Now don't you start using words again," said his wife. "I'm not
accustomed to them, being a Stanley, and I reckon the young lady
ain't, either, for all her uncertificated ideas. If you wants to go to
sleep—go."

"I'm going," said Mr. Dalrymple.

"Then take back your coat. I've dried under it nicely."

"I don't want any coat. I'm warm as a bug."

"You want it, and you'll take it. Here now."

An amiable tussle followed, which ended in Mr. Dalrymple putting
on his coat, while his wife had the piece of sacking in addition to her
share of the rug. They took no more notice of Meave Anstey and Bob
Pettigrew, but were soon asleep, with the queer, stiff, silent sleep of
animals who rest among foes.

"Rum old pair," said Bob, under his breath. "I'm sorry you've been
let in for this, Meave, but it's better than being swamped upstairs."

"Oh, they're all right! I rather like them, though of course they're
frauds. They're decent to each other, which is odd. I rather thought
that type of man always bullied his wife."

"Men aren't quite such rotters as you think—even tramps."

He spoke irritably, for the sordid side of the adventure was un-
pleasantly obvious on this night of wind and rain without, and stuffi-
ness and teasing smoke within. To his surprise, she did not take up
his challenge. She sat watching the old couple as they lay huddled in
the corner, a confused blot of rags and shadows.

"It's love that holds them together," she said, in her debating-society
voice, hushed down to a whisper, "not the mere fact of marriage."

"I dunno," said he, truculently. "I don't believe they'd be together
now if they weren't married—anyhow, not together like this."

"Why not? Why shouldn't lovers be faithful?"

"It's different, as I've told you a hundred times. Especially when
you're old. I'd think nothing of it if they were young or middle-aged.
But they're old, and there must have been lots of times when they

were tired of loving and tired of life, and 'u'd never have gone on if they hadn't belonged to each other."

"That's just it—they were tied."

"And the tie kept them together over the bad places. It's like being roped on a climb; when one or another of them went down, there was always the rope, and as soon as they were on their legs again they didn't notice it. I believe people who aren't married—no matter how they love each other—somehow they're hardly ever in together at the finish. . . . You generally find that if the going's rough they drift apart. Why, you, yourself, say you'd hate to belong to a man all your life; you want the one great Moment, and then not to spoil it by going on together. I think there's a good deal to be said for that, though, as I've told you a dozen times, I want to marry you."

He looked very young as he sat there beside her in the dying firelight. He was only a boy or he wouldn't have come with her—he wouldn't have let her force her adventure on him like that. He was very young—but he would grow old, like Mr. Dalrymple. That soft brown lick of hair of his forehead would be gray—his face a little worn, perhaps. Should she see it then, or would they have gone their separate ways? She wondered what he would look like when he was old—what he would be like—kind, protective, unselfish, like Mr. Dalrymple—a strong arm to lean on when she needed it most? . . . Growing old together . . . together not only at the start, but at the journey's end . . . but tied . . . as Mr. and Mrs. Dalrymple were tied . . . by the memories of struggles and toils together, by adventures and hardships shared, by long years of companionship in wayfaring, by the love of their children. . . .

She bowed her head suddenly over her lap and tears fell into her hands.

"Meave—darling—what is it? Tell me."

His arm was round her, his shoulder under her cheek.

"Bob . . . Bob . . . will you always love me—when we're old?"

"Of course I shall always love you."

"As much as that?" and she waved her hand toward the indefinite mass of Mr. and Mrs. Dalrymple.

"I should hope so," with a little contempt.

"Then Bob . . . let's go back."

"Go back where?"

"Home. I want us to get married."

"My little Meave! . . . But you said—"

"It's seeing them. They're so happy—they're so true. They're dirty, terrible, shameless old things, but they're happy; they've got something we haven't got—that we can't ever have, unless we're married."

He had wisdom to be silent, hugging her without a word.

"Let's go back home. It's not ten o'clock yet, and we can tell mother we were caught in the rain and waited to see if it would stop. She need never know."

"And we'll get married?"

"Yes, though you know she'll make us go in for everything—bridesmaids and rice and church bells and all that."

"Never mind; it'll make Mrs. Dalrymple's fortune come true."

They both laughed a little.

"When shall we start?" he asked her.

"Oh, soon—now."

"But it's coming down in buckets."

"Never mind; we're only an hour from home. We haven't got to face all that walk into Rye and then the journey to London."

She shivered a little, and he drew her close in sudden, fierce protection.

"I shouldn't have let you come. I've been a fool about all this. I didn't believe in it, and yet I gave way because I was afraid of losing you. I should have had sense enough for both of us, and made you go my way instead of yours."

"Is that what you're going to do in the future?"

"Yes—when you're a silly little thing."

She laughed, and their lips came together.

It was he who remembered the need for quick action.

"Come, we must be getting off, or we sha'n't be home till it's too late to explain. Are you ready?"

"Quite. I'm glad we didn't bring any luggage, except in our ulster pockets. It would have been difficult to explain why we'd gone for a walk with two suitcases."

They giggled light-heartedly, and went out on tiptoe.

They were off. But just as they were leaving the mockbeggar she remembered something that had been left undone.

"Bob, we ought to tell them. I want them to know."

"For Heaven's sake don't go back and wake them up! What d' you want them to know?"

"That we're going to be married."

"What on earth has that got to do with them?"

"Oh, nothing, of course . . . but I thought . . . Give me a leaf out of your pocket book, there's a darling."

He gave it, and she scribbled on it, "We are going to be married," and, creeping back into the room, put it on the mantelpiece beside the pictures of the blowsy girl and the sailor.

"And look here," she added, "as we're not going to London, we might just leave the price of our tickets with them. It may help them a lot."

"They'll probably spend it on drink."

"Well, let them. I don't care. I can't bear to think of people without proper boots on their feet."

The firelight was playing reproachfully on the toe of Mr. Dalrymple's shoe.

"Nor can I. Well, here's the money. It'll be a surprise for them when they wake up."

He put it beside the paper on the mantelpiece, and they went out.

It was daylight when Mr. and Mrs. Dalrymple woke. The storm had ceased.

"Hullo! They've gone," said he.

"Not taken any of our things with them, have they, Reg?" asked his wife, looking anxiously round.

"Not they. They're gentry. Gentry don't take poor people's things without a lawyer."

"You never know. Besides, they was queer gentry. All that talk she had about marriage . . . it was shocking. If I'd ever heard my Sue using such words I'd have—"

"Wot's this?"

Her husband had found the treasure on the mantelpiece.

"I'm blowed if they haven't left their money behind 'em! Ten bob if it's a tanner! Well, I'm blowed!"

"That's luck for us, anyway, if it ain't exactly luck for them."

"Oh, I reckon they done it on purpose. They'd never have put their dough there by our Jack's likeness. It's Christian charity, that's what it is."

"I don't believe it's Christian charity—that 'u'd be tuppence. Ten bob's nothing but an accident. Howsumever, it makes no difference to me what it is as long as it's there. I could do with a plate o' ham."

"A plate o' ham and a cup o' coffee, and a bottle o' whiskey to come along with us to Tonbridge."

"That's it. But look here, Reg—there's writing on the paper."

"So there is. Pity we ain't scollards."

"Maybe it's a word for us."

"That's what it is, I reckon."

She picked up the paper and inspected it solemnly, then passed it on to her husband, who did the same.

"Pity we never got no school learning, Reg."

"I've never felt the want."

"But I'd like to be able to read the word they've left us."

"That's because you're a woman and made of curiosity. I, being a man, says let's take the money and be thankful. And now, old lady, pack up your traps, for, thanks to this bit of luck, we'll have our breakfast at the Blue Boar."

Katherine Mansfield

THERE WAS in Katherine Mansfield a relentless drive for perfection; reading her Journal one hears the accent of the unyielding idealist— "marks of earthly degradation still pursue me. I am not crystal clear. . . . There is so much to do, and I do so little. . . ." But she "did," in all, eighty-eight stories, the best of which the world will be slow to let die. With fastidious, but ruthless delicacy she sought to reveal human attitudes, some of them lovely, others calling for the cautery of the satirist. Not for her the smoothly-turned plots, the stock characters of the fiction market; she wrote from her own view of life. Her view was the intent, doomed vision of those who seize experience before it is too late.

Her range was not wide nor was her genius robust. Her weaker stories are finical; and she came to feel a tormenting self-distrust. But no one can read her collected stories without feeling that she set standards which—to paraphrase T. S. Eliot—it is desperate for story-telling to ignore.

She was born Kathleen Beauchamp in New Zealand in 1888. Educated in London, and returning there after two years at home, she sought a career in music and literature. In 1913 she married the English critic, J. Middleton Murry, editor of the London Athenaeum, a periodical for which she wrote both criticism and fiction. After a long struggle against ill health, she died at Fontainebleau in 1923. Her several volumes of short stories were published in a collected edition by Alfred A. Knopf in 1933.

TAKING THE VEIL *
Katherine Mansfield

IT SEEMED impossible that anyone should be unhappy on such a beautiful morning. Nobody was, decided Edna, except herself. The windows were flung wide in the houses. From within there came the sound of pianos, little hands chased after each other and ran away from each other, practicing scales. The trees fluttered in the sunny gardens, all bright with spring flowers. Street boys whistled, a little dog barked; people passed by, walking so lightly, so swiftly, they looked as though they wanted to break into a run. Now she actually saw in the distance a parasol, peach-coloured, the first parasol of the year.

Perhaps even Edna did not look quite as unhappy as she felt. It is not easy to look tragic at eighteen, when you are extremely pretty, with the cheeks and lips and shining eyes of perfect health. Above all, when you are wearing a French blue frock and your new spring hat trimmed with cornflowers. True, she carried under her arm a book bound in horrid black leather. Perhaps the book provided a gloomy note, but only by accident; it was the ordinary Library binding. For Edna had made going to the Library an excuse for getting out of the house to think, to realize what had happened, to decide somehow what was to be done now.

An awful thing had happened. Quite suddenly, at the theatre last night, when she and Jimmy were seated side by side in the dress-circle, without a moment's warning—in fact, she had just finished a chocolate almond and passed the box to him again—she had fallen in love with an actor. But—fallen—in—love. . . .

The feeling was unlike anything she had ever imagined before. It wasn't in the least pleasant. It was hardly thrilling. Unless you can call the most dreadful sensation of hopeless misery, despair, agony and wretchedness, thrilling. Combined with the certainty that if that actor met her on the pavement after, while Jimmy was fetching their cab, she would follow him to the ends of the earth, at a nod, at a sign, without giving another thought to Jimmy or her father and mother or her happy home and countless friends again. . . .

The play had begun fairly cheerfully. That was at the chocolate

* Reprinted from *The Doves' Nest and Other Stories* by Katherine Mansfield, by permission of and special arrangement with Alfred A. Knopf, Inc., authorized publishers.
573

almond stage. Then the hero had gone blind. Terrible moment! Edna
had cried so much she had to borrow Jimmy's folded, smooth-feeling
handkerchief as well. Not that crying mattered. Whole rows were in
tears. Even the men blew their noses with a loud trumpeting noise
and tried to peer at the program instead of looking at the stage.
Jimmy, most mercifully dry-eyed—for what would she have done
without his handkerchief?—squeezed her free hand, and whispered
"Cheer up, darling girl!" And it was then she had taken a last
chocolate almond to please him and passed the box again. Then, there
had been that ghastly scene with the hero alone on the stage in a
deserted room at twilight, with a band playing outside and the sound
of cheering coming from the street. He had tried—ah! how painfully,
how pitifully—to grope his way to the window. He had succeeded at
last. There he stood holding the curtain while one beam of light, just
one beam, shone full on his raised sightless face, and the band faded
away into the distance. . . .

It was—really, it was absolutely—oh, the most—it was simply—in
fact, from that moment Edna knew that life could never be the same.
She drew her hand away from Jimmy's, leaned back, and shut the
chocolate box for ever. This at last was love!

Edna and Jimmy were engaged. She had had her hair up for a
year and a half; they had been publicly engaged for a year. But they
had known they were going to marry each other ever since they
walked in the Botanical Gardens with their nurses, and sat on the
grass with a wine biscuit and a piece of barley-sugar each for their tea.
It was so much an accepted thing that Edna had worn a wonderfully
good imitation of an engagement-ring out of a cracker all the time
she was at school. And up till now they had been devoted to each
other.

But now it was over. It was so completely over that Edna found it
difficult to believe that Jimmy did not realize it too. She smiled wisely,
sadly, as she turned into the gardens of the Convent of the Sacred
Heart and mounted the path that led through them to Hill Street.
How much better to know it now than to wait until after they were
married! Now it was possible that Jimmy would get over it. No, it
was no use deceiving herself; he would never get over it! His life was
wrecked, was ruined; that was inevitable. But he was young. . . .
Time, people said, Time might make a little, just a little difference.
In forty years when he was an old man, he might be able to think of
her calmly—perhaps. But she,—what did the future hold for her?

Edna had reached the top of the path. There under a new-leafed tree, hung with little bunches of white flowers, she sat down on a green bench and looked over the Convent flower-beds. In the one nearest to her there grew tender stocks, with a border of blue, shell-like pansies, with at one corner a clump of creamy freezias, their light spears of green criss-crossed over the flowers. The Convent pigeons were tumbling high in the air, and she could hear the voice of Sister Agnes who was giving a singing lesson. *Ah-me,* sounded the deep tones of the nun, and *Ah-me,* they were echoed. . . .

If she did not marry Jimmy, of course, she would marry nobody. The man she was in love with, the famous actor—Edna had far too much common-sense not to realize that would never be. It was very odd. She didn't even want it to be. Her love was too intense for that. It had to be endured, silently; it had to torment her. It was, she supposed, simply that kind of love.

"But, Edna!" cried Jimmy. "Can you never change? Can I never hope again?"

Oh, what sorrow to have to say it, but it must be said. "No, Jimmy, I will never change."

Edna bowed her head; and a little flower fell on her lap, and the voice of Sister Agnes cried suddenly *Ah-no,* and the echo came, *Ah-no.* . . .

At that moment the future was revealed. Edna saw it all. She was astonished; it took her breath away at first. But, after all, what could be more natural? She would go into a convent. . . . Her father and mother do everything to dissuade her, in vain. As for Jimmy, his state of mind hardly bears thinking about. Why can't they understand? How can they add to her suffering like this? The world is cruel, terribly cruel! After a last scene when she gives away her jewellery and so on to her best friends—she so calm, they so broken-hearted— into a convent she goes. No, one moment. The very evening of her going is the actor's last evening at Port Willin. He receives by a strange messenger a box. It is full of white flowers. But there is no name, no card. Nothing? Yes, under the roses, wrapped in a white handkerchief, Edna's last photograph with, written underneath,

The world forgetting, by the world forgot.

Edna sat very still under the trees; she clasped the black book in her fingers as though it were her missal. She takes the name of Sister Angela. Snip! Snip! All her lovely hair is cut off. Will she be allowed to send one curl to Jimmy? It is contrived somehow. And in a blue gown with a white head-band Sister Angela goes from the convent to the chapel, from the chapel to the convent with something unearthly in her look, in her sorrowful eyes, and in the gentle smile with which they greet the little children who run to her. A saint! She hears it whispered as she paces the chill, wax-smelling corridors. A saint! And visitors to the chapel are told of the nun whose voice is heard above the other voices, of her youth, her beauty, of her tragic, tragic love. "There is a man in this town whose life is ruined. . . ."

A big bee, a golden furry fellow, crept into a freezia, and the delicate flower leaned over, swung, shook; and when the bee flew away it fluttered still as though it were laughing. Happy, careless flower!

Sister Angela looked at it and said, "Now it is winter." One night, lying in her icy cell she hears a cry. Some stray animal is out there in the garden, a kitten or lamb or—well, whatever little animal might be there. Up rises the sleepless nun. All in white, shivering but fearless, she goes and brings it in. But next morning, when the bell rings for matins, she is found tossing in high fever . . . in delirium . . . and she never recovers. In three days all is over. The service has been said in the chapel, and she is buried in the corner of the cemetery reserved for the nuns, where there are plain little crosses of wood. Rest in Peace, Sister Angela. . . .

Now it is evening. Two old people leaning on each other come slowly to the grave and kneel down sobbing, "Our daughter! Our only daughter!" Now there comes another. He is all in black; he comes slowly. But when he is there and lifts his black hat, Edna sees to her horror his hair is snow-white. Jimmy! Too late, too late! The tears are running down his face; he is crying *now*. Too late, too late! The wind shakes the leafless trees in the churchyard. He gives one awful bitter cry.

Edna's black book fell with a thud to the garden path. She jumped up, her heart beating. My darling! No, it's not too late. It's all been a mistake, a terrible dream. Oh, that white hair! How could she have done it? She has not done it. Oh, heavens! Oh, what happiness! She is free, young, and nobody knows her secret. Everything is still possible for her and Jimmy. The house they have planned may still be built, the little solemn boy with his hands behind his back watching them plant the standard roses may still be born. His baby sister . . . But when Edna got as far as his baby sister, she stretched out her arms as though the little love came flying through the air to her, and gazing at the garden, at the white sprays on the tree, at those darling pigeons blue against the blue, and the Convent with its narrow windows, she realized it now at last for the first time in her life—she had never imagined any feeling like it before—she knew what it was to be in love, but—in—love!

Seán O'Faoláin

Since James Joyce's Dubliners was published in 1914, a number of younger writers, among them Seán O'Faoláin, Liam O'Flaherty, and Frank O'Connor, have contributed memorably to a great heritage of story telling. O'Faoláin's first stories Midsummer Night Madness (1932) were accorded high praise by the critics, some of whom remarked a Joycean influence in their sensitive rhythms. His vigorous and original talent has gone on in a direction of its own. Two novels Nest of Simple Folk and Bird Alone were published within the next four years, and in 1938 O'Faoláin published another collection of short stories A Purse of Coppers, a strange and exciting work. He has also recently edited an anthology of old Irish lyric verse The Silver Branch.

Seán O'Faoláin was born in Cork in 1910, and is a graduate of the National University of Ireland. After taking "the left side" in the Irish Civil War, he came to America for study at Harvard where he held fellowships in 1926 and 1928. His first story in this country was published in Hound and Horn. He has also been a frequent contributor to Story. He is a charter member of the Irish Academy of Letters.

LONELY LIVES *

Seán O'Faoláin

FROM BETWEEN the little wayside platforms the railway shot two shining arrows off into the vast bogland where they vanished over a rise that might have been imperceptible without them. It was just before sunset in early spring, a soft evening of evaporating moisture

* From Story, October, 1936. Copyright, 1936. Reprinted by permission of Seán O'Faoláin and Curtis Brown, Ltd.

and tentative bird-song; for the birds seemed to be practising rather than singing, twirling and stopping, and twirling and stopping, and when the bold thrush rolled out a whirl of sound he might have been mocking all the other eager, stupid little fellows like the bullfinch or the tits who had not yet learned their songs.

The three men, leaning on the wooden railing along the platform, looked at the blush of the sun on the last drifts of snow on the far-off mountains, and though every rail was cut into an A shape on top, uncomfortable for arm or elbow, they found it restful to lean and look over the bog, speaking hardly at all. They had been walking all day on the bogs and now were dog-tired. They were waiting for the last train to take them into the country town where they all three taught in the Diocesan College.

The priest stood in the middle, a young man, too fat for his years, with drooping lids, puffed lips, and a red face as if he suffered from blood pressure. The same features on another man might have suggested a sensual nature but there was in his heavily lidded eyes a look that was sometimes whimsical and sometimes sad, and that look, with the gentle turn to his mouth when he smiled, gave him the appearance of a man who had gone through many struggles and finally solved his problems in a spirit of good-humored regret. So, now, as he pulled at his pipe and looked down into a cold bog-stream that flowed beneath them, his chin and his piggy jowls rested on his Roman collar, expanded around his little mouth as if he might at any moment break into a little, silent chuckle. Only, you might have felt, those tired eyes would not even then have changed: they would have mocked his own smile.

On his left, carrying the haversack, was a small dark man, with a slim small body and a button of a head and clipped dark mustaches. The main thing about him was that he did break occasionally into sudden talk, and when he did he banged the hard railings repeatedly or lifted his two fists in the air and slapped his forehead. He did all these things, suddenly, when he cried out:

"Why on earth is this ten-thousand times accursed station three miles from the village? What's it here for at all? My God, what a country! What—is—it—for?"

"To take us home," said the third man, and the priest's belly shook a little, too tired to expel laughter.

There was nothing remarkable about this third man except that he had handlebar mustaches and a long black coat and a black hat that came down low on his forehead and shaded his melancholy face; when he spoke, however, his face was gentle as the fluting of a dove. There was nothing resigned about him; his oblong face was blackberry-colored where he shaved and delicate as a woman's where he did not. His eyes were lined with a myriad of fine wrinkles. They were cranky, tormented eyes, and his mouth was thin and cold and hard.

"I know," cried the small man. "It's some bloody Czar that did it. Some fool of an Under-Secretary long ago or some ass of a flaming Lord Lieutenant who took a ruler and drew a line across Ireland and said, 'That shall be the route of the new railway!' God, what a flaming country!"

"I wonder," said the sad man, Hanafan, in his slow voice, "do the common people ever admire scenery?"

"Now, that's very interesting, Hanafan," cried the small man across the priest's chest. "That's a most extraordinary thing. I often thought of that. Isn't that a coincidence?"

"Well," said the sad Hanafan, blushing modestly, "it's a common enough idea, you know."

"Of course they do," said the deep basso of the priest.

"But do they, do they, do they?" shouted the little man, hammering the railing.

The priest nodded, never taking his eyes from the stream or his pipe from his little mouth.

"How do you know?" demanded the small man, leaping backward and whirling his head left, right, and up in the air, as if the answer were a bird.

"Why wouldn't they?" grunted the priest.

"I know what you mean," interrupted the small man and he wagged his finger into the priest's face. "I know. I met men like that. Our gardener at home, for example. I'd say to him—he was an awful old drunkard—he'd be lying of a hot summer's afternoon under an apple-tree—a lazy old ruffian, 'Grand day, Murphy,' I'd say. 'Oh, a grand day, God bless it,' he'd say, 'and isn't it good to be alive?' But, that's not admiring the scenery," went on the small man. "It's not being *conscious* of it. It isn't, if you understand me, projecting the idea of the beauty of the scene, the idea, into one's own consciousness. Is it, now, Hanafan? And that's what you mean by admiring the scenery."

"Well," said Hanafan, and his words were like prize pigeons that he released one by one from his hands, "I don't know. I'm not sure I mean that."

"Then what the hell *do* you mean?"

"If a man said to me," went on Hanafan, in his downy voice, " 'I do be sometimes sitting here, Mr. Hanafan, enjoying the cool of the evening,' I'd say that that man was enjoying the scenery even though he might not know he was doing so at all."

The priest nodded. The small man looked contemptuously at Hanafan who now began to quote from Gray's "Elegy" in his round, womanly voice, all the time looking sadly at the warmth of the sun fading from the distant grains of snow, and the mountains becoming black and cold:

The lowing herd winds slowly o'er the lea. . . .

"I know, I know," interrupted the other, but Hanafan went on quietly,

The ploughman homeward plods his weary way;
And leaves the world to darkness, and to me.

"You see I feel," he said, "that the ploughman responded to the sense of the end of the day, and the way the fields were all gentle, and dark, and quiet. Just like the bog there . . . is . . . all. . . ." His voice died out.

"Ah, damn it," said the small man in disgust, "that has nothing to do with it."

"It has, Mr. Governey," murmured the priest. "In a sense it has."

"Every man," cried Hanafan, aroused with such vigor that the other two glanced at him, "lives out his own imagination of himself. And every imagination must have a background. I'll tell you a queer thing. It's about the station master in this station a few years ago."

The priest nodded and chuckled aloud.

"He was nearly sixty-five," said Hanafan. "And he was married, and had a grown-up son in New York, and a daughter, a nun in South America."

"I sent her there," said the priest. "A nice poor girl she was, God rest her."

"Did she die?" asked Hanafan, and when the priest said, "Yes," he fell silent and forgot his story until the teacher reminded him crossly.

"Yes," said Hanafan. But, again, he stopped because the station porter came out with two oil lamps, one of which he put into the frame of the standard near them.

"It's a grand evening, father," he said as he turned up the wick.

"Is she late again?" asked the priest, and the porter looked up the line at the signal, and said:

"Aye, she's a trifle behindhand, I'm thinking."

He got down and drew a great silver watch from his corduroy vest and held it up to the setting sun, peering through the yellow celluloid guard.

"She's due, bedad. Ah, she'll be here in a quarter of an hour all right."

The small man groaned and said, "What a country!" The other two looked up at the lamp and then away, and Hanafan said,

"Isn't it dark!"

The porter had walked away.

"Well," resumed Hanafan suddenly, "this old station master! His name was Boyhan. He thought he had a great voice for singing. He was stationed at N—" (he mentioned the town where they all lived and taught in the college) "and he used to come and sing in the choir with us. That was before your time, Mr. Governey. And he sang in the parish choir. And he'd have sung in the Protestant choir and the Wesleyan choir and the tin-hut choir if they let him. There was not a concert in N— that he wasn't the head and tail of it, and he always sang twice and three times and it was all they could do to keep him from giving encores all night long. For," sighed the teacher, "he had no sense and the people used to make a hare of him. He couldn't sing any more than I could. He had a small little voice, a small range too, but it had no strength or sweetness; there was no richness in it."

The teacher said these words, *strength, sweetness, richness,* with a luscious curl of his thin lips around the fruit of sound. His eyes widened. Clearly he was seeing nothing but the old station master. Earnestly he went on, a small glow on each cheek:

"That was all right until they shifted poor Boyhan to this God-forsaken place. And if N— is a lonely hole, this is the back of beyond. At the same time they started the new Broadcasting Station in Dublin and Boyhan conceived a great ambition to sing there. He formed the idea that some day or other a passenger would be on his way to Dublin, or from Dublin, and he would hear him singing and say, 'My Heavens, who is that with the grand voice?' And he would make inquiries— some director or government official—and stop the train and seek out Boyhan and say to him, 'What's the meaning of this neglect? Why haven't you been asked to sing over the Radio?' Then there would

be paragraphs in the newspapers about, Discovery of Great Irish Baritone, and Romance of a Chance-heard Voice, and so on.

"The result of this was that whenever a train rolled in, Boyhan used
always to come out of his office singing. He'd be singing little trills
up and down the scale, or a bar of *The Moon hath raised her Lamp
Above.* He was known to all the passengers and, sure, they used to be
looking out for him. And there he would always be, rubbing his hands
and pretending he was doing his *Dohsohmedoh,* just for delight and
jollity. And even if it was a miserable wet day he'd be at it, up and
down the train.

"Well, one hard, moonlight night in December, I was here, like this,
waiting for the last train back to N—. The snow was white on the
hills. It was blazing. There wasn't a sound but the wind in the telegraph wires. The clouds were in flitters, in bits. I well remember it.
A rich night. A deep, rich night, and no harm in the winds but they
puffing and blowing."

Again Hanafan's cold thin lips sucked the sound of those words,
rich, deep, and his eyes dilated under his black hat with the image
of his memory. His eyes were not cranky now, but soft and big.

"I was here with a– a–. I was here with a– a– friend."

He stopped for a second. The small man's eyes pounced on him,
observing at once his strange embarrassment. He glanced at the priest
but he had lowered his face and his mouth was clamped. In that
hesitant second he saw at once a piece of Hanafan's secret life revealed,
a memory of something known also to the priest; the thought of a
dead friend—or perhaps a woman—something or somebody that made
the memory of that night so precious to Hanafan that he could not
speak of it openly.

"Was this long ago?" probed the small man inquisitively.

"We walked up and down," said Hanafan, looking at the snow
under the moon and the clouds tumbling. Then Boyhan came out
and he took us across the line. He had a fire and we sat around it.
The smell of the peat, thick and slab, was struck into everything in
the room."

"Was it only two of you?" prodded the small man, eager to know
if it was a woman.

"He showed us photographs of his daughter, the nun, and of his son,
Timsy, with, as he said, a lawn-tennis in his hand. He had no wife.
She was dead. And there he was living alone, in the station, three miles
from the village and his only two children in the world away in exile.

I quoted Sir Thomas Browne for him, the passage in *The Quincunx*. We all looked out the little window. 'Think!' said I '*The quincunx of heaven runs low and 'tis time to close the five ports of knowledge. . . . To keep our eyes open longer were to act our Antipodes. The huntsmen are up in America and they are already past their first sleep in Persia. But who can be drowsy at that hour which freed us from everlasting sleep, or have slumbering thoughts at that time, when sleep itself must end, and as some conjecture all must wake again?'*

"Then, by way of no harm, he began to talk about music and singing and he gave us one song after another. He sang us, *Oft in the stilly night*—and, you know, he sang it well. He sang, *The moon hath raised her Lamp Above.* I heard the signal bell ring as he was in the middle of it and far away the train began to purr. He was singing it so heartily we didn't like to interrupt him and as the train became a roar across the bog and the lights went flashing across the window, he rose and went out to the platform. By Heavens, that man saw the trainload as a vast audience whirled before him. He stood out on the platform singing like mad to them.

"We rushed for the bridge, we had no tickets, he gave us no tickets, and as I ran I shouted back to him, 'Hold the train!' He paid no heed and when we were up on the middle of the bridge he got to the grand burst, the last crescendo, of—

I come! . . . My heart's delight

and waved the train on. We were left looking at it vanishing up the line. I roared at him for a fool, and a vain fool, but he only bowed to us, and he bowed to the porter, and he bowed his way backward to the office like a Caruso. The train purred into the distance and there we two were with the wind in the wires and the white moon on mountains.

"I went back to abuse him—it was the last train—but he only looked at me like a child you'd strike and said he couldn't hold back a train for anyone. The porter paid no heed to us. He outed the lamps and locked the place up. We left the old fellow alone in the station. We had to walk home. It was a grand, bright night. A lovely, thick night. . . ."

Hanafan's voice broke. Just then a signal bell rang. It was dark over the bog where far away the train murmured and it could easily be heard because the birds had stopped singing. There was nothing but the deep scent of the night air, and below them in a marsh, still deep from the March rains, a prattling as of a thousand tiny frogs.

"This is a lonely place he lived in," whispered Hanafan. "A lonely life. No children. No wife."

The priest rose up and knocked out the ashes of his pipe as the train roared nearer.

"Yes," he agreed.

"But," cried Governey, "what has all that got to do with admiring the scenery?"

"He sang to the night," cried Hanafan passionately. "He sang to the whole night. The moon was up. The moon!"

His voice fell and they barely heard him over the rumbling train at the end of the platform.

"We saw the moon in the flags of the Liffey as we left the station. In the flags of the river, through the trees. So must he."

"Still and all," cried the small man, "he didn't form any intellectual concept. . . ."

The train drowned his voice and its lights flitted across their faces. When they climbed into a carriage the windows were speckled with rain and the three men inside, who leaned back to let them pass, had a cold, damp look. They had been talking when the train stopped but when they saw the priest they fell silent; looked at him under their brows; and shyly tipped their hats.

"Raining up the line?" asked the priest in a friendly voice.

"Oh, pouring in Dublin, father," said one of the three men—an elderly, soldierly-looking man, probably a warder in the jail at M—.

The three teachers fell silent, sensing that they had interrupted a conversation. Then they were rolling through the night, looking at the lights racing along the little hedges beside the line. Suddenly the rain that had hit Dublin half an hour before swept down on them across the mountains, slapping the windows like a bucket of water. It kept trickling and shining on the windows.

"He died there last year," said Hanafan suddenly, looking at the trickle outside the pane.

"I once asked him," the priest leaned forward to say to the small man, "what his favorite song was. Do you know what he said? *Scenes that are brightest.*"

The priest leaned back and gave a merry little laugh.

"Still," cried the small man, thumping his knee, "I can't see what this has to do with the question we were discussing!"

The priest looked at him, and kept looking at him, as he swayed with the carriage, but he said nothing. Angrily the small man looked back, and then he looked angrily at Hanafan whose eyes had become cranky and tormented once more. He began to wonder why Hanafan was always so sour, and why he remained on in N— if he didn't like the place, and why he had never married. His eye lit up a bit at that and he determined to get it all out of the priest when they were next alone. He tapped Hanafan on the knee and he began to ask him some question, but when he saw that Hanafan's eyes were closed he leaned back again. The priest was still looking at him so he nodded toward Hanafan and winked. The priest's lidded eyes were as immovable as an owl's.

As they rolled on through the bog the small man kept looking around him restlessly, and at last he shifted over to the three countrymen, determined to find out if the common people really do admire the scenery. He started a conversation about turf-cutting, but before he could lead up to the question the train halted at a small station and the strangers got out. Then the three friends were left alone in the cold, damp carriage, listening to the battering rain. Tired and sleepy, nobody noticed that, in his corner, Hanafan was weeping silently through his closed eyes.

Continental Stories

ℋonoré de ℬalzac

Of all makers of fiction Balzac came the closest to creating a world of his own—the world of his titanic series of novels and stories, The Human Comedy, in which some two thousand characters appear and reappear like familiar acquaintances. Only Tolstoy could approach him in sheer scope and power. Power is the word for him, a creative power that drove him to write endlessly, often for twenty hours at a stretch. Such great novels as Old Goriot (1834) or Eugenie Grandet (1833) are most representative of his work, but his many short stories are not asides; they, too, attest his brilliance of conception, his boldness of execution. His best stories are timeless, as fresh today as the hour they were written.

Honoré de Balzac was born in Tours in 1799. As a youth he studied the law at his father's behest, broke free to write, piled up no less than thirty-one volumes of inferior fiction in mere apprenticeship, turned in 1824 to the publishing business, in which he failed, and in 1830 launched fully upon the prodigious series of works which were to establish his greatness. His health broke under his furious labors, and he died at Paris in 1850 at the age of fifty-one.

A PASSION IN THE DESERT *

Honoré de Balzac

"WHAT A terrifying sight!" she cried, as she came out of Monsieur Martin's menagerie. She had just been watching that fearless adventurer "rehearsing" his hyena, to adopt the vocabulary of the billboard.

---

* Translated by Barbara Coney Silber and Gordon R. Silber from *Oeuvres complètes de Honoré de Balzac* (Paris: Conard, 1914–1920), Vol. XXII.

"How can he have trained his animals to the point of being sure enough of their affection to—"

I interrupted her. "This fact, which seems unbelievable to you," I answered, "is perfectly natural."

"Really?" she exclaimed incredulously.

"Do you think that animals are entirely free from passions?" I asked. "Just let me tell you that we can give them every one of the vices for which our state of civilization is responsible."

She looked at me in amazement. I went on, "The first time I saw Monsieur Martin I confess that I uttered an exclamation of surprise like you. An old, one-legged soldier had come in at the same time and happened to be standing near by. His appearance had made a strong impression on me. He had one of those fearless heads, stamped with the seal of war and having written on it the story of Napoleon's battles. The first thing that struck one was his expression of frankness and jollity, qualities which always predispose me in favor of a stranger. He was doubtless one of those old warriors who are never caught off guard, who find something to laugh at in the last convulsion of a dying comrade, who bury him or strip him gaily, defy bullets with an air of authority, speak briefly and to the point, and in general fraternize with the devil. After looking very attentively at the owner of the menagerie as he came out of the cage, my companion pursed his lips in such a way as to indicate derisive scorn with the kind of significant expression in which superior individuals indulge in order to show others that *they* are not taken in. So when I exclaimed over the courage of Monsieur Martin, he smiled and said, wagging his head with the air of an expert, 'Old stuff.' 'What do you mean, "Old stuff"?' I asked. 'If you will explain this mystery I'll be obliged to you.' After a few moments during which we got acquainted, we went off to take dinner in the first restaurant we came to. When we reached the dessert a bottle of champagne restored to the memories of this remarkable soldier all their clarity, he told me his story, and I saw that he had been right when he exclaimed, 'Old stuff!' "

When I took her home she coaxed me so much, and made me so many promises, that I consented to write down for her what the soldier had confided to me. The next day, therefore, she received this episode of an epic which might be entitled "The French in Egypt."

At the time of the expedition undertaken in Upper Egypt by General Desaix, a soldier from Provence fell into the hands of the

Maghrebi Arabs and was carried off by these Arabs into the desert above the cataracts of the Nile. In order to put a reassuring distance between themselves and the French army the Arabs made a forced march and did not stop until nightfall. They camped around a well screened by palm trees, near which they had earlier buried some provisions. Not imagining that the idea of flight would occur to their prisoner they contented themselves with tying his hands, and after eating a few dates and giving some barley to their horses, they all went to sleep. When the bold Provençal saw that his enemies were no longer guarding him, he used his teeth to get hold of a scimitar, and holding the blade steady between his knees, he cut the ropes which bound his hands, freeing himself. Then he seized a rifle and dagger, took a supply of dried dates, a little bag of barley, gun powder and shot. He buckled a scimitar around his waist, mounted a horse, and spurred him in the direction in which he supposed the French army must be. Impatient to reach an outpost, he pushed the already weary steed so hard that the poor beast, his flanks rowelled by the spurs, expired, leaving the poor Provençal in the middle of the desert.

After walking for some time through the sand with all the courage of a galley slave who is making his escape, the soldier was forced to stop because night was falling. In spite of the beauty of the oriental sky at night, he did not feel that he had the strength to continue his journey. Fortunately he had been able to reach the top of a hill where stood several palm trees whose foliage, seen much earlier, had stirred hope in his heart. He was so exhausted that he lay down on a ledge of granite freakishly shaped like a camp-bed, and fell asleep without bothering to take any precautions for his own safety. He had made the sacrifice of his life. His last thought was actually one of regret. He already repented having left the Arabs whose vagabond life began to seem attractive to him now that he was far away and helpless. He was awakened by the sun, whose pitiless rays falling vertically on the granite were beginning to make it unbearably hot, for he had carelessly lain down to the east of the trees and so had not taken advantage of the shadow cast by their verdant, majestic foilage. He looked at these solitary trees and shuddered. They reminded him of the elegant pillars, crowned with long leaves, which characterize the Saracen columns of the cathedral of Arles. But when, after contemplating the palm trees, he looked around him, deep despair flooded his soul. He saw a limitless ocean. The dark sand of the desert stretched as far as the eye could see in every direction and glistened like a steel blade struck by a bright light. He did not know whether it was a sea of ice or a string of lakes, quiet as a mirror. Fiery hot vapor rising up in billows eddied over the shifting sands. The sky had an oriental brilliance, intense to the point of inspiring despair in the beholder, for it left nothing to the imagination. Heaven and Earth were on fire. The silence was terrifying in its wild and awful majesty. Infinity and immensity weighed down upon the soul from every side. Not a cloud in the sky, not a breath in the air, not an irregularity in the surface of the sand, which was covered with tiny ripples. Finally the horizon ended in a line of light, as clear-cut as the blade of a saber, such as one sees on a clear day at sea. The Frenchman clasped the trunk of one of the palm trees as if it were the body of a friend; then sitting down in the straight, slender shadow which the tree cast on the rock he wept and remained there contemplating with deep sorrow the pitiless scene which stretched out before him. He shouted as if to test the solitude. His voice, lost in the hollows, gave out but a weak sound which awoke no echo. The echo was in his own heart. The Provençal was twenty-two years old. He loaded his rifle.

"There will always be time," he said to himself, putting down on the ground beside him the weapon which could set him free.

Looking at the darkish sand and the blue sky by turns the soldier dreamed of France. He seemed to smell with delight the gutters of Paris; he recalled the cities through which he had passed, the faces of his comrades, and the smallest incidents of his past life. Finally, his southern imagination brought before his eyes a glimpse of the stones of his dear Provence in the movement of the heat which was wavering over the expanse of the desert. Fearing all the dangers of this cruel mirage, he went down the slope opposite that by which he had mounted the hill the night before. His joy was great on discovering a kind of grotto cut out by nature in the immense fragments of granite which formed the base of the hillock. A dilapidated piece of matting showed that this retreat had once been inhabited. Then several steps away he saw palm trees laden with dates. Then the instinct which attaches us to life flared up afresh in his heart. He hoped to live long enough to await the passage of some Arabs—or perhaps he would soon hear the noise of cannon!—for at this moment Bonaparte was sweeping over Egypt. Revived by this thought, the Frenchman knocked down several clusters of ripe fruit under the weight of which the date trees seemed to be bending over, and when he tasted this unexpected manna he became convinced that the former inhabitant of the grotto had cultivated the palm trees. The fresh, tasty flesh of the date revealed, in fact, the care which his predecessor had expended. The Provençal passed suddenly from somber despair to almost mad joy. He climbed up again to the top of the hill and spent the rest of the day cutting down one of the barren palm trees under which he had slept the night before. A vague memory made him think of desert animals, and foreseeing that they might come to drink at the spring which came to the surface amid the sand, he resolved to protect himself against their visits by putting a fence across the entrance to his retreat. In spite of his eagerness, in spite of the strength which a fear of being devoured while he slept lent him, he was unable to cut the palm tree into pieces that day, but he did succeed in felling it. When, toward evening, this king of the desert crashed, the noise of its fall echoed afar and seemed like a groan uttered by the desert. The soldier shuddered as if he had heard a voice predicting misfortune, but like an heir who does not feel sorry for himself very long after the death of a relative, he stripped the tree of the broad, long green leaves which are its poetic ornament and used them to repair the mat on which he was going to lie. Tired out by the heat and labor, he went to sleep in his damp grotto whose reddish walls and ceiling looked as if they were of moulded plaster.

In the middle of the night his sleep was disturbed by an extraordinary noise. He sat up, and the deep silence which reigned allowed him to perceive the alternating accents of breathing whose wild energy could not belong to a human. Deep fear, heightened by the darkness, by the silence, and by the confusion of his awakening, chilled his heart. He hardly felt the sharp prickling of his scalp when, after straining his eyes, he perceived two faint yellow gleams in the obscurity. First he attributed those light spots to some reflection of his own pupils, but soon, as the brilliance of the night helped him to distinguish more and more clearly what was in the grotto, he saw an enormous animal lying a few feet away from him. Was it a lion, a tiger, or a crocodile? The Provençal was not well enough up on zoology to know to what sub-genus his enemy belonged, but his terror was all the more violent since his ignorance made him apprehend all kinds of misfortunes at once. He bore the cruel torture of listening to catch the peculiar qualities of this breathing without losing a sound and without daring to make the slightest movement. An odor as strong as a fox's, but more penetrating, heavier, so to speak, filled the grotto, and when he had become aware of this his terror was at its height, for he could no longer doubt the existence of this terrible companion whose royal cave was his camp. Soon the rays of the moon, which was fast setting, lighted the den and caused an almost imperceptible gleam to play over the spotted skin of a panther. This Egyptian lion was sleeping rolled up like a big dog, peaceful inhabitant of a commodious niche in the façade of a mansion. Its eyes opened for a second and closed again. Its face was turned towards the Frenchman. A thousand confused thoughts passed through the soul of the prisoner. His first impulse was to kill it with a rifle shot, but he realized that there was not space enough to take aim. The barrel would have reached beyond the animal. And suppose he woke it up! This thought rooted him to the spot. As he listened to his heart beating amid the silence he cursed its thumping, which he feared might interrupt this sleep which gave him time to think of a means of salvation. Twice he put his hand on his scimitar with the idea of cutting off his enemy's head, but the difficulty of piercing this smooth, hard skin compelled him to give up this bold expedient. Suppose he missed? That would be certain death, he thought. He preferred the uncertainty of a combat and resolved to wait for dawn. And the day did not keep him waiting long. The Frenchman could then examine the panther. Its jaws were spotted with blood. "She's eaten well!" he thought without concerning himself whether or not the banquet had consisted of human flesh. "She won't be hungry when she wakes up."

It was a female. The fur of the belly and the haunches was flecked with white. Tiny spots, like velvet, formed pretty bands around the paws. The sinewy tail was white, likewise, but tipped with black rings. The upper part of this costume, yellow like dull gold, but smooth and soft, bore those characteristic flecks which serve to distinguish panthers from the other varieties of *felis*. This tranquil and fearsome hostess was snoring in a pose as graceful as that of a cat lying on a sofa cushion. Her head, with its sparse whiskers straight as silver wires, rested on her outstretched paws, which were bloody, sinewy and tipped with sharp claws. If she had been lying like this in a cage, the Provençal would certainly have admired the animal's grace and the vigorous contrasts between the bright colors which lent her costume imperial brilliance; but under the circumstances he felt that his capacity to appreciate them was inhibited. The presence of the panther, even though asleep, made him experience the effect which they say the hypnotic eyes of a serpent produce on a nightingale. The soldier's courage finally disappeared completely in the presence of this danger, whereas he would doubtless have risen to heights of heroism under the mouth of a cannon belching grape shot. Then his boldness returned and at once dried up at its source the cold sweat which was rolling down his brow. Acting like those who, driven to the wall through misfortune, come to the point of defying death and present themselves to its blows, he saw without realizing it a tragedy in this adventure and resolved to play an honorable rôle therein up to the last scene.

"After all, the Arabs might have killed me day before yesterday," he said to himself. Looking upon himself, therefore, as already dead, he awaited bravely and with eager curiosity the awakening of his enemy. When the sun rose, the panther opened her eyes suddenly. Then she stretched her paws violently as if to take the numbness out of them and get rid of cramps. Then she yawned, revealing the frightening apparatus of teeth and forked tongue, tough as a file. "She's like a coquette," he thought as he watched her roll over and over and make the gentlest and most delicate little movements imaginable. She licked the blood from her paws, licked her snout and scratched her head with repeated pretty gestures. "Good! go ahead and primp," thought the Frenchman, who had recovered his gaiety when he recovered his courage. "We are going to wish each other good morning." And he grasped the short little dagger which he had stolen from the Arabs.

At this moment the panther turned her gaze toward the Frenchman and looked at him fixedly, without advancing. The steadiness of her metallic eyes and their insupportable brilliance made the Provençal tremble, above all when the animal started toward him, but he looked at her in a caressing way, ogled her as if to hypnotize her, and let her come near him. Then with a movement as gentle, as loving as if he were trying to caress the loveliest of women, he passed his hand along her whole body from head to tail, scratching with his nails the flexible spine which divided her yellow back. She raised her tail voluptuously, her eyes softened, and the third time the Frenchman performed this act of purposeful flattery she uttered one of those purrs by which cats express their pleasure. But this murmur came from a throat so powerful and so deep that it echoed in the grotto like the final chord from a church organ. Understanding the importance of his caresses, the Provençal redoubled them so as to appease, to stupefy this imperious courtesan. When he thought that he had surely lulled the ferocity of his capricious companion, whose hunger had so fortunately been satisfied the night before, he got up and started to leave the grotto. The panther let him leave, but when he had climbed the hill she started after him, bounding with the agility of a sparrow hopping from branch to branch, and came up and rubbed against his legs, arching her back as cats do. Then, looking at the visitor with an eye whose gleam had become less inflexible, she uttered that wild cry which naturalists compare to the sound made by a saw.

"She's very exacting!" exclaimed the Frenchman with a smile. He ventured to play with her ears, pat her belly, and scratch her head hard with his nails. Observing that he was successful, he next tickled her skull with the point of his dagger, watching for a chance to kill her, but the strength of the bones made him fear that he would not succeed.

The Sultana of the desert accepted the services of her slave by raising her head, stretching her neck, and betraying her intoxication by her relaxed attitude. The Frenchman realized suddenly that to assassinate this fierce princess with a single blow he had only to stab her in the throat, and he was just raising his blade when the panther, doubtless satiated with caresses, lay down gracefully at his feet, from time to time casting up at him glances in which, despite her natural fierceness, good-will was vaguely to be seen. The poor soldier, leaning against one of the palm trees, ate his dates, but by turns scanned the desert for rescuers and kept a wary eye on his terrible companion to make sure of her uncertain clemency. The panther kept watching the date seeds every time he threw one away, and her eyes then would express unbelievable distrust. She looked the Frenchman over in a businesslike fashion, but the examination proved favorable, for when he had finished his scanty meal she licked his boots and with that rough, strong tongue miraculously removed the dust that clung to them.

"But when she gets hungry—?" thought the soldier. In spite of the shudder which this thought caused him, he idly began to estimate the dimensions of the panther. Certainly one of the finest specimens of the animal, she stood three feet high and four feet long, not counting the tail. This powerful weapon, round as a club, was almost three feet long, and the head, as thick as that of a lioness, was remarkable for its unusual expression of intelligence. Cold, tigerish cruelty was dominant, but there was also a vague resemblance to an artful woman. In fact, the face of this solitary queen showed at this moment a kind of gaiety reminiscent of Nero in his cups. She had slaked her thirst for blood and wanted to play. The soldier tried walking about and the panther left him free, contenting herself with following him with her eyes, which resembled less those of a faithful dog than of a big angora cat, concerned about everything, even its master's movements. When he turned around he saw beside the spring the remains of his horse. The panther had dragged its body all that distance. About two thirds of it had been devoured. This sight reassured the Frenchman. It was now easy for him to explain the absence of the panther and the respect that it had for him while he was asleep. This first piece of good luck encouraged him as he looked into the future. He conceived the mad hope of getting along with the panther the whole day long by neglecting no means of taming her and winning his way into her good graces. Approaching her again he had the pleasure of seeing her tail move almost imperceptibly. He then sat down fearlessly beside her and the pair of them began to play. He took hold of her paws, her muzzle, twisted her ears, turned her over on her back and scratched roughly her warm, silky flanks. She let him do as he pleased, and when he tried to smooth down the hair on her paws, she carefully drew in her claws, curved like scimitars. The Frenchman, who kept one hand on his dagger, was still planning to plunge it into the belly of the too-trusting panther, but he felt that he would be immediately crushed in her final convulsion. And besides, he felt in his heart a kind of remorse which called upon him to respect the inoffensive creature. It seemed to him that he had found a friend in this limitless desert. He thought involuntarily of his first mistress, whom he had nicknamed Cutie as a joke because she had been so wildly jealous that throughout their entire relationship he had reason to fear the knife with which she continually menaced him. This youthful memory gave him the idea of trying to make the young panther, whose agility, grace and softness he could now less fearfully admire, answer to that name.

Toward the end of the day he had become familiar with his dangerous situation, and he almost liked its uncertainties. His companion had finally become used to looking at him when he shouted "Cutie" in a falsetto voice. At sunset Cutie uttered several times over a low, melancholy cry.

"She's well brought up," the light-hearted soldier thought. "She's saying her prayers." But this inward joke occurred to him only after he had noticed the peaceful attitude which his comrade was maintaining. "Go ahead, my little blond. I'll let you go to bed first," he said to her, counting on the activity of his legs to escape as quickly as possible after she had gone to sleep, in order to search out another refuge during the night. The soldier waited impatiently for an opportunity to escape and when it came, he hurried in the direction of the Nile, but hardly had he covered a quarter of a league through the sand when he heard the panther bounding up behind him and uttering that cry that sounded like a saw, more terrifying still than the heavy sound of her leaps.

"Well," he said to himself, "she has taken a shine to me. Perhaps this young panther has never met a human being before. It's flattering to be her first love."

At this moment the Frenchman fell into one of those quicksands so terrifying to travelers, from which it is impossible to escape. When he felt himself sinking he gave a cry of alarm and the panther seized him by the collar; then, jumping vigorously back, she drew him from the pit as if by magic. "Ah! Cutie!" he cried, caressing her enthusiastically, "we're bosom companions from now on!—But no tricks, now!" And he turned back with her.

From then on, it was as if the desert were populated. It contained an individual to whom the Frenchman could speak, whose fierceness had been softened toward him without his being able to explain the reasons for this incredible friendship. Great as was the soldier's desire to remain up and about and on his guard, he went to sleep. When he woke up, Cutie was gone. He climbed the hill and in the distance saw her bounding along, as those animals who cannot run on account of the extreme flexibility of their spinal columns must do. Cutie arrived with her jaws covered with blood. She accepted the necessary caresses from her companion, going so far as to indicate by several deep purrs how happy she was. Her soft eyes turned with even more affection than the night before to the Frenchman, who talked to her now as if to a domestic animal.

"Ha ha, Mademoiselle, you're a respectable girl, aren't you? Just look, you like to be petted, but aren't you ashamed? You've eaten some Arab all right. That's the way you animals behave—but don't go and eat up any Frenchmen! I wouldn't love you any more."

She played as a young puppy plays with its master, letting herself be rolled over, scratched and petted by turns, and sometimes she would even make advances by stretching out her paw to him in a pleading gesture.

Several days passed thus. This association allowed the Frenchman to admire the sublime beauty of the desert. From the moment he discovered hours of fear and of calm, food, and a creature about which to center his thoughts, his soul was stirred by contrasts. His life was full of antitheses. The solitude revealed all its secrets to him, wrapped him in its charms. He discovered in the rising and the setting of the sun sights unknown to the world. He came to tremble on hearing above his head the faint beating of a bird's wings,—a rare passer-by! —on seeing the clouds mass together—ever-changing, varicolored travelers! At night he studied the effects of the moon on the ocean of sand, on which the wind produced waves, undulations, swift changes. He lived with the Orient, admired its brilliance, and often, after enjoying the dreadful spectacle of a windstorm in this plain where the simoon would stir up red, dry fog, deadly clouds of it, he saw night come with delight, for then the beneficent coolness of the stars would rain down. He listened to imaginary music in the heavens, and this solitude taught him to unfold the treasures of revery. He passed hours at a time remembering trifles, comparing his past life to this present life. Finally he came to love his panther passionately, for he had to feel affection for something. Whether his will had modified the character of his companion, or whether she found abundant food, thanks to the war then being waged in the desert, she respected the Frenchman's life and he ended by no longer distrusting her when he saw her so well tamed. He spent most of his time napping, but was compelled to watch like a spider in the middle of its web so as not to let the moment for his rescue slip by if someone should pass in the circle bounded by the horizon. He had sacrificed his shirt to make a flag which he hoisted to the top of a palm tree bare of foliage. Taught by necessity, he had found a means of keeping it spread out by stretching it on sticks, for the wind might not be shaking it at the moment when the long-awaited traveler happened to look.

It was during the long hours when hope left him that he played with the panther. He had finally come to know the different inflexions of her voice, how she reacted. He had come to know the peculiarities of all the spots which were scattered over her golden coat. Cutie did not even scold any longer when he held the tuft on the end of her tail so as to count the black and white rings which glistened like jewels in the sunlight. He enjoyed looking at her smooth contours, her white belly, her graceful head, but it was above all when she was frisking around that she was delightful to watch, and the agility and youth of her movements continually surprised him. He admired her suppleness when leaping, crouching, gliding, rolling and curvetting about. However swift her spring, however smooth a block of granite might be, she would stop short when he called "Cutie!"

On one brilliantly sunny day a huge bird was soaring through the air. The Frenchman left his panther to look at this newcomer, but after a moment of waiting, the deserted Sultana gave a deep roar. "For Heaven's sake, I believe she's jealous!" he exclaimed on seeing her glaring eyes. "Virginia's soul must certainly have passed into her body."

The eagle disappeared in the sky while the soldier was admiring the rounded hind quarters of the panther. But how much grace and youth in her outlines! She was pretty as a woman. The blond fur of her costume passed by imperceptible shades into the white which clothed her haunches. The abundant light cast by the sun made this living gold, these brown spots gleam, so that they had indescribable charm. The Frenchman and the panther looked at each other in an understanding way. The coquette trembled when she felt her friend's nails scratch her skull, her eyes gleamed like two flashes of lightning, and then she closed them tight.

"She has a soul," he said, studying the tranquillity of this queen of the sand, golden, white, solitary and burning like the sand. . . .

"Well," she said, "I've read your argument in favor of animals, but how does the story end? How did two people so made for each other . . ."

"Oh, it ended as all great passions end. In a misunderstanding, you know. Both parties think they have been betrayed, out of pride they make no explanations, and out of obstinacy they separate."

"Of course. Sometimes in the loveliest moments a look, an exclamation is enough . . ." she agreed. "Well, will you tell me how it ended?"

"It's horribly difficult, but you will understand what the old veteran had already confided when, finishing off his bottle of champagne, he cried, 'I don't know what I did wrong, but she turned, furious, and bit my thigh with her sharp fangs—not hard, of course. And thinking that she meant to eat me up I plunged my dagger into her neck. She rolled back, uttering a cry that pierced my heart. I watched her struggle and she looked back at me without anger. I'd have given anything in the world—my medal even, but of course I didn't have it then—to save her life. It was as if I had assassinated a real person. And the soldiers who had seen my flag and arrived to rescue me at that moment found me in tears.' "

"Well, Monsieur," he went on after a pause, "I've fought since that time in Germany, Spain, Russia, and France. I've been around, and I haven't seen anything comparable to the desert. . . . Ah, it's beautiful. . . ."

"Just what was it you felt in the desert?" I asked.

"Young man, you can't describe that. Anyway, I don't long for my cluster of palms and my panther all the time. . . . Only when I'm blue. . . . You see, in the desert there's everything and there's nothing."

"But can't you explain?"

"Well," he said with a gesture of impatience, "it's God without men."

Alphonse Daudet

IN HIS career as a novelist Alphonse Daudet was associated with the great French naturalists of the nineteenth century, but in his graceful short stories he is essentially the romanticist, even when, occasionally, his themes are grim. It is not surprising that after he abandoned teaching to come down to Paris from Provence his first publication was a volume of lyric poetry. Many of the stories in his second book Letters From My Mill (1868) have the wistfulness and the gaiety of old ballads.

Daudet's mastery of prose can not be fully conveyed in translation; but his quick sympathy for the joys and sorrows of his characters speaks a universal language. He is like Dickens in his power over tears and laughter, unlike him in precision and flexibility of structure. Daudet's work had a marked influence on American short story writers of the Eighties, especially Thomas Bailey Aldrich and Frank R. Stockton.

Daudet was born at Nimes in 1840. He came to Paris in 1857 and won fame quickly with his short stories, his Tartarin trilogy, and a number of naturalistic novels, of which the best known is Sapho (1848). He died in Paris in 1897.

M. SEGUIN'S GOAT *
TO M. PIERRE GRINGOIRE, LYRIC POET IN PARIS.
Alphonse Daudet

YOU will always be the same, my poor Gringoire!
What! a place is offered to you as reporter on one of the best Parisian newspapers, and you have the coolness to refuse it? Look

* From *Letters From My Mill* by Alphonse Daudet. Reprinted by permission of Little, Brown & Company.

at yourself, you luckless fellow! Look at your shabby jacket, those dilapidated breeches, and that thin face that cries out hunger. It is to this that your passion for noble verse has brought you! This is what your loyal ten years' service as page to Sire Apollo has won! On the whole, are you not ashamed of it?

Come, make yourself a reporter, imbecile; make yourself a reporter. You will earn good crown-pieces, and have your knife and fork at Brébant's, and you can exhibit yourself at all first nights with a new feather in your cap.

No? What, you won't? You insist on living free and as you please to the end of the chapter? Well, then! listen to the history of M. Seguin's goat. You will see what is gained by wishing to live at liberty.

M. Seguin never had any luck with his goats. He lost them in all kinds of ways. One fine morning they broke their tether and wandered away to the mountain, where a wolf ate them. Neither the caresses of their master nor fear of the wolf, nothing could restrain them. They were, it appeared, independent goats, wanting at any cost free air and liberty.

The worthy M. Seguin, who did not understand the nature of his animals, was shocked. He said:

"That's enough; goats are bored by living with me; I won't keep another."

However, after losing six in that way, he was not discouraged, and he bought a seventh; but this time he was careful to get her quite young, so young that she might the better get accustomed to live with him.

Ah! Gringoire, she was pretty, that little goat of M. Seguin's, so pretty with her soft eyes, her little tuft of beard like a sub-officer, her black and white shiny hoofs, her ribbed horns, and her long, white hair which wrapped her like a mantle! She was almost as charming as that kid of Esmeralda's—you remember, Gringoire?—and then, so docile, so coaxing, letting herself be milked without budging, and never putting her foot in the bowl! A love of a little goat!

Behind M. Seguin's house was a field hedged round with hawthorn. It was there that he put his new boarder. He fastened her to a stake, at the very best part of the meadow, taking care to give her plenty of rope; and from time to time he went to see if she was satisfied. The goat seemed very happy, and cropped the grass with such heartiness that M. Seguin was delighted.

"At last," thought the poor man, "here's one at least that isn't bothered by living with me!"

Mr. Seguin deceived himself; the goat was bored.

One day she said to herself, looking at the mountain:—

"How nice it must be up there! What a pleasure to skip in the heather, without this cursed rope, which rubs my neck! It is all very well for asses and cattle to browse in a field, but goats! why, *they* want the open."

From that moment the grass of the meadow seemed to her insipid. Ennui seized her. She grew thin, her milk was scanty. It was really piteous to see her, straining at the tether all day, her head turned to the mountain, her nostril flaming, and she saying "Ma-ë" so sadly.

M. Seguin saw that something was the matter with his goat, but he did not know what. One morning, after he had milked her, the goat turned round and said to him in her patois:—

"Listen, M. Seguin; I am so weary here with you; let me go on the mountain."

"Ah! *mon Dieu!* She, too!" cried poor M. Seguin, stupefied, and he let fall the bowl; then, sitting down on the grass at the side of his goat he said:—

"Oh! Blanchette, would you leave me?"

And Blanchette answered:—

"Yes, M. Seguin."

"Isn't there grass enough here to please you?"

"Oh! plenty, M. Seguin."

"Do I tie you too short? Shall I lengthen the rope?"

"It isn't worth while, M. Seguin."

"Then what's the matter? what do you want?"

"I want to go on the mountain, M. Seguin."

"But, you unhappy little thing, don't you know there are wolves on the mountain? What would you do if a wolf attacked you?"

"I'd butt him with my horns."

"A wolf wouldn't care for your horns. He has eaten up goats of mine with much bigger horns than yours. Don't you remember that poor old Renaude who was here last year? Strong and spiteful as a ram. She fought all night with the wolf, but, in the morning, the wolf ate her."

"*Pecaïre!* Poor Renaude! But that does not matter, M. Seguin; let me go to the mountain."

"Merciful powers!" exclaimed M. Seguin, "What *is* the matter with my goats? Another one for the wolf to eat! Well, no, I shall save you in spite of yourself, you slut! and for fear you should break your rope I shall put you in the stable, and there you will stay."

Whereupon M. Seguin led the goat into his brand-new stable, and double-locked the door. Unfortunately, he forgot the window, and hardly had he turned his back before the little one was out and away.

You laugh, Gringoire? *Parbleu!* I suppose so; you take the side of the goats against that good M. Seguin. We'll see if you laugh presently.

When the white goat reached the mountain there was general delight. Never had the old fir-trees seen anything so pretty. They received her like a little princess. The chestnut-trees bent to the ground to kiss her with the tips of their branches. The golden gorse opened wide to let her pass, and smelt just as sweet as it could. In fact, the whole mountain welcomed her.

You can imagine, Gringoire, how happy she was! No more rope, no stake, nothing to prevent her from skipping and browsing as she pleased. My dear fellow, the grass was above her horns! and such grass!—luscious, delicate, toothsome, made of all sorts of plants. Quite another thing from that grass in the meadow. And the flowers, oh! Great blue campanulas and crimson foxgloves with their long calyxes, a perfect forest of wild-flowers giving out an intoxicating sweetness.

The white goat, a little tipsy, wallowed in the thick of them with her legs in the air, and rolled down the banks pell-mell with the falling leaves and the chestnuts. Then, suddenly, she sprang to her feet with a bound, and hop! away she went, head foremost, through thicket and bushes, now on a rock, now in a gully, up there, down there, everywhere. You would have said that ten of M. Seguin's goats were on the mountain.

The fact is, Blanchette was afraid of nothing.

She sprang with a bound over torrents that spattered her as she passed with a dust of damp spray. Then, all dripping, she would stretch herself out on a nice flat rock and dry in the sun. Once, coming to the edge of a slope with a bit of laurel between her teeth, she saw far below, far below on the plain, the house of M. Seguin with the meadow behind it; and she laughed till she cried.

"How small it is!" she said; "how could I ever have lived there?"

Poor little thing! Being perched so high she fancied she was tall as the world.

Well! it was a good day for M. Seguin's goat. About noon, running from right to left, she fell in with a herd of chamois munching a wild vine with all their teeth. Among them our little white-gowned rover made quite a sensation. They gave her the choicest place at the vine, and all those gentlemen were very gallant. In fact, it appears—but this is between ourselves, Gringoire—that a young chamois with a black coat had the great good fortune to please Blanchette. The pair wandered off in the woods for an hour or so, and if you want to know what they said to each other, go ask the chattering brooks that are running invisible through the mosses.

Suddenly the wind freshened. The mountain grew violet; it was dusk.

"Already!" said the little goat; and she stopped, quite surprised.

Below, the fields were drowned in mist. M. Seguin's meadow disappeared in the fog, and nothing could be seen of the house but the roof and a trifle of smoke. She heard the little bells of a flock that was on its way home, and her soul grew sad. A falcon, making for his nest, swept her with his wings as he passed. She shuddered. Then came a howl on the mountain:

"Hoo! hoo!"

She thought of the wolf; all day that silly young thing had never once thought of it. At the same moment a horn sounded far, far down the valley. It was that good M. Seguin, making a last effort.

"Hoo! hoo!" howled the wolf.

"Come back! come back!" cried the horn.

Blanchette felt a wish to return, but remembering the stake, the rope, the hedge of the field, she thought that she never could endure that life again and 'twas better to remain where she was.

The horn ceased to sound.

The goat heard behind her the rustling of leaves. She turned and saw in the shadow two short ears, erect, and two eyes shining. It was the wolf.

Enormous, motionless, seated on his tail, he was looking at the little white goat and smacking his lips in advance. As he knew very well he should eat her up, the wolf was not in a hurry; but when she turned round and saw him he began to laugh wickedly: "Ha! ha! M. Seguin's little goat!—" and he licked his great red tongue round his wily chops.

Blanchette felt she was lost. For an instant, remembering the story of old Renaude, who had fought all night only to be eaten in the morning, she said to herself that 'twas better, perhaps, to be eaten at once; but then, thinking otherwise, she put herself on guard, head low, horns forward, like the brave little goat that she was. Not that she had any hope of killing the wolf,—goats can't kill wolves,—but only to see if she, too, could hold out as long as old Renaude.

Then the monster advanced, and the pretty little horns began the dance.

Ah! the brave goatling! with what heart she went at it! More than ten times—I'm not exaggerating, Gringoire—more than ten times she forced the wolf back to get breath. During each of these momentary truces the dainty little thing nibbled one more blade of her dearly loved grass; then, with her mouth full, she returned to the combat. It lasted all through the night. From time to time M. Seguin's goat looked up at the stars as they danced on the cloudless sky and said to herself:—

"Oh! if I can only hold out till dawn."

One after another, the stars went out. Blanchette redoubled the blows of her horns, and the wolf the snap of his teeth. A pale gleam showed on the horizon. The hoarse crowing of a cock rose from a barnyard.

"At last!" said the poor little goat, who had only awaited the dawn to die; and she stretched herself out on the ground in her pretty white fur all spotted with gore.

Then the wolf fell upon her and ate her up.

Adieu, Gringoire!

The story you have now heard is not a tale of my own invention. If ever you come to Provence, our farmers will often tell you of *la cabro de Moussu Seguin, que se battégue touto la neui emé lou loup, e piei lou matin lou loup la mangé.*

You will understand me, Gringoire: "And then, in the morning, the wolf ate her up."

Guy de Maupassant

Guy de Maupassant, born in 1850 but a few months after the death of Poe, has meant as much to the advance of the short story as his great predecessor. Like Poe he was always the craftsman, intent, not on theories or pronouncements about life, but on rendering what he saw with conscious, delicate workmanship. But while Poe could rarely escape the introspection of his own darkening mind, Maupassant—destined to actual insanity—nevertheless possessed the strength to maintain a cool objectivity which did honor to his literary task-master, the great Flaubert.

Maupassant was a realist with a mind which could see stories in all the life he knew, whether it were the peasant world of Normandy, the antics of the boulevard, the cruelties of war, or the struggles of the conscience. He saw much that was unpleasant, and his sardonic temperament made the most of what "Man has made of Man," but it is not sufficiently remembered that in his novels and in some of his short stories he conveys a deep sympathy for life's tragedies. His cleverness is not callousness. More than two hundred tales came from his pen with a mastery that has not been surpassed.

Maupassant's days of greatness were in the Eighties, after he had served an arduous apprenticeship under Flaubert. In the next decade his nervous disorders, aggravated by the use of drugs, completely destroyed his health, and he died in pitiable circumstances in 1893.

TWO FRIENDS *

Guy de Maupassant

Paris was blockaded, starved, in its death agony. Sparrows were becoming scarcer and scarcer on the roof-tops and the sewers were being depopulated. One ate whatever one could get.

As he was strolling sadly along the outer boulevard one bright January morning, his hands in his trousers pockets and his stomach empty, M. Morissot, watchmaker by trade but local militiaman for the time being, stopped short before a fellow-militiaman whom he recognized as a friend. It was M. Sauvage, a river-side acquaintance.

Every Sunday, before the war, Morissot left at dawn, a bamboo pole in his hand, a tin box on his back. He would take the Argenteuil railroad, get off at Colombes, and walk to Marante Island. As soon as he arrived at this ideal spot he would start to fish; he fished until nightfall.

Every Sunday he would meet a stout, jovial little man, M. Sauvage, a haberdasher in Rue Notre-Dame-de-Lorette, another ardent fisherman. Often they spent half a day side by side, line in hand and feet dangling above the current. Inevitably they had struck up a friendship.

Some days they did not speak. Sometimes they did; but they understood one another admirably without saying anything because they had similar tastes and responded to their surroundings in exactly the same way.

On a spring morning, toward ten o'clock, when the young sun was drawing up from the tranquil stream wisps of haze which floated off in the direction of the current and was pouring down its vernal warmth on the backs of the two fanatical anglers, Morissot would sometimes say to his neighbor, "Nice, isn't it?" and M. Sauvage would answer, "There's nothing like it." And that was enough for them to understand and appreciate each other.

On an autumn afternoon, when the sky, reddened by the setting sun, cast reflections of its scarlet clouds on the water, made the whole river crimson, lighted up the horizon, made the two friends look as ruddy as fire, and gilded the trees which were already brown and beginning to tremble with a wintery shiver, M. Sauvage would look at Morissot with a smile and say, "Fine sight!" And Morissot, awed,

* Translated by Gordon R. Silber from *Oeuvres complètes de Guy de Maupassant* (Paris: Conard, 1908).

would answer, "It's better than the city, isn't it?" without taking his eyes from his float.

As soon as they recognized one another they shook hands energetically, touched at meeting under such changed circumstances. M. Sauvage, with a sigh, grumbled, "What goings-on!" Morissot groaned dismally, "And what weather! This is the first fine day of the year."

The sky was, in fact, blue and brilliant.

They started to walk side by side, absent-minded and sad. Morissot went on, "And fishing! Ah! Nothing but a pleasant memory."

"When'll we get back to it?" asked M. Sauvage.

They went into a little café and had an absinthe, then resumed their stroll along the sidewalks.

Morissot stopped suddenly. "How about another, eh?" M. Sauvage agreed, "If you want." And they entered another wine-shop.

On leaving they felt giddy, muddled, as one does after drinking on an empty stomach. It was mild. A caressing breeze touched their faces.

The warm air completed what the absinthe had begun. M. Sauvage stopped. "Suppose we went?"

"Went where?"

"Fishing, of course."

"But where?"

"Why, on our island. The French outposts are near Colombes. I know Colonel Dumoulin; they'll let us pass without any trouble."

Morissot trembled with eagerness: "Done! I'm with you." And they went off to get their tackle.

An hour later they were walking side by side on the highway. They reached the villa which the Colonel occupied. He smiled at their request and gave his consent to their whim. They started off again armed with a pass.

Soon they passed the outposts, went through the abandoned village of Colombes, and reached the edge of the little vineyards which slope toward the Seine. It was about eleven.

Opposite, the village of Argenteuil seemed dead. The heights of Orgemont and Sannois dominated the whole countryside. The broad plain which stretches as far as Nanterre was empty, absolutely empty, with its bare cherry trees and its colorless fields.

Pointing up to the heights M. Sauvage murmured, "The Prussians are up there!" And a feeling of uneasiness paralyzed the two friends as they faced this deserted region.

"The Prussians!" They had never seen any, but for months they had felt their presence—around Paris, ruining France, pillaging, massacring, starving the country, invisible and all-powerful. And a kind of super-stitious terror was superimposed on the hatred which they felt for this unknown and victorious people.

Morissot stammered, "Say, suppose we met some of them?"

His Parisian jauntiness coming to the surface in spite of everything, M. Sauvage answered, "We'll offer them some fish."

But they hesitated to venture into the country, frightened by the silence all about them.

Finally M. Sauvage pulled himself together: "Come on! On our way! But let's go carefully." And they climbed over into a vineyard, bent double, crawling, taking advantage of the vines to conceal them-selves, watching, listening.

A stretch of bare ground had to be crossed to reach the edge of the river. They began to run, and when they reached the bank they plunged down among the dry reeds.

Morissot glued his ear to the ground and listened for sounds of anyone walking in the vicinity. He heard nothing. They were indeed alone, all alone.

Reassured, they started to fish.

Opposite them Marante Island, deserted, hid them from the other bank. The little building which had housed a restaurant was shut up and looked as if it had been abandoned for years.

M. Sauvage caught the first gudgeon, Morissot got the second, and from then on they pulled in their lines every minute or two with a silvery little fish squirming on the end, a truly miraculous draught.

Skillfully they slipped the fish into a sack made of fine net which they had hung in the water at their feet. And happiness pervaded their whole being, the happiness which seizes upon you when you regain a cherished pleasure of which you have long been deprived.

The good sun was pouring down its warmth on their backs. They heard nothing more; they no longer thought about anything at all; they forgot about the rest of the world—they were fishing!

But suddenly a dull sound which seemed to come from under ground made the earth tremble. The cannon were beginning.

Morissot turned and saw, over the bank to the left, the great silhou-ette of Mount Valerien wearing a white plume on its brow, powder-smoke which it had just spit out.

And almost at once a second puff of smoke rolled from the summit, and a few seconds after the roar still another explosion was heard.

Then more followed, and time after time the mountain belched forth death-dealing breath, breathed out milky-white vapor which rose slowly in the calm sky and formed a cloud above the summit.

M. Sauvage shrugged his shoulders. "There they go again," he said.

As he sat anxiously watching his float bob up and down, Morissot was suddenly seized by the wrath which a peace-loving man will feel toward madmen who fight, and grumbled, "Folks sure are stupid to kill one another like that."

M. Sauvage answered, "They're worse than animals."

And Morissot, who had just pulled in a bleak, went on, "And to think that it will always be like this as long as there are governments."

M. Sauvage stopped him: "The Republic wouldn't have declared war—"

Morissot interrupted: "Under kings you have war abroad; under the Republic you have war at home."

And they started a leisurely discussion, unravelling great political problems with the sane reasonableness of easy-going, limited individuals, and found themselves in agreement on the point that men would never be free. And Mount Valerien thundered unceasingly, demolishing French homes with its cannon, crushing out lives, putting an end to the dreams which many had dreamt, the joys which many had been waiting for, the happiness which many had hoped for, planting in wives' hearts, in maidens' hearts, in mothers' hearts, over there, in other lands, sufferings which would never end.

"That's life for you," opined M. Sauvage.

"You'd better say 'That's death for you,' " laughed Morissot.

But they shuddered in terror when they realized that someone had just come up behind them, and looking around they saw four men standing almost at their elbows, four tall men, armed and bearded, dressed like livried servants, with flat caps on their heads, pointing rifles at them.

The two fish lines dropped from their hands and floated off down stream.

In a few seconds they were seized, trussed up, carried off, thrown into a rowboat and taken over to the island.

And behind the building which they had thought deserted they saw a score of German soldiers.

A kind of hairy giant who was seated astride a chair smoking a porcelain pipe asked them in excellent French: "Well, gentlemen, have you had good fishing?"

Then a soldier put down at the officer's feet the sack full of fish which he had carefully brought along. The Prussian smiled: "Aha! I see that it didn't go badly. But we have to talk about another little matter. Listen to me and don't get excited.

"As far as I am concerned, you are two spies sent to keep an eye on me. I catch you and I shoot you. You were pretending to fish in order to conceal your business. You have fallen into my hands, so much the worse for you. War is like that.

"But—since you came out past the outposts you have, of course, the password to return. Tell me that password and I will pardon you."

The two friends, side by side, pale, kept silent. A slight nervous trembling shook their hands.

The officer went on: "No one will ever know. You will go back placidly. The secret will disappear with you. If you refuse, it is immediate death. Choose."

They stood motionless, mouths shut.

The Prussian quietly went on, stretching out his hand toward the stream: "Remember that within five minutes you will be at the bottom of that river. Within five minutes! You have relatives, of course?"

Mount Valerien kept on thundering.

The two fishermen stood silent. The German gave orders in his own language. Then he moved his chair so as not to be near the prisoners and twelve men took their places, twenty paces distant, rifles grounded.

The officer went on: "I give you one minute, not two seconds more."

Then he rose suddenly, approached the two Frenchmen, took Morissot by the arm, dragged him aside, whispered to him, "Quick, the password? Your friend won't know. I'll pretend to relent."

Morissot answered not a word.

The Prussian drew M. Sauvage aside and put the same question. M. Sauvage did not answer.

They stood side by side again.

And the officer began to give commands. The soldiers raised their rifles.

Then Morissot's glance happened to fall on the sack full of gudgeons which was lying on the grass a few steps away.

A ray of sunshine made the little heap of still squirming fish gleam. And he almost weakened. In spite of his efforts his eyes filled with tears.

He stammered, "Farewell, Monsieur Sauvage."

M. Sauvage answered, "Farewell, Monsieur Morissot."

They shook hands, trembling from head to foot with a shudder which they could not control.

The officer shouted "Fire!"

The twelve shots rang out together.

M. Sauvage fell straight forward, like a log. Morissot, who was taller, tottered, half turned, and fell crosswise on top of his comrade, face up, as the blood spurted from his torn shirt.

The German gave more orders.

His men scattered, then returned with rope and stones which they tied to the dead men's feet. Then they carried them to the bank.

Mount Valerien continued to roar, its summit hidden now in a mountainous cloud of smoke.

Two soldiers took Morissot by the head and the feet, two others seized M. Sauvage. They swung the bodies for a moment then let go. They described an arc and plunged into the river feet first, for the weights made them seem to be standing upright.

There was a splash, the water trembled, then grew calm, while tiny wavelets spread to both shores.

A little blood remained on the surface.

The officer, still calm, said in a low voice: "Now the fish will have their turn."

And he went back to the house.

And all at once he caught sight of the sack of gudgeons in the grass. He picked it up, looked at it, smiled, shouted "Wilhelm!"

A soldier in a white apron ran out. And the Prussian threw him the catch of the two and said: "Fry these little animals right away while they are still alive. They will be delicious."

Then he lighted his pipe again.

Anatole France

ANATOLE FRANCE, born *Jacques Anatole Thibault in Paris in 1844,
the son of a book-seller, was the great inheritor of the intellectual
tradition of Voltaire and Renan. A Nobel Prize winner in 1921, he
died three years later at the age of eighty, a novelist and satirist who
had carried his immense learning gracefully, even negligently, and
whose profound scepticism had not disturbed his ironic pity for the
human spectacle, or prevented him from offering his support to those
more positive in revolutionary faith than he. He had lived long
enough to see the younger generation of literary men turn from his
leadership, but there can be no doubt of his major place in French
letters.*

*He made his debut as poet and critic, and achieved international
renown with his first novel The Crime of Sylvestre Bonnard (1881)
which was crowned by the French Academy. His mastery of the short
story was demonstrated in such volumes as Balthasar (1889), Mother
of Pearl (1892), and The Merrie Tales of Jacques Tournebroche
(1909). His most enduring works are probably the great satires
Penguin Island (1908) and The Revolt of the Angels (1914). And
there are other great titles not to be mentioned here. "One escapes in
his books," said Stuart Sherman, "from the shallow and savorless
modernity of contemporary literature."*

THE MANUSCRIPT OF A VILLAGE DOCTOR *

Anatole France

DOCTOR H—, who recently died at Servigny (Aisne), where he had
practised medicine for more than forty years, left behind him a
journal never intended for the public eye. I should not feel justified in

* From *Mother of Pearl* by Anatole France. Used by permission of Dodd, Mead &
Company.

publishing the manuscript *in extenso,* nor even in printing fragments of any considerable length, although, like Monsieur Taine, there is a large number of persons nowadays of the opinion that it is above all things desirable to print and circulate what was never planned for publication. Whatever these worthy folk may say, the fact that a writer is an amateur does not afford any guarantee that what he has to say will be interesting. The memoirs of Doctor H— would be wearisome from their mere monotonously moral note. And yet the man who wrote them, in his lowly environment, possessed an intellect quite out of the ordinary. This village doctor was philosopher as well as physician. Perhaps the closing pages of his journal might be perused without any exceptional distaste. I venture to transcribe them here:—

Extract from the Journal of the late Doctor H—,
Physician at Servigny (Aisne).

"It is an axiom of philosophy that nothing in this world is either altogether bad or altogether good. Pity, the tenderest, the most natural, the most useful of the virtues, is not at all times in place either with the soldier or the priest; both with priest and soldier there are occasions when it must be held in restraint—when confronted by the enemy, for instance. Officers do not make a practice of recommending it on the eve of battle, and in some old book I have read that Monsieur Nicole held it in distrust as the motive principle of concupiscence. There is nothing of the priest about me, and still less of the soldier. I am a doctor, and amongst the most insignificant of that profession, a country doctor. I have practised my art for long years and in obscurity, and I would assert that if pity alone can be a worthy stimulus to the adoption of our profession, we must lay it aside finally when we encounter those miseries which it has inspired us with the desire to alleviate. A doctor whom pity accompanies to the bedside of his patients will find his observation not sufficiently acute, his hands not sufficiently steady. We go wherever compassion for the human race calls, but we must leave pity behind us. Moreover, doctors for the most part find it an easy task to attain the callousness which is so necessary to them. That is a mental condition which cannot long elude them, and there are moral reasons for this. Pity speedily becomes blunted when brought into contact with suffering; there is less disposition to deplore those misfortunes for which alleviation can be procured; finally, to the physician an illness offers a succession of interesting phenomena.

"From the time when I began the practice of medicine I flung myself into it with ardour. In the bodily ills disclosed to me I saw only opportunities for the practical application of my art. When a complaint developed without complications, I was able to see beauty in its conformity to the normal type. Those phenomena of disease, which offered apparent anomalies, awakened curiosity in my mind; so that I was enamoured of disease. What am I saying? From the point of view I espoused disease and health were possessed of indisputable personality. As an enthusiastic observer of the human mechanism, I found as much to admire in its more baleful affections as in its most healthy compliance with law. Willingly should I have exclaimed with Pinel: 'What a magnificent cancer!' That was a fine attitude of mind, and I was on my way to become a philosopher-physician. I only needed to have a genius for my art in order to enjoy completely, and enter into possession of, the full beauty of the theory of disease classification. It is the privilege of genius to unveil the splendour of things. Where the ordinary man would see only a disgusting wound, the naturalist worthy of the name stands enraptured before a battlefield on which the mysterious forces of life struggle for supremacy, in an encounter more inexorable, more terrifying than any that the strenuous abandon of Salvator Rosa ever depicted. I only caught glimpses of that spectacle of which the Magendies and Claude Bernards were familiar witnesses, and it was a distinction for me to do so; but though resigned to the career of a humble practitioner, I fortified myself, as a professional duty, in the habit of confronting grievous situations unemotionally. I gave my patients my energies and my intellect. I did not give them pity. God forbid that I should place any gift, howsoever precious, above His gift of pity! Pity is the widow's mite; it is the incomparable offering of the poor man, who with generosity outstripping that of all the wealthy in this world of ours, gives with the gift of his tears a piece torn from his heart. For that very reason it is that pity must be dissociated from the carrying out of a professional duty, how noble soe'er that profession may be.

"To enter upon more particular considerations, I would say that the folk in whose midst I am living evoke in their misfortunes a sentiment which is not pity. There is something of truth in the theory that a man cannot inspire in another an emotion which he is incapable of experiencing himself. Now the peasantry in our part of the country are not tender-hearted. Harsh to others as to themselves, they drag out an existence morose in its gravity. That gravity, too, is contagious, and in their company sadness and dejection affect one's mind. What is fine about their moral outlook is that they preserve unscathed the nobler features of humanity. As they are not accustomed to think with any frequency or profundity, their thoughts assume naturally in certain circumstances a solemn tone. I have heard some of them give utterance at the point of death to brief, forcible speeches worthy of the patriarchs of the Old Testament. They can call forth one's admiration, but do not awaken one's sympathies. With them everything is quite simple, even their illnesses. Their sufferings are not accentuated by their imagination. They are not like those over-sensitive creatures who construct from their ills a monster more harassing than the ills themselves. They meet death so much as a matter of course that it is impossible to be greatly disturbed. To sum up, I might say that they are all so much alike that no shred of individuality vanishes as each one passes away.

"For the reasons which I have just set down it follows that I practise my profession of village doctor very peacefully. I never regret having chosen it. I sometimes think I am a little above it; but if it is vexatious to a man to feel himself above his position, the annoyance would certainly be greater if he felt unequal to it. I am not rich, and never shall be so long as I live. But of what use would money be to one who leads a solitary village life? My little grey mare, Jenny, is as yet only fifteen years old, and she still trots as easily as in the days of her first youth, especially when we are going in the direction of the stable. I do not, like my illustrious fellow-physicians in Paris, possess a gallery of pictures for the entertainment of my visitors, but I can show pear trees which the townsmen have nothing like. My orchard is famous for twenty leagues round, and the owners of the neighbouring châteaux come to beg cuttings from me.

"Now on a certain Monday—it will be a year ago this very day— as I was busy in my garden inspecting my espaliers, a farm servant came to beg me to call as soon as possible at Les Alies.

"I asked him whether Jean Blin, the farmer at Les Alies, had sustained a fall the previous day as he came home in the evening. For in my part of the country a sprain is a common Sunday occurrence, and it is not at all rare for a man to break two or three ribs that day on leaving the public-house. Jean Blin is not exactly a bad sort, but he likes drinking in company, and more than once he has known what it is like to wait for Monday's dawn at the bottom of a miry ditch.

"The farm servant replied that there was nothing the matter with Jean Blin, but that Éloi, Jean's little son, was seized with fever.

"Without another thought for my espaliers, I went in search of my hat and stick, and set out on foot for Les Alies, which is only twenty minutes' walk from my house. As I walked, my thoughts were on ahead with Jean Blin's little boy in the grip of a fever. His father was a peasant much like every other peasant, with this peculiar difference, that the Intelligence which created him forgot to provide him with a brain. This great hulking Jean Blin has a head as thick as his fist. Divine wisdom has only furnished that ·particular skull with what was strictly indispensable, there's no getting over that. His wife, the best-looking woman in the place, is a noisy, bustling housewife, stolidly virtuous. Well, well! To this worthy couple a child had been given, who was easily the most delicate, the most spiritual little being that ever adorned this old world of ours. Heredity is responsible for some of the surprises in nature, and it has been well said that nobody knows what he is about when he fathers a child. Heredity, according to our honoured Nysten, is the biological phenomenon which is responsible for the fact that, in addition to the normal type of the species, ancestors transmit to their descendants certain peculiarities of organization and of aptitude. I admit it. But what peculiarities are transmitted and what are not, that is what is not very clear, even after a perusal of the learned works of Doctor Lucas and Monsieur Ribot. My neighbour, the notary, lent me last year a volume by Monsieur Émile Zola, and I observe that that author takes credit for particular discernment in this respect. 'Here,' he says, in substance, 'is an ancestor afflicted with neurosis; his descendants will show neuropathic tendencies, that is to say, when they do not do so; amongst them will be found some foolish and some intelligent individuals; one of them may even be a genius.' He has gone to the trouble of drawing up a genealogical chart to make his idea more easily apprehended. Well and good! The discovery is not particularly novel, and its expounder would unquestionably be ill-advised to vaunt himself upon it; it is none the less true, however, that it embraces practically all we know on the subject of heredity. And this is how it came about that Éloi, Jean Blin's little son, was an embodied intellect. He had the creative imagination. Many a time, when he was no higher than my walking-stick, I have come across him playing truant with the village urchins. Whilst they were reaching after nests, I have watched the little fellow constructing model mills and miniature syphons with pipes of straw. Inventive and unsociable, he turned to nature. His schoolmaster despaired of ever making anything of so inattentive a child; and, to tell the truth, at eight years old Éloi was still ignorant of his letters. But at that age he learned to read and write with astonishing rapidity, and in six months became the best scholar in the village.

"He was the most affectionate and the most clinging child. I gave him a few lessons in mathematics, and was astounded at the fertility that his mind displayed at this early age. In fact—I own it without any fear of being ridiculed, for in an old man cut off from civilization some exaggeration is pardonable—I rejoiced to have detected in this little peasant the premonitions of one of those enlightened spirits which at long intervals shine forth in the midst of our purblind race, and, impelled alike by the need of lavishing their affection and the desire for knowledge, are bound to effect something useful or beautiful wherever fate may assign them a place.

"My mind was occupied with musings of this kind as far as Les Alies. Entering the low-ceiled room, I found little Éloi ensconced in the big bed with cotton hangings, to which no doubt his parents had removed him on account of the gravity of his condition. He was lethargic; his head, though small and delicate, nevertheless made as great a dent in the pillow as if it had been of enormous weight. I stole near. His forehead was on fire; there was a disquieting redness about the conjunctive membrane; the temperature of the body was altogether too high. His mother and grandmother kept close to him, anxiously. Jean Blin, whose uneasiness prevented him from working, not knowing what to do, and being afraid to go away, stood with his hands in his pockets looking inquiringly first at one and then at another. The child turned his drawn face towards me, and scrutinizing me with an affectionate but heartbreaking glance, said in reply to my questions that his forehead and his eyes were both very painful, that he could hear noises which he knew were imaginary, and that he knew perfectly well who I was, his dear old friend.

" 'First he has shivering fits, and then he is feverishly hot,' said his mother.

"Jean Blin, after ruminating for several minutes, remarked—
" 'My belief is that what ails him is his inside.'
"Then he relapsed into silence.

"It had been only too easy for me to diagnose the symptoms of acute meningitis. I prescribed revulsive applications to the feet, and leeches behind the ears. I drew near to my little friend a second time, and tried to say something cheerful to him, more cheerful, alas! than facts warranted. But I was suddenly aware of an entirely new personal experience. Although I was completely self-possessed I seemed to see the sick child through a veil, and at such a distance that he appeared quite, quite small. This upsetting of my ideas of space was speedily followed by an analogous upheaval of my ideas of time. Although my visit had not lasted above five minutes, I received the impression that I had been in that low-ceiled room, in front of that bed with its white cotton hangings, for a long time, for a very long time, and that months and even years had rolled by whilst I was held motionless.

"By a mental effort which is perfectly natural to me, I there and then put these singular impressions under analysis, and the cause of them became quite clear to me. It was simple enough. Éloi was dear to me. At the sight of him so unexpectedly and so seriously ill I could not 'get my bearings.' It is the popular phrase, and it is appropriate. Moments of anguish appear to us unnaturally long. That is why I received the impression that the five or six minutes I had passed beside Éloi had something interminable about them. As to the fancy that the child was at a distance from me, that came from the idea that I was about to lose him. This idea, impressed on me against my will, had from the first moment assumed a character of absolute certainty.

"The following day Éloi was in a less alarming condition. The improvement continued for several days. I had sent into the town to procure ice, and this had had a good effect. But on the fifth day I recognized that he was in violent delirium. He talked a great deal, and amongst the disconnected words I heard him pouring out I could distinguish these—

" 'The balloon! the balloon! I have hold of the helm of the balloon. It rises. The sky is inky. Mamma, mamma! why won't you come with me? I am steering my balloon to a place where it will be so beautiful! Come, it is stifling here.'

"That day Jean Blin followed me up the road. He slouched along with that air of embarrassment a man has who wants to say something and is yet afraid to say it. At last, after walking some twenty paces with me in silence, he stopped, and laying his hand on my arm said—

" 'See here, Doctor, it's my belief that what ails the little chap is his inside.'

"I continued my way sorrowfully, and for the first time in my life my eagerness to see once more my pears and apricots did not avail to mend my pace. For the first time in forty years of practice I found the plight of one of my patients heartrending, and in my inmost self I bewailed the child I was powerless to save.

"Distracting pangs soon came to magnify my grief. I feared that my treatment had contributed to the development of the disease. I caught myself forgetting in the morning what I had prescribed the night before, uncertain in my diagnosis, nervous, and worried. I called in one of my fellow-practitioners, a clever young fellow, who had a practice in the next village. When he arrived, the poor little fellow, whose sight was already gone, was plunged in a profound coma.

"The following day he died.

"A year having elapsed after this misfortune, it happened that I was called in consultation to the county town. The fact is singular. The causes which led up to it are extraordinary; but as they have no connection with what I am relating, I do not record them here. After the consultation, Dr. C—, physician to the prefecture, did me the honour to invite me to lunch with him and two other members of the profession. After lunch, where I found refreshment in conversation at once erudite and diversified, coffee was served to us in the doctor's sanctum. As I approached the mantelpiece to put down my empty cup, I saw hanging upon the mirror-frame a portrait which aroused in me so profound an emotion that it was with difficulty I refrained from crying out. It was a miniature, the portrait of a child. The child resembled in so striking a fashion the one I had been unable to cure —the child of whom I had been constantly thinking for a year past— that for a moment I could not avoid the thought that it was he himself. That supposition, however, was of course absurd. The black wooden frame, with the circlet of gold surrounding the miniature, proclaimed the taste of the end of the eighteenth century, and the child was depicted in a vest of pink and white striped material such as the little Louis XVII might have worn; but the face was out-and-out the face of my little Éloi. The same forehead, imperious and powerful—the forehead of a man beneath the curls of a cherub; the same fire in the eyes, the same suffering grace on the lips! Indeed, to the very same features was joined the identical expression!

"I had probably been examining this portrait for quite a long while when Dr. C—, clapping me on the shoulder, said—

"'Ah, my friend, you have before you a family relic which I am proud to possess. My maternal grandfather was the friend of the illustrious man whom you see painted there in the days of his early boyhood, and it was from my grandfather that that miniature came into my possession.'

"I asked him to be good enough to tell me the name of his grandfather's illustrious friend. Upon this he unhooked the miniature and held it out to me:

" 'See,' he said, 'on the exergue . . . *Lyon, 1787.* Doesn't that recall anything to you? No? Well, that child of twelve was the great Ampère.'

"Then, in a flash, I had an exact perception, an unequivocal estimate of what death had swept away one year previously in the farmhouse of Les Alies."

August Strindberg

A GREAT and unhappy genius, August Strindberg had, by the time of his death in 1912, become Sweden's greatest literary figure, and one of the most influential writers in modern European literature. It was felt, wrote Edwin Bjorkman, that "he, more than any other writer, appeared to be the incarnation of the past century, with its nervous striving after truth, its fear of being duped, and its fretting dread that evolution and progress might prove antagonistic terms." With more than half a hundred plays he challenged comparison with Ibsen as an innovating force in the drama, but he found time, too, for realistic novels such as The Red Room (1879), for autobiographical studies of terrifying intensity, such as Inferno (1897), and for short stories, often satiric and sombre, which appeared in Swedish Fates and Adventures (1882–83) and Married (1884–86).

Although Strindberg's corrosive cynicism deeply affected his work, and his contempt for women amounted to an obsession, he had great powers of insight, and his strength is tonic. He was born poor in 1849, the son of a shopkeeper, had to struggle for social position, made two unhappy marriages, and for a time came close to insanity. It is no wonder that his writings are turbulent with the bitterness of his own experience.

AUTUMN *
August Strindberg

THEY HAD been married ten years! Happily? As happily as circumstances had permitted. They had pulled along as smoothly and steadily as two bullocks of equal strength, each at its place in the team.

In the first year, naturally, many illusions about marriage were

---

* Translated by Charles Wharton Stork. Reprinted by permission of Erik Lidforss, representative for August Strindberg.

dispelled, that of absolute bliss, for instance. With the next year children began to arrive, and the drudgery of life did not leave much time for reflection.

He was very domestic, extremely domestic, one might say; finding in his family his miniature world, of which he was the middle point. His children were the radii, and his wife sought likewise to be a middle point, but never in the centre of the circle, since that was where the husband was; for which reason the radii sometimes ran to him, sometimes to her, intersecting each other.

In this tenth year the husband was appointed a secretary of prison inspection, and had therefore to travel about. This was a blow to his domestic habits, and he felt a genuine repugnance at the thought that now he would have to be away a whole month. He could not tell for sure whether it was his wife or the children he would miss most; perhaps it was all of them together.

On the evening before his departure he sat on the sofa watching his wife pack his portmanteau. She was on her knees on the floor, putting in his linen. She then dusted off his black clothes and folded them carefully so that they should take as little room as possible; he wasn't very handy at that sort of thing! She had not taken a place in the house as his maid-servant, scarcely as his wife. She was mother, mother to the children and to him. She never felt humiliated at darning his socks, and never asked for thanks. Nor did she consider him indebted to her for such things, when he in return gave her and her children both stockings and many other things which she would otherwise have had to go out and get, while her children were left at home alone.

He sat in the corner of the sofa watching her. Now that the departure drew near, small intimations of regret began to stir in him. He surveyed her figure. The shoulder blades had grown more prominent, and the back was bent with work over the cradle, the ironing board, and the stove. He too was bent with work at his desk, and his eyes needed the help of glasses. But just now he was really not thinking of himself. He saw that her hair was thinner than formerly, and that the part between the braids was growing brighter. Was it for him she had lost her beauty, only for him? No it was for the little community which consisted of them all, for she had worked for herself too. And his hair had also become thinner on the crown in the fight for them all. He would perhaps have had more youth if there had not been so many mouths to feed, but not for a moment did he wish he had been alone.

AUGUST STRINDBERG

"It'll do you good to go about a bit," said his wife; "you that have always sat too much crouched up in the house."

"You're glad to be quit of me, you are," said he, not without a touch of bitterness; "but I shall be missing you a lot."

"You're like the cat; you'll miss your warm corner, but I don't believe you'll miss me so dreadfully."

"And the children?"

"Oh, when you're away; but when you're home you're always picking at them; not seriously, of course, but still picking. Oh, you're really fond of them, I believe; I don't mean to be unjust."

At supper he was very gentle and felt in low spirits. He did not read the evening papers, but wanted only to talk with his wife. She, however, was so busied with chores that she did not give herself much time to chat, and, besides, her feelings had been pretty well blunted by her ten years' campaign in the nursery and the kitchen.

He was more emotional than he cared to show, and the disorder about him made him restless. He beheld bits of his daily life, of his existence, tossed higgledy-piggledy on chairs and bureaus, and the black open portmanteau gaped at him like a coffin. White linen was wrapped about black clothes, which still retained the shape of knee and elbow, so that it seemed to him as if he himself were stretched there in his white laying-out shirt ready to have the lid put on and be carried off.

Next morning—an August morning it was—he hurried out of bed, dressed breathlessly and was very nervous. He went into the nursery and kissed all the children, who were rubbing the sleep out of their eyes, and after embracing his wife sat himself in a cab to go to the railway station. The journey in company with his chiefs diverted him, and he felt it was really a good thing to stir himself up a bit. His home behind him seemed like a stuffy bedroom, and he was thoroughly glad when he got to Linköping.

The rest of the day was taken up with a fine prison dinner at the big hotel, where they drank the health of the provincial governor, but not that of the convicts, for whose sake the trip was made. But then came the evening in his lonely room. A bed, two chairs, a table, a wash-stand and a tallow-candle which spread its feeble light on the naked wallpaper. The secretary felt ill at ease. Everything was lacking: Slippers, dressing-gown, pipe-rack, desk; all the little things that were the constituents of his life. And his children and wife. How were things with them? Were they well? He grew restless and extremely depressed. When he was going to wind up his watch, he could not find the key. It hung at home on the watch-frame his wife had embroidered for him when they were engaged. He went to bed and lighted a cigar. But then he had to get up and hunt for a book in his portmanteau. Everything was so neatly packed that he was afraid to disturb it. But as he dug about he found his slippers. She thought of everything! And then he got hold of the book. But he did not read. He lay and thought of the past, of his wife in the last ten years. With that appeared the picture of old times, and the present vanished in the bluish-brown cigar smoke which rose in spirals toward the rain-splotched ceiling. He was conscious of an infinite remorse. Every hard word since those days came back to him, and he regretted every bitter moment he had caused her. At last he went to sleep.

On the following day, work and another dinner, with healths to the prison governor, but still none for the convicts. In the evening, loneliness, desolation, chill. He ached with the need of talking to her. He therefore got some paper and sat down at a writing-table. He paused at the first stroke of the pen. How was he to address her? It was always "Dear Mama" when he sent home a note to say that he should be out for dinner. But now it was not to mama he wrote, it was to his former *fiancée*, his sweetheart. So he wrote "Lily, my darling," as he used to. At the start it went laboriously, because so many words of endearment had vanished from the dry, dull speech of their common, everyday life; but soon he grew ardent, and with that the forgotten melodies rose up in his remembrance: waltz-beats and bits of novels, lilacs and swallows, evening moments of sunset across the mirroring bays; all of life's vernal memories danced out amid golden clouds and grouped themselves about her. At the bottom of the page he put a star, as lovers do, and wrote beside it—just as of old—"Kiss here!" When he had finished and read through his letter, he felt a glow on his cheeks, and was somewhat embarrassed. Why, he could not exactly say. It was like giving out his innermost thoughts to some one who might perhaps not understand them.

Still he sent the letter.

A couple of days passed before the answer came. During the interval of waiting he went about with a feeling of childish discomfort and bashfulness.

But then the answer came. He had struck the right note, and from cooking smells and children's din rose a song, bright and harmonious, warm and pure as that of first love. From now on there began an interchange of love letters. He wrote every evening and sometimes would also send a post-card in the course of the day. His companions did not recognize him. He began to give such attention to his clothes and the details of his outward appearance that he was suspected of a love affair. And he was in love, afresh! He sent her a photograph of himself without spectacles, and she sent him a lock of her hair. They were childish in their expressions, and he bought tinted writing-paper with doves upon it. But at the same time they were persons of middle age, not far past forty, though the struggle of life had made them feel older. In the past year he had also given up his conjugal privileges, not so much from coldness as from respect, for he saw in her always the mother of his children.

The end of his trip drew near. He now began to experience a certain unrest at the thought of the reunion. He had corresponded with a sweetheart; should he rediscover her in the mother and the house-wife? He feared to find himself disappointed at the homecoming. He did not want to see her with a cook's apron on or with the children at her skirts when he was to embrace her. They ought to meet at another place, alone. Could he bring her into tune with him at Vax-holm, for instance, in the inn where they had spent so many happy hours in their engagement time? That would be an idea! To re-capture there in memory for a couple of days the first glad period of their springtime, which would never return.

He sat down and presented his plan in a long glowing letter, which she answered by return mail with her assent, delighted that he had lit upon the same thought as she.

Two days later he was in Vaxholm, putting in order their room at the hotel. It was a beautiful day in September. He ate his dinner alone in the big hall, drank a glass of wine, and felt himself young again. It was so bright and airy here. Outside the bays spread shining and blue; only the birches on the shore had changed their colour. In the garden the dahlias were still in full bloom, and the mignonette breathed its perfume from the borders. Now and then a bee would still visit the withering blossoms, but would turn back to its hive in dis-appointment. In the channel there were sail-boats passing in and out before a light breeze. As they came about, the sails flapped and the sheets threshed, while the frightened gulls flew screaming away from the herring-fishers, who sat in their skiffs with rod and float.

He took his coffee on the veranda, and began to look forward to the coming of the steamer, which was due at six o'clock.

Restlessly, as if he were going toward an uncertain event, he promenaded up and down the balcony, looking out across the bay and the channel in the direction of the city to catch sight of the boat.

At last a puff of smoke rose across the fir woods of Tenö. His pulse quickened and he drank a liqueur. Then he went down to the shore. The funnel now appeared in the middle of the channel, and soon he could see the flag at the bow. Was she there, or had she been prevented from coming? It would only need that one of the children should be ailing to keep her at home, and then he would have to spend the night alone at the hotel. The children, who had been in the background during the past weeks, now came forth as something that stood between him and her. In their last letters they had spoken but little of the children, as if they wished to keep out a disturbing element, something they did not want as witness to their present state of feeling.

He paced the landing, which creaked under his feet, till he finally paused irresolutely near a pile, gazing continuously out at the boat, whose hull grew ever larger, while her wake spread a flood of molten gold across the rippling blue expanse of water. He could now see people moving on the upper deck and sailors busy with ropes at the bow.

Then something white flutters beside the pilot house. As he is alone on the dock, no one can well be waving to anybody but himself; and no one can be waving to him but she. He takes out his handkerchief and answers the signal. But he notices that his handkerchief is not white, for he has long since changed to coloured ones from motives of economy. . . . The steamboat whistles, and its engine slows down. On up to the landing the vessel glides; and he catches sight of her. They greet with their eyes, but cannot as yet exchange words because of the distance. The boat is warped in, and he sees her quietly leaning forward over the gangway. . . . It is she, but it is not she. Ten years are between! The style has changed, the cut of dresses is different. Formerly he saw her dark delicate features half enclosed in the then popular bonnet, which left the forehead free; now it is shaded by a poor imitation of a man's hat. Then her pretty figure was outlined in sportive curves under the graceful drapery of a cloak, that roguishly hid and revealed the roundness of the shoulders and the motions of the arms; now her entire form is distorted by a coachman's ulster which displays the dress but not the figure. And as she takes her last step on the gangway, he sees her little foot, of which he had been so fond when it had been in a buttoned boot that followed its shape, now prolonged in a pointed Chinese slipper which prevents the ball of the foot from rising in those dancing rhythms that had formerly enchanted him so.

It was she, but it was not she! He embraced her and kissed her. They asked each other how they were and how the children were. Then they went up on the shore.

Words came—broken, dry, forced. So strange! They were as if shy before each other, and there was no allusion to their correspondence.

At last he took courage and said, "Shall we take a walk before the sun goes down?"

"I should love to," she answered, and took his arm.

They went up the street into the little town. All the places of summer amusement were closed and shuttered up, and the gardens were despoiled. An apple or so that had hidden behind the leaves was still left on the tree, but the beds were stripped of every flower. The verandas, which had lost their awnings, looked like skeletons, and where faces and happy laughter had been all was silent.

"It has an autumn look," he remarked.

"Yes, it's forlorn to see the summer amusements like this." And they strolled on.

"We ought to go and see where we used to lodge," she said.

"Yes, that will be nice."

They went along the row of bathhouses.

There lay the little cottage wedged in between the gardener's and the chief pilot's places, with the red fence around it, the veranda and the garden plot.

Memories of the past sprang up. In that room their first child had been born. Jubilation and festivity, song and youth! There stood the rose-bush they had planted. There was the strawberry bed they had laid out; but it was there no more, for it was grown over and become a grassplot. There in the cinders were the traces of the swing which had hung there, but was no longer to be seen.

"Thanks for your lovely letters," she said, and pressed his arm.

He blushed and made no answer. Thereupon they turned back to the hotel, while he related the details of his trip.

He had had the table set in the big hall where they used to eat in the old days. They sat down without saying grace.

There they were *tête-à-tête* again. He took the bread-tray and passed it to her. She smiled. It was not yesterday that he had been so polite. But it was very novel and pleasant to eat away from home, and soon they started an eager conversation, as in a duet, each in turn bringing out a memory, and in these memories they lived. Their glances shone, and the little wrinkles were smoothed away. Oh, the rose-and-golden times which we live but once, if live them we may, and which many, many never live! At dessert he whispered to the waitress, who straightway brought in a bottle of champagne.

"My dear Axel, what are you thinking of?" said his wife, half reproachfully.

"Of the spring that is gone but will return."

But he did not think of it exclusively, for, disturbed by his wife's reproach as if a cat had gone through the room, he had a dark vision of the nursery and the porridge-dish.

However, things brightened up again, and the rose-red wine touched again the strings of memory, until they threw themselves once more into the magic intoxication of the past.

The hours flew swiftly. They got up and went into the parlor, where the piano stood, to drink their coffee.

"I wonder how my little ones are," said the wife, awakening for the first time from the enchantment.

"Sit down and sing!" he bade, opening the piano.

"What shall I sing? You know I haven't sung for ever so long."

Oh, he knew that, but now he would have a song.

She sat down and played a prelude. It was a shrill hotel piano that sounded like loose teeth.

"What shall I sing?" she asked, turning around on the stool.

"You know, Lily," he replied, not daring to meet her look.

"Your song! Yes. If I remember it."

And so she sang, "Where lies the happy country Where my true lover dwells."

But alas! the voice was thin and sharp, and emotion made it untrue. At times it was like a scream from the depths of a soul which feels its noon is over and the evening drawing near. The fingers which had been busied with heavy work did not easily find the right keys, and the instrument was played out, the cloth on the hammers being worn so that the bare wood clacked against the metal strings.

When the song was done, she did not dare to turn around for a while, but sat as if waiting for him to come to her and say something. But he did not come, and there was silence in the room. When she turned around on the stool, he was sitting in a corner, weeping. She wanted to run to him, take his head in her hands and kiss him as of old, but she remained sitting motionless, her eyes on the floor.

He held an unlighted cigar between his thumb and forefinger. When he heard that all was quiet, he bit off the end and struck a match.

"Thanks, Lily!" he said, and lighted the cigar. "Will you have coffee now?"

They drank their coffee and talked about summer amusements in general and where they should go next year. But the conversation soon began to lag and repeat itself.

Finally he said, in the middle of a long unsuppressible yawn, "I'm going to bed."

"I'll go too," said she, rising. "But I'll go out a little while first—on the balcony."

He went into the bedroom. His wife stopped a while in the dining room to talk to the landlady about pickled onions, from which they digressed into washing woolens, so that the conversation lasted half an hour.

When she returned, she stood at the bedroom door and listened. Everything was quiet within, and her husband's boots were outside. She knocked, but there was no answer. Then she opened the door and went in. He was asleep.

He was asleep!

Next morning they were at coffee together. The husband had a headache, and the wife looked uneasy.

"Bah! what coffee," said he with a grimace.

"It's Brazilian," said she.

"What shall we do today?" he asked, taking out his watch.

"You ought to take some bread and butter instead of fretting over your coffee," opined his wife.

"Yes, I'll do that," said he, "and a little nip to finish with. That champagne, brr!"

He got a bread-and-butter tray with a brandy flask and brightened up.

"Now we'll go to Pilot's Hill and see the view."

They got up and went out. The weather was splendid, and the promenade went well. But when it came to climbing the hill their pace was slow; the wife was short of breath and the husband stiff in the knees. They drew no comparisons with former times.

They then went out into the meadows.

The fields had been mown long since and afterwards grazed over, so that not a flower was to be seen. They sat down each on a separate stone.

He began to talk about the prison inspection and his work, she about the children.

Next they went on a bit further without talking. He took out his watch.

"It's three hours to dinner," he observed.

At the same time he thought, "I wonder what we shall do to-morrow."

They turned back to the hotel. He began to look for newspapers. She smiled and sat by him without speaking.

Dinner was quite silent. Finally the wife broached the subject of servants.

"Oh, for heaven's sake don't let us start on servants," he burst out.

"Yes, we haven't come here to quarrel," she replied.

"Have I started quarreling, I'd like to know?"

"Or I, either?"

Then came a fearful pause. He would have been glad now if there had been some one to come between them. The children? Oh, by all means. This *tête-à-tête* began to be tiresome. But with that he felt a pang as he thought of the bright hours yesterday.

"Let's go to Ekbacken and pick wild strawberries," she suggested.

"There are no strawberries this time of the year, my good lady; it's autumn."

"Let's go, anyhow."

So they were walking again. But they found nothing to say to each other. He sought with his glance for an object, a place on the road that they could talk about, but everything was dried out, talked to death. She knew all his opinions on every subject and disapproved of many of them. Furthermore, he was now longing for home, home with the house and the children. It was too silly to go about here like a pair of idiots liable any moment to get into a quarrel. At last they stopped, for the wife was tired. He sat down and began to trace on the ground with his stick, only wishing she would give him some opening for an outbreak.

"What are you thinking?" she asked finally.

"I?" he responded as if released from a weight; "why this is what I think: we're old, mama; we've played out our play, and we'd best be content with what has been. If you agree, we'll go home by the evening boat. Eh?"

"That's what I've been thinking all along, dear old boy, but I wanted you to say so first."

"Well, come along, we'll go home then! It's not summer any more, it's autumn."

"Yes, autumn it is."

They went back with lighter steps. He was somewhat abashed at the awkward prosaic turn matters had taken, and felt the need of giving a philosophic interpretation to the situation.

"You see, mama," he explained, "my lo—" (the word was too strong) "my affection for you has in the course of years undergone an evolution, as they put it nowadays. It has developed, amplified itself, so to speak, so that from concentrating on an individual as in the beginning, it has now broadened itself to include in the family, as it were, a collective object. It refers not to you as a separate person, or to the children, but to the whole combination. . . ."

"As uncle always says, the children are lightning conductors."

After his philosophic exposition he had become himself again. It was good to get out of the frock-coat attitude and into a dressing gown again.

And as soon as they got back to the hotel, his wife started on the portmanteau, and then she was in her element.

When they boarded the steamer they went down at once to the dining room. To save his face he had first asked if they should watch the sunset, which she had declined. As they ate supper, he helped himself first, and she asked the proprietress what the bread cost. When he had eaten to his heart's content and was about to put the beer-glass to his mouth, he could no longer restrain a thought that had been amusing him for some time:

"Old fools, eh?" he exclaimed, smiling at his wife, who looked up at him in the middle of a bite.

But she did not smile back at his shining fat face. On the contrary, her eyes flashed like lightning for an instant, and then assumed an expression of such withering dignity that he became embarrassed.

The enchantment was now broken, the last trace of the sweetheart had vanished; he was sitting only with the mother of his children, and he felt himself crushed.

"Because I was silly a while, you needn't forget to respect me," she said severely. "But there's a good deal of contempt in a man's affection; it's a funny thing."

"And in a woman's?"

"Much more, that's true. But then, she has greater provocation."

"Lord knows, it's about equal, though in different ways. Probably they're both in the wrong. A thing one has over-estimated because it is difficult to get may easily become an object of contempt."

"Why should it be over-estimated?"

"Why should it be hard to get?"

The steamer's whistle above their heads interrupted the conversation. They had arrived at their destination.

When they were back in their home, and he saw her in the midst of the children, he soon felt that his "affection" for her had gone through a transformation, and that hers for him had flowed over and been distributed among all these little cry-babies. Perhaps it was only as a means to these that he possessed her affection. His *rôle* then was transitory, and he therefore felt himself set to one side. If he had not been necessary to provide bread, he would now presumably have been discarded.

He went into his work-room, put on his dressing gown and slippers, lighted a pipe, and felt at home again. Outside the wind-gusts lashed the rain, and there was a whistling in the stove-pipe.

His wife came in when done with the children.

"This is no weather for strawberry-picking," she remarked.

"No, old lady; the summer's done, and autumn's here."

"Yes, it's autumn," she responded, "but it isn't winter yet. That's one comfort."

"That a comfort! Not much comfort when we live only once."

"Twice, when one has children; three times, if one lives to see one's grandchildren."

"But after that it's really all up."

"Unless there's another life after this."

"There's no being sure of that. Who can tell? I believe in it, but my faith is no proof."

"Yes, but it's nice to believe it, so let's believe, let's believe there may be another spring for us! Let's believe it!"

"All right, we will believe it," said he, putting his arm around her waist.

Theodor Storm

In America Theodor Storm is known to thousands of students who have responded to the gentle sentiment of "Immensee," a favorite of classes in German. "Immensee," written in 1852, is Storm's most famous story, his first, and perhaps the most characteristic of the fifty he wrote. "Veronika," the story selected here, is a subtle, concentrated study of the heart which might easily have been expanded into a novel. "My stories have developed from the lyric," Storm once remarked, and most of them are romantic mood-pictures recalled from the scenes of his youth. He had a genius for turning reminiscence into literature.

Born at Husum, Schleswig, in 1817, Theodor Storm studied jurisprudence at Kiel and Berlin, and began the practice of law in his native town. For ten years he was a political exile in Prussia during the period when possession of Schleswig-Holstein was disputed between Denmark and Prussia. In his busy life he continued to practice law and to hold a judgeship while he reserved his evenings for the poems and the stories which won an enduring position in German letters. Some of his later stories, such as "Psyche" (1875) and "Aquis Submersus" (1875), are psychological studies in more extensive form than his earlier work. One of his most effective stories "Der Schimmelreiter" appeared in the year of his death, 1888.

VERONIKA *

Theodor Storm

I. At the Mill

IT WAS at the beginning of April on the day before Palm Sunday. The mild rays of the late afternoon sun shone on the young grass at the side of the path which led down gradually along a mountain slope. At this moment one of the most respected jurists of the city, a man of middle age, with calm but distinctive features, was walking leisurely, exchanging only an occasional word with the clerk at his side. Their destination was a water-mill not far off whose owner, troubled by age and illness, wished to make over his property to his son.

A few paces behind followed another couple; beside a young man with fresh, intelligent features walked a beautiful, still very youthful woman. He spoke to her, but she did not seem to hear. Her dark eyes gazing straight ahead, she walked silently, as though unaware of anyone at her side.

As the mill became visible in the valley below, the counsellor turned his head. "Well cousin," he called, "you write a passable hand; how would you like to learn a little about making contracts?"

But the cousin waved his hand in protest. "Go on!" he said and looked questioningly at his companion. "Meanwhile I'll have a conversation-lesson with your wife!"

"Well, at least don't teach him too much, Veronika!"

The young woman only inclined her head as in assent. Behind them, from the towers of the city, the sound of the evening chimes came spreading over the country-side. Her hand, which had just stroked back the black hair beneath her white satin hat, glided down over her breast and, making the sign of the cross, she began softly to recite the Angelus. The glance of the young man who, like his relative, belonged to a protestant family, followed the uniform movement of her lips with an expression of impatience.

Several months ago he had come to the city as an architect to work on the addition to a church and since then had been an almost daily guest in the house of the counsellor. He had entered immediately into a lively and friendly association with the wife of his cousin. The two

* Translated by Charles H. Stubing from Storm's *Sämtliche Schriften* (Braunschweig: G. Westermann, 1868).

were drawn together through the youth which they had in common as well as through his accomplishment in drawing, which she also practiced with enthusiasm and skill. Now she had found him a friend and teacher at the same time. Soon, however, as he sat beside her evenings, it was not so much the drawing lying before her upon which his eyes rested, as it was her small, busy hand; and she who had been wont to cast aside her pencil at any given moment, now drew silently and obediently without looking up, as though caught in his gaze. It may be that they hardly realized themselves, that, every evening when saying "Good night," their hands remained together a little longer and their fingers were clasped a little tighter. The counsellor, whose thoughts were usually with his business, thought still less about it; he was glad that his wife had found stimulation and understanding for her favorite occupation, which he himself was unable to give her. Only once, just after the young architect had left their house, the dreamy expression in her eyes had surprised him. "Vroni," he said, holding her back by the hand as she tried to pass, "It's true then, isn't it, what your sisters say." "What is, Franz?" "Of course," he said, "now I see it myself, you have spiritual eyes." She blushed and submitted without speaking as he drew her closer and kissed her.

Today, in the fine weather, she and Rudolf had been invited by the counsellor to accompany him on his official errand to the near-by mill.

Since yesterday's social gathering, when she had displayed, at the request of her husband, a drawing which had been completed under his eyes, everything had become different between them. Rudolf felt it only too well; he recalled how it had come about that he had opposed the excessive praise of the others with such sharp and passionate criticism.

Veronika had long ended her prayer, but he waited in vain for her to turn her eyes toward him.

"You are angry with me, Veronika," he said at last. The young woman nodded slightly, but her lips remained firmly closed.

He looked at her. Obstinacy still lay upon her brow.

"I should think," he said, "you might know how it could happen! Or don't you know, Veronika?"

"I know only," she said, "that you have hurt me." "And," she added, "that you wanted to hurt me."

He remained silent for a while. "Did you not notice," he asked hesitantly, "the knowing eye of the old man who stood opposite you?"

She turned her head and glanced up at him fleetingly.

"I had to do it myself, Veronika. Forgive me! I can't bear to have you criticized by others."

It seemed as though a veil drew over her eyes, and long black lashes sank upon her cheeks; but she did not answer.

A short time later they had reached the mill. The counsellor was led into the house by the miller's son; Rudolf and Veronika entered the garden lying at the side, and continued to walk silently up the long incline; it was almost as though they were angry with each other, as though they had to stop for want of breath when they tried to speak an occasional word.

When they had wandered through the garden, they passed over a narrow foot-bridge into the lower door of the mill-building, which stood by a swift stream at the edge of the garden. Through the clattering of the works and the roar of the falling water which drowned every sound coming from outside, a strange sense of separation reigned in the almost dusky room. Veronika had walked over to the door which led to the mill-race and gazed down into the thrashing wheels upon which the water glistened in the evening sun. Rudolf did not follow; he stood within, beside the big cogwheel, his gloomy eyes unswervingly upon her. Finally she turned her head. She spoke, he saw how her lips moved, but he did not understand her words.

"I don't understand!" he said and shook his head.

As he was about to go to her, she had already stepped back into the inner room. In passing she came so close to the wheel beside which he stood, that the teeth almost touched her hair. She did not see it, since she was still blinded by the evening sun; but she felt her hands seized and herself drawn quickly to the side. As she looked up, her eyes met his. They remained silent; a sudden unmindfulness dropped like a shadow over them. At their heads thundered the mill works; from outside came the monotonous rushing of the water, plunging over the wheels into the depths. Gradually, however, the young man's lips began to move, and, protected by the deafening noise, in which his voice was lost, he whispered intoxicated, maddening words. Her ears could not discern them, but she read their meaning from his lips, from the impassioned pallor of his face. She threw her head back and closed her eyes; only her mouth smiled and betrayed life. Thus she stood holding her face toward him helplessly, her hands obliviously in his.

Then suddenly the roaring ceased; the mill stood still. They heard the mill-hands walking above, and outside, the dripping water fell from the wheels, tinkling into the pond. The lips of the young man became dumb, and when Veronika withdrew from him, he did not try to hold her back. Not until she had gone out through the door into the open, did he seem to regain his speech. He called her name and extended his arms to her, pleadingly. But she shook her head, without turning to look at him, and walked slowly through the garden to the dwelling.

As she went in through the door which had been left partly open, she saw opposite her the old miller, with folded hands lying in his bed. Over it a wooden crucifix was attached, from which hung a rosary. A young woman with a child in her arm had just come over to the bedside and was bending over the covers. "He only needs air," she said. "He enjoys his food well enough."

"Who is your doctor?" asked the counsellor, who was standing close by, holding a document in his hand.

"Doctor?" she repeated, "We have no doctor."

"You're doing wrong there!"

The young woman let out an embarrassed laugh. "It's old age," she said, as she wiped her chubby boy's little nose with her apron, "The doctor couldn't help that."

Veronika listened breathlessly to this conversation. The old man began to cough and put his hand to his eyes.

"Is this your will, Martin, as it is written here?" the counsellor now asked. But the sick man seemed not to hear him.

"Father," said the young woman, "Is that right as the counsellor has just read it?"

"Of course," said the sick man, "Everything is all right."

"And you have considered everything well?" asked the counsellor.

The old man nodded. "Yes, yes," he said, "I have worked hard; but the boy shouldn't have it too bad. . . ."

The son, who until now had been sitting in the corner smoking, entered into the conversation. "Of course, the old man's part has to be considered too," he said, and cleared his throat several times, "The old man will live away a neat sum yet."

The counsellor cast his gray eyes down upon the coarse peasant. "Is that your son, Wiesmann?" he asked, pointing at the child playing at the bed side. "Send him out, if you expect to do any more talking!"

The man was silent; but his eyes met those of the counsellor with an almost threatening expression.

The old man stroked his hard hand over the cover. And said quietly, "It won't be so very long, Jakob!—But," he added, turning to the counsellor, "in keeping with the village customs, he will have to bury me; that will cost something, too."

The young lady disappeared without a sound, just as she had come, from the open door in which she had been standing during these proceedings.

Outside she saw Rudolf on the other side of the garden in conversation with the mill-hand, but she turned away and followed a footpath, which led below the mill down to the stream. Her eyes strayed unconsciously into the distance; she did not notice how dusk was sinking upon the mountains ahead of her, nor how, gradually, even while she was strolling up and down, the moon was rising behind them and pouring its light over the silent valley. Life in its naked poverty confronted her as she had never before seen it; an endless, arid way,— at the end, death. She felt as though she had been living in a dream until now, and as if she were now wandering in a reality without solace, in which she did not know how to find her way.

It was late when the voice of her husband called her back to the mill where he awaited her at the door. On the way home she walked silently at his side, without feeling his understanding eyes upon her. "You have been frightened, Veronika!" he said and laid his hand upon her cheek. "But," he added, "these people live according to different standards; they are harsh, not only towards their kin, but also towards themselves."

She looked up at her husband's calm face for a moment; then she cast her eyes upon the ground and walked humbly at his side.

Just as silently Rudolf walked at the side of the old clerk. His eyes hung upon the hand of the woman, illuminated by the moonlight, which had only a short time ago rested so weakly in his own. He hoped that he would be able to hold it once more, if only for a moment when saying good night.—But it was to be otherwise; for, as they approached the city, he noticed the small hands, one after the other, slip into a pair of dark gloves, which, as he well knew, Veronika usually carried only for the sake of completing her costume.

Finally they had reached the house; but before he was quite aware of it in his dejection, he felt the hasty touch of her covered fingers upon his own. With a distinctly spoken "Good night" Veronika had opened the door and had disappeared into the darkness of the hall ahead of her husband.

II. PALM SUNDAY

The morning of Palm Sunday had arrived. The streets of the city were thronged with country-folk from the neighboring villages. Here and there in the sunshine in front of the house-doors stood the children of protestant inhabitants, gazing down toward the open door of the Catholic Church. This was the day of the great Easter procession.— Now the bells were ringing, and the procession became visible under the Gothic arch, and surged out into the street. At the head the orphan boys with black crosses in their hands, behind them in white veiled hoods, the Sisters of Mercy, then the various public schools and finally the whole endless train of country and city folk, of men, women, of children, and old people, all singing, praying, dressed in their best clothes, men and boys bare-headed, their caps in their hands. Over-head at measured intervals, carried upon shoulders, the colossal religious pictures: Christ at Calvary, Christ jeered by the soldiers, in the center, high above everything, the tremendous cross, finally the Holy Sepulchre.

The ladies of the city did not customarily participate in the public festivities.

Veronika sat half dressed in her bedroom at a small dressing table. Before her lay open a small, gilt-edge Testament, such as the Catholic Church permits its members. She seemed to have forgotten herself over her reading, for her long black hair hung loose over her white night-gown, while her hand, holding a tortoise-shell comb lay idly in her lap.

As the din of the approaching procession reached her ears she raised her head and listened. Ever more distinctly came the dull sound of steps, the singing, monotonous murmuring of prayers. "Holy Mary, Mother of Mercy!," it came from outside, and from the rear of the procession resounded a subdued: "Pray for us poor sinners, now, and in the hour of death."

Veronika recited the familiar words softly. She had pushed back her chair; with her arms at her sides, she stood in the back of the room, her eyes steadfastly directed toward the window. New people came and went continuously, new voices spoke, one picture after the other was carried by. Then suddenly a heart-rending tone penetrated the air. The *castrum doloris* approached, accompanied by the sound of trumpets, surrounded by people, followed by the acolytes and the highest priests in festive vestment. The ribbons fluttered, the black crepe of the canopy rippled in the air; underneath it in a garden of flowers lay the image of the Crucified One. The metallic peal of the trumpets was like a summons to the Day of Judgment.

Veronika was still standing motionless; her knees trembled; beneath the accentuated black eyebrows her eyes lay as if extinguished in the pale countenance.

When the procession had passed, she sank to the floor beside the chair upon which she had been sitting, and covering her face with both hands, she cried, with the words in Luke: "Father, I have sinned against Heaven, and I am not worthy of being called your child!"

III. In the Confessional

The counsellor belonged to that ever increasing community of those who saw in the appearance of Christianity not so much a miracle, but rather the natural result of the spiritual development of humanity. He himself, therefore, did not go to any church; nevertheless, he permitted his wife to retain the habits of her youth and parental home, perhaps in the expectation of her gradual, independent liberation from them.

Since their wedding two years before Veronika had gone to confession and communion only at Easter-time, which had now begun again. He was already acquainted with the way in which she went about in the house on the preceding days, quiet and apparently indifferent; therefore, it had not struck him that the enthusiastically undertaken drawing lessons had ceased ever since that evening walk. But the time passed, the May sun began to beam warmly into the room, and Veronika put off her confession again. At last it could escape him no longer that her cheeks became paler from day to day, that little shadows became visible under her eyes, left there by sleepless nights. Thus he found her one morning upon entering the bedroom unnoticed, standing at the window lost in thought.

"Vroni," he said, putting his arm around her, "Won't you try holding up your little head again?"

She shuddered, as if he had surprised unguarded thoughts in her, but she sought to control herself. "Go, Franz!," she said, taking his hand tenderly and leading him back to the door.

Then, soon after he had left her alone, she dressed and departed from the house, prayer-book in hand.

A short time later she entered St. Lambert's. Meanwhile the morning was advancing. Outside the windows of the vast hall the leaf-covered branches of the Linden trees cast their shadows; in the choir, upon the doors of the reliquary, a broken sunray fell through the stained glass panes. In the confessionals in the nave of the church here and there people sat or kneeled before opened prayer-books, preparing for confessions. There was no sound but the whispering from the confessionals, now and then a deep breath, the rustling of a dress, or a soft footfall upon the flagstones. Soon Veronika, too, was kneeling in one of the confessionals, not far from the picture of the Holy Mother, who looked down upon her, smiling compassionately. Her completely black costume made the transparent pallor of her face still more striking. The priest, a robust middle-aged man, leaned his head against the screen which separated him from his penitent.

Veronika began the introductory formula in a half whisper: "Forgive me, Father, for I have sinned," and with wavering voice she continued: "I confess to Almighty God and to you, Father, . . ." Her words became slower and slower, less and less understandable; then she stopped.

The dark eye of the priest was calm and directed upon her with an expression almost of fatigue, since he had been hearing confessions for hours. "Turn ye to the Lord!" he said mildly. "Sin is death; but repentance is life."

She tried to collect her thoughts. And again, as so often since that hour, her inward ear heard the turbulent roar of the mill; and again she stood before him in the mysterious twilight—her hands caught in his, closing her eyes under the stress of the overwhelming emotion, transfixed in mortification, not daring to escape, and even less, to remain.—Her lips moved, but she could not get it out; she tried in vain.

The Priest remained silent for a moment. "Courage! my daughter!" he then said, raising his head with the rich black hair. "Think of the words of the Lord: 'Receive ye the Holy Spirit; those whom ye free from sin, their sins shall be forgiven!'"

She glanced up. The flushed countenance, the powerful bull-neck of the man in vestments was close before her eyes. She began once more; but an unconquerable resentment came over her, a reluctance, as before something unchaste, worse than that which she had come here to confess. She was frightened. Was not this revolt in her a temptation of the deadly sin from which she wanted to be released? She bowed her head in silent conflict upon the prayer-book lying before her. Meanwhile, the expression of fatigue had vanished from the face of the priest. He began to speak, earnestly and forcibly, and then with all the magic of persuasion; softly, yet sonorously the tone of his voice came to her ears. At any other time she would have sunk to the dust, enraptured; but this time the newly awakened emotion was stronger than all the power of rhetoric and all the habit of her youth. Her hand fumbled at her veil which was thrown back over her hat.

"Forgive me, father," she stammered. Then, silently shaking her head, she drew the veil down without having received the sign of the cross, stood up, and went hastily down the aisle. Her clothes rustled past the church benches; she gathered them in her hand; it seemed to her as though unseen hands were reaching out to keep her there.

Outside, beneath the high doorway she stood still, breathing deeply. She was troubled in spirit; she had rejected the redeeming hand which had led her since childhood; she knew no other which she might grasp now. Then, as she stood undecided on the sunny square, she heard the voice of a child beside her, and a small brown hand offered her a bouquet of primroses for sale. It was indeed spring outside in the world. As though she had not known it, like a messenger it came to her heart.

She bent down to the child and bought his flowers; then, the bouquet in her hand, she walked down the street towards the city gate. The sun glittered on the stones; from the open window of a house a canary sent forth its loud song. She walked slowly on and soon reached the last houses. From there a foot-path led off to the side up toward the hills which bounded the city. Veronika breathed more freely; her eyes rested upon the green of the fields which bordered the path; now and then the air stirred and brought the gentle fragrance of the cowslips growing at the foot of the mountain. Farther on, where, at the border of the fields the forest began, the path rose steeper, and physical effort became necessary although Veronika had been used to mountain climbing since her early youth. Now and then she stopped and gazed from the shadows of the firs into the sunny valley which sank deeper and deeper below her.

When she had reached the summit she sat on the ground among the wild thyme which had spun itself over the mountain at this spot. As she breathed the spicy air of the forest her eye swept over toward the blue mountain-chain which lay on the horizon like a haze. Behind her, at short intervals, the spring wind was blowing through the tops of the pines. Now and then the call of a blackbird sounded out of the depths of the forest, or above her the cry of a bird of prey which floated invisible in the immeasureable vastness of space.

Veronika removed her hat and supported her head with her hand. Thus in solitude and quiet a period of time passed. Nothing approached her but the pure breezes which touched her brow and the calls of the birds which reached her ear from the distance. At times a bright glow flushed her cheeks and her eyes became large and shining.

Now the bells sounded up from the city. She raised her head and listened. They rang shrilly and hastily. "Requiescat!," she said softly, for she had recognized the little bell from St. Lambert's tower which informed the community that beneath one of its roofs the grim messenger of the Lord had entered.

At the foot of the mountain lay the cemetery. She could see the stone cross towering over the grave of her father who, but a few years before, had passed away in her arms as a priest intoned his prayers. And farther on, there, where the water glistened, was that ugly barren patch of earth which she had so often entered as a child, full of shy curiosity, where, according to the commandment of the church, those who had not received the sacrament of the altar were buried beside those who had taken their own lives. This would now be her resting place, too, since Easter confessions were at an end for her.

An expression of pain crept about her mouth and then disappeared. She stood up, a decision firm and clear in her soul.

A moment longer she looked down upon the city and let her eyes wander over the sunlit roofs as if in search of something. Then she turned and walked through the pines down the mountain the way she had come. Soon she was in the green of the fields again. She seemed to hurry, walking erect with firm steps.

Thus she reached her house. From the maid she learned that her husband was in his room. As she opened the door and saw him sitting calmly at his desk she remained hesitantly on the threshold.

"Franz," she called softly.

He laid his pen aside.

"Is it you, Vroni?," he said, turning to her. "You're late! Was your list of transgressions so long?"

"Don't joke!" she said pleadingly as she stepped up to him and took his hand. "I did not confess."

He looked up at her, surprised. She, however, knelt before him and pressed her lips upon his hand.

"Franz," she said, "I have hurt you!"

"Me, Veronika?" he asked, and took her face softly between his hands.

"And now you have come to confess to your husband?"

"No, Franz," she replied, "Not to confess, but to confide in you, in you alone,—and you,—help me, and if you can,—forgive me!"

For a moment he gazed at her earnestly, then he raised her with both arms and laid her head upon his breast. "Then speak, Veronika!"

She did not stir, but her mouth began to speak and, as his eyes hung upon her lips, she felt how his arms tightened about her.

Hermann Sudermann

SUDERMANN's great year was 1889, marked by the beginning of the realistic movement in the German theatre to which he contributed his first play Honor, and in which he and Gerhart Hauptmann became national leaders. From that time to his death in 1928, Sudermann was a dominant and controversial figure in German literature, although in his last years he evinced little sympathy for post-war writing, and was in turn felt by the younger critics to have been arbitrarily sensational in developing his career.

Sudermann's reputation was hard won. Born in Matziken, East Prussia in 1857, the son of a brewer, he knew poverty, and was obliged to serve a term as an apothecary's apprentice. He managed, however, to get an education at the University of Koenigsberg, went to Berlin, tutored for a while, and then turned to journalism. His first book, Twilight Tales (1887), from which "The New Year's Eve Confession" is taken, shows considerable French influence, and his next work Dame Care (1887), a novel based upon personal experience, better reveals his own qualities of warm characterization and dramatic intensity. His play Magda (1893) won international fame, its title role being interpreted by the world's greatest actresses, Modjeska, Bernhardt, Duse, and Mrs. Patrick Campbell.

Other collections of Sudermann's short stories are Brothers and Sisters (1888), The Indian Lily (1911), and Lithuanian Tales (1917). His later novels The Song of Songs (1908) and The Mad Professor (1926) were widely read in this country.

THE NEW YEAR'S EVE CONFESSION *

Hermann Sudermann

A H, DEAR LADY, it's good to be here, with you again, sitting so peacefully in this comfortable chair, ready for a cozy chat. Thank goodness, the holiday hubbub is over and done with, and you have a little leisure for me again.

Oh, the Christmas season! I do believe it was invented by the devil especially for the annoyance of us bachelors, to impress upon us the dreariness of our homeless lives. The thing that is a source of delight to others is a torture to us. Of course, of course, we're not all of us lonely. The joy of bestowing joy blooms for most of us, too. But the pure pleasure of sharing pleasure with others is embittered partly by a dose of ironical self-criticism, partly by that acid yearning which I might call, instead of homesickness, marriage-sickness.

Why did I not come and pour my heart out to you? you ask, you sympathetic soul, who bestow consolation as generously as most of your sex bestow petty spite. Ah, but you see, the matter is not so simple. Don't you know what Speidel says in his charmingly chatty *Lonely Sparrows,* which you, correctly divining the state of my soul, sent me on the third day of the holiday? He says, "The genuine bachelor does not *want* to be consoled. Once having become unhappy, he wants to indulge his unhappiness."

Besides Speidel's lonely sparrow, there is also a species of confirmed old bachelors, family friends. I do not mean those professional destroyers of the family who insinuate themselves hypocritically with evil intent while making themselves comfortable at the hospitable hearth. I mean the good old uncle, papa's whilom schoolmate, who dandles baby on his knees while respectably reading aloud to mamma the story in the evening paper—with omission of the indecent passages.

I know of men whose whole life goes in the service of a family with which they have become friendly, men who pass their days without desire beside a lovely woman whom they secretly adore.

You are skeptical? Oh, it is the "without desire" that you object to? You may be right. In the depths of even the tamest heart there probably lurks a wild desire, but a desire—it is understood—that is held in check.

I should like to give you an example and tell you of a conversation

* From *Great German Short Novels and Stories,* edited by Bennett A. Cerf. Translated by Adele Seltzer. Reprinted by courtesy of Random House, Inc.

that two ancient gentlemen had with each other this very New Year's Eve. You must not ask me how I found out about the conversation, and you must not tell it to any one else. May I begin?

Picture, as the scene, a high-ceilinged room furnished in an old-fashioned style and dimly lighted by a green-shaded, brightly polished, hanging lamp, such as our parents used before the era of kerosene; the light falling upon a round table covered with a white cloth and set with the ingredients for mixing a New Year's punch, and in the center a few drippings of oil spreading slowly.

My two ancient gentlemen sat half in the dimness cast by the green shade. Moldy ruins they were of a time long past, each tremulously sunk in himself, and each staring into space with the dim eyes and dull look of old age. The one, the host, was a military man, as was clear at first glance from his close-fitting stock, his pointed mustache, shaved off under the points, and his eyebrows knitted in a martial frown. He sat huddled in a rolling chair and clutched the handle of the steering rod with both hands like a crooked walking-stick. Nothing about him stirred except his lower jaw, which went up and down incessantly with a chewing movement. The other, who was sitting beside him on the sofa, was tall and thin, with narrow shoulders and the head of a thinker, angular and broad of brow. He drew skimpy clouds of smoke from a long pipe that was about to go out. Snowy white curls framed his face, and in the thousand fine lines of his smooth, dried-up skin nestled a soft, quiet smile, such as nothing but the peace of renunciation can impress upon an aged countenance.

They sat without talking. In the silence you could hear the slight bubbling of the burning oil mingled with the slight bubbling of the tobacco juice. Then the clock on the wall in the dark background wheezed and struck eleven.

"This is about the time you usually brew the punch," said the man with the thinker's head. His voice sounded soft and quavered a little.

"Yes, this is the time," the other rejoined. His tone was harsh, as if again resounding with the strident shouts of command.

"I should never have thought," the guest continued, "that it would be so sad without her."

The host nodded and chewed on.

"She made the New Year's punch for us forty-four times."

"Yes," the old soldier put in, "ever since I have been living here in Berlin and you have been coming to see us."

"Last year at this time," the guest continued, "we three were still together, so happily. She sat there in the easy chair, knitting socks for Paul's oldest child, and hurrying as fast as she could. They had to be finished by twelve o'clock, she said. And they were. Then we drank the punch and very comfortably discussed death. And two months later she actually was carried out to the cemetery. You know, I wrote a thick volume on the immortality of the idea. You never could bear it. And I cannot bear it any more either, since your wife died. As a matter of fact, I don't give a fig for any ideas any more."

"Yes, she was a good woman," said the husband of the deceased. "She took good care of me. When I had to be out for service by five o'clock in the morning, she was always up ahead of me and saw to it that I had a good cup of coffee before I left. To be sure, she had her faults, too. When once she got to philosophizing with you— whew!"

"You simply never understood her," murmured the guest, something like restrained resentment quivering about the corners of his mouth, though the look he allowed to rest on his friend a long time was mild and sad, as though his soul carried the secret consciousness of guilt.

After a period of silence, he began:

"Listen, Franz, I must tell you something—something that has been gnawing at me a long time. I cannot possibly go down into the grave carrying it along with me."

"Fire away, then," said Franz, picking up the long pipe leaning against his rolling chair and stuffing its bowl with tobacco.

"Once—something happened—between me and—your wife."

"Please don't joke, Doc," said Franz.

"I'm in grim earnest, Franz. I have been carrying it round with me for more than forty years, and now the time has come at last to make a clean breast of it."

"Do you mean to say my wife deceived me?" the old soldier shouted in a rage.

"Shame on you, Franz," said the philosopher, with his sad, mild smile.

Franz mumbled and muttered a little, and then lighted his pipe.

"No, she was pure as an angel," the philosopher went on. "You and I are the criminals. Listen to me. It was forty-three years ago. You had just been ordered to Berlin as a captain, and I was teaching at the University. You know what a wild fellow you were then."

"Hm," said Franz, and raised his shaking hand to twist the points of his mustache.

"There was a beautiful actress with big black eyes and small white teeth. Do you remember?"

"Do I remember! Bianca was her name." A feeble smile flitted across the old man's weather-beaten countenance with the marks on it of hard and fast living. "She could bite, I tell you, she could bite!"

"You deceived your wife, and she suspected it. But she never said anything, and suffered in silence. You did not notice it, but I did. She was the first woman I got to know after my mother's death. She came into my life like a shining star, and I looked up to her as to a shining star. Finally I summoned up the courage to ask her what was troubling her. She smiled and said she was not feeling quite well yet. You remember, it was only a short while before that that Paul had been born. Then came New Year's Eve—exactly forty-three years ago this very night. I came to your house at about eight o'clock, as usual. She sat embroidering, and I read to her while we waited for you. The hours passed, one by one. You did not come. I saw how uneasy she became and how she began to tremble, and I trembled with her. I knew what was keeping you, and I was afraid that you would forget twelve o'clock in that woman's arms. It was getting very near the hour. She stopped embroidering, and I stopped reading, and an awful silence descended on us. I saw a tear creep out slowly between her lashes and fall down on her embroidery. I jumped up and wanted to go out, and bring you home. I felt capable of tearing you by force from that woman's side. But at the same instant your wife jumped up, too, from this very seat I am sitting on.

"Where are you going?" she cried. There was unspeakable dread in her face.

" 'I am going to get Franz,' I said.

"At that she fairly screamed.

" 'For goodness' sake, stay with me. At least *you* stay with me. Don't *you* leave me.'

"And she threw herself on me and laid her hands on my shoulders and hid her wet face on my chest. My whole body quivered. Never before had a woman been so close to me. But I held on to myself and spoke to her comfortingly. She so needed comforting. Soon after, you came back. You did not notice my confusion. Your cheeks were flushed and there was a love-drunken weariness in your eyes.

"That New Year's Eve produced a change in me which filled me with alarm. Since I had felt her soft arms around my neck and had drawn in the perfume of her hair, the star had fallen from heaven, and instead of the star it was the *woman,* the woman, beautiful, and breathing love. I knew there was ardor in my glances; and I denounced myself as a blackguard, a deceiver; and to make at least partial atonement to my conscience, I went to work to separate you from your mistress. Fortunately, I had some money, which I had inherited, and she was satisfied with the sum I offered her, and—"

"By Jingo," the old soldier interjected, "so you're the one to blame for Bianca's writing me that touching good-by letter in which she told me it was with a breaking heart that she had to forego my love?"

"Yes, I am the one to blame for it. But listen. I had expected to purchase peace with the money I gave her. I was mistaken. The wild thoughts kept going round and round in my brain worse and worse. I buried myself in my work. It was just then that I conceived the central thought for my *Immortality of the Idea.* No use. Peace did not come that way.

"And so a whole year went by, and another New Year's Eve arrived. I was sitting beside her on this seat once again. This time you were at home, but you were lying asleep on the sofa in the next room, tired out by a jollification at the club. Sitting there, close beside her, looking at her pale face, the recollection of the New Year's Eve before came back and overwhelmed me irresistibly. Just to feel her head at my neck once again, just to kiss her once again, and then let come what may! Our glances met for an instant. It seemed to me that a secret understanding flashed into her eyes. I could not control myself any longer. I dropped at her feet and hid my burning face in her lap.

"I lay there like that, motionless, for possibly two seconds, when I felt her hand cool on my head and heard her say softly and gently:

"'You must be good.'

"Yes, I must be good. I must not deceive the man sleeping in the next room so trustfully. I jumped up and looked about, disconcerted. She picked up a book from the table and handed it to me. I knew what she meant, and opened the book at random and started to read aloud. I do not know what I read. The letters danced before my eyes. But gradually the storm in my soul subsided, and when it struck twelve, and you, with a sleepy look in your eyes, came in to wish us a Happy New Year, I felt as though that instant of sin lay far, far behind me, in an era long past.

"From that time on I became calmer. I knew she did not return my love, and I had nothing to hope for from her but compassion. The years went by. Your children grew up and married. We three grew old. You gave up sowing wild oats and lived for only the one woman, like myself. I did not stop loving her. No, that was impossible. But my love took on other forms. It discarded earthly desires and turned into a spiritual communion. You often used to laugh when you heard us philosophizing. But had you divined how my soul became one with hers, it would have made you very jealous. And now she's dead. Perhaps by next New Year's Eve we shall have followed her. That is why it is high time for me to unburden myself of my secret and say to you, 'Franz, I once did you a wrong. Forgive me!' "

He held out his hand to his friend pleadingly, but Franz answered testily:

"Bah, stuff and nonsense! A lot to forgive! This news of yours, this confession, is stale. I've known it for ages. She herself told me all about it forty years ago. And now I'll tell you the reason I ran after women the way I did until I was an old man—because, when she told me, she also said that you were the only man she had ever loved."

His guest stared at him in silence. The clock on the wall wheezed and struck twelve o'clock.

Arthur Schnitzler

To THE American reader Arthur Schnitzler is best known for his graceful, ironic studies—in both play and story—of men and women under the evanescent illusion of love. But it would be a mistake to suppose that such writing as the frivolous and witty escapades of Anatol (1893) is most typical of Schnitzler's genius. The erotic is but one of the impulses which moved his imagination to interpretations of delicate artistry. In human lives, outwardly commonplace, he sensed the inward drama of desire and frustration. As he grew older Schnitzler turned to the profounder implications of man against death, and his posthumous Flight into Darkness is one of his most brilliant books. He seems, as Pierre Loving remarked, to be "peculiarly a child of the age of Freud."

Arthur Schnitzler was born in Vienna in 1862, the son of a famous laryngologist, and was himself trained for medicine at the University of Vienna. Receiving his degree in 1885, he established a successful practice before he suddenly turned to writing for the stage. His first work Anatol was immediately popular, and Schnitzler had found his life work. Other plays followed, and then novels and short stories, Schnitzler often working on several productions at once. Among English translations of his works are Bertha Garlan (1918), The Shepherd's Pipe and Other Stories (1922), Fraulein Else (1925), Rhapsody (1927), and Casanova's Homecoming (1922).

THE BLIND GERONIMO AND HIS BROTHER*

Arthur Schnitzler

THE BLIND Geronimo rose from the table and took his guitar where it lay beside his wineglass. Hearing the faint rumble of the early coach, he felt his way over to the open door and down the narrow wooden steps which opened into the sheltered courtyard. His brother came with him, and they quickly placed themselves near the steps, huddled close to the wall for protection against the cold, damp wind that blew through the open gate into the muddy area where they waited.

Under the gloomy archway of the old inn, travellers from Italy to the Tyrol took their last rest before reaching the summit. Here the coaches going over the Stelvio Pass stopped but briefly, for the road ran on a level between bare hills with no outlook. Here the blind young Italian and his brother Carlo were as well off in the summer as at home.

Before long the postchaise was followed by other coaches, and while most of the passengers kept their seats, wrapped up in rugs and coats, a few got out to pace back and forth between the gates. The weather grew worse, with a cold rain splashing down. After a stretch of beautiful days, autumn had come suddenly, and all too soon.

Taking up his guitar, the blind man began to sing, and his voice, betrayed by the wine, was uneven and shrill. Though at times he lifted his head with an air of fruitless searching, his features with the black stubble beard and bluish lips were quite without expression. His older brother stood quietly at his side until someone dropped a coin into his hat; then he nodded his thanks with a sudden confused look, turned furtively away, and like his brother stared again into space. He seemed ashamed that his eyes could see the light but impart no ray of it to his blind brother.

"Bring me some wine," ordered Geronimo, and Carlo went obediently away. As his brother mounted the steps, Geronimo began again to sing. For a long time he had been so accustomed to his own voice that he could notice what went on around him. Now he heard nearby the voices of a young man and girl whispering together, and he wondered how often these two might have walked back and forth

* Translated by Dorothy Blodgett from *Sterben und andere Novellen*. Printed by permission of Heinrich Schnitzler and Curtis, Brown, Ltd.

over the same road. Indeed, in his blindness and drunkenness it often seemed to him that the same people travelled day after day over the pass, now toward the south, and now to the north. And so he had known this young couple for a long time.

Carlo came back and handed Geronimo a glass of wine. The blind man raised it to the young couple and said: "Your good fortune, ladies and gentlemen!"

"Thank you," said the youth, but the young woman drew him away, for she felt there was something uncanny about this blind man.

Next came a coach filled with a rather noisy party—father, mother, three children, and a nurse.

"A German family," Geronimo whispered to Carlo.

The father gave coins to the children, and each was allowed to throw his own into the beggar's hat. Geronimo nodded his head every time in thanks. Carlo observed the oldest boy who was looking at the blind man with anxious concern. The sight of such children always reminded Carlo that Geronimo had been just that age when he had lost his eyesight. For even now after twenty years he remembered that day with perfect clearness. Even now the shrill cry of a child sounded in his ear, the cry with which little Geronimo had fallen on the grass,—even now he saw the sun flicker lightly on the white garden wall and again heard the Sunday bell which had sounded at just that moment.

He had been shooting his dart towards the ash tree by the wall, and when he heard the cry he realized at once that he must have hurt his little brother who had just run past. He let the blowpipe slide out of his hands, sprang through the window into the garden and dashed toward the little boy who lay crying on the grass, his hands pressed against his face. The blood was flowing down over his right cheek and neck. At that moment their father came home from the field in through the little garden gate, and together they knelt help-lessly beside the crying child. Neighbors came running up; old Vanetti it was who first succeeded in drawing the child's hands away from his face. The smith, to whom Carlo was then apprenticed and who knew a bit about cures, came over too, but he saw at once that the right eye was lost. Nor could the doctor who came evenings to Puschlav do anything more to help; indeed it was too true, as he said, that the other eye was already in danger.

A year later Geronimo's world was lost in night. At first they tried to persuade him that he might be cured and he seemed to believe it. But Carlo, who knew the truth, wandered day and night over the country roads, through the vineyards and in the woods on the verge of suicide, until the priest to whom he confessed made him see that it was his duty to live and devote his life to his brother. Then Carlo was consumed with a great pity. Only when he was near the blind youth, when he might stroke his hair, tell him stories, or lead him over the fields behind the house and through the vineyards, was his pain lessened. From the first he had neglected his hours in the smithy in order not to be separated from his brother, and as time went on he could not bring himself to take up his work again in spite of his father's anxiety. One day Carlo noticed that Geronimo had stopped talking about his misfortune altogether, and he soon realized why: the blind man was at last aware that he would never again see the sky, the hills, the streets, the people, nor daylight itself. Now Carlo suffered even more than before, trying hard to console himself with the thought that the misfortune had been unintentional. But time and again when he looked at his brother lying beside him in the early morning he was seized by such a dread of watching him waken that he ran out into the garden. He could not be there when the blank eyes opened hopefully toward the new light of day that was lost to him forever. It was then that Carlo thought of having Geronimo, who had a pleasant voice, take some lessons in music. The schoolmaster, who sometimes came over from Tola on Sundays, taught him to play the guitar. To be sure, Geronimo did not then suspect that his new art would one day be his means of livelihood.

On the sad summer day of the accident, misfortune, it seemed, took up her abode in the home of old Lagardi. The harvest turned out badly year after year; the old man was cheated, by a relative, out of his small savings; and when one hot August day he was taken with a stroke in the fields and fell over dead, he left behind nothing but debts. The small piece of property was sold, and the two brothers, poor and with no roof to shelter them, left the village.

Carlo was then twenty, Geronimo fifteen, when they began the wandering life of beggars that they had led until today. At first Carlo had hoped to find some way of supporting them both but he met with no success. And Geronimo was always restless, too, and must be forever on the road.

For twenty years they had wandered about on roads and mountain passes in northern Italy and the southern Tyrol, always where the stream of travellers was thickest. And though by now Carlo was no longer tortured when he saw a bit of sunshine or a pleasant landscape, he was still filled with an involuntary pity like his heartbeat and his breath. He was happy when Geronimo could lose himself in drink.

The German family had driven away. Carlo sat down to rest on the lowest step of the stairway, but Geronimo stood listening intently.

Maria, the maid, came out of the taproom. "Have you earned much today?" she called down. Carlo did not turn around, but the blind man bent down for his glass and drank to Maria. Often she sat beside him in the taproom of an evening, and he knew that she was beautiful.

Carlo bent forward and looked down the road where the rush of the wind and the rain had quite drowned out the sound of an approaching wagon. As it drew up, Geronimo began to sing again while the driver quickly unharnessed his horses and dashed into the taproom. A single passenger stayed in the corner of the wagon, wrapped in a gray raincoat and scarcely seeming to hear the song at all. When presently he climbed down to pace back and forth, rubbing his hands to get them warm, he noticed the beggars for the first time and stopped to study them more closely. He was a very young fellow with a pretty, beardless face and restless eyes. Carlo nodded his head slightly in greeting, but the traveller hurried back to the gate to look with annoyance at the forlorn picture of rain and mist.

"Well?" asked Geronimo.

"Nothing now," answered Carlo. "He will probably give us something when he goes away."

The traveller returned to lean upon the wagon shaft, and to listen attentively as the blind man began to sing. The house boy appeared to harness the horses again, and as though he had just bethought himself, the young man reached into his pocket and gave Carlo a franc.

"Oh, thank you! Thank you!" Carlo said.

The traveller sat down in the wagon and again wrapped himself in his coat while Carlo picked up his glass and went back up the wooden steps. Geronimo sang on. The traveller leaned out of the wagon and shook his head with an air of condescending pity. Suddenly an idea came to him and he smiled. He said to the blind man, standing close at hand, "What is your name?"

"Geronimo."

"Well, Geronimo, don't let anyone cheat you." At this moment the driver appeared at the top steps.

"How cheat me, kind sir?"

"I have given your companion a twenty franc piece."

"Oh sir, thank you, thank you!"

"Yes; so watch out!"

"He is my brother, sir; he will not cheat me."

The young man was taken aback for a moment, but while he was thinking it over, the driver had climbed into his seat and started the horses. So he leaned back with a movement of his head as though to say, "Fate, take your course!," and the wagon drove off.

Lifting both hands in an excited gesture of thanks, the blind man turned as he heard Carlo cry at the door of the taproom, "Come, Geronimo, it's warm in here! Maria has built a fire."

Geronimo nodded, took his guitar under his arm, and felt his way up the steps, calling out to his brother: "Let me feel it! How long since I have felt a goldpiece!"

"What's that?" asked Carlo. "What did you say?"

At the top step Geronimo reached with both hands for his brother's head, a favorite gesture in moments of joy or tenderness.

"Carlo, dear brother, there are still good men alive!"

"Of course," replied Carlo. "So far there are two lire and thirty centesimi, and here is some Austrian money besides,—perhaps half a lira."

"And twenty francs—twenty francs, you know!" Geronimo insisted. "I'm sure of it!" He stumbled into the room and sat down heavily on the bench.

"What are you sure of?" asked Carlo.

"Now stop joking; put it in my hand. How long since I have had a goldpiece in my hand!"

"What do you want, then? Where should I take a goldpiece from? There are two or three lire here."

The blind man struck the table. "That's enough now, enough! Are you hiding it in front of me?"

Carlo looked at his brother in anxious wonderment. Sitting down beside Geronimo, he moved close and took his arm soothingly. "I hide nothing from you! How can you think such a thing? No one has given me a goldpiece!"

"But he told me he did!"

"Who?"

"Why, the young man, who was running back and forth."

"What? I don't understand you."

"Why, he just said to me, 'What is your name?', and then, 'Take care, take care, don't let anyone cheat you!'"

"You must have dreamt it, Geronimo, that's nonsense!"

"Nonsense? But I heard it, and I hear well. 'Don't let anyone cheat you; I have given him a goldpiece . . .'—no, he said: 'I have given him a twenty franc piece.'"

The landlord came in: "Well, what's the matter with you? Have you gone out of business? A four span has just driven up."

"Come along," cried Carlo, "come on."

Geronimo remained seated. "Why should I come? What good will it do me? You stand right beside me and—"

Carlo touched his arm. "Be quiet and come on down now!"

Geronimo obeyed, but on the steps he spoke again: "We'll talk later, we'll talk later!"

Carlo did not understand what had happened. Even when he was angry Geronimo never spoke like this. Had his brother suddenly gone mad?

In the carriage that now arrived were two Englishmen. Carlo raised his hat to them and the blind man sang. One of the Englishmen climbed out and threw some coins into Carlo's hat. Carlo thanked him and said as if to himself: "Twenty centesimi." Geronimo's face was unmoved. He began a new song, and the carriage with the two Englishmen drove on.

The brothers went up the steps in silence. Inside Geronimo sat down on the bench, while Carlo remained standing by the stove.

"Why don't you say something?" asked Geronimo.

"Well," answered Carlo, "it's just as I told you." His voice trembled a little.

"What did you say?" asked Geronimo.

"Perhaps it was a madman."

"A madman? That's very likely! If someone says: 'I have given your brother twenty francs,' then he is a madman!—Eh, and why did he say: 'Don't let anyone deceive you'—eh?"

"Well, perhaps he wasn't mad . . . but there are men who play jokes on us poor people. . . ."

"Yes, jokes!" cried Geronimo. "You did have to say that; I've been waiting for that!" He finished his glass of wine.

"But Geronimo!" Carlo was almost too amazed to speak: "Why should I . . . how can you believe. . . .?"

"Why does your voice tremble . . . eh . . . why . . .?"

"Geronimo, I tell you, I—"

"Yes, yes—and I don't believe you! And now you're laughing . . .
I know you're laughing!"

The servant called up from below: "Hey, blind man, there are
some people here!"

From force of habit the brothers joined each other and went downstairs. Two wagons had arrived together, one with three gentlemen
in it, and the other occupied by an elderly couple. Geronimo sang:
Carlo stood beside him all distracted. What was he to do now? His
brother did not believe him! Impossible!—And he looked around
anxiously at Geronimo as the blind man went on singing his songs
with an unsteady voice. Strange new thoughts seemed to flit across
the blind man's face.

The wagons had gone but Geronimo kept on singing. Carlo did not
venture to interrupt him, for he hardly knew what to say and he
was afraid that his voice would tremble again. Then there was a
laugh from above, and Maria called out: "Why do you keep on
singing? You'll certainly get nothing from me!"

Geronimo stopped in the middle of a song, as though his voice and
the guitar string had broken together. He went up into the taproom
again and Carlo followed sitting down beside him. What was he to
do? Nothing but to try once more to make his brother understand.

"Geronimo," he began, "I swear to you . . . just think, Geronimo,
how can you believe that I. . . ."

Geronimo said nothing, his blank eyes seeming to gaze out into
the gray fog. Carlo went on: "Of course, he needn't have been crazy,
he may have been mistaken . . . yes, he made a mistake . . .," feeling
almost as if he himself could not believe what he was saying.

Geronimo turned away impatiently, but Carlo talked on with sudden
animation. "For what reason would I . . . but you know that I
do not eat and drink any more than you, and when I buy myself a
new coat you know that . . . why would I need so much money?
What would I do with it?"

Then Geronimo fairly hissed, "Don't lie, I can tell that you're
lying!"

"Geronimo, I'm not lying, I'm not!" cried Carlo in a shocked voice.

"Eh!, have you given it to her already? Or does she get it later?"
cried Geronimo.

"Maria?"

"Well, who but Maria? Oh you liar, you thief!" And unable to sit beside him at the table any more, Geronimo jabbed his elbow into his brother's side.

Carlo stood up. He stared briefly at his brother, then left the room and crossed the steps into the courtyard. He gazed wide-eyed down the road where it disappeared in the brownish fog. The rain had abated, and thrusting his hands in his pockets, he walked out into the open air. He felt as if his brother had driven him away. What could have happened? He could not understand it. What kind of man could that have been—to give one franc and say it was twenty? He must have had some reason for it . . . And Carlo searched his memory for some possible enemy somewhere who might have sent another man for revenge. But as far as he could recall, he had never offended anyone, had never even seriously quarreled with anyone. For twenty years he had done nothing but stand in courtyards or at roadsides with his hat in his hand. . . . Was someone angry with him because of a woman? . . . But it had been long since he had been interested in anyone . . . the waitress at "La Rosa" had been the last the spring before, but certainly no one was envious on her account. He couldn't understand! What kind of people were in the strange world outside? They came from everywhere; what did he know of them? To this stranger there was doubtless some reason for saying to Geronimo, "I have given your brother twenty francs." Yes, yes, but what was to be done now? . . . Suddenly it was clear that Geronimo distrusted him! . . . He could not endure that! He must do something about it! And he hurried back.

When he stepped back into the taproom, there lay Geronimo stretched out on the bench seemingly unmindful of his brother's entrance. Maria brought them food and drink. They said nothing during the meal, but when Maria cleared away the plates, Geronimo all at once laughed aloud and exclaimed to her, "What will you buy with it?"

"With what?"

"Well, what? A new coat or earrings?"

"What does he want of me?," she turned to Carlo.

Just then the courtyard below echoed with a heavy dray, loud voices sounded up, and Maria hurried downstairs. After a moment three travellers came in and took places at a table. The host went over to greet them, and they complained about the weather.

"You'll have snow tonight," said one.

The second one told how ten years ago he had been snowed in

on the yoke in mid-August and had almost frozen to death. Maria sat down with them, and the servant came over, too, to ask for news of his parents who lived down in Bormio.

Presently another carriage came up, and the two brothers went down, Geronimo singing and Carlo holding out his hat, while the travellers gave their alms. Geronimo seemed now quite composed, asking frequently, "How much?" and nodding lightly at Carlo's answers. But Carlo tried hard to collect his thoughts, with the heavy feeling that something dreadful had happened, and that he was entirely helpless.

When they climbed the steps again they heard a babble of voices and much laughing among the travellers. The youngest one called out to Geronimo, "Sing us something over again, we will pay you, won't we?" as he turned to the others.

Maria, coming in with a bottle of red wine, said, "Don't get him started today, he's out of humor." Without answering Geronimo took his place in the middle of the room and began to sing. When he finished, the travellers clapped their hands.

"Come here, Carlo!" one of them called. "We want to put some money in your hat as they did down stairs." And he took a small coin and lifted it high in his hand as if to let it fall into the hat that Carlo held out to him. But the blind man grasped the driver's arm: "No, to me, give it to me! It might fall outside, you know!"

"What do you mean—outside?"

"Well, at Maria's feet!"

Everyone laughed, the innkeeper and Maria along with the rest. Only Carlo stood there quite still. Geronimo had never made such a joke before. . . .

"Sit down with us," urged the travellers, "you're a merry fellow!" And they moved closer to make room for Geronimo. The babble grew louder and more confused, Geronimo in the midst of it noisier and merrier than ever before, and drinking all the time. When Maria came in again he wanted to pull her over his way, but one of the company jested, "Maybe you think she is beautiful? She's just an ugly old woman!"

The blind man drew Maria down to his lap. "You're all blockheads," he said. "Do you think I need my eyes to see? And I know where Carlo is, too—he's standing there by the stove, his hands in his trouser pockets, laughing."

All eyes turned to Carlo beside the stove, leaning there with his mouth open and now actually distorting his face to a grin as if he must bear out his brother's story.

The servant came in to say that if the travellers still wanted to get into Bormio before nightfall they must stir themselves. They got up and went out noisily. Now the two brothers were alone in the tap-room. This was the hour when they usually took a nap; indeed the whole inn slept during the early afternoon. While Geronimo drowsed with his head on the table, Carlo walked back and forth and then sat down on the bench. How tired he was! It seemed as if he were caught in a bad dream. He thought of all sorts of things—of yesterday, the day before, and other yesterdays, but especially of warm summer days and white country roads over which he had always wandered with his brother, and everything seemed strange and far away as if it could never be the same again.

In the late afternoon the post came in from the Tyrol, and then wagons for local stops going south. Four times the brothers had to go down to the courtyard. When they came back the last time, dusk had fallen and the oil lamp, hung from the wooden ceiling, was sputtering. Some stonecutters who lived in wooden huts near by came in from the quarry. Geronimo sat down with them, but Carlo stayed alone at his table. It seemed as though his loneliness had already been with him a long time. He could hear Geronimo over there, speaking loudly, almost crying, telling of his childhood: how he still remembered quite clearly all sorts of people and things that he had seen with his own eyes: of his father working in the field, of the little garden with the ash tree by the wall, of the little house that belonged to them, of the cobbler's two little daughters, of the vineyard behind the church,—yes, of his own childish face as it had looked back at him from the mirror.

How often Carlo had heard all that! Today he could not bear it. It had a strange new sound; every word that Geronimo said took on a new meaning and seemed aimed at him. He slipped out to walk in the country road, now lying in darkness. The rain had stopped, the air was chill, and Carlo had the fleeting temptation to wander on and on further into the night, to lie down in some roadside ditch, to fall asleep and never waken.

Suddenly he heard the rumble of a wagon and saw the glimmer of two lanterns coming toward him. Two men drove past. One of them, a thin beardless fellow, jumped with fright when Carlo's form loomed up out of the darkness in the light of the lantern. Standing quite still, Carlo stopped and lifted his hat. When the wagon and its lights disappeared, he stood again in darkness. All at once he started, afraid of the dark for the first time in his life. He couldn't bear it a minute longer, for in some strange way his own fears were mixed in his sombre thoughts with a hurting pity for his blind brother, and drove him back home.

When he returned to the taproom he saw the two travellers sitting at a table with a bottle of red wine and talking earnestly. They hardly noticed him when he came in. At another table Geronimo still sat among the workmen.

"Where were you, Carlo?" the innkeeper called from the door. "Why did you leave your brother alone?"

"What's the matter?" Carlo was frightened.

"Geronimo is treating the crowd. It's all the same to me, but you ought to remember that harder times will come again before long."

Carlo hurried over to his brother and took his arm. "Come!", he said.

"What do you want?" cried Geronimo.

"Come to bed," Carlo said.

"Let go, let go! I earn the money. I can do what I want with it—ha!—you can't pocket it all yet! Maybe you think he gives it all to me! Oh no! I am just a blind man! But there are people—good people —who say to me, 'I have given your brother twenty francs!' "

The workmen laughed aloud.

"That's enough," said Carlo, "come along!" And he pulled his brother with him, almost dragging him upstairs to the bare attic where they slept. All the way Geronimo cried: "Yes, it's clear now, I see now! Oh, but wait! Where is she? Where is Maria? Or did you put her in the savings bank? Oh, I sing for you, I play the guitar, you live on me—and you are a thief!" He fell back on the pallet.

Through the passage a weak light shone from the guest room where Maria was making up the beds for the night. Carlo looked down at his brother. Lying there with swollen face, bluish lips, and moist hair clinging to his forehead, he looked much older than he was. And slowly it dawned on him that the blind man's distrust had not started to-day, that it must have slumbered in him a long time, and that he had lacked only the occasion or perhaps the courage to speak out. All that Carlo had done for him had been fruitless; in vain the regret, in vain the sacrifice of his whole life. What was he to do now?—Should he continue to lead his brother day after day for Heaven knew how long through this eternal night, care for him, beg for him, and have no other reward for it than distrust and abuse? If his brother believed him to be a thief, then any stranger could do as well or better than he. Actually the wisest way would be to leave him and go away forever, for then Geronimo would soon realize how unjust he had been and would find out what it really was to be deceived and robbed, alone and miserable. And where should he himself begin? True, he was not old, and by himself could do many things; he could always find work as a servant.—But all this time he stood looking at his brother, and he suddenly had a picture of him sitting alone on a stone at the side of a sun-flooded road, with his white eyes wide open staring at the bright sky and his hand reaching into the night which was always around him. And he felt that even as the blind man had no one but him, so too he had no one but his brother.

He realized that his love for his brother was now the whole purpose of his life, and it occurred to him with sudden clarity that only the hope of his brother's love and forgiveness had let him bear all this misery so patiently. He could not abandon this hope. He needed his brother as much as his brother needed him. He could not, he would not leave him. He must either endure the distrust or find some way to convince Geronimo of his mistake. What if he could get a goldpiece somewhere! Then he could say to the blind man early in the morning: "I kept it just so you wouldn't drink it up with the workmen, so people wouldn't steal it from you" . . . or something. . . .

Steps sounded on the stair, the travellers were going to bed. All at once the idea occurred to him to knock on their door, tell them all that had really happened to-day, and ask them for the twenty francs. But no,—that would be hopeless! They wouldn't believe the story at all. And now he remembered that one of them had jumped with fright when he, Carlo, had suddenly appeared in the darkness in front of the wagon.

It was dark in the room when he stretched himself out on the strawsack. He could hear the workmen talking loudly as they went out with heavy tread. Before long the doors were closed, the servant went up and down stairs once more, and then all was quiet. Now Carlo heard nothing but Geronimo's snoring, and he was soon lost in his own bewildering dreams. When he awoke it was still dark but for the grey square that was the window. As Geronimo slept on with the heavy breathing of a drunken man, Carlo thought with a shudder of the day which was tomorrow, of the night after that day, the next day, and all the future that lay before him; and horror filled him at the thought of the loneliness which was in store for him. Why had he not had the courage the evening before to go to the strangers and ask them for the twenty francs? They might have taken pity on him. No—maybe it was as well that he hadn't asked them. Hm, why was it as well? . . . Suddenly he sat up with his heart beating fast. Of course it was better; if they had refused him, he would always have remained suspicious of them—but. . . . He stared at the grey spot that was beginning to show a dull light. . . . The thought that went through his head in spite of himself was impossible, altogether impossible! . . . The door over there was bolted—and besides, they might wake up. . . . Yes, there—the grey, shining speck in the darkness was the new day.

Carlo stood up, drawn to the light, and touched his forehead to the cold pane. Why had he stood up? To think it over? . . . To try it? . . . What for? . . . It was impossible—and besides it was a crime. A crime? What do twenty francs mean to people who ride a thousand miles for pleasure? Surely they wouldn't miss the money. He went to the door and opened it slowly. Two steps across was the other door— shut. On a nail hung garments. Carlo went over them with his hands. . . . If people would leave their purses in their pockets, life would be very simple and soon no one would ever need to go begging again. . . . But the pockets were empty. Now what? Back to his strawsack in the room? Maybe there was a better way to get twenty francs—a little less dangerous and a bit more honest. If he just kept back a few centesimi from the alms each time until he had saved twenty francs and then bought the gold piece! But how long would that take—months, perhaps a year. Oh, if only he had the courage!

He was still standing in the passage. He looked across at the door. . . . A line of light the length of the door! Was it possible that the door was just ajar, not bolted at all? That was not surprising, considering that the door had not been shut for months. He recalled that only three times during the summer had the room been used, twice by journeymen and once by a tourist with an injured foot.

Well, the door is not shut. Now all he needs is courage—yes, and luck! The worst that can happen to him is that they should both wake up and even then he can think up some excuse. He peeks through the crack into the room. It is still so dark that he can just barely see the outlines of two figures lying on the bed. He listens: their breathing is quiet and regular. He opens the door gently and with bare feet steps into the room. The two beds stand endwise along the wall opposite the window. Carlo creeps to the table in the middle of the room. With his hand he feels over the surface: a bunch of keys, a pocketknife, a little book—nothing more. Naturally! Why should they leave their money on the table? Well, now he can get away again! . . . And yet perhaps only a lucky move is needed to bring it off! And he comes near the bed beside the door. Here on a seat lies something . . . he feels of it . . . it is a revolver . . . Carlo starts! . . . Should he take that too? Why does this fellow have a revolver lying ready? If he should wake and look up . . . But no, Carlo would just say, "It is three o'clock, sir, get up." . . . And he puts the revolver down.

And he creeps on into the room. Here on the other seat under the clothes. . . . Heavens, that's it, a purse! He takes it in his hand. . . . Now he hears a slight creaking. With a quick movement he stretches himself out flat near the foot of the bed. . . . Again the creaking— a heavy sigh—a cough—then again deep silence. Carlo lies waiting on the floor, the purse in his hand. All is quiet, but the dawn is already glimmering palely in the room. Carlo creeps forward on the floor to the door and out into the passage where he gets up slowly and draws a deep breath.

He opens the purse. It is divided into three parts, with nothing but small silver in the left and right sides. Now he opens the middle part which is fastened by another clasp, and feels three twenty-franc pieces. For a moment he considers taking two of them, but he quickly thrusts this temptation aside, takes out a single gold piece, and closes the purse. Then he kneels down, peers through the doorway, and slides the purse along under the bed. When the stranger awakes he will think that it has fallen down from the seat. Just as Carlo is getting up, the floor creaks and he hears a voice from within, "What is it? What's the matter?" He steps back and with bated breath glides into his room. Safe at last, he listens again. . . . Once more the bed creaks in the other room, and then everything is still. He holds the goldpiece in his fingers. It's done—he has succeeded! He has the twenty francs, and he can say to his brother, "Now you see that I am no thief!" And they will still start on their trip today—south towards Bormio, then through the Valtellina, then to Tirano . . . Edole . . . Breno

. . . and to Lake Iseo as they did last year! . . . That will not look at all suspicious because day before yesterday he himself had said to the innkeeper, "In a couple of days we are going away."

Now the whole room has filled with a gray half-light. If Geronimo would only waken soon! It's so good to walk out in the early morning! Well, they will get started before sunrise. A good morning to the innkeeper, to the servant, to Maria, and then away, away. . . . And not until they are two hours away, down near the valley, will he tell Geronimo.

Geronimo stretches and stirs and Carlo calls, "Geronimo!"

"Well, what's up?" Geronimo props himself up with both hands.

"Geronimo, we're going to get up."

"But why?" And he turns his blank eyes to his brother.

Carlo is aware that Geronimo recalls the event of yesterday, but he also knows that his brother will not mention it until he is drunk again.

"It is cold, Geronimo, and we must get started. There'll be no more good weather here this year; I think we should be off. We can be in Boladore by noon."

Geronimo got up as the noises of the awakening house reached their ears. Hearing the innkeeper talking with the servant down in the courtyard, Carlo went down. He enjoyed waking early and going out of doors at dawn. He approached the innkeeper and said, "We're going to say goodbye now."

"Oh, are you going today?" asked the host.

"Yes, it's begun to be too cold standing in the courtyard; we feel the wind."

"Well, remember me to Baldetti when you get to Bormio; tell him not to forget to send me the oil."

"Yes, I'll do that. Now about last night's lodging." He reached into his sack.

"Let it go, Carlo," said the innkeeper. "I'll give the twenty centesimi to your brother. I've listened to his songs, too. Goodbye, then."

"Thanks," said Carlo. "Of course, we're in no hurry. We'll see you again when you get back from the huts. Bormio will wait for us, won't it?" He laughed and went up the stairway.

Geronimo was standing in the middle of the room. "Well, I'm ready to go."

"So am I," answered Carlo.

From an old chest of drawers in a corner of the room, he took their few belongings and packed them in a bundle, saying, "A beautiful day but very cold."

"I know," said Geronimo, and together they left the room.

"Walk softly," said Carlo, "those two who came last night are sleeping in there." They went down cautiously. "The innkeeper told me goodbye for you," Carlo went on. "He gave us the twenty centesimi for last night. He's out at the huts now and won't be back for a couple of hours. We'll see him again next year."

Geronimo made no answer. There before them lay the country road in the early morning light. Carlo took his brother's arm as they began descending into the valley. After a bit they reached the place where the road began to wind in long drawn-out curves. The fog climbed up toward them and above them the mountain tops were hidden in clouds. And Carlo thought: "Now I'll tell him."

But he said nothing—just took the goldpiece out of his pocket and handed it to his brother. Geronimo took it between the fingers of his right hand, touched it to his cheek and forehead, and at last nodded. "I knew it," he said.

"Yes?" Carlo looked at Geronimo in astonishment.

"Even if that stranger had said nothing to me, I'd still have known it."

"Oh, yes," said Carlo, puzzled. "But you understand why I said up there in front of the others . . . I was afraid that you would spend the whole amount at once. . . . and you see, Geronimo, I said to myself that it would be for the time when you buy yourself a new coat and shirt and shoes, and so I. . . ."

The blind man shook his head and smoothed his hand over his coat. "What for?" he said. "This is good enough, and warm enough; we're going south now."

Carlo did not understand why Geronimo was still unsatisfied. He went on, "Geronimo, I did the right thing, didn't I? Then why aren't you happy? Now we have it, you see—we have it all! If I had told you up there, who knows. . . . Oh, it's lucky indeed that I didn't tell you!"

"Stop lying, Carlo," Geronimo cried out, "I've heard enough!"

Carlo stood still and dropped his brother's arm. "I'm not lying."

"But I know you're lying! . . . You lie all the time! . . . You've lied a hundred times! . . . You just wanted to keep it for yourself, but you got worried—that's it!"

Carlo dropped his head, but without a word he took his brother's arm and walked on. Although he disliked hearing Geronimo speak this way, he was actually surprised not to feel more depressed.

Now the fog rose and out of a long silence Geronimo spoke: "It's getting warmer." He said it indifferently as he had said it a hundred times, and in a flash Carlo realized that for Geronimo nothing had changed: for him Carlo had been a thief all the time.

"Are you hungry?" he asked.

With a nod Geronimo took bread and cheese from his pocket, and they went on. The post from Bormio met them and the coachman called out, "Down already?" Then came other wagons, all going upward. "Valley air," said Geronimo, and right there after a sharp turn lay the Valtellina at their feet.

"Actually, nothing has changed," thought Carlo. . . . "Now I've really stolen for him, and not a thing has been gained!"

Presently the sun's rays broke through the thinning fog, and Carlo mused: "Maybe it wasn't wise to leave the inn in such a hurry. . . . The purse lies there under the bed, that's suspicious in any event." . . . But what difference did it make! What bad luck could happen to him now? Geronimo, whose eyesight he had destroyed, thought himself robbed by his brother, had believed it for many years, and always would. What greater evil could befall him now?

There below them lay the great white hotel bathed in the morning light, and still further below where the valley widened, the little village sprawled. Silently they walked along, Carlo's hand as usual on the blind man's arm. As they passed the hotel park, Carlo saw guests sitting at breakfast in light summer clothes.

"Where do you want to rest?" asked Carlo.

"Why, at the 'Eagle' as usual."

They walked to the little inn at the end of the village. Going inside, they sat at a table in the taproom and asked for wine.

"How is it that you have come to us so early?" the innkeeper inquired.

Carlo was startled a bit at the question. "Is it so early?" he said. "It's the tenth or eleventh of September, isn't it?"

"You came down much later last year."

"It was so cold up there," Carlo responded. "Last night we were frozen. Oh, by the way, I'm supposed to tell you not to forget to send up the oil."

The air in the taproom was close, and a strange uneasiness stole over Carlo. He wanted to be out in the open air again, on the great road which led toward Tirano, Edole, and Lake Iseo—to everywhere away! Suddenly he stood up.

"Are we going already?" asked Geronimo.

"We can still get into Boladore by noon. The wagons stop at the 'Stag,' and it's a good place, you know."

And on they went. The barber, Benozzi, smoking in front of his shop, called out, "Good morning! Well, how does it look up there? Did it snow last night?"

"Yes, yes!" said Carlo, and hastened his footsteps.

Now the village lay behind them, the road stretching white between meadows and vineyards along the roaring river. The sky was clear and blue. 'Why did I do it?' thought Carlo. He glanced sidewise at the blind man. 'Does his face look any different? He has always believed it—I've always been alone—and he has always hated me.' He felt burdened as he walked along with a load that he could not throw off, and he also sensed the night in which Geronimo walked by his side while the sun shone everywhere.

And they walked on, walked and walked by the hour. From time to time Geronimo sat down on a milestone, or they both leaned on a bridge railing to rest. Again they passed through a village. Wagons stood in front of the inn, and travellers had alighted to walk around, but the two beggars did not stop. They were away again on the open road. The sun kept climbing higher; it must be nearly noon. It was a day like a thousand others.

"The tower of Boladore!" said Geronimo. Carlo looked up and wondered how Geronimo could reckon the distance so exactly: the tower of Boladore had indeed appeared on the horizon. Now someone came toward them from a distance—someone who, it seemed to Carlo, had been sitting there and had suddenly stood up. The figure came nearer. Now Carlo saw that it was one of the gendarmes that he often met on the highway; nevertheless he was a bit frightened. But when the man drew still nearer, Carlo recognized him and was reassured. It was Pietro Tenelli. Only last May the two beggars had sat with him in the inn of the Raggazzi in Morignone, and he had told them a horrible story about how he had nearly been stabbed once by a tramp.

"Someone is standing there!" Geronimo said.

"Tenelli, the gendarme," Carlo explained.

Now they had come up to him.

"Good morning, Herr Tenelli," Carlo said.

"It so happens," the gendarme spoke directly, "that I must take you both to the station at Boladore for the present."

"What?" cried the blind man.

Carlo grew pale. 'How can that be?' he thought. 'But it can't have anything to do with that. Surely they can't know anything down here yet.'

"You seem to be going this way anyway," said the gendarme laughing, "you won't mind going with me."

"Why don't you say anything, Carlo?" asked Geronimo.

"Oh yes, I will speak. . . . I beg of you, Herr Gendarme, how does it happen . . . what shall we . . . or rather, what shall I . . . honestly, I don't know. . . ."

"That's the way it is this time. Perhaps you're not guilty at all. How do I know. At any rate, we've had a telegram at the station to detain you, because you are suspected, definitely suspected, of having taken people's money up there. Now of course, it's possible that you're not guilty. So forward!"

"Carlo, why don't you say something?" begged Geronimo.

"I'll talk—oh yes, I'll say something. . . ."

"Now go along!" said the officer. "What sense is there in stopping on the road! The sun is scorching and in an hour we'll be on the spot. Go ahead!"

Carlo touched Geronimo's arm in the old familiar way, and they moved slowly along, followed by the gendarme.

"But Carlo, why don't you talk?" Geronimo asked again.

"What do you want me to say, Geronimo? It will all be cleared up; I myself don't know. . . ."

And again he reflected: "Shall I explain it to him before we are brought to justice? . . . That won't do,—the gendarme would hear us. . . . Well, what's to be done? I'll certainly tell the truth in the courtroom. 'Herr Judge,' I'll say, 'this is no ordinary theft. That is to say. . . .' And now he tried to find the words to present the matter to the court in a clear and plausible way. 'A gentleman drove over the pass yesterday. . . . it may have been a madman—or he may have just made a mistake. . . . and this man. . . .'"

"But what nonsense! Who would believe it? . . . They wouldn't even let him talk that long.— No one could believe this stupid story . . . not even Geronimo believed it . . ."— And he gave him a sidelong glance again. The blind man's head moved up and down in his old custom as if in time with his walking, his face a blank and his eyes staring into space.—And Carlo suddenly knew what thoughts were running along in his head. . . , "So this is the way things stand," Geronimo must certainly think.— "Carlo robs not only me, but he steals from other people too. . . . Well, he is lucky, he has eyes that see and he makes the most of them." . . .—Thus Geronimo must surely be thinking. . . . And besides, it won't help me any that they don't find any money on me,—either with the judge or with Geronimo. They will lock us both up . . . yes, him as much as me, for he has the goldpiece.— And he was too confused to think any further. He felt as though he had lost his way in the whole affair and was sure of but one thing: that he would gladly remain a whole year under arrest. . . . or ten years, if Geronimo could only know that he had been a thief for him alone.

And then Geronimo stopped so suddenly that Carlo had to pause too.

"Come, what's the matter?" said the gendarme impatiently. "Forward, go ahead!" But then to his astonishment he saw Geronimo let his guitar fall to the ground, raise his arms and with both hands feel for his brother's cheek. Then he kissed Carlo who didn't know at first what had happened to him.

"Are you crazy?" asked the gendarme. "Go ahead, I tell you! I have no inclination to stand here and bake."

Geronimo picked up his guitar from the ground without a word. Carlo drew a deep breath and put his hand again on his brother's arm. Could it be possible? His brother had faith in him once more? He understood at last—? And once more he looked doubtingly at him from the side.

"Forward!" Once again the gendarme spoke. "Will you get on with it!" And he gave Carlo a poke in the ribs.

Now at last Carlo, guiding the blind man with a firm pressure on his arm, struck up a much faster pace than before. And when he saw Geronimo smile in a gentle happy way as he had never seen him do since his childhood days, Carlo smiled too. It seemed now as though no misfortune could ever again befall him,—either from the law or from anywhere else in the world.—He had his brother again. . . . No, he had him now for the first time.

Arnold Zweig

Now UNABLE to live in Nazi Germany, as Ignazio Silone is unable to live in Fascist Italy, Arnold Zweig is best known in this country for the exciting series of novels about the war years and after, called A Triology of the Transition. The first of them The Case of Sergeant Grischa (1928) is widely regarded as the greatest novel to come out of the world war. The other two, Education before Verdun (1936) and The Crowning of a King (1938), have not failed the expectations aroused by the first.

Although most readers think of Arnold Zweig as the chronicler of vast social movements affecting the whole future of civilization, he has written many short stories which deal easily and simply with unexceptional themes. Such a collection, Playthings of Time, was published in 1935. The story here printed is one of a series of episodes about a cultured young German girl which appeared under the title Claudia in 1930.

Arnold Zweig was born in Silesia in 1887. Trained in several German universities for a career of teaching, he is deeply versed not only in Germanic studies but in the literature of France and England as well. During the World War he was a soldier in a German Labor Corps. It is expected that in his future works he will continue to depict the struggle between the forces of oppression and liberty in modern states.

THE PARCEL *

Arnold Zweig

"Pray don't trouble, my dear doctor," said Claudia in her deep soft voice, as he eagerly offered to fetch her things from the cloak-room. "James will have seen to that already"; and, in fact, as she spoke, a youthful footman in livery—yellowish-gray coat, white breeches, and top-boots—appeared with his mistress's pink evening cloak and a thin shawl. Doctor Rohme stood helplessly among the chattering groups in the foyer. Beyond the aesthetic excitement of the evening, he still felt the resolve that had brought him there, like the note of a taut harp string, ringing in his mind, though as yet it was a resolve and nothing more; and as Claudia stood for the footman to arrange the cloak about her with a deftness that betrayed long practice, he brooded with set lips and vacant dreamy eyes, under the hostile looks of the audience now struggling for their coats and wraps, upon the wave of weary depression that had fallen upon him yesterday, and now once more swept over him as the sea flings a swirling wave against a cliff. When he noticed the announcement of that night's performance of Goethe's *Götz*, he picked up the play and began to read it, at first idly and then with growing dismay, for Weislingen's vaccillation had struck him like a blow in the face. A choking feeling of disgust and contempt rose in his throat at the thought that for three weeks he had known that he must reach some definite understanding in his relations with this girl, whom he loved to adoration, without finding the courage to bring matters to a decision. Her calm and friendly attitude towards him seemed to show that she did not in the least know how impossible it all was. His sense of order would not let him rest; he felt he was degrading himself and her, so he prescribed himself the torment of this performance, and the specific had worked. He would end it all this very evening, open his soul to her, at the risk of being dismissed for ever and thrust out into the darkness and the cold. That was what he must do, and he would do it.

Claudia's face seemed altered as she smiled at him over the white silk about her throat; she slipped her hand without a word under her companion's arm, and let him appear to lead her to the door,

---

* From *Claudia* by Arnold Zweig. Copyright, 1930, by The Viking Press, Inc., New York.

though it was really she who guided him. James had already beckoned to the chauffeur, and the familiar blue car stood, panting like a great beast, among the crowds that surged into the streets. He felt her guidance with a sharp thrill of shame, which he at once saw was futile, and would have preferred to go away, but could not; and when she disappeared into the dark vehicle without a word that would have given him excuse for departure, he had to get in after her. The chauffeur started almost before he sat down; so he sank back onto the leather cushions, looking suspiciously for a smile on that mobile mouth that would have made him unhappy. But the lovely pale face remained unchanged in its expression of gentle kindliness as she smoothed her frock and turned her bright gaze to his, and he felt his purpose quail under the spell of those perilous great black eyes that so glowed with understanding. For a few moments the faint hiss and throb of the speeding car stirred the stillness of their thoughts, that still lingered with enjoyment over the play they had just left. The curtain had fallen, but they could still hear the clash of brandished weapons and hear the ring of that crisp and soldierly prose. *Götz von Berlichingen* had been played as though to give two great actors the opportunity to prove their art upon the creations of the youthful Goethe: the forceful talent of the older man made a vigorous living figure of the bluff Knight, while the younger with countless nervous subtle touches tried to present the unstable Weislingen as a man of to-day, and his abrupt uncertain gestures appealed strongly to an audience whose minds were not dissimilar to his. The balance between the two characters was presented in a fashion that thrilled and delighted the audience, and at the end their enthusiasm burst forth in a torrent of applause that swept on to the stage.

While these now vague recollections were hovering in his mind, he tortured himself to discover some means, some way, in which, without shocking her by blurting out his position—how well he could imagine her raised eyebrows and contemptuous curled lips!—he might make his mind clear to her, and say, in effect: "This is what I am like—now decide." But it was not easy and the words would not come.

At last Claudia said in a light conventional tone: "An interesting performance, Herr Doctor, don't you think?"

To Rohme, it was as though that murmurous silence were a living entity that her words had shattered; he collected himself and answered,

in a high voice with a touch of hoarseness that concealed his intonation, and a slightly formal air:

"Most interesting, indeed. Old-fashioned and yet modern, one might
say. I wonder whether Goethe saw his Weislingen like that?"

She smiled faintly. "So you are thinking of Weislingen? It is Götz
that is in my mind. . . . But I will ask the same question: I wonder
whether he saw Götz like that?"

He took off his glasses and polished them with a white handkerchief
as he observed slowly:

"I rather doubt, Fräulein Claudia, whether Götz is the center of
interest just now. I'm sure the people who were sitting round us this
evening will be talking much more about Weislingen, just as you
caught me doing. He is one of them—of us. The Götz we saw was a
possible embodiment of Goethe's idea of him, but as to Weislingen—
I am at least doubtful. Goethe's age would certainly have regarded a
man so easily swayed and so . . ." he hesitated for an instant and
brought out his succeeding word in an emphatic tone . . . "unmanly,
as a pitiable object. This kind of Weislingen is reserved for us. . . ."
He concluded with peculiar bitterness.

Claudia Eggeling thought that she could grasp all that was implied
by his tone; she had not failed to notice her old friend's intense
interest in Weislingen's character during the performance of the play.
But as she wanted to postpone a discussion that was not at all unwelcome to her, until their relation had become easier and more man-
ageable, she said lightly:

"Well, we must talk about that later; I don't agree with you. You
condemn poor Weislingen, I see."

"Condemn him? Nothing was further from my mind. . . ."

"Well, you disapprove of him. But how do you reconcile the unmanly man with your philosophy, my learned friend?"

She hoped a touch of banter might enliven his answers, but in
vain; he answered just as gloomily as before.

"Perfectly well. . . . One can imagine a type, Man, possessing all
the characteristics that constitute manhood, can't one?—and possessing
them in the highest degree. The individual falls short of this type,
and in specially unfortunate cases, so far short that manhood is no
longer there. And yet he still walks about on two legs."

The car suddenly swept into a broad avenue. After bumping wildly
for a minute or two on the slightly uneven paving, the wheels seemed
to leave the asphalt surface altogether and shoot through a whirl of

white and red lights. And the faint hum of traffic, and the glitter of the great highway flooded that little rushing room and made the faces of the two stand out, pale and sharp, in a kind of intenser actuality.

Claudia forgot her resolve, and took up the theme once more with her usual reluctance to abandon an idea: "I wish," she said, "you would describe the type to me a little." And she wondered whether he would describe his own character.

"So you agreed with me," he said, shading his eyes against the speeding lights. "We need not go further than Götz, for Götz is very much a man. I need not mention every quality that distinguishes a man—such as kindness, simplicity, courage and so on. Weislingen, too, can be kind—but from weakness. Fundamentally man is a creative, productive creature. . . ."

"And woman?" she asked.

"Conceives, transmutes, and gives forth: brings, in fact, to birth. But the man sows the seed. He has the power of vision, he creates because he sees the world anew. . . . Weislingen sees what is to be, and understands it—he has intelligence. But he never builds a bridge from one point to another, he only sees the result. Götz never realizes that there are difficulties. . . . Götz takes things piecemeal, as warring elements that need a unity, and yet has more respect for them than Weislingen who blindly surrenders to a circumstance or a situation and is continually lost."

Claudia felt suddenly baffled. At first he seemed to be talking about himself, disparagingly. Was he not, preeminently, intelligent—like Herod and Kandaules, typically manly characters, and much more akin to him than Götz, who was his opposite? Then it flashed across her mind that there was a ring of deeper purpose in his hesitating speech, and she had been listening not so much to what he said but to his tone, which was strangely moving and suggested a burdened soul finding its deliverance. However, he had rather overweighted the conversation, so she decided to turn the subject. What she wanted to say was: "You are being deliberately unfair to yourself"; but she took refuge in a generality and said:

"I think this type of yours is unjust to our present society. However, we can talk about that later on; at present all I know is that I'm vulgar enough to be terribly hungry, and Mamma made it quite clear that there would be some bread and butter for you, if you would give us your company so late."

He listened eagerly; it was, indeed, a torture to him to talk just then of what he felt so deeply. He let his mind dwell on what she had just said. What joy!—one more hour in her company. Then a stab of uneasiness went through him: could he be sure they were expecting him as a welcome guest, or did his enjoyment of that lovely house blind him to the fact that his was the pitiable role of an intrusive visitor?

"Your mother is very kind," he said gently, ". . . but I don't know . . . I had tried to make up my mind not to come to your house so often. . . ."

A bitter loathing of himself and a burst of fury against his unlucky tongue exploded within him. He ought to have put and said this quite differently—now it rang quite false.

From time to time the klaxon gave forth a loud deep roar, full of the power and purpose of a mighty beast that is certain of its way and will not harm those weaker than itself. Shrill rasping answers came from other cars as they shot across the road ahead, or came up behind, plunging from darkness into darkness. On either side of them was blackness, against which stood out a few lamps, trees, and foliage; they had almost imperceptibly left the city and were speeding along the asphalt highway that seemed to undulate before them under the flooding glare of the headlights, as they neared the villas and gardens. Claudia turned her face once more to her companion:

"Do we bore you?" she asked in an astonished tone, but with an air of unbelief that softened it. She understood him pretty well, and by way of reply, she thought to herself with not a little satisfaction: How charmingly gauche such a clever man can be! If only he wouldn't torment himself so. . . .

He passed his hand over his forehead and said: "You know that is unfair, Fräulein Claudia. But I am so often at your house now, and stay so long . . ." he began to speak at last with rather less constraint . . . "that I don't understand how you and your mother. . . . After all I am not a very presentable sort of person . . . and you're so considerate of me. . . ."

He was cut short by a ripple of laughter, the dear delightful laughter of a girl, to which she gave herself more gladly as it was just what she wanted to relieve the situation. She could not have him shamed, or, even faintly, humiliated. She shook her head quickly.

"Considerate, my dear Doctor Rohme? And what for? You have never broken a vase, or spilt your tea or your wine on the table cloth at our house. Don't you want us to be glad to see you? Really. . . ."

"But I might do one of those things at any moment, indeed I'm quite surprised I haven't," he said with a smile. Her cheerfulness did him good, and shifted the conversation into a lighter and less highly charged atmosphere.

"Ah, don't be always thinking of what might happen. You think too much about yourself in that way, you know—you must be careful," and she assumed a maternal tone that went through him with an almost physical sweetness. Good God, how he loved her—far too much. But perhaps it was true that they did find him quite a tolerable guest. There was something like joy in his voice as he asked:

"Did your mother really expect me?"

"She certainly did, and I ventured to expect you too. Didn't I invite you to our box? I could not suspect that you would make up your mind to neglect us or me."

She knew quite well that he would understand her jesting tone; he did, and helped her to lighten the conversation. He shook his head smilingly, and a long wisp of reddish hair fell down over his broad white forehead, now freckled by the summer sunshine; he smoothed his thick fair mustache, took up her tone of persiflage which he turned against himself.

"Well, I must confess you were too strong for me. While I was dressing, I proved to myself with algebraic exactitude, that what I was doing was foolish because I did not intend to come to your box."

"That was very wrong of you, Doctor Rohme," she said reprovingly. She appeared to be calmly listening, but she was, in fact, watching him with some care. He was clearly in a state of nervous tension.

"As I finally found myself at the theater," he continued, "and even at the box-office, I tried to buy a seat, but they were all sold out." He explained that he had made up his mind not to read so much. It did him no good, and did not help him, for he had, in the end, to think everything out for himself.

"Ah." She smiled; her lovely gray eyes were strangely expressionless that day.

"There was only standing-room, and boxes. Neither was any good: I did not want to stand, and I could not take a box—it would have been almost an insult."

"Certainly it would," she interjected. "I should never have forgiven you."

She realized she must be careful, but she could not help looking at him again. Could she imagine that he was no longer there? She struggled; of course! Hardly fair, certainly. Meanwhile, she heard him say:

"So I decided to go home."

"Oh!" said she indignantly.

Lights began to flash through the windows; they were near their destination. Then the glasses of his spectacles clouded and she could no longer see his eyes. It was almost discourteous to sit there without a word, absorbed in his thoughts. Perhaps he was pondering on her own inattention. . . . If he only knew! However, he soon went on. . . .

"And then I discovered as I walked up and down the foyer once or twice that for some days I had inwardly made up my mind to spend this evening at the theater and . . . with you, and I felt the force of that tyrannical resolve. Besides the place was crowded with people coming in, not a soul was going out. So I let myself be carried on and found myself outside your box just as I was finally deciding that I had better go home. If I had had to open the door myself, I should probably have found it impossible and retreated to the street; but at that instant an attendant opened it—and you gave me a whispered greeting, for the piece had of course begun. But you gave me your hand, Fräulein Claudia."

She would not let his words sink far into her mind, and she merely replied:

"And why not? You weren't disturbing any one. Boxes are so agreeable because one can do as one likes. Theaters and concerts are only possible when one can listen in peace. But I think we have arrived. At last!" And she gave a sigh of satisfaction. In a room there was space to move about and use one's voice, and the four familiar walls made companionship and conversation easy. . . . The car swept in a grinding curve through the iron gates and stopped at the front door of the villa. The footman opened the door; the air was cool, and their breath was faintly visible.

Doctor Rohme walked up and down alone in the lovely drawing-room, and pondered—a black conventional figure with broad black necktie and white shirt-front. He knew every piece of furniture and every picture, although his enthusiasm for the latest pictures was somewhat artificial. His restless pacing feet sank silently into the thick blue carpet. He thought of Claudia. His lips moved excitedly as though he were speaking silently to himself. He loved her—that he could no longer doubt. When he was with her, she filled his heart, and then at least he ceased to think of her. Indeed he often had to rouse himself from his absorption, but she had always been so kind. At first he had put it all down to the house, the lovely rooms, where he came to tea with the two of them, and then with one of them alone; and then to the delightful mother; but at last he had discovered that it was the daughter who attracted him and held him fast. Well, he knew his duty: he would go, and go at once. For what would come of it? He could not marry her. He was a young university teacher, making very little money, with a certain reputation in academic circles for a polemical and drastic treatise on the "Will," and no more; and she, Claudia Eggeling, was generally reputed to be excessively rich. A fortune-hunter, eh? Of course, it was utterly impossible . . . there was nothing for it but to go, irrevocably, and at once. For how could he explain his reasons? Should he begin: "Claudia, I love you, but. . . ." There now—he broke off in desperation, he was thinking of himself as he had always done. Presumably she had to give some sort of consent before a man could marry her. How fatuous and stupid he was!

He stopped before the mirror to confirm the fact that it was absurd and hopeless for him, Walter Rohme, to look for a wife. Not merely because he was red-haired, with a complexion like a copper kettle, and freckled into the bargain—his appearance was merely comic; and he glared with impotent fury at the object in the mirror that he so longed to be able to destroy—the commonplace familiar image of a broad-shouldered man, with thick bushy eyebrows and mustache, rather like the conventional representations of a pirate—an impression that was on second glance destroyed by the blinking gray eyes behind the thick glasses of the fragile gold spectacles, the pale and hesitating lips beneath the mustache, the high thin voice, the rounded chin, and pensive forehead. Indeed this counterpart might well provoke to laughter when he reminded himself that all his gestures were clumsy and ill-turned, emphatic and yet meaningless, and would never be otherwise. Never in his life had he been so disgusted with his appearance. . . . Claudia had indeed warmly maintained not long before that she cared little for a man's appearance, that Adonis and Absalom had probably been stupid—still, he must go. She hardly knew him, quick-witted as she was. Indeed how should she, deeply as he now knew her? For only sorrow gives men vision and unlocks the soul. He walked at her side, unknown and eternally a stranger. For he could not talk about himself, and when he tried, shame and self-hatred thrust a distorting mask upon his face. She could not have guessed whom he was condemning when he proclaimed Berlichingen as the type of manhood—how could she? And if she did not know him, he ought not to stay with her, and if she saw him as he was, their relation was equally at an end. Had she even an idea how unreliable he often was, and that in the affairs of daily life he was often guided by the last piece of advice he had been given, she would of course very soon control him, and in everything his will would soon be hers. Inevitably: and the certain result would be that she would first find him ridiculous, and then contemptible. She called him her friend, it was true; they read agreeable philosophic books together, they went to concerts together now and then, she played to him, and they went to the theater or to the Opera as they had done this evening—but that proved nothing. No, Claudia was a determined young woman, she rode, she knew her own mind and thought at once of Götz. What was it she had said not long ago when her mother was late? "I am punctual myself and I demand punctuality in others." It was true, she had a horror of undependable people. . . . The blood throbbed in his throat and he clenched his hands; he was condemned, and despair seized and shook him.

Thus, in his honest fashion, he tormented his soul with this monstrous psychology.

"You must excuse Mother, my dear Doctor, she has already gone to bed," said Claudia's voice behind him. During the few minutes he had been waiting, she had put on a favorite frock of his, a loose brown house-frock edged with gray-green at the neck and sleeves. This was the image of his dreams, this slim soft being with her quiet movements and her clear quick eyes, in whose irises the brown hue of her dress shone and was transfigured, while the pupils were black with the deep glowing blackness of her hair. Her nose was bold yet delicately molded; Roman she was from head to heel, with the liquid voice of a warbling bird. Yes, this was the woman whom he loved and must give up.

"You will have to put up with me," she went on.

Then he decided upon a sudden and abrupt departure: he would say nothing, rush from the house, and settle the affair in a letter—that would be the easiest way.

"I think it would be better if I went home now, Fräulein Claudia," he said, and tried to steady his voice so that it should not betray his misery: "It's time now. . . ."

The girl walked quietly to the threshold of the dining-room, turned with her fingers upon the door handle, and observed:

"I think it would be better if you stayed and had some supper with

me. There are only eggs, I'm afraid. We always have them when we
go to the theater."

She opened the door and went in; he hesitated, shrugged his shoulders helplessly, and followed.

Under a strong light from the white ceiling, the black paneling and
the black wood of the furniture looked somewhat formal, but the gay
grass-green of the carpet, chairseats, and curtains softened the gravity
of the beautiful room and made it look sedately cheerful. It was a
pleasant place in which to sit and eat. The table at which they sat
opposite each other was covered with a fine white linen cloth and laid
with dishes of inviting bread and rolls, various sorts of red and reddish
sausages, glasses for beer and tea, silver cutlery, goblet-shaped egg-cups
of thin porcelain, and plates, large and small, of the same fine white
china. At this bright delightful table they sat down opposite each
other—Claudia Eggeling and Doctor Rohme, she unconstrained and
cheerful, bending slightly forward as she ate, a gay and animated
figure in her faintly rustling silk frock, he still stiff and starched and
angular, black with a white shirt-front, high collar, and red shock of
hair that somehow recalled a woodpecker's crest. . . . They both ate
assiduously; it was late—though time had no existence in that shining
room—and they were hungry, and even if Claudia had wanted to
start a conversation she would have had to rouse her companion. His
expressionless fixed vacant gaze betrayed but too clearly that only his
bodily self was present, his spirit was ranging over fields unknown. . . .
Claudia smiled a little roguish smile, because in the meantime she
could indulge herself by gazing at him to her heart's content. She
thought him still at the play or somewhere in the world of Goethe; but
how startled she would have been if she could have heard her companion's thoughts! He had not gone far, indeed he was in that very
room, wandering slowly and gloomily round those two seated figures.

"Why do I feel so mean and full of faults when I am with you,
Claudia? Why do you sit there so clear and confident while I humble
myself before you? Because I have reached up to you from the lowly
place where I was born, entered an air in which my soul can breathe,
and because my intellect is greater than yours though it is housed in
the body of a slave; because in every problem I see many possible
solutions, because I will not let some element within me make a blind
choice, because I reflect, and am in the meantime overborne? Because
I cannot help smiling, a little contemptuously, I think, at decisions and
deeds; because these people so full of pompous energy and so wanting

in intelligence are grotesque in their crudity. . . . They have more strength and more success—but since when do success and strength count for anything in the region of the spirit? No, my little Claudia, though they who conquer me laugh, I am the higher type, weaker, subtler, and more spiritual, and what gives your class power over me, what allows Götz to triumph over Weislingen, is no more than the brute force of nature."

But this outburst of pride died down as the meal proceeded, and as he watched her hands, moving so nimbly and gracefully to serve him, the convulsions of a soul thus damned to solitude passed into a peaceful melancholy; nothing remained of it but a soft sad look behind those glittering glasses. This pleasant life would soon be over. Perhaps this was the last time—and he shuddered at his empty rooms which he once looked on as a refuge. They now meant banishment.

While they ate, only a few brief words passed between them, a little joke, a request for bread, the offer of a dish. But when their first hunger was stayed, the conversation grew more personal. Claudia now decided to open the subject that she had hitherto avoided. While she chose some of the cold sausage from the dish at her side, she observed:

"Well, you found your way to our box at last—but do you often change your mind so many times as that?"

He sighed gently.

"Ah, Fräulein Claudia, I have given up counting these absurd moral defeats. It is not worth the trouble. Have I ever told you the story of the parcel I once sent from Freiburg?"

He started with astonishment as the words fell quite unexpectedly from his lips. How on earth had this foolish and forgotten story suddenly occurred to him? Perhaps it was the prompting of a subconscious search beneath the surface of his mind that had produced so apt an instance of his folly. But he greeted it with grim exultation. It was none the less welcome and timely: by it she would know him, and all would be at an end.

"Never; you must tell it to me. Shall I like it? Tea or beer?"

What was all this about a parcel? His demeanor that evening had been eloquent of tension and excitement. She must find out what his trouble was; she felt so much at ease with him that he must not be allowed to torment himself for nothing.

"Tea, please; not too strong, thank you. It's a very foolish and tedious story, and I can't tell it properly, but I'll try. After that I'm sure you won't want to hear anything more of me." And he gloomily enjoyed the double meaning that only he could understand.

"Ah well, we shall see, Doctor," she said gayly.

How small and white her hands were. She wore no ring. And this was the woman he was to lose! A surge of self-pity threatened to overwhelm his resolve, but he beat it down. He felt his fate upon him, and he began bravely.

"Well then, I had been living for a time in Freiburg. It rained a great deal and I thought I would move elsewhere. I packed all my things into trunks and cases to be sent on by a firm of forwarding agents, Sabelberger & Co., who seemed efficient people and accepted liability." He stopped, as he noticed her lips were slightly parted as though she were about to speak, and he was glad to stop.

"Had you all your books at that time?" She was just peeling an egg, and her fingers moved with the light grace of dancing children—he could do nothing but watch them. . . . He recovered himself with a start, and answered:

"Indeed I had, do you suppose I could have endured it otherwise? Besides it is not so very long ago. The books were in a large case, carefully packed as you may imagine. But I could not get them all in, and as I reflected that the case would take some time to reach me, I chose my favorite books and made a parcel of them, a good stout parcel, stiffened with cardboard and securely tied with string. It contained the *Critique of Pure Reason* in a large volume bound in leather, a first edition of Schopenhauer, a *Meditationes* of 1650, a handsome edition in vellum"—he smiled slyly—"you know, Descartes—three or four old French editions of Montaigne and others, a volume of Shakespeare in English, and so on. Books that I really valued."

What if he stopped and changed the subject before it was too late? No that would be cowardly.

"Did they include the La Rochefoucauld you lent me?"

"Yes, that was there. So I took the parcel under my arm (it seemed very heavy), and carried it to the post office on a Saturday afternoon. The official I saw had red and dirty hands but a good heart, for he weighed the package sympathetically and advised me to make it a little lighter, for it weighed twenty-five pounds and would cost a lot of money to send by post. He suggested that I might send it by express instead. So I took back the parcel, thanked him, and went off to the express-office."

"So you took his advice?" She asked the question with an almost dream-like air, for she said to herself meanwhile: If he is so careful of his beloved books, a . . . person that he loved would be very safe with him. . . . And she blushed in confusion.

"I did. As I now knew I was carrying a weight of twenty-five pounds my burden seemed all the heavier. The office was at the railway station about twelve minutes away from the post office. I was received rather hastily, as on Saturday afternoon about half-past five the men are about already contemplating their well-earned Sunday rest. The man said he would see that the parcel went off, but did I know what it would cost? And he told me, for railwaymen are kindly fellows. It was twice the postal rate. 'Ah,' said I thoughtfully. 'Yes,' said he, 'that is what it will cost'; and he suggested I might as well save my money and send it by post or by ordinary freight. For which purpose I had only to cross over to the freight station."

He was in for it now and must go on, however much he longed to stop.

"So you went to the post office again?" she asked with a little laugh. How meticulous men were sometimes; but it was just that which made him so deliciously ingenuous.

"No, I thought I would send it by freight, Fräulein Claudia. I went to the freight station. It was some distance outside the town as such places usually are. I shifted my five and twenty pounds from one arm to the other, but it still weighed just the same. Ah, now you're laughing at me," he said, and laughed too. Perhaps it would be all right after all. And he prayed, to what power he could not tell, that it might be so.

"But didn't it occur to you to pay some one to carry it?" He looked very boyish when he laughed.

"Yes, as a matter of fact it did, in a vague sort of way, but in the first place there wasn't any one about, and secondly, the two of us and the parcel would have looked so silly marching through the streets. So at last I reached the freight station."

"And there I hope your poor soul found peace?"

The dreadful truth, that his hopes and half-serious tone had covered up, now stood forth dark and menacing; he gave himself up for lost.

"Yes, Claudia, in a certain sense at least. Well, there I was, and all around me was a complicated system of sheds, and inclines, and vast sliding doors. But all shut. It was, indeed, a quarter past six; I could hear the Cathedral bell ringing for vespers. I walked along an interminable wall, and turned a corner, for I reflected that a place like this is never entirely deserted. Not a dog barked, at which I was relieved, for dogs make me nervous. At last I heard the sound of knocking and tramping feet, and I came upon a few men in railwaymen's caps, lazily pushing some cases about, and in charge of them a man who did not look at all professional, wearing a short jacket and a traveling cap, a sort of jockey's cap. To him I addressed myself. Ah, said he, with immense affability, I need only leave the stuff there, and he would look after it, and see it went off on Monday without fail. I thanked him warmly, left my precious volumes, which he had described as 'stuff,' in his charge, and went home."

His rather thin high voice sounded even hoarser than usual. Claudia noticed it.

"So all was well," she said, smiling. "Will you have some more tea?"

"Yes, I thought so too. Just one more cup, if I may, and that must be the last. I felt quite cheerful; shortly afterwards the sun set, the air was delightfully cool, and I seem to remember whistling as I walked back home."

He stopped for a moment, and turned his hungry eyes away from her face. They had finished supper some while before. What a pity, he thought, as he surveyed the table, now strewn with used plates and dishes, that our needs are fated to leave ugliness behind them. How pretty the little table looked before they started with all its shining white linen and porcelain—and what an uninviting sight it was now. . . . Claudia stood up.

"One moment, my friend, I propose an adjournment; this table disturbs me. Let us take our cups and smoke a cigarette in the next room."

His delight at finding that she felt as she did left him without a word to say; he merely picked up his cup and followed her slowly and cautiously into the red drawing-room. And as they went backwards and forwards once or twice to fetch what they needed, these casual acts seemed to awaken in him the phantom of a hope. They had something in common, perhaps more than they knew—why should he not make plain to her that in those days he had lived the life of the mind, and had been quite blank and indifferent to the world outside? Why should he merely accuse himself, why shouldn't he excuse and explain himself as well? Why shouldn't he confess that for her sake he would act, and act without compunction or delay? No! he must not. When she had seen him as he was, then she could decide. He need not be certain she would reject him; but hope had nearly gone.

Between them was a small table on which stood a lamp with an orange-colored shade; they sat down in two deep arm-chairs, and round them the room and all that it contained seemed vague and far away in the red half-light. A tall clock ticked with admonitory persistence.

"Please—you prefer cigars," said Claudia, already blowing white fragrant cigarette smoke from between her lips.

"I really oughtn't to smoke. . . . Thank you, I have a match. Where was I? . . . If you really want me to go on. As I warned you, it is a tedious story."

If she had had enough and turned the subject, then he could in honor break off the matter and stage the farewell scene for another day. All he wanted now was to enjoy this hour, and watch the lovely creature smoking, her face flecked with golden light behind the veil of smoke.

"Not in the least, go on; though I don't see that there can be any more to tell. The story's over, and you are going cheerfully home."

Yes, the story was indeed over, utterly and absolutely over, and the very word seemed to quiver in his mind.

"Very well then. I was whistling, and suddenly I stopped—it was the *Tannhäuser March,* I remember—and I shuddered at a thought that had come into my mind. I suddenly realized how careless I had been. The man had given me no receipt, no paper to show that he had received a parcel from Doctor Rohme. And he bore no recognizable sign of being a railway official. After all, the fact of being in charge of a few men in railway-caps, or rather of watching them while they worked, was no proof of respectability. The fellow had only to open the parcel to scatter my beautiful books among all the dealers in the town the very next day, and I did not even know his name; all I could say about him was that he had worn a short jacket and a jockey-cap, which was not much. I had already gone some distance, but I stopped and tried to decide to go back—"

"Which would have been a very sensible thing to do," put in Claudia reprovingly.

"Then I remembered that the men in railway-men's caps who had been working in such an such a place at a quarter past six could certainly be traced. They were witnesses, three reliable witnesses. That would be enough. They would, if necessary, have to swear that I had given a large round parcel into the charge of jockey-cap. Comforted at last, I again pursued my way home, for I was tired and hungry." And he smiled faintly as the memories of the past came over him.

"But you would not have got your books back through them either," she said, in a matter-of-fact tone. It was now too late, she noticed, for the talk that she had put off once before; well, to-morrow would do.

"Probably not, or at any rate not easily. But I reckoned on the man in the short jacket thinking of them too. They constituted a moral quantity. But the adjective gave a new turn to my thoughts. Moral? But money was stronger than morality; workmen are poor people; consequently. . . ." He had to stop for a moment. While he was speaking, he became aware that from thenceforward he was condemned to monologue and silence; and he caught his breath. He looked at her; she thought he wanted her to speak, and she innocently drew the inference, while she reflected that his eyes were very kind. "Consequently, he would pay them to say nothing." (And his forehead was finely shaped as well as intelligent.)

"Of course," he cried, with rather exaggerated emphasis, "they could be bribed. Jockey-cap would get a respectable sum for my books, he could afford to sacrifice a few marks and my witnesses would be as silent as the grave, as the phrase goes. The probability of this so impressed me that I stopped, overcame my hunger and weariness, and tramped back again. Shortly after a quarter to seven I reached the place where I had handed over my package. Not a soul to be seen. I wandered through all the warehouses. Not a sign of any one. I shouted, but in vain. At last, at a quarter past seven, full of disgust and misery at my carelessness, twice as tired and hungry as before, I turned to go home. At eight o'clock I reached the town. I thought of consulting my landlord's mother, or the police, but I was ashamed to, and besides I was sick of the whole business."

She found herself wondering faintly why he was telling her all this; it was not very amusing. But she was ashamed of her thought and made up for it by saying with obvious sympathy:

"I quite understand."

He silently flicked the ash from his cigar, and went on, more rapidly as the story hurried to the precipice that must engulf it, and as he spoke, his eyes rested on her hands that were lying quietly on the table.

"That night I slept badly. Next morning I got up at six o'clock, though it was Sunday, and even on week-days I used not to get up before ten, as I was staying in Freiburg for a rest after an illness. Well, I got up at six, and went to the freight station. Naturally I did not find a soul. I repeated this futile journey at ten, half-past eleven, and four, each time with the same result. I had ceased to think; I was simply obsessed with the idea of getting back my own."

Again he was silent and inspected his cigar which was near its end.

She was watching him with a reflective and faintly mocking expression; he was really making a great deal of fuss about all this.

"Well?" she said at last. He started.

"I have nearly finished," he said, and looked down once more from her face to the carpet. "My train went at shortly after nine on Monday. On Monday at half-past six I was standing in the office of the freight station, and of course I saw my parcel as soon as I came in. It lay in its proper place; the man had done what was necessary, and it was ready to send off."

He stopped and did not look up.

"Then all was well," she said indifferently, for she felt he was waiting for a word. He propped his head on his hand and looked down at the table.

"And what do you think I did then?"

"You made your excuses and went to the railway station feeling much relieved in mind," she answered without hesitation.

"Well, I didn't. I took back the parcel, saying it was urgent, and carried it off to the post office."

Claudia seemed to stiffen as she sat, and sank back slowly in her chair.

"You carried it to the post office?" she said in amazement, and nearly burst into mocking laughter, but restrained herself.

"Yes, to a different post office. I didn't like to go to the first one, you see." And he nodded several times without lifting his head from his hand or raising his eyes from the table, smiled sadly, and once more said "Yes."

Claudia's eyes were eloquent of the fear that sank slowly into her soul like a bucket into a well, and mockery and shocked contempt wrote a wry line round her mouth. She was angry, and in her heart flung him a question that she did not utter: Why had he told her such a futile story? She stared at him with hard eyes and saw nothing. The great clock ticked unceasingly; Doctor Rohme sat with bent head looking at the reddish reflection of the lamp on the tablecover. There sat the hero of this exploit, she thought angrily. Why didn't he defend himself? Where was all his cleverness and charm? He, who had so often led her to believe that he could preserve her life from ugliness, and let nothing vex or disquiet her, why was he displaying himself to-day as so feckless and so weak? There he sat, with bent head, like a man condemned, and did not stir. . . .

And then she knew. A sudden flash illuminated everything; she saw him as he was, clear and undisguised. Her joy rose up within her like a bucket from a sunlit fountain, brimming with golden water. She felt a warmth and soft pressure at her heart and knew that it was joy. Slowly she lifted her hand and stretched it towards him across the table, until her delicate finger-tips touched the back of his hands. He started out of his dead despair, looked uncomprehendingly into her happy eyes, caught his breath in a choking gasp as he understood, and kissed her hand with a long burning kiss of deliverance.

"You must go now," she said, and got up: "Thank you for your story, I liked it very much."

Her eyes still shone, and he still held her hand; for he was saved.

"Come to tea to-morrow, and we will talk about Weislingen, and play some music, or do whatever you like."

There was a deep thrill in her voice that he had never heard before, and he pressed the beloved hand.

"I will," he said.

Thomas Mann

AWARDED the Nobel Prize for Literature in 1929, self-exiled from Hitler's Germany, and now awaiting American citizenship, Thomas Mann is regarded by many as the greatest living citizen of the world of letters. With the recent publication of the third volume in his profound interpretation of the Biblical legend of Joseph (the three books are Young Joseph (1934), Joseph and his Brothers (1935), and Joseph in Egypt (1938), he has won such homage as is usually accorded to writers whom posterity has adjudged classic. While the "Joseph" series plunges into the mists of antiquity, much of Thomas Mann's writing—especially The Magic Mountain (1927)—has explored the structure of twentieth century civilization. More than any other author Mann is engaged by the attempt of the civilized spirit to find an answer to the gigantic problems of modern living. Many of his short stories, collected under the title Stories of Three Decades (1936), deal with the spiritual adventures of the creative artist. When he was only twenty-six, he published his first long novel Buddenbrooks, the study of a family group, and largely autobiographical.

Thomas Mann was born in Lübeck, Germany, in 1875, his father being a senator of a patrician merchant family. Before turning to the study and writing of literature, he worked for a while in a Munich insurance office, and then travelled for some months in Italy. Ludwig Lewisohn has described him as "a supremely kind and earnest man, utterly untempted to make either kindness or earnestness or stylistic stringency the 'notes' of his personality." Behind his unobtrusiveness, says Bruno Frank, "is a dark and tremendous consciousness of evil, a terrible knowledge of the abysses of the spirit."

THE HUNGRY *

Thomas Mann

THERE CAME the moment when Detlef was struck by the sense of his own superfluity; as though by chance he let himself be borne away by the bustling throng and disappeared from the sight of his two companions without taking leave.

He gave himself to the current which bore him the whole length of the splendid auditorium; not until he knew that he was far away from Lily and the little painter did he resist the tide and stop in his tracks. He was by then near the stage, leaning against the heavily gilt projecting front of a proscenium box, between a bearded baroque caryatid with neck bent to his burden and his female counterpart whose swelling bosoms were thrust out into the hall. He put on as well as he could the air of a complacent observer, lifting his glasses now and then to his eyes—but in the brilliant circle which they swept he avoided one single point.

The fête was at its height. At the back of these swelling boxes eating and drinking were going on at laden tables, gentlemen in black and coloured dress suits, with mammoth chrysanthemums in their buttonholes, bent over the powdered shoulders of fantastically garbed and extravagantly coiffed ladies, talking and pointing down upon the motley and the bustle in the hall below as it formed eddies and currents, got choked and streamed on again, in quick and colourful play.

There were women in flowing robes, with barge-shaped hats fastened in outlandish curves beneath their chins, leaning on tall staves, holding long-handled lorgnons to their eyes. The puffed sleeves of the men came almost to the brims of their grey top hats. Loud jests mounted to the upper tiers, healths were wafted thitherwards in brimming glasses of champagne and beer. People pushed their way up closer to the stage and stood craning their necks to see the screaming turn then being performed. When the curtains rustled together, everybody pushed away again amid laughter and applause. The orchestra blared. The crowd wreathed and sauntered in and out and to and fro. The golden-yellow light, far brighter than day, gave brilliance to every eye; every breast heaved with quickened breath, idly yet avidly drinking in the intoxication of an atmosphere reeking with odours of food and drink, flowers and scent, dust and overheated human flesh.

* From *Stories of Three Decades* by Thomas Mann. Reprinted by permission of and special arrangement with Alfred A. Knopf, Inc., authorized publishers.

The orchestra stopped. People stood where they were, arm in arm, looking up at the stage, where a new turn was beginning with a din of sound. Four or five actors in peasant costume were parodying with clarinets and stringed instruments the chromatic wrestlings of the *Tristan* music. Detlef closed his eyes a moment, the lids burned. His senses were so keen that even this wanton distortion of the music could not fail to bring home to him poignantly that yearning for unity which it supremely expresses. It evoked in him overwhelmingly the suffocating melancholy of the lonely man who has lost himself in love and longing for some light and common child of life.

Lily. His soul, in imploring tenderness, shaped the name; his gaze, do what he would, turned towards her distant form. Yes, they were still there, they stood on the spot where he had left them and as the crowd thinned he would catch glimpses of her figure, leaning against the wall in her milk-white, silver-trimmed gown; her head slightly on one side, she talked with the little artist and looked into his eyes with lingering, mischievous gaze. And his eyes were just as blue, just as wide apart and unclouded as her own.

Ah, that prattle of theirs, flowing so blithely from an inexhaustible fount of simple, artless, unassuming gaiety—how could he share in it, he, a slow and serious man whose life was compact of knowledge and dreams, of paralysing insight and the inexorable urge to create! So he had left them, stolen away in a spasm of defiance and despair, in which there mingled a queer sort of magnanimity; stolen away and left these two children of life to themselves. But even at this distance came the strangling jealousy in his throat with the knowledge that they had smiled with relief at being freed of his oppressive presence.

Why had he come, why had he come here again? To move, with his tormented soul, among these carefree throngs, knowing himself to be with but not of them? Ah, well he knew! Why then this craving for contact with them? "We lonely ones," so he had written once in a quiet hour of self-communing, "we isolated dreamers, disinherited of life, who spend our introspective days remote in an artificial, icy air and spread abroad a cold breath as from strange regions so soon as we come among living human beings and they see our brows marked with the sign of knowledge and of fear; we poor ghosts of life, who are met with an embarrassed glance and left to ourselves as soon as possible, that our hollow and knowledgeable eye may not blight all joy . . . we all cherish a hidden and unappeased yearning for the harmless, simple, and real in life; for a little friendly, devoted, familiar human happiness.

That 'life' from which we are shut out—we do not envisage it as wild beauty and cruel splendour, it is not as the extraordinary that we crave it, we extraordinary ones. The kingdom of our longing love is the realm of the pleasant, the normal, and the respectable, it is life in all its tempting, banal everydayness that we want. . . ."

He looked over at them again as they stood there talking. The whole hall rang with shouts of laughter and the whining of the clarinets, as the passionate, cloying music was being distorted into shrieking sentimentality. "That is you," he thought. "You are warm, mad, sweet and lovely life, that which stands in eternal opposition to the spirit. Think not that it despises you. Think not it feels one single motion of contempt. Ah, no, we abase ourselves, we denizens of the profound, mute with our monstrous weight of knowledge, we stand afar and in our eyes there burns an avid longing to be like you.

"Do we feel pride stirring? Would we deny that we are lonely? Does our self-respect make us boast that the motions of the spirit bring to love a loftier union with life, at all times and in all places? Ah, but with whom, with what? Always only with our like, with the suffering and the yearning and the poor—never with you, you blue-eyed ones who have no need of spirit!"

Now the curtains had fallen again, dancing began afresh. The band crashed and lilted. Couples turned and glided, wove in and out upon the polished floor. And Lily danced with the little painter. How pricelessly her dainty head rose out of the stiff chalice of her silver-embroidered collar! They moved in a constricted space, with effortless, elastic turnings and pacings. His face was turned towards hers, they continued to talk and smile as they moved in obedience to the sweet and trivial measures from the band.

Suddenly the lonely man felt his spirit reach out to grasp and form as with hands. "After all, you are mine," he thought, "and I am above you. Can I not see through your simple souls with a smile? Do I not observe and perpetuate, half in love and half in mockery, each naive motion that you make? The sight of your artless activities arouses in me the forces of the Word, the power of irony. It makes my heart beat with desire and the lustful knowledge that I can reshape you as I wil' and by my art expose your foolish joys for the world to gape at." B· then all his defiance collapsed again quite suddenly, leaving only ꜀ longing in its wake. Ah, to be not an artist but a man, if only onꞁ only on a night like this! If only once to escape the inexorable which rang in his ears: "You may not live, you must create; yꞁ not love, you must know." Ah, just once to live, to love and to give thanks, to feel and know that feeling is all! Just once to share your life, ye living ones, just once to drink in magic draughts the bliss of the commonplace!

He shuddered and turned away. As he looked at all these charming, overheated faces it seemed to him that they peered into his and then turned away in disgust. He was overpowered by a desire to avoid the field, to seek out stillness and darkness—yes, he would go away, withdraw without a word, as he had withdrawn from Lily's side; go home and lay his burning, throbbing head upon a cool pillow. He strode to the exit.

Would she see him go? He was so used to this sensation, this going away, this silent, proud, despairing withdrawal from a room, a garden, from any place where society was gathered, with the secret hope of causing even one pang in the light heart of her for whom he longed! He paused, looked across at her again; he implored her in his thoughts. Should he stay, stick it out, should he remain near her, though separated by the length of the hall, remain and await some unhoped-for bliss? No, it would all be vain. There would be no approach, no understanding, no hope.—"Go out into the darkness, put your head in your hands and weep, if you can—if in your world of rigid desolation, of ice, of spirit, and of art there are tears left to shed."—He left the hall.

He felt a burning, gnawing pain in his breast and at the same time a wild and senseless expectation. She *must* see him, must understand, must come, must follow him, even if only out of pity; must come half-way and say to him: Stay here, be glad, I love you. He moved very slowly, although well he knew, was certain to the point of absurdity, that she would not come at all, that little laughing, dancing, chattering Lily!

It was two o'clock. The corridors were empty and behind the long tables in the cloak-room the attendants nodded sleepily. No one but himself thought of going home. He wrapped himself in his cloak, took his hat and stick, and left the theatre.

Long rows of carriages stood on the square; lamps illumined the white mist of the winter night. The horses stood blanketed, with hanging heads; groups of well-bundled coachmen stamped the hard snow to warm their feet. Detlef beckoned to one, and as the man uncovered his horse he waited in the vestibule and let the cool dry air play about his throbbing temples.

The flat after-taste of the champagne made him want a smoke.

Mechanically he drew out a cigarette and lighted it. But at the moment when the match went out he saw something strange. He did not at first understand it and stood there puzzled and aghast, with hanging arms. He could not get over it, could not put it out of his mind.

Out of the dark, as his vision recovered from the blindness caused by the flame from the match, there came a red-bearded, hollow-cheeked, lawless face, with horribly inflamed, red-rimmed eyes that stared with sardonic despair and a certain greedy curiosity into his own. The owner of this anguished face stood only two or three paces off, leaning against one of the lamp-posts which flanked the entrance of the theatre, with fists thrust deep into his trouser pockets and the collar of his tattered jacket turned up. His gaze travelled over Detlef's whole figure, from the opera-glass round the neck, down over the fur coat to the patent-leather shoes, then back again to search the other's face with that avid stare. Once the man gave a short, contemptuous snort; then his body relaxed, he shuddered, his flabby cheeks seemed to grow even hollower, while the eyelids quivered and closed and the mouth drooped at the corners with an expression both tragic and malign.

Detlef stood transfixed. He struggled to understand. He had a sudden insight as to how he must look as he stood there; his air of prosperity and well-being as he left the gay gathering, beckoned to the coachman, took the cigarette from his silver box. Involuntarily he lifted his hand in the act to strike his brow. He took a step towards the man, he drew breath to speak, to explain—but what he did was to mount silently into the waiting carriage, almost forgetting, in his distraction, to give the coachman his address. He was confounded by the inadequacy of any explanation he might make.

My God, what an error, what a crass misunderstanding! This starving, outcast man had looked at him with the bitter craving, the violent scorn that spring from envy and longing. Had he not put himself there to be looked at, this hungry man? Had not his shivering body, his tragic and malignant face, been deliberately calculated to make an impression, to give him, Detlef—as an arrogantly happy human being—one moment of misgiving, of sympathy, of distress? But you mistake, my friend—that was not the effect they had. "You thought to show me a horrifying warning out of a strange and frightful world, to arouse my remorse. But we are *brothers.*

"Have you a weight here, my friend, a burning weight on your breast? How well I know it! And why did you come? Why did you not hug your misery in the shadow instead of taking your stand under the lighted windows behind which are music and laughter? Do not I too know the morbid yearning that drove thee hither, to feed this thy wretchedness, which may just as well be called love as hate?

"Nothing is strange to me of all the sorrow that moves thee—and thou thoughtest to shame me! What is mind but the play of hatred? What art, but yearning in act to create? We are both at home in the land of the betrayed, the hungering, the lamenting, the denying; and common to us both are those hours full of betraying self-contempt, when we lose ourselves in a shameful love of life and of mad happiness.

"Wrong, all wrong!"—And as this pity wholly filled him he felt kindled somewhere deep within an intuition at once painful and sweet. "Is it only he who errs? Where is the end of error? Is not all longing on earth an error, this of mine first of all, which craves the simple and the instinctive, dumb life itself, ignorant of the enlightenment which comes through mind and art, the release through the Word? Ah, we are all brothers, we creatures of the restlessly suffering will, yet we do not recognize ourselves as such. Another love is needed, another love."

And when at home he sat among his books and pictures, and the busts ranged along the wall looked down upon him, he felt moved to utter those gentle words:

"Little children, love one another."

Anton Chekhov

ALTHOUGH he always insisted that the artist be objective, and strenuously practiced his own credo, Chekhov's stories (he wrote more than one hundred and fifty) are alight with the strange, poignant illumination of his own temperament. They are stories as inconclusive as life itself; yet somehow complete with the precision of a craftsman who knows exactly what he sets out to do. Their themes often reflect the inescapable loneliness of every human being, and their note is minor, held in the mind long after the reading is over. His writing, it has been said, is alien to the Russia of today, but in the western world generally he is regarded as a great master.

Anton Chekhov was born of peasant parents in southern Russia in 1860. Educated for a medical career at the University of Moscow, he practiced little as a physician, but began about 1879 to write sketches for the magazines. His stories and his great plays gave him commanding position in Russia's literary world, and he was most generous with advice and encouragement to younger, aspiring writers. He died from tuberculosis at the age of forty-four. Among his great short stories are "Grief"; "The Chorus Girl"; "The Darling"; "The Bet"; "The Duel"; and "The Lady with the Dog." His best loved plays are "The Sea Gull" and "The Cherry Orchard."

GRIEF *

TO WHOM SHALL I TELL MY GRIEF? . . .

Anton Chekhov

IT IS TWILIGHT. A thick wet snow is slowly twirling around the newly lighted street-lamps, and lying in soft thin layers on the roofs, the horses' backs, people's shoulders and hats. The cabdriver, Iona Potapov,

* From *The Steppe and Other Stories* by Anton Chekhov. Translated by Adeline Lister Kaye. Reprinted by permission of William Heinemann, Ltd., London.

is quite white, and looks like a phantom; he is bent double as far as a human body can bend double; he is seated on his box, and never makes a move. If a whole snowdrift fell on him, it seems as if he would not find it necessary to shake it off. His little horse is also quite white, and remains motionless; its immobility, its angularity, and its straight wooden-looking legs, even close by give it the appearance of a ginger-bread horse worth a kopeck. It is, no doubt, plunged in deep thought. If you were snatched from the plough, from your usual grey surroundings, and were thrown into this slough full of monstrous lights, unceasing noise and hurrying people, you too would find it difficult not to think.

Iona and his little horse have not moved from their place for a long while. They left their yard before dinner, and, up to now, not a "fare." The evening mist is descending over the town, the white lights of the lamps are replacing brighter rays, and the hubbub of the street is getting louder. "Cabby, for Viborg way!" suddenly hears Iona. "Cabby!"

Iona jumps, and through his snow-covered eye-lashes, sees an officer in a greatcoat, with his hood over his head.

"Viborg way!" the officer repeats. "Are you asleep, eh? Viborg way!"

With a nod of assent Iona picks up the reins, in consequence of which layers of snow slip off the horse's back and neck. The officer seats himself in the sleigh, the cabdriver smacks his lips to encourage the horse, stretches out his neck like a swan, sits up, and, more from habit than from necessity, brandishes his whip. The little horse also stretches his neck, bends his wooden-looking legs, and makes a move undecidedly.

"What are you doing, were-wolf!" is the exclamation Iona hears, from the dark mass moving to and fro as soon as they started.

"Where the devil are you going? To the r-r-right!"

"You do not know how to drive. Keep to the right!" calls the officer angrily.

A coachman from a private carriage swears at him; a passer-by, who has run across the road and rubbed his shoulder against the horse's nose, looks at him furiously as he sweeps the snow from his sleeve. Iona shifts about on his seat as if he were on needles, moves his elbows as if he were trying to keep his equilibrium, and gapes about like someone suffocating, and who does not understand why and wherefore he is there.

"What scoundrels they all are!" jokes the officer; "one would think they had all entered into an agreement to jostle you or fall under your horse."

Iona looks round at the officer, and moves his lips. He evidently wants to say something, but the only sound that issues is a snuffle.

"What?" asks the officer.

Iona twists his mouth into a smile, and with an effort says hoarsely: "My son, barin, died this week."

"Hm! What did he die of?"

Iona turns with his whole body towards his fare, and says:

"And who knows! They say high fever. He was three days in hospital, and then died. . . . God's will be done."

"Turn round! The devil!" sounded from the darkness. "Have you popped off, old doggie, eh? Use your eyes!"

"Go on, go on," said the officer, "otherwise we shall not get there by to-morrow. Hurry up a bit!"

The cabdriver again stretches his neck, sits up, and, with a bad grace, brandishes his whip. Several times again he turns to look at his fare, but the latter has closed his eyes, and apparently is not disposed to listen. Having deposited the officer in the Viborg, he stops by the tavern, doubles himself up on his seat, and again remains motionless, while the snow once more begins to cover him and his horse. An hour, and another. . . . Then, along the footpath, with a squeak of goloshes, and quarrelling, come three young men, two of them tall and lanky, the third one short and hump-backed.

"Cabby, to the Police Bridge!" in a cracked voice calls the hump-back. "The three of us for two griveniks!" (20 kopecks).

Iona picks up his reins, and smacks his lips. Two griveniks is not a fair price, but he does not mind if it is a rouble or five kopecks—to him it is all the same now, so long as they are wayfarers. The young men, jostling each other and using bad language, approach the sleigh, and all three at once try to get on the seat; then begins a discussion which two shall sit and who shall be the one to stand. After wrangling, abusing each other, and much petulance, it was at last decided that the hump-back should stand, as he was the smallest.

"Now then, hurry up!" says the hump-back in a twanging voice, as he takes his place, and breathes in Iona's neck. "Old furry! Here, mate, what a cap you have got, there is not a worse one to be found in all Petersburg! . . ."

"Hi—hi,—hi—hi," giggles Iona. "Such a . . ."

"Now you, 'such a,' hurry up, are you going the whole way at this pace? Are you? . . . Do you want it in the neck?"

"My head feels like bursting," says one of the lanky ones. "Last night at the Donkmasovs, Vaska and I drank the whole of four bottles of cognac."

"I don't understand what you lie for," said the other lanky one angrily; "you lie like a brute."

"God strike me, it's the truth!"

"It's as much a truth as that a louse coughs!"

"Hi, hi," grins Iona, "what gay young gentlemen!"

"Pshaw, go to the devil!" indignantly says the hump-back.

"Are you going to get on or not, you old pest? Is that the way to drive? Use the whip a bit! Go on, devil, go on, give it him well!"

Iona feels at his back the little man wriggling, and the tremble in his voice. He listens to the insults hurled at him, sees the people, and little by little the feeling of loneliness leaves him. The hump-back goes on swearing until he gets mixed up in some elaborate six-foot oath, or chokes with coughing. The lankies begin to talk about a certain Nadejda Petrovna. Iona looks round at them several times; he waits for a temporary silence, then, turning round again, he murmurs:

"My son . . . died this week."

"We must all die," sighed the hump-back, wiping his lips after an attack of coughing. "Now, hurry up, hurry up! Gentlemen, I really cannot go any farther like this! When will he get us there?"

"Well, just you stimulate him a little in the neck!"

"You old pest, do you hear, I'll bone your neck for you! If one treated the like of you with ceremony one would have to go on foot! Do you hear, old serpent Gorinytch![1] Or do you not care a spit?"

Iona hears rather than feels the blows they deal him.

"Hi, hi," he laughs. "They are gay young gentlemen, God bless 'em!"

"Cabby, are you married?" asks a lanky one.

"I? Hi, hi, gay young gentlemen! Now I have only a wife: the moist ground. . . . Hi, ho, ho . . . that is to say, the grave! my son has died, and I am alive. . . . A wonderful thing, death mistook the door . . . instead of coming to me, it went to my son. . . ."

Iona turns around to tell them how his son died, but at this moment the hump-back, giving a little sigh, announces, "Thank God, they have at last reached their destination," and Iona watches them disappear

---

[1] A character in Russian tales.

through the dark entrance. Once more he is alone, and again surrounded by silence. . . . His grief, which had abated for a short while,
returns and rends his heart with greater force. With an anxious and a
hurried look, he searches among the crowds passing on either side of
the street to find if there is just one person who will listen to him.
But the crowds hurry by without noticing him or his trouble. Yet it is
such an immense, illimitable grief. Should his heart break and the
grief pour out, it would flow over the whole earth it seems, and yet,
no one sees it. It has managed to conceal itself in such an insignificant
shell that no one can see it even by day and with a light.

Iona sees a hall-porter with some sacking, and decides to talk to him.

"Friend, what sort of time is it?" he asks.

"Past nine. What are you standing here for? Move on."

Iona moves on a few steps, doubles himself up, and abandons himself to his grief. He sees it is useless to turn to people for help. In less
than five minutes he straightens himself, holds up his head as if he
felt some sharp pain, and gives a tug at the reins: he can bear it no
longer, "The stables," he thinks, and the little horse, as if he understood, starts off at a trot.

About an hour and a half later Iona is seated by a large dirty stove.
Around the stove, on the floor, on the benches, people are snoring; the
air is thick and suffocatingly hot. Iona looks at the sleepers, scratches
himself, and regrets having returned so early.

"I have not even earned my fodder," he thinks. "That's what's my
trouble. A man who knows his job, who has had enough to eat, and
his horse too, can always sleep peacefully."

A young cabdriver in one of the corners half gets up, grunts sleepily,
and stretches towards a bucket of water.

"Do you want a drink?" Iona asks him.

"Don't I want a drink!"

"That's so? Your good health! But listen, mate—you know, my son
is dead. . . . Did you hear? This week, in hospital. . . . It's a long
story."

Iona sees what effect his words have, but sees none—the young man
has hidden his face, and is fast asleep again. The old man sighs, and
scratches his head. Just as much as the young one wanted to drink,
the old man wanted to talk. It will soon be a week since his son died,
and he has not been able to speak about it properly to anyone. One
must tell it slowly and carefully; how his son fell ill, how he suffered,
what he said before he died, how he died. One must describe every

detail of the funeral, and the journey to the hospital to fetch the defunct's clothes. His daughter Anissia remained in the village—one must talk about her too. Was it nothing he had to tell? Surely the listener would gasp and sigh, and sympathize with him? It is better, too, to talk to women; although they are stupid, two words are enough to make them sob.

"I'll go and look at my horse," thinks Iona; "there's always time to sleep. No fear of that!"

He puts on his coat, and goes to the stables to his horse; he thinks of the corn, the hay, the weather. When he is alone, he dare not think of his son; he could speak about him to anyone, but to think of him, and picture him to himself, is unbearably painful.

"Are you tucking in?" Iona asks his horse, looking at his bright eyes; "go on, tuck in, though we've not earned our corn, we can eat hay. Yes! I am too old to drive—my son could have, not I. He was a first-rate cabdriver. If only he had lived!"

Iona is silent for a moment, then continues:

"That's how it is, my old horse. There's no more Kuzma Ionitch. He has left us to live, and he went off pop. Now let's say, you had a foal, you were the foal's mother, and suddenly, let's say, that foal went and left you to live after him. It would be sad, wouldn't it?"

The little horse munches, listens, and breathes over his master's hand. . . .

Iona's feelings are too much for him, and he tells the little horse the whole story.

Ivan S. Turgenev

OF ALL the great Russian writers, Turgenev, exiled in Paris for most of his writing life, had most care for the beauty of form and most sensitivity for the poetical values of his themes. Tolstoy is greater in his tremendous spiritual power, Dostoyevsky looks deeper into the abysses of the soul, but Turgenev was inimitable in his ability to tell a story with simplicity and quiet naturalness. His first successful book of stories A Sportsman's Sketches (1852), from which "The District Doctor" is taken, was a sympathetic study of the serfs whom he liked better than their masters. Later he was to portray his people in a series of novels, the greatest of which, Fathers and Sons (1862), presents an unforgettable portrait in Bazarov, the nihilist. Of himself he wrote "I am, above all, a realist, and chiefly interested in the living truth of the human face. . . . Everything human is dear to me."

Turgenev was born in Orel in 1818. Of distinguished family, he had opportunities for education in Moscow, St. Petersburg, and Berlin. The first Russian to be greatly admired in western Europe, he came to find most appreciation for his work in France rather than in his native country. Maupassant said of him, "No more cultivated, penetrating spirit, no more loyal, generous heart than his ever existed." He died in 1883 at Bougival, near Paris.

THE DISTRICT DOCTOR *

Ivan S. Turgenev

ONE DAY in autumn on my way back from a remote part of the country I caught cold and fell ill. Fortunately the fever attacked me in the district town at the inn; I sent for the doctor. In half-an-hour

* From *Best Russian Short Stories*, compiled and edited by Thomas Seltzer. Reprinted by courtesy of Random House, Inc.

the district doctor appeared, a thin, dark-haired man of middle height. He prescribed me the usual sudorific, ordered a mustard-plaster to be put on, very deftly slid a five-ruble note up his sleeve, coughing drily and looking away as he did so, and then was getting up to go home, but somehow fell into talk and remained. I was exhausted with fever-ishness; I foresaw a sleepless night, and was glad of a little chat with a pleasant companion. Tea was served. My doctor began to converse freely. He was a sensible fellow, and expressed himself with vigour and some humour. Queer things happen in the world; you may live a long while with some people, and be on friendly terms with them, and never once speak openly with them from your soul; with others you have scarcely time to get acquainted, and all at once you are pouring out to him—or he to you—all your secrets as though you were at confession. I don't know how I gained the confidence of my new friend—anyway, with nothing to lead up to it, he told me a rather curious incident; and here I will report his tale for the information of the indulgent reader. I will try to tell it in the doctor's own words.

"You don't happen to know," he began in a weak and quavering voice (the common result of the use of unmixed Berezov snuff); "You don't happen to know the judge here, Mylov, Pavel Lukich? . . . You don't know him? . . . Well, it's all the same." (He cleared his throat and rubbed his eyes.) "Well, you see, the thing happened, to tell you exactly without any mistake, in Lent, at the very time of the thaws. I was sitting at his house—our judge's, you know—playing preference. Our judge is a good fellow, and fond of playing preference. Suddenly" (the doctor made frequent use of this word, suddenly) "they tell me, 'There's a servant asking for you.' I say, 'What does he want?' They say, 'He has brought a note—it must be from a patient.' 'Give me the note,' I say. So it is from a patient—well and good—you understand—it's our bread and butter. . . . But this is how it was: a lady, a widow, writes to me; she says, 'My daughter is dying. Come, for God's sake!' she says, 'and the horses have been sent for you.' . . . Well, that's all right. But she was twenty miles from the town, and it was midnight out of doors, and the roads in such a state, my word! And as she was poor herself, one could not expect more than two silver rubles, and even that problematic; and perhaps it might only be a matter of a roll of linen and a sack of oatmeal in payment. However, duty, you know, before everything: a fellow-creature may be dying. I hand over my cards to Kalliopin, the member of the provincial commission, and return home. I look; a wretched little trap was standing at the steps, with peasant's horses, fat—too fat—and their coat as shaggy as felt; and the coachman sitting with cap off out of respect. Well, I think to myself, 'It's clear, my friend, these patients aren't rolling in riches.' . . . You smile; but I tell you, a poor man like me has to take everything into consideration. . . . If the coachman sits like a prince, and doesn't touch his cap, and even sneers at you behind his beard, and flicks his whip—then you may bet on six rubles. But this case, I saw, had a very different air. However, I think there's no help for it; duty before everything. I snatch up the most necessary drugs, and set off. Will you believe it? I only just managed to get there at all. The road was infernal: streams, snow, watercourses, and the dyke had suddenly burst there—that was the worst of it! However, I arrived at last. It was a little thatched house. There was a light in the windows; that meant they expected me. I was met by an old lady, very venerable, in a cap. 'Save her!' she says; 'she is dying.' I say, 'Pray don't distress yourself—Where is the invalid?' 'Come this way.' I see a clean little room, a lamp in the corner; on the bed a girl of twenty, unconscious. She was in a burning heat, and breathing heavily—it was fever. There were two other girls, her sisters, scared and in tears. 'Yesterday,' they tell me, 'she was perfectly well and had a good appetite; this morning she complained of her head, and this evening, suddenly, you see, like this.' I say again: 'Pray don't be uneasy.' It's a doctor's duty, you know—and I went up to her and bled her, told them to put on a mustard-plaster, and prescribed a mixture. Meantime I looked at her; I looked at her, you know—there, by God! I had never seen such a face!—she was a beauty, in a word! I felt quite shaken with pity. Such lovely features; such eyes! . . . But, thank God! she became easier; she fell into a perspiration, seemed to come to her senses, looked round, smiled, and passed her hand over her face. . . . Her sisters bent over her. They ask, 'How are you?' 'All right,' she says, and turns away. I looked at her; she had fallen asleep. 'Well,' I say, 'now the patient should be left alone.' So we all went out on tiptoe; only a maid remained, in case she was wanted. In the parlour there was a samovar standing on the table, and a bottle of rum; in our profession one can't get on without it. They gave me tea; asked me to stop the night. . . . I consented: where could I go, indeed, at that time of night? The old lady kept groaning. 'What is it?' I say; 'she will live; don't worry yourself; you had better take a little rest yourself; it is about two o'clock.' 'But will you send to wake me if anything happens?' 'Yes, yes.' The old lady went away, and the girls too went to their own room; they made up a bed for me in the parlour. Well, I went to bed—but I could not get to sleep, for a wonder! for in reality I was very tired. I could not get my patient out of my head. At last I could not put up with it any longer; I got up suddenly; I think to myself, 'I will go and see how the patient is getting on.' Her bedroom was next to the parlour. Well, I got up, and gently opened the door—how my heart beat! I looked in: the servant was asleep, her mouth wide open, and even snoring, the wretch! but the patient lay with her face towards me, and her arms flung wide apart, poor girl! I went up to her . . . when suddenly she opened her eyes and stared at me! 'Who is it? who is it?' I was in confusion. 'Don't be alarmed, madam,' I say; 'I am the doctor; I have come to see how you feel.' 'You the doctor?' 'Yes, the doctor; your mother sent for me from the town; we have bled you, madam; now pray go to sleep, and in a day or two, please God! we will set you on your feet again.' 'Ah, yes, yes, doctor, don't let me die . . . please, please.' 'Why do you talk like that? God bless you!' She is in a fever again, I think to myself; I felt her pulse; yes, she was feverish. She looked at me, and then took me by the hand. 'I will tell you why I don't want to die; I will tell you. . . . Now we are alone; and only, please don't you . . . not to anyone. . . . Listen. . . .' I bent down; she moved her lips quite to my ear; she touched my cheek with her hair—I confess my head went round—and began to whisper. . . . I could make nothing out of it. . . . Ah, she was delirious! . . . She whispered and whispered, but so quickly, and as if it were not in Russian; at last she finished, and shivering dropped her head on the pillow, and threatened me with her finger: 'Remember, doctor, to no one.' I calmed her somehow, gave her something to drink, waked the servant, and went away."

At this point the doctor again took snuff with exasperated energy, and for a moment seemed stupefied by its effects.

"However," he continued, "the next day, contrary to my expectations, the patient was no better. I thought and thought, and suddenly decided to remain there, even though my other patients were expecting me. . . . And you know one can't afford to disregard that; one's practice suffers if one does. But, in the first place, the patient was really in danger; and secondly, to tell the truth, I felt strongly drawn to her. Besides, I liked the whole family. Though they were really bad off, they were singularly, I may say, cultivated people. . . . Their father had been a learned man, an author; he died, of course, in poverty, but he had managed before he died to give his children an excellent education; he left a lot of books too. Either because I looked after the invalid very carefully, or for some other reason; anyway, I can venture to say all the household loved me as if I were one of the family. . . . Meantime the roads were in a worse state than ever; all communications, so to say, were cut off completely; even medicine could with difficulty be got from the town. . . . The sick girl was not getting better. . . . Day after day, and day after day . . . but . . . here. . . ." (The doctor made a brief pause.) "I declare I don't know how to tell you." . . . (He again took snuff, coughed, and swallowed a little tea.) "I will tell you without beating about the bush. My patient . . . how should I say? . . . Well she had fallen in love with me . . . or, no, it was not that she was in love . . . however . . . really, how should one say?" (The doctor looked down and grew red.) "No," he went on quickly, "in love, indeed! A man should not over-estimate himself. She was an educated girl, clever and well-read, and I had even forgotten my Latin, one may say, completely. As to appearance" (the doctor looked himself over with a smile) "I am nothing to boast of there either. But God Almighty did not make me a fool; I don't take black for white; I know a thing or two; I could see very clearly, for instance that Aleksandra Andreyevna—that was her name—did not feel love for me, but had a friendly, so to say, inclination—a respect or something for me. Though she herself perhaps mistook this sentiment, anyway this was her attitude; you may form your own judgment of it. But," added the doctor, who had brought out all these disconnected sentences without taking breath, and with obvious embarrassment, "I seem to be wandering rather—you won't understand anything like this. . . . There, with your leave, I will relate it all in order."

He drank off a glass of tea, and began in a calmer voice.

"Well, then. My patient kept getting worse and worse. You are not a doctor, my good sir; you cannot understand what passes in a poor fellow's heart, especially at first, when he begins to suspect that the disease is getting the upper hand of him. What becomes of his belief in himself? You suddenly grow so timid; it's indescribable. You fancy then that you have forgotten everything you knew, and that the patient has no faith in you, and that other people begin to notice how distracted you are, and tell you the symptoms with reluctance; that they are looking at you suspiciously, whispering. . . . Ah! it's horrid! There must be a remedy, you think, for this disease, if one could find it. Isn't this it? You try—no, that's not it! You don't

allow the medicine the necessary time to do good. . . . You clutch at
one thing, then at another. Sometimes you take up a book of medical
prescriptions—here it is, you think! Sometimes, by Jove, you pick
one out by chance, thinking to leave it to fate. . . . But meantime a
fellow-creature's dying, and another doctor would have saved him.
'We must have a consultation,' you say; 'I will not take the responsibility on myself.' And what a fool you look at such times! Well, in
time you learn to bear it; it's nothing to you. A man has died—
but it's not your fault; you treated him by the rules. But what's
still more torture to you is to see blind faith in you, and to feel
yourself that you are not able to be of use. Well, it was just this
blind faith that the whole of Aleksandra Andreyevna's family had
in me; they had forgotten to think that their daughter was in danger.
I, too, on my side assure them that it's nothing, but meantime my
heart sinks into my boots. To add to our troubles, the roads were in
such a state that the coachman was gone for whole days together to
get medicine. And I never left the patient's room; I could not tear
myself away; I tell her amusing stories, you know, and play cards
with her. I watch by her side at night. The old mother thanks me
with tears in her eyes; but I think to myself, 'I don't deserve your
gratitude.' I frankly confess to you—there is no object in concealing
it now—I was in love with my patient. And Aleksandra Andreyevna
had grown fond of me; she would not sometimes let any one be in
her room but me. She began to talk to me, to ask me questions; where
I had studied, how I lived, who are my people, whom I go to see.
I feel that she ought not to talk; but to forbid her to—to forbid
her resolutely, you know,—I could not. Sometimes I held my head
in my hands, and asked myself, "What are you doing, villain?" . . .
And she would take my hand and hold it, give me a long, long look,
and turn away, sigh, and say, 'How good you are!' Her hands were
so feverish, her eyes so large and languid. . . . 'Yes,' she says, 'you
are a good, kind man; you are not like our neighbours. . . . No, you
are not like that. . . . Why did I not know you till now!' 'Aleksandra
Andreyevna, calm yourself,' I say. . . . 'I feel, believe me, I don't
know how I have gained . . . but there, calm yourself. . . . All will
be right; you will be well again.' And meanwhile I must tell you,"
continued the doctor, bending forward and raising his eyebrows, "that
they associated very little with the neighbours, because the smaller
people were not on their level, and pride hindered them from being
friendly with the rich. I tell you, they were an exceptionally cultivated
family; so you know it was gratifying for me. She would only take

her medicine from my hands . . . she would lift herself up, poor girl, with my aid, take it, and gaze at me. . . . My heart felt as if it were bursting. And meanwhile she was growing worse and worse, worse and worse, all the time; she will die, I think to myself; she must die. Believe me, I would sooner have gone to the grave myself; and here were her mother and sisters watching me, looking into my eyes . . . and their faith in me was wearing away. 'Well? how is she?' 'Oh, all right, all right!' All right, indeed! My mind was failing me. Well, I was sitting one night alone again by my patient. The maid was sitting there too, and snoring away in full swing; I can't find fault with the poor girl, though; she was worn out too. Aleksandra Andreyevna had felt very unwell all the evening; she was very feverish. Until midnight she kept tossing about; at last she seemed to fall asleep; at least, she lay still without stirring. The lamp was burning in the corner before the holy image. I sat there, you know, with my head bent; I even dozed a little. Suddenly it seemed as though some one touched me in the side; I turned round. . . . Good God! Aleksandra Andreyevna was gazing with intent eyes at me . . . her lips parted, her cheeks seemed burning. 'What is it?' 'Doctor, shall I die?' 'Merciful Heavens!' 'No, doctor, no; please don't tell me I shall live . . . don't say so . . . if you knew. . . . Listen! for God's sake don't conceal my real position,' and her breath came so fast. 'If I can know for certain that I must die . . . then, I will tell you all—all!' 'Aleksandra Andreyevna, I beg!' 'Listen; I have not been asleep at all. . . . I have been looking at you a long while. . . . For God's sake! . . . I believe in you; you are a good man, an honest man; I entreat you by all that is sacred in the world—tell me the truth! If you knew how important it is for me. . . . Doctor, for God's sake tell me. . . . Am I in danger?' 'What can I tell you, Aleksandra Andreyevna, pray?' 'For God's sake, I beseech you!' 'I can't disguise from you,' I say, 'Aleksandra Andreyevna; you are certainly in danger; but God is merciful.' 'I shall die, I shall die.' And it seemed as though she were pleased; her face grew so bright; I was alarmed. 'Don't be afraid, don't be afraid! I am not frightened of death at all.' She suddenly sat up and leaned on her elbow. 'Now, . . . yes, now I can tell you that I thank you with my whole heart . . . that you are kind and good—that I love you!' I stare at her, like one possessed; it was terrible for me, you know. 'Do you hear, I love you!' 'Aleksandra Andreyevna, how have I deserved—' 'No, no, you don't—you don't understand me.' . . . And suddenly she stretched out her arms, and taking my head in her hands, she kissed it. . . . Believe me, I almost screamed aloud. . . . I threw myself on my knees, and buried my head in the pillow. She did not speak; her fingers trembled in my hair; I listen; she is weeping. I began to soothe her, to assure her. . . . I really don't know what I did say to her. 'You will wake up the girl,' I say to her; 'Aleksandra Andreyevna, I thank you . . . believe me . . . calm yourself.' 'Enough, enough!' she persisted; 'never mind all of them; let them wake, then; let them come in—it does not matter; I am dying, you see. . . . And what do you fear? why are you afraid? Lift up your head. . . . Or, perhaps, you don't love me; perhaps I am wrong. . . . In that case, forgive me.' 'Aleksandra Andreyevna, what are you saying! . . . I love you, Aleksandra Andreyevna.' She looked straight into my eyes, and opened her arms wide. 'Then take me in your arms.' I tell you frankly, I don't know how it was I did not go mad that night. I feel that my patient is killing herself; I see that she is not fully herself; I understand, too, that if she did not consider herself on the point of death, she would never have thought of me; and, indeed, say what you will, it's hard to die at twenty without having known love; this was what was torturing her; this was why, in despair, she caught at me—do you understand now? But she held me in her arms, and would not let me go. 'Have pity on me, Aleksandra Andreyevna, and have pity on yourself,' I say. 'Why,' she says; 'what is there to think of? You know I must die.' . . . This she repeated incessantly. . . . 'If I knew that I should return to life, and be a proper young lady again, I should be ashamed . . . of course, ashamed . . . but why now?' 'But who has said you will die?' 'Oh, no, leave off! you will not deceive me; you don't know how to lie—look at your face.' . . . 'You shall live, Aleksandra Andreyevna; I will cure you; we will ask your mother's blessing . . . we will be united—we will be happy.' 'No, no, I have your word; I must die . . . you have promised me . . . you have told me.' . . . It was cruel for me—cruel for many reasons. And see what trifling things can do sometimes; it seems nothing at all, but it's painful. It occurred to her to ask me, what is my name; not my surname but my first-name. I must needs be so unlucky as to be called Trifon. Yes, indeed; Trifon Ivanich. Every one in the house called me doctor. However, there's no help for it. I say, 'Trifon, madam.' She frowned, shook her head, and muttered something in French—ah, something unpleasant, of course!—and then she laughed —disagreeably too. Well, I spent the whole night with her in this way. Before morning I went away, feeling as though I were mad. When I went again into her room it was daytime, after morning tea.

Good God! I could scarcely recognize her; people are laid in their grave looking better than that. I swear to you, on my honour, I don't understand—I absolutely don't understand—now, how I lived through that experience. Three days and nights my patient still lingered on. And what nights! What things she said to me! And on the last night—only imagine to yourself—I was sitting near her, and kept praying to God for one thing only: 'Take her,' I said, 'quickly, and me with her.' Suddenly the old mother comes unexpectedly into the room. I had already the evening before told her—the mother—there was little hope, and it would be well to send for a priest. When the sick girl saw her mother she said: 'It's very well you have come; look at us, we love one another—we have given each other our word.' 'What does she say, doctor? what does she say?' I turned livid. 'She is wandering,' I say; 'the fever.' But she: 'Hush, hush; you told me something quite different just now, and have taken my ring. Why do you pretend? My mother is good—she will forgive—and I am dying. . . . I have no need to tell lies; give me your hand.' I jumped up and ran out of the room. The old lady, of course, guessed how it was.

"I will not, however, weary you any longer, and to me too, of course, it's painful to recall all this. My patient passed away the next day. God rest her soul!" the doctor added, speaking quickly and with a sigh. "Before her death she asked her family to go out and leave me alone with her."

"'Forgive me,' she said; 'I am perhaps to blame towards you . . . my illness . . . but believe me, I have loved no one more than you . . . do not forget me . . . keep my ring.'"

The doctor turned away; I took his hand.

"Ah!" he said, "let us talk of something else, or would you care to play preference for a small stake? It is not for people like me to give way to exalted emotions. There's only one thing for me to think of; how to keep the children from crying and the wife from scolding. Since then, you know, I have had time to enter into lawful wedlock, as they say. . . . Oh . . . I took a merchant's daughter—seven thousand for her dowry. Her name's Akulina; it goes well with Trifon. She is an ill-tempered woman, I must tell you, but luckily she's asleep all day. . . . Well, shall it be preference?"

We sat down to preference for halfpenny points. Trifon Ivanich won two rubles and a half from me, and went home late, well pleased with his success.

Maxim Gorki

MAXIM GORKI, born Alexey Maximovich Peshkov at Nizhni-Novgorod in 1868, took a pen name which means "the bitter one," but the strength and penetration of his work does not suggest bitterness so much as the exultant, varied energy of a man who found life romantic with possibilities. In him the literature of social protest is undoubtedly sincere—no one can mistake the wrath of his indictment—but it is also temperamental. He knew at first-hand the homeless and the dispossessed; he had belonged to them. Turned out into the world at the age of nine, he tried to earn his bread in many ways which furnished a remarkable background for the genius that was to appear in his first great story Chelkash, published in 1895. Two years later Gorki published his first book of stories, and his success was immediate. Presently his play The Lower Depths was given a long run in Berlin, and Gorki began to earn a thousand rubles for each printed page.

Probably Gorki's most enduring work is to be found, not in his novels and plays which often seem to lack constructive skill, but in his strong and moving short tales and his extremely interesting reminiscences—such books as Twenty-six Men and a Girl (1902); Pogrom and other Stories (1909); My Childhood (1915); In the World (1917); and Reminiscences of my Youth (1924).

Gorki was exiled by the Tsar on Bloody Sunday (January 22, 1905), returned to Russia in 1914, served in the World War, and after the Revolution accepted a government post from Lenin, with whom he sometimes differed. He left Russia in ill-health and returned in 1928 to be hailed as a patriarch of the Revolution. He died in his villa near Moscow in 1936.

ONE AUTUMN NIGHT *

Maxim Gorki

ONCE IN the autumn I happened to be in a very unpleasant and inconvenient position. In the town where I had just arrived and where I knew not a soul, I found myself without a farthing in my pocket and without a night's lodging.

Having sold during the first few days every part of my costume without which it was still possible to go about, I passed from the town into the quarter called "Yste," where were the steamship wharves—a quarter which during the navigation season fermented with boisterous, laborious life, but now was silent and deserted, for we were in the last days of October.

Dragging my feet along the moist sand, and obstinately scrutinising it with the desire to discover in it any sort of fragment of food, I wandered alone among the deserted buildings and warehouses, and thought how good it would be to get a full meal.

In our present state of culture, hunger of the mind is more quickly satisfied than hunger of the body. You wander about the streets, you are surrounded by buildings not bad-looking from the outside and—you may safely say it—not so badly furnished inside, and the sight of them may excite within you stimulating ideas about architecture, hygiene, and many other wise and high-flying subjects. You may meet warmly and neatly dressed folks—all very polite, and turning away from you tactfully, not wishing offensively to notice the lamentable fact of your existence. Well, well, the mind of a hungry man is always better nourished and healthier than the mind of the well-fed man; and there you have a situation from which you may draw a very ingenious conclusion in favor of the ill fed.

The evening was approaching, the rain was falling, and the wind blew violently from the north. It whistled in the empty booths and shops, blew into the plastered windowpanes of the taverns, and whipped into foam the wavelets of the river which splashed noisily on the sandy shore, casting high their white crests, racing one after another into the dim distance, and leaping impetuously over one another's shoulders. It seemed as if the river felt the proximity of winter, and was running at random away from the fetters of ice which the north

* From *Best Russian Short Stories,* compiled and edited by Thomas Seltzer. Reprinted by courtesy of Random House, Inc.

wind might well have flung upon her that very night. The sky was heavy and dark; down from it swept incessantly scarcely visible drops of rain, and the melancholy elegy in nature all around me was emphasized by a couple of battered and misshapen willow-trees and a boat, bottom upwards, that was fastened to their roots.

The overturned canoe with its battered keel and the miserable old trees rifled by the cold wind—everything around me was bankrupt, barren, and dead, and the sky flowed with undryable tears. . . . Everything around was waste and gloomy . . . it seemed as if everything were dead, leaving me alone among the living, and for me also a cold death waited.

I was then eighteen years old—a good time!

I walked and walked along the cold wet sand, making my chattering teeth warble in honour of cold and hunger, when suddenly, as I was carefully searching for something to eat behind one of the empty crates, I perceived behind it, crouching on the ground, a figure in woman's clothes dank with the rain and clinging fast to her stooping shoulders. Standing over her, I watched to see what she was doing. It appeared that she was digging a trench in the sand with her hands—digging away under one of the crates.

"Why are you doing that?" I asked, crouching down on my heels quite close to her.

She gave a little scream and was quickly on her legs again. Now that she stood there staring at me, with her wide-open grey eyes full of terror, I perceived that it was a girl of my own age, with a very pleasant face embellished unfortunately by three large blue marks. This spoilt her, although these blue marks had been distributed with a remarkable sense of proportion, one at a time, and all were of equal size—two under the eyes, and one a little bigger on the forehead just over the bridge of the nose. This symmetry was evidently the work of an artist well inured to the business of spoiling the human physiognomy.

The girl looked at me, and the terror in her eyes gradually died out. . . . She shook the sand from her hands, adjusted her cotton head-gear, cowered down, and said:

"I suppose you too want something to eat? Dig away then! My hands are tired. Over there"—she nodded her head in the direction of a booth—"there is bread for certain . . . and sausages too. . . . That booth is still carrying on business."

I began to dig. She, after waiting a little and looking at me, sat down beside me and began to help me.

We worked in silence. I cannot say now whether I thought at that moment of the criminal code, of morality, of proprietorship, and all the other things about which, in the opinion of many experienced persons, one ought to think every moment of one's life. Wishing to keep as close to the truth as posible, I must confess that apparently I was so deeply engaged in digging under the crate that I completely forgot about everything else except this one thing: What could be inside that crate?

The evening drew on. The grey, mouldy, cold fog grew thicker and thicker around us. The waves roared with a hollower sound than before, and the rain pattered down on the boards of that crate more loudly and more frequently. Somewhere or other the night-watchman began springing his rattle.

"Has it got a bottom or not?" softly inquired my assistant. I did not understand what she was talking about, and I kept silence.

"I say, has the crate got a bottom? If it has we shall try in vain to break into it. Here we are digging a trench, and we may, after all, come upon nothing but solid boards. How shall we take them off? Better smash the lock; it is a wretched lock."

Good ideas rarely visit the heads of women, but, as you see, they do visit them sometimes. I have always valued good ideas, and have always tried to utilize them as far as possible.

Having found the lock, I tugged at it and wrenched off the whole thing. My accomplice immediately stooped down and wriggled like a serpent into the gaping-open, four cornered cover of the crate whence she called to me approvingly, in a low tone:

"You're a brick!"

Nowadays a little crumb of praise from a woman is dearer to me than a whole dithyramb from a man, even though he be more eloquent than all the ancient and modern orators put together. Then, however, I was less amiably disposed than I am now, and, paying no attention to the compliment of my comrade, I asked her curtly and anxiously:

"Is there anything?"

In a monotonous tone she set about calculating our discoveries.

"A basketful of bottles—thick furs—a sunshade—an iron pail."

All this was uneatable. I felt that my hopes had vanished. . . .

But suddenly she exclaimed vivaciously:

"Aha! here it is!"

"What?"

"Bread . . . a loaf . . . it's only wet . . . take it!"

A loaf flew to my feet and after it herself, my valiant comrade. I had already bitten off a morsel, stuffed it in my mouth, and was chewing it. . . .

"Come, give me some too! . . . And we mustn't stay here. . . . Where shall we go?" she looked inquiringly about on all sides. . . . It was dark, wet, and boisterous.

"Look! there's an upset canoe yonder . . . let us go there."

"Let us go then!" And off we set, demolishing our booty as we went, and filling our mouths with large portions of it. . . . The rain grew more violent, the river roared; from somewhere or other resounded a prolonged mocking whistle—just as if Someone great who feared nobody was whistling down all earthly institutions and along with them this horrid autumnal wind and us its heroes. This whistling made my heart throb painfully, in spite of which I greedily went on eating, and in this respect the girl, walking on my left hand, kept even pace with me.

"What do they call you?" I asked her—why I know not.

"Natasha," she answered shortly, munching loudly.

I stared at her. My heart ached within me; and then I stared into the mist before me, and it seemed to me as if the inimical countenance of my Destiny was smiling at me enigmatically and coldly.

The rain scourged the timbers of the skiff incessantly, and its soft patter induced melancholy thoughts, and the wind whistled as it flew down into the boat's battered bottom through a rift, where some loose splinters of wood were rattling together—a disquieting and depressing sound. The waves of the river were splashing on the shore, and sounded so monotonous and hopeless, just as if they were telling something unbearably dull and heavy, which was boring them into utter disgust, something from which they wanted to run away and yet were obliged to talk about all the same. The sound of the rain blended with their splashing, and a long-drawn sigh seemed to be floating above the overturned skiff—the endless, labouring sigh of the earth, injured and exhausted by the eternal changes from the bright and warm summer to the cold misty and damp autumn. The wind blew continually over the desolate shore and the foaming river—blew and sang its melancholy songs. . . .

Our position beneath the shelter of the skiff was utterly devoid of comfort; it was narrow and damp, tiny cold drops of rain dribbled through the damaged bottom; gusts of wind penetrated it. We sat in silence and shivered with cold. I remembered that I wanted to go to sleep. Natasha leaned her back against the hull of the boat and curled herself up into a tiny ball. Embracing her knees with her hands, and resting her chin upon them, she stared doggedly at the river with wide-open eyes; on the pale patch of her face they seemed immense, because of the blue marks below them. She never moved, and this immobility and silence—I felt it—gradually produced within me a terror of my neighbour. I wanted to talk to her, but I knew not how to begin.

It was she herself who spoke.

"What a cursed thing life is!" she exclaimed plainly, abstractedly, and in a tone of deep conviction.

But this was no complaint. In these words there was too much of indifference for a complaint. This simple soul thought according to her understanding—thought and proceeded to form a certain conclusion which she expressed aloud, and which I could not confute for fear of contradicting myself. Therefore I was silent, and she, as if she had not noticed me, continued to sit there immovable.

"Even if we croaked . . . what then. . . ?" Natasha began again, this time quietly and reflectively, and still there was not one note of complaint in her words. It was plain that this person, in the course of her reflections on life, was regarding her own case, and had arrived at the conviction that in order to preserve herself from the mockeries of life, she was not in a position to do anything else but simply "croak"—to use her own expression.

The clearness of this line of thought was inexpressibly sad and painful to me, and I felt that if I kept silence any longer I was really bound to weep. . . . And it would have been shameful to have done this before a woman, especially as she was not weeping herself. I resolved to speak to her.

"Who was it that knocked you about?" I asked. For a moment I could not think of anything more sensible or more delicate.

"Pashka did it all," she answered in a dull and level tone.

"And who is he?"

"My lover. . . . He was a baker."

"Did he beat you often?"

"Whenever he was drunk he beat me. . . . Often!"

And suddenly, turning towards me, she began to talk about herself,

Pashka, and their mutual relations. He was a baker with red moustaches and played very well on the banjo. He came to see her and greatly pleased her, for he was a merry chap and wore nice clean clothes. He had a vest which cost fifteen rubles and boots with dress tops. For these reasons she had fallen in love with him, and he became her "creditor." And when he became her creditor he made it his business to take away from her the money which her other friends gave to her for bonbons, and, getting drunk on this money, he would fall to beating her; but that would have been nothing if he hadn't also begun to "run after" other girls before her very eyes.

"Now, wasn't that an insult? I am not worse than the others. Of course that meant that he was laughing at me, the blackguard. The day before yesterday I asked leave of my mistress to go out for a bit, went to him, and there I found Dimka sitting beside him drunk. And he, too, was half seas over. I said, 'You scoundrel, you!' And he gave me a thorough hiding. He kicked me and dragged me by the hair. But that was nothing to what came after. He spoiled everything I had on—left me just as I am now! How could I appear before my mistress? He spoiled everything . . . my dress and my jacket too— it was quite a new one; I gave a fiver for it . . . and tore my kerchief from my head. . . . Oh, Lord! What will become of me now?" she suddenly whined in a lamentable overstrained voice.

The wind howled, and became ever colder and more boisterous. . . . Again my teeth began to dance up and down, and she, huddled up to avoid the cold, pressed as closely to me as she could, so that I could see the gleam of her eyes through the darkness.

"What wretches all you men are! I'd burn you all in an oven; I'd cut you in pieces. If any one of you was dying I'd spit in his mouth, and not pity him a bit. Mean skunks! You wheedle and wheedle, you wag your tails like cringing dogs, and we fools give ourselves up to you, and it's all up with us! Immediately you trample us underfoot. . . . Miserable loafers!"

She cursed us up and down, but there was no vigour, no malice, no hatred of these "miserable loafers" in her cursing that I could hear. The tone of her language by no means corresponded with its subject-matter, for it was calm enough, and the gamut of her voice was terribly poor.

Yet all this made a stronger impression on me than the most eloquent and convincing pessimistic books and speeches, of which I had read a good many and which I still read to this day. And this, you see, was because the agony of a dying person is much more natural and violent than the most minute and picturesque descriptions of death.

I felt really wretched—more from cold than from the words of my neighbour. I groaned softly and ground my teeth.

Almost at the same moment I felt two little arms about me—one of them touched my neck and the other lay upon my face—and at the same time an anxious, gentle, friendly voice uttered the question:

"What ails you?"

I was ready to believe that some one else was asking me this and not Natasha, who had just declared that all men were scoundrels, and expressed a wish for their destruction. But she it was, and now she began speaking quickly, hurriedly.

"What ails you, eh? Are you cold? Are you frozen? Ah, what a one you are, sitting there so silent like a little owl! Why, you should have told me long ago that you were cold. Come . . . lie on the ground . . . stretch yourself out and I will lie . . . there! How's that? Now put your arms round me? . . . tighter! How's that? You shall be warm very soon now. . . . And then we'll lie back to back. . . . The night will pass so quickly, see if it won't. I say . . . have you too been drinking? . . . Turned out of your place, eh? . . . It doesn't matter."

And she comforted me. . . . She encouraged me.

May I be thrice accursed! What a world of irony was in this single fact for me! Just imagine! Here was I, seriously occupied at this very time with the destiny of humanity, thinking of the re-organisation of the social system, of political revolutions, reading all sorts of devilishly-wise books whose abysmal profundity was certainly unfathomable by their very authors—at this very time, I say, I was trying with all my might to make of myself "a potent active social force." It even seemed to me that I had partially accomplished my object; anyhow, at this time, in my ideas about myself, I had got so far as to recognise that I had an exclusive right to exist, that I had the necessary greatness to deserve to live my life, and that I was fully competent to play a great historical part therein. And a woman was now warming me with her body, a wretched, battered, hunted creature, who had no place and no value in life, and whom I had never thought of helping till she helped me herself, and whom I really would not have known how to help in any way even if the thought of it had occurred to me.

Ah! I was ready to think that all this was happening to me in a dream—in a disagreeable, an oppressive dream.

But, ugh! it was impossible for me to think that, for cold drops of rain were dripping down upon me, the woman was pressing close to me, her warm breath was fanning my face, and—despite a slight odor of vodka—it did me good. The wind howled and raged, the rain smote upon the skiff, the waves splashed, and both of us, embracing each other convulsively, nevertheless shivered with cold. All this was only too real, and I am certain that nobody ever dreamed such an oppressive and horrid dream as that reality.

But Natasha was talking all the time of something or other, talking kindly and sympathetically, as only women can talk. Beneath the influence of her voice and kindly words a little fire began to burn up within me, and something inside my heart thawed in consequence.

Then tears poured from my eyes like a hailstorm, washing away from my heart much that was evil, much that was stupid, much sorrow and dirt which had fastened upon it before that night. Natasha comforted me.

"Come, come, that will do, little one! Don't take on! That'll do! God will give you another chance . . . you will right yourself and stand in your proper place again . . . and it will be all right. . . ."

And she kept kissing me . . . many kisses did she give me . . . burning kisses . . . and all for nothing. . . .

Those were the first kisses from a woman that had ever been bestowed upon me, and they were the best kisses too, for all the subsequent kisses cost me frightfully dear, and really gave me nothing at all in exchange.

"Come, don't take on so, funny one! I'll manage for you to-morrow if you cannot find a place." Her quiet persuasive whispering sounded in my ears as if it came through a dream. . . .

There we lay till dawn. . . .

And when the dawn came, we crept from behind the skiff and went into the town. . . . Then we took friendly leave of each other and never met again, although for half a year I searched in every hole and corner for that kind Natasha, with whom I spent the autumn night just described.

If she be already dead—and well for her if it were so—may she rest in peace! And if she be alive . . . still I say "Peace to her soul!" And may the consciousness of her fall never enter her soul . . . for that would be a superfluous and fruitless suffering if life is to be lived. . . .

S. Sergeev-Tzensky

As John Cournos, the translator of "The Man You Couldn't Kill,"
has noted, very little is known of S. Sergeev-Tzensky's personal history, even in Russia. Although he was born in 1876, and, like such
contemporaries as Gorki, Andreyev, and Artzybashev, achieved literary
reputation before the World War, he has entered upon a new period
of vigorous creative energy since the Revolution.

He began his literary career in 1904 with exuberant stories which
were distinguished for their vivid use of peasant dialect. In most of
his work he is concerned with the fundamentals of existence—life,
love, and death—and in his more recent writing a characteristic
elaboration of style has been abandoned for directness and simplicity
of expression. His novel Transfiguration, the first part of which has
been translated into English, has been highly praised by Gorki.
Among his other works are The Forest Quagmire (1907), The Sadness
of the Fields (1909), and The Professor's Narrative (1924).

THE MAN YOU COULDN'T KILL *
S. Sergeev-Tzensky

ONE MAN beats another with none too great assurance. He may
even entertain a fear that the other, whom he is beating, should
suddenly play a trick on him.

He beats his victim with the bigger half of his being, while the
smaller observes and weighs the act.

The smaller whispers: "Enough!" The bigger goes on beating. The
smaller says unmistakably: "It's folly! Stop it!" The bigger goes on
beating, but more weakly, with some restraint. The smaller, at last,

* From _Short Stories out of Soviet Russia_, translated by John Cournos, published and
copyrighted by E. P. Dutton & Co., Inc., New York.

commands: "Stop it, I tell you!"—and in an instant takes the place of the bigger. The man who did the beating walks away, outwardly righteous and indignant, but is inwardly sometimes even ashamed.

Not so the crowd. Delicate feelings are unknown to it. When a crowd shouts, it does not shout but judges; does not discuss but pronounces; does not beat but punishes, and anyone whom the crowd has beaten knows he will not rise again.

And Feodor—Feodor Titkov, from the Cossacks' village, Ouriupin-skaya—knew this. He was of low stature and inconspicuous, but compact of body and with bright red face, still young and slenderish, his small eyes not set into eyes' hollows but resting, as it were, on the immediate surface of his angular cheeks.

But he saw, as did another comrade, Manolati, a Bessarabian gypsy, whose dark face was marked with white scars; and a third, a cobbler from Akhtirka, named Karavanchenko, otherwise comrade Semyon, a lugubrious fellow with caved-in chest, loud voice and eyes which shone.

When they were seized in the village and their arms bound, they were asked curtly:

"Bolsheviks?"

They replied with equal curtness:

"Bolsheviks."

And Manolati, only stretching out his neck, added vehemently: "Never mind! Just wait and see. We'll be on top yet!"

Then they were led to a well with a very high crane on it, and no one shouted nor mocked at them; only a thick dust rose from heavy boots, and someone sneezed, or coughed, or spat. Now Cossack women appeared on either side, standing by their homes, and scampering small boys.

Just before he had been caught here at work, Titkov had been eating a herring, and hadn't had time to quench his thirst; then, with his comrades, he was locked for the night in a barn.

The day had been very hot and he craved water. As he approached the well, he felt with his whole compact, swollen body that he was being led precisely where he needed to be led, and his eyes sought the pail.

The pail was large enough to be a tub, and stood, as it happened, with its wet-gleaming chain, on the well shelf and he could not take his eyes from it.

They were near it now: it was full to the brim. Someone had just given his horse a drink and had refilled the pail, but the horse wouldn't drink any more.

Around the well the sand was damp: there was a smell of cattle. A gad-fly settled on Titkov's cheek; he got rid of it by wiping his face against his left shoulder, never once removing his gaze from the pail. When they had come to a halt, he said, without pleading, but simply yet audibly:

"Comrades, let us have a drink!"

To this the Cossack nearest to him, a red-bearded fellow with blue veins on his nose and wet locks showing under his cap, responded no less simply:

"Drink to your content!"—and vigorously struck him across the cheek from which the gad-fly had just been brushed off.

And at the same moment he saw that they had knocked down comrade Semyon, whose feet, in the upset, kicked his own; and it seemed to him that Manolati's dark head flew upward, above the other heads, as if it actually flew; and just as he observed this something struck him on the back of his head and brought him to his knees, and he murmured distinctly:

"So this is the end of us!"

And he drew in his head into his shoulders, like a turtle, and stretched out his legs. He lay flat, upon his face; he felt the wet sand upon his lips, and it smelt strongly of the water of horses.

He tried to work his hands round under him, but they were bound tight and the rope resisted his most desperate efforts.

They kept beating him, except for brief interjections, in silence: and did it in earnest, as if they were killing a pig.

At first Titkov was able to tell where it hurt him most: afterwards, it pained equally, no matter where they struck. He merely gritted his teeth and swallowed spittle.

The shrill outcries of Semyon could no longer be heard. Titkov thought: "They've killed him!" and drew his head in further. But Manolati still managed to make himself heard. Again and again he cried:

"Ours! They'll be on top yet! They will! . . . They will! . . . On top! . . ."

Titkov had time to think about him: "He's a tough one. . . . He'll have to get it a hundred times! . . ."

Then, suddenly, he was hit on his right arm, so hard, the pain went to his head, and was hit again on the head, so he ceased to hear Manolati and everything else.

The cold woke him.

He was wet from head to foot.

He could not at once recall what had happened to him: then remembered the well, and the Cossacks, and how they had beaten him. He thought: "They have thrown me into the well!" But quickly corrected himself: "Why soil the well? It would have to be cleaned out afterwards. . . ."

And, opening the eye which was higher above the ground than the other, he saw the wet tawny point of a boot almost at his very nose, and understood someone's quite good-natured words:

"Eheh! . . . This devil's still alive!"

Then he heard another voice:

"The gypsy, too, is stirring!"

He scarcely had time to think that men had come to their rescue when the boot, with a hard crack, struck him just under his eyes.

Again he lowered his face and drew in his head.

"On top!" came the stertorous sound somewhere near Manolati.

Then they began to hammer with their boots, and someone heavy sprang on his back and jumped up and down.

Titkov tightened his stomach, but the iron-shod heels with their sharp points tore the skin from his arms. . . . At last, the other arm, as yet unhurt, cracked above the wrist under the onslaught.

Titkov was in the act of moistening his lips with his tongue when he ceased to feel.

Once more they poured ice-cold well water on his body. Again he opened one eye—the other was filled and would not open—and again he saw the huge wet point of the boot.

They turned him over. Someone's beard, as it were a paternal one, bent over him, and he murmured into it:

"A drink! . . ."

Then, simultaneously, a deafening concord of voices:—

"Alive! . . . The devil himself! . . . The gypsy, and the other, have pegged out, but this one's still alive! . . ."

He lay thus for a few moments and saw above him fragments of beards, and red noses, and, as if the men were not at all the ones who had been trying to beat him to death, he again whispered:

"A drink . . . brothers!"

Then, above his eye, a fist flashed out and broke his teeth.

Someone asked, with astonishment and not a little distress:

"Where did he get it all? The strength of an anathema! Whew!"

And no matter how Titkov braced his stomach, he felt the full force of the iron-shod boot.

Five minutes later the three bodies near the well were motionless.

The Cossacks washed, coughed intermittently, and blew their noses, as they did in the morning after sleep; one even wetted his hair and drew a small metal comb through it.

Cossack women with infants in their arms approached to have a look. The sun was inclining toward mid-day when a cart drove up. The three bodies were dumped into it and were borne four versts from the village—towards a ravine.

Two young Cossacks walked beside the cart. Their shouldered rifles gleamed in the sun.

They never left the village without their rifles, even a small matter of four versts. It was a turbulent time—the 'eighteenth year.

And it so happened that when Titkov, lying uppermost of the others, opened his eye, he was blinded instantly by the gleam of the rifles at the backs of the Cossacks walking side by side.

Cossacks and rifles—he remembered them afterward—he had seen them before, but the gleam seemed extraordinary, had something unearthly about it. . . .

And the pain, all at once, went through his whole frame: his throat, and every organ in his body burned unbearably.

He had come to himself just as the horses were approaching the ravine, and once more tried to recover his memory, to find out what was the matter with him, where he was, and why he felt pain everywhere, when he heard one Cossack say to the other:

"Here's a nice slope. . . . They'll fly like jackdaws. . . ."

And the second voice said:

"Here, of course! The very place. . . ."

Titkov could make neither head nor tail of this. And when, all wet, he was being dragged from the cart by four hands, amidst curses, he groaned with his whole broken body, and looked with his single eye, so that the four superstitious hands perceptibly relaxed, and as he struck the earth he groaned even louder.

Then the horses snorted and moved their heads about, and the pair with the rifles sprang back twenty paces. . . .

He listened, and heard one of the Cossacks, after prolonged cursing, add:

"And you, unholy power, when will you give up your accursed
breath?"

And when Titkov looked again, he saw how the other snatched his
rifle off his back, aimed and fired. . . .

Titkov trembled as he lay. It was as if someone had driven a hugh
nail into his breast. . . . And here, a jot higher, another nail was
driven in: a bullet fired by the second Cossack.

His mouth opened to let the blood out; twice he jerked his head,
then grew quiet.

The Cossacks dragged the stiffened body of Semyon, with its broken
head, toward the chasm, and, swinging it first by the feet and shoulders, flung it down in silence. The corpse of the gypsy Manolati, with
its head to one side, they threw after it, with the remark:

"Well, that's where your 'On top' will be!"

As for Titkov's body, when they had dragged it to the edge of
the ravine, they paused:

"Suppose, suddenly, this devil . . ." began one.

"D'you think he's alive?" said the other.

They even pulled up his wet shirt to see where the bullets were.
But when they saw the whole body blue with bruises, and that the
bullets had pierced the right breast, they merely shook the tufts of
hair at the edge of their caps and pushed him down genially and
watched the body turning somersaults, now catching vegetation by
the feet, now by the head, until, at last, it lay at the bottom of the
slope beside the first bodies.

Evening was coming on. The sun was no longer shining in the
valley. There were shadows and coolness.

Three women from a neighbouring farm descended into the ravine
for wood. At the bottom, and here and there on the slopes, there
were bushes hacked down each year, and not the less persistent in
growing again. And the women brought with them knives and rope.

When they stumbled on the corpses, they fled in fright. They looked
behind and paused. Each pushed the other forward until again they
confronted the bodies.

They gazed, shook their heads, and held the ends of their head-
kerchiefs against their eyes.

"They must stink by this time?" asked one, doubtfully.

"They look fresh, I think," said the second, feeling her nose.

"An' yesterday I was rummaging here, my dears—them wasn't here then!" said the third, clasping her hands. "What kind o' scoundrels did it to them?"

Corpses should lie quiet. It is terrifying when a corpse tries to lift its head. It is enough to frighten anyone.

And when, slightly opening an eye, Titkov's head weakly turned, the women groaned and screamed all together, and the place was full of gleaming white ankles and running feet.

Scarcely a quarter of an hour had passed when, one encouraging the other, the women returned for the third time, and heard the whisper:

"Little women, a drink, please. . . ."

A tiny spring had broken a way through the ravine two hundred paces below. The women knew this, but they had neither jugs nor cups, only knives and rope.

They suddenly noticed a blood-stained cap on the slope. It had fallen off Semyon Karavanchenko when his body had been flung down. They washed it as best they could and brought water to Titkov, and, bending over him, with the cap full of water in their hands, they thirstily watched as he thirstily drank it.

He drank the whole contents of the cap and, breathing with difficulty, glanced from woman to woman.

"My poor man, what kind of villains beat you like this?" one of the women asked, but in a whisper, which came as it were from his vitals, he responded:

"My dears . . . mayn't I have a little more water?"

It had grown dark when the women, at last, lifted him and bore him from the ravine.

Several times they paused wearily, while he again lost consciousness, and they said one to the other, reproachfully:

"What was the good of disturbing the poor soul? . . . Better had he died there, in the night. He'll only suffer now. . . ."

Nevertheless, they dragged him out, unbound his hands, and took him to the hospital in town, some twelve versts away.

And all, during the journey, went on reproaching one another. They said it would have been better if they had let him alone, if they had not brought him water, if they had left him to die back there in the ravine. They said they would never get him to the hospital alive, and that it was all for nothing. They'd only lose their sleep, and tire out their horse.

If they comforted themselves at all, it was that there were but few moujiks left on the farm, and their households were without any, and they could do as they pleased: it pleased them to be taking this man to the hospital, that was all there was to it . . . they'd take him there. . . . Let him die in the hospital if he must: there was something good in that, he'd at least have a proper burial.

To the questions asked them in the hospital: "Who is he?" and "Who beat him up?" the women answered:

"An' how should we know? . . . We found him like that . . . in the ravine. . . ."

"What's the good of bringing him here?" they said. "It's all the same, he'll die in the end!"

"If he dies, we'll fetch a wreath to put on his grave," said the women. "We've got to hurry home now, and be there by morning. There are cows to feed. . . ."

The women returned home in time, just as the first light showed in the sky. That morning the physicians in the hospital sought and marked off Titkov's broken ribs with the same dispassionateness with which the ribs had been broken in the village, by the well.

2

A month had passed.

It was a holiday—there was little to do.

The three women from the farm journeyed to town, bringing with them a wreath of simple country flowers to put on the grave of the man whose thirst they had quenched and whom they had rescued from the ravine.

Much had happened during the month, and everyone knew all about the corpses and how they came to be in the ravine.

It was a summer day, and the women, having started at luncheon time, thought to return in the evening. They had no business of any kind in town. Their one thought was to pay a visit to the grave, place the wreath there, and return home.

They harnessed a pair of horses, both well-fed beasts.

And while the hoofs and the wheels sounded their measured pace along the little frequented road, the women recalled how but a month before they had covered the same ground with the man in their cart.

"Did anyone ever carry in a cart such a cripple?" said the eldest, who

was about forty years of age and was called Lukerya and had faded
eyes. "That shaking-up was enough to be the end of him!"

"Yes, pulling at the reins, it was all I could do to keep my eyes off
him, lying there so pitiful-like. . . ." said Aksinya, who was somewhat
younger and had dark arched eyebrows.

"An' he lying there with his head on my knees all the time, and
me never moving for fear of disturbing him, though my legs did
ache. . . ." said Likonida, the youngest of all, grief in her grey eyes. "If
we just knew his name!"

Thus rode the women with the wreath, and on their sides there
stretched first the Cossack fields, then the peasant fields. The boundary
of the district lay not far from the farm; they were across the frontier
of another province.

Hordes of men had not long since passed over these fields and in
places had trod the wheat down. The women observed these traces of
indifferently treading feet.

The sun, however, shone friendly, and the earth, like a warm body,
exhaled odours comprehensible to the women—was not the earth like a
woman's body?

A hawk circled overhead, a mere dot in the blue. A cuckoo sounded
its note in the ravine. Flies settled on the horses, who vigorously
switched their tails but could effect nothing and had to depend on the
reins to drive the flies off.

There had been a fire on one of the farms. The women knew of
this, they had seen the flames a week before; and now, fastening their
eyes on the spot where some charred cottages and barns were standing:

"Cattle must have been lost, too!" said Aksinya, holding the reins.

"How long do you think it will keep up?" said Lukerya, arranging
the straw under her.

Likonida, who was holding the wreath, tore off a leaf that seemed to
her superfluous, held it between her lips; then, throwing it on the road,
said sadly:

"Fool-ish, fool-ish women. . . . What's the good of going? Why
go?"

But the belfries of the town were already appearing from behind the
dark green of the gardens, and the other two said:

"It's all the same now—it won't take long."

As it happened, in approaching the hospital they had to pass the
graveyard, which lay to the right of the road. And the women said one
to the other:

"If we just knew his name! You'd get down and ask the watchman. He's obliged to know the names of the dead."

They stopped the horses, but found no one they could ask.

They drove on, and at two o'clock reached the hospital.

They left the horses at the gate after giving them hay. For fear someone passing by would steal the wreath, grey-eyed Likonida took it with her. And thus the trio, carrying it, marched across the hospital court-yard, to ask where they should find the grave of him they had brought a month before, and what his name was.

Simple people remember their illnesses and the illnesses of those near them during holidays—never on workdays. And now amid the bustle in the hospital courtyard, with grass between the cobbles, the three women with the wreath wandered, not knowing of whom to ask what they wanted to know.

They ran into a stocky figure in an apron, and asked him, but he only grunted angrily:

"Can't you see? I am the cook."

They met another, this time a bareheaded man, also in an apron, carrying an ill-smelling pail. He listened to them, then said that he hadn't been long here, and went off at a trot.

They turned to a woman, all in white with a red cross, and she answered by asking:

"And what's his name?"

"An' how should we know, my dear?" said the women, in astonish-ment.

"If you don't know, what's the good of looking?"

And she hurried away from them on her high heels.

Then they stopped an old woman, who chanced to be the matron. She did not know, but conducted them to the assistant-surgeon, a red-moustached, beardless man, in a white smock.

He greatly astonished them.

"You say he died a month ago? . . . It sounds simple, but to say a month ago! It'll take a little searching. You couldn't count them. . . . Do you know what it's like now? Do you know how many people die here? You can't imagine it!"

"But you see, this man of ours—he was killed," they tried to jog his memory. But the assistant-surgeon, staring at them, said:

"Everybody's killed nowadays. . . . There's no such a thing as a live man."

In any case, they'd look up the books.

The women looked to their horses, who were standing where they had left them, munching their hay. They made a complete circuit of the courtyard, glanced into the laundry, into the kitchen, into the cess-pool (Likonida holding on to the wreath), and walked into the garden to sit in the cool for a while, until the assistant-surgeon should find in the books what they wanted to know.

The garden was small; it had but two narrow pathways. There were a few patients sitting on forms painted yellow. They were in white—dressed all alike; only their caps were their own. One lay on a folding stretcher and read a newspaper—they looked at him critically—while another sat in a wheel-chair and gazed high at the foliage; his arms were bandaged, and his head was also bound in white. . . . Two patients had relatives sitting with them; near one of them a tiny girl sucked at a sweet in a rose paper.

Timidly, holding to one another, the women went along one of the paths, staring hard with country eyes: such were the patients, such was the three-flounced frock worn by one woman, such were the brown stockings worn by the little girl. . . .

They walked past the man who was reading the newspaper. They studied him attentively, each for herself noting his thin fingers—like straws, they thought—however did he manage to hold the paper with them!—what keen eyes he had. . . . Then they walked past the one in the chair, and they scrutinized him as well. His eyes were sunken and large, and his arms supported from the neck by a sling . . . and they noticed another thing, that the wheel-chair was in the full sun, and they thought it might better have been in the shade. . . . And they went farther.

It was impossible to go very far in this small garden. They had come to the green fence, and so they retraced their steps along the same path, past the little girl with the sweet, past the stretcher, past the wheel-chair.

They pushed back their kerchiefs on their heads to allow coolness to reach them, while Likonida bore the wreath over the crook of her elbow, like a basket. As they approached the wheel-chair, it occurred to her to look at the flowers and say regretfully:

"See, they've withered, dragging 'em about. . . ."

The patient with the white swathe around his head, and his arms bandaged as far as the neck, darted a perturbed look at them suddenly, and said in a low voice:

"My d-dears. . . . Is it you . . .?"

And the women stopped short.

"It's you—yes! my dears! . . ." he repeated with an uncommon joy, all radiant.

"It's our man! . . . Our man! In God's truth, ours! . . ." the women cried it loud enough for everyone in the garden to hear. "Our very own! . . . And we, with a wreath for your grave. . . . Look, it's he! . . . come to life again! . . ."

It was so unlooked-for, so marvellous, so exquisite, it transported their very souls, and unable to do otherwise, they fell each after the other on their knees by the wheel-chair, full of prayer and praise.

ℒuigi 𝒫irandello

For Luigi Pirandello, whose great achievements as dramatist, novelist, and short story writer won the Nobel Prize in 1934, the life of man is full of subtleties which make a mock of his intentions, however brave. No resolution, he seems to say, is proof against deception; no man really knows who he is, or where he is going. "My art," he said in 1920, "is full of bitter compassion for all those who deceive themselves; but this compassion cannot fail to be followed by the ferocious derision of destiny which condemns man to deception."

It is noteworthy that Pirandello drew much of his material, not from the intellectuals who are all too aware of their predicament, but from people in lower walks of life in whose experiences the comic spirit finds its richest expression. Pirandello considered Boccaccio the greatest of short story writers. He has some of Boccaccio's pungency himself. While he considers life to be full of clownish uncertainty, the craftsmanship by which he expresses that uncertainty is very sure and confident.

Luigi Pirandello was born in Girgenti, Sicily, in 1867. At eighteen he went to Rome for study, and later attended the University of Bonn in Germany, returning to take a position at Rome as teacher of Italian literature at the Normal College for Women. Here he remained for thirty years. Although he is best known in America for such immensely successful dramas as Six Characters in Search of an Author (1921) and As You Desire Me (1930), he has written twenty volumes of short stories, three novels, and five volumes of poetry. In 1925 Pirandello founded his own theatre in Rome. He died December 10, 1936.

THE HOUSE OF AGONY *

Luigi Pirandello

THE VISITOR had certainly given his name on entering, but the bent old negress, like a monkey dressed up in an apron, who had come to open the door, either hadn't understood it or had forgotten it. And so he had been sitting for three quarters of an hour in that silent house, nameless—"a gentleman who is waiting in there."

"In there" meant in the parlor.

In the house, except for the negress, who must have retired to the kitchen, there was no one. The silence was so deep that the slow tick-tock of an old clock, possibly in the dining-room, was heard distinctly in all the other rooms, as though it were the heart-beat of the house. It seemed that in each room, even the farthest, the pieces of furniture, worn but well cared-for, slightly ridiculous because they belonged to an earlier era, were listening to this tick-tock with the certainty that nothing would ever happen in that house and that therefore they would remain forever useless, for the sole purpose of admiring one another, or commiserating with one another, or better still of drowsing.

Even pieces of furniture, especially old ones, have souls, souls derived from their memories of the house where they have been for so long. To become aware of it, you have only to put a new piece among them.

New furniture is still soulless. Naturally so, if only because it has been picked out and bought with the eager desire for ownership.

Well then, just notice how the old pieces look askance at it. They consider it a pretentious intruder, who as yet knows nothing and can tell nothing. And who knows how many illusions it may have. The old pieces no longer have any and that is why they are so sad. They know that in time memories begin to fade, and that along with them their souls, too, will gradually fade. For that reason they are allowed to stand there, discolored if upholstered, darkened if of wood, without saying anything more, not even they.

If ever, through some mischance, an unpleasant memory clings to them, they run the risk of being thrown away.

That old armchair, for instance, feels a real uneasiness on seeing the dust on the surface of the little table in front of it. It is devoted to that

* Translated by Barbara Coney Silber from *Una Giornata* (Milano: A. Mondadori, 1937). Printed by kind permission of the publishing house of A. Mondadori.

table, and knows that the moths, which have been feeding on the chair's upholstery for years, are the cause of that unsightly dust. The chair realizes that it is too heavy, knows the weakness of its short legs, particularly the two back ones. It is afraid of being seized by the back and thrown out: Heaven forfend! With the little table in front of it, it feels safer, more protected. It wouldn't like to be responsible for having the table thrown in the attic, too, just because those moths and their dust make it cut such a ridiculous figure.

All these observations and considerations were made by the anonymous caller, sitting forgotten in the parlor.

Was he a part of the silence of that house, he wondered,—had he really a name? Intent on listening to the clock's slow tick-tock, which could be heard even there in the parlor across from the half-closed hall door, it seemed to him as though he had lost his identity and had actually become one of those pieces of furniture.

Slight of figure, he was lost in the deep easy-chair upholstered in purplish velvet into which he had sunk. He was equally lost in the suit he was wearing. His spindly arms and legs could hardly be seen in his sleeves and trousers. He was just a bald head with two bright eyes and a small mousy moustache.

Of course his absent host had never thought again of the fact that he had invited someone to call. Already the little man had asked himself several times whether he still had the right to keep on waiting, since the appointed hour was long past, but as a matter of fact he was no longer waiting for his host. Even if he had finally appeared, it wouldn't have mattered.

Sitting there sunk in the chair, with a convulsive fixity shining in his bright little eyes, and a gradually mounting anguish stopping his breath, he was waiting for something else, something terrible: a scream from the street below. A scream announcing the death of someone passing by at a certain time, the death of that person among all those men—young and old—, women and children, whom he could hear coming and going five floors below the parlor window.

And all this because a big grey cat had come into the parlor through the half-closed door and, without taking any notice of the caller, had jumped up on the sill of the open window.

Of all animals, a cat is the one which makes the least noise. It was inevitable that there should be one in such a silent house.

A pot of red geraniums stood out against the rectangle of blue sky framed by the window. The sky, a vivid blue at first, had gradually become tinged with violet, as though the evening had blown a slight shadow on ahead to announce its coming.

The swallows, flashing by in swarms, apparently frenzied by the fading daylight, voiced their shrill cries from time to time and swooped with a thunder of wings toward the window, as if they were going to burst into the parlor, but when they reached the window-sill, swerved away again. Not all of them. Each time, first one, then another darted mysteriously under the window-sill.

Before the cat had walked in, the visitor, his curiosity aroused, had gone to the window, moved the pot of geraniums aside and leaned out. Then he had discovered a swallow's nest directly underneath.

The ominous situation now was this: that none of the many pedestrians, concentrating on their own affairs, could possibly be expected to think of a nest perched under a fifth floor window-sill in one of the many houses on the street, and of a pot of geraniums placed on that window-sill, and of a cat that was stalking the two swallows which had built the nest. Still less could the cat be expected to think of the people below. The cat, crouching behind that flower-pot for concealment, barely moved its head to follow with blank eyes those flying flocks of swallows, who, drunk with air and light, twittered as they passed the window. And each time, at the regular passage of the flight of swallows, the cat barely twitched the tip of its pendant tail, ready to pounce with its sharp claws on the first of the two swallows to light on the nest.

He, he alone was aware that the cat had only to jerk and that pot of geraniums would be precipitated from the window down on some unsuspecting head. Twice already the pot had been jostled by the cat's impatient movements. It was resting now on the very edge of the window-sill. The agony of suspense was choking him and his whole head was covered with great beads of sweat. The torment of expectancy was so unbearable that he had had the diabolical thought of going to the window, bent over and silent, with one finger extended to give that flower-pot the final touch, without waiting for the cat to do it. Certainly a mere touch would be all that was needed. But he was helpless.

In the state to which the silence of that house had reduced him, he no longer had any will power. He actually was that silence, defined by the slow ticking of the clock. He actually was those pieces of furniture, mute and impassive in the face of the disaster which was bound to befall someone in the street below, and of which they would be ignorant. He himself only knew of it by chance. He should have gone long before. He could reason that there really wasn't anyone in the parlor at all. The easy chair, to which he seemed riveted by the hypnosis of the fatality hanging over the head of some unknown, was really empty.

It was useless for him to meddle with the fateful but natural combination of the cat, the pot of geraniums, and the nest of swallows.

The flower-pot was meant to stand in that window. If, to prevent the accident, he moved it, he would prevent it today; tomorrow the old negress would replace it on the window-sill, just because the window-sill was where those geraniums belonged. And the cat, if driven away today, would return tomorrow to stalk the two swallows.

It was inevitable.

There! the pot had been jostled again. It was already a finger's length over the edge of the sill.

He couldn't bear the suspense any longer and fled. Throwing himself down the stairs, it came to him in a flash that he would arrive just in time for the pot of geraniums, which just at that moment was falling from the window, to land on his own head.

Ignazio Silone

Italian

IN HIS first novel Fontamara (1934) Ignazio Silone wrote of experiences which his own career has authenticated. It was a story of Fascist persecution in an Italian peasant village, and Silone wrote it in exile after years of underground activities against the dictatorship. His own suffering went into the harshness of that book, with its violence and its passionate sympathy for the people of Italy. During his exile his mother and brothers were killed in an earthquake in Southern Italy, and a remaining brother died in a Fascist prison.

Silone lives today in Zurich where he is editor of a newspaper and carries on his activities against Fascism. Fontamara, widely translated, made him famous in Europe. In 1935 appeared his Mr. Aristotle, a group of five short stories about the peasants whom he, a man of aristocratic birth, loves and understands. His second novel Bread and Wine (1937), the story of Pietro Spina, a young revolutionary, brought him the widest recognition. "His is clearly the most authentic voice," wrote one critic, "which has yet been raised against the present regime in Italy." His most recent work, The School for Dictators (1938) is a satiric dialogue on the technique of Fascism.

In Silone the propagandist and the artist are a single, powerful force. No doctrinaire, he projects his theme with great artistry and great understanding; and his theme—the possibility of human freedom—is the most momentous in the world of today.

THE TRAP *

Ignazio Silone

DANIEL was still out at the pig-sty, looking after the sow who was having young ones, when someone called to him from the house thirty yards away. He had much to do yet, and had told them once that he did not care to be disturbed; so he did not answer. It was Daniel's wife, Filomena; she had called him two or three times.

"Daniel! Oh, Daniel! There's someone wants to talk to you." When she received no reply, she was silent.

Daniel had done all he could to see that the sow had an easy time of it; but that is the sort of thing you can never be sure about. The night before, he had put the animal on a strict diet and, by way of further precaution, had given her a strenuous castor-oil enema. What he feared more than anything else was that she would become constipated, which might result in a paralysis of the lower regions and the drying up of her milk. He had summoned to help him one Agostino, a native of Bergamo, who had lived at Ticino for a number of years. Agostino was a mason by trade, but in the off-season he was a man of all work.

Things had started off well. Three pigs, looking like three enormous rats, had already made their appearance. Agostino's chief concern was with finding a suitable name for each. The fourth one was slow in coming, and while Agostino held its snout, Daniel put up his bare arm, smeared with oil, to draw it out, leaving the way open for others.

"We ought to call this one Benito," suggested Agostino.

"Nothing doing!" replied Daniel. "These pigs have already been sold to an Italian firm."

"You haven't the nerve!" said the man from Bergamo.

At this point, the voice of Daniel's younger daughter, Luisa, was heard.

"Daddy! There's someone wants to talk to you!"

Daniel meanwhile went on with the umbilical dressings of the young pigs, which was to avoid infection. Had he not already told them at the house that he did not want to be bothered by anything but his work? Again he made no reply. He put the young animals in a large wooden crate lined with straw and covered them over with a woolen

* From *Mr. Aristotle* by Ignazio Silone. Translated by Samuel Putnam. Robert M. McBride and Company, New York, 1935. Reprinted by permission of Robert M. McBride and Company.

blanket, while Agostino saw to the cleaning of the pig-sty and the removing of the evidences of the obstetrical operation. Silvia, Daniel's elder daughter, now called from the path which ran down to the pig-sty.

"Daddy! There's someone here who wants to speak to you!"

Silvia was accompanied by Caterina, the seamstress, an old lady from the province of Florence, who had been a dressmaker at Minusio for years, but who earned the better part of her living by going around from house to house and doing mending. When Daniel saw Caterina, he was annoyed.

"Is that why you've been yelling at me for the last hour?" he demanded. For Caterina was not exactly what you would call a person of few words.

"Caterina wants to talk to you," Silvia went on, taking no notice of her father's reproof. Agostino and Silvia went off toward the house, and Caterina was left alone with Daniel.

"You know very well," Caterina began, "that I have always attended strictly to my own business—"

"That's no business of mine," said Daniel; his tone was anything but encouraging.

"Well, you know, don't you, that all the years I've lived at Ticino I've never meddled with other people's affairs?"

"That doesn't concern me," said Daniel as he made for the house.

When she saw that he had no intention of listening to her, Caterina abandoned all preliminaries and got down to facts.

"An Italian gentleman has just been to see me," she said; "he made me a proposition; he wants me to play the spy!"

Daniel stopped short. Caterina caught her breath and then went on to tell about the call she had received from this gentleman, whom she had met once by chance in an office at Locarno.

"'You've lived here at Ticino for a good many years,' he said to me, 'you ought to know everybody. Your business takes you everywhere, into any number of homes; you listen to any number of conversations. You're an old woman and alone in the world; no one is afraid to talk in front of you—' I told him that everybody certainly did respect me, because I've always minded my own business. He kept talking that way, and then at last he said: 'If you've a mind to get certain information for me concerning the activities of some of the anti-Fascist Italians here in Ticino, between Ascona and Bellinzona, you can earn a little something that will make it easier for you in your old age—'"

Daniel had recovered from his surprise and was watching Caterina closely as, trembling and sighing, she went on with her story.

"Why did you come to me?" he wanted to know.

"Why did I come to you?" Caterina echoed.

"I am a native of Ticino," said Daniel, "and the affairs of these Italians don't interest me; that's the reason I'd like to know why you came to me. Who sent you?"

The old lady was taken aback.

"What do you mean?" she stammered. "You've known me for thirty years. You know that I've always been a hard worker and have always minded my own business!"

"What I want to know," Daniel broke in on her, raising his voice, "what I want to know is, who sent you here?"

"Nobody!" Caterina insisted. "I'm sorry to have bothered you; I'll be going."

Caterina took the foot-path which skirted Daniel's house and which came out on the Gordola-Minusio highway. Daniel followed her and, after a bit, resumed the discussion.

"If no one sent you, then why did you come?"

"I wanted some advice," said Caterina, and she kept on walking.

"What kind of advice?"

"Whether or not I should accept the gentleman's offer." The old lady came to a stop. "I don't know what to do. I never was in such a predicament in all my life. If I accept, I'll earn something substantial, but by doing harm to those who have never harmed me. If I refuse, they're sure to look on me as an anti-Fascist and persecute me every way they can. You've known me for thirty years. You know that I'm neither a Fascist nor an anti-Fascist. You know that I've always been a hard worker and minded my business."

Daniel was lost in thought for a moment. Caterina started to walk away again, sighing resignedly. Once more he followed her. At the end of the path, Agostino was waiting.

"I'll tell you what," Daniel suddenly said to her, "You needn't be afraid. So long as you're honest, you have nothing to fear. Tell Agostino what you've just told me and do as he says."

He watched the pair as they went down the road in the direction of Gordola; then he turned back to the pig-sty, to look after the sow.

It was one morning while Daniel was at work with his daughter Silvia on the vines in the arbor that Agostino went past again for the

first time. The vines were being eaten by an insect which had bored its
way through the bark, and Daniel had wanted to take advantage of a
free morning to get at them. He would run a metal scraper over the
ailing stalks in such a manner as to remove the bark and lay bare the
hidden chrysalisis, and Silvia would come after him to sprinkle the
shoots with boiling water. It was at this time that Agostino went by
upon a truck-load of brick and shouted to Daniel:

"Did you hear about it? That business is coming along!"

"What business?" Daniel answered him, although he understood
well enough what Agostino meant.

"Those Italians are all right," he remarked, turning to his daughter.
"Big-hearted, impulsive, never think of danger—but they talk too
much!"

"Listen, Daddy," said Silvia, plucking up courage at this point to
voice a wish she had been cherishing for a long time, "I know that,
though you don't say anything about it, you are doing a great deal to
help free Italy, and I too would like so much to help!"

"Silvia," was her father's reply, "I wish you would pick up the
pieces of bark which I have chipped off the vines, and which are lying
around on the ground here, and burn them. That is all you have to do
just now!"

His daughter obeyed. Daniel watched her as she went about the
arbor, bending down at the foot of each vine and gathering up in her
apron the tiny pieces of bark. Silvia had been twenty last November.
And there was pride and trepidation in her father's glance as it rested
on her. She was the dearest thing in his life, and the one over which
hung the greatest threat.

Some days afterward Agostino came past a second time, one Sunday
morning. Daniel and Filomena were talking with a woman who was
telling them how, at Cadenazzo and at Robasacco, the night before, a
number of hen-houses had been raided by foxes.

"They found fifty hens with their throats slit and their blood
sucked!" The woman was precise regarding details.

"If that's the case," Daniel disagreed, "then it's not a fox but a pole-
cat."

At this point, a chauffeur from Cadenazzo came past and they put
the question up to him.

"It's a fox," declared the chauffeur, "and maybe more than one. In
one hen-house, all they found left was a bunch of wing-feathers."

"We'll have to be looking after our hens," said Filomena to Daniel. "Last year they were sick, and this year, of course, it would have to be foxes!"

"The thing to do," suggested Daniel, "is to set a trap."

Agostino now arrived on the scene.

"It's coming to a head," he said to Daniel, calling him over to one side. "Caterina did what I told her to, and that fellow from the police has swallowed the hook. We'll have to be on the watch now!"

"What are you thinking about doing?" inquired Daniel.

"The thing to do is to set a trap," Agostino answered.

Daniel burst out laughing when he heard the word trap, and Filomena, who had caught nothing more than the word, now took a hand in the conversation.

"A trap's not always enough," she observed, turning to Agostino. "The fox is too wise for that. Almost always, before nibbling at the bait, he feels all around it, and he doesn't take it in his mouth right away but joggles it about and draws it over to him with his paw. It's all right to set a trap, but it's a good thing to put a little poisoned food around the hen-house at the same time."

Agostino did not get the drift at first.

"But you can't be sure of poison, even," said Daniel to his wife; "a fox has to be pretty hungry if, when he's near a hen-house, he wastes any time in picking up what's lying around on the ground. And even if he eats a piece of poisoned meat or a few chestnuts soaked in strychnine, you can't be sure then. No one has ever yet found just the right dose of strychnine to give a fox, when you don't know what kind of a fox it is. If he's big and strong, and there isn't much strychnine, all he gets is a little belly-ache, which doesn't keep him from eating the hens; but if it's a strong dose, he'll vomit it up right away, get it off his stomach, and have all the keener an appetite for chickens."

"It seems, then, there's no chance of catching a fox!" Agostino had finally realized what it was they had been talking about before he came.

"There is a chance," said Daniel, "but it's not easy. And anyway," he added, "no fox ever yet was caught by talking about it."

Filomena now went back into the house, for Luisa, the younger daughter, had called her; and the two men went out into the garden back of the house to continue their conversation.

"Caterina," Agostino was saying, "after many qualms and no end of

holding back, has finally taken the job of spying on the work that we
are doing here in Locarno. That fellow from the Italian police came to
see her again yesterday and left her an address in Pallanza to which
she is to write in case she has any information to give him."

"He didn't tell Caterina who the persons are she is supposed to spy
on?" asked Daniel.

"It seems not, for the present," said Agostino, "but he told her in a
general way that she was to get the names of all those Italian migratory
workers who are all the time crossing the border into Switzerland and
who there are in touch with revolutionary circles. He told her also
that she could make a nice little sum of money if she would help him
track down those who are responsible for smuggling revolutionary
books and publications into Italy."

"He didn't say who it was he suspected of doing that?"

"Apparently not," said Agostino, "from the story that Caterina gave
me." And then he went on: "I had to promise Caterina that, in case of
any trouble, we'd see to it that she got out all right; I told her we'd
provide her with the means to go to Zurich and live. For the thirty
years she's been here in Ticino, as you know, that's all she's dreamed
of, to be able to live in Zurich."

"Does Caterina suspect that I have any connection with the Italian
revolutionists?"

"You can put that out of your head," Agostino assured him. "Every
time she's talked to me—you know Caterina, with a sigh after every
other word—she's told me how she has always minded her own affairs
and always means to, and how Mr. Daniel, fine man that he is, is one
Ticinese who has never meddled in politics, she can swear to that—"

Silvia, from the window of her room, had caught sight of her father
and Agostino at the far end of the garden.

"May I come down?" she called to her father.

"Of course!" the two men replied.

The girl left the house and came down the garden path. As she
reached them, the pair changed the conversation and began talking
about the weather.

Every night Daniel set a trap at the entrance to the hen-house and
put some poisoned food about, but no fox came. And Agostino's fox
seemingly was in no more of a hurry to set foot in the man from
Bergamo's trap, for Daniel had heard no more about it.

"A farmer's life," he would say, "is one continual war with the weather and with animal parasites, but the hardest war of all is the one against the fox."

The work of scraping the vines had been finished, and he now began on the fruit trees. He would clean the trunks of their dried branches, dead bark, and moss, by way of uncovering the parasites' nests. Wherever there was a hole surrounded by a little streak of red, Silvia would then insert an iron wire to kill the wood-worm hidden at the bottom. When the cleaning was finished, Filomena came with a pail of lime, and each trunk was given a whitewashing to the height of a man's head.

"The trees," observed Daniel, "are now protected the earth side, but who is going to protect them from the heavens?"

Agostino, exchanging pleasantries with Luisa, was waiting for Daniel at the door of the house.

"What's new?" was Daniel's question.

"The trap is ready!" the man from Bergamo replied.

"And the fox, what about him?"

"He'll be there tonight!"

"If only we could finish off all the foxes at once!" Daniel exclaimed.

Agostino then proceeded to inform Daniel of the way in which the provocateur was to be trapped.

"Caterina has written him that she has important information to give him, and she's made an appointment for nine o'clock tonight, at Rivapiana, down by the lake, opposite the old chapel of San Quirico. Caterina will be there, and I mean to be there too, with a couple of others."

"But don't you think," said Daniel, "that it might be well to notify the police?"

"That wouldn't be wise at all," said Agostino. "The consulate might get wind of it right away, and the fox wouldn't show up."

Daniel could not very well offer an objection to this, seeing that a number of subordinates among the police were suspected of being disloyal. The thing that worried him more than anything else was the possible trouble that might be caused the Italian emigrants.

"It ought to be done by Ticinesi!" said Daniel; but Agostino was not of this opinion.

"Too many people would be in on it then; and what's more, an Italian fox—an Italian trap!"

That evening Daniel took the train for Locarno; and along about ten o'clock he started strolling along the lake toward Saleggi, as he waited for Agostino, who was to let him know how the thing had turned out. About half-past ten, in place of Agostino, there appeared one Lucca, an Italian carpenter who lived at Minusio.

"Agostino," he told Daniel, "has been slightly wounded in one hand, and so he did not come, because he did not want to attract attention by going around with a bandaged hand."

"And what about the other man?"

"We left him lying on the ground! He came to keep the appointment with a couple of others, who went off and left him alone with Caterina, saying they would be back in an hour. We were in behind San Quirico, and we waited until they were a good distance away—they left in the direction of Navigna. In the meantime, Caterina, with her usual tears and sighs, was filling the informer with all sorts of foolishness, telling him over and over again how she had never in all her life meddled with anyone's business but her own and never would, but how all the same she had discovered, beyond any doubt, that revolutionary books and magazines to be taken into Italy were being deposited in the Franciscan Convent at Madonna del Sasso, up above Locarno."

Daniel had a good laugh at this.

"Agostino went up alone at first," Lucca went on, "leaving us there behind the church. It had been agreed that he was to make use of his revolver only in case the fellow tried to take him. He acted as if he just happened to be passing. As it was dark, he lighted a cigarette, and pretended to recognize the stranger by the glow of the match. 'Ha!' he called out, and then the rumpus began. We came out of our hiding place, while Caterina took to her heels."

"Did you have a hand in it, too?"

"Oh, there wasn't any need of that. All we did was keep a watch to see that nobody came. Agostino soon enough had the best of him. He threw him to the ground and held him with his knee and then started pounding his face as if he were crushing stone. We knew how strong Agostino was, but we never knew how much hate he had in him—"

"You mustn't forget," Daniel reminded Lucca, "that the Fascista killed Agostino's brother! You say he was wounded in the hand?"

"Yes, the spy bit him. He got Agostino's hand between his teeth and wouldn't let go. With his free hand Agostino was pounding the fellow on the jaw like a madman, but the spy held on with his teeth. Then

Agostino took him by the throat and choked him just about to death."

"Did he finish him?" Daniel was alarmed.

"I think he did."

"Then Agostino in all probability will have to clear out of the country," Daniel said. "He may have to go to France—"

In view of the unforeseen turn which events had taken, Daniel made up his mind to spend the night at Locarno and to go to Bellinzona the following morning. In order that his family might not be worried about him, he went into a café and telephoned to Silvia.

"It's a lucky thing you called," his daughter said. "I've been trying for an hour to reach you, everywhere in Locarno where you're known—"

"Why, what's happened?" Daniel asked in some alarm.

"Nothing at our house," Silvia hastened to reassure him. "But not far away, on the Gordola road, there's been an automobile collision and one man was seriously injured. They got a doctor as quick as they could, and the doctor said his injuries were so serious that it would be dangerous to move him very far. They inquired in a number of houses whether they could take him in; but you know very well that, here in our neighborhood, there are nothing but hovels, like stables. And so the neighbors assured them that our house was the only possible one. Mother, to tell the truth, was rather put out about it; she said that, you being away from home, we couldn't very well take in a stranger, but I told her that I knew you would approve of it—"

"Certainly!" Daniel interrupted her. "Where did you put him?"

"In my room, on the second floor," said Silvia. "I'll sleep with Luisa; she'll be only too glad to have me."

"Is he in danger of death?"

"The doctor wouldn't say as to that. He said that he would send a nurse in this very night, although I told him that I could do everything that was necessary without any help."

"Where is he from? What's his name?" Daniel questioned her further.

"The poor fellow can't talk yet," his daughter explained. "He must come from a well-to-do family, though, for the doctor insisted that mother accept something as a deposit, to cover any expense that we might be put to."

"I'm really very sorry," said Daniel in conclusion, "that I can't come home tonight; but I'm staying over in Locarno, and tomorrow morn-

ing I'm going to Bellinzona, on some business that can't be put off.
I leave everything to you; be a good girl and do whatever the doctor
tells you to."

Daniel telephoned from Bellinzona the next day to find out if the
injured man was still alive. It was Luisa who answered the phone, as
Silvia had gone out to make a few purchases.

"He's a little better," said the young girl. "A nurse came in an automobile last night, but Silvia insisted on staying up anyway—and now
the doctor's here again."

The doctor came to the telephone.

"Doctor, I want you to make yourself perfectly at home in my
house," Daniel said to him. "I regret very much having to be so far
from home at a time like this."

"I think the patient may be considered out of danger," the physician
replied. "He's had rather a severe cerebral shake-up, but I don't look
for any complications. So far as your family is concerned, I will take
care of everything."

"Who is he?" inquired Daniel. "Where are his people?"

"He is Umberto Stella, an Italian engineer from Bologna. You may
have heard the name. He came to Switzerland to make a study of
certain hydro-electric plants."

"Whoever he may be," said Daniel, "I want you to feel that my house
and my family are at your disposal."

At Bellinzona Daniel at once set about endeavoring to find out just
what course the authorities might have taken in their investigation of
the semi-homicidal affair at Rivapiana. He prudently refrained from
bringing up the subject himself, leaving it to others to speak of it first.
With such an object in view, he called on his lawyer and went with
him to the courthouse, by way of settling certain formalities which, as
it happened, were not at all pressing. He stopped everyone he knew on
the street. He bought a couple of morning newspapers but found in
them not the slightest allusion to what had occurred the evening before.
It was evident that nothing whatever was known of the affair at
Bellinzona. Upon finding himself alone with his lawyer, he finally
ventured a hint.

"I hear," he began, "that there was some kind of a political fracas
among the Italians, not far from Locarno, last night—"

"Nobody's heard anything of it around here," replied the lawyer. "It
must have been one that didn't get anywhere. If it had been anything

serious, they would have known of it here at once. The tension between the two parties is very high in this town!"

This answer confirmed Daniel in a suspicion he already had, to the
effect that Lucca's imagination had been working overtime and had
dramatized a comparatively unimportant incident.

"Those Italians," said Daniel, by way of bringing the conversation to
a close, "are fine fellows, big-hearted and impulsive, but they don't
know when to stop talking."

"It's better the way it is," he thought to himself, "or otherwise,
Agostino and Caterina would have had to leave Switzerland." Nevertheless, the fact that he had spent a night away from home and lost a
day on account of such an affair annoyed him more than a little. On the
train going back, he found himself in the company of a number of
farmers who were talking of the fox and how it was massacring the
chickens at Magadino.

"That fox is pretty clever," one of them was saying; "he's too clever
for any trap!"

"But there's a new kind of trap," a second one put in, "an Italian
invention—"

"It makes a lot of noise, but it doesn't catch anything!" was the first
speaker's rejoinder.

"That's true enough," said Daniel, joining in the discussion, "it does
make a lot of noise, and it doesn't catch a thing. All you have is a
fracas that doesn't get anywhere."

Upon reaching home, Daniel went up at once to the second floor to
see the patient. But on the threshold of the room Silvia barred his way,
putting a finger to her lips for him to be silent.

"He has need of complete rest," the daughter whispered in her
father's ear; "no visitors, no formalities, nothing that can disturb him
mentally, the doctor says."

"Then there's nothing that I can do?" Daniel was a bit crestfallen.

"Before you go back downstairs, you can take your shoes off so as
not to make so much noise," Silvia advised him in a hushed tone.

Daniel took off his shoes and went back down the stairs and out into
the garden. He entered the tool-shed and started sharpening stakes
with a hedge-knife. He had no sooner begun than Silvia came running
out in her slippered feet.

"Are you crazy?" she said. "Here we have a sick man in the house,
and you're making all this noise."

Daniel put down the hedge-knife.

"I suppose I may at least eat?" he plaintively inquired.

Silvia nodded and ran back upstairs. Daniel took the spade and began digging up a corner of the garden. In a little while he saw Silvia leave the house with a market-basket. He then went back into the house, took off his shoes, and hastily crept up to the second floor. At the door he met the nurse, who told him that he might enter, "but only for a moment."

There in Silvia's little white bed, Daniel had a glimpse of an enormous head all bandaged in white. Although he was not naturally of a humorous turn of mind, he could not help thinking of the head of St. Nicholas of the Snows. In that huge expanse of white, there was a tiny hole for an eye, and another one a little larger which probably represented a mouth.

"There, that will do," the nurse said, ushering Daniel to the door. Going down stairs, shoes in hand, the latter met Silvia coming back.

"Where have *you* been?" Silvia demanded in a tone of reproof.

"Is that any way to speak to your father?" said Daniel, and he went back to digging in the garden. As he was digging away, Filomena came out to him.

"Silvia's lost her head!" Filomena complained to her husband. "Ever since yesterday, she hasn't shut an eye nor touched a morsel of food."

"Silvia has found her head!" Daniel answered; "she is one girl who has a heart."

"Too much of a one!" responded Silvia's mother.

"Too much of a one? You can never have too much heart," said Daniel. He was well satisfied with his daughter. His glance, always, as he gazed at her was one filled with pride and trepidation.

At the foot of the garden wall there were a few cowslips growing. Silvia came out and plucked them all, for the patient's room.

"But he can't see them! He has his eyes bandaged!" Filomena objected.

"Mother," said Silvia, "you know very well that you can see flowers with your eyes shut."

Daniel spent a good part of the following day in a vineyard which he had on the hillside. Upon coming home in the evening, he inquired after the patient's condition and learned from Silvia that their guest was improving rapidly. They had let the nurse go, and Silvia had taken the care of the patient upon herself. Daniel had a glimpse of the man only two or three times, and the impression he received was an altogether favorable one. He had, moreover, a good many other things on his mind, and so failed to notice the profound change that was taking place in the girl.

"You might give a little less thought to others and a little more to your own daughter!" his wife reproved him one evening.

"Silvia is not a child any longer, and she has a good head on her," was Daniel's curt response.

"She has a head all right, but no experience," replied his wife, who had resolved to unburden herself of what had been on her mind for a number of days past. Daniel reflected.

"You think I ought to speak to her?" he asked.

"I think you had better before it is too late!"

The next day Daniel had to go to bring a bag of seedling peas to a friend of his who lived at Comuna, in Val Verzasca, and Silvia went with him. At Comuna it did not take him long to get through with what little business he had, and he refused all invitations to go to the café.

"I prefer a little walk with my daughter," he explained to his acquaintances; "she's getting a trifle pale lately and needs the exercise."

Father and daughter then set out in silence along the road to Gordola. The wagon-road at this point ran at a considerable elevation above the stream, which could be heard tumbling down below them.

"Couldn't we walk along it?" Silvia asked.

"I don't believe so," said Daniel; but with the desire of giving in to any whim his daughter might have, he added: "We have plenty of time, though; we might go down to the river."

They found a small foot path, steep as a stair, and after many windings and turnings, they came to where the torrent was foaming against a wall of rock. The water was clear-running, and they could see every stone at the bottom. Up to this time father and daughter had exchanged only the briefest and most insignificant of words. This more than anything else gave Daniel a sense of the change which had taken place in their relations.

"Oh, look!" cried Silvia, pointing down at her feet to a strip of sand a dozen inches or so under water, "how pretty!"

"That is spawn," her father informed her. "At the end of September the trout leave the lower part of the river and come up toward the source, and the females, full of eggs, start looking for a well-protected sandy spot. With the aid of their tails they displace the gravel and drop their eggs, which are mixed with the sand."

"And is that the way trout are born?"

"The fertilizing is done by the males, which come along after the females and sprinkle over the spot where the eggs have been deposited a thick white milky fluid. The eggs ought to be hatching about now."

Silvia looked in wonderment at the strip of sand where this mystery was accomplished.

"How beautiful," she said, "and how simple!"

"Trout, my dear girl, don't go to church!"

That was all that was said between them during this jaunt.

"Did you speak to her?" Daniel's wife asked him when they came home.

"Yes."

"What did you say?"

"Nothing."

The engineer had left his room for the first time one day and was lying stretched out on a reclining chair in the garden, when Caterina arrived from Gordola at the same time as Daniel.

"Miss Silvia!" the engineer was calling.

Caterina stopped instantly. Going up to the hedge which hid the garden from the street, she strove to see who it was that had called.

"Mr. Daniel," she said trembling all over, "that man whom you've taken in is the spy who came to Rivapiana that evening!"

"You're out of your senses!" Daniel exclaimed; and he went on to tell Caterina how it was, in his absence, the stranger had come to be brought there. Caterina went up to the hedge again and studied the convalescent intently, as he sat in the garden jesting with Silvia.

"That's the one!" she repeated; "I'm going away before he sees me."

"Very well," said Daniel, who had turned pale. "Tell Agostino to come here tomorrow at this same time; tell him, I'll make sure that no one sees him."

Silvia came running up to meet her father.

"Now that our patient is better," she said, "I think it would be nice of you to have a little talk with him. You will see what a really fine person it is that chance has thrown our way."

"Yes, I should be very much interested in having a talk with him," said Daniel, who was doing his best to keep from showing how disturbed he was; "we can have lunch together today."

At the table, however, as he saw the man sitting there between Silvia and Luisa, the situation became unbearable to Daniel, and, pretending that he was feeling slightly ill, he excused himself and went outside. The others joined him in the garden.

"What's new in the papers?" the self-styled engineer inquired of Daniel. "It's been weeks since I've seen a newspaper."

"There's a fresh tragedy every day," replied Daniel. "Yesterday it was a big railroad wreck in France, with hundreds of dead."

"Every day a tragedy," said the alleged engineer, "but the most tragic thing of all is the way in which men go to meet their tragedies. Think of all those hundreds of persons killed in that railroad disaster. In the same train were farmers and merchants, doctors and lawyers, students, army officers, fashionable modistes, what not. They were all on the same train, and they were not on the same train. The farmer was thinking of the prices he would get from the merchant, the lawyer was thinking of the Cross of the Legion of Honor, the army officer was thinking of his wealthy fiancée, the doctor was engaged in a mental lawsuit with the mayor of his village, and the student, out of the cornor of his eye, was admiring his new necktie. Each was thus traveling in his own train. And each of us has his own train in society, until, of a sudden, we all find that we are on the same train, the train of death. The student's necktie ends up under the country-man's clogs, the officer's sword is run through the traveling salesman's belly, and the modiste's latest model goes up in smoke. For all were on the same train, and they did not know it."

"But the railroad company soon enough saw to that," said Daniel; "they soon saw to it that the unity which had been reëstablished by death was broken, by putting the fur-coated corpses on one side and those in plain workmen's blouses on the other."

"Can it be," said Silvia, "that human beings are condemned to be set over against one another like that, even after death?"

"There is a vast gulf," replied the convalescent, "between man's nature, his destiny, and the thing that society makes of him. During these past days, when I was fighting off death, that subject became an obsession with me. Each of us is traveling on his own train, and we are all on the same train!"

"Present-day society," said Daniel, "is based upon keeping men divided and set against one another. The vast majority of them are separated from and set against the fruit of their own labor. For no sooner does it leave their hands than the product of men ceases to belong to those who have made it but becomes instead their enemy;

the thing produced is set over against the human beings who produced it, the inanimate object becomes the fetish before which living man must bow."

"But must it always be like that?" persisted Silvia.

"When I was young," the invalid went on, "I too hoped for a society that would be different from the one we have."

Daniel rose and went back to his spading. Spring was coming on, and it was time that the work was getting under way. It was with an unwonted vigor that he sank the spade in the earth, throwing the entire weight of his body upon his right foot and tossing the clods into the air. Behind him came Filomena, breaking up the clods with a three-pronged rake. A pleasing odor of moist earth hung over the garden. The sweat was trickling down Daniel's face; internally, he was very much upset. The invalid remained in the garden, stretched out in the armchair, until the first evening stars appeared from behind Monte Ceneri.

"It's been so long," he said, half to himself, "it's been so many, many years since I've had a glimpse of the sky."

Silvia rose and returned shortly with a book.

"There is a similar case here," she told him, "in this first volume of Tolstoy's *War and Peace*. Prince Andrei, in November, 1805, had fallen wounded in the outskirts of Pratzen, in a battle between the Russian troops and those of Napoleon. Here is what Tolstoy has to say about it:

"'Then he opened his eyes, to see what the outcome of the struggle between the two Frenchmen and the artilleryman had been, whether the red-haired artilleryman had been slain or not; he also wanted to know whether the cannon had been saved or captured. But all he could see was the high heavens up above him, no longer filled with light, but immeasurably far above, and covered over with tranquil-gliding gray clouds. "How calm and still and restful it all is," thinks Prince Andrei. "All that has no resemblance whatsoever to this running, shrieking and fighting of ours; the tranquil gliding of those clouds over the high unending heavens has nothing in common with this struggle of the Frenchmen and the artilleryman, as with grim, distorted faces they strive for the possession of a cannon swob. How does it happen that I have never seen these heavens before? How happy I am to have seen them at last. Yes, all is as naught, it is all a mistake and a lie, all except that endless expanse of blue. There is nothing, nothing beyond that. Yet even it does not exist; there is nothing but stillness and peace. And God be thanked for it!" ' "

The moon came up, flooding the Magadino plain with an eerie light.

"The moon," Luisa observed, "has eyes and a nose like us."

"Those things," Silvia explained to her younger sister, "are seas and mountains."

Their guest took it upon himself to round out the explanation.

"If the inhabitants of the moon," he said, "happen to be looking down at the earth at this moment, we probably look much the same to them as the moon does to us. Seen from up there, what are the great cities of the earth? Italy must look like a comma and Switzerland like a period."

"And how does Mussolini look from up there?" Luisa wanted to know.

"You'd better watch out," said Daniel, "or you'll be straining your eyes."

A general laugh went round at this.

The next day, when Daniel saw Agostino coming, he went out to meet him and brought him into the house from the side opposite the garden, where the engineer was seated out in the sun. The two men went up to Luisa's room, and there, from behind the Venetian shutters, Agostino was able to take a good look at the man without being seen.

"That is the one!" he said softly; and rubbing his hands, he added: "This time he's not going to get away from us!"

"What do you mean?" said Daniel with a frown.

"I mean just that, that he's not going to get away from us this time."

"You're joking." The tone of Daniel's voice took his friend from Bergamo by surprise.

"The fox is in the trap," said the latter; "do you mean to say, you're going to let him go? We've got in our hands at last, without his knowing it, one of those who in Italy have been massacring our people, in prison and on the deportation islands; and should we let him get away?" Agostino was wrought up about the matter.

"That man is a guest in my house," Daniel calmly announced.

"He's a spy!" said Agostino.

"He was a spy," answered Daniel, in the same calm voice, "but now he's a guest. He came to my house at the point of death and sought hospitality, and he has been cured in my house."

It was all Agostino could do to believe his ears.

"I can't understand such scruples as that," he said. "You know as well as I do the methods that the Fascists use against us; you know, don't you, there are no moral scruples where they are concerned?"

"I know it," was Daniel's response; "that's why I'm not a Fascist."

"And that's why we're always beaten!"

"That's why we'll win out in the end!" This was Daniel's last word. Agostino could only shake his head, in the face of such stubbornness as this.

"How long is he going to be here yet?"

"Another week, perhaps; he's not very strong yet."

"Then we'll have time to talk it over before he has a chance to get away."

Daniel decided to say nothing about it to the other members of the family, so as not to alarm them or arouse their guest's suspicions. It was at this time that one of Filomena's sisters who lived at Vira had a child, and Daniel with his wife and Silvia went to pay her a visit, leaving Luisa at home with the invalid.

"You've been here all these weeks," said the little girl, "and you haven't yet seen our house."

"That's because I've been in bed all the time," said the engineer.

Luisa then proceeded to show him the storeroom, where they kept the potatoes, the onions, their fruit, and the garden tools. On the second floor she showed him her own room, which her sister Silvia shared with her for the time being. The guest's attention was attracted by a photograph fastened up on the wall with a tissue paperflower on either side.

"Who is that?" he asked.

"That's Matteotti," Luisa informed him.

The engineer dropped down on a chair.

"Who is Matteotti?" was his next question.

"He was the man who stuck up for the poor people, and for that reason he was killed by Mussolini."

"Are you an anti-Fascist?"

"I most certainly am!"

"And Silvia, what about her?"

"She's more of a one than I am."

"And your father?"

"More than any of us—not in what he says, but in what he does."

Luisa then showed the guest the third floor.

"This is my parents' room," she said.

"And what's this?" The engineer pointed to a small room adjoining.

"Oh, you mustn't go in there; Daddy doesn't allow it. He has a lot of papers in there, and he doesn't want us to muss them up."

Luisa and the guest went back to the garden. The invalid began striding up and down the path and kept it up for a good half hour. Then, as if he had made up his mind to something, he came up to Luisa.

"Would you mind running down with a telegram for me?" And when he had given the little girl the wording of the telegram and a few pennies, he added: "I'm tired; I am going to bed at once."

It was in vain that Silvia knocked at their guest's door the next morning, when she came to bring him his breakfast. Her repeated knocking brought not the slightest response. The door was locked. Feeling certain that something dreadful had happened, Silvia began calling at the top of her voice, and the whole family came running up. When Daniel had taken the door off its hinges, it was found that the guest was not in his room. The bed had not been slept in. His suit-cases had disappeared.

"He's gone!" Silvia cried.

"He left without saying good-by!" wailed Luisa.

"He's been gone ever since yesterday," Filomena declared, pointing to the bed.

In a couple of bounds, Daniel was on the third floor, and a moment later, the other members of the family were terror-struck by his furious outcries:

"Thief! Crook! Traitor! He's taken all my papers with him! He's taken away all my papers!"

It was like a mortal blow to Daniel. When the women came up, their eyes fell on the disordered room; all the drawers had been overturned on the floor. At this point, Agostino came in. He did not know what had happened yet, but he was very pale and he seemed excited.

"Yesterday evening," Daniel explained to him, "the spy left the house while I was away and took all my papers with him, among others, those about the smuggling. Quick! There's not a minute to lose; we must let the ones concerned know."

"This morning," said Agostino, "at Luino, a score of seasonal laborers, who are in the habit of coming over to work in Switzerland during the daytime and going back into Italy at night, were arrested."

Silvia stood staring at her father and Agostino, as if all this were some kind of play which they were putting on for her benefit.

"No! No!" she moaned, "it's not true! It's all a joke! Agostino, for heaven's sake, tell me that it's not true!"

Daniel was on his feet.

"We've got to think of saving the others before that spy gets his hands on them!"

And he and Agostino were off in a hurry.

It was late in the evening when Daniel came home. Filomena and Luisa were seated by the hearth, while Silvia sat on a chest, over in one corner of the dark kitchen.

"The smugglers," announced Daniel from the kitchen door, "were arrested early this morning. A consignment of books at Brissago was seized at noon today. The police have been to Caterina's house. I hear that Agostino has been arrested, and that he will probably be expelled from the country. Haven't they been here yet?"

"No," said Filomena.

Daniel dropped down on the doorsill. The night wore slowly on, with the slow procession of the stars. The cock crowed for the first time, but no one so much as thought of going to bed, no one thought of going up to the second floor where *that man* had lived until yesterday. The cock crowed a second time. Mother and daughter still sat by the hearth, the elder daughter on a chest over in a corner of the kitchen, and the father there on the doorsill. It was like a wake for the dead. The cock crowed a third time.

Then came an animal's shrill cry, like the yelp of a dog in pain, and the squawking of hens broke in upon the silence of the night. Daniel leaped to his feet and ran across the garden to the hen-house. In front of it he saw a fox with one paw in the trap; planting its remaining feet upon the ground and arching its back, the animal was doing its utmost to free the prisoned member. When it saw the man approaching, it began leaping furiously from side to side, tugging on the chain by which the trap was securely fastened.

"At last!" said Daniel in a ferocious tone of voice. And snatching up an ax which lay beside the hen-house, as if he were hewing at an oak, he began raining terrible blows upon the animal's head, its back, its belly, its legs—blow after blow, the blows of a madman, death-dealing blows continued to rain down, even after the little beast had been hacked to tiny bits and reduced to nothing more than a puddle of blood-soaked mush.

Appendix

NOTES AND SUGGESTIONS

THE ADVENTURE OF THE GERMAN STUDENT

To one of his friends Irving wrote, "For my part I consider a story merely as a frame on which to stretch the materials; it is the play of thought, and sentiment, and language, the weaving in of characters, lightly yet expressively delineated; the familiar and faithful exhibition of scenes in common life; and the half-concealed vein of humor that is often playing through the whole,—these are among what I aim at, and upon which I felicitate myself in proportion as I think I succeed."

Criticize "The Adventure of the German Student" in the light of this conception.

The reader should note that this story is one of a number of tales told by a group of travellers to each other. It is anecdotal, like many a ghost story, little attempt being made at probability. Indeed Irving cleverly emphasizes the air of frank incredulity by the sequel, which engagingly informs us that the tale came from a madman.

Note that the interest depends upon an extreme oddity of circumstance which does not need to be rooted in character. The student and the girl are simply romantic types. Would the story have been improved if Irving had individualized them?

MR. HIGGINBOTHAM'S CATASTROPHE

Poe said of this story that "it is vividly original and managed most dexterously." Do you agree with this criticism, and would you add to it? Certainly it shows Hawthorne in an unaccustomed, some would say, an uncharacteristic mood. But he had his own humor which preserved him from morbidity.

Consider whether this story conforms to all the requirements of the modern detective story, posing, as it does, the chief narrative question: "Was Mr. Higginbotham murdered, or not?"

Note Hawthorne's skillful use of dramatic suspense—the teasing of the reader with the withholding of the solution until the end. Yet notice that while the story has a surprise ending, it is not a trick ending: the solution is consonant with all that has gone before.

Is the implied love story an advantage to the tale? Would a story writer bother today with the explanations in the last paragraph? Does it seem an entirely superfluous sequel?

For Hawthorne's general theory of the short story, read his preface to the *Twice-Told Tales,* written at Lenox, January 11, 1851.

THE CASK OF AMONTILLADO

Since Poe was the great exemplar of the principle of economy in the short story, the reader will profit in studying how much in this story is left out. We are not told what the thousand injuries of Fortunato are; nor do we hear more than a word about the insult which precipitated the revenge. It seems sufficient—so effective are Poe's phrases—that we witness the terrible punishment alone. Poe was capable of verbosity, but in this story the economy is as effective in expression as it is in structure. Every word is directed to the advance of the story.

Do you think that the same story could have been told effectively in the third person? Or would you agree that the use of the first person is essential in portraying an egocentric personality obsessed with desire for revenge?

Note the effectiveness of repetition of phrase—especially the sardonic echoing of "Amontillado!"

For Poe's complete statement of his theory of the short story, see both his review of Hawthorne's *Twice-Told Tales* and his essay *The Philosophy of Composition.*

TENNESSEE'S PARTNER

In his general introduction to *The Luck of Roaring Camp and Other Tales,* first written for the English edition of his tales, Bret Harte defends himself against the charge of implausibility and sentimentality. Read his remarks and make your own judgment upon the issue.

Note that most of the action of this story—the trial and the hanging—is concerned with Tennessee himself rather than the partner. Nevertheless Harte skillfully centers the interest on his title character.

Since this is a character story, it is interesting to decide whether or not its events proceed inevitably out of the dominant trait of the chief character.

Is the point of view confused? The story begins in the first person, the narrator relating events in which he has taken part. Yet the story seems to be predominantly in the third person. The narrator does not put himself in the trial scene or tell how he knew of the events of the trial. He does indicate his presence at the funeral scene. Is Harte to be accused of technical clumsiness, or is his story sufficiently free of confusion?

One of the Missing

C. Hartley Grattan, one of Bierce's biographers, says that "Bierce was only moved to write a story when he discovered a case where the extraordinary impinged upon the ordinary tenor of events." Does the extraordinary in this story win your full acceptance? Does it in such stories as "An Occurrence at Owl Creek Bridge" or "A Horseman in the Sky?"

Would you call this a "thematic" story, written chiefly to point the truth that fate rules human lives?

Note that Bierce avoids the familiar "author talking to reader" attitude so common in the stories of Harte or Irving. He enters the mind of his chief character, but he does not intrude his own comment. What is the advantage of this attitude?

Is it true to say that the final section of the story, dealing with Lieutenant Adrian Searing, is sheer sequel?

Compare Bierce's story telling with that of Poe.

Paste

In his preface to the volume containing this story, Henry James writes that he had set out to reverse the situation in Guy de Maupassant's famous story "The Necklace." "It seemed harmless sport simply to turn that situation round—to shift, in other words, the ground of the horrid mistake, making this a matter not of a false treasure supposed to be true and precious, but of a real treasure supposed to be false and hollow. . . ." Compare James' story with Maupassant's.

More than any other modern craftsman, Henry James has been influential in his use of the technical device of keeping the author out of the story: that is, of refusing to comment on his situation or telling about his characters, but allowing them to reveal themselves in a myriad subtle ways. Study his stories with this technique in mind.

Note the effectiveness of the disturbing question which James puts in the mind of the reader in the next to the last sentence of the story.

Define the conflict in this story.

The Two Churches of 'Quawket

All of Bunner's stories are based upon the anecdote, the story which is odd or remarkable in circumstance. In this respect he anticipated the vogue of O. Henry, whose dazzling surprises were chronic. In so far as such stories have placed a premium upon manipulation of plot, their influence has been unfortunate, as witness the ubiquitous and empty "short-shorts" in the magazines.

The masters can not be greatly blamed for their unsought or inept disciples. Bunner himself had more than plot agility to give to the reader: his characters are accurately, if broadly, drawn; his satire, as in "The Two Churches of 'Quawket," can be pointed indeed; and his humor is unforced.

Who is the chief character of this story, the Reverend Mr. Pursly or Brother Joash Hitt? Is the characterization typical or individualistic? Do you feel that the plot requirements of the story make for superficiality of character interpretation?

Bunner's command over story structure is notable. Analyze the plan of this story, and of such stories as "The Love Letters of Smith," "A Letter and a Paragraph," "A Sisterly Scheme," and "As One Having Authority."

My Platonic Sweetheart

Mark Twain was fascinated by dreams, and often recounted how strong a part they played in his life. At first glance this story may seem like a mere transference from a notebook, the materials of a story but not the story itself. As a matter of fact he first wrote it in the summer of 1898, and then laid it away for rewriting. He did not return to it, and it was first published two years after his death in *Harper's Magazine* for December, 1912.

The probabilities are that Mark Twain had done his best with "My Platonic Sweetheart." Do you regard it as a completed work of art, a real story; or is it merely a fragment? Does it possess an essential unity, a singleness of mood which preserves it from being a mere series of anecdotes?

Would the story be improved by the omission of the last paragraph?

Mrs. Ripley's Trip

How the story-teller's mind will sometimes work under the insistent pressure of a theme is told by Hamlin Garland in his foreword to the volume containing this story. "My mind teemed with subjects for fiction, and one Sunday morning I set to work on a story which had been suggested to me by a talk with my mother, and a few hours later I read to her . . . the first two thousand words of "Mrs. Ripley's Trip."

Is this primarily a story of atmosphere, of local color?

Do you think of the dramatic conflict as being between Mrs. Ripley and her husband?

Study the structure of the story. It is unusually effective for analysis into scenes.

Roads of Destiny

This is a brilliant example of the "contrived" story, a story which deliberately ignores considerations of probability in order to illustrate its theme that man can not escape his destiny. No matter whether young David take the road to the left, to the right, or straight ahead, he is fated to die by the pistol of Monseigneur, the Marquis de Beaupertuys. Perhaps the discerning will see autobiography in this apologue.

Discuss the legitimacy of the surprise endings in O. Henry's stories. When does this device offer artistic satisfaction; when does it cheapen the story by seeming a mere theatricalism? To what extent is the story-teller justified in manipulating the apparently incredible if he is not writing out-and-out legend?

What essential distinction would you make between the stories of O. Henry and those of Sherwood Anderson?

A most interesting criticism of O. Henry is that by O. W. Firkins in the September, 1919, number of *The Weekly Review*. Among the best of his stories are "A Municipal Report," "The Furnished Room," "The Last Leaf," and "The Gift of the Magi."

There Are Smiles

Nearly all of Ring Lardner's stories carry a high proportion of dialogue. Study the way in which dialogue is made to forward the action of the story and characterize its speakers. Does the dialogue seem entirely natural, or does it become a "line"?

Note that although this story is written in third-person, it has almost the same effect as first-person narration—as if the author were talking to the reader directly.

Who is the chief character—the girl or the traffic cop?

When tragedy is not inherent in a story, it falls flatly and shockingly because the reader is not emotionally prepared. Does the story avoid this difficulty? How?

For an interesting example of a story told entirely by letter, read Lardner's "Some Like Them Cold."

Your Obituary, Well Written

Note that while the narrator of this story seems at first to be the chief character, the story is remembered in terms of Reine Wilson. Is it a tenable dictum that every story contains a *single* chief character, or is it possible to divide a story's interest equally between two or more people? In other words can you successfully shift the focus of a story?

In this study of artistic sensitivity do you detect a satiric note in the author's interpretation? Does the sensitivity become mere preciosity?

Is there any legitimate objection to the unusually long introduction?

The narrator thinks of his "odd little adventure with Reine Wilson" as being, for him, his most revelatory experience. What, after all, does the story reveal?

How Beautiful with Shoes

Wilbur Daniel Steele's mastery over the possibilities of his material is so pervasive that it becomes a nice point of discussion whether his emphasis is chiefly on situation, character, "atmosphere," or theme. "How Beautiful with Shoes" may be called—to borrow Thomas H. Uzzell's phrase—a multiphase story.

Is the focus upon the girl or upon the lunatic, and do you remember the story chiefly because of these two, or because of its theme?

In bare situation the story is common enough—many a newspaper clipping tells about escaped lunatics and abductions. But here such common stuff of melodrama is made to move the reader with the spectacle of a man mad with adoration of beauty, hunted by the world, and able briefly to bring the wonder of love and passion to a primitive country girl who can then no longer be satisfied with the clumsy attentions of her rustic lover. The theme is difficult, treading the thin line between the sublime and the ridiculous.

The technical devices by which the author makes his story plausible— for instance the necessary deafness of Mrs. Doggett and the way antecedent information about Humble Jewett is conveyed—repay close study.

In the sketch of Mr. Steele contributed to the book *Living Authors,* the student will find interesting information about his writing habits.

That Evening Sun

This story is told as it is recollected fifteen years after it happened, when the narrator was a child of nine. What special advantage does this point of view give to the tale?

Faulkner's stories are noted for their power of evoking atmosphere. Is it an analyzable power? That is to say, can you indicate any technical means by which it is achieved?

This story affords a brilliant illustration of the effectiveness of omission, of leaving the thing unsaid. The *real* story is implied, and the horror and suspense of the situation is greatly intensified by the author's refusal to dwell upon its denouement.

Faulkner's work has often been discussed in connection with that of two other Southern writers, Erskine Caldwell and Thomas Wolfe. Read the stories of all three and make your own comparisons.

BLIND EVE

Such a story as this is a good peg on which to hang a discussion of the adjectives "romantic" and "realistic." Does their usefulness justify such labels, and would it be merely confusing, or clarifying to call Edmonds a romantic realist—romantic in his turning to the past for the magic of the remote, realistic in his sense of fact?

The student will notice how strong a role "atmosphere" or setting plays in this story, not only in its evocation of early spring in the Kill Gorge but also in its infusion of the whole tale with a legendary, almost idyllic quality.

Note the author's skillfulness in making credible the happenings of the fifth section of the story. All within a lunchtime and in one conversation, a man and a girl, known to each other for the first time, arrange for a marriage. Notice especially the dialogue.

Of manner in writing Edmonds has said: "Style is not a mechanical service—it is purely an involuntary result of the point of view of the writer." Discuss this dictum in relation to the stories that seem to you especially distinguished in style.

A DAY IN NEW YORK

The craftsmanship of this story will repay study. The idea of it, baldly stated, seems merely anecdotal, and a cruel anecdote at that: a young couple sleeping through the big day of their lives. But as it is developed, the "trick" of the situation is made to seem wholly natural and the story becomes plausible and appealing, reflecting, not disappointment, but the pleasant qualities of an average American couple.

Note how the structure of the story is balanced by its theme, announced in the first paragraph and restated in the last.

Does the characterization of Dan and Rosy depend mainly upon direct explanation, or upon their conversation and behavior?

AFTER THE STORM

What would this story lose if it were told—as are many stories of unusual incident—in objective third-person narration?

Does the value of the story lie chiefly in the remarkable experience itself, that is, in its anecdotal interest alone? Or is there another value which makes it worth the telling? If so, what is it?

What have you to say about the effectiveness of Hemingway's style? Has the author caught the natural rhythm of talk, or is his style too mannered to be wholly natural? Although this story happens to be monologue, Hemingway is noted for his ability to express the very rhythm of personality in dialogue. Study his other stories and make your own judgment.

Read and comment upon Hemingway's strictures on American writing in the first chapter of his *Green Hills of Africa*.

Golden Wedding

The strength of this story rests in its faithful truth to character and its accurate interpretation of the drama of every day. No "plot" controls the characters; the characters, rather, make the plot. The story deals with the unusual—a golden wedding—in a usual existence, and its artistic pleasure is that of recognition. No further departure from the kind of story that Poe wrote could be imagined; yet Poe, one believes, would have praised this story. Each good story of whatever kind has its own excellence, and must succeed by observing the laws of its own being.

Note that the focus of the story is on Mrs. Willey, whose hopefulness has for years been tried by the small complaints of her husband. How would you define the dramatic conflict of the story?

The structural balance of the story is expert. Note how the strictly chronological selection of scenes develops narrative suspense within the natural order of events.

Miss Suckow has discussed the technique of the short story in the two articles "I Could Write If Only—" (*Outlook*, March 21, 1928) and "The Short Story" (*The Saturday Review of Literature*, November 19, 1927).

The Ladies Call on Mr. Pussick

For the student who has to look for a plot, who feels that he has "nothing to write about," nothing is more instructive than the Scribner series *Life in the United States* from which this story is taken. "The Ladies Call on Mr. Pussick" is the stuff of direct, intimate, sympathetic observation of the drama of everyday. It is a good story because its author has enough power and insight to fashion the material he knows into effective art without resort to formula. Any intelligent student has the same opportunity for imaginative commentary on the life he knows.

The underlying theme of the story—the silly futility of a certain kind of reform—is obvious but unlabored, and the conflict between Pete and the reforming ladies is simple and complete. What quality in the story gives its distinction?

Owen Francis has written a brief account of himself in the "Editorial Notes" of *The American Mercury* for November, 1929.

THREE BITES AT A STORY

It is one thing to present an interesting situation—for instance, a holdup in a barroom—and another to "resolve" it, the solution developing plausibly from the events. Many students find it hard to "go on from there," to find an artistically satisfying outcome for their situation; and "Three Bites at a Story" was deliberately written as an object lesson in dealing with this difficulty.

Harkness, a frustrated artist whose mind naturally moves in terms of story, finds himself in the midst of a situation, and his imagination ponders three ways—"three bites"—out. Only the third way satisfies him; only the third really makes a story. And at the end is an added fillip which removes the charge of mere trickery, providing a plausible "out" for the whole story.

What are "the three bites"? What is the implication of the ending?

THE PARDON

In this story of the loneliness of a man who has been segregated from his familiar human world and tries again to return to it, notice how the pardon itself becomes an ironical symbol.

Is the dramatic conflict primarily between Adams and his wife, or rather between Adams and society at large? How is the conflict resolved? What is the essential role of Jackie, the child?

Note exactly the means employed by the author to increase the emotional effect of the story. Notice also the structural excellence of the story—its strict limitation of time, place, and action.

An interesting "Literary Profile" of Marjorie Kinnan Rawlings was written by Elizabeth Shepley Sergeant for the New York Herald-Tribune *Books* of June 18, 1933.

ARCADIA RECALLED

In "Arcadia Recalled" nothing unusual "happens"—nothing except the rare, the complete happiness of four young girls on the farm in the summer time. The title is an exact statement of the story's theme. It has no "plot" in the traditional sense; its events are ordinary day-to-day happenings, made dear and familiar by the transfiguring power of recollection.

Note that while the story deals with the experiences of four characters—

three sisters and their cousin—it is mainly presented through the conscious-ness of one of them, ten year old Mary Josephine.

Compare this story with the childhood reminiscences of another Mis-sourian, Mark Twain, as told in his *Autobiography*.

A Cold Day

In the traditional sense "A Cold Day" is not a short story at all. A young man writes a letter about how cold it is in San Francisco, so cold, indeed, that he can't write a good story and so turns to writing a complaint instead. As a student will write a theme about theme writing, so Saroyan writes a story about writing a story. Make an argument for or against its inclusion under the term, "short story."

Notice that "A Cold Day" has more pattern than at first it seems to have. Does it achieve artistic unity, completeness of effect?

Read Saroyan's two prefaces to his first book *The Daring Young Man on the Flying Trapeze* and discuss his "rules" for story writing.

His most solid advice for a writer is, he says: "Try to learn to breathe deeply, really to taste food when you eat, and when you sleep, really to sleep. . . . Try to be alive."

With the Fog

This story begins with a description of "the known world of the average Brushy Mountain family"; and it is this world and the Gentle family which make the story—a telling about a "borning," a usual event, on an early April day when the fog is beginning to roll into the clearing. The effective-ness of the tale is in the whole "picture" of the situation; yet it is more than a description, more than a sketch. It is a narrative with dramatic rise of event, but the drama, as in such stories as "Ten" or "Grief," is the drama of the natural pattern of life.

Note how the story is focused upon a single character, the child, Jettie; and yet the writer conveys with artistic economy the disturbing currents of a whole swarming family.

Do you remember this story, in the last analysis, for its place, its "setting," so to speak, or for its people? Or is such a distinction equivocal?

Deep Water Man

In "Deep Water Man" the author is concerned with the full characteriza-tion of an eccentric personality. He is also concerned with showing that character under the stress of dramatic circumstances which give opportunity for just and triumphal mastery over an enemy. Here is that "reversal of the situation" which is so satisfying a principle in many good stories. Do you find the emphasis of the story to lie chiefly in characterization, or in situation?

Note how the dramatic suspense of the situation is so accompanied by the rising fury of the flood that Mr. McAusland's Nemesis becomes, not Captain Tuttle alone, but the roaring tumult itself; and as the deep water man takes joyous farewell he has demonstrated his mastery over both his enemy and the elements.

What is the advantage in this story of first-person narration from the point of view of a minor character?

JOB'S TEARS

Like other stories in this collection, such as "Arcadia Recalled," "Ten" and "With the Fog," this story not only tells about a specific situation but conveys the quality of a whole region and way of life. Although Uncle Jolly, incorrigible and faithful, is the chief character whose situation gives point to the narrative, the reader is likely to remember with equal vividness the dramatic conflict between the lean winter and the little family—the boy of seven and the indomitable grandmother of eighty-four.

Mr. Still has written another story about Uncle Jolly—the title is "Uncle Jolly"—in *The Atlantic Monthly* for July, 1938. His work beautifully illustrates the truism that a man writes best of that which he best knows.

SOPHISTICATION

In his introduction to the Modern Library edition of *Winesburg, Ohio,* Ernest Boyd writes: "The stories are written out of the depths of imagination and intuition, out of a prolonged brooding over the fascinating spectacle of existence, but they combine that quality with a marvellous faculty of precise observation." Do you agree with this estimate? In this study of two typical young Americans—George Willard and Helen White—is Anderson's intuition unerring? Is he a true interpreter of adolescence? Compare his discernment with that of Katherine Mansfield in "Taking the Veil."

Is the story impeded by Anderson's exposition upon "the moment of sophistication" beginning with the phrase "There is a time in the life of every boy . . ."?

Note that the author takes the omniscient point of view, entering the minds of both his characters. Could the story have been told as well from a limited point of view?

Do you feel any clumsiness or unnaturalness in the characterization of Helen White's guest, the young man from the college?

For the fuller understanding of Sherwood Anderson's aims in story-telling, the student should read *Sherwood Anderson's Notebook* (1926) and the remarkable autobiography *A Story Teller's Story* (1924).

TEN

This story of a country lad and a fifty-cent piece is in a great tradition of American writing, the tradition which embraces the close, tenacious observation of a Thoreau recording life in Concord, or a Mark Twain evoking the memories of a Mississippi childhood. That tradition is both romantic and realistic, concerned with the whole pattern of experience.

In "Ten" the chief event—the earning, the losing, and the finding of the fifty-cent piece—is simply the means of dramatizing a crisis in character. What is that crisis? What is the bearing of the story's ending upon Eric's problem?

"The only magic available to an artist," writes Mr. Nuhn in his essay "Art and Identity," "is the latent magic of his own mind-working; the only secret worth anything to him is his own secret; what he learns from some one else is to that extent no secret anyway."

RACHEL AND HER CHILDREN

The distinction of this story, both in style and structure, rewards study. As in her two novels, Miss Newman rejects direct presentation with its dialogue and description to narrate her story through retrospection in the mind of the chief character—in this case, old Mrs. Overton. Even the immediate occasion—the funeral itself, to which the story returns at intervals—is not presented directly, but told about.

This method is dangerous in the hands of the amateur because it may convey the effect of mere synopsis, but in Miss Newman's hands it becomes a perfect instrument. She can "tell about" because she illuminates her telling with witty inference and cool cynicism. The story stands alone; its sardonic irony can hardly be matched in all American fiction.

Of her much discussed style, Miss Newman has remarked: "I write long sentences because I like inferences, not flat-footed declarations, and of course that requires a protasis and an apodosis." Of herself she said: "I am mentally cynical and personally sentimental." Much excellent talk of literature is in her *Letters*, edited by Hansell Baugh in 1929.

A TRIP TO CZARDIS

In bare situation this story would be almost too painful to endure, as the reader will realize if he attempts to summarize it. But under the reticence and discipline of its treatment the situation does not become explicit until the end, and as the implications of the trip to Czardis gradually dawn upon the older boy, Jim, a mounting narrative suspense is resolved and the reader is greatly moved.

The workmanship of the story is beyond the mechanics of analysis, but note how artfully the author arouses sympathy in his characterization of the little boys, his delicate delineation of their waking and their coming down to breakfast; and how the language itself, poised and cadenced, conducts the story fittingly to its tragic end.

No One My Grief Can Tell

This story is brilliantly successful in its use of a much abused technique. Even before Freud began the investigations which have made commonplaces of such terms as "free association" and "stream of consciousness," certain writers—witness Dostoevsky—had explored the hidden impulses beneath conscious behavior, and within the last twenty years Joyce's *Ulysses* has enormously influenced the interest of creative artists in presenting the unspoken drama of the mind.

For the beginning writer the danger of psychological exploration is that he may know too little of psychology, that in recording a welter of impressions he may avoid dramatic conflict altogether, and that he may not have the expressive power to make his reverie significant and moving.

The artistic discipline of "No One My Grief Can Tell" will repay study. The external action, unimportant though it may seem, is clearly patterned. The all-important internal action is equally definite in its structure.

But above all, this story of a young mother whose mind is filled with a torment of emotions—possessive love for her child, the realization that he will grow and leave her, and beyond this the realization of her husband's growing indifference,—all this is moving because it is the reflection of an interesting mind which is acquainted with beauty as well as with grief.

Compare this story with those of Conrad Aiken, Katherine Mansfield, and William Saroyan included in this collection.

A Terribly Strange Bed

Wilkie Collins is said to have pronounced the dictum that the way to hold one's readers is to "make 'em laugh, make 'em weep, make 'em wait." His ability to accomplish the last of these effects is undeniable; and the student should study his manipulation of narrative suspense. Notice how each advance in the story is designed to raise the question: what will happen next?

In his *The Short Story in English* Henry Seidel Canby remarks of this story: "Collins did not know how to begin his story, he did not know how to end it, but he distributed his incidents with the most excellent care." Discuss this opinion.

The student should compare this story with Joseph Conrad's "The Inn of the Two Witches" which contains another terribly strange bed. Conrad has written that he did not know of Collins' tale when he wrote his own.

The Signal Man

This story is one of "Two Ghost Stories," written in 1865 and 1866 for Dickens' series of Christmas stories. The second story, "The Trial for Murder," a psychological study of mounting horror, is a worthy companion.

The special problem of the ghost story is to induce belief without the sacrifice of intelligence. The reader will not be satisfied with oldwife anecdotes. Notice how from the first startling cry of "Halloa! Below there!" Dickens induces a mood of grim premonition which leaves the climax completely acceptable.

Is the last paragraph necessary to the story, or is it likely that an author of today would dispense with it?

The technique of this story is unusual with Dickens. "It should be read," says Henry Seidel Canby, "in an edition of his works, for only then does one realize, by contrast, how foreign to the methods of the free-and-easy writer is this single example of the new short story."

A Lodging for the Night

Although Stevenson himself made an often-quoted distinction between the three chief elements of the short story—plot, character, and setting— it is not always easy to decide which one of these elements is the chief motivating principle in his own stories. Is "A Lodging for the Night" motivated chiefly by the atmosphere of medieval Paris, by the character of Francois Villon, or by the complication of events? Or is it chiefly a thematic story, setting forth the principle that, as against conventional morality, roguery has its code of honor, too? Or are all these elements so evenly balanced that the question remains open?

Stevenson said, "I never use an effect when I can help it, unless it prepares the effects that are to follow; that's what a story consists in."

Study the logic of this story to see how Stevenson follows his principle.

For his theory of the story read his essays: "Gossip on a Novel of Dumas"; "A Gossip on Romance"; "A Humble Remonstrance"; "The Morality of the Profession of Letters"; and "A Note on Realism." Also read the two volumes of *Vailima Letters*.

Tony Kytes, The Arch-Deceiver

Although it is artistically complete, this lighthearted story is part of a larger composition entitled "A Few Crusted Characters" and labelled by its author as "colloquial sketches." It is told by a carrier to a group of town-folk riding in a van from a market town to Longpuddle. Like some of the stories in Chaucer's *Canterbury Tales,* it has the easy informality and casualness of the oral tradition, and belongs to the company of the myriad stories told before the invention of printing.

How much plausibility does the reader require in a story of farcical incident? Is Hardy true to character as well as to the probabilities of his situation?

Is there any essential difference between the first-person point of view, as employed here, and the omniscent third-person point of view?

Hardy has often been criticized for overemphasis upon irony of circumstance. Read some of his other short stories for a discussion of this charge.

Books about Thomas Hardy include *Thomas Hardy: Poet and Novelist* by S. C. Chew, and the two-volume biography by his wife, Florence Hardy.

The Pig and Whistle

Gissing did not write a great number of short stories, and those he wrote do not lend themselves to labels. He did not contrive elaborate plots: his characters simply walk into the ordinary urgencies of living and make a story in which neither atmosphere, event, nor characterization is strikingly preponderant.

"The Pig and Whistle" is more cheerful than many of Gissing's stories, and it is felicitous in its homely humor. Note especially its characterization. Many a writer might enviously admire Gissing's ideas for characters in his stories—such characters as an innkeeper whose whole life turns on the issue of whether or not he had really entertained His Royal Highness.

Good studies of Gissing may be found in "An Introductory Survey" by T. Seccombe which prefaces the 1906 edition of *The House of Cobwebs* and in the biography *George Gissing* (1912) by Frank Swinnerton.

Salta Pro Nobis

The student will notice the subtitle of this story. In music a variation is defined as "the presentation of a musical thought in new and varied aspects," and Galsworthy probably meant this story to have the effect of a musical mood—a tune gay and sad, expressing beauty lost, but not conquered by death. The immediate situation may have been suggested by the execution of the famous dancer and World War spy, Mata-Hari.

In his foreword to the collection *Caravan,* Galsworthy, always the idealist, warns the beginning writer against surrender to the immediate fashion of the fiction market: " 'Ev'yone that talk about Heav'n ain't goin' there!' and those who dutifully confection the short story to the sacred pattern of the hour may well become of the company which shakes its tambourines in hell."

For the study of Galsworthy's literary principles the student is referred to his book of essays *The Inn of Tranquility* (1912).

A Little Cloud

Frustration is so common a condition in life that most stories deal with it in one or another of its multitudinous forms, but it has rarely been embodied more memorably than in the portrait of Little Chandler. Its skill is beyond strict analysis, but the reader will note how scrupulously the author refrains from judgment, and how he limits the story's unfolding to Little Chandler's point of view. Ignatius Gallaher is the moving spirit of the story, but we know all we need to know of him through his conversation. His thoughts are not entered into, but the thoughts of Little Chandler are the stuff of the story.

The other stories in Joyce's *Dubliners* observe the same artistic detachment. They will repay renewed study.

Note the effective simplicity of structure in "A Little Cloud," its division into three scenes: Little Chandler at the office, at the bar, and at home.

The student who wishes to know Joyce must read, above all, his *Portrait of the Artist as Young Man* wherein Stephen Dedalus (Joyce) goes forth "to encounter for the millionth time the reality of experience and to forge in the smithy of my soul the uncreated conscience of my race."

The Blind Man

This story is a brilliant exemplification of psychological analysis. A study of the inward relationship of three people, the wife, the husband, and the friend, it deals with no special crisis, save that of human awareness. Lawrence is not interested in the bold melodrama of the traditional triangle,

Is the author objective in his characterization, or does he "take sides"? Where do your sympathies lie?

In its way "The Handsome Lady" is a ghost story, with a fancifulness, a gentle irony not usually associated with tales of the supernatural. Does the author ask you to believe the incredible, or is such an issue entirely gratuitous?

THE NAP

There can be no question in this story about the identity of the chief character, or of his dominant trait. The whole tale moves through the consciousness of Mr. Thripp, who on a Saturday afternoon when he wants to have his tea alone and doze by the fire is confronted by the worries and demands of his swarming family.

Is the dramatic conflict between Mr. Thripp and his family, or rather between himself and his *alter ego,* that inward monitor which rages at the shortcomings of those to whom he is an unfailing comforter?

Note how beautifully the structure of this story is unified in time, place, and action—a single afternoon in a family kitchen, and a single action built up by a natural series of encounters.

Is "The Nap" primarily a character or a thematic story?

About poetry, Mr. de la Mare has written: "It seems to me that our one hope is to get away from realism, in the accepted sense. . . . An imaginative experience is not only as real but far realer than an unimaginative one." Do his stories also illustrate this dictum?

MRS. PACKLETIDE'S TIGER

So deftly does Munro write his stories that the student is likely to take their superb technique for granted. It does not mar his tales to subject them to analysis, and it would be a good use of time for the student to copy one of his stories to get a "feel" for its structure. Since Munro, partly because of journalistic exigencies, wrote within sharply restricted limits, he practised notable economy. Note how the first sentence of "Mrs. Packletide's Tiger" launches the reader into the story.

Is the story chiefly interesting for its complication or for its satirical implications?

Note the effectiveness of the sequel.

The one-volume, complete collection of the stories of Saki includes a "Biography of Saki" by his sister, Ethel M. Munro, which contains many of his letters and delightfully reveals his personality.

in *Trente ans de Paris* (1887). An interesting English criticism of Daudet may be found in Arthur Symon's *Studies in Prose and Verse.*

Two Friends

Maupassant was a master of the *conte*—a form seldom exceeding fifteen hundred words. Within this limit he could expand an anecdote into a brilliant, hard, effective interpretation of the real world. In "Two Friends" the action is swift and terrible. Two old men go fishing in war time and are senselessly shot as spies. Note the cruelty of the sequel. Compare the story with Bierce's "One of the Missing."

Maupassant has written of the advice given to him by Flaubert, who said: "When you pass a grocer sitting in his doorway, a porter smoking his pipe, or a cab horse,—show me that grocer and that porter, their attitude and their whole physical aspect, including, as indicated by the skill of the portrait, their whole normal nature, in such a way that I could never mistake them for any other grocer and porter; and by a single word, give me to understand wherein one horse differs from fifty others, before and behind it."

Like Flaubert, Maupassant sought for the *mot juste:* "Whatever thing we wish to say, there is but one word to express it, but one verb to give it movement, but one adjective to qualify it."

For an understanding of Maupassant's art the student should read his own preface to *Pierre and Jean* (1888), and Henry James' essay in *Partial Portraits* (1888).

The Manuscript of a Village Doctor

The classic grace and serenity of Anatole France's prose—of necessity imperfectly conveyed in translation—seems effortless and spontaneous, but he was one of the most laborious of writers. He confessed that he "rarely felt the gust of inspiration," and his secretary, Jean Jacques Brousson, has recounted how the Master would insist on correcting and revising to the eighth proof. His prose is great art, and greatly artful. "Caress your phrase tenderly," he would say, "it will end by smiling at you."

Note how carefully the author has selected the point of view in this story. We are led to believe that the child Eloi is really a genius because his story is told in the journal of an objective, sceptical scientist who has disciplined himself against sentiment or enthusiasm.

Is Eloi the chief character of this story, or is it the village doctor himself? Compare the story with Turgenev's "The District Doctor."

For two differing views of Anatole France, read *Anatole France: The*

Man and His Work by J. Lewis May and *Anatole France* by Barry Cerf. A most interesting personal reminiscence is *Anatole France Himself* by Jean Jacques Brousson.

AUTUMN

Strindberg was a misogynist, and unhappily married. This is a story of a married couple in their early forties, who find that after ten years a second honeymoon is really impossible, that romantic sentiment has been destroyed by the routine of domesticity. Do you feel that Strindberg's interpretation may be affected by a personal bias? If so, would you agree, nevertheless, that his characterization is acute and his situation powerfully presented?

Note how carefully the author, telling the story of two people of equal importance to the narrative, focuses it on the husband alone. Compare its technique with that of "Golden Wedding."

In his famous preface to the play *Miss Julia,* Strindberg wrote: "Everybody is clamouring arrogantly for the 'joy of life.' . . . I find the joy of life in its violent and cruel struggles, and my pleasure lies in knowing something and learning something." In the same essay he testified that the novels of the French naturalists, the brothers de Goncourt, "have appealed more to me than any other modern literature." An English biography of Strindberg was written by Miss L. Lind, London, 1913.

VERONIKA

"Veronika" is a dramatic study of inward conflict more subtle and complex than most treatments of a relationship which too often becomes a stereotype in life as well as in literature. Note that the struggle takes place entirely within the soul of Veronika, who wages her fight alone without the help of husband or of lover. The delicacy and power of Storm's interpretation is extraordinary and refreshing.

What significant part do the mill people play in the story? What part the Church?

How would you define the story's theme?

Note the symbolism of the gloved hands.

THE NEW YEAR'S EVE CONFESSION

"The New Year's Eve Confession" is an adroit example of the society tale written as a story within a story, and showing traces of the structural dexterity of such masters as Maupassant and Daudet who influenced the young Sudermann when he was beginning his literary experimentation.

An excellent story of its type, it is not especially characteristic. In his autobiography *The Story of My Youth* Sudermann remarks: "In those days (1880) the masters of literature had laid down stringent rules for the tying of literary posies, the neglect of which was met inevitably with scorn and outlawry or, what was worse, laughing neglect. . . . In my nature, however, impetuosity and lack of skill were engaged in a mad battle. I foamed with fury against the narrowness of the forms prescribed, and yet I felt flattered when I got a perfect strophe."

Note with what economy "The New Year's Eve Confession" achieves its single effect of irony, and how it uses the familiar situation of the "triangle" with a surprising, but entirely plausible denouement. The sardonic humor of the telling and its psychological penetration minimizes the effect of literary trickery.

Is it clear that the bachelor talking to the lady is also one of the gentlemen of the confession?

The Blind Geronimo and His Brother

German authors have long been fond of the "Novelle," a narrative more extensive and slower-paced than the average short story and yet limiting itself to the dramatic interpretation of a single episode. Schnitzler's "The Blind Geronimo" is an excellent illustration of the form. In America and England such narratives are likely to be labelled "long short stories." The label doesn't matter; it is clear that such stories, despite their length, are not to be confused with novelettes.

It is interesting to observe that in "The Blind Geronimo" an author who is famous for his portrayals of men and women in love chooses to interpret a deeply-felt, deeply pitiable relationship between two brothers in a situation in which women play no vital part whatever.

The misunderstanding which arises between the two brothers depends, apparently, upon sheer chance. What part may the element of sheer chance legitimately play in the construction of a narrative?

What is the underlying theme of the story?

The Parcel

This story of a man who is determined to tell the girl whom he loves about his own weakness is a masterful illustration of the drama of psychological exploration. The external action is of no importance except as it serves for background in a penetrating analysis of character. Note how skillfully the author builds up narrative suspense to the point where Dr. Rohme, quite to his own astonishment, suddenly risks his whole standing by telling the absurd story of the parcel, and how the denouement, when Claudia all at once sees the doctor for what he is—faithful, generous, and honest—is as decisive and exciting as any drama of outward event.

What significant part does Goethe's play take in the story?

Do you think this story could have been as effectively told from Claudia's point of view?

The Hungry

"The Hungry" is narration in the mood and rhythm of meditation, the dramatic interest arising from an ironical interpretation of the artistic temperament. As in many psychological studies in story form, the external action is extremely simple. Detlef turns from the theatre, pitying himself that he cannot partake of the thoughtless joy of the merry-makers within. As he starts home without his "Lily" who is enjoying another's company, he meets an outcast whose scorn he feels that he does not merit, whom he calls—to himself—"brother."

Does Mann intend satire in his pointed contrast between the spiritual loneliness of the well-dressed, well-fed artist and the physical loneliness and hunger of the street waif?

In his introduction to *Stories of Three Decades,* Mann says that this story is among those tales, written in his twenties, which "wear the impress of much melancholy and ironic reflection on the subject of art and the artist: his isolation and equivocal position in the world of reality, considered socially and metaphysically and as a result of his double bond with nature and spirit."

Among Mann's great short stories are "Death in Venice," "Tonio Kröger," "Mario and the Magician," and "Disorder and Early Sorrow."

Grief

In his preface to *East and West* Somerset Maugham has remarked that Chekhov, unlike Maupassant, was unable to invent a story interesting in itself. In "Grief" we have a cabdriver who wants to tell his grief to somebody, but nobody will listen; and so he tells the whole story to his little horse. Is this situation interesting in itself, or does its whole effectiveness consist in the atmosphere of pathos with which the writer surrounds the story?

Chekhov did not try to resolve or "solve" the situations he created. He had no answer, because life has no answer. But does that mean that his stories failed in intrinsic interest? Do you feel a greyness or a dreariness in his stories, as some readers have confessed?

In his letters and notebooks Chekhov has made many absorbing comments upon the problems of literature. See the *Letters of Anton Chekhov* (1920); *The Notebooks of Anton Chekhov, together with Reminiscences of Chekhov by Maxim Gorki* (1921) and *Letters on Literary Topics* (1924). A characteristic entry is that of August 6, 1891: "I got into difficulties and often tore up what I had written, and for days at a time was dissatisfied with my work. . . . How awful it is. I must rewrite it! . . ."

The District Doctor

In this story, like that of Anatole France which also deals with the experiences of a physician, the point of view is of great technical importance. What is its advantage?

Note how skillfully Turgenev heightens the pathos of the story by his emphasis, both at the beginning and the end, upon the unromantic qualities of the narrator of this affecting experience, a man who now hopes only to keep the children from crying and his wife from scolding.

Is it true that this story universalizes its experience, that the reader's interest is less in the doctor and the girl as individuals than in the conflict between love and death?

What is the dominant characteristic of the doctor?

Henry James tells us that Turgenev always found the idea for his stories in character: "to this end he wrote out a sort of biography of each of his characters, and everything that they had done and that had happened to them up to the opening of the story."

Interesting studies of Turgenev will be found in Henry James' *Partial Portraits*, Conrad's *Notes on Life and Letters*, and James Huneker's *Overtones*. The best biography is Avrahm Yarmolinsky's *Turgenev, The Man, His Art, and His Age*.

One Autumn Night

Many of Gorki's stories have the intimacy of personal confession, and, characteristically, "One Autumn Night" reads like a chapter of autobiography. Its action is simple—a man and a girl seek for food and shelter on a cold night along the wharf—but Gorki is not content with the objective recital of circumstance. The boy of eighteen is no ordinary waif; he is an intellectual, and his mind is bitterly alive to the irony that he, occupied with the problem of humanity's destiny, has to depend for warmth upon a poor girl. The story is strong because it deals eloquently with the fundamentals of existence—with the need for food, the need for shelter, and the need of the heart. Note how powerfully the weather furnishes a fitting background for the action. What is the emotional effect of the story?

In a remarkable sketch of Gorki (*The Yale Review,* Spring, 1937) Ivan Bunin says: "I learned that he was capable of reciting monologues from morning to night, and always with the same skill and sincerity. He could completely enter into his role, and at pathetic moments, when he wanted to be particularly touching, tears came easily to his green eyes. . . ."

The Man You Couldn't Kill

Note how this powerful story symbolizes a universal conflict—that between the life-giving forces of love and the death-dealing forces of brutality, the prize in this particular contest being the sturdy body and indomitable soul of a Bolshevik soldier. In this sense the tale might be considered an apologue upon the radiant kindness of women, and the impersonal, almost jaunty, savagery of men. Yet the author avoids fable: his is the particular story of an individual, Titkov, told in realistic detail.

Judging by your general reading, does the characterization and the theme seem peculiarly Russian? Why?

Do you find the story plausible? What slight references convince the reader that the almost unbelievable treatment of Titkov by the Cossacks could still let him remain alive?

A brief comment upon the work of S. Sergeev-Tzensky may be found in Prince D. S. Mirsky's *Contemporary Russian Literature,* pp. 141–144.

The House of Agony

Pirandello's stories, usually concerned with simple situations and quite ordinary people, are extraordinary in quality. The author's talent is highly skilled in artful and unexpected suggestion. The analysts who fit stories to the specifications of a formula would have trouble, one suspects, with "The House of Agony." Its only human character is anonymous and passive; its action is suspended until the end, and it uses no dialogue whatever.

Is the chief character the atmosphere of the house itself, quiet, intent, and capable of inducing a hypnotic sense of fatality which overpowers the luckless occupant? Just how does Pirandello succeed in creating dramatic suspense? Is the whole emphasis upon the point of the story? What is the point? What part does the characterization of the furniture play in the story's economy?

Two studies of Pirandello are *Luigi Pirandello* (1926) by Walter Starkie and *Luigi Pirandello* (1927) by F. Pasini.

THE TRAP

This remarkable story is strong because it is projected against a background whose implications are of profound importance to every human being. Silone is not concerned with spinning a yarn for entertainment; he writes to dramatize an eternal conflict, a conflict not so much between Daniel, the farmer, and Umberto, the engineer, as between human idealism and human treachery.

Is the story equally strong because of its artistic values? What characteristics save it from becoming an anti-Fascist tract, a piece of propaganda merely? To generalize, is there any essential, unresolvable conflict between the aims of the artist and those of the propagandist?

Note the powerful use of symbolism in this story: the parallel between the fox in the trap and the spy in the house.

A biographical sketch of Silone may be found in the *Wilson Library Bulletin* for March, 1935.

SELECTED BIBLIOGRAPHY

BOOKS

Beach, Stewart, *Short-Story Technique*. Houghton Mifflin Company, Boston, 1929.

Bement, Douglas, *Weaving the Short Story*. Long and Smith, New York, 1931.

Besant, Sir Walter, *The Art of Fiction*. Cupples, Upham, London, 1885.

Bildersee, Adele, *Imaginative Writing*. D. C. Heath and Company, Boston, 1927.

Brande, Dorothea, *Becoming a Writer*. Harcourt, Brace and Company, New York, 1934.

Canby, Henry Seidel, *A Study of the Short Story*. Henry Holt and Company, New York, 1913.

Canby, Henry Seidel, *The Short Story in English*. Henry Holt and Company, New York, 1909.

Clark, Glenn, *Manual of the Short Story Art*. The Macmillan Company, New York, 1922.

Fothergill, John, *Mr. Fothergill's Plot*. Oxford University Press, New York, 1931.

Fagin, Nathan B., *Short Story Writing*. Seltzer, New York, 1923.

Gallishaw, John, *The Only Two Ways to Write a Story*. G. P. Putnam's Sons, New York, 1930.

Gallishaw, John, *Twenty Problems of the Fiction Writer*. G. P. Putnam's Sons, New York, 1930.

Gallishaw, John, *Advanced Problems of the Fiction Writer*. G. P. Putnam's Sons, New York, 1931.

Hale, Edward Everett, Jr., *The Elements of the Short Story*. Henry Holt and Company, New York, 1915.

Hamilton, Clayton, *A Manual of the Art of Fiction*. Doubleday, Doran and Company, New York, 1918. (Revised, 1939, by Clayton Hamilton and Burges Johnson.)

Hamilton, Clayton, *The Materials and Methods of Fiction*. Doubleday, Doran and Company, New York, 1912.

Hoffman, Arthur Sullivant, *Fundamentals of Fiction Writing*. The Bobbs-Merrill Company, Indianapolis, 1922.

Hoffman, Arthur Sullivant, *The Writing of Fiction*. W. W. Norton and Company, New York, 1934.

Howells, William Dean, *Criticism and Fiction*. Harper and Brothers, New York, 1892.

Joseph, Michael, *How to Write a Short Story*. Henry Holt and Company, New York, 1921.

Marks, Percy, *The Craft of Writing*. Harcourt, Brace and Company, New York, 1932.

Matthews, Brander, *The Philosophy of the Short Story*. Longmans, Green and Company, New York, 1901.

Mirrielees, Edith, *Writing the Short Story*. Doubleday, Doran and Company, New York, 1929.

Newman, Frances, *The Short Story's Mutations*. B. W. Huebsch Company, New York, 1925.

O'Brien, Edward J., *The Advance of the American Short Story*. Dodd, Mead and Company, New York, 1923.

O'Brien, Edward J., *Dance of the Machines*. Macaulay Company, New York, 1929.

O'Brien, Edward J., *Short Story Case Book*. Farrar and Rinehart, New York, 1935.

Pattee, F. L., *The Development of the American Short Story*. Harper and Brothers, New York, 1923.

Perry, Bliss, *A Study of Prose Fiction*. Houghton Mifflin Company, Boston, 1902, 1920.

Perry, F. M., *Story Writing: Lessons from the Masters*. Henry Holt and Company, New York, 1926.

Smith, C. A., *The American Short Story*. Ginn and Company, Boston, 1912.

Uzzell, Thomas H., *Narrative Technique*. Harcourt, Brace and Company, New York, 1923, 1934.

Wharton, Edith, *The Writing of Fiction*. Charles Scribner's Sons, New York, 1925.

Williams, Blanche Colton, *A Handbook on Story Writing*. Dodd, Mead and Company, New York, 1930.

ARTICLES

Anderson, Sherwood, "Why Men Write," *Story*. January, 1936.

Aden, M., "The Short Story," *London Mercury*. April, 1934.

Buck, Pearl, "Fiction and the Front Page," *Yale Review*. March, 1936.

Burnett, Whit, "Hammock Writing," *Story*. August, 1936.

Colum, M. M., "Short-story Formulas," *Forum*. December, 1935.

Chenery, W. L., "Picking Popular Fiction," *Saturday Review of Literature*. June 18, 1938.

DeVoto, Bernard, "Writing for Money," *Saturday Review of Literature*. October 9, 1937.

Fitzgerald, F. Scott, "One Hundred False Starts," *Saturday Evening Post*. March 4, 1933.

Gerould, K. F., "Feminine Fiction," *Saturday Review of Literature*. April 11, 1935. See also reply to this article, "The Problem of Popularity," by Margaret Culkin Banning, *Saturday Review of Literature*. May 2, 1936.

Leach, Henry Goddard, "A New Deal in Fiction," *Forum*. December, 1935.

Leonard, Jonathan Norton, "Short Story Schools," *Saturday Review of Literature*. June 8, 1935. See also reply to this article by Thomas H. Uzzell, *Saturday Review of Literature*. June 29, 1935.

Lowe, O., "American Literature of the Short Story," *Scholastic*. December 7, 1935.

MacPhail, Andrew, "The Short Story," *Quarterly Review*. July, 1934.

Maugham, William Somerset, "How I Write Short Stories," *Saturday Review of Literature*. July 28, 1934.

O'Brien, Edward J., "The American Short Story," *Story*. December, 1935.

Suckow, Ruth, "The Short Story," *Saturday Review of Literature*. November 19, 1927.

Suckow, Ruth, "I Could Write If Only . . . ," *Outlook*. March 21, 1928.

Strong, L. A. G., "Short Stories," *Nineteenth Century*. October, 1932.

Strong, L. A. G., "Concerning Short Stories," *Bookman*. November, 1932.

Warren, C. H., "The Modern Short Story," *Bookman* (London). April, 1933.

Williams, H. E., "Permanence in Short Stories," *Canadian Bookman*. August, 1930.

Wylie, I. A. R., "As One Writer to Another," *Harper's Magazine*. February, 1937.